CHAD HANNA

CHAD HANNA

WALTER D. EDMONDS

THE REPRINT SOCIETY
LONDON

FIRST PUBLISHED, OCTOBER 1940
THIS EDITION PUBLISHED BY THE REPRINT SOCIETY LTD.
BY ARRANGEMENT WITH WM. COLLINS AND CO., LTD.

1942

FOR
GRACE ROOT

ACKNOWLEDGMENT

I CANNOT let this book out of my hands without acknowledging my indebtedness to the aid, suggestions, and encouragement of several people. Definite facts of early circus history are hard to come by. Wages, for instance, have been worked out largely through inference. But, though the first purpose of *Chad Hanna* is the entertainment of the reader, I have taken some pains to make the daily routine of Huguenine's Great and Only International Circus as accurate as I might.

In this I have been enormously helped by Mr. Robert W. G. Vail, librarian of the American Antiquarian Society in Worcester, Massachusetts, who not only opened the library's collection of posters for my edification, and put me on the right trail more than once, but also read the entire manuscript for errors of fact. What errors may come to light are bound, however, to be mine, not his.

A stirring contribution also was made by Miss Lilian Achilles of the Swann Library in Albion, New York, who discovered the Philadelphia rhinoceros, the extensive advertising employed by the Institute's Menagerie and Aviary, and fixed Huguenine's pitch in that town, where Oscar slowly died.

Also to Mr. M. V. Atwood, of the *Times-Union*, Rochester, New York, who dug up the advertisement which was the model for Burke and Walsh, who lent me books, and made many fertile suggestions ; to Mr. Nelson Greene of Fort Plain, author of the best and most extensive history of the Mohawk Valley ; and to Mr. George Freedley, librarian of the Theatre Collection of the New York Public Library, go my most grateful thanks.

W. D. E.

CONTENTS

BOOK I

CANASTOTA

BOOK II

THE LOCKET

BOOK III

THE TENTING SEASON

BOOK IV

OSCAR'S SLOW DECLINE

BOOK V

THE RETURN SWING

BOOK VI

THE BAND BEGINS TO PLAY

Book I

CANASTOTA

THE CIRCUS AGENT

THE Yellow Bud Tavern had a long porch fronting on the canal with a rail about hip-high. Sitting with his feet on the rail, Chad Hanna discovered that he could frame the face of the young woman on the canal boat with the toes of his boots. He twisted on his chair to hold her face there as long as he could, but she went by just the same. After she was gone he wondered what kind of girl she was ; whether she was a married woman or just hired.

Elias Proops, who never did anything but sit on the porch anyway, said, " That there was a pretty girl," right in the middle of what he was talking about. His voice didn't even break off. He and Judd Parsons were having an argument. Judge was a Democrat and Jackson man—he worked in Spencer and Eaton's mechanic's shop where they made mechanical instruments. Mechanics were always Jackson men, Elias Proops said, even if they wasn't Democrats. " By God," he said. " I didn't vote for Andrew Jackson, even the first time. I voted for Adams. And I ain't going to vote for no Van Buren neither."

" You poor Federalists ain't going to have anybody to vote for," said Judd. " You're too dead to even stink."

Elias Proops said in a dignified voice, " You dumb mechanics don't have the eyesight to see around your own backsides. Business ain't a chicken you can fatten by caponising. Crimus, if a man can't make all the money he wants, what's going to become of men like me ? "

" I expect you'll just keep setting here." Judd Parsons got up. " You never did a lick of work your whole life, did you ? "

" I was in the Revolution," said Elias. " I got a pension."

Judd Parsons hawked scornfully. He didn't appear to have heard. He said, " I bet you when you die they'll have to build you an L-shape coffin. I'll draw the plans for it." He looked over at Chad. " And I'll make a copy of them plans for Chad, so he can use 'em when his time comes."

Chad wiggled his big toe through the hole in his boot and grinned. " I ain't got no pension, Juddy," he said..

Judd hawked again and went around the corner without saying anything more.

" These-here mechanics think they're all-fired smart," Elias said. He spat over his boots. He was the only man in Canastota who could spit sitting from the Yellow Bud porch into the canal. He turned his old wizened head to look at Chad. " What you doing to-day, Chad ? "

Chad didn't answer, but Elias didn't seem to mind that. The two of them sat there, looking out, hazy-eyed. It was getting to be hot even for June. The grass was coming up rank in Siddley's pasture over the canal. Chad noticed there was a rail down in the towpath fence. A boat came by from the west behind a poor team. You saw a lot of poor teams hauling on the canal nowadays. A lot of canallers thought it was easier to buy horses cheap and drive them till they wore out than buying good and taking care of them. Chad thought lazily that the captain looked like a hog.

There wasn't any sound in the tavern back of them except where Mrs. Mott and the black girl were washing up the dishes and Mrs. Mott was wishing she lived in a Southern state so Diney would be a slave and she could give her what-for when her feet hurt the way they did now. Mott was reading the paper in the taproom and a bluebottle fly was butting the windowpane.

" Bobby Gray wants me to go fishing," Chad said. " Maybe I'll go if he brings the worms."

" Ain't no real fishing like there was in my time," said Elias. " Don't hardly pay to go after them now, when you got to look for the things."

" You got to know where they are," said Chad.

" You got to find out though,"said Elias. " I don't call that fishing."

" That's right, Elias."

The boat was unloading at Marvin's forwarding house. They watched the men working. One of the men was in his undershirt. Elias said, " It's getting pretty warm."

" Yeah."

That was when they saw the horseman cross the bridge and head down the canal bank. They looked him over. He was riding a rat-tailed light brown horse with a white nose. Strapped to his saddle were two long pouches that slapped against the horse's forelegs as he walked. He had a fast walk, Chad saw; pretty good horse even if he didn't look like much.

The man himself was a little like the horse. He had a light reddish-brown coat, not well taken care of He had on a grey hat with a slight bell of the crown that made his face lengthen down; and his eyes seemed to set at an angle to the high bridge of his nose and they looked nearly as smart as the horse's. Chad thought the two of them must have done a lot of travelling.

" Medicine peddler ? " he said out of the side of his mouth.

Elias let go a spit. " They wear black," he said, in some scorn. " Like preachers, or doctors, or undertakers."

The man stopped his horse and said, " Hallo."

" Hallo," said Elias.

" How many taverns you got in this town ? "

" Four."

" This the best one ? "

" It's where I set," said Elias.

The horseman grinned.

" That'll do to begin on," he said. He swung a long leg over the saddle and got down. Chad cussed, and got up. " You want him to have a feed ? "

" Two quarts of oats, and some hay. If you clean him good, I'll give you a free pass."

" Pass to what ? "

" Circus. Huguenine's Great and Only."

" I never heard of that one," said Elias. " Cheap show, hey ? "

" Twenty-five cents to you, Granpa," he said. " Who runs this hotel ? "

" Paul Mott. Hey, Paul ! "

They heard Mott put his paper down and come to the door.

" Mr. Mott ? " said the traveller. " My name's Bisbee. B. D. Bisbee. I'm agent for Huguenine's Great and Only International Circus."

" That so ? "

Mott advanced a cautious hand. The agent shook it.

" I want to route the circus through this town," he said. " It's a handy stop between Vernon and Cicero. Is it a good town ? "

" I make out all right," said Mott.

" How many people live here ? "

" About eight hundred," said Mott.

" I've got that right, then. Is there a decent lot ? "

" I guess you could hire a piece of my brother-in-law's pasture. That's just over the canal bridge."

" No free lots ? How's the supervisor ? "

" He's a nice man," Mott said. " You want a bed here, Mr. Bisbee ? "

" I've got to post the other taverns," said Bisbee. " Hey you," he said to Chad. " Hand me those pouches, will you ? "

Chad drew them off the horse's withers and tossed them on to the porch. Bisbee caught them, opened them, and drew out some posters. " I'm tacking two kinds," he said. " One of them's a world-beater. The other's just the regular. I'll show you them first. I'm putting only one of the good ones up in this town. Six-by-three feet. Look at it, Mr. Mott. Wouldn't that look handsome in your bar ? "

Both posters said HUGUENINE'S GREAT AND ONLY INTERNATIONAL CIRCUS across the top. But the small ones had only one cut of a high-rider. " You don't want to look at that," said Bisbee. " This is the one that counts."

" You can put the big one up here," said Mott.

" I'll be glad to do it," replied Bisbee. " And put myself up here at the same time. It don't cost you a cent either, Mr. Mott."

" What are you talking about ? " Mott said. " Nobody ever paid money for letting a circus man post a bill in his bar."

" Well, it's this way," said Bisbee. " You put me up here free and you get the big poster in your bar. It's a dandy. Look at that picture of the lion. Look at the lady rider in her English riding clothes. Look at that acrobatic act. It damn' near beats the real thing."

" I never see the picture that didn't," said Elias.

" Why in hell should I board you free and let you tack your bill up here for nothing too ? " demanded Mott.

" Because if I take this big one to another tavern where they've got more sense," Bisbee said good-naturedly, " all the people will want to go there to look at it. This ain't just an ordinary wafer, Mr. Mott. This-here's artistic. It's educational. It's as good as the circus itself, pretty near. Why, Mr. Mott, after the circus has gone, people will still want to come into your bar and look at the poster so they can remember the circus better." He reached in his pocket and pulled out a stogie. "How about it, Mr. Mott? Ain't that sense?"

"All right," said Mott.

Bisbee lit the cigar.

Elias said, " I like the smell of a Conestogie myself."

"Do you, Granpa?" said Bisbee.

"I set here a whole lot of my time," continued Elias, " and everybody in this town passes a word with me. Now if I had a Conestogie and they said where did you get that smoke, I'd say (natural) that the circus agent passed it out to me. They'd say what agent of what circus. I'd say Huguenine's Circus. See the pictures inside."

"That sounds fine."

"Then," said Elias, arching a high one over his toes, " I could say I seen the poster and I could say the high-rider picture's a lie."

"Well, Granpa?"

"Seeing as how it's a picture of Hunter, made out for the posters I seen five years ago in Albany, and it ain't Signor Rossello at all."

Bisbee grinned.

"You win, Granpa. Want a pass, too?"

"I don't mind. I don't go to circuses much unless they're good. I've been round, mister."

"This one's good. This-here's the biggest tent show ever came to this town, Granpa."

"It's the first," said Elias.

"It's a dinger just the same. Five wagons, a covered tent, seats for three hundred people."

"That so?"

"It is. Rossello's better than Hunter ever was."

"You ever see Hunter?"

"No."

"I thought not," said Elias. "But I guess you got a good show. This ain't a bad Conestogie, either."

Mott had decided he was doing a pretty smart deal getting the big poster. "You say I can keep this-here when the circus is gone?"

"Yes. If I post here I got to see the supervisor and then I've got to get a lot."

"You give my brother-in-law a free pass for his family and he'll let you have it. Same for the supervisor, and he'll get you a permit. If he don't, tell him to come up here and have a drink."

"You're a smart man, Mr. Mott. Thank you. You, boy, you take that horse in and treat him good."

Chad Hanna had been leaning in over the porch rail, studying the big poster. He could read a little and he had made out the HUGUENINE'S GREAT AND ONLY INTERNATIONAL CIRCUS part, but he couldn't understand the & EQUES-TRIOLE under it.

"What's that?" he said, pointing to it.

"That's Lady Lillian's academy act. She's the best lady rider in America. She's worth paying the whole twenty-five cents to look at, let alone her horse and her on it," said Bisbee. "*Equestriole* means school for horses. Get the idea?"

"I guess so," said Chad. He took another good look at the lady in the picture before he ambled off with the agent's horse.

2

CHAD HANNA HIMSELF

CHAD took the agent's horse around to the Yellow Bud barn and put him in the end stall where he got the benefit of the cool side of the building. He had to move out Mott's horse to put him there, but he didn't think much of Mott's horse. He did it really because he liked the look of the white-nosed brown, ratty tail or not.

He gave him a short one from the stable pail and then he washed his eyes and nose out with a piece of damp rag, cleaned his ears, and gave him a going over with the corn brush. The horse took it all as if he were used to it ; but Chad was willing to bet that he hadn't been in a barn for a week where his ears had been cleaned out, and he thought Bisbee must be one of those easy-going people who knew their way around but had no idea about a good horse. Maybe, he thought, he wouldn't take the time to fuss over a horse himself if he had money enough to own one.

When he was through and had put a measure of oats and a fork of bluejoint in the manger, he dumped some more hay in the manger of the loose stall and lay down in it with his legs hanging over the edge.

Once, talking about Chad, Elias Proops had made a speech.

"Vegetables has got mushrooms," Elias said, "animals have got rabbits, birds have got eggs, humans have people like Chad there. One minute you don't know there is such a thing, and the next minute they've got born, Lord knows how."

Chad himself didn't know how or when he had got born. The nearest he could figure was that he was about twenty—but he might be anywhere from sixteen to twenty-five for all he knew. At the orphanage in Troy they said he had come out of a bad-house. He didn't know about that either. It was a funny thing that in a place where the children were all in the same fix anyway, they should set up a kind of law as to who was better than who else. There was one little girl that the superintendent's wife liked picking on, which made the other children pick on her too. Because she was supposed to have come from the same house as Chad, the two of them used to stand together against the other children. She had black curling hair and skinny legs with big red knees. He had forgotten her name, but he remembered how she held up her fists.

A farmer named Humphrey, near Mechanicsville, had taken him out of the orphanage as an indentured apprentice "for the business of farming." Before the year was out Chad had run away from the place. He had taken to the canal and had got a job driving.

The canal was a bad place for a little boy who didn't have any relations. Captains didn't hire boys of that kind to give them a living; they hired them to drive boats. They worked two six-hour tricks a day. In the off time they had to clean their teams, mend their harness, cook their own food, and harness the team again. The rest of the time they slept. Plenty of boys got used up, like the underfed horses. Half of them didn't get paid. They drifted from boat to boat when they could get away from the one they were working on. It didn't do them any good to go along with a missionary. If a captain found out, he would generally half kill them. All the missionaries wanted them to do anyway was to find steady work and keep away from gin and liquor.

Some boys did get killed. Picking on a driver was about the only kind of fun some captains could think up on a long, fast haul. Some of them were tough articles. Chad used to figure that the only reason he managed to get along as well as he did was because he always could get a lot of pulling out of even a poor horse.

In summer driving wasn't so bad except for the flies. But in spring and fall, when the rain was cold and there was frost in the ground, driving was hard. Especially during the night hauling, when a boy had to keep awake. The first trick wasn't so hard because he could watch out for the lit windows of houses, and see things to keep him thinking. A driver boy could see a lot of things going on that the people never thought about themselves. But in the early morning trick it was different. Then it was all dark and he didn't see anything but the back ends of the team in front of him, or maybe a boat passing. Even the packet boats during that trick didn't carry more light then the bow lantern.

Then he had to hold on to the towline to keep himself walking. Some boys, when they had steady teams, learned to do that and sleep while they walked. But that was a risky business, because you might start sliding back along the towline into the canal and get pushed under by the boat. Or the clevis might break and the evener slap back at you. Chad was on a boat where that happened to a boy the captain had been picking on. The boy had both his legs broken at the knees. The captain started whaling him on the edge of the twopath, but he left off when he saw the boy didn't know anything and left him in a hay barn near the towpath.

Chad quit that boat and signed on a line boat ; and he quit that one night when the captain and the steersman had a fight and the steersman got killed. Chad thought the captain was figuring to fix the murder on him ; he couldn't get rid of a steersman the way you could a driver boy. Chad jumped a boat heading back east, the other way ; he buried himself in the loose wheat of the cargo and stayed there a whole day and most of a night. He slipped off when the boat was tied up and started walking along the towpath.

A little after breakfast time he came into Canastota and he was walking by the Yellow Bud as old Elias Proops came out to pick his teeth in the sunshine. Proops said good-morning to him and asked him where he was going. Proops then said did Chad know how to mind horses ; and when Chad said he did, Proops hollered for Mott, who asked him if he wanted to take care of his horse, mind the tavern barn, and help out with the glasses when business got too big for Mrs. Mott. He offered eleven dollars and board, and Chad had been there ever since.

It wasn't a bad place to work in. There wasn't much work for one thing ; and he liked the horses, when they did show up. Otherwise he had time to fish, or do a little trapping in winter, or sit around the barn or on the porch, as much as he wanted to. Mott was easy-going. Chad figured to stay there for a while longer.

Chad stretched himself and shifted his legs and listened to the agent's horse snuffling for a loose oat. The barn was a nice dry cool place and the loose stall was as good as a sitting-room. He had tacked up a couple of pictures on the walls. One was called " Eliza and her little Sparrow." It was a picture of a young woman with her hair down her back and a sparrow standing on her finger. The other was a picture little Bobby Gray had brought to show him. Bobby had found it in the minister's wastebasket. It was called " The Murderers." It showed two Indians in their leggings. One of them was holding a scalp of a young girl, with the ribbons still in the hair. The other was staring down at the body. Chad thought the clothes ought to look more mussed up. The girl's shoulders were on the ground, but she was lying on one hip. She had a big hip even for a girl, and her petticoat was nice and smooth. Bobby used to come down and stare at it sometimes. Sometimes it made him look as if he wanted to cry. He was a funny little fellow.

Once he asked Chad how the Indians took off a scalp and Chad told him what Elias Proops had said. They made a cut around the crown and took hold of the loose flap and pulled. If it bled a lot to make the fingerhold slippery they used their teeth. Chad thought it would interest Bobby but he went away without saying anything and the next morning Reverend Gray came down to the Yellow Bud and stood outside and told Mr. Mott through the window just what he thought of him, and the loafers that told Bobby stories to give him a screaming fit at night, and what he would like to do to all saloons and the Yellow Bud in particular. Mr. Mott said he was sorry but he couldn't help it if the minister let his son run around saloons.

It was too bad. He didn't know who had told the story to
Bobby, but he knew he hadn't. He didn't aim to go running
down people or telling stories.

The minister was a tall man and he got red in the face. Old
Elias Proops said if he was a minister of the Gospel he would
think burning down saloons would be a bad business. If all the
saloons and all the houses of bad women (he didn't want to
offend Mr. Gray on a public street, he said) went out of business,
how would people like Mr. Gray make their living ?

The minister swallowed a couple of times, without answering
Proops. He just told Mott he hadn't meant wrongfully to
accuse anybody of anything, but he did think Chad Hanna was
a no-good kind of boy and a lot of people in the parish had been
complaining of him.

" He's lazy all right," said Mott, " but I don't know as he does
any harm. He tends my horse and barn, that's all I know about
him."

That was when old Elias made his remark about mushrooms
and birds' eggs and rabbits and Chad Hanna.

3

AL HEENEY

MOST of the people in Canastota took Chad the way Proops did—
he was something that just happened ; or else they took him the
way the minister did. When he first came there they saw he
was a tall, thin, freckled boy with long arms and big hands,
who looked poor, and for a while men kept offering him odd
jobs of extra work. But Chad was better off working for Mott
than he had been on the canal and he didn't see why he should
do anything else. So they started saying he was no good. They
weren't the kind of people who figured that they thought the
work they offered Chad was too dirty for themselves to do. It
got to be a regular saying in some families that if the boys
didn't clean the privies out well every January and July they'd
grow up to be do-nothing no-accounts like Chad Hanna.

Most of the boys wished they were like Chad Hanna just the
same, without any parents, without having to go to school or

do what they didn't want to do. A lot of them didn't dasst be seen anywhere near the Yellow Bud. They met up with him out in the woods to go fishing, if they could persuade him to show them a good hole. Usually they had to pay him money to do it. Bobby Gray was the only one he would take along free any time. He liked Bobby Gray and felt sorry for him, too. First because he was little and scared easy, second because he was the son of Mr. Gray and had to live with him and Chad thought that would mean a hard time for any boy, and mostly because he liked Bobby and he liked the way, even if he was scared by something, he still wanted to find out about it. The funniest thing about him was that he was always telling Chad what his father said. He seemed to think his father knew a lot about things Chad didn't know and if it came to a direct haul of one against the other on any idea except fishing or trapping, Chad had to take the back seat with Bobby.

About four o'clock Chad climbed out of his manger and decided he would sneak down by Purvis's woodshed. If there were any worms in the box of dirt where Purvis kept a stock of worms Chad thought he'd try the riffle. He had closed the back door behind him and was getting set to jump over the manure pile when he heard somebody walk into the barn ; and he turned the door open again, thinking it might be Bobby after all

But it wasn't. It was Al Heeney. He was nosing round at the foot of the hayloft ladder. The door didn't make any noise so Heeney didn't hear him. His head was lifted, and his nose pointed up the ladder, and he looked like a snipe-nosed, under-sized bird dog hitting the scent of a quail on a fence.

Then he said, " Chad. Hey, Chad." But he said it quietly. He looked round once, a quick look, and started to take hold of the ladder rungs with his hand, and then he caught sight of Chad by the door.

He acted foolish, letting go the ladder. His hands bothered him for a minute. Then he tried grinning back at Chad and said, " I didn't hear you nowhere, Chaddy, and I was just going to see if you was in the loft." He made a kind of coughing laugh and said, " And there you was by the back door. It makes me feel kind of comical."

" I guess it does, the way you look."

" I've been meaning to stop and see you sometime, Chaddy."

" Well, now you've done it, ain't you ? "

Al Heeney looked at him awhile. He had yellow-brown eyes and his lips looked as if they lay right on his teeth. He kept moving his lips all the time, even when he wasn't talking, or he touched them with his fingers.

" Yeah," he said.

Chad said. " Looks to me as if you'd got yourself some new clothes since I saw you the last time."

Al said, " Yes, I have." He raised his arm to look at the sleeve of his coat, then he took hold of the lapels and held on. His lips shifted themselves, and he said, " You're trying to make a laughing-stock of me, ain't you ? "

" I don't have to do that," Chad said.

" Now, Chaddy," Al said. " What you acting mad at me about ? "

" Me ? I ain't mad. I just don't like people sneaking into my barn and sticking their nose into my business."

" What business have you got ? " Al asked curiously.

" I've got business putting food into one end of a horse and carrying what he don't want out on a fork," said Chad. " It ain't any business of yourn, that I ever heard of."

Al Heeney made his little cough-laugh. " Now, Chaddy," he said, " I just thought I'd pass a little time with you. There's no harm in looking in a hayloft, is there ? "

" If you still want to look up there, go ahead. I won't stop you."

" What's the sense of me looking up there now I've found out where you are ? "

" That's what I ask you."

" Have a little drink ? " asked Al Heeney.

He pulled a bottle of Lucky Horseshoe whisky out of his pocket and pulled the cork and stuck it under Chad's nose. Chad took it and put some in his mouth. He had never tasted any of that brand. It was rank.

" Thanks," he said, handing it back. " Where'd you get it ? Steal it off a nigger ? "

Al Heeney almost lost hold of the bottle. He didn't say anything for a minute, but just stared with his head turned and his lips drawn over his teeth. He put the bottle to his own mouth and took a long pull without taking his eyes from Chad.

" That's a funny thing you said." His voice sounded careful.

" What was funny ? "

" About stealing whisky off a nigger."

" That's what it tasted like to me," Chad said.

Al Heeney put the bottle back under the tail of his coat.

" What would you say if I did ? " he asked.

Chad sat down on the edge of the manger and let his legs hang. He could tell that Al Heeney was worried, first at having got caught sneaking round the barn, and then at what Chad had said about stealing whisky. But the funny thing was that he should come back with that question. Chad realised that Al wanted to learn something, and the best way for him to find out what was to act dumb-headed. He grinned at Al and said, " Why, if you did, I guess you won't do it again. Not after tasting it."

Al Heeney put his finger to his lips. When he took it away his lips were parted.

" Maybe it ain't too bad."

" Maybe it ain't bad." Chad was agreeable. " It just tastes so."

" Well, you needn't drink any more." Al Heeney leaned himself against what looked like the cleanest part of the stall post. He said, " You're a smart boy, Chad. Ever since I seen you I've always thought you was smart. I've told Cisco more than once, ' Chad's a boy that knows how to keep his mouth shut if he wants to. Chad sees a lot,' I told Cisco, ' but he don't let on about it.' "

Chad didn't say anything.

" That's gospel," Al Heeney said, after a minute.

" I don't talk more'n I have to," Chad said then.

" That's it," said Al Heeney. Chad noticed he was still keeping his voice down. " That's just it. Me and Cisco have been talking about it." He looked round him. It was quiet in the barn. There wasn't a sound except from the agent's horse, which had turned out to be a weaver. The halter rope rubbed the wood as he swung.

" Listen here, Chaddy. What is it a young feller like you wants the most ? "

" I don't know. What is it, Al ? "

" How about money ? "

Chad's lip got long, making his freckled face look solemn. " You offering me money ? " he asked.

" Yes, if you can keep your mouth shut."

" I don't want work," Chad said.

Al Heeney laughed. "Who does? All you got to do is keep your eye open and answer me a question when I come around. Or stop in at Cisco's when anything turns up."

" That sounds all right," Chad said slowly. He had got an idea but he didn't let on. " I guess you wanted to find out something when you came in here, didn't you? "

" That's it," Al Heeney said. " I wanted to look around. But you can tell me better." He fished inside his pocket and brought out a worn piece of paper.

As soon as Chad saw it he knew what it was, and he knew what Al Heeney wanted and how he made his money. A lot of people round Canastota had wondered about Al Heeney. Now and then he or Cisco Trid would disappear from the town, sometimes for as long as two or three months. Sometimes both of them would disappear together. People never saw them leaving town; but when they returned they almost always had money. They didn't throw it around. It was only the fact that they had any money at all that was queer. Neither one of them ever worked; and in a place like Canastota, if a person had a job, someone was bound to know what it was and how much it paid. Chad and Mott and Elias Proops had discussed it once or twice; but they hadn't got ahead any. Now Chad knew.

The paper showed a lithograph of a black man, in a little white jacket and dark trousers, running. He carried a stick on his shoulder with a bundle on the end of it. Chad had often seen the same picture smaller in newspapers. It was a crazy picture, he thought, because the small tree at the negro's back was blowing the way he was going, and the grass at his feet was blowing towards him. Underneath the picture it said :—

$200 REWARD

RAN AWAY from my plantation in Charlotte County, Virginia, on April 27th, the negro man, Henry Prince, aged 28 years ; 5 feet 10 inches high ; chestnut colour ; strong built ; last seen wearing jean trousers and a blue shirt with holes in it ; some marks of the whip and a scar in left leg, made by a scythe, I believe. Middle finger of his right hand is bent into the palm from an old knife wound. Answers quick and likes to talk religion.

Liable to be dangerous. I will give $50 if taken in this
state and $200 if taken out of the state and secured
in jail so I can get him again.

FREDERICK L. SHURTLIEFFE.

He handed it back to Al Heeney without saying anything.
Al took the paper from him, read it through himself as if he
were refreshing his memory, and then put it in his pocket.

" This one ought to be easy to pick out," he said. " That
finger."

Chad said, " Yeah."

" He's worth working for, too," said Al Heeney. " They
don't often run over a hundred. Mostly fifties." He rested one
leg by putting the foot flat against the wall. A look of disgust
came into his narrow face and he took hold of his lip a couple of
times to control it. " Twenty-five dollars ! My God, when you
get the nigger and take him to a sheriff that's friendly and get
the papers made out by a magistrate and then sometimes have
to hire a carriage to get him started out of the town so people
won't see you, and then take him across two states maybe—
and you got to feed him so he won't give out, you know—and
then hire your own way back again—why, for God's sake you
haven't got enough left to buy a spit box."

" I guess maybe that's right," said Chad.

Al Heeney had to get mad. " And you know what a lot of
them twenty-five dollar niggers sell for ? Yes, sir. I've seen 'em
sold right off after delivery. You get twenty-five dollars and
what does the Esquire get ? Well, I've seen him get nearly six
hundred dollars once. That's God's truth. And you ought to
seen the house he lived in. Three stories high and columns
raising right to the top. Him sitting on the porch drinking his
ice drink and a cream coloured gal fanning him with a turkey
fan. He claps his hands and another gal comes out as good
looking as the first one. ' Send for the overseer,' he says. And
when the overseer comes, he says, ' Take them back to the
office,' he says, ' and give this man his money. And Jenkins,'
he says, ' see he leaves by the lower gate. I'm expecting the
cunnel and his friends,' he says. Did he offer me a drink ? Did
he say thank you ? No, twenty-five dollars and get the hell out."

Al Heeney looked over at Chad expecting him to say something so Chad said, " My, my."

"No, sir," Al Heeney said. "I don't deal in any more of this fifty dollar trash. Me nor Cisco both. But two hundred dollars is a chance for profit. You seen anything of a nigger like him?" he asked out and out.

"No," said Chad. "I ain't."

It was the truth. He looked down at his hands which lay on his knees and counted the knuckles.

Al Heeney said, "That's too bad."

"What makes you think you'd find him here?"

"He came through Franklinville," Al Heeney said. "He was in Peterboro four days ago. Cisco picked up word of him there. He didn't turn off to Clinton—I was watching. He come this way sure. Cisco's girl thought she seen a big buck nigger hiding out back of Murphy's hog yard last night. He's bound to be here—the rate he's travelled the last week he's going to need rest. Listen, Chad. You see him and you just drop down to Cisco's. Tell the girl or the old woman if him or me aren't round. If we catch him it'll be worth five dollars to you."

Chad said, "Thanks."

"Don't talk about it," Al Heeney said. "The main thing about this business is for people not to know about it. These God damned abolitionists. Some of them will even help the niggers get away." He buttoned up his coat. "Sometimes it's a lot of work for me and Cisco cornering one. But your five dollars don't mean work—just like I said. Well, I got to find Cisco. He's watching the Cicero road. Come around sometime, even if you don't see this feller. There's always some whisky round the place."

Chad said, "Thanks."

Al Heeney stepped out of the stall, looked round, and went to the door. He looked pleased with himself. Just before he went out, he turned back and said, "That finger."

4

BOBBY GRAY

FOR two or three minutes after Al Heeney had gone Chad sat
still thinking about him. He thought Al Heeney didn't have
much to do with the actual cornering of a runaway negro ; Al
was always a scared shrimpish man if anything noisy started up.
Most likely Cisco Trid was the man who did the final running
down of any negro they were after. Cisco Trid was big enough
to handle a good sized negro by himself.

When he was driving on the canal, Chad had met more than
one negro walking the towpath. They always drifted off into
the brush or the high grass and lay low. They were like rabbits
or nesting guinea hens the way they would just flatten themselves in a piece of grass. It had never occurred to him that
good money could be made picking them up. He always felt
kind of sorry for them.

He unfolded himself off the side of the manger and went to
the door of the barn. He stood there blinking against the sunlight, wiggling his big toe slowly in the hole of his boot. Some
people said he was sly looking, some said he was dumb looking ;
but he thought it would be too bad if he ever looked as sly or as
dumb as Al Heeney. He put his hands into the pockets of his
old black trousers that he wore rolled over the top of his boots.
They'd never been pressed since he put them on and they had
teacup shaped bulges over the knees that gave him a sagged,
shuffling look when he walked.

From the door he could see the canal, the line of forwarding
houses beyond the Yellow Bud, the white canal bridge which
with its reflection made a kind of flat sided circle. A packet boat
was coming through, and the towline was like a small thread
in the eye of a big needle.

The packet boat steersman blew on his bugle and the notes
were so clear Chad felt he could darn near see them. The sound
of them brought Mott out on the porch of the Yellow Bud. It
was a double porch, painted brown. In the bright sunshine it
looked nice against the yellow side walls. Mrs. Mott came out
of the top floor bedroom with a bucket of mop water and threw
it away wide across the towpath and it made a scattered splash

in the canal. Then she leaned on the rail of the porch just above where Mott was standing and asked him if it was the *Henry Clay*. He said so. They went in and the boat hauled right through Canastota, the tandem hitch going well, and the little driver boy riding the back horse cracking his whip like a hundred dollars. He must be new, Chad thought, and he was feeling as big as the President and Congress.

Just as the boat passed, the circus agent came out and sat down next Elias Proops. Diney followed him with a glass of liquor and a sandwich. Without any warning a robin began calling rain in the maple next Chad, and he started back round the barn corner and said, " He's gone. But you better come in the back door."

He went back into the barn and sat down in the manger again, and in a minute Bobby Gray came in barefoot, carrying his shoes in his hand. He took the bucket of water and washed his feet and put the shoes on. And all the time Chad watched him get redder in the face.

" Last time Mamma smelled the manure," he explained.

Chad didn't say anything and Bobby said, " I didn't know you heard me."

" You keep sticking your eye through a knothole that way and someday somebody is going to cut the end off," said Chad.

Bobby giggled. He was a thin little boy, about twelve years old. He had straight brown hair which his parents kept cut long so it flopped over his ears. But he wasn't at all fancy in the clothes he wore. They looked nearly as old as Chad's, though a good deal cleaner.

" I been waiting for you a long time," Chad said. " What's the use of me planning to go fishing with you if you don't show up ? "

" I couldn't help it. Papa asked me a geography question and I didn't remember the answer. And he whopped me and made me study till half an hour ago."

" What's he whop you for all the time ? Don't you have to go to school anyway ? "

" He says I don't work enough. I don't learn good. I get tired listening to Miss Mapes."

" What did he want to know ? " Chad asked curiously.

" He asked me if there were any lions in Madagascar. I said there were."

" Ain't there ? "

" No, of course not. There's nothing bigger than caymans and catarrhine monkeys."

" Did he lick you for that ? "

" No, he asked me how I was going to remember about them, now I'd learned ; and I said I could remember the catarrhine monkeys by Miss Mapes."

Chad laughed, and Bobby felt better. He sat himself down on some straw, shifted for a less uneasy position, and asked, " What did Al Heeney want around this place ? "

Chad said, " I get tired of Al Heeneys and Bobby Grays and the way they stick their noses into my barn."

Bobby looked flushed. " I wasn't trying to nose any."

" You was spying on me through that knothole," Chad said.

" I was not. I was just going to come in when I heard somebody was here and I went around to that old hole so I could tell when he left. Only I couldn't see well, because you moved your back against it. I only heard him say something about a black man."

Chad made no comment.

" Honest I wasn't going to spy." He got himself off his hunkers and squatted instead with his bottom off the floor. His thin pale little face looked all eyes. " I wouldn't do anything to spoil our being friends, Chad. You know that."

Chad looked awful as a judge, not saying a word, sitting up on the manger with his big feet and big hands dangling.

" Chad," Bobby said after a minute. " I—I thought this was sort of both our place. That's why I brought the picture down. But I won't come around any more if you don't want."

" Oh, quit bellering," said Chad. " I ain't mad at you. Only you hadn't ought to take chances of somebody like Al Heeney seeing you. All Heeney wouldn't like it. Cisco Trid and him are mean people."

He looked down at Bobby and saw that he had got very white and was shaking.

" You don't have to be scared though. He didn't notice."

" I'm not scared," Bobby said. " But Chad, I did hear what he said to you. You—you wouldn't do it, would you ? "

" Well, God damn," Chad said. " Do what ? "

" Help out a nigger-chaser," said Bobby.

" Why not ? If I don't somebody else will catch them."

"No they won't. Not when they get this far. Papa says there's nothing to be scared of except Al Heeney and Cisco Trid."

Chad sat up.

"What does your Pa know about those two?"

Bobby turned white. He looked up beseechingly.

"Chad, you won't tell them. I'm not supposed to know about it. If my father thought I'd told you, and you'd told Al, he—he'd be hurt about it."

Chad studied his big toe. He wasn't wiggling it.

"I can't pay you five dollars—not all at once, I can't."

"You shut your mouth." Chad got up. "Who said I was going to hand over niggers? I don't even know where this one is. Though I can get a notion now."

Bobby drew back.

"I didn't say that."

"Look, Bobby. Your Pa don't preach abolition, but you tell me true, is he one?"

"You won't tell them?"

"For God's sake, no."

Bobby nodded his head, looking scared.

"Why don't he preach it then?" Chad asked.

"I heard him telling Mamma he didn't dare. He said if people knew he was he wouldn't be able to help runaways."

"Don't he know that it's breaking the law?"

"I don't know," Bobby said. "He says slavery's sin. He told *me* that, I think so too."

He looked solemn, and Chad thought for an instant that maybe someday Bobby would turn out to be a preacher like his father. He almost had to laugh, though. He couldn't think Reverend Mr. Gray had ever taken off his shoes to walk over a manure pile.

Chad said, "Well, I ain't seen the nigger so I couldn't tell Al about him if I wanted to. But you better tell your Pa that if there's a buck nigger around, a big one, with a bent finger on his right hand, that Al Heeney and Cisco Trid's looking for him. Tell him I said the nigger better lay low."

Bobby got up and looked worried. "Papa's going to be mad. I said I wouldn't come down to the barn any more."

"Well, then, don't tell him. I don't care."

"We can't let them catch the negro, Chad."

" I could tell him," Chad said. " Only then he'd know you told me about him."

Bobby said, " All right, Chad."

He followed Chad to the door and stood to one side while Chad looked out to see if the coast was clear.

" Nobody's round," Chad said, " You better sneak now."

" G'bye," Bobby said. He scurried out and ducked over the fence where the burdocks were showing their ground leaves. They made good cover for a diminutive piece like Bobby later on, but now even a mole could have been seen. He went like a little, scared rabbit, close to the ground and looking, Chad thought, as if a whole pack of Cisco Trids were after him.

Chad waited until he was back of the graveyard fence and then he ambled out himself, with the pockets of his old black pants housing his hands, and his shoes dragging in the warm dust.

He stopped halfway to watch a misguided night crawler trying to rectify his mistake in coming out into sunlight. " Jeepers," he said to himself, " I never told him anything about the circus." Probably Bobby hadn't heard about it yet. Well, he could tell him to-morrow or next day. He put his foot down right on the night crawler, straddling him with heel and sole, and went on looking over his shoulder and laughing to himself.

5

TACKING THE PAPER

As Chad came round the corner of the Yellow Bud, Elias Proops was in the act of jacking himself out of his chair, and Chad gave him a haul on the suspenders. Elias yelped for the buttons' sake, but they held. When he was on his feet and had got his breath moving right, he explained : " That circus feller, Bisbee, says he's going to stick up his poster in the bar. Want to come along ? "

" All right," Chad said. " He's routing it through here, then ? "

" God A'mighty," Elias said scornfully. " It's been coming

all the time, only he was trying to play cute getting his board and the circus lot for nothing. He says they'll per-form in Vernon June eleven, he says, and they'll drag over here that night and per-form here on the thirteenth."

" Why don't they do it the twelfth ? "

" My God," says Elias, " you're an ignorant pup. They don't per-form on Sundays. Ministers don't like it. They think the circus is horning in on their own show if they do that. Bisbee went and told Mr. Gray they wouldn't per-form Sunday and said he hoped Gray would come to the show on Monday. Gray told him he'd never been to a circus and didn't think he'd come now. Imagine that ! A grown man like him never seen a circus per-form in his life."

" That's a new word you've got, ain't it ? " Chad said.

Elias got mad and stopped to tell Chad something, but then he heard a hammer striking inside and he nearly fell down trying to get through the door.

" You said you'd wait till I got inside," he said accusingly.

Bisbee turned his smart, horse's eyes on Elias and said, " It's all right, Granpa. I was only sinking a nail in the bar."

" I wanted to see it go up," said Elias. He worked his stiff knees hard, crossing the room in a hurry, and let himself down on a chair in the corner. " Go ahead," he said.

Mott was behind the bar, slicking it with a rag ; and Mrs. Mott stood in the kitchen door with a boiled-turnip smell breezing in past her.

Bisbee gave her a sort of bow as he unrolled the poster.

" I been thinking that between the windows is the best place," he said, " What do you think, ma'am ? "

Mrs. Mott's thin face got red. She said, " That would be real nice, I think," and her voice went way up and broke apart so comically, that Chad put his hand in front of his mouth. But nobody would have noticed him if he hadn't. Mott said, " Yeah. It would look good between the windows. There's room for it there. But maybe if it set on the other wall the lamp would shine on it better."

" That's right," said Bisbee.

Mrs. Mott turned on Mott and said, " You fool, then the sun would shine on it and fade the print."

Mott wiped his hands on the wet rag and looked foolish, and the circus agent looked admiringly at Mrs. Mott, and said, " I wouldn't have thought of that, either. Though this poster is printed with good ink, you don't want to chance it."

The circus agent unrolled the poster as far as he could and held it up in the space between the windows and everybody admitted it filled the wall nice there but that it was hard to see. Mott asked Chad whether he had any ideas about it and Chad said may be they ought to tack it up in the corner so Elias Proops wouldn't have to unbend his knees to read it, and Bisbee laughed politely because it was a joke and then stopped laughing because Proops looked mad, and Mrs. Mott said Chad had a loose tongue. Bisbee stood there with his arms stretched like somebody ready for a fancy dance, his long face patient and intelligent. Nobody seemed to know what to do for a minute and then Diney, the coloured girl, came in and said it was pretty and why didn't they tack it back of the bar, at the end.

Right away everybody realised that was the place they would have thought of themselves if she hadn't interupted them. In the first place it got enough light in the daytime, and in the second place the bar lamp would shine on it at night. Besides, as Diney said, " You leave it where de men come close an' read it with dey fingers, an' they're gwine dirty it all up." But Elias pointed out the real advantage, which was that it could only be seen from the end of the bar, and was far enough back so only one man at a time, standing at the end, could read the small print. " When they make a line starting from there," he said, " the natural Adam in them's going to make them line along the bar. And a man can't lean against a bar without he's got a glass in his hand."

So Bisbee went behind the bar and Mott held the hammer for him and Mrs. Mott came round front to hand him tacks. Bisbee was handy, he had it on the wall in two minutes, and then he and Mott came out front and Elias even got out of his chair, and they all looked at it. It looked beautiful. In a strange way it brought into the room's dull, brown-painted walls a feeling of excitement and movement. Entering by the door from the canal porch, a solitary, fat bluebottle fly buzzed the length of the room, headed right, and disappeared into the turnip smell in the kitchen.

Mrs. Mott's face was invaded by a strange look of hunger. " It seems a long time off," she said, and swallowed. Then she laughed self-consciously. " What am I doing standing here ? "

she wanted to know. " You, Diney, you get back where you belong."

The coloured girl started. The whites of her eyes showed suddenly and she passed her pinkish tongue over her lips. Then, without a word, she turned, her thin hollow back preceding Mrs. Mott's bent shoulders into the kitchen. The door closed on them, leaving a kind stillness in the turnip smell and the men looked at each other as though somebody had picked up their lives for them.

Bisbee said, " I better get out and get my posters tacked before dark. Want to come along ? " he asked Chad.

Chad said he wouldn't mind. While Bisbee was assembling his tacks and hammer, Chad went over to the end of the bar and had another good look at the picture of Lady Lillian on her academy horse, and he realised that the picture didn't show what she looked like at all. It might have been the figure of any woman on any horse, sitting a little stiff, too, on the sidesaddle. Once or twice outside one of the big places like Albany or Utica he had seen a woman riding a horse like that, but never close to. He began to feel curious about her, not as something merely to look at, but as to what kind of person she was ; and as he went out with Bisbee he would have liked to ask him about her.

Like his horse, Bisbee had a fast walk. He seemed in a hurry to get his posters tacked up. " I want to go to the taverns, the groceries and the stores, and the busiest blacksmith, he told Chad. " And then we'll stop at the church sheds and the feed stores. How many does that make ? "

Chad figured.

" Fourteen, I guess, Mr. Bisbee."

Bisbee sounded impressed. " It's quite a town, ain't it ? "

It didn't take much time to post the grocery stores. He handed out a free pass in each. " A woman always believes what a grocer tells her," he explained to Chad, " so long as it ain't about groceries." It took him longer at the taverns ; he emerged each time with the gin on his breath refreshed. Chad, lounging against a tree outside, got surly waiting for him. But Bisbee took hold of his arm in a friendly way and walked beside him to the next place. " Yes, sir," he said. " You take the bar-keeps and the storekeeps, and between them they know every-body there is in a town and they know how to talk to them too."

" Then what's the use of putting up the posters in the horse sheds ? " Chad asked.,

" They're for the horses to look at," said Bisbee. " Did you ever stop to think how sick a horse must get of studying a cure for human piles ? "

They went round the corner of the Methodist Church and Bisbee sat on the hitch rail while Chad tacked the poster for him. Then they stopped at Luther Frank's blacksmith's shop and put up a poster over the row of nail boxes by the front window. Luther Frank was cold-shoeing a canal horse from the relay stable of the Insured Transportation Line. The hostler explained sourly that the poor brute had been in only two hours but would have to go out on another boat because the stable was short. The animal looked as though the wind must moan when it blew against his ribs. The loafers and the hostler came over to look at the circus poster, but the smith kept on with his work until he was done with the rasp. Then he came over too, looked the poster over, and untied the strings of his leather apron.

" How many horses does the circus have ? " he asked.

" Thirteen," said Bisbee.

" Well, maybe there'll be some business for me." He hung the apron on a nail and said to the hostler, " Take that horse out of here. The only decent thing on him is the shoe."

One of the loafers asked, " Is there wimmen in it ? "

" Can't you see the picture ? " one of the others said.

" I don't mean her ; she's a lady," said the loafer. " I mean Wimmen. I heard a preacher once. I mean wimmen like them."

Bisbee said, " I don't know what the preacher said."

" It was something ! " said the loafer.

" We have female performers," Bisbee said. " All of them are celebrated in their acts."

" By God, I'm going to it."

A farmer came down the street with an old horse and the smith cursed and put his apron on and started blowing up his fire with a sad hand on the bellows. Bisbee went oustide.

Apparently word about the posters had got around, for a string of small boys came down the street and ran into the shop. The blacksmith started whanging his hammer on the anvil and yelling at them, and in a minute they came streaming out into the street, where they scattered, then bunched again, and lined out towards the centre of town yapping like a bunch of puppies.

" They didn't see us," Bisbee said to Chad. " Generally they catch on quicker. There'll be two or three show up when I tack the first card, and then they'll commence gathering and tag me all around the town. It's a funny thing. I travelled fifteen years ago for a little one wagon show. We had three acrobats and a man that could only just stand up on a pad. Five horses—the pad horse, two to pull the wagon, one I rode on, and one we had that had gone lame. Imagine that, only five horses. But I wasn't telling you about the show. It was about boys. I used to go half a day ahead of the show, to pick a yard or a barn to play in if it looked like rain because we didn't have no tent in those days. All I had was wafers, about four by ten inches, and when I stuck them up on the notice boards in bars and canal offices they hardly showed at all and the print was so small a fly could read it sitting down." Bisbee walked with his long nervous stride for a while as if he had forgotten where he was or what he was talking about, and Chad went along without listening. It was getting dark, and people had finished their suppers and he wished he had his.

" We hadn't done much business," continued Bisbee, " and we didn't hardly have enough to eat, so we stopped at every place where there was a store or a tavern to get us enough to live on—if we could—till we got to the next place. We had got up into the hills in Allegany County, and I tell you that was a wild place in those days and the roads so bad you couldn't have taken a four-horse hitch round some of the corners. Well, I came into a funny little place they call Centre Almond about one o'clock one day and there was a gristmill, and a tavern and two houses, and I thought I'd post it, because the show couldn't reach the next place, Angelica, before night. I stuck up one of those wafers on the tavern porch before I went inside to see if I could use the yard, and a little boy saw me tack it up. We called the show BOSWORTH'S FAMOUS COLUMBIAN EX-HIBITION *and* CIRCUS, and the boy could read the big print, and he yelled at me, ' Where's the clown ? ' " He turned his long face to Chad and regarded him gravely. " You can't believe it. There'd never been a circus there. What did he know about one ? But he did. He was back at four o'clock with about eight other boys and quite a lot of settlers and we had a crowd of twenty-five waiting on the tavern porch when the wagons pulled in and the clown—Lord, he was a terrible clown—started playing the hurdy gurdy. They didn't even have twenty-five cents, a lot of them, and part of our money was a ham, seven eggs, and a string of beads a half-breed Indian girl had brought along."

Chad said "Yeah" mechanically and Bisbee turned his face front. But after a minute he asked, "What's on your mind?"

"Nothing," said Chad.

"All right," Bisbee said. "It don't bother me." But whether it was the gin or because he was going back with Chad to get his supper or something else he seemed to want to talk.

"It's surely changed since then," he said.

"What has?"

"Circuses."

"Oh," said Chad.

Bisbee gave it up. "Ain't you listening to me?"

"Yes, I am. Is this Signor Rossello good?"

"Didn't you read the poster?"

"I read some."

"I bet you read about Lady Lillian, hey?"

"I read about her. Is she good?"

"My God," said Bisbee. "They're both of them better than anything *you* ever saw."

"What's her last name?" Chad asked.

Bisbee smiled.

"Vail. Lady Lillian Vail."

"What's the Lady part of it for?"

"I don't know. But it sounds good. It sounds the way she looks. High toned. And she can ride, too. You better go see her."

"I figure to," Chad said.

They were close up to the Yellow Bud now. It was nearly dark and a boat, hauling through town, had its bow lantern lit. The yellow globe of light, seen through the porch posts, appeared to wink on and off, like a deliberate firefly.

"Well," said Bisbee, taking the roll of posters from Chad's hands, "thanks for coming along. Here's your pass. Don't lose it."

"Thanks," said Chad.

He wandered round to the back door, thinking about Bisbee.

He thought Bisbee must have been around the country a lot
in his life. He didn't tell you anything, even when he was
talking, except just what he wanted you to know. He hadn't
said anything about Lady Lillian that Chad wanted to know.
Even if Chad had had more time, Bisbee wouldn't have said
more than what you could find out from the posters.

Chad dragged his foot to get a little road dust in through
the hole in his boot where he could work it around with his big
toe. The dust felt cool. He would just plain have to wait to find
out what she really looked like. He didn't mind. Waiting was
something he never minded doing. He felt lazy all over anti-
cipating that time.

Still hanging on, the turnip smell made a kind of barricade
round the kitchen porch that he entered from the outside. He
was right in the middle of it when he heard a noise beside the
little knoll where Mott had a hogshead sunk in the ground for
smoking hams.

" Chad."

He stopped, one foot on each step of the porch, and turned
his face slowly.

" It's me, Bobby."

" What are you doing here ? " Chad said.

Bobby said, " Shhh ! Come out here, Chad." And as Chad
lingered, he said, " Please," in his high urgent voice.

Inside the kitchen Mrs. Mott suddenly went on the rampage.
" You Diney," she said. Then louder, " *Diney !* " Then Chad
heard her feet slap into the kitchen. " DI-NEY ! " He heard her
wrench the pantry door open. " Where are you ? " she said.
She called out, " Paul ! You seen Diney ? " " No," Mott
answered from the bar. " She ain't here," said Mrs. Mott.
" Send Chad up to her room," Mott suggested.

" Chad," yelled Mrs. Mott. " You, Chad."

Chad came down off the porch steps with a greased easiness
of feet that made no sound. He slunk into the shadows towards
where the hogshead was. " Chad," whispered Bobby.

" Keep your mouth shut," Chad said. " Lay down."

He lay down beside Bobby behind the low mound just as
Mrs. Mott opened the back door and came out with the light
on to the porch. She stood there with her tired slouched shoulders
straining her eyes against the darkness.

" Diney ! " she called. Then, " Chad ! "

It struck Chad as comical and he put his face down into his hand and snickered. He was all relaxed on the dewy rough grass, his body fitting the ground. Beside him Bobby Gray quivered like a little nervous dog. There was a faint smell of crystallised soot from the charred smoke barrel, as if in the course of years a suppuration had gradually occurred and even the grass roots had become impregnated.

Mrs. Mott shaded her eyes against the light that came past her, holding her hands like blinders on a headstall, and moved her head right and left, peering into the dark.

" I can't see either one of them anywheres," she complained loudly.

Behind her through the lighted doorway they saw Mott enter the kitchen, and come past the new stove.

" No use hollering. Bisbee's waiting for his supper. You better fetch it in yourself. He picked a friedcake out of the jar, bit into it, and went back past the stove. Mrs. Mott reluctantly went into the house. When she had got Bisbee's plate, she stopped again by the open door, looked out, and said, " That black lazy bitch. No wonder they whip them."

Chad let go of Bobby, who rolled on to his knees.

Bobby said, " Papa wants to see you right away."

6

ON THE TOWPATH

CHAD waited till they had stepped into the inky dark made by the projecting upper story of Reeder's Feed Store. Then he stopped so short that Bobby bumped into him.

" He does, does he ? " he said.

" Yes," Bobby said. " He said for me to fetch you right away. I've been waiting for a long time, Chad." He sounded anxious and strained.

Chad felt like worrying him.

" I don't see what business *he's* got sending for me, the way he came down here and called me names. I ain't had any supper either."

Bobby was miserably silent. He could see how Chad felt

C.H.   B 2

about it ; he had thought the same way himself earlier in the
evening, but he hadn't known how to explain the awkwardness
to his father. Finally he said, " It isn't about you, Chad. It's
about that negro. I told him."

Chad jumped on that. " Oh, I'm not good enough so he
wants to see me. It's only because there's a black nigger mixed
up somewhere, so he wants me to come. That makes it just
dandy."

He felt pleased with himself. He could tell how bad Bobby
was feeling, too. Bobby was so easy to devil Chad couldn't help
acting up. He felt fine. He had always been curious to see the
inside of the minister's house, and now that the minister had
had to send for him, he could go in owing nobody nothing.

Bobby Gray could just make him out against the faint shine
on the canal water. He had his hands in his trousers' pockets
and was slouching his weight on one foot. In the darkness his
shape was long and thin, like a thoughtful bittern, and to the
boy he looked just about as sympathetic.

" He didn't say anything real bad about you, Chad. He
only said you were lazy. . . ."

Chad didn't move, but his voice came down at Bobby like a
hand in the dark. " Keep quiet."

Bobby pressed back into the corner made by the loading
platform, and suddenly Chad moved in with him. " Stay tight
against the wall," he whispered.

There was nothing out of the ordinary to see in the darkness.
The bar windows of the Yellow Bud shone out over the towpath on to the canal basin, making a shadow pattern of their
frames, the porch rail and the posts with braces large as tree
limbs. The Yellow Bud itself was just a darker block against the
sky.

Bobby could see the shape of the towpath, which cast a
shadow of its own on the water. Beyond that line the water
showed smooth and dark, and the opposite berm stood out plain
with its grass, new mullein leaves, and thistle growth, where the
window light touched it. Farther along the canal was Eliab
Joslin's Canal House. There was only one lit window and it was
so far away it seemed to cast no light.

Nothing moved anywhere. It was so still that Bobby could
hear the late peepers along the rush banks of the wide water to
the east. And it struck him queer that he had not seen a boat

for a long time. He looked up at Chad, but Chad was invisible against the wall.

Chad must have felt him move for his hand came down on Bobby's shoulder, warm and large ; and it made Bobby feel pleased and excited. Then he heard the feet coming rapidly towards the canal.

They stopped a moment with a faint shuffling sound before the person stepped out on to the towpath. It was a woman. The skirt and the thin ankles showed against the light from the Yellow Bud. Then, as the woman moved forward, they saw her for an instant entire, Mott's negro wench, Diney.

Chad wondered where she had been. She had a piece of towel in one hand, which she suddenly stuffed inside the breast of her dress. She went towards the Yellow Bud quickly and furtively. She moved like an animal, bent from her hips, her head turning first to one side and then the other. She had gone only a few steps when she stopped short.

A man walked right out of nowhere on to the towpath and took hold of her arm. Diney uttered a queer bleating sound and froze.

The man said, " Where you been ? "

But she didn't say anything.

He said again, " You tell me where you been."

She said then, " I don' know." Then she flinched and turned her face to the man, and he said, " Don't make no noise. You tell me what you been doing and I won't hurt you."

Chad whispered to Bobby, " You sneak round back and go home. I'll be up there pretty soon." He felt Bobby shaking. " You don't need to get scared. Don't let anybody see you." Bobby nodded. He watched Chad's figure emerge from the darkness and move down along the towpath. Chad made no noise. Then Bobby himself sneaked round the feed store and went for home.

Chad moved down the towpath and got within twenty feet of the man and the negress. The man was twisting her arm and she wasn't saying a thing.

Chad said, " That you, Diney ? " and started to run. The man turned without looking and jumped off the towpath. He went like a scared horse. Chad let him go. He didn't see any sense to running in the darkness after somebody he didn't know the identity of. Instead he took out after Diney, who was making tracks herself. She didn't go for the kitchen but headed round it for the back-house. She bolted into it and shut the door.

Chad moved cautiously up to the side wall and said " Diney," quietly. He heard her stir like a fluttered hen. Then she was still. He said, " It's me, Chad. Who was that feller ? " He could hear her breathing.

She said, " You go way."

He said, " Did he hurt you ? "

" No, he didn'. Not much."

" Didn't you see who it was ? "

" I ain' sayin'. I ain' sayin' nothin'." He could tell she was getting over her fright.

" You better stick around home," he said.

" I am, *sir* ! " she said. " Don' catch this nigger out no mo'. I ain' riskin' my place again for no black niggers no mo'."

" Mrs. Mott's been yelling for you. She'll have your hide if you don't think up a good story," Chad said.

Diney giggled inside the back-house.

" I been sick," she said. " I been sick here."

Chad grinned and ambled away towards the bridge. He went along the south side of the canal as far as the creek and then struck down into its bank, went through some brush, and waited.

Diney was a queer girl, he thought. The way the man had been twisting her arm would have made any ordinary girl yell, but she had been like a dumb sheep suffering it. Maybe it was because she was coloured. Coloured people had a queer silent ability to stand hard luck ; most of them would hole up out of sight if they got sick or got hurt. Diney wouldn't think of telling on that man, even to Chad.

When he had stood still for about ten minutes and heard nobody behind him in the brush, Chad decided that he had not been followed. He began moving himself. He went as quietly as an Indian, setting his feet lightly, and followed the creek shore for about a hundred yards before he came out into the open again.

There he waited for another five minutes, not trying to see through the darkness, but listening. The woods behind him were quiet. He could hear the full sound of the creek well back of him, but there was nothing in between.

He struck out across the open, heading on a slant towards

Peterboro Street. He walked along that until he was a hundred yards from the Gray house, then turned through Fay's land and came out on Main Street. Most of the places had been dark, but there was a light in Hitchcock's store, and through the window he made out Mr. Sam Hitchcock in back working over his books. He looked at him a minute, thinking if he had money enough he wouldn't mind having to keep track of it in books. Then Mrs. Hitchcock came in in a kind of wrapper. She was carrying a dipper and he saw her fill it from a sugar barrel and return towards the rear of the store. The wrapper made her shapeless. She didn't look as handsome as she did in a dress.

Chad watched with a curious sort of interest to make out how people carried on together. He saw Mr. Sam look up suddenly from his books. Sam had a solemn face and it looked real solemn as he talked. Chad couldn't hear a sound. The whole thing went on in dumb show. Mrs. Hitchcock was saying something. She had let her wrapper slide open and her face looked scornful. She held out the dipper as if to show Sam what she had in it. And he got down off his stool and picked up his candle and took the dipper out of her hand and went back with it into the store. He poured the sugar out on the scale tray and weighed it and Mrs. Hitchcock stood behind him and laughed. When he had weighed it he got some more in the dipper and sifted it out. Chad thought he must be making up a pound by the looks of the pile. Then Sam put the sugar back in the dipper and handed it to Mrs. Hitchcock and she laughed again and put her hand through his hair, quite rough, and kissed him and went out of sight, while Sam returned to his stool, reached for a paper, and made a note with his pen. He looked sleepy, and Chad thought all of a sudden that Hitchcock was a poor damn fool wasting his time.

Thinking about a man wasting time made Chad realise he was wasting time himself, even if it wasn't as pleasurable a kind of it. He moved round the store and gave a low whistle so Hitchcock's rabbit dog would know who he was. Most of the dogs in town did. Most of them would rather go off with Chad than with their own people. Hitchcock's old dog was one he depended on. The dog hauled himself out from his barrel in the back shed and came over to smell of Chad's ankles with a cool nose. Chad heard his tail whipping in the dirt and reached down and took hold of his nose and squeezed it. It made the dog sneeze. It was a big noise and Mrs. Hitchcock cried to him from the back window to go to bed.

The dog and Chad both stood still looking at the dark window—knowing they couldn't be seen. They could just make out a pale shape of her standing by the cool open window in her nightgown. It made Chad realise all at once that she was a young woman. Only a young woman would stand that way in an open window, and be bothered by a dog's sneezing. It was comical to think of ; with her husband back in the store figuring out how much money he had made that month.

Chad heard the dog's tail whip the dust again and he eased himself away from the shed and headed for the back of the minister's house. He had to go through Hitchcock's back yard— he knew that well enough to dodge the manure pile and the trash heap ; but when he crossed through into the Grays' yard he was in strange ground, and had to go slow.

It was dark there. He could not make out the rabbit dog, which had no white spot on him to mark. The window that was lit in the back of the house had a curtain over it and made only a brown square, that shed no light outdoors.

The yard was neat. There was a clean lime smell from the back-house and the walks in the garden patch were raked smooth. Chad went easy, letting the old dog snuffle along ahead. The old dog was doing a good deal of scent-eating, taking it in in gulps and swallowing about it. It wasn't a rabbit, Chad decided all at once. The old dog would hit a rabbit track and go off like a four-horse mail coach whipping the wheelers. The old dog wasn't liking what he got out of the smell at all. He considered the minister's back yard, which had no dog, just as much his own as Hitchcock's. He growled a couple of times and then suddenly bored off for the lilac bush beyond the well. His barking was mad and short and he came to whatever he was after almost at once because he stopped dead and the other thing yelped and then the barking started all over and the two of them lit out for glory round the house.

Chad ran round the other side and got there in time to see them passing down the street towards the canal. When they went through the light in front of Hawley's house the rabbit dog was reaching for the man's heels at every jump, and at every other jump he seemed to be getting home. The man was Al Heeney.

Chad had to laugh. He was still chuckling a minute or two later when the old dog came trotting back through the light rolling a little from side to side, and obviously feeling big.

As he returned to the back of the house it occurred to him as strange that nobody had come out to see what all the ruction was about. He looked up at the windows as he went by, but he couldn't see so much as a curtain edged open. It seemed to him a queer way to act. He climbed the porch steps and knocked on the kitchen door.

7

THE MINISTER'S HOUSE

THE door was opened at once by Bobby Gray.

"Gee, it took you a long time, Chad," he said.

Chad stepped inside and closed the door after him.

"I didn't want people to see me coming here," he said. He looked round him. The kitchen was just like plenty of other kitchens he had been in. But it made him feel vaguely uneasy, and after a moment he took his hat off. As he did so he caught Bobby staring at him and asked him what he was staring for. Bobby flushed and said he wasn't.

"Papa's in his room," he said. He led the way through the door out into a narrow hall where there was a coat tree and a pretty lithograph of " Rachel at the Well."

The hall made Chad more uneasy than the kitchen had and he felt annoyed. He didn't see why he should feel troubled by any house, least of all this one where he had been asked to come to help the minister out. But he wondered if there were any mud from the garden on his shoes.

He didn't have time to look because Bobby had knocked on the left-hand door. Beyond it the minister's voice told them to come in and Bobby opened the door and signed to Chad to enter.

Mr. Gray was sitting at a narrow walnut desk with pigeon-holes of light maple. His shirt-sleeved shoulders rose high above his coat, which was hung neatly over the chair he sat on. Though he bent a little to his writing, his gaunt back remained straight, and the uncompromising action of his shoulder-blades was visible through the waistcoat. He finished his paragraph, the pen stopping on a periodic squeak, before he rose and, only when he was erect, turned to face them.

There was a top-heavy look to his long face ; the brow was wide and full-templed, the jaw pointed, the mouth repressed. His deep-set, thin-lidded eyes had a nervous brilliance, and his natural voice was like his praying voice, high-pitched but flat.

" Good-evening," he said. " Sit down if you want to." He pointed to the second chair, but stayed erect himself, resting the fingers of his left hand on the corner of the desk, and listened with a kind of restrained relish to Chad's mumbled reply. He revealed no embarrassment himself as he went on, " I've never had a high opinion of you, Hanna. But it seems from what Robert has told me that I may not have judged you altogether justly."

Chad did not say anything. He supposed that this might be Mr. Gray's way of saying he was sorry. He didn't want to make Bobby uncomfortable by looking at him, so he looked round the room. It was a little like an office, with dark brown wallpaper and three small engravings on the walls—one of " The Dead Sea," one of " The Shipwreck," and one of " The Tomb."

Mr. Gray said suddenly, " I never suspected that you might be one of us," and Chad was so surprised he said, " One of who ? "

" One of those who have enough clear sight to see that slavery is an abomination before God. Born free and equal ! Life, Liberty and the Pursuit of Happiness ! " The minister's voice was bitter with scorn. " How long will it be before people open their eyes, if not their hearts ? Here I have to work with one or two people, and who are they ? A hired girl at a local saloon ! She's willing to carry food to one of her own race. A freighter on a local stage, who'll only help when his wagon has no other riders. Now you."

He looked over Chad's head so fixedly that Chad felt he should say something. He said, " Diney swears she won't take any more food. She nearly got caught by a man to-night. He scared her bad."

" Who was it ? " Mr. Gray asked with sudden practicality.

" I don't know, Mr. Gray. He ran off when I came up."

" Was it this Heeney fellow ? "

"No, he was outside your house. That racket was him being chased by Hitchcock's dog."

"They're watching me, then," said Mr. Gray. "I thought there was someone last night. He drew his breath. "I've lost Diney apparently. Well, it's lucky I've found that you think the way I do."

"I never thought about it," Chad said awkwardly.

"You refused his bribe."

"I didn't know where the nigger was and I don't like Al Heeney."

Mr. Gray stared at him. His voice dropped and he said, "Are you willing to help me?"

"Yes," said Chad. "But I'm not no abolitionist."

"Then what did you come here for?"

"Bobby asked me and he's a friend of mine. Besides," Chad grinned, "I wouldn't mind cheating a feller like Al."

Mr. Gray made a gesture with his hands—as if he called the Lord to witness the help that he was sent.

"I can't pay you anything," he said.

Chad said, "You needn't."

"If only some of the people who could help, who have the money and the position to be leaders of thought in this town . . ."

Chad waited for the sentence to end, but Mr. Gray let it drop. So he asked, "How about Reverend Snell at the Reformed Church?"

"He agrees with us in theory. But he can't do anything. He can't afford to risk losing his church. The feeling's very strong in his church against breaking the Slave Law. For that matter," said Mr. Gray, "it is in mine. I worked hard to get this church, and I've got to keep it if I can for my family's sake. I'd have a hard time getting another."

Chad looked at him. He didn't understand him very well. He had never thought of a minister's work as a job, but it was probably so.

"I've had to be careful," said Mr. Gray. "I've not even subscribed to the *Freeman* for fear people would start talking. I have to live like a criminal. I am a criminal under this abominable law. Did you read the handbill for Henry?" he asked Chad.

"Robert said you had."

"Yes, sir."

"He's to be identified by marks like a branded animal. I've

seen others too—worse marked than he. Cropped ears, a joint cut off a finger. Do you suppose God thinks it wrong to help abused beings like that ? "

He stared at Chad again, and swallowed suddenly. Chad thought for a minute he was going to cry, but his mouth stayed tight and his face was cold. Chad had never talked to a man like Mr. Gray. He wondered whether it was religion that made a man like that. Then he saw Bobby out of the tail of his eye, and Bobby had a tense whiteness on his small face.

" Where is this nigger, Mr. Gray ? "

" He's safe enough for now," said the minister. " But I can't go to him myself as long as they're watching me. I'll have to depend on you, now that Diney's been scared. If you're willing to help."

He seemed to be trying to make up his mind if Chad was safe. Chad understood. " I won't tell on him, or you either," he said, " seeing Bobby here's a friend of mine. If you'll tell me where the nigger is I'll go down to-night and start him for wherever you say."

Mr. Gray gave a thin smile.

" Thank you, Hanna. The trouble is the poor fellow can't walk. He was shot at when he was leaving Peterboro. He was hit in the leg. And he barely managed to get here. I had a hard time making him go as far as the hideaway. If we had a decent hiding place in this house, I'd have kept him here. I was tempted, it's lucky I didn't do it." He paused. " Now I don't see what in the world we can do."

Chad thought swiftly. It seemed to him this business might have fun in it. He said, " You get Mrs. Gray to give Bobby lunch enough for him and me to go fishing. We'll go, but we'll give it to the nigger. I'll see how he is and maybe I can work out some way we can get him going. Where'll he go to when he leaves ? "

" He'll go to Cicero. He knows the name of the farm."

" Well," said Chad, " you ain't told me where he is yet."

Mr. Gray looked at him hard.

" He's in an old potato hole on the edge of the hickory grove near the Jarvis place. You know those pines along the brook ? " Chad nodded. " And you know where the north corner of Jarvis's east field is ? It's planted to wheat, I think."

" Barley," said Chad.

" Perhaps," Mr. Gray said. " You head for it from the pines

The hole is about halfway." He paused. "What do you plan to do?"

"I'll have to see the nigger first. That's what I want the lunch for. Of course," he said slyly, "me and Bobby will have to *go* fishing. He wants to sneak down into the barn just as if you still didn't want him to waste his time with me. He met the minister's eye with a blank face. "We don't want Al Heeney to figure you and me are getting together in this, Mr. Gray. And I'll have to talk to Elias Proops about it."

Mr. Gray jerked his shoulders. "That . . ." he began, but checked himself and an expression of bitter humility passed over his face. "You do what you think best." Chad felt like hugging himself inside—it was a wonderful idea getting all the people the minister had run down to help him out. But his long lip remained sober.

"There's one thing more," he said. "If I have to move the nigger quick, I'll need a horse. Mott's horse is no good, so I'll have to borrow yours. You still keep him in Turner's pasture, don't you?"

"Yes," said Mr. Gray. "But he's an easily marked horse, and he might be recognised."

"Don't worry." Chad grinned. "Nobody'll know about it. You won't yourself."

Mr. Gray held out his hand. "Be careful," he said. A little colour came into his face. "I wish I were young and could come with you."

He sounded as if he meant it. Chad shook hands dubiously. As he and Bobby stepped into the hall, they were confronted by Mrs. Gray in the kitchen door. "Bobby told me you hadn't had anything to eat to-night. I've got something for you." She was a pleasant-faced, small woman with a very low voice. She smiled as she gave him a cup of tea and a plate of beans from a hot pan, with tomato relish and a wedge of blackberry pie. "Bobby tells me a lot about you, Chad," she said. "I'm glad he has such a good friend."

Chad turned red to the ears. "Bobby's all right," he said. "He can look out for himself." She did not make him embarrassed, only shy. He got a different idea of the kitchen, too, with her in it. It was a nice place, the food was good, and the very clean smell seemed like something kind. Bobby was smiling too, lounging on the ettle by the stove. His older sister came in and sat down beside him with a piece of family sewing in her hand. Chad only flicked a glance at her, finding her level eyes on him. She looked a little like her mother, except in height, which she inherited from the minister. She was about fifteen or sixteen, with a braid down her back ; but she was beginning to look like a woman dressed up as a girl.

Chad wasn't usually shy of girls ; but she wasn't like the girls a driver could pick up along the towpath. He wondered why he hadn't ever noticed her before. Bobby didn't talk about her much—Chad didn't even know her name. Looking through his sandy lashes he could make out that she was keeping on with her sewing. " She thinks I'm just a big galoot," he thought, conscious of his heavy boots, probably with mud on them, and Lord knew what else, trailing through back yards the way he had been that night.

To Chad the three made a kind of picture together. They didn't need conversation to make themselves appear happy. Of course, there was the presence of the minister beyond the door to account for their quiet ways ; but they didn't seem uncomfortable about it. Chad felt happy watching them as he ate. He didn't let them know he was watching ; and they paid no attention to him, except when Bobby explained that his father had said he could go fishing with Chad to-morrow, and could his mother fix them a lunch. She said Yes, smiling, and said Edith could fix it for them while she herself was getting breakfast, so Chad learned the girl's name.

When he was through he thanked Mrs. Gray and got up to go. She said for him to come again. Edith got up too. She gave a cool smile. When she did he saw a dusting of freckles across her nose. She had one of those pale skins that go sometimes with light brown hair, but that look alive. She had very dark grey eyes, like her mother. After he had seen that he didn't look above her hands.

He said to Bobby on the stoop, " Don't open the door again till I get away."

" All right," whispered Bobby. He moved stiffly like an excited pup smelling game. " Where'll I meet you to-morrow ? "

" Back of the barn, same as usual."

" When ? "

" Early." Chad made his voice heavy : " You better show up or you'll get whopped for *not* going fishing with me."

Bobby giggled as he watched Chad drift off the porch into the dark of the yard. In only a minute he couldn't even hear him, so he went inside.

Chad was leaning on the coping of the well, with the cool updraught against his face, thinking about the Gray family. They had surely been nice and he had got to feeling almost homey there in the kitchen ; but now, outside, it began to seem different to him, as if they were being nice to him as well as just being nice. He couldn't put his finger on it ; but the thought troubled him.

It wasn't that he wished he was the same as them, though they were nice people. " Hell," he thought, " they don't even know how to have fun." But that wasn't so. He knew it.

The light went out of the kitchen window. It came on in two upstairs rooms, then in the peak under the eaves. The last was Bobby's room, he knew. He wondered which was Mrs. Gray's and which the girl's. He waited till they went out too. There wasn't anybody in the yard. Nothing stirred at all except bats and you couldn't see them. He started off, flat-footed, towards the canal.

8

POTATO PIT

ELIAS PROOPS, his thin hair sticking around his weazened skull like winter straw, lay on his bed and wrestled with his second boot. Chad gave him a hand to loosen it.

" You in the minister's house," said the old man. " Talking to the Reverend ? Squatting in the kitchen and eating with the Missis ? "

" Honest to God," said Chad.

Elias Proops crossed his leg over the other upraised knee and dangled the loose boot with his toes. It made his ankle look as if it were hinged the wrong way. " Well, you can shave my butt with a crosscut saw," he said. He rolled his eyes sideways at Chad till he looked like a gander with ambition.

Chad shoved the chair, which had lost its back, against the wall beside the window and looked out. He saw three bow lanterns coming east from New Boston. While he watched the second light caught up and passed the first.

"How'm I going to get this Henry away from here, Elias? He can't walk."

"Hand me my tobacco," said Elias. He caught the plug and worked on one corner with his teeth, holding his head down to get at it with the back ones. Getting the corner off he tossed the plug back at Chad, who put it where it belonged in the soap dish. "I never knew the nigger as couldn't walk if he was scared enough," he said.

"Me and Bobby are going to look at him to-morrow," Chad said. "I guess I couldn't get you to go along, could I?"

"*Me!*" Elias raised up on his elbows. "I ain't walked that far since the Fourth of July. God, I was tired."

"I couldn't get a doctor to go see him. I thought if he was hurt bad maybe you could fix him up. You ought to know how to do it."

"Salt and whisky," said Elias. "Them are the two best things, Chad. You put the salt on the man that's hurt, and you drink the whisky. We done it in the Revolution all the time, and it never done us any harm."

Chad grinned. He got up and looked out of the window at the sound of horsehoofs. Two bow lanterns were still down the canal, their slow lights like fireflies through the trees; but the first was coming into the basin, the horses trotting. The steersman gave a few low toots on his bugle.

"*Red Bird Packet,*" Elias said from the bed. "They're early to-night. Hauling through."

"Yeah," said Chad.

The boat slid under the windows at the end of the towline, its light glancing on the wake ripple and finding a ring in the bugle mouth. The windows were dark. The hoof beats echoed rapidly off the front of the Yellow Bud, seeming to change direction abruptly, as though they were ascending the wall. Then they jumped off into space and there was no more sound.

"Those boats are fliers," Elias remarked, letting his head down on the smudged pillow. "Who the hell wants to go faster? These railroad men with their big mouth, fifteen miles an hour."

"Uh hunh."

"The kind of people want that," said Elias, "let them ride

on the damn things if they want to. Get out of here, Chad. I want to rest my mind."

Chad went to the door. Downstairs he could hear Mott closing up.

" Where's Bisbee ? "

" Who ? "

" The circus agent."

" Oh, that feller," said Elias. " He went to bed. Says he's going to start early."

Bisbee was as good as his word. At half-past five o'clock when Chad had finished going over the horse, Diney brought word down from the Yellow Bud that he was ready to start.

She was a thin negress, with a long neck carrying her head well back. She moved quick and a little wild. When Chad said " Hey, Diney," she took hold of her arms hard, squeezing them in front of her, so the sharp points of her breasts were drawn together under the calico.

" What you want ? " she whispered.

" How bad hurt is that nigger ? "

She moved her head right and left, showing white in the corners of her eyes.

" You hush up, for God's sakes."

" Ain't nobody here. Can he walk ? "

" He's a hurt man," she said.

" Get me some salt in a paper," Chad said. " I'm going to fix him up."

" You ? " she said. " How does you know where he's at ? "

" The minister told me. It's all right."

" I'll get you the salt," she said. " I ain' going there no mo' myself."

" And Diney. I want a good mess of cornbread or beans or something. You know. To keep him a couple of days. And I'll need whisky, too. You get it."

" I cain't get no liquor," said Diney. " Mrs. Mott watch me too close."

Chad grinned.

" I'd hate to tell Mott about the way you run around."

" Oh, God, Mr. Chad, don' you do that." She whirled and fled, her flat dark feet reaching way out from her skirt.

Chad knew she would have what he wanted. He saddled Bisbee's horse and led him up to the canal porch. The circus agent was waiting with his saddlebag and the cases of posters. He looked over his horse approvingly.

"You've fixed him up fine. He hasn't looked good like this for a week."

"He's a good horse," Chad said.

Bisbee, having arranged his bags and cases, swung up on the saddle.

"You're wasting your time in a place like this," he said. "You ought to look around."

"Say," said Chad. "You ain't got another of those free passes, have you?"

"Sure. Want to take your girl?" Bisbee handed him another. Then he settled his lank hams and the horse started without being spoken to. He went off at his long walk towards Peterboro Street, with a steady tramp of hoofs in the stillness of the early morning.

Chad felt sorry when he had gone. He didn't often have a decent horse to mind. He went to the kitchen for his breakfast and sat by the open door eating friedcakes, broiled ham, and hominy grits and tea. While he watched the mists being pushed back along the wet places by the sunlight, he was aware of Diney hovering breathily behind him. She couldn't keep still.

"Hell, Diney," he said to her suddenly. "You ought to get married or something."

"What fo' me?" she demanded.

"To stop having the damn fidgets."

She let out a squawk.

"Lawd, Mr. Chad," she said. "A girl can get into trouble enough without gettin' herse'f no husband."

Mrs. Mott poked an outraged face through the bar-room door. "You pinching that girl again, Chad?"

"No," he said.

"Then what you hollering about? Stop it."

"Yas'm," said Diney. She began to giggle.

"You'll get me killed, Mr. Chad," she said. "Who'd I marry?"

"How about this Henry?"

"That black man? He's all mahked up." She dropped her words and stared. "You quit such talk," she whispered in angry panic. "You make me say things. You finished? Go way."

" Where are those things I asked for ? "

" They're in the barn. You go on. Go," she said.

Chad left. He found Bobby waiting in the box stall. He had a big splint basket that looked heavy.

" You got some worms ? " Chad asked.

" Yes, but are we really going to fish ? "

Chad grunted. He went into the harness stall and looked round it till he found the food left by Diney, done up in an old headcloth.

" What's that, Chad ? "

" You ask too many questions," Chad said, and led the way out of the back door, Bobby silenced at his heels.

They crossed the bridge and went west, keeping away from the canal bank until they were beyond the village. Then on the other side of a fence they hit a cowpath that led them through a small grove and down to the edge of the water, where a solid gravel cow ford crossed the canal bottom.

Chad took off his trousers and shirt and gave them to Bobby, and then took him and all their paraphernalia on his shoulders. He waded across fast. The water climbed up on him until it reached his short ribs and Bobby asked whether it was cold. Chad swore. " Someday if I can get around to it I'll have me a raft along here."

He dumped Bobby on the far side and wiped his wet flanks with his hands, combing the water off the way he would comb a lathered horse with a sweat knife. Bobby watched him with the queer prickling fascination of a small boy. Cold and wet, with the warming sunlight all over his body, Chad stripped well. He had little of the slouched look his clothes put on him. He was lean and hard and white-skinned. A canal boat coming round the bend of the grove surprised them. The woman who was putting out wash on the deck yelped and pointed a red hand. The drowsing driver caught hold of his horse's tail and stared and began grinning.

Chad yanked up his blue jeans and slid the suspender strap over his shoulder. The woman shook with a raging modesty. She kept yelling in a shrill voice and pointing her hand. The steersman yelled back at her to stop yelling and then he shouted across at them asking what in a pig's—— Chad thought he was anyway. Didn't he have any decency ? His voice sounded foreign. The woman, no longer able to restrain herself, ran up

on to the bow to get opposite to them and then went marching
back as the boat passed, hiking her skirts, and yelling at them in
her un-understandable language until she got near the stern,
where the steersman whanged her rear with the flat of his hand.
Her holler brought up the captain from the cabin and he asked
what was going on and the boat went away with her and the
steersman and the captain all yelling at each other.

Chad laughed and said they were pea-soupers, French
Canadians, from the Champlain Canal, and thumbed his nose
after them. It made Bobby feel the whole business was all right
because they were foreign, and he thumbed his nose, and still
laughing they picked up their bundles and headed into the
knee-high marsh grass below the berm.

Red-winged blackbirds made a great to-do, slinging themselves out of the yellow-green grass with rapid charr-notes, and,
looking up at them in the pale blue sky, Chad said it was fine.
Anybody could see where they were going by the birds. He
kept heading a little west of north all the time, as if they planned
to strike the Cowasselon below the Canastota.

He didn't head east till after they had crossed the Cicero
road and were down on the edge of the big marsh where some
summers the grass reached over eight feet tall. Now it was only
waist-high and utterly still on this windless day. A long line of
dying trees marked the course of the Cowasselon. A marsh
hawk swept down over the grass at them, and seemed to stand
upright in the air for one outstretched instant before it turned.

They were now out of sight of the road, and Chad thought
fairly safe from any followers. He kept a straight line, cutting
across the angle the Canastota made with the Cowasselon, and
in twenty minutes they got sight of the pine grove and then,
pushing through some sumac, came out on the fence marking
Jarvis's east field, where the barley showed a soft clear green on
the red soil.

They followed the fence, bringing Jarvis's frame barn into
view for a while, and then struck into the hickory woods. Here it
was cool, the ground nearly clean of brush and sweet-smelling
with its damp winter's leaves. Chad followed a line for the
pines. The line cut across a slight roll and dip of the ground
and on the farther rise they found a spring.

" Funny place for a potato cellar," Chad said. " Must've
been one of the Palatine cabins the Indians had cleared out."

"Probably," said Bobby. He didn't know about the Palatines or the Indians sending to Albany to get them put off the land. He was staring round everywhere for a sign of the cellar.

At the top of the rise a few maples maintained themselves and in among them witch hobble cast a green net of broad leaves. Chad said, "It'll be in there, I guess," and headed into it. He didn't try to thresh around. He stood still, with his face in the leaves, and called the negro.

"Henry," he said. "Hey, Henry Prince. We're friends."

A red squirrel started scolding them and then a weasel slipped out near by and looked at them and didn't bother. He lifted his nose towards the scolding squirrel and slid over some leaves towards the tree. In the stillness Bobby heard his own heart pounding.

Then from their left came a scared voice.

"Yes, boss. Here's Henry."

They turned that way and went about thirty feet before they saw him. He was sitting on the ground, but his feet were out of sight in the hole. It made him look legless—a big, brownish negro, in a sweat-stained, dirty blue shirt. He had a limp straw hat on his head, and the brim hung on one side like a hound's ear-flap.

9

FUGITIVE

THE negro kept staring at them. Even in the cool of the woods there was a glisten of sweat on his brown face. He had to lick his lips before he managed to ask huskily if they were from the Reverend.

"Yes," said Chad. "This is Mr. Gray's son."

The negro held out his hand towards Bobby. The middle finger lay crooked in his palm like a trinket he had just picked up. "You wouldn' lie to me, white boy?"

He was a badly scared negro. Sitting the way they had found him, he told them how he had come to be shot.

"It was dark. The man step out in the road and he say, 'You name Henry Prince?' and I jump for the bushes but he lammed with his gun and he hit my leg."

" Did you get a look at him, Henry ? " asked Chad.

" No, sir. He jes' look monstrous big."

" I bet it was Cisco Trid."

" He seem like the devil to me, boss."

He started to shake as he thought of it. Bobby could see his eyes roll under the shadow of his hat brim. Chad said, " How are you feeling ? "

" Pretty bad. That black girl didn't come this morning, boss. And las' night there was a little black rabbit houn' kept chasing a rabbit roun' and roun' these woods. Seems to me like that rabbit keep jumping over the top of this hole every other minute, boss."

" Did you see anybody ? "

" No, sir. I wa'n lookin'. I jes' put my face in the back of the bottom of that hole and stay there."

" Didn't you hear anybody ? "

" I heard someone beatin' through the bresh. But it might have been the devil, boss, I don' know. He come and he go. I didn' say nothin'."

" Well, we've got something to feed you," Chad said, " but I guess first we better fix your leg. Let's look at it."

The negro obediently started hiking the leg of his blue jean trousers up. He had a long scar along one side of the shinbone. " Nigger name George done that with a scythe," he explained. " We was mad."

The bandage began above the knee and as soon as he bared it a couple of flies buzzed up out of the potato pit and got curious. " It was clean yesterday," he apologised. " That black girl she give hit to me. But that leg keeps mattering."

Chad said, " I got some more wrapped round your food. You can use that."

" Thank you, boss."

The negro began picking gingerly at the end of the bandage. It was stuck solid. He worked at it a minute and then looked away and mumbled. " I jes' cain't make the resolve, boss."

" We'll have to soak it off down at the spring. You can use the old bandage to wash it out and then we'll put the salt on it."

" Salt, boss ? "

" Sure, salt."

" Oh, my Lawd ! "

But he got up and went hobbling down to the spring with Chad and Bobby following with the food.

"Cripus," said Chad. "We can't move him far. It's bad."

Bobby whispered, "Do you think he'll lose his leg, Chad?" His eyes looked round and big in his white face.

"No," Chad said. "He's a nigger and niggers are tougher than frogs."

But soaking off the bandage was a slow process, and when Chad first started piling the salt on the torn flesh the negro bucked so that he had to give him the whisky. He was disgusted.

"You ain't even cleaned the spring out," he said.

Henry Prince hung his head. "Ol' marster always say I'se a no-'count nigger," he mumbled. Bobby watched him with fascinated eyes. He had never seen any one drink straight whisky like that. It seemed to give the negro a jolt, for he sat up after a second with the sweat beading all over him and by the time Chad got the rest of the salt on his leg and tied it up with the calico he was ready to eat.

He said it was the best feed he had had all the way north. "You gemmun do take care of me fine," he said. He looked so friendly that Bobby asked him how he had managed to find his way to Canastota.

"I jus' kept headin' no'th," he said. "They sent me along from one place to the next but it was mostly no'th, boss. I got my eye on the No'th Star and kept walkin', tha's all."

"Did they treat you bad where you were, Henry?"

"Yes, siree. Ol' marster was mighty strict with us niggers but that overseer was plumb mean. He told ol' marster I was makin' trouble and for him to sell me off the plantation, so I lit out from there one night. I jes' put my eye on that star and come along. The star's easy to find when you're thirsty, boss. Canady's underneath that star, they say." He looked down at himself and all of a sudden his brown face puckered. "I mos' got there, too."

Bobby felt like crying himself. He glanced at Chad; but he could tell by the way Chad was finishing up the preserve pie that he was studying some kind of idea, and he did not want to disturb him. Chad, however, looked up and said to Henry, "Don't worry We ain't going to let two beggers like Al and Cisco get hold of you"

"Thank you, boss" Henry Prince wiped his eyes with the

back of his hand and then drew his wrist across his lips. " You sho is good to me."

Chad got up.

" You think you could walk some this evening ? " he asked.

" Depends on how far," Henry said.

" Maybe a mile."

" If I had a crutch maybe I could, boss. I'd make myself one only I los' my knife when that man shot me."

" You make yourself one," Chad said. He fished in his pockets and found his knife, which he handed over to the negro. " I'll come back for you after sunset. You'll be all right ? "

" Hit's lonesome here."

" You better be glad it is," Chad said dryly. " Bobby, you come along with me now. We got to get some fish and get back."

Bobby said good-bye to Henry Prince. He felt mean, leaving him. The negro looked wistful. He was still sitting by the spring when Bobby looked back, his back hunched as he stared down at his leg. The broken flap of his hat made him look like an old hound after a day's running. Bobby thought he seemed like a nice man. He said so to Chad.

" Him ? He's just a lazy nigger," Chad said. " I don't know why I'm bothering about him anyway." He kept a fast pace through the woods until they struck the Canastota.

" You going to try the springhole ? " Bobby asked, breaking out of the brush behind him.

" I got to catch fish in a hurry," Chad said. He turned unhesitatingly towards the village until they came opposite the crossing place. Bobby would have thought it was downstream from where they hit the creek, but he had learned that Chad always knew exactly where he was.

They crossed the Canastota and struck due east.

In half an hour they came out on the Cowasselon above the big curve, and Chad began to go south. Suddenly he turned west again and headed across an opening full of beaver grass, clumps of dead cattails, and a few old tamarack stubs. They stirred out a ratty black cow that snorted at them and Chad said, " Must be the one Dagget's missing. You'd think he'd be proud to lose her."

A bittern squawked at them and hopped clumsily out of the grass, using its wings as though they were crutches. Chad took a sight on a big hemlock a little south and went for it. Half-way to it the grass began to feel swaley underfoot. Then, all of a sudden, they came out on a small brook running through alders and bush willow and Chad swung right. " Walk easy," he said.

He borrowed Bobby's knife to cut a pole and fixed the line on the end. Then he baited the hook and told Bobby to sneak up on his belly and drop the worm over the edge of the grass. " Let him drop right down. The water will slide him under you. And don't get up if you hook one. Just swing him back to me and I'll unhook him and bait for you."

Bobby stared incredulously.

" It don't look like much of a place to me," he said. " You never told me about it either."

" I don't use it except when I want to catch a big one in a hurry. I want a couple of big ones," Chad said. " So's everybody can see we went fishing. If they ask you where we got them, say we got them down the Cowasselon. They come from there, anyhow." He lay down on a high dry hummock of grass, cradling his bony shoulders between two roots of an overgrown stump. He laid the sock he carried worms in handy beside him and put his hands back of his head.

He watched Bobby through half-closed eyes and grinned. Bobby did not look much convinced, but he was moving up like a snake through the grass. Bobby was always that way. Though he might not believe a thing, he would always give it a fair try. Chad doubted if Bobby's father was the same way. Well, he figured Bobby was going to get a surprise. The sky was clouding some and the fish ought to bite after this good weather. There was a cold spring that rose under that grass and the hole was a good six feet deep. He didn't mind giving Bobby a treat ; Bobby wouldn't ever find the place by himself anyway, coming the way Chad had brought him. He lay back a little easier and began to figure on just how he was going to handle Al Heeney. There wasn't any sense in letting five dollars go past you.

Bobby didn't think much of the place but he sneaked up on his belly and edged the pole through the grass and raised the tip to let the worm swing out. The worm was pink and clean from being carried in the old coffee grounds Chad always kept the sock full of. It was a good worm, too, with plenty of kick. He dropped it upstream a little and was surprised to see how much slide the water had. Then he inched his face through the grass and looked down. He could see no bottom, only the dark surface of the water and the line making a fine V on it. It hung there quite steady for an instant, then began to wave just a little. Bobby realised there must be an eddy underneath the sod. Maybe it was a better place than it seemed. He began to feel prickles in the back of his neck. A cloud stuck itself over the sun and the water turned almost purple and the tip of the pole took a fling so fast he just saved it breaking the water.

It wasn't any mere jerk. It was as though the line had turned into an iron rod with a couple of horses on the end. He couldn't handle it without getting up on his knees and he rose up shaking, and lifted the pole.

The pole was bent uneven. It bucked like a lame cow and then the tip went down again and the line went straight across the narrow pool, lifting a slice of clear water. Behind Bobby, Chad's voice said quietly, " When he's straight away, heave him. Don't monkey with the fool."

The line and the pole and Bobby's arm made an arc. He heaved. The fish came even on its turn. When it broke the water, Bobby gave a yip, seeing the red and black-edged white stripe. It was a real deep-water trout. It went over his head, lighting square on Chad's belly, and Chad grabbed it with his freckled hands just as Bobby turned over on his hunkers.

" My Jewish God ! " said Bobby.

Chad was wrenching the hook loose and muttering about bellyhooking a fish. " He's eighteen inches," he said, spreading out both hands with joined thumbs over the bulging side. " Maybe three pounds." He broke the fish's back and baited up. " Get me another," he said.

Bobby didn't say anything. He was speechless. He fouled the worm in the grass before he got it over the water, and lay down so close he could feel the grass roots against his wishbone.

The second one was not so big, but he must have weighed a pound and a half. Bobby was half crazy with excitement and begged to have one more try. It was like dropping your line into the bowels of the universe, he thought, and Lord knew what might not take hold of it.

Chad said all right. He wanted to think anyway, and Bobby had to wait a long time before he got a nibble. It was a cautious pull and let go before he could raise the tip. But after a minute it came again, and then it laid hold like perdition.

Even Chad got up on his knees and started for the edge.

" That's the old one," he said. " Heave him. Don't let him get across. Heave him."

It was too late. Bobby got a glimpse of one big fin and a flash of red and the fish bored and hit the far bank. The line anchored. A boil of water came out from under the sod and a big ripple went up and over and returned downstream and Chad said, " That's another one of my hooks. Break the line."

Bobby was just about weeping.

" He just bent the pole which way," he said.

" Sure," said Chad. " I got to bring down a tree for him."

He stood close to Bobby and emptied the worms into the water. " He'll keep," he observed. " Must be a quarter pound of my hooks in him already. I bet he looks like a bullhead."

Bobby said, " How much do you figure he weighs, Chad ? "

" I guess maybe five pounds." Chad looked down into the water. He was grinning. " Ain't he a lunker, though ? "

Bobby said, " He felt like a thousand of brick when he took it."

Chad nodded. " It's quite a hole. We better get going." He picked up the fish. " If you ever tell anybody where this place is I'll black your face and hand you over to Cisco Trid." He strung the two fish on a hooked stick and started straight off across the swale, found a log to cross the brook, and went south. They struck the canal near Miller's, waded his cattle ford, and went openly down the towpath.

As soon as they got in sight of Canastota, Chad handed the fish to Bobby. " Here," he said, " you caught 'em."

Bobby said, " Thanks." He was numb with pride. When they reached the Yellow Bud, Mott and Elias and Al Heeney were on the porch, watching a boat unload barrels at Reeder's Feed Store. Elias saw them first and said, " You got something."

Bobby mutely held up the fish. Even Al Heeney got excited. " That's the best fish I seen in two years," he said. " Where'd you get him ? "

Bobby wanted to tell about the old lunker, but Chad caught his eyes in time and said, " In the Cowasselon."

" You better take them home," Chad said. He sat down beside Elias. " Don't tell your Pa you been with me."

Bobby blushed bright red and went off round the corner. When he had crossed the bridge he took the sunny side of the street so the light could catch the fish.

10

IN THE YELLOW BUD

AL HEENEY kept looking Chad's way. His yellow-brown eyes were casual, but his lips kept moving uneasily on his teeth. After a few minutes of it, to devil with him, Chad said, " I bet you two buffaloes can't guess what me and Bobby came across."

It was comical to see Al stiffen up ; but Elias Proops, who wasn't interested, said, " Cow cakes, probably," and spit.

" Aw gee," said Chad. " How'd you guess it ? "

Al sat back in his chair for a minute and then he made his mouth smile, showing his teeth, and got up.

" Well, a man can't set still all day, can he ? " he said.

" He can try pretty hard," said Elias.

Al said, " Well, 'bye, boys. See you pretty soon maybe, Chad ? "

" Maybe." Chad watched him walk off the porch and go along the towpath towards the bridge. Elias grunted.

" It got so I couldn't hardly tell whether it was him or me sitting in my pants," he complained.

" Been around all day ? "

" Honest to God. I forget *when* he come. I can remember when General Abercrombie's army come marching into Albany, but I can't remember when that bucktoothed frog sat down." Elias's mouth opened, with a sort of shocked delight. " Think of remembering that far back, will you ? "

" How far ? "

" That far." Elias looked as if he had been struck down by the powers of his own brain. He was solemn. " I only just thought of it. I was three years old. It was 1758. Say, can you figure out how old that makes me ? "

" What's the use ? "

" It might come handy," Elias said. " If I was borned in 1756, I would be eighty years old, wouldn't I ? But I was three years old in 1758, so I must have got borned in 1755. That is one more than 1756, so I must be eighty-one years old. That's awful old for a man to be, Chad. My God, I remember that girl in the barn up Guilderland way. I was twenty-one. Katsie Vrooman was her name. It was on account of old man Vrooman I joined the army. That's how I came west. I seen this country when there wasn't only Indian women in it. I wonder what she called him—Vrooman, maybe. If she did, does that make me a Vrooman?" He rolled his eye at Chad, but Chad was staring along the canal. It was a pretty, soft-looking sunset, with a considerable piece of pink cloud.

Elias said, "You ain't listening. You don't even see that the whole history of this country is right in my insides. You don't care. You're ignorant, Chad."

Chad turned and grinned.

"Sure," he said. "I'm ignorant."

Elias spit.

"Yes, you're ignorant. What you figuring on?"

"Where a man could hide a nigger so he could claim the reward for catching him."

Elias sat up straight.

"You going to let them bug-wits catch him?"

"Naw," said Chad. "He's a decent nigger. I want to collect five dollars, though."

"You better not mix up with Cisco, Chad."

"I ain't scared of him. It all depends on where I can hide that nigger."

Elias grunted at him. "I'm telling you to watch out," he said. "You better watch out for Mrs. Mott, too. She's feeling mean about the pig slops." He hoisted himself out of his chair and said he was going to go upstairs and get some rest before supper. Chad let him go, then went round to the kitchen and sneaked the pail of slops off the porch and took it down to the hog pen. He flung it in to the hogs and watched them sort it over, balancing potato peels on their lower jaws, and wondered if a darkey could nourish himself on that stuff. It would be simple if he could. But probably the hogs would raise a row. Mott's boar was pretty ugly.

He rinsed the pail in the canal, got it back on the porch and himself into the kitchen before Mrs. Mott came in. She started dressing him down about the garbage but he said he'd taken care of it a long time ago and went on eating out of the plate Diney had set for him. When Mrs. Mott found the pail empty and realised that she hadn't caught him out to his face, she went ramping back into the bar and picked on Mott. Mott told her to leave him alone. If she didn't like Chad, tell Chad so, not him. So Mrs. Mott came back to the kitchen and laid into the black girl. But suddenly she said her feet hurt and she started to cry.

Diney, who had been taking the tirade with a sullen, subdued bend of her neck, switched round and said, " Ah, you po' lady. You go upstairs and lay your head on the pillow and I'll fetch some tea and cake." She led Mrs. Mott out, and Mrs. Mott still cried softly. But when Diney came down she said to Chad he ought to be ashamed.

" What've I done to her ? " he asked.

" Nuthin'," said Diney. " But you ought to be ashamed. All you men ought."

She folded up into a dark silence, getting the tea and making up a tray. She even went outside and got a couple of the Johnny-jump-ups that grew on the off side of the steps and put them into a glass and put it on the tray. She wouldn't hear Chad at all.

He thought women were queer, old women and niggers especially. He draped himself over the table, dawdling, because he knew it would annoy Diney, but when she came down the second time she paid no attention at all.

Diney went into the bar and laid Elias's supper out with Mott's and presently the two started eating. She went back and forth, peddling their plates. Somehow she seemed restless to Chad, troubled, and full of hatred. He felt it get under his own hide. He quit thinking about Henry Prince and what he was going to do with him. He found himself watching the coloured girl ; and she, knowing he was, began to go soft on her feet. She was like a cat moving back and forth between the kitchen and the bar. When there wasn't anything else for her to do, she stood in the open kitchen door, leaning one hip against the jamb, and hugging her breasts. She just waited. The curve of her back was submissive ; the square her shoulders made from her neck was somehow sad ; and Chad had a queer thought that he could see the hip getting heavy against the jamb. Heavier and heavier, so that he almost expected to hear her suddenly cry out.

It was getting darker outside. A boat went by with a light in the cabin. A woman was singing in there and her voice passed with the lighted window, making the whole world seem dreary. Chad got up abruptly, shoving the plate back so it crashed against the cup and the knife slid over the rim and made its own clatter. Elias and Mott stopped jawing in the bar. Chad stood still, surprised by the noise he had made. A fly came straight out of the bar and lit on the sugar bowl. It was the only living thing, with purpose, in that house.

Chad saw it light and then he jumped for the door. He elbowed Diney over. " What did you say ? " he asked her angrily.

Her face didn't change. She was looking past his ear, her eyes narrowed down, and her flat nostrils expanded.

" Men ! " she said.

He ought to have had sense enough to get out without bandying with her. But he said, " What about it ? "

She didn't move.

" What about it? " he demanded.

She looked at him. Her eyes flew open and as he stared at them he thought he saw the pupils contract as if by a muscular feat.

" Oh, Lawd Jesus," she said.

He thought she was crazy, or he was, and he stamped out on to the canal dock and went east towards the bridge. He climbed up its ramp and stopped a minute to look along the canal.

" What's into me ? " he thought. What was the matter with Diney and Mrs. Mott ? He hadn't done anything. He tried to figure it out, draping his long arms over the rails and letting his hands hang. He felt the blood run into his hands and swell his fingers. A breath of cool air came off the canal, as though it welled upwards after coming under the bridge. The water was all dark except the slight sky colour along the northern bank and the reflected windows of the Yellow Bud.

For an instant Mott's head showed in the reflected window light ; then a ripple from an unseen cause jellied it ; and the window light was empty when it re-formed. Staring at it, Chad wondered how he had happened to stay so long at the Yellow Bud. Four, five years, it was now. It made him feel almost festered, as if he had just been swelling there, doing nothing. But now he was all tied up with getting this nigger free. That was the trouble, of course, having to get something done.

He saw Elias tramping along the towpath.

" Mott wants you back," he said. " You got to help in the bar. Business has got started already."

News of the big poster had gone all over town since last night, and by eight-thirty the bar was crammed full. Chad had a permanent place in the kitchen washing up what Diney handed to him, except when he went out to pump water. With the stove going to heat the water, the kitchen felt hot enough to fry steam, and the talk coming through the bar-room door was like a fog, half smoke, half liquor.

He listened to the blurred voices admiring the lion, but hardly any one admired the picture of Lady Lillian. By the end of the bar two men were discussing how much it would cost to take their families along. They used the argument that the minister was against circuses, and they agreed they had better go by themselves. Then Elias, who was an authority on circuses, piped up to say that anybody could look at one. The show was all right for the smallest child to see, he said. It was the people who were that way. Like gypsies, he went on. Why, he'd seen circus girls washing their underclothes and hanging them out right in front of a bail of men.

Judd Parsons, the mechanic, pushed over to ask Elias where he had seen that ; and Elias said it was in Troy, though he couldn't see what difference it made where he had seen it happen. That seemed to still Judd's argument. After a minute, just to show he was still there, probably, Judd said he had seen Sam Hitchcock getting on the packet that afternoon. Sam said he was going to Troy. He wanted to compare nail prices at the factories.

Chad perked up his ears and for once he got a good dry shine on a glass. Judd's statement brought back a small idea that had been working in his head ever since last night. Sam Hitchcock was violent against all abolitionists and everybody in Canastota knew it. When Judd went on to say that Sam planned to be gone several days, the idea took solid form ; he began to think about what he might know of Hitchcock's barn ; and by a little after nine he remembered a boy named Cahill who used to live in Canastota.

· Mr. Cahill had had an interest in the mechanic's factory, and once Mrs. Mott's talking about him, said he was gentry, which, Chad supposed, meant that you didn't have to work to make money. If you were gentry you had the kind of money that made more. But the boy was the kind that liked seeing people do things without knowing they were being watched. It didn't matter what it was, so long as he knew they thought they were alone. He had told Chad once about seeing old Sam Hitchcock blow his nose on a piece of flannel he was tying a ham in, and when Chad asked him how he had seen that he told Chad about an old grain box under the hay in Sam's barn. This box, he said, had a slide for a chute that led into the back of the barn where there used to be cows, but which Sam now used for a store-room. Cahill said he had spent the whole afternoon there hoping Sam would come back again or that Mrs. Hitchcock would come in. She had, as a matter of fact, but only to get pickles out of the firkin. However, it was a good place to hide in because there wasn't any hay and you could shift around in it without making any noise.

It was queer how things would come into your mind. The Cahills had left Canastota over a year ago and it had been a good deal longer than that since young Cahill had told him about the grain box. Chad supposed that with Sam only keeping one horse the hay had never got low enough to uncover it. Probably Sam himself had forgotten its existence. It sounded to him like about as perfect a place as a runaway darkey could expect to find, and by the time he was wiping the last round of glasses, Chad had made up his mind it was the place he was going to move Henry Prince to.

II

MRS. HITCHCOCK

IT was pitch-black in the woods. A mist was working in off the marsh and the underbrush had pretty well soaked Chad by the time he broke through it and started calling Henry Prince's name. It was some time, however, before he got an answer. Then it came from right in front of him, and thinking of the way he had been making circles and getting wet for nothing made him mad.

"Didn't you hear me hollering?" he demanded.

"Yes, boss."

"Why didn't you answer?"

"I didn't know it was you, boss."

"I kept telling who I was," Chad said.

"I know that. I heard you saying it. But I done forgot your name, boss."

Chad gave it up. "Did you make a crutch?" he asked.

"Yes, *sir*." Henry Prince sounded proud. "I cut it right after you'd gone, boss. And I whittled on it till plumb dark. I wrapped up the crotch in some of them rags and she fits fine. Guess I can get along all right now." He floundered up and hitched the stick under his arm, and Chad could imagine him standing there to be admired.

"That's fine," he said. "You better start using it now. You're moving house."

"You got a place for me?"

"Yes."

"Where's this place?" the negro asked.

"In town. It's a nice dry barn."

"You got a wagon, boss?"

"No."

"You ought to fotched me a wagon."

Chad swore. "Who do you think you are, anyway?"

"I'm a hurt man," Henry Prince said with a kind of dignity. "If they sees me, I can't run, boss."

"They won't see you, not if you're walking. It's dark to-night. There's a thick mist. It's clean over the canal. The boats are just creeping and the drivers are carrying lanterns. Anyway, you said this morning you'd try it."

"Maybe I did, and maybe I didn't. You say so. But this leg hurts me when I walk." His voice turned plaintive.

Chad said, "Listen here. A big strong nigger like you ought to be able to walk that far. Why, I bet you'd fetch a heap of money in Virginia."

"Twelve hundred dollars in the market." Henry Prince spoke with wistful pride. "I'm valuable, boss."

"Twelve hundred dollars!" Chad was incredulous. "Why, Mr. Shurtlieffe is only offering two hundred dollars."

"Maybe he is, maybe he ain't." Henry Prince fell back on his stock rhetorical retort. "But the overseer tol' me what was the use of keeping me on the plantation when they could sell me to an Arkansas dealer any day for twelve hundred dollars."

"Is that the truth?"

"Honest, boss. The dealer ain't going to know I'm shif'less. He jus' sees how strong I am. I'm powerful, boss."

" Why, that's more than anybody else I know is worth," Chad said sceptically. " If I was worth that much money, I wouldn't be scared trying to walk a mile. I could make a decent crutch. I wouldn't be afraid of no Al Heeney. I'd say, what's the sense of hiding out in a wet hole like this with my leg getting stiff and nobody bringing me food ? No ham, no friedcakes, no pickles. Just getting hungrier and hungrier till Cisco Trid comes along with his double-barrel gun to pick me up."

" He done been here once," said the negro.

" He didn't know where to look."

" You ain't goin' to tell him."

" Why not ? If you're going to lay out here and die I might as well get paid something for tramping round the country. It won't hurt you none." Chad stepped back into the brush. " It's too bad, Henry. But I might just as well say good-bye, now."

He heard the negro breathing hard. Suddenly he made a clumsy one-legged rush, missing Chad by a dozen feet, tripping himself in the underbrush and going down. He groaned, then floundered up and said softly, " Just let me get my hands on you, white boy."

" You won't," said Chad. He started off towards town, making plenty of noise. Behind him the blackness was still. He could imagine the negro leaning on his crutch, trying to make up his mind.

" Boss, I dropped my crutch. You wouldn't leave me without my crutch ? You come back and help me find it. Please, sir."

" It will show up in daylight," Chad said, moving away.

There was another silence.

" Don't go way. Boss, don't leave me here. I'll try it. Yes, I will. I didn't mean nothing."

He came stumbling after Chad in the darkness.

" Boss," he said. " Boss, you wait a minute. I'm coming."

Chad kept just a little ahead of him, leading him away from the potato hole. He could hear the negro's rough breathing over the noise he made in the underbrush. He made little moaning sounds, like a lame dog tagging a man. He fell down again but got up at once and said, " Excuse me, boss. I'm coming."

Chad had no mercy on him till they had gone past the Jarvis farm. Then he said, " You be quiet. There's dogs round here."

The negro came up with him, breathing hard and reeking sweat.

C.H.   C 2

Chad backed off and said, " Now, Henry, you're going to do what I tell you ? "

" Yes, sir, boss."

" And no more back talk, either ? "

" No, sir."

Chad thought he sounded licked, and he was. He made no more trouble and the only difficulty was getting him over the fences. But in about an hour they struck the Cicero road and came out on the canal.

The mist was thick. From the bridge, which he scouted first, Chad saw that the Yellow Bud was closed. The only light came from Mott's room. There wasn't a soul stirring except a boat hauling west.

The bridge inclines made hard going for the negro. He panted, fluttering his lips, and wiping them with his free hand.

" You're doing all right," Chad said. " It's not far, now."

They went slowly up Peterboro Street and stopped opposite Hitchcock's store. The house was dark, a shadow under the shadow of the elms. Chad whispered, " Come quiet. We're going in." As they headed into the yard he gave a low whistle, to warn the hound.

The dog came out of the shed and sniffed Chad and then went over to Henry Prince, who stiffened at the hostile touch of the cold nose on his ankles. " I sho likes rabbit dogs," he whispered. " I sho does. He's a fine dog, ain't he, boss ? Yes, sir."

Chad told him to be quiet. The yard was dead still. The mist pressed against their faces. The old hound finished his inspection and went over to the barn door, dropping on his hunkers. But suddenly, as though the African smell had proved too much for him, he blasted it out of his nostrils with a sound like clapping hands. Chad swore, caught the negro's arm, and dragged him over to the barn wall.

" Keep still," he whispered. " Don't you move."

The negro began to say prayers under his breath.

Chad couldn't tell how he knew that Mrs. Hitchcock had come to her ground-floor window, but he knew she was there, listening, just as she had been last night. Her voice came into the yard. " Go to bed," she told the dog. The hound started growling. He got up again and came over to the negro, who said, " Oh, Lawd Jesus," faintly and leaned back. He lost his hold on his crutch, which started to tap from his shaking against the barn boards. Chad grabbed it too late. Then they waited to see what she would do.

They couldn't hear her, not even when she opened the kitchen door. But the porch boards squeaked. She said then, " Who's that ? " Her voice was taut, dry, and sharp. Chad felt a sneaking admiration for her. Nine women out of ten would either have locked themselves in or run out the front door for a neighbour. He gripped hard on the negro's arm to keep him quiet. There was still a chance that, hearing nothing, she would go back into the house. But the hound sniffed loudly at Henry's ankles and growled again ; and she said sharply, " Who's that ? I've got a gun and I'll shoot it if you don't answer."

" Don't shoot," Henry Prince begged in a loud voice.

Chad said, " You damn' fool," and then walked towards the porch. " It's me, Chad Hanna," he said to her.

When he got near the porch he could make her out leaning against the rail. She had on a loose dark coat but it was un-buttoned, showing the faint white of her nightdress.

She said, " Chad," in a relieved tone.

He leaned against the rail close to her.

" You ain't got a gun," he said, raising his voice enough for Henry Prince to hear.

" No. What are you doing round here ? You were here last night," she said. He realised that she was not frightened ; she was excited. He tried to get a look at her face, but he could not see anything except the pale oval framed in her hair.

" How do you know I was here ? "

" You were out by the shed. I heard the dog sneeze and told him to go to bed."

" I was standing there," he admitted. " I seen you in the window."

She didn't seem bothered that he had seen her. She didn't seem bothered now to be out of the house talking to him, with only one of her husband's coats over her nightgown. She said calmly, " You haven't told me what you were doing."

" Nothing," he said. " I'm just moseying around."

" Who's that with you ? " she asked.

" Nobody."

" You didn't say, ' Don't shoot.' And the hound wouldn't growl at you, either."

"He's just a durn-fool dog," Chad said.

"No, he's not. There's somebody out there. If he don't come here, I'll get a lantern and find out who he is." Her voice hardened. "I haven't accused you of trying to break into the storage room to steal, Chad. But it looks suspicious."

He admired her. She had nerve.

"I don't steal, Mrs. Hitchcock." .

"Did you know Sam's away?"

"Yes, Judd Parsons said so."

"And you came round the barn knowing it."

"Yes, ma'am." He tried to figure out the best thing to do. "I'd rather you didn't know what I was doing," he said after a minute. "It would be better for you not to know."

He could see she was trying to make him out. She had always been pleasant to him. He liked her, but he knew the way Sam felt about negroes and it seemed logical she would feel the same way. She said, "Whatever it is you can't do it now without my knowing, can you? I want to know."

"Mrs. Hitchcock, will you promise not to tell anybody? If you don't like it, I've got to stop. But I'm in a pinch right now and I guess I'll have to tell you."

She said, "You mean not to tell Sam?"

"Yes."

"All right," she said after a minute.

"Henry Prince," Chad called softly. "You come here."

The hound growled instantly, but after a moment Henry got up his nerve and came shuffling and hobbling through the yard.

They could both make out that he took off his hat in the darkness. "You can't see him very good," Chad said. "He's coloured."

"Yes, ma'am." Henry's voice was softly wheedling. "I'm coloured." He bowed on his crutch. "You mighty kind to let me come here."

"Shut up, Henry." Chad tried to discover Mrs. Hitchcock's reaction. He heard her draw her breath slowly. "He's a runaway nigger," he explained. "Al Heeney and Cisco Trid are after him. He's shot in the leg, probably by Cisco. He's been hiding out in a potato cellar over beyond Jarvis's. I wanted to get him a place to rest in till he can run again. I heard Sam's away, so I thought of your barn."

She said slowly, " Don't you know. Sam's against the abolitionists ? He says runaway negroes ought to be shot."

Chad was conscious of Henry's jump. He nearly lost his
balance. Only the hound's growl at the back of his legs kept
him on his feet. " You better keep still," Chad said to him. Then
he turned to the woman. " Everybody knows how Sam feels.
That's what made me think of his barn."

She said, " Yes. It's a smart idea."

Chad said, " Well, it's up to you. You won't tell. If you're
against it, we'll have to hunt some other place. That's all."

" Sam would find him when he went up for the mare's hay."

" No, he wouldn't." Chad had caught a change in her voice.
He explained about the grain box and the slide into the store-
room.

" I didn't know about it," she said. She was obviously
thinking about going into the storeroom sometime, Chad thought,
and he told her about Cahill. It seemed to relieve her. " It's a
wonderful place to hide anybody, isn't it ? " she said. " Why,
I could go in there any time and just hand him up food and
water."

" You'd feed him ? " Chad asked. " I didn't figure you
doing anything."

" Yes, I'll feed him." She sounded quite calm, as if she had
settled the whole business in her mind. " Tie up the hound
while I go in and get a jug of water and some food. I've got
some cheese and pie."

As she slipped back into the house, Henry said unexpectedly,
" This-here's going to be a good place for Henry Prince."

He sounded glib. Chad said, " It will be if you get into it.
You'll have to climb a ladder."

The negro turned meek.

" Yes, sir. I'll climb it."

By the time Chad had tied up the dog and got Henry Prince
into the barn, Mrs. Hitchcock came out again with a basket and
a jug. She had taken time to pull on a dress. She crossed the
yard swiftly, passing through the faint shine from the open door
with a slight sway of her skirts, like someone floating. She
handed Chad the jug. " I'll bring the basket."

There was plenty of hay in the loft and they crossed it together to the rear corner of the mow, the negro making heavy
weather with his crutch, but Mrs. Hitchcock moving lightly over

the mounds. In the corner where Cahill had described it, Chad started burrowing for the grain box, and after a moment he found it and got the door open. It was warm and dry inside and the negro admired it, pulling in great armfuls of hay after him. Chad showed him the slide after he had found it, taking hold of his hand to guide him, and said that Mrs. Hitchcock would pass him up food through it.

"It sho is fine, boss," the negro said.

Chad climbed back into the hay where Mrs. Hitchcock waited and handed down the basket. He told Henry to close the door, and when he had done so shoved hay down against it. As he stood up again, Mrs. Hitchcock said, "It's a perfect hide-hole. It would almost be fun to be him, wouldn't it?"

They stood a moment listening to the negro settling himself in his armfuls of hay like a dog making his bed.

Chad said, "He ought to be all right in a week or two."

He went down the ladder and waited while she fumbled in the dark.

"Sit down and slide," he said. "I'll catch you."

"Here I am."

He reached for her, swinging his arms over the hay until his hand struck her ankle. It was bare. He held her there for an instant, then he put her feet against his chest and told her to let go.

"Shall I come?"

"Sure?"

He caught her by the waist as she came down.

"I am heavy?"

"You're light."

"Oh?" She gave a soft laugh.

Letting his arms slide up under her armpits, he lifted her to show how light she was. She let him hold her. She neither moved nor made a sound; but suddenly he felt her hang like a dead weight in his hands and set her down. She went right out of the barn, but she was waiting in the yard when he came out and closed the door gently behind them.

"It's late," she said. "But me, I am hungry. Aren't you?"

"I could eat a little.".

She said with a little laugh, "I have some scraps left after the black man's supper."

She had left a single candle on the kitchen table, but the

curtains were drawn over the windows. " You sit down," she said. " Will you drink milk with the pie ? I do not want to light a fire. They might smell smoke."

He said he would drink milk and sat down at the table, watching her bring it in a brown earthenware pitcher, and then lay out two plates and fetch the pie. It made him feel queer to be in the house with her like this. Hitchcocks were supposed to be quality folks; Sam was a deacon.

She sat down across the table from him and lifted her glass of milk. " Success to our black man," she said. Her hair down her back was a bright dark brown, with reddish lights brought out by the candle shine. Her grey-brown eyes met his frankly.

" It tastes good, eh ? " She smiled.

" Yes," he said. " Did Sam say what day he'd get back ? "

" Yes, he said he'd be back the fourteenth."

" That's after the circus," Chad said in some surprise. " It shows here the thirteenth. Didn't Sam know that ? "

" Yes. I wanted him to take me, but he said business has to come first."

" That's kind of too bad."

He felt sorry for her. It must be bad sometimes for a young woman, being married with an old yardstick like Sam. She didn't seem like a happy person, either. All of a sudden he thought he would like to see her dressed up and having fun.

" I got two tickets," he said. " You can have one."

" Me ? " She laid a fingertip on her breast, still looking at him. When he nodded, her colour rose slowly. Watching her, Chad realised that she wasn't a woman who coloured easily. Perhaps she wasn't used to it.

" I'd like to take you, if you'd come with me."

" Oh." Her lips parted and her face grew softer. " I couldn't," she said hurriedly. " It would make a scan-dal."

The way she said it gave the word a queer foreign sound. She noticed his surprise with a little run of laughter.

" You didn't know I was a foreigner ? Sam does not like me for it. I'm French. I was brought over by a factory to work in a mill. They brought us to Cohoes. It was not a good place to live. Sam came there one day, and he came again on his way home. He asked me to marry him." She shrugged her shoulders. " I did not like the place."

Chad said, " Yeah."

She glanced at him quickly. Her flush had gone away and her eyes were calm again. " You see, he had to buy my contract. That is why I am sorry for the black man."

" Why don't you clear out ? This is a free country."

She gave a small smile. " For a man. Even a poor black one. But what could I do ? He makes me comfortable."

Chad reached into his pocket. French people were queer anyway, Elias Proops had told him often. They would marry Indians or negresses or vice versa. Just the same he had offered her a ticket. He handed it over the table to her.

" You can set by yourself, if you don't want to come—with anybody."

" You are nice. I don't think I can go. But I like to have the ticket."

He could tell that she was bursting to go. He would like to see her face when she went into the tent.

" I could meet you down the street and walk over with you," he said.

She shook her head.

" Sometimes Sam comes home ahead of time."

Chad got up. " Damn Sam," he said. She was looking up at him and it made him feel tall, to stand over her. It was natural for Sam to be jealous, her being French and all. He wondered how she would have acted if he had kissed her in the barn as he had thought of doing. But now, looking down at her face, he didn't want to try it. He had a shrewd notion you couldn't make her step over the shafts she was used to without having some pretty good sugar of your own. A circus ticket wasn't much.

" Thanks for supper. You'll look after Henry ? "

" Yes," she said, smiling.

" I wouldn't go into the haymow, though. Sometimes niggers get over being scared."

" The poor black man ? " She shook her head. " Oh, no."

" I'll come down night to look at his leg."

" Yes."

" Well," he said, " I'd better get along."

She came to the door with the candle in her left hand.

" I'll blow it out before you open the door," she said. " Goodnight, Chad. I think you are smart, and you are nice. If Sam does not come home to take me, I'll use the ticket for the circus."

She held out her hand. It was a warm hand with thin

quick fingers. It made him think of what Elias had once said : " A dandified French, kiss-her-fingers, butter-bottomed little slickster," about a travelling salesman who had sold him a nightshirt without tails.

He bent over and kissed her fingers.

As he straightened up he saw she was just about giggling, and he felt himself get hot. " Elias Proops says that's what they do in France," he mumbled.

She suddenly thrust the candle behind her at arm's length and, reaching on tiptoe, put her right arm round his neck.

" This is what they do in America," she said solemnly and kissed his mouth.

She gave him a little shove on the shoulder, blew the candle, and opened the door.

" Good-night, Chad," she said.

12

CAROLINE

" IF you ask me, you missed a trick when you had her that way in the barn."

Sunny mornings, Elias Proops liked to shave himself on the upper porch of the Yellow Bud. Mrs. Mott didn't approve of the idea ; she said it gave the house a loose appearance, which was quite true. Anything looser-looking than Elias Proops with his nightshirt stuffed into his trousers and ogling himself in the mirror he had hung to the corner post wasn't easily encounterable between Buffalo and Troy, let alone in Canastota. But there was nothing she could do about it. A hotel couldn't afford to lose a customer with a government pension.

Chad, who was squatting with his back against the arm clap-boards, said sleepily, " I didn't ask you."

Elias rolled his eyes.

" When a woman lets a man hold her up off her feet in a haymow, Chaddy, she ain't generally thinking about her mamma at the time." He let go of the strop and lifted a long slice of lather off his cheek. It piled up nice on the razor and he looked at it a minute and then flipped it off into the canal.

Chad said, " If I had a face like that I'd let the hair grow."

" Who in hell is the God-damned son-of-a-bitch who done that ? ".

Elisa leaned over the rail and said, " Excuse me, ma'am," and raising up again remarked to Chad, " Missed the crow but flushed the pigeon."

The voice below continued, passing slowly from left to right.

" If I wasn't working for a bunch of lousy, turtle-backed bastards one of them would be eating your greens for you, you old goat."

Chad said, " She's quality, I think. It's funny, her being French and coming over to work for a factory and all."

Distance was robbing the voice of emphasis, but it still sounded pretty erect.

" That woman must have something on her mind," Elias observed. " Ain't you getting ambitious, Chad ? First you have supper with the minister's family and now it's Mrs. Hitchcock. Next thing I know you'll be building a house on Quality Hill." He pinched up the skin and started down the neck.

Chad grinned. " Better watch out for the wattles," he said. " You seen anything of Cisco Trid lately, Elias ? "

" No. And I don't want to."

" Ever been to his place ? "

" No." Elias rinsed the razor in the bowl that Chad had put on the stand with the bamboo legs, and then wiped the blade carefully on the tail of his nightshirt. The warm air came in against his nut-shaped belly and he rubbed it gratefully. " You won't listen to an old man, but just the same I'm telling you, Chad. Don't go mixing with Cisco or Al. You got the nigger away ; if you had the sense of a pig's whistle, you'd let it go at that."

Chad stretched his arms over his knees, spread his fingers, and yawned.

" I ain't scared of Cisco or Al," he said, getting up. " They won't hurt me."

" Well," said Elias, taking up the bowl, " I've told you."

He slung the water out and handed the bowl to Chad to take down to the kitchen. Chad told Mott that he was going to do some cleaning up in the barn. He didn't do much. He gave Mott's old horse a few licks with the brush and swept out the back of the stall and let it go at that. He was just putting away the broom when he heard Bobby Gray come in the manure door.

" Papa wants to know where Henry Prince is," Bobby said.

" I'm not telling."

" Then you've moved him."

" Smart, ain't you ? "

" Well, you just about said so, didn't you ? "

" I didn't say anything," Chad said. " The less people know about that nigger the better."

" What will I tell Papa ? "

" You tell him to forget about that nigger. No matter what happens. You forget him, too."

Bobby looked dejected. He swallowed two or three times, and then said in a muffled voice, " Mother told me to thank you for the trout. She said she never saw such fine ones."

" I didn't catch them."

" I told her we caught them in your private hole," Bobby said. " She said you must be wonderfully smart."

Chad allowed himself to be mollified. " Pshaw," he said.

" I didn't tell about *where* we caught them, though," Bobby said.

After Bobby had cleared out, Chad waited alone in the barn for ten minutes, but nobody showed up. Nothing seemed to be happening at the Yellow Bud either, except for Elias Proops's coming out on the porch to pick his teeth in the sunshine and read the paper.

The paper was the June number of the *Ladies' Repository*, which Mrs. Mott subscribed to, and it had just come. Elias was excited by a series of stories in it about a beautiful girl of poor but quality people. Her name was Fanny Preston and the stories had told how her family had got poor just when she was getting seventeen, and how her rich girl-friends stopped coming to see her and young Alfred Fortune had broken their engagement. Then in the middle of the worst blizzard of the winter when they were all very poor, a man had fallen for dead on the doorstep. Poor old Mr. Preston had dragged him in, and Fanny had given him her bed because it was on the ground floor. She had fallen in love with him while she nursed him faithfully, though he was almost middle-aged. As soon as he was cured, he had gone away on business. But he had come back on the coldest day of the year and declared his love for her. He was Wilbur Lovell, the great Philadelphia banker. Last month the piece had been called " The Honeymoon at the Spa." This month it was to be " Mrs.

Lovell at Home, or Love's Ministries," and Elias was in a lather to see if Fanny was going to have children.

Elias Proops would tell what had happened when Judd Parsons and three or four other interested parties came around in the evening to find out. Chad wondered whether Fanny Preston was a real girl. She was nice. Miss Eveleen Bell, the author called her a ladylike blonde, so he supposed she might look a little like Bobby's sister.

Thinking about Edith Gray, it occurred to him to wonder what a writer like Miss Eveleen Bell would tell about her, and if he himself would be put into such a story, or somebody like Henry Prince. You didn't find runaway niggers in stories. But Mrs. Hitchcock might be in it. She was genteel. In the story, maybe, Edith would be worried about his going to see Mrs. Hitchcock. But in real life she didn't know about it. He found the notion pleasurable ; it made him feel important. In a story they might both be in love with him, and he would be about to make his fortune. Then all the high-class people in Canastota would come to the wedding and Elias would be disgusted.

He was delighted figuring out how it would happen, and he hardly noticed how far along the towpath he was till he heard dogs barking and looked up to see Cisco Trid's house set back under the trees across the canal.

It had a broken-down look, no paint, and a good many shingles missing. There was no bridge, only a small scow tied to the bank. Three or four pigs were wallowing in the mud close to the boat and the dogs alternately barked at them and at Chad.

After a minute three children came out from behind the cedar at the corner of the house to see who it was. As soon as they saw Chad, they straggled down to where the boat was and stood looking at him.

He said, " Hey. Is your Pa home ? "

The two smallest just stared, but the oldest, a girl who was pretty near grown, rubbed one bare foot up her leg and said he wasn't. All three looked ragged and dirty, and the littlest one had no pants on.

Chad asked, " Who are you ? "

" Caroline."

" Is Mrs. Trid home ? "

" Yes, Ma's home. You want to come over ? "

When Chad said that he did, she put the oars in the boat and shoved off. The heavy oars made clumsy rowing, but it was only a few yards, and Chad got in and was pulled back among the pigs, children, and dogs.

Caroline drove back the dogs with an oar while the little boy without trousers watched gravely, one finger up his nose; but when the first dog yelped he pulled it out and yelped too. Then he put his finger in his nose again and walked ahead of Chad and Caroline towards the house.

"What's his name?" Chad asked.

Caroline answered, "Andrew. He's a seven months' baby an' he ain't ever quite caught up."

She wore a tattered gingham dress with, as far as Chad could tell, not a stitch under it. Her eyes had a queer, wise expression; Chad thought she probably knew more than she ought to. She looked him up and down a minute, smiled deliberately, and said not a great many people came out to their house in daylight. Then she opened the kitchen door and led him inside.

The kitchen was cluttered up with a mess of things, from boots and old bags to a black Spanish hen on the back of a chair. Caroline said, "Here's a young man, Ma. He wants to see Pa but he says you'll do."

She shoved a bird's nest of clothes and clothespins off a table, perched herself in its place, and cocked her big toes one after the other, slowly, like a cat. A thin woman in a sleazy dress rose up from behind the chimney. "You wanted to see me, mister?" She shoved back a straggling lock of hair and said apologetically, "I was making butter."

Chad said who he was and asked whether Cisco Trid or Al Heeney had mentioned him.

"I don't know," said Mrs. Trid. "They're always mentioning people." She dumped a cat and three kittens off a chair, wiped the seat with a dishcloth and asked him to sit down. "They're always coming in and going out. It's hard enough to tend to men anyway." She pulled aside the clothes Caroline had dumped from the table and picked up a baby who had just begun crying. "This-here's Paul," she said. "We want to get money enough to send him to college. What did you want to see Cisco about?"

"Didn't he tell you?"

She shook her head.

"That's queer," he said. "I don't understand it."

" It wasn't about Caroline, or anything ? " asked Mrs. Trid.

" No," said Chad. He knew Caroline was staring at him. When he turned, he saw the curious look leave her eyes and her mouth turn sullen. She stretched her legs out again and started cocking her toes. She had high arches.

" Al Heeney told me him and Cisco were looking for a nigger."

" Oh, the nigger ! " It was Caroline who said that, but Mrs. Trid's face was marked by a passing comprehension.

" Yes," she said wearily, " that blamed nigger had give us a lot of worry. Cisco's spent money looking for him. If he don't catch that nigger it'll be a dead loss."

Chad said, " Al told me to come down here if anything turned up."

" You know something about him ? " asked Caroline.

" I know where he's been hiding," Chad said.

Mrs. Trid perked up right away.

" My ! " she said. " That's a relief to my mind. Them two poor men out hunting day and night. It would make your heart bleed, Mr. Hanna."

Caroline said briefly, " Where ? "

" I'd like to see the five dollars," Chad said blandly.

" Five dollars ? So would I ! "

Mrs. Trid said, " It costs such an awful lot, Mr. Hanna. Pigs is different."

Caroline said, " How do I know you ain't fooling ? "

" You don't," he said grinning. But she didn't smile back. Her forehead was puckered. After a minute, she said slowly, " How do you know it was the same nigger ? "

" He's just the same as the handbill Al showed me. He's got a bent finger."

" Yes," she said. " It does seem so."

She thought some more, leaning her chin on her fists.

" Why didn't you let on last night ? "

" There was a lot of people in the Yellow Bud. I had to help." She nodded.

" Well," he said, " that's how it is. I want the money before I tell. If you people don't want to pay, that's all right, too."

He got up.

Mrs. Trid said, " Maybe you could wait for Cisco, Mr. Hanna ? "

" No I couldn't. I've got a job."

Caroline said, " I'll tell them to come down and see you."

" All right," said Chad. " If I'm there, I'll tell them. Of course, they'll lose time, but that's their business."

She agreed. " Pa'd want to know quick," she said. " You wouldn't lie ? "

" I'm telling you the truth," Chad said. He felt pleased with himself.

Caroline still looked suspicious. But she eased her long legs off the table and went over to the china cupboard and felt around among the bottles and broken cups on the top shelf. She had to stretch, and her dress hiked a little. She came back to Chad with some money in her hand. " Here's the five dollars," she said. " But you'll tell me before you leave here."

Chad told her about the potato hole back of Jarvis's barley field. She nodded. " It sounds all right," she said.

She asked whether he would have a drink, but remembering Al's sample of whisky, he said no. He had to get back to the hotel. Mrs. Trid asked him to come again. It was too bad he had found them all mixed up in housework, but next time they'd try to make him feel more at home. She gave her tired smile. The hen squalled and flew out of the door, scaring the pigs who had come up to see what was going on. One of the hounds caught hold of a sow's ear, and the sow screeched murder, and the whole shebang went bucketing round the house in the hot sunlight.

Caroline set Chad back on the towpath. She didn't say good-bye. She still looked sullen. When he looked back she was rowing the boat up the canal and the steersman of a west-bound freight was hollering at her. She wasn't paying attention.

13

APPROACH OF THE CIRCUS

THERE was another good crowd that night, and Mott preened
himself about how smart he had been to get the one big poster
for the Yellow Bud. Patronage at the bar was so steady that
Mrs. Mott had been forced to help Diney wash glasses to that
Chad could act as second barkeep.

Over the heads of the men lined up to study the poster, he
was able to keep track of the session Elias and Judd Parsons were
holding on the adventures of Fanny Lovell. They all agreed that
she was making a first-class wife for Wilbur, especially when she
told Mrs. Euphemia D'Arcy that her first interest was to please
her husband. But there was no sign of any children. " Hell,"
said Elias, " it's generally them quiet, bashful girls that have
babies the quickest." He didn't understand it at all, and the
announcement of the next chapter, to be called " The Philo-
sophies of Marriage," gave him no clue.

Chad expected Cisco Trid might show up, but he didn't.
Al Heeney came in about ten o'clock, though. He took his place
in line along the bar and when he came opposite Chad he called
for a double whisky. He swallowed it plain, his buck teeth
clicking against the glass.

" Pretty busy," he remarked.

Chad said they were. He hadn't been able to leave his place
since seven. But it had been a nice day.

Al looked reproachful. He said he didn't hold the weather
against anybody.

" That's nice," Chad said. " How's Cisco these days ? "

Al said Cisco wasn't feeling well. He'd just been cheated on
a deal.

Chad said that was too bad.

Something to do with a horse, Al said. A black horse that
Cisco had paid five dollars down on. But when they got around,
the horse wasn't even there. Didn't Chad think that was a
dishonest way of doing business ?

Chad said it was always a risk where a horse was concerned.
Probably everybody had to make a living the best way he could.
He grinned. Al Heeney's Adam's apple quivered a little, but he ·

managed to stretch his lips over his buck teeth in some sort of grin. He said Cisco Trid didn't look at it that way. It was too bad there was a woman mixed up in it. It hadn't made things pleasant. When Cisco felt this mean it wasn't pleasant in the house at all. So Al had come down to town till things wore off a little.

Chad said he was sorry to hear that. He poured out a gin and lemon for the next man, who remarked that he had had a brown mare he would sell if Cisco Trid was interested. Al Heeney looked disgusted. He backed out of the line and left the bar-room.

Chad wondered what was going on up at Cisco's and the man with the gin said they were a queer bunch and he didn't really care about selling a mare to a man like Trid. Why didn't Mott get rid of his old skate and buy a decent horse? If Chad could persuade him to deal, the man said he would give Chad five per cent of the money.

Chad wasn't interested in that proposition. He knew Mott.

Outside the open door a canal boat scraped against the dock and a man with a big bag entered the Yellow Bud. Announcing that he was travelling for the New York and Brooklyn Crown Glass Company, he presented Mott with a tumbler of pressed fancy glass. He said it was worth two dollars, but when Mott said he didn't want it, the traveller returned it to his bag and agreed to pay cash for his room. Nobody paid any attention to him until, having had a drink, he announced that if that poster was for Huguenine's Great and Only International Circus, he had seen it in Utica yesterday.

That got him an immediate audience. He said it wasn't a big circus, not like some of the real rolling shows you saw in the southern tier—but it wasn't too bad either. He said the lion act was something to see. He had never seen anything quite like it himself, he said, and he had seen Herr Driesbach in New York City dozens of times, and Van Amburgh more than once. In this Huguenine show, the lion was in a small cage, not more than a good-sized calf box that he had room enough to turn around in. A man got in with him; yes, sir, it beat all. A man got in with that lion in that little box and they lay down together just like man and wife and a damned sight more peaceable than some he knew, too. He looked knowing when he said that and he got a big laugh and half a dozen men offered him drinks, so he was kept active for quite a while, telling this and that, and bringing the talk back to the lion act so he could repeat his remark about lying down like man and wife.

After a while, since nobody else had, Chad asked about Lady Lillian and the equestriole act. The traveller in glass said now that was a cute and pretty piece and with the lion it went to make this show better than the average one-horse breakdown it would otherwise have been. It was high-class, see? It was refined. It was a nice thing to watch. And it was cute. She rode the cutest horse he ever saw.

Chad wanted to ask what Lady Lillian looked like but he didn't like to in the bar. It stood to reason, however, that Lady Lillian must be pretty good or the traveller wouldn't mention her the way he had. Chad decided he would get himself a new shirt to wear to the performance. He would buy it at Hitchcock's to-morrow and that would give him an excuse to go down there in daylight.

Mrs. Hitchcock started when he came openly into the store. She said he ought not to come in daytime; but he said he was just aiming to get a new shirt, so they picked out a cotton shirting together and a cravat to go with it; and Mrs. Hitchcock offered to make the shirt up. She said it would be fun making a shirt for somebody besides Sam. She pinned the cloth on him, and while she was cutting it, she told him that the negro was giving no trouble. Nobody had been around, though the hound had barked a couple of times last night.

Halfway down the block Al Heeney stepped up beside him looking curious and asked what he was doing in town. Chad told him. It was fun telling Al the truth. Al didn't know what to believe. Al said, after a minute, that he and Cisco had been hunting for signs of Henry Prince and Chad said he felt mean about the nigger having escaped before they got to the potato hole. He was positive he had seen the nigger there. If he had been wrong, of course, he couldn't keep the five dollars.

Al admitted there was no doubt about somebody having been in that potato hole for some days and he and Cisco were willing to believe it was Henry Prince. They wanted Chad to feel satisfied and to tell them anything else that came up.

During the night Chad heard somebody in the grass behind the barn. He had chained the doors so he didn't bother to get up. But he knew they were watching him. Though it rained during the night, the man hung round and in the morning Chad felt so fine he decided he would go to church.

He went to Mr. Gray's church. The Grays all saw him there. Mrs. Gray smiled at him, Bobby turned red, and Edith, after one glance, studied her hymn book. Mr. Gray noticed him when he was starting the sermon and lost his text for a minute. But he found it again quickly, announcing the third and fourth verses of the thirty-fifth chapter of Isaiah :—

> Strengthen ye the weak hands, and confirm the feeble knees. Say to them that are of a fearful heart, Be strong, fear not . . .

He spoke in good voice. Watching him, Chad thought that he seemed fitted to a pulpit. The wide brow, from below, no longer looked toplofty, the repressed lips became alive and mobile, shaping the prepared sentences. " Behold, your God will come with vengeance, even God with a recompense ; he will come and save you." Mr. Gray was walking hand in hand with God. For a moment Chad lost consciousness of the bare painted walls. Then he put the high flat voice out of his mind and began to study the congregation. The first person he saw was Mrs. Hitchcock.

She sat erect in the pew, hands folded about the prayer-book in her lap. Though her face was lifted to the preacher, her bonnet, set with its Sabbath decorum, managed to convey a sense of week-day gaiety. Her eyes slowly came round to Chad's, glancing from the pointed corners, and moved back. Not a muscle moved in her face. But he could tell she was amused and interested, and through the rest of the service he was conscious of her awareness of his presence. Just as Edith Gray was, except that Edith, the one time she looked towards him, coloured slightly.

He realised that he had become important in the lives of several people. Bobby, of course, had always depended on him. But now there were in this church Mr. Gray, Bobby, Edith and Mrs. Gray, and Mrs. Hitchcock, all concerned in what he might not do. And outside it, though he would never know it, there was Sam Hitchcock, and Al Heeney and Cisco Trid, and Caroline and her mother, and even, if you stretched it out a bit, the baby, Paul Trid, whom they wanted to send to college. Then there was Henry Prince, the most concerned of all, but he was just a runaway darkey.

Chad, looking over the unsuspecting faces of the congregation, found himself enchanted with the idea. Here he was engineering all this business and concerning these people in it, and nobody else in Canastota had any idea. He wriggled into the corner of the uncompromising pew. His body wasn't adapted to pew-sitting. Up in front the minister was still talking about God and not being scared. Chad folded his hands, composed his freckled face into unaccustomed attentiveness, and realised that Mr. Gray had finished his discourse.

There was a hymn, and a prayer, and then people started getting up and filing out. Mr. Gray disappeared and reappeared and stood on the doorsill shaking hands. As Chad started to slide out with the rest, Bobby signalled him to stay. So he went back and sat down in the corner pew where the light was dimmest until Mr. Gray returned.

"This is a surprise, Hanna. I didn't know that you ever attended divine worship."

"We used to have to go to church when I was in orphanage," Chad said easily.

Mr. Gray gave a thin smile. "Did you? That's fine." He sat down abruptly on the pew at Chad's side. "What have you done with that poor negro?"

"Hid him. He's safe."

"Where?" Mr. Gray made a motion of washing his hands; they sounded dry. "That man put himself in my care, Hanna. I ought to know."

"You don't want to know. It's better for you and your folks if you don't." It's better for Henry Prince, too, he said to himself. Mr. Gray was on the ragged edge of his nerves. If he knew he would be likely to betray the whole affair. That sermon had been preached to the minister himself more than to the congregation.

Mr. Gray was saying, "It's a duty for me to know."

Chad couldn't help thinking what Mr. Gray would say if he told him where the negro actually was, two hundred feet behind his house.

But he shook his head. "No, sir. I don't see it that way. Nobody ought to know where Henry is. Then nobody gets blamed for anything. The only trouble I've got is getting him out of town when the time comes."

" When do you think that will be ? "

" Maybe in a week." Chad hadn't worked over that problem yet to any extent, but now the idea jumped whole and
solid into his mind. " I've been thinking I'll move him out the
afternoon the circus is here. " It was a wonderful idea. He began
to embroider it. " Has your house been watched, Mr. Gray ? " he
asked.

The minister said bitterly, " There's been someone all the
time for two days. I hear him at night. I don't see him, but I
know he's there. It's enough to drive one mad."

Chad nodded. " Yes, I guess so. But that's what we want.
As long as they figure you know, they've got to watch you. You
don't know, but that's how you can help Henry Prince get out
of here." Chad could feel a pleasant crawling in his stomach.
" The thing for you to do is to take Mrs. Gray and Bobby and his
sister to the circus. Then whoever's watching you will go there too."

" I take my family to the circus ? " exclaimed Mr. Gray. " I
can't do that. Why, I've talked against it."

" You can change your mind. You can say you've talked with
the circus manager."

" It's impossible. Besides, if they're watching me, why
won't it be just as valuable to you to have them at my house ? "

Chad was expecting that question.

" Witnesses," he said. " At the circus there'll be the whole of
Canastota to say you wasn't concerned in anything." He made
his voice solemn. " I don't expect anything will go wrong, but
these people are pretty set on capturing that nigger, Mr. Gray."

" It's impossible."

" Elias says a nursing baby couldn't see anything bad in a
circus per-formance." Chad was watching the minister's face.
By holy, Bobby was going to get in to the show after all. But
it took working. It was quite a while before Mr. Gray would
admit that he would even consider the idea. . . .

Chad felt fine. A couple of times during the day he went for
a short walk, just to see if anybody was watching him. Once it
was Al Heeney who ambled down the street behind him. The
second time he saw nobody till he got nearly to Jarvis's. Then
he heard someone tailing him in the woods. When he turned
round the man cleared out. Chad only got a look at his back,
but that was enough to tell him that Al and Cisco had brought
in outside help. They were getting pretty desperate, he thought.

14

RETURN OF MR. BISBEE

HENRY PRINCE was doing well. Three meals a day had filled him out ; his leg was healing nicely. He told Chad that if it weren't for the nigger-chasers, he wouldn't mind living in Canastota. "This-here's a nice town, boss. Mis' treats me fine." She had even washed his clothes for him one night.

Squatting across the barn lantern from Henry, Chad saw how he had filled out. He looked bolder. His eyes had gained a kind of slyness.

"Ever hear anybody round the barn ? " he asked.

"One day. Last Sunday. I guess Mis' was in church. The rabbit dog bark and bark. A man come in here. I heard him in the hay. But he went away." Henry snickered at his own astuteness. "That man he holler, ' Henry Prince. Here's yo' friend.' But I ain't saying nothin'."

He wished he could send word about it to some other darkies he knew. He was a little stiff in his bad leg, but he could walk. Chad told him he would have to limber up every night now. To-day was Saturday. To-morrow the circus was due to arrive. It was going to show on Monday.

"Circus ? Boss, I'd mighty like to see that circus."

"What do you know about a circus ? " Chad said. "You ain't been to one, have you ? "

"No, sir. But I seen one going by along the road. The over-seer wouldn't let us quit the rows. But I could see the red wagons with the gold on 'em, boss. Yes, sir, and two spotted hawses. They sure did look pretty. Right then I said, ' Henry Prince, the first time you're a free man you're gwine to see a circus.' " He looked at Chad from under his brows. "Cain't you fix it so I see this one ? "

"No."

"Don't cost but two bits for the pass, does it, boss ? " His voice was wheedling. "I been a good nigger, ain't I ? You give me two bits, boss."

"You ain't free yet," Chad said. "What do you want to do?

Walk right in among Cisco and Al and the constable there
handy for them and maybe the county sheriff? You crazy? "

" It do seem like I ought to see that circus," Henry muttered.
Chad turned down the flame of the lantern.

" Listen here," he said. " You can't see that circus because
when that circus starts performing you're going to light out for
Canada."

" In the afternoon? "

Chad nodded. " I got it all figured out. There's going to be a
crowd round here. All kinds of people. Likely some other
niggers will show up. People ain't going to notice one more.
Anyway, Al and Cisco are going to be at the circus watching me
and Mr. Gray. Mrs. Hitchcock is going to give you a bundle of
food and Mr. Gray is going to give you two dollars. Half an
hour after you get it you're going to walk right out of this barn.
You'll cross the canal bridge and walk north along the road.
You'll get to Ridgeville. It's just a corners' post office and you
take the left fork and keep going till you reach Cicero. It's a
good road, good walking all the way."

He felt pleased with the plan as he told Mrs. Hitchcock
about it in the back of the store. She was making him try on
his new shirt and they both thought it looked handsome. She
tied the cravat for him, and then brought a mirror for him to
see himself in.

" You look so nice, Chad," she said. " You ought to keep
yourself better."

Chad, grinning self-consciously at himself in the glass, lifted
his eyes. The frame of the mirror was under her chin. She was
smiling and her eyes were bright.

He felt embarrassed.

" I ought to pay you for making the shirt," he said. " But
I guess you don't want to be."

She shook her head. " It was fun to make it. When you go
to the circus I shall feel proud. You're smart, Chad. You could
earn money to have a dozen shirts if you wanted. You could be
very rich."

" Me rich? How could I make money? "

" I don't know." She pursed her lips, making a mouth at
him. " But see how smart you are thinking how to get Henry
Prince away from here."

" It ought to work all right. Don't you think so? "

"I do not know. Perhaps." She shrugged. "But it is a lovely plan. You make each one think different things, so you know what every one is thinking. Then the black man walks out of the town in the middle of the day, and nobody knows."

"Except you. You know all about it."

He tried to persuade her to come to the circus with him.

But she refused. "You are a smart boy, Chad," she said. "I think you have a good heart, though you are so lazy. Some day you will want to work hard, maybe because you are in love and not because you are excited because she is French and married to some old Sam. I think then you will be a big success. Maybe you'll remember Berthe Hitchcock and wonder how you could have been so foolish." She smiled for a moment, then reached up and kissed him as she had that first night, putting one arm round his neck. "There," she said. "To-morrow I go to church again. Monday the black man goes away. Tuesday Sam returns. It is finished. But it was fun and we have done a good thing together. Good-night, Chad."

He walked back slowly, thinking about her. As he rounded the Yellow Bud, he made out a shadowy figure in the garden patch. They were still on the watch; so much the better, he thought. He wedged the latch on the barn door after closing it, lit his lantern, and slapped the rump of Mott's horse as he passed. Then he pulled up short.

There were three new horses in the stalls. One look at the brown coat of the first was enough to identify the circus agent's horse. He was glad to have him back. Then he glanced at the next two.

The second was a heavy iron-grey, with full quarters and a broad back. Not quite as heavy as a Conestoga, Chad thought; he would move easier.

The third animal was coal black, about fifteen and a half hands, well-ribbed. It turned to meet the lantern light, pricked ears, and nickered softly. For a minute Chad stood still; then slowly hung the lantern from a nail and went into the stall, using both his hands.

"Where'd you come from, boy?" he asked softly.

His hands had never touched a horse they fancied so immediately. He hadn't a reservation to find. He couldn't have put him together better if he had been God and God had been Chad Hanna. The horse was sweeter in front, if any part of him was better than another. The drop of the leg from the point of the shoulder, the deep chest. Even in the stall he kept his weight well under himself. He had finish, he had style. God damn it, he was perfect.

Chad hoisted himself on to the manger, and the horse lifted the cravat with his lips and sniffed at the opening of the shirt.

"Kind of a pet, ain't you?" Chad rescued his tie, but the horse hadn't mussed it. "Who cleaned you?" he asked. There was no mark of harness or saddle. He was still puzzling about it when he went to sleep, but he slept well. Three fine horses in your barn beat monkeying with runaway niggers and visiting a storekeeper's French wife.

He woke before sunrise and did a good job on the three horses. It was a clear dawn, a south wind pulling in through the barn door, just strong enough to feel. When he had finished, Chad wandered up to the Yellow Bud to see what it all meant. Diney wasn't down yet, so he went round front.

A faint dawn-colour down the canal turned the water pink and grey. A crow crossed it, solitary, unvoiced. The door opened to let out Mr. Bisbee.

"Hallo," he said. "We missed you last night."

"Hallo," Chad said. "I didn't expect to see you back here."

"I didn't myself." Mr. Bisbee slapped his leg with the poster case. "There's been some trouble along the line," he said. "Burke and Walsh are tearing our paper. I guess we've been going too good to suit them."

"Burke and Walsh?"

"Sure. They're bigger than us; one of the Flatfoot shows. They've got the syndicate money behind them," he said. "Who'd think they'd bother showing the bush towns? They must be counting on a dry season for their heavy stock. Well, I better get down and see if A.D. is up yet."

"Who's A.D.?" Chad asked.

Mr. Bisbee had stepped off the porch and now with easy long strides was making along the towpath. "A for Alonzo. D for Dent. Alonzo Dent Huguenine. He's the boss, owner, equestrian director, but he rides with the wagons and sleeps on the cashbox when we're on the road. At least him and Mrs. Huguenine do it together."

Chad hurried after him.

" You mean the circus, Mr. Bisbee ? Why, I aimed to see it come in."

" Well, all you had to do was walk out and look. There she lays."

He extended a lean hand. His intelligent eyes softened for an instant, and a kind of glow came over his face. He leaned against a post in the derailed fence and looked across the pasture lot of Mott's brother-in-law.

All Chad saw was five wagons, irregularly spaced on the uneven grass. The unharnessed teams were grazing contentedly towards a far corner. The harness sweat still marked their hides. They looked like decent animals, but nothing extra. The teamsters were sleeping, curled up in blankets under the wagons. If it hadn't been for the colour and shape of the wagons, Chad wouldn't have given the outfit a second look.

But the wagons were painted red and yellow, and two of them were great boxed affairs that would make heavy hauling on a wet road.

" It looks better when the tent's up," Mr. Bisbee said.

" Where's the other horses ? You said there were thirteen."

Mr. Bisbee smiled. " Haven't forgot much, have you ? Well, they're in some of the hotel barns. Rossello's at the Graham House. He always goes to the best hotels. Pamplon's at the Canastota House. So's Fiero, the juggler. Ike Wayfish is at the Yellow Bud. I wrote him about it being a nice place when I was here before. And Lillian's there too, Kind of surprise to me. Generally she goes to the same place Rossello does. They must have had a bust-up. Well, it's none of my business."

" Lillian ? You mean Lady Lillian ? " Chad asked. " Then that's her horse ? The black one ? "

" Yep."

" He's the one in the poster ? "

" Yep. Nice animal, ain't he ? " Mr. Bisbee replied casually.

" Yep," said Chad. He felt sarcastic. Mr. Bisbee smiled and gave a hitch to his pants.

" Well," he said. " I got to get down and break the bad news to A.D."

Chad stood still, watching him across the pasture. He went to the smallest of the wagons, put one foot on the step at the rear, lifted a lean hand, and knocked. After a minute, a stocky man emerged buttoning his trousers. He sat down on the steps,

taking a stogie from Mr. Bisbee, and the two of them talked and
smoked.

Chad hesitated between going down to them and returning
to the black horse. It seemed incredible that Lady Lillian should
have put up at a place like the Yellow Bud, but Bisbee had said
she was there, and the horse in the barn proved it.

Back towards town roosters began crowing. Mechanically,
Chad looked east. The sun was coming up over the canal. Fiery
in the horizon haze, it dented the edge of the world.

The fields and woods seemed to move as the light gained
force, as if the land breathed. A bittern appeared from the north,
cutting east, with lazy wing strokes, and slowly dwindled against
the sunlight. The sun completed its round, and in an instant the
horizon had healed. Chad heard a thin horn note. The *Red
Bird Packet* was coming at a trot behind its tandem hitch.

He waited till the team passed, watched the towline slip by,
and then the boat—the windows curtained, the shutters white
against the red cabin walls, smoke issuing from the stovepipe.
The steersman leaning against the rudder stick raised his horn
and blew again, a long flat note.

As if to answer the horn, a deep catarrhal roar broke out,
filling the flat land from end to end. The packet steersman was
transfixed. He turned to look at Chad, his horn still held an inch
from his lips. Chad, delighted, waved his hand. That steersman
didn't know about the circus. Probably the dumb bezabor had
never heard a lion. Neither, apparently, had Jarvis's brown bull.
His bellowing was thinned by the distance but full of bluster.
Another bull took it up. Dogs started barking.

Chad looked at the wagons. Mr. Huguenine and Mr. Bisbee
were still talking unconcernedly ; but one of the blanketed men
had waked up. He crawled from under his blankets, stretched,
walked to the farthest wagon, and hammered on the side with
a heavy stick. Then he dropped the stick, said a few words to
Huguenine, and came towards the fence.

" 'Morning," he said to Chad.

" 'Morning," Chad said.

" I got to find a butcher."

" It's Sunday." Chad said.

" Don't I know it ? God damn that lousy horn tooter. Now I
got to find eight pounds of beef, or lamb, somewhere."

Chad said, " Probably Allen's will give you some."

He decided to walk back with the circus man.

"You going to put the tent up to-day?"

"Naw. It's Sunday. It's a day of rest, see? All a canvasman has to do is to tear her down and load the show and drive the God-damn wagons over from Vernon. And get up at sunrise to hunt eight pounds of fresh meat because a fool thistle-chin happens to have a tin horn in his hand and thinks he's a wind-jammer. He's waked the cat, see? That wakes the gaffer, so the gaffer remembers he's got to order meat for to-morrow. Cats don't eat Sunday, but they're hungry Monday. And that God-damn kinker that works the act rots in his bed in a hotel. Seventy-five cents a day expense allowance for him. That's what I get for wages. The hell with it. Where is this town?"

"Over the bridge," Chad said. "You'll see Allen's round the first turn to your left."

The skinner stamped on to the bridge, paused to spit from the top, wiped his mouth, and stamped down the other side. Chad eased past the Yellow Bud, but Mrs. Mott caught him and set him to carrying up cans of hot water. He had to leave cans outside of three doors, besides taking up Elias Proops's basin. The old man was already out of bed and peering through the door that led on to the upper porch.

"Mrs. Mott says you can't shave outside to-day or to-morrow."

"That woman would talk if she had bugs between her teeth. Don't she give me credit for no manners when a lady's in the next room? Ain't I got my pants on?"

"Well, that's what she says." Chad obeyed orders by sitting on the bed until Elias had begun shaving over the washstand. But he kept his own eye on the porch. He didn't see anything worth seeing, however. Circus people seemed to be heavy sleepers. There wasn't a sound from the next room.

"You didn't get a look at her, did you?"

"Looks like a female," Elias said. He was mad.

"So did your grandmother."

"Must have two legs. I didn't see 'em. But she's got the same number of feet."

"Yeah."

"Well," said Elias, "she's got two eyes, and two arms, two hands, two bubs, and two . . ."

"You dumb old goat."

Elias Proops snickered.

"Yes, Chaddy, she adds up to be a woman all right. Looks to me she's got two everywhere she ought to have two, and most likely she's got one of all the other essentials, including a tongue."

Chad disgustedly walked downstairs. He went to the barn before Mrs. Mott could find out anything else for him to do, and just to have an alibi started shining the black horse with his hands.

He was still at it when he heard a light footfall on the barn floor, and glancing along the horse's side he saw a woman's shadow in the sunlight.

15

LADY LILLIAN

"Good-morning."

Her voice was clear, low-pitched, and cool. At the sound the horse turned his head, ears pricked tight so that they both looked out together. Chad said, "Hallo," but the horse whinnied, drowning the word.

She stopped short at the stall post and Chad saw that her good-morning had been for the horse, not for him.

Her shadow had given no warning of how small she was ; she would hardly reach Chad's shoulder. She was wearing an old riding habit, of a dull and slightly faded green, the skirt caught up in her left hand. Above it the short jacket fitted snugly to show her erect slender waist and the small high curve of her breast. At the sight of the two faces, the horse resting his chin lightly on Chad's shoulder, she smiled widely.

"You've done a lovely job," she said. "Are you the hotel groom ? "

Chad nodded, still looking at her.

He didn't think then that her face was beautiful, but he had never seen anything like her, either. She wore a long-vizored and weather-stained jockey cap set jauntily on her dark hair. It was gathered behind and a cluster of loose curls came forward over her right shoulder. He thought she had the widest smile he had ever seen on a girl. But it was her eyes that held him most. They were a clear grey.

He said, " If you call it a hotel, maybe I'm the groom. My name's Chad Hanna."

" Mine's Albany Yates," she said. Lifting her skirt high enough to show the ankles of her half boots, she came into the stall beside him and the horse immediately craned farther over Chad's shoulder and started nuzzling the bow of her stock. " I've been in all sorts of hotels, Mr. Hanna, but I've never seen any one groom Buck as well as you have."

" He's a fine horse," Chad said.

" Isn't he ? " she said quickly, and reached over Chad to bat the horse's nose gently with her whip. " It's not often we get a free Sunday morning like this, is it, boy ? Wouldn't you like a good gallop ? "

" You going to take him out, Miss ? "

She nodded.

" Yes. It does him good to have a real run. Is there a patch of open woods anywhere near ? "

He could see that she was as excited as the horse at the notion of a ride. " I could show you, Miss."

" Where is it, Mr. Hanna ? "

" There's a small stand of hard maple down beyond Jarvis's. It's cleared and the ground's level. I could borrow Mott's horse and go along with you to it." Her grey eyes were speculative. He explained, " There's three or four high-barred gates. You'd want somebody to take them down."

It would be worth while going along, he thought, even on Mott's old plug.

" All right," she said. She stepped past him to unfasten Buck's halter rope. She wore no perfume ; but she carried an indefinable healthy sense of freshness that was more heady to Chad than any scent.

" I'll get him out for you," he said quickly.

" No thanks. He likes me to."

The horse backed out rapidly, spreading his hind legs as if he knew what was up, and started dancing as soon as he was out on the run, lifting both forehoofs together and making a play on the halter rope. The girl looked tiny under his head. She stood at ease, one brown hand firm on the rope, the other still holding her skirt off the floor, and looking back towards Chad.

"We'll have to get the saddle from the wagons," she said. "Is the lot far off?"

"Just the other side of the road." He came out of the stall. He hated thinking how he and Mott's horse would look passing the Yellow Bud along with those two.

The girl kept eyeing him. As she went into the stall, she said, "I tell you what. You take Jerry. It won't hurt him, though you mustn't gallop him hard. You don't mind riding bareback?"

"No, miss."

He had the iron-grey out in a moment. The horse handled easily. He was careful. He was as different from the black as any horse could be, unless he was dead. But he looked like a horse, which was more than you could say of Mott's horse. As they started out of the barn, however, Chad stopped and looked back at the girl. "Is it all right to take them out this way?"

She glanced up in annoyance.

"What do you mean?" she asked. "Why shouldn't we?"

"That black horse belongs to Lady Lillian. I oughtn't to let him out without her say-so."

"Oh, *she* won't mind," she said carelessly.

"I ought to ask," Chad said with unaccustomed virtue. "I'm responsible for this barn."

"I tell you she won't mind at all. She's only too glad to have the horse exercised. She said to me this morning she wished I'd get up and take Buck out."

"Cripus," Chad said. "Do you know her?"

"Yes."

"She lets you take the horse out? That a fact?"

"Honest," she said. She looked honest. But Chad couldn't quite make her out.

"Why don't she take him out herself? I should think she'd want to."

"Oh, she's really a lazy sort of girl. She likes to lie in bed late. You wouldn't think much of her, Mr. Hanna." She beamed on him.

"She must be something to own this horse, though. What do you do, Miss Yates?"

"I ride a little. And I hold things for Mr. Pamplon when he's on the rope. I want to be a lady rider someday," the girl said confidingly. Somehow they were out of the barn and walking the horses along the towpath.

In spite of the hampering skirt, Albany Yates moved easily. She was sure on her feet. She had a free stride for a girl. She had class, just like the horse. And she was liking it, just like the horse. She kept looking right and left over the fields, and suddenly she looked at Chad, bright-cheeked, bright-eyed, and friendly.

" My, it's fun ! A whole day with no show. And we're out in the best of it, the very best. Aren't we ? "

He nodded.

" Not even Fred's around yet," she said.

She didn't mind his being along. It made him feel proud. He wondered who Fred was. He didn't like him. By God, he felt jealous. He felt fine to feel jealous. The grey whickered in his ear and then snorted, and Chad pointed out the circus wagons in the lot. Who the hell is Fred, he wondered.

She said, " Fred's mad at me. He's our top star, he gets the last spot for his act."

" You mean Sig-nor Rossello, the high-rider ? "

" Yes. He's crazy about Lillian, you know." She was looking at him solemnly. Then she laughed. " But we don't care, do we, Buck ? "

" Does Lillian think anything about this Fred Rossello ? " Chad asked elaborately.

" She's been crazy about him. All the troupe expects them to get married. His real name is Fred Shepley, though he's billed as Rossello. And he really is good. Wait till you see him. Mr. Hanna. But he has got a nasty temper at times." They were turning into the lot, and she drew a deep breath, arching her breast in the tight little jacket. " Let's forget Fred. Let's forget everything ; do you hear Buck, Jerry ? I want to get on my saddle and ride ! I don't want to see a tent or smell a cat, or hear anybody even whisper ' circus.' " She lifted her chin. " I want to hear birds and see flowers and smell the woods."

" Sure," Chad said. " I get that way sometimes."

" Do you ? What do you do for it, Mr. Hanna ? "

" Oh, go fishing maybe."

She said, " Fishing ! That's lazy. I despise it." She pushed ahead of him towards Mr. Huguenine's wagon, where Huguenine and Mr. Bisbee were still in conference. " Good-morning," she said in her clear voice. Mr. Bisbee grinned at her, but Mr. Huguenine merely looked up to say, " Hallo, there . . ." in a moody voice.

She interrupted him gaily. " You don't know me," she cried.
" I'm Albany Yates and I'm playing hooky. You don't see me,
you don't hear me, you don't know where I'm going." Her •
cheeks were pink. " I want my saddle and I want a bridle and
circingle for Jerry. Mr. Hanna's showing me the way."

Mr. Huguenine looked to Chad just like a farmer whose
pasture was drying up. His broad hands hung over his knees, he
had milker's wrists ; and his chunky red face was exasperated
and confounded. He just stared at the girl, but Mr. Bisbee said,
" All right, Albany. Have a good time."

She led the way to another wagon, which was loaded solid
with chests and boxes and blue-painted planks. A side-saddle
hung from a cross rod and wall hooks carried bridles, halters,
and harness replacements. In five minutes she had put her small
boot in Chad's palm and swung up. The black stepped giddily
sideways as she adjusted her skirt, and Chad bridled the grey and
tightened the circingle with its hand grips. He started him across
the grass, keeping his hand on the grey's withers, caught his
spring with the horse's stride, and vaulted clean.

The girl brought the black alongside. " You did that
nicely," she said.

Chad didn't answer. He could have told her of scrambling
on and off the backs of tow horses when he didn't reach above the
elbow. He swung the grey towards the opening in the fence. By
the time he reached it, the black was waiting for him.

" Where ? " asked Albany.

" Towards town," he said. " Then turn right at the foot of
the bridge."

She was off with the word ; he saw her round the corner
ahead, the horse changing his lead. By the time the grey had
reached the same place, she was far down the road.

But she came back before he was half-way to Jarvis's, swinging
the curve close, and passing him, the horse dancing as she pulled
up, then turning and dropping into place alongside.

" We feel lots better," she said. " Buck couldn't wait, but
we'll be polite now."

They rode till they came in sight of the Jarvis farm, companionably side by side, saying nothing, but they couldn't hold
back for long. As soon as they had passed the buildings, the
black sprang away.

She rode like a feather, her hands light, her back pliant and straight. She was nothing on the horse's back ; he hardly felt her ; and this time she really let him out. After trying to kick a slow gallop out of the grey, Chad resigned himself, and they fell back into his lolloping canter that was as easy to sit as a chair with arms. He went straight ahead down the middle of the road, his neck arched soberly, minding his own business. He wouldn't have shied on any account.

Chad fancied that she had offered him the grey, knowing he would keep his own gait. With Chad safely ambling in her wake she could be alone when she felt like it. He would be handy to take down bars and put them up, and she could play with him, as a swallow would play with a cat. If it pleased her, he didn't care. He dismounted when they came to the fence he had in mind, and he and the grey waited amiably till she returned.

The run had warmed the black. He was easy now, blowing deep as he minced through the bars. And the girl's colour was high.

" Did you wait long ? " she asked.

" Only time enough for Jerry to catch his wind," Chad said.

She laughed. " He's an honest sobersides," she said.

She kept pace beside him over the low roll of the pasture. But at the next bars she told him to take down only the top, and Buck, seeing, pointed his ears, turned back with a quarter lift, turned again, and took the jump, well put together, and danced back.

" That was pretty," Chad said.

She dropped the tip of her whip to the withers. The black placed his forefoot, and bowed. Then as Chad stared he came up, started his mincing, and threw his head up and down.

" Does he do that in the show ? "

" I don't want to hear the word ' circus,' " she said. " Remember ? "

" All right," said Chad. " Who trained him, though ? "

" I don't want to talk show."

Chad took down the bars, led Jerry through, replaced the bars, and mounted. He was getting the hang of vaulting pretty well, and he felt pleased with himself. Jerry had a trick of giving, too, leaning against the vault, that made it easy. The girl said, " I bet you could ride."

" I've done it some. But I never rode a good horse." He looked at Buck ; then raised his eyes to her face. She kept it in profile, so that he saw it against the sky. Her lips were closed, and her eyes looked straight between the ears of her horse, as clear and impersonal as the look of a young hawk.

"Albany's a queer name for a girl," he observed.

"Yes, isn't it?"

"It sounds nice, though, when you say it." He repeated it— "Albany."

She would not turn her head.

"It's your real name, ain't it?"

"Of course it is. I told you. But I didn't pick it out. Why do you ask?"

"I like it better than Lillian," he said. "It—it kind of goes with you."

She turned sharply on him. "Didn't you hear me say I wanted to forget about the circus?" she demanded imperiously.

Chad grinned at her.

"What made you have such a silly idea?" she asked.

"That horse wouldn't do tricks for just anybody. I've handled enough horses to see that."

"Oh?"

"Then what you said about Lillian wanting you to exercise the horse while she stayed in bed. I think that was kind of cute."

"It's true."

"Yes, but there wasn't any conversation going on when I was in the next room. You can hear a lot through those walls."

"That old man makes dreadful noises."

"Elias? Yes, he got a powerful catarrh."

"Well, I don't want to think about Lillian and her affairs. What I said was true, too. You wouldn't like her. Albany's a nice enough girl."

"Yes, she is. But I ain't seen Lillian."

She smiled, "Well, you'll see her to-morrow. Let's forget her now."

"Sure. Now I know who she is." He kicked the grey round into a cow track and they headed down a slope towards the maple grove. "There's your woods, Miss Yates."

"Oh," she said. "They're perfect."

The cows had kept the ground brushed. The clear grey boles grew straight and close, covering perhaps three acres.

"You stay here," Albany said. "And you can watch Buck. It's the prettiest thing he does, though we can't do it in the show. It's what a horse ought to do, not shake hands, and bow and waltz. Watch us."

She put him into a canter down the maincow track which ran straight through the grove. Then, without visible manipulation, she turned the horse into the thickest part of the growth. Without losing pace he began threading the trees, taking a line alternately on his right and left. As soon as he was well warmed to the work she began changing his turns, starting him on figure eights. He kept his neck arched close ; his ears pricked back and forth catching the least whisper she had to give. She sat him like a fairy, her face gaining the same absorption as the horse in their evolutions. The turn, the quarter pivot, the change of lead, the sidestep from one alley to the next, the backward pacing, the full pivot, followed each other, adapted to the spacing of the trees, figures of a mystery.

Sitting on the broad, complacent, unmoving back of the grey, Chad thought he had never seen two living beings so completely one. And he had never seen anything more beautiful : the black horse, all fire, perfectly controlled, absorbed ; the girl, with her black hair, in her faded soft green habit, entranced by the figures they performed ; the grey straight boles of the trees, the brown leaf mould, the green sun-filtering canopy of leaves. His ears were full of the cushioned thud of hoofs, and even as he listened and watched, seeing the white spatter of froth against the horse's chest, and the clear grey shining in the girl's eyes as she passed, he knew it was something he would never be able to forget. When she finally brought up before him, her eyes exalted, he hadn't a thing to say.

The shine dimmed in her eyes ; she saw him ; and her eyelids drooped. She became shy, waiting for praise, for her horse and for herself. Finally she asked, " Was it nice ? " And he said " Yes." It was enough for them both. They rode out of the woods into the clear heat : the green pasture, the bars, the road, the turn at the bridge, the wagons to restore the saddle and bridles, and so back to the barn, walking the towpath side by side.

At the porch of the Yellow Bud she turned Buck's lead over to him. " I'll have to go in and change."

" I'll rub him down."

She said, " I think it's the best ride I ever had."

As she went in through the door, passing under Diney's

rolling stare and Mrs. Mott's curious and disdainful eyes, it gave Chad a start to see again how small she was.

Elias Proops hawked at him from the bar-room door.

" My, my," he said. " Our little Chaddy."

" You go to hell," said Chad.

16

THE SHOW

By ten o'clock on Monday morning, Elias Proops admitted that Canastota looked like a real metropolis. Wagons were hitched all along the street. They said the church sheds were jam full of horses ; the barn at the Yellow Bud was packed ; and because of the big poster, there were plenty in the Yellow Bud bar ; even some people you would not expect to find there, like the Honourable Spencer. " Me and him had quite a conversation," Elias told Chad. " He gave me this-here Albany cigar."

Chad was alternating between the bar and the barn. He had more to do than he could rightly handle. A circus hand had come after the horses, but Chad had insisted on leading Buck himself. Elias had gone along and they had had an early view of the white tent with its red and yellow banner floating from the centre pole.

He didn't see Albany Yates anywhere around, so he and Elias trudged back to the Yellow Bud. Elias said he felt tired. He ought to have saved his strength for the performance. It had been a long morning for Chad, too. Before sunrise he had gone down to Hitchcock's to give Henry Prince final directions and make sure that Mrs. Hitchcock would have the negro's food ready for him.

The day was perfect ; circus weather, Mr. Bisbee said, pulling complacently on his after-breakfast stogie. The sky was deep blue and high white clouds rode lazily on a warm wind. Everywhere through the village out-of-town folks were visiting on the front porches. Their voices up and down Peterboro Street made a sound as steady as flowing water. Once in a while the pitch changed, and then you would see a circus performer threading his way along the footpath.

Down beyond Hitchcock's a Professor Arganave had set up a Hydro-Oxygen Gas Microscope. He had five slides, which cost ten cents to look at. One was a sample of blood from a young unmarried girl ; the second was from a married woman ; the third was the blood from a healthy man ; after it you saw the blood from a man who died of drink. (The professor said he had got it from Bellevue Hospital in New York. Judd Parsons, ordering a double whisky in the Yellow Bud, declared it was enough to shake a strong man's nerves.) The most interesting to see was the fifth—the blood of a man-eating lion. The professor explained that it had been taken from the lion in Huguenine's Circus. If you looked close you could see islands of human blood in the slide, proving the fact beyond a doubt. For twenty-five cents you could see the blood of half a dozen celebrated people, like Byron, or Benjamin Franklin, or Alexander Hamilton (procured at Weehawken just after he was shot by Aaron Burr). For fifty cents the professor would take a sample of your blood and let you compare the slide with those of the others. Canastota had never seen anything like it.

A little before eleven, Bill Jones, the constable, began clearing people off the canal bridge. Two minutes later, the whole town heard the circus coming.

A string of yelling boys preceded it. They were followed along the towpath by a man mounted on a mule, and even at that distance the redness of his nose was like a ball of fire. Every few paces the mule would stop short, and the man would tilt forward and make a wild grab for the ears. He wore a long frock-coat with a patched tail, a flowing purple cravat, and an enormously high top hat.

Behind him rolled the largest of the wagons, hauled by four horses. The driver, who turned out to be Mr. Huguenine himself, wore a scarlet jacket and a shiny, high, black, stiff, military cap. On top of the wagon the band, in similar attire, were whanging out the tune of " Long-Tailed Blue " on a fiddle, a bugle, and a drum.

The mule turned up on the bridge and the drunken man yelled, " Hey, mister, can you tell me the road to Canastota ? "

The constable got embarrassed. The crowd howled. A small boy shinnied along the outside of the railing and piped up, " Straight ahead, sir."

The drunken man said, " Thank you, my boy," in a deep

grave nasal voice and took off his hat. The mule stopped, and the man slammed forward against his neck, dropping his hat in the effort to grab the ears. The mule then picked the hat up, twisted his neck back, but just as his rider reached for the hat he straightened his neck. The band behind struck up " Clare de Kitchen," and to that tune, the drunken man still trying to recover his hat, the circus rolled down the bridge into town for its parade.

Chad, standing beside Mr. Bisbee on the upper porch outside Elias's room, felt his blood quickening. As the big wagon made the turn by the Yellow Bud, he saw that the tail gate had been chained horizontal to make a platform. On it, sitting unsteadily on a gilded chair was the fattest woman Chad had ever seen. She wore a magenta silk dress, with a scarf of blonde gauze round her throat. The scarf did nothing to protect the rolls of flesh that bulged from the square-cut low corsage and back. At each lurch of the wagon, she gave the impression of being about to flow over one edge or the other of the chair, and each time, recovering her ponderous balance, she gave a hearty laugh and waved her fringed parasol at the bystanders. As her dark roving eyes spotted Mr. Bisbee on the upper porch, she screeched a greeting.

Mr. Bisbee waved his hat and kissed his hand. " That's Bettina Billings—Mrs. Huguenine in private life. Billings was her maiden name. She weighs two hundred and eighty. ' America's Own Fat Woman : She Stands Against the World.' It was my idea."

" Who are those two walking ? "

They were both dressed in raspberry-coloured tights. The man was swarthy, a foreigner by his looks. He kept flashing his teeth in a nervous brilliant smile. The woman was thin. She also smiled, but on her colourless face the smile looked strained.

" Those are the Pamplons," Mr. Bisbee said. " She's bad scared. He wrenched his ankle in Vernon and she's afraid of a fall. Ah, here comes Rossello."

Chad would have known him anyway. Anybody would have known him who had seen the poster. He wore a costume of vivid green tights and leotard, like Mr. Pamplon's, but his were covered from neck to ankle by spangles. His arms were folded across his chest, his seat was erect, graceful, and negligent, and at every motion of his body the spangles seemed to catch fire

from the sun. But though he must have been aware of the
impression he made, he looked neither right nor left, but straight
between the ears of his cream-coloured horse, with a sullen,
disdainful expression on his mouth.

Chad said, " He's young."

" Twenty-four ; but boy, he's good. And he knows it all
right, too."

Rossello was followed by the juggler tossing balls from time
to time. Behind him came Lady Lillian ; not at all like the
Albany Yates of yesterday. Her habit of light blue velvet was
the epitome of elegance with its puffed sleeves and snow-white
stock. Her gloves were white and so was Buck's bridle. A shiny
top hat tapering to the crown sat stylishly on her dark hair, the
effect softened by a three-foot floating pale blue gauze.

It was obvious that Buck was enjoying himself, and that she
was enjoying him. He went up the bridge sidewise, pirouetted
and reared on the top, and went down the other side facing the
other way, and at the foot of the incline he made a bow, to the
great delight of the populace.

" Ain't she a picture, though ? " asked Mr. Bisbee.

Lady Lillian was followed by the cat wagon. The sides had
been removed. Through slats, Chad had a glimpse of a crouching
brown animal. He seemed perfectly shapeless ; he seemed asleep.
But he was a lion, a genuine lion ; you could smell him ; and the
foot-high gilt lettering proved it.

Chad did not see the parade complete the circuit of the town.
But from time to time he heard the music of the band. He was
down in the barn taking care of half a dozen newly-arrived
horses, when the parade returned over the bridge. The band
was playing the patriotic air, " Champlain." From the door,
Chad had a glimpse of the big wagon on the arch of the bridge,
the drummer beating his drum, against the blue June sky. Behind
them came the crowd.

He went into the loose stall he slept in and put on his new
shirt and cravat and wondered whether Mrs. Hitchcock had
given the negro his bundle of food yet. Well, he had done all he
could do himself. The rest was up to her and Henry Prince.

Al Heeney was waiting on the porch when Chad came by.

" Hallo, Chaddy," he said. " Quite a parade."

" Yeah. You going to the show ? "

" I ain't made up my mind. You going ? "

" Yeah. I'm just about going now. I want a good seat."

" Say, that's a good idea," said Al. " Guess I'll move along pretty quick. They say the tent holds over three hundred people. I call that mammoth." He drew his lips over his teeth in a smile that he meant to look careless. His small restless eyes wandered away. For a minute neither he nor Chad had anything to say, but stood there like two dogs working out a mutual idea, listening to the thud of people's feet, the shuffle of boots in the dust, the steady hum of voices . . . " I seen a sample of that lion's blood." . . . " Yes, sir, the spots of human showed up plain." . . . " I wouldn't have believed blood had all that stuff in it." " What stuff, George ? " " Them spots. Kind of like dead wigglers in a swamp puddle." " You mean my blood's got wigglers ? I think it's disgusting." " Science is science, the professor says. You can't go against it." . . . " And a man gets right in with that lion." . . . " I won't look." . . . " Leony had a sample of her blood took. Jed tried to see it but she wouldn't let him." " Serves her right. That girl always was a hussy, is what I say. Trying to hook a man like Jed after being five years on the canal. Can you imagine ? "

" Hallo," Chad said to Al Heeney. " Don't tell me Reverend Gray is going to the circus."

Al perked up.

" I'll be durned," he said.

They were coming down the bridge. Mr. Gray looked pretty self-conscious, but Edith and Mrs. Gray were laughing at him, teasing him. Chad thought the minister was just as excited as they were but didn't want to have it show. He heard a whistle tootling and saw Bobby galloping after them.

Bobby was too excited to notice anything or anybody. He bumped right into his father and was caught up short by Mr. Gray's hand. But even then, walking at the Reverend's pace, he managed to look like someone prancing.

A little way behind Bobby, Chad saw Cisco Trid. He had heavy jutting hairy brows over narrow dark eyes. His face was mostly chin and jowls. He rolled a little as he walked, and he kept looking round him all the time. When his eyes passed over Chad and Al they gave no sign, and Al acted as if he hadn't seen him at all.

Chad grinned at him. " Well, well," he said. " You coming too ? "

"I might as well."

The people were already thinning out along the towpath, but Al kept reluctantly looking back all the time. It was obvious that Chad's brisk pace didn't suit him, but at the same time he didn't dare let Chad out of his sight. When they were half-way to the lot, however, he turned his head, and now he began to hurry Chad. "We'll be late," he said. "We'll miss the march around the ring. It's all in historical costume."

Chad glanced back at the bars and saw Mrs. Hitchcock walking by herself among the last stragglers. But behind her was a man whom Chad felt sure was following her, because he kept looking at everybody else without ever seeming to see her at all. They were all accounted for.

They were late. There were only a few at the ticket wagon where Mr. Huguenine was making change. "I got a pass," Chad said. "See you inside, maybe." He had to laugh at the way Al hustled for his ticket, his eyes agonizingly following Chad inside.

The band was playing beyond the performers' fly. "Long-Tailed Blue" was the tune again. Mr. Bisbee took Chad's pass. "We're just about due to commence," he said. He smiled. "Three hundred people here. It's a good stand."

The tent was circular, nearly seventy feet across, with tiers of seats ranged round the red curb of the ring and a small square wooden platform ; the centre pole, like the trunk of a tree, straight up to the canvas peak. The canvas curved down to the side walls just over the heads of the topmost spectators. It was white and soft with the sun on it, but the air inside seemed like the heart of a green lake, as though the spring grass of the pasture lot gave out a light of its own. The wind was just strong enough to put small bellies in the canvas top. It seemed to Chad not like a roof held up by poles, but like a shaped and hovering cloud ; and as it moved and dipped it seemed to catch cupfuls of sunlight and then to run them off, as though the light were a kind of rain.

It took him some time to find a seat, and when he did he never noticed Al's entrance. Al was swinging his head, working this way and that around the ring ; and when he finally spotted Chad he was exactly like a pointing dog. Then he relaxed, found himself a seat, and seemed to disappear.

Chad did not even notice Mrs. Hitchcock. He sat like the rest of the crowd, who were in line to see, staring at the performers' entrance. And a long moment of silence settled over the audience.

It was broken by the bugle in an uncertain rendition of the opening bars of "Anacreon in Heaven." The roll of the drum followed. Then the fife opened the stirring notes of "Champlain"; the fly parted; and the band appeared preceded by the red-nosed clown in his unsteady shabby elegance. He tripped as he entered and fell flat, so that the four players had to step over him. He scrambled up and ran helplessly for the nearest tier of seats. Anybody could see that he had made a fearful mistake and gone to the wrong entrance. He tried to wedge himself between a young farm lad and his girl, but the lad indignantly shoved him out. Chad laughed. He was so busy watching the antics of the clown that he did not notice the rest of the performers until then.

When he saw them, he felt baffled. All but the Pamplons were on foot; but they had a queer ineffectual appearance, as if they were tired and felt that the tramp around the ring would never end. Their bows were stiff, and when the women made gestures of kissing their hands, they looked like animated dolls. Their smiles meant nothing. Only their eyes showed a kind of defensive estimation of the audience.

He saw it even on the face of Lady Lillian. She was not wearing her blue habit, or if she was, it was hidden by a long red cape. She was meant to look like a queen, he thought, or a princess, for she wore a crown and carried a ball and a golden rod. It must have been the historical costume. He felt worried, sensing the same apathy in the crowd.

They brightened momentarily when the Pamplons passed, walking cautiously on high stilts. Mrs. Pamplon kept straight ahead, her colourless face intent. Her husband occasionally did a kind of shuffle, two steps forward, one step back; but he didn't impress the crowd. Then the red-nosed clown appeared from the end of the tiny arena on stilts of his own. He seemed almost to run, taking incredibly long strides, seeming on the point of a fall a dozen times, but jerking himself erect again. His stilts were the tallest of the three, and he overtook the procession just as they reached the fly. But his stilts were too high to let him out. Half a dozen times he tried, but at each attempt his head struck the canvas and he staggered back. The audience hooted. Then Mr. Huguenine, dressed up in tails and a very flowery waistcoat, appeared, holding the ringmaster's whip and whistle. He nearly collided with the clown. " Get out," he roared. " I'm trying," the clown cried shrilly. " Give me my hat, mister."

" I'll give you something hot ! " shouted Mr. Huguenine, and he began cracking his whip behind the drunken man. " Get down," he commanded. " I can't," howled the clown. It became suddenly excruciating to the small boys. Clouds of flour dust erupted from the clown's seat. He took one foot out of a stirrup, lost his nerve, and fumbled frantically to regain it. All of a sudden he began to sway. His face struck the canvas and he jerked himself back. Then he yanked himself forward and hit the canvas again. He gave a wild yell as he came back the next time. Every one could see he was going to fall and the ring-master mechanically shielded his eyes from the sight. But the clown struck on his shoulders, came up on his feet, and then fainted dead away. At a final cut of the whip, after every one thought he must have been hurt, he jumped up and ran fran-tically to the main entrance.

The ringmaster wiped his brow with a handkerchief. Seeing it, the clown pulled his own handkerchief out of his pocket. It was a long handkerchief, it kept coming ; he started pulling with both hands, hand over hand. Yards and yards emerged. It changed colour—white, blue, green, yellow, purple, red. At the red the clown cried, " Nosebleed," dropped it, and fled. Through the laughter Chad heard a packet horn blowing for the landing.

Mr. Huguenine, unnoticing, his collar riding low on his thick shoulders, bawled " LAdies and GENTlemen," in a tremendous voice, and drew breath. " I welcome you, one and all, man, woman, and cheeild, to Huguenine's Great and Only International Circus and Equestri*ole*. I address my introductory observation particular to those ladiees and gentlemen who have felt scrupular about attending the pleasing recreations of the CIRCUS. In order to meet this objection at once I pledge myself that in this establishment there will be nothing to en-courage an unpure idea or awaken a thought to disturb the infant mind. Here," he wiped his forehead again, " are—are mirth and skill commingled, without a painful blush to the fairest cheek. Fathers, mothers, sisters, brothers, we welcome you one and all. Ladiees and GENTlemen." With obvious relief he blew on his whistle. " I now pree-*sent* the Pamplons, Mounseer and

Maydam, the premeer gymnasts in Europe, in their first American tour, exclusive with Huguenine's Great and Only International Circus."

The Pamplons, still with the anxious look, ran out of the fly, jumped up on the platform, where Mr. Pamplon executed some backward flips and Madam Pamplon jumped up and down with little kicks of her toes. The band struck up. They went into a series of acts, somersaulting together, the woman standing on the man's shoulders, somersaulting to the ground. It all seemed to go easily, and as he watched Chad saw the colour come into their faces. Suddenly they were lost in the concentration of their work. It became increasingly exciting. It worked up to a climax, as Mr. Huguenine announced the journey on the slack wire ; Mr. Pamplon taking his position on one of the platforms, Mrs. Pamplon on the other.

He remembered what Mr. Bisbee had said about the man's ankle being wrenched, but Mr. Pamplon swung across the wire with a quick run of his feet, swung round and smiled at the audience and then at his wife. Then he started doing wonderful things on the wire.

Chad was so absorbed that he had not noticed Albany Yates standing in the fly. Now she came forward to hand things either to Mrs. Pamplon or to Pamplon himself. First a sword that he balanced on the edge of a wineglass as he kept his own balance in the middle of the wire, his feet swaying from side to side. Then a hoop, which he stepped through and worked over his body. Then a musket, with which he did the manual of arms, the climax coming when he fired it.

At this point concentration held every performer motionless, and Chad realised that this was how Mr. Pamplon must have injured himself. His flinch after the recoil was noticeable, his feet shuffled rapidly, for a moment he seemed about to fall ; then he caught the sway of the wire, dropped the gun into Albany's waiting hands, and everybody smiled and the audience clapped for the first time, though it did not know quite why it did.

The finale, when he walked the wire in full swing, seemed somehow easy to them all, and Mrs. Pamplon's face showed such obvious relief that the audience applauded wildly. The journey on the moving globe was a distinct anti-climax. Chad drew a deep breath and looked at Albany Yates, met her eyes, and to his amazement got a smile. It seemed incredible that she should

have picked him out of the crowd. He watched her run lightly
to the flies. Then in the lull between the acts, as Mr. Huguenine
was drawing wind for his next announcement, Chad looked
round the tent.

The Grays sat together on an upper tier. A little to the left
of them was Cisco Trid. Chad found the man who had been
trailing Mrs. Hitchcock, but it took him a moment to find her.
She was looking for someone in the audience. He saw her eyes
pass over the row he sat in without finding him. It gave him
an odd feeling of helplessness, as if something in his plans had
gone wrong. He did not hear Mr. Huguenine bellowing that
the next act would be Señor Fiero, the juggler and magician,
with his unbelievable and graceful feats of pure dexterity, the
delight of the crowned heads of Europe, including the King and
Queen of England. He wondered how far out of town Henry
Prince would be by now. And then, as the clown stumbled in,
Chad saw Bill Jones, the constable, moving towards Mrs.
Hitchcock.

As the constable spoke to her, she turned pale, rose hurriedly,
and followed him out. The same man who had trailed her to
the circus also got up. Glancing towards the Grays, Chad saw
that Cisco Trid had vanished. Al Heeney was working his way
out of his seat. Something had happened ; something down at
Hitchcock's, or they wouldn't have sent for her.

The juggler was already doing his tricks with bottles, balls,
hoops. He was pretty good, but Chad had seen jugglers as good
or better. He hitched himself over the back of the seat and
dropped to the ground. The sudden clapping was like a storm
over his head. It would be a long way round, under the seats.
He ducked under the canvas wall, came up in the bright outer
sunlight, and ran round to the entrance.

Mrs. Hitchcock, with the constable, was hurrying along the
towpath. Some distance behind her, Cisco Trid, Al Heeney, and
the third man made a group, like trailing dogs, but Mrs. Hitchcock wasn't looking back.

" You leaving too ? "

Mr. Bisbee stepped quietly out of the tent.

" Do you know what's happened ? "

" That woman's husband's been hurt, they say."

" Sam Hitchcock ? " Chad was incredulous.

" That was the name. They say he'd just got home. Somebody heard a noise in his store and went in and found him. He's hurt bad. He said a nigger did it."

" My God, Henry Prince ! "

" Yes, boss. Please, sir."

A slouching figure in faded blue jean cloth worked towards them round the curve of the tent wall. Henry Prince was a badly scared darkey once more. He took off his hat humbly and stood beside Chad, his eyes averted.

" I didn't mean to hurt him, boss. He come jes' as I's a-going. He say where did I come from. He try to stop me. I done hit him, I guess. I put him in the house. A white man heard me, but I got here first." His teeth began to chatter. " They'll come after me, boss. Maybe they'll turn the dogs on me."

" Did you kill him ? "

" 'Fo' God, I didn't try to."

" You're a murderer, Henry," Chad said in an awed voice.

" He's not completely dead if he can tell the colour of the man who hit him," Mr. Bisbee observed dryly. He raised his brows as he studied Henry. " Fugitive ? "

Chad nodded. " Cisco Trid and Al were after him. They're nigger-chasers," he explained. " I was trying to get him loose."

" I don't like nigger-chasers," Mr. Bisbee said.

" You were a fool to hit him, Henry. Why didn't you just run ? "

" My leg's too stiff. He cotched me." He drew a slobbering breath. " I thought maybe I could hide in the circus wagon."

" Go ahead," Mr. Bisbee said suddenly. " In the big one. Get up front and lie down under the patching canvas. Let them load on top of you. You'll be all right."

Henry made a gasping sound ; he went without a word, running with a stiff limping stride.

" Nigger-chasing is a dirty business," Mr. Bisbee said. " He can drop off the wagon to-morrow in Cicero. They won't look for him here and you and me can forget we saw him. But there's going to be a ruction in Canastota," he added thoughtfully. " That woman's smart. She'll shift the blame. Who else is in it ? "

" Her and the minister and me. That's why we all came to the circus. They can't prove anything."

" Mr. Bisbee nodded. " It was a good idea. It ought to have

worked, except for the husband coming home. Why didn't you allow for that?"

"He was due to-morrow," Chad said. "Maybe old Sam got jealous, or maybe he wanted to take her to the circus after all."

"Old man, eh? She's not old. She's damned handsome, I'd say. That makes it worse for you."

"Me?"

"Yep. Somebody's going to be set up for the old man to blame. You're the logical choice." Mr. Bisbee began tapping his leg with a stick. "There's one of those three coming back. He's got his eye on you. It's not going to be healthy for you in Canastota. If I were you, I'd plan to move."

Chad watched Cisco Trid lean his arms on the fence rail at the entrance to the lot.

"Maybe I will. I'm getting tired of this place."

The south wind blew warmly on them, popping the canvas softly at their backs. Inside the business of clapping broke out again.

"What will you do?" asked Mr. Bisbee.

"I'll look around."

"How would you like to work for the circus?"

"For this circus?"

"Yep. You'd start as a canvasman. But maybe I could use you tacking paper, with this Burke and Walsh business going on."

"I might try it."

"Seventy-five cents a day to start with. One of the canvasmen has quit."

"All right."

"Then get inside and see the show. You've missed the vaulting. You'd better learn what you can about it. Hang around afterwards. I'll talk to Huguenine."

17

THE SHOW, PART II

CHAD decided to sit near the performers' entrance, and he found an empty seat at the very end of the fourth tier from which he could look down on the performer's heads as they came in. The ringmaster's whistle was shrilling an end of a demonstration on the parallel bars by the Pamplons and Fiero. His voice was raised laboriously in the "Ladies and GENTlemen" as they ran off to brief applause. "We now present the outstanding talent in schooled riding in the World to-day, procured by the management at immense cost direct from the British Empire. Lady LILLIAN and her educated horse, BUCEFFLUS . . ." Mr. Huguenine wiped his brow . . . "in their Equestriole, an act acclaimed throughout the universe."

Chad heard her voice. "Let go of him, Fred."

"Still high-and-mighty?" The man laughed. "You'll come down, my lady."

The whistle shrilled. The flap was lifted. Buck appeared at a hand gallop, ears up, neck arched, perfectly in hand. As she passed, Chad saw Lady Lillian compose her face for the audience-smile. The band, a bit late, struck up a tune as they went round the open, then changed to a kind of wheezy dance in which the drummer marked the beat emphatically, and Buck began to dance, changing his lead, and bringing his quarters from one side to the other.

The audience took to him, and in a moment they took to the girl in her ladylike blue habit. Farmers, used to walking the furrows behind tired teams, were entranced to see an animal that knew what he was up to. Woman admired the dress and the girl's face. Someone near Chad said, "She ain't painted or nothing. She looks real nice."

He drank it in, as if he were already a part of the show. The fixed smile had left Lady Lillian's face, she was concentrating on her riding now, and the horse was dipping his ears back to her. As they finished a new step, she would smile, and the horse would toss his head. He went through most of the paces she had showed off for Chad in Jarvis's maple grove, walking sidewise, walking backwards, rearing, turning close round the centre pole, but it wasn't as free a sight ; it wasn't half as much fun to watch as the close riding through the trees, though the audience didn't know that.

Then she made the horse step into the ring and kneel and lie down, while she slipped off. She made him play dead and stood on his side. She batted him with the whip, but he would not move. She called Mr. Huguenine over and asked for help, but Mr. Huguenine got nowhere.

She turned to the audience and spoke a little piece :—

> " My horse lies dead apparent in your sight,
> But I'm the girl can set the thing to right,
> Speak when you please, I'm ready to obey,
> My faithful steed knows what I want to say.
> Please, Mr. Ringmaster, just lift his foot.
> You see, the horse is dead beyond dispute.
> This shows how horses by heaven were designed
> To be in full subjection to mankind.
> Arise now, Buck, and stop your sham and fun.
> Salute your National Hero, General Jack-SON."

She saluted, hand to vizor of her hat. Behind her the horse heaved up on his haunches and raised a forefoot. The cheers broke out, loudest from Judd Parsons and his fellow mechanics. Lady Lillian blushed brightly, stepped to the horse, caught her knee over the pommel. They made a circuit of the tent and went out through the flap.

Chad let out his breath. Making a horse lie down and sit up didn't seem fun to him, but if the audience liked it, he supposed it was necessary. There was no doubt about their liking it. Even the girl beside him was applauding. The energy of her clapping unloosed a cloud of heavy perfume. Chad took notice of her for the first time. It was Cisco Trid's daughter, Caroline.

She was dressed in what might have been something that had belonged to her mother, a limp, flowered cotton. It had been altered to fit tight to her narrower breast, and her tanned face had been rouged and powdered. Her hair was fixed in curls that were still damp and she wore a locket on a chain—cheap pedlar's jewellery full of bright glass—that hung suggestively

to the almost invisible cleft of her breasts. Over her shoulders
was a thin shawl with a hole badly mended.

"Hallo," he said.

She turned slowly to look at him and looked away without
speaking. "Didn't you like it?" he asked.

She did not answer.

He said, "If you'll be a good girl, I'll buy you some sugar-
candy."

"I don't want sugar-candy."

"Didn't you like the act?"

"Oh, yes." She hardly breathed. "She was beautiful."

Chad said "Yes," and looked down to see if he could catch a
glimpse of Albany. But she had gone. "I took care of her
horse," he said.

"Did you? That's fine. You're good at taking care of things,
aren't you?" she said grimly.

"What do you mean?"

"I mean I believed what you said. I gave you the five
dollars."

"I told the truth," Chad said. He chuckled. "I bet Cisco
was mad?"

"Mad? Some. You want to see? I can't show you all of it,
but you can see a little."

She let the shawl slide off her shoulders.

At the edge of her dress was a long livid welt.

"You told the truth all right, Mr. Hanna."

"He licked you like that?"

"That's the top one," she said.

He said, "I'm sorry. I didn't know he was that mean."
Being the cause of it, his anger became self-righteous. "By
God, I'll fix him some day for that."

"You're a brave man, aren't you?" she said scornfully.
"You'll do a lot. You know a lot." She was talking in a low
voice, so that only he could hear. She seemed to have lost her
sense of shame. "Perhaps you'd want to knock me down, even."

"He let you come to the circus, though."

"He made me. I didn't want to come. He told me I'd have
to earn the money back. Perhaps you know how, Mr. Hanna.
Perhaps you'd like to help me earn it. Perhaps you'd think that
was being real smart. He said there would be plenty of men up
to anything if I hung around."

"Don't cry," Chad said. "I'm sorry."

"I'm not crying about that," she said angrily, fishing for a handkerchief. "I just hate to see people like her, who can do what she wants. Who's nice and goes with nice people. That's all. Leave me alone." She drew a deep breath. "But I ain't going back. I ain't going. I'm going to quit. He's after that nigger now."

Chad said, "Yes, the nigger's run away." He fumbled in his pocket. "Here," he said. "Here's the money, most of it."

"I don't want your dirty money. I don't want to see you. Leave me alone."

A couple of women near by were staring furiously at Chad. "Stop it," he said. "You've got to stop it."

"I believed you," she said. "I thought you were real nice."

Chad swore helplessly.

Neither of them had seen what was going on ; neither had heard Mr. Huguenine's announcement of the high-riding act, and now Signor Rossello was doing his stunts, making his running jumps from board to horse's back, doing his pirouettes and leaps over ribbons. The applause drowned their voices, her crying. She was properly crying now.

Then Chad felt someone touch his leg. Albany Yates, her face concerned, was standing below him.

"What's the matter, Mr. Hanna?"

He said that the girl was upset. She had been misused. He didn't know what to do.

"Poor thing." Albany gave him a long look, then leaned forward and said to Caroline, "Won't you come down with me? We can get outside, away from these people. I'd love to help you if I could."

The girl stopped crying, and stared at Albany. "You mean it?" she asked. "You'd let *me* come with you?"

"Of course," Albany said.

They disappeared through the performers' entrance, a warning glance from Albany having told Chad to stay where he was. He felt glum, alone, and watched Rossello with sour eyes. The drunken clown had come through the flap and was trying to catch the ringmaster's attention. "Hey!" he shouted. But Mr. Huguenine took no notice until everybody had had time to see the clown. Then he cracked his whip at him.

The clown ducked back, but instantly reappeared, to repeat

the pantomime. The third time, however, he held a huge whistle to his lips. He swelled his cheeks ; he blew, and a tiny pipe was emitted. Instantly, clapping his hands, the clown rushed to the ring, hit the jump-up board, and made a tremendous leap at the cream-coloured horse.

He went clean over, turning a single somersault, rising to his feet, and then falling down. The ringmaster jumped after him, and a chase ensued, with the clown always returning to the board and attempting his leap.

Signor Rossello, having finished his act, stood outside the ring with folded arms and open scorn on his face. The fourth time the clown hit the pad and fell on his knees. He rode that way shouting, " Look at *me* ! Look at *me* ! "

The ringmaster now proceeded to try to dislodge the clown, but, failing, decided to employ guile. They began to bargain. The clown would come down if he could join the circus. He said he could do anything. The ringmaster said he had no room for another performer. There was no place for any one else to sleep. The clown said he would sleep anywhere. He lay down on the pad to prove it while the horse still continued his amiable lollop. The ringmaster said all right, if he didn't mind sleeping with the lion, he could stay. But he would have to get himself a costume. The clown jumped up and clapped his hands. " I got one," he cried. " I'll show you." He unbuttoned his coat and threw it away. He took off his waistcoat, and dropped it ; he took off another, then he took off his cravat. Then three pairs of trousers, while at each new garment the audience guffawed. At the last pair of trousers, the shirt turned out to be a full-length nightshirt. The clown gave a drunken start round and hid his face. Then he whipped the nightshirt over his head, and showed himself in red and white striped tights with a leotard of blue, bearing white stars. It was only then that people realised that all this time he had been standing erect on the back of the lolloping horse.

" Bring on your lion," he yelled. " He dasn't touch me now."

Two bandsmen hauled in the cage wagon, turning it to face the entrance, then with poles poked through the bars, driving the lion away from the small end gate.

People could really see him now. He moved torpidly, swinging his shaggy head. He looked to Chad like an old animal, but he was big, and when he sat down and yawned, showing his immense jaws, Chad couldn't help a shiver. As the clown in his stars and stripes approached the cage, the lion's hide rippled once or twice. The clown giggled.

"There is where I sleep," he announced. "Lay down, you big bezabor."

One of the bandsmen slid back the gate and, moving cautiously, the clown approached it. He growled. The tip of the lion's tail twitched. His yellow eyes blinked and narrowed.

"Lay down," said the clown. "Here I come."

With lethargic indolence the lion allowed himself to lean against the bars and slowly lie down. The clown crawled in. The cage was too small for him to stand erect in. He had to stoop as he approached the lion and laid a hand on his shoulders. The lion lifted his head, looked at the man, opened his mouth, and yawned.

It was unbelievable. The man-eating lion allowed his paw to be lifted. He let his head down. He gave a lazy flip, exposing his belly, and the clown tickled his side so that the hide twitched responsively.

Then, as deliberately as the beast had, he stretched out beside him, rested his head on his hand, and asked the ringmaster, with a hiccough, "Do I get the job?"

"You do," said Mr. Huguenine.

"Then I'll come out now." He got up as slowly as he had lain down, petted the beast, and said, "See you to-night."

He backed out of the bars, dropped to the ground, and gave a little spring. A storm of clapping greeted him. The band struck up "Yankee Doodle," and the show was over. . . .

Chad watched the people file out. For a minute he was all alone in the green and white stillness of the tent. It was broken by the sound of mauls on stakes outside. Then a hand came in, took off his red jacket, and started knocking the seats apart. When he saw Chad, he said, "There ain't any more, bub. No more at all."

"I know," Chad said. "I'm waiting to see the boss."

"He's busy."

"Mr. Bisbee told me to wait."

"Oh, you're taking Jim's place. My name's Joe Duddy."

"Mine's Chad Hanna."

" Pleased to meet you."

They shook hands.

Joe Duddy said, " Well, you might as well do something to keep warm. How about helping me lug out these blocks ? Rossello's supposed to do this work, but he's late and the boss wants to get an early start. This is the damn'dest circus you ever saw. What did you join it for ? "

Chad said, " What's the matter with it ? "

" Oh, it's been doing all right, but we've had no competition. It'll be different from now on. You'll see. Huguenine don't know nothing. You know what he is ? He's a farmer. Yes, sir. Just a rube like you were till he signed on. He comes from Herkimer. This show broke down there last fall on his place and the manager asked Huguenine to take a mortgage on the show so he could get down to Putman County after some new talent. And poor old Huguenine done it. Yes, sir."

They were lugging out a section of the seat boards as Rossello came in.

" Hallo, Fred," Joe greeted him. " Been getting a nice nap ? "

" Don't get chesty," Fred said. " I'll help you with the rest. Who's the helper ? "

" Chad Hanna, meet Fred Shepley, the greatest top-rider in America—when there ain't too many others around."

Fred Shepley shook hands casually. He was about Chad's height, but he looked all muscle. His straight blond features were handsome. He had a good opinion of himself, and Chad, having seen him perform, didn't blame him. But he didn't like Fred. He didn't like anybody that looked that sure of himself. It wasn't healthy.

But Fred was willing to work and he lifted one end of a seat stringer a good deal easier than Chad could.

" Feeling tired, gillie ? "

" He ain't no towner," Joe said. " He's joined out."

" Not much heft for a roustabout," Fred said as though Chad were somewhere else. " He won't last. Hand me the gimmix, Hanna."

" The what ? "

" The sledge," Joe put in quietly. " Don't let him do his high-riding act on *your* back, bub."

Chad, however, picked up the sledge and tossed it, helve rst. " Catch," he said.

It took Fred by surprise. He had to jump to save himself, and he lost his footing, sitting down solid in the dirt bank of the ring.

Chad said calmly to Joe Duddy, " He ain't very quick when it comes to work, is he ? "

Joe said, " Easy, bub. Go easy."

Fred had got up.

" What do you mean by doing that ? " His voice was truculent.

" If you want to find out, come over here," Chad said.

He felt mad enough to fight anybody. He didn't like Fred Shepley, and he was still mad at himself about the trouble Caroline Trid had got into, on account of him.

Joe Duddy said quickly, " No fighting on the tear-down, Fred. You can comb him later if you feel like it, but Chad didn't mean harm, I guess."

" I'm the kind of horse bucks if a man gets fresh on my back, see ? " Chad said. " Next time I'll hand it to you, Mr. Shepley."

" All right," Fred said. " So long as you don't throw it. I can't afford to get crippled by a sledge. The show can't afford it either."

" Pardon," Chad said. " I didn't know you was that valuable."

Duddy broke in again. " Don't be damn fools. Here comes the gaffer."

Huguenine entered with Mr. Bisbee. He looked around irritably. " Why ain't Pamplon here ? Him and Fiero ought to have the wire down by now. How the devil are we going to reach Cicero if you boys don't work ? "

Bisbee said soothingly, " They'll be along. The old rag will come down on time. Here's the lad I told you about. Come over here, Hanna."

Mr. Huguenine said, " Bisbee tells me you'll join out."

" Yes," said Chad.

" All right. I see you're working. Keep at it, Hanna. By God, we need somebody that will work." His square face was troubled.

He was an older man than Chad had at first imagined. But he liked his face and the honest way he chewed tobacco. " Can you write your name ? "

Chad said he could.

" Then go along with Bisbee and sign up. I don't know what

you want to sign up a roustabout for, but if you want to it's all right. You people drive me crazy. First Albany wants to take along that girl just because her Pa licked her, and now you've got this feller. What is it? The French Revolution? He looks useful anyway."

He was peeling off his coat, showing his heavy shoulders bulging the shirt. When they left, he was already at work knocking the seats apart.

Mr. Bisbee took Chad down to the treasury wagon, got out a paper, and showed him where to sign. "Now," he said, "you're a legal member of the troupe. They can't get you without a warrant. Mr. Hitchcock is raising hell in town. If I was you, I'd sneak down and get your things and go out along the road. You can pick us up as we go by."

Chad said "all right. . . ."

It was near sunset when he stood at the crossroads at Ridge-ville. The light wagon with the performers had already gone by behind the trick mule and an odd horse. Chad had had a glimpse of Albany, Fred, the Pamplons, Fiero, and Caroline Trid. The clown was driving. None of them had seen him. He hadn't wanted them to.

He felt a little mean, not having had a chance to say good-bye to Bobby Gray. Bobby and Elias were the only people he was going to miss. Mrs. Hitchcock had disturbed him. Elias had said that she had foisted everything off on his shoulders. She said Chad had come around and threatened her. It had been all she could do to keep him out of her house. She hadn't dared say anything, because the negro was so close. He was a murderous man. That was why she had gone to the circus, to keep safe in the crowd. If she had only known Sam would be home.

"Does he believe it?" Chad asked.

"An old man like him with a pretty wife has got to believe it or the town will laugh him silly," Elias said. "When you go to get married, Chad, pick out a steady, hard-working woman, who's willing to support you. That is, if you can't get you a pension somewhere. Hell, boy. It ain't going to seem right in this town without you helling around. I wish I was going with you."

Chad asked about the Reverend Gray.

"Have they talked about him being into this business?"

Elias said he hadn't heard anything. "You let God worry about Mr. Gray," he said, "and the rest of the same he will do for himself."

"I'd like to have you say good-bye to Bobby. I'd like you to give him my knife."

The old man promised. He would also explain things to the Motts. They would be glad enough to be rid of him, now.

"I'll kind of miss Diney, though," Chad said.

"No you won't. You won't miss nobody. You'll have a hell of a time, Chaddy. Maybe you'll be a fool and marry the circus Queen. Maybe you'll get rich. By God, you might even work. It's time you done something for yourself. Why, when I was your age, I had got two girls into trouble, and fought the British, and earned me a pension. . . ."

In the crossroads store a couple of checker players, glancing up between moves, kept curious track of him. He didn't mind them, poor old dodderers ; they probably didn't even know there was a circus. They'd have a shock when the big wagon with the four-horse hitch came by. He leaned his shoulders against the finger-post with the flat rays of the setting sun warm on his freckled face. His bag rested beside his feet. He held his battered hat in his hands.

He wondered how far the first wagon had got, and whether Albany and Fred had made up their trouble. They might go to the same hotel in Cicero. He didn't know how many there were in that town. Then he remembered Caroline. He had been upset to think of her coming along. Now he saw that for a while she might keep Albany's attention away from Fred. His mouth sobered. A lot of fat that would be for him, though, sleeping with the wagons.

Then he saw dust down the road that led from Canastota, and turning out of the trees came the treasury wagon with Mr. Huguenine holding the lines. The team were hauling against the slight grade, putting a jerk in Mr. Huguenine's big wrist, hammering their heads up and down.

"Hallo," he said. "Where's the sign ? "

He peered at the finger-post when Chad pointed. "Cicero," he said. "It don't tell how far."

"Eighteen miles," said Chad.

"No toll bridges, are they ? "

"No," said Chad.

" Hup," said Mr. Huguenine. " Come, girls, we'll get to bed yet to-night."

The kingbolt screaked as the wagon made the turn. " You kin ride with Budlong," Mr. Huguenine shouted over his shoulder.

The led horses, Buck, Jerry, and the cream, with the mule, followed docilely behind the wagon. They were out of sight by the time the big wagon hove in sight. It took the grade slowly, the four horses down against the collar, almost kneeling, and the driver walking alongside the wheelers, the four reins in his fists held high. Their hoofs dug thunder out of the hard dirt, and the wheels rumbled in their boxes.

They stopped at the corner and Budlong asked, " Cicero. How far ? "

" Eighteen miles," repeated Chad. " I'm riding with you. The gaffer told me." He was picking up their language.

Budlong, a loose-jointed man, climbed on to the eveners, put his foot on a broad rump, and jumped to the seat. Chad followed. The leaders took up the slack of the traces, the wheelers heaved, puckering their haunches. Looking down on them, you could see their power, the necks, the shoulders, the swell of the backs to the squared-off quarters.

The wheels rolled far under them. Chad looked out over the country. He looked back to see the fourth wagon make the turn and the two old checker players squeezing noses against the windowpane.

" We ought to get to bed to-night," he said.

" That's all right by me, roustabout," said Budlong.

Roustabout. He said it over to himself. He liked the word. It made him feel tough, ornery, up to pretty near the whole shebang that was the universe.

18

ROADSIDE

HALF an hour after they had left Ridgeville, Budlong observed,
" Might rain."

" Yeah ? " said Chad. " It don't seem likely to me, though."

" Well, maybe not." Budlong put a twist of the reins round
his right knee, sat on the ends, and used both hands to get a
paper out of his pocket. " Chewing tobacco ? " he asked.

Chad said no.

Budlong fished himself a nice chew with the ends of his
fingers, gauged it against his open mouth, and engulfed it like
a trout inhaling a first-grade grasshopper. He replaced the
paper and took up the reins again.

" Don't ever want to do that with a four-horse hitch yourself, bub. Now you seen me do it, that ought to be enough."

" No ? " said Chad.

" Nope," Budlong shook his head. " Seen a man do that once
on a mountain trace. Nigh wheel hit a pothole. Pole bucked
and eveners slugged the wheelers in the rump. Had a runaway
before he got the tobacco in his mouth. Reached to put it back
in his pocket when the bolt broke and the team yanked him off
the seat slicker than spit. Four horses and Pasco at the end,
bucketty, down Clinch Mountain. Wagon broke off on the first
bend and went over the bank. Ran over Pasco's wrist with the
off wheels, when he reached for the lines he didn't have no
hand. Made him helpless."

Budlong got his chew salubriated and let go the first spit. It
marked up plain in the road dust, and he worked on the reins
and brought the broad wheel spang over it. It made pretty
driving.

" Pasco must have had a bad time," Chad remarked.

" Kind of. He was killed. Know what he died of ? "

" No," said Chad.

" Strangulation."

" By the lines ? "

" Tobacco."

The ice being broken, Budlong let the conversation go. The

wagon lumbered steadily westward. Now and then Chad thought
he had glimpses of Oneida Lake, but he could not be sure with
the dusk laying heavy on the flat land. It was getting dark fast.

Budalong, however, seemed to have owl's eyes and it was
some time after Chad had given up trying to follow the road
that the driver remarked, " Getting kind of dark. Better light a
lantern. We kin eat, too."

He had picked out a hard turnout at the side of the road. He
swung the team into this space, leaving room behind for the
following wagons. Then he climbed down.

" How about Huguenine ? " Chad asked.

" The gaffer ? Always wants to get right into the next stand,
if he can make it afore bedtime," Budlong said. " If we're
hauling all night he stays with us. Pertection for the treasury
wagon," he explained. " Fidgety old bastard."

He had got out a big oil lamp from the toolbox at the off side
of his wagon. He lit it now with a locofoco, adjusted the wick
and handed it to Chad."

" Hang her on the nigh side bracket," he directed.

Chad had to balance himself on the tyre of the front wheel to
reach the bracket. When the lamp was set, it made a warm amber
glow on the road and picked out the leaves of a young elm against
the thick sky. The darkness was shoved back, but the sounds
in it came closer : frogs hollering in the swamp, whippoorwills
down the road, bugs humming in the grass—so that the wagon,
the four horses, and the two men seemed cut off from an outer
world. Only the mosquitoes whined in across the gap.

Budlong mechanically brushed them off his neck. " Get the
smudge pot out," he said. " I got her hanging from the tail
gate."

While Budlong was putting a light feed in the nose bags,
Chad unhooked a blackened kettle. He tested the air with a wet
finger, set the kettle beside the road, gathered dry grass and
twigs enough to start the fire, and then built up the smoke
with green stuff. By the time he had a decent smudge the wagon
behind them was coming up, the horses' ears pricked for the
light. Joe Duddy hollered a greeting and swung them into the
turnout.

" Say," he said, " this is all right."

He got out a small feed for his team.

" Bastock's coming along," he said.

He brought a parcel with him to the big wagon and sat down in the thick of the smudge.

" Now if we had a chicken to fry it would be just like home," he said. " You got any food, bub ? "

Chad said he hadn't thought of getting any ; but he wasn't hungry.

" Never seen a man your build didn't have appetite," said Budlong. " Here Joe, spread your vittles long of mine. When Bastock comes we'll share four ways."

They seemed to take it as a matter of course. Chad felt friendly towards them.

" I'll know better next time," he said. " I'll make it up."

" Don't bother," Joe said. " Everybody has got to find out once that it's eating keeps a man from being hungry."

Budlong, sitting with his hands on his knees, cocked his lean face. " Bastock's coming," he said. " Someone else, too. Horseback. Who'd they be ? "

Chad listened. He could pick out the wagon now ; then he got the sound of three or four horses. They were coming right along. He looked at Budlong and Joe. He felt embarrassed.

" Might be the sheriff coming after me," he said.

" You ? "

" Yeah. I'll climb over the fence and keep out of sight."

" Take your time, bub," said Joe. " What they after you for ? "

In a few words, Chad told them about Henry Prince. " It's either me or the nigger they're after."

" What did you do with the nigger ? " Budlong asked.

" He's in the bottom of the small wagon."

" Well, for God's sake," said Joe.

" Ain't time to get him out. Couldn't get him out without unloading the wagon," Budlong said.

" Well, you better get over the fence till we see what's what. But lay close," Joe said. " If we holler, you come running, see ? "

" Bring a fence rail," said Budlong.

Chad eased himself over the fence and found a top rail loose down the line. He left it where it was and lay down flat. He was a little behind the two wagons so he could see Bastock's team come in, the wide curve of their bellies black-shining with sweat.

Joe and Budlong helped Bastock get out the feed bags.

Bastock said, " Someone's coming along."

" Yep," said Budlong. " Nigger-chasing, or after this new gillie we got along. He's over the fence. The nigger's inside your wagon. You don't know nothing, Pete."

Bastock was a little man with bowlegs and a limp in one. He wore a moustache which made a kind of oddity of his face. He rolled his eyes and said, " I just been driving along."

The three of them sat down on the side of the road and started eating. They were sitting that way when the horsemen walked their horses into the light. They were Al Heeney and Cisco Trid and Constable Jones and a fourth man who wore a hard hat and a black coat. Chad knew him. He was Sheriff Wylie.

He picked on Joe Duddy. " Seen a young fellow named Hanna ? "

Budlong answered. " How'd he know what the feller's name was ? "

The sheriff turned on him.

" Maybe you do."

Bastock said, " Budlong don't know nothing."

Budlong grinned.

Joe Duddy said, " What do you want him for ? "

" Assisting a fugitive negro. Did you see him ? "

" I seen a passel of young fellers in Canastota," said Budlong. " Why don't you look there ? "

" He's got sandy hair and a freckled face. He doesn't look like much," said the constable.

" Neither do you, mister," said Bastock.

The sheriff said, " They said in Ridgeville that Hanna had got on to one of your wagons."

" Mabe he went with the gaffer."

" Gaffer ? "

" The boss, Huguenine. He owns this show."

Cisco Trid said, " They told us he got on the wagon with four horses."

Budlong shook his head. " Ain't no four horses got on any of these wagons," he said.

There was a moment of silence. The three skinners looked up at the sheriff and the constable and Cisco and Al. Their faces were blank.

The sheriff made a gesture.

"Do you know what the penalty is for assisting a fugitive negro?"

"Nope."

"Five hundred dollars fine."

"My," said Bastock.

"You seen anything of this nigger?" asked Al Heeney.

Budlong got up.

"If I had I wouldn't tell you."

Al Heeney backed his horse. Its quarter hit the side of the second wagon, jarring it. There was a scuffling sound inside; then a snarling cough. The horse reared and plunged and Al cried, "What's that?"

"Lion," said Budlong.

Joe Duddy said, "He gets meat-hungry when he smells hot horse.

The sheriff looked down at the three skinners. They looked tough. He didn't want to mix with them. He had no warrant. He said, "Mind if we look in your wagons?"

"Yep," said Budlong.

Cisco broke in. "There's only three of them. Why don't we just pile in?"

"Why not?" Bastock asked.

The sheriff said, "We've got no reason to doubt these men. What would they want with a nigger?"

Bastock said, "I tell you what, Mr. Sheriff. I'll let you look in the back of the wagons and if you can figure how we could get a bedbug in after we get them loaded, why, you're welcome to look."

The sheriff said, "That's fair enough for me."

The tail gates were let down and the doors opened. What Bastock had said was evident to any one. Al said, "He might be way in."

"Sure," said Bastock. "With half a ton on top of him."

Cisco Trid's face was ugly.

"You got to get hold of Huguenine," he said to the sheriff.

Sheriff Wylie flushed up. "Huguenine's out of Madison County by this time. Get the Onondaga sheriff to do your work for you, Trid. Come along, Jones," he said to the constable. The two of them turned their horses.

Cisco Trid and Al Heeney remained. Cisco scowled down at

the circus hands, but Al Heeney moved his lips over his buck teeth and fashioned a smile.

He said, " Maybe if we shared up some with these gentlemen, they might know something, Cisco."

" All right," Cisco said after a moment. " How much do you want ? "

Budlong was listening to the fading hoof-beats. There was a turn in the road he wanted them to get around. Al Heeney must have sensed what was passing through his lean mind. His lips closed painfully over his teeth ; suddenly he kicked his horse, forcing him along the road past the wagons. " Come on," he said urgently. " No use staying here all night."

Cisco, finding himself deserted, thought better of it. He yanked his horse back, out of reach. He said, " We'll keep our eyes on you, anyway."

The three skinners stood together in the road, listening. After a while, Bastock said, " All right, bub, you can come out." They went over and sat down together and began parcelling out the food, making up Chad's share.

Budlong remarked, " Heeney feller got windy."

" Kind of a disappointment all around," Joe Duddy said. " Tell us about it, Chad."

Chad told them, except for the part that Caroline had taken. He was ashamed of that. But the rest of it made a good story. Joe said, " So that's why you joined out. Thought you was just another damn fool."

Chad grinned.

" Maybe I was."

" It's nothing new. Everybody has to go through it with her."

" With who ? "

" Albany Yates. She cocks 'em all when she gets up on that Buck horse," Bastock said. " But it won't do you no good, Chad. Top acts ain't sociable with roustabouts. Fred Shepley's got that place surveyed, anyway."

Chad flushed. But they didn't pay any attention to him.

Budlong said, " We got this show weeded out pretty good."

" Jim was no use," Bastock agreed. " He was nervous. If Burke and Walsh is getting after this show, we won't want nervous people."

" What can they do ? " Chad asked.

"Well, we probably won't be showing the same towns against them," Joe said. "But pretty soon there will be people seeing Burke's and then our show won't look like much. They got a real band."

"But Huguenine's has good people in it," Chad said. "How about Lady Lillian's act? That's good, isn't it?"

Bastock pursed his lips.

"Albany's got class. She's pretty. Her horse is pretty. She'd go good anywhere, but these bush-country twerps don't know *how* good she is. It's just pretty to them."

"Well, take Rossello," Chad said.

Bastock said, "Fred Shepley thinks he's good all right. But he don't do any somersets, does he?" He threw away a bread crust and fished for tobacco. "You ain't a high-class principal rider till you can do that. Jumping on and off a horse looks handsome if you ain't seen nothing else. Jumping over a ribbon is all right, but, hell, Shepley's is only three foot. And what does he do besides? I don't mean standing on one foot."

"What else is there to do?" Chad asked. "I don't like Shepley but I had to say he was good."

"Ask Budlong," Bastock said. "He was with Brown's Circus down south two years ago. Tell him about Mateer."

"Rides three horses at once. Jumps over twelve-foot sheets. Jumps through a frame of daggers. Throws a back somerset. Does a flying leap through the body of a mail coach."

Chad said, "Jeepers," in an incredulous voice.

"Fact," said Budlong.

Bastock said, "Take the Englishman, Hunter; he rides bareback. Without no pad. So does DeForest. I wouldn't hold out against Fred, only he thinks he's so all-fired good he don't have to improve. Huguenine don't know any better than you. He thinks the show is going fine and that Fred's the thing that's doing it. Pamplons and Fiero, they're all right. And so is Ike Wayfish. They're the start-off. They ain't what they was or they wouldn't be with this show, but they try. But a show has got to have a principal act." He paused. "We ain't got it. We got a lion, but I don't think he's healthy. And what have we got on the side of the show? Mrs. Huguenine ain't no world-beater, though she does the best she can. We ought to have a ossified man or a transparent girl, something they ain't seen before."

"Well," said Chad. "We made money in Canastota, didn't we?"

"Sure, bub. But we ain't tied up against Burke and Walsh yet. There's lots more a big show can do to a little one. They can tear down paper. They can put stories in the newspapers. They can send a man ahead warning the town boards we're gypsies and horse thieves."

"Kidnappers," said Budlong.

"Yeah. They all believe that. Then what happens? You either get run out of the town or they start a clem and stop the show. Or they set fire to the tent."

Chad thought it over.

Then he asked, "How did you fellers get into this business?"

Duddy said, "Pete's always hung around circuses."

"Yep," said Budlong. "We just join out."

"When it's going good," said Duddy, "it ain't bad. You ride around the country, and you get food and some pay; but when it's bad it's no fun."

It wasn't much of an explanation. Pete Bastock seemed to feel that. He tried to make sense of it:

"Well, you get watching even a crumby show like this and you got to hang around to see how somebody's going to make out at the next stand. Take Pamplon, now. He's got a bad ankle. I don't feel easy till he gets the swing of it back. Or take Albany. I want to see if she don't get off on to a big show. Or Shepley: he might break his neck. I wouldn't cry."

Chad said, "Yeah. But what is there for you and me in it?"

"Us? Well, we put up the big rag, then we take it down; then we load it, unload it, and put it up again. We don't know no better than that." He grinned.

Chad had one more question.

"How much does a real top high-rider get in cash?"

"Well," said Bastock, "it's different, depending on the show. But a rider like Hunter in a big show might get a hundred dollars."

"A month?"

Bastock stared at him.

"You are a gillie, for sure. A week."

Chad sucked in his breath. After a minute he said, "You and me, we get how much?"

"Well, I guess we don't get as much as that. But we're skinners, not canvasmen. We get a dollar a day."

Chad let it go; but he stayed thoughtful while they re-bridled the horses. He was still thinking when they rolled out of the turnout.

It was complete black night now; and the lamps on the wagons behind were like eyes on the road. In Bridgeport a dog ran out at them, barking till he smelled the lion; then he raised a hullabaloo, fleeing behind a house and yelling to himself round and round the yard. The rumble of the heavy wheels echoed off the house walls as they came out into open country again. Budlong said suddenly, "Thinking about maybe being a high-rider yourself, bub?"

"I don't know."

"Ain't built bad for it." Budlong's lean face turned towards Chad, and the eyes glowed for a moment in the light of the night lamp.

"I don't know nothing about it," Chad said.

"Watch Shepley. Does vaults good enough." He let Shepley go with a spit. "Pete can teach you all of it, though."

"Pete Bastock?"

"Used to be a clown rider. He's come down. Broke his leg." He dropped the conversation there.

It was nearly eleven o'clock when the wagons rolled into Cicero. Budlong had been right about one thing, anyway. It was raining softly, a misting rain, and they had trouble picking up Bisbee's rail signs for the lot. The house eaves dripped as they rolled along the street; all the windows were dark. And the treasury wagon was a lonely blot on the lot.

19

GOOD-BYE TO HENRY

" Whose place you supposed to go to here, Henry ? " Chad asked.

They had managed to extract the negro from Joe's wagon without completely unloading it. The three skinners were stuffing the canvas back in, and Henry Prince, his shoulders hunched against the fall of rain, stared disconsolately at the ground at Chad's feet.

" I done lost the paper the Rev'n'd gave me," he mumbled. " Seem like I disremember the name, too. It might be Clap, or it might be Trap. I jes' ain't sure of it, boss."

Budlong closed the tail gate and he and the other two left the wagon and joined Chad and Henry in the corner of the lot.

" You can't stay here," Bastock said. " Huguenine wouldn't stand for it, and those twerps will likely have a constable hanging round here with them to-morrow. Maybe they'll get a warrant. Didn't anybody tell you where this Clap feller lives ? "

" Seem like somebody must," Henry agreed apologetically. " Seem like they say take the north road about a mile out. Yes, sir, boss." His voice brightened. " I remember now, hit was a brown house and they's a skin of a no-tail coon nail' on the barn door. Yes, sir."

" You sure ? "

" I don't remember the name—I done forgot, boss. But I remember 'bout the no-tail coon."

" Did the Reverend tell you about it ? "

" No, sir. They told me that in the place in Peterboro. That was about the coon, boss. They had a no-tail hide like it there. Yes, sir. Just the same *as*. Mr. Gray he know the name all right, but I done forgot."

Chad said, " All right. I'll go find that coon hide with you, Henry."

" You ain't going along with him ? " Joe asked.

Chad lowered his voice. " I want to see he gets there." He drew Joe Duddy aside. " I got the feeling if I don't get shut of him myself I'll have him on my neck for the next ten years."

" Yeah, he wants to stay with the circus. God, niggers are fools. The minute they ain't being actually chased, they think everything's just dandy. But the minute somebody shows up, all they can think of is going underground the first hole they see. I feel sorry for them," said Joe. " Want for one of us to go with you, Chad ? "

" No," said Chad. " You fellers done enough. I'll be back, maybe in an hour."

He took hold of Henry's sleeve and steered him away. As they passed the cat wagon, Henry drew deep breaths. " I'd sho like to see that lion, boss. He got a mighty big smell."

" Maybe you'll see a lion in Canada."

They went straight into the village and found the centre cross-road with no difficulty. A providential cat distracted the only dog that seemed to be nigger-conscious. She treed outside a small house and the dog barked her ; and then an irate man banged a window open and started throwing firewood. In the middle of it he stopped and yelled back into the room, " God damn your honesty." By that time Chad and Henry were a couple of houses away.

They had the road to themselves all the way out of the village. The farms on the outskirts were set close, but when they got into open country, the houses were harder to spot, except when the pig-pen was close to the road. Henry went slow, but he got along well enough, and Chad didn't try to hurry him.

His mind was absorbed by what Bastock had told him about a high-rider's earnings. Fabulous as it sounded, he didn't think Bastock had been running a rig on him ; the bowlegged little fellow had sounded too scornful for that. Of course, a show like Huguenine's playing the back-country villages wouldn't pay anything like such a wage ; but suppose it paid as much as twenty-five dollars a week : that was a hundred a month or seven hundred for the rolling season. Probably Shepley made that much ; maybe Albany Yates did too.

But the point that stood out in Chad's mind as he matched his pace to the limping negro's was not the high-rider's salary ; it was the notion that no employer he had ever heard of was willing to pay his hired hand bigger money than he made himself. That was something that an old performer like Pete Bastock would never think of. To him, being a high-rider was like being the Emperor of Russia. Nobody took much notice of an owner,

not even if he acted as equestrian director the way Huguenine
did ; it was the high-rider they paid to see.

" Yes, sir, boss. That house look brown to me."

Henry Prince was pointing to a dark square shape set back
from the road.

" You think it's brown ? " Chad asked.

" Yes, I does."

Chad told him to stay beside the road while he went over to
the house. It showed no lights in front ; but in the back the
door opening to the shed showed him a yellow wall. He returned
to Henry with the information, and they resumed their slow
progress.

" Your leg holding out all right ? " he asked.

" It's doin' all right, boss. Hit ache some when I hit a hole."
Henry's voice was eager for conversation. He said, " Hit mighty
good to have company. I used to get lonesome on the road
coming no'th, boss. You been good to me."

" Pshaw," Chad said.

" Yes, sir, you surely has," the negro persisted. "Ain't nobody
else thought this nigger was worth taking no place. They been
good, but the first thing they wanted most was to see the last of
me. But you done found me a hay barn to stay in, and then you
found me a wagon to ride in, and now you've come a walkin'
along with me, like I'se pretty near white." Henry Prince's
voice dropped, but its resonance deepened. " ' And went to
him, and bound up his wounds, pouring in oil and wine . . .
and brought him to an inn, and took care of him.' " He waited
for a moment, but as Chad took no particular notice, he asked,
" Ain't it the truth ? "

" What is ? "

" What I just done texted from the Bible at you. About you,
boss, and it might be about me, too. I wa'n coming down from
Jerusalem to Jericho. It's the other way round and seem like
it's Jerusalem I see ahead. Jerusalem. Canady. But I fell among
that Cisco Trid and Al Heeney, and he wounded me, didn't he ?
There was the priest ; he didn't pass on the other side, exactly,
boss, maybe ; but he didn't come so close, neither. And that
Diney gal, she might have been the Levite. But you come along
and you put in the salt and the whisky and you fotch me to the
hay barn. Hit like Lord Jesus say in the Bible mighty near
exact, and it say somewheres else there that the righteous man

has got the everlasting reward. Yes, it does. I surely hopes so, boss."

" You know quite a lot for a nigger, Henry. You talk just like a preacher."

" Yes, sir, our preacher he say I got a scripture mind even if'n I cain't spell." In the darkness Henry pursed his lips. " I cain't read any, boss, but when I hear the words, my head grab right hold on them, and I got them, and there they is, just like I done texted you now."

" It's a pity your head couldn't have grabbed hold of that man's name," Chad said. He had spotted a crossroad. It was no more than a cart track with a high bone of grass between the ruts.

Henry Prince, who had fallen into a humiliated silence, studied it for a moment. There wasn't anything to see in that darkness beyond the bare fact of the road's existence. But suddenly he said, eagerly, " Yes, sir. Here's the place. They tell me to turn to the left and here it is. We go down this-yer road till we get to the brown house and hit got a barn. . . ."

" All right," Chad said. " With a no-tail coon's hide nailed on the barn door. You said it before. But we might as well try."

There was a house, anyway, about two hundred yards down the side road. They smelled the barnyard as they came up to it, and a long-haired dog approached them, growling defensively, but making no outcry, as if he were accustomed to nocturnal visitors. Henry was positive now, and he led Chad to the barn, finding the door and sweeping his brown hands over the surface of it, whispering to himself all the time.

" Yes, sir. Here de hide. Hit ain't got no tail. Didn' I say ? "

He took Chad's hand to show him, and Chad agreed. The dog, which had become anxious, gave a low warning bark. After a moment a door opened in the back of the house and a man's voice asked who was there.

" Is this Clap's place ? " Chad asked.

" No, it ain't. It's Dave Pratt's. I'm him. What do you want ? "

Chad explained that he had heard of Mr. Pratt through Mr. Gray in Canastota and also from people in Peterboro.

" You don't sound like no nigger," the man said.

" I'm not. But there's one here."

" Well, you better come inside."

They went towards the house, following the man into the kitchen, which smelled warm and close. The man was fumbling for a light; they couldn't see him, but he said, " This is the second one to come along this spring. Must be a power of niggers down South."

He got his light. He was a scrawny looking man. He shook hands with Chad and with Henry Prince, examining the latter with the objective eyes of a farmer at a horse sale.

" He's in bad shape. He'll have to be wagoned, I guess."

When Chad explained about Cisco Trid and Al Heeney, Mr. Pratt said Al Heeney had been along early in the evening; a neighbour down the main road had told him of it.

" It's a nuisance," he said. " I ought to be getting after my corn, too. Told my wife I wouldn't go to the circus on account of it. I had my shovel plough all laid out for it. But, gol darn it, there ain't no government going to tell me what I can do, nor no men from some furrin state is going to walk in on my township and run my doings. My Pap fit the British and the Indians, and gol darn if I don't do it to Virginia. Reckon if I took my chuck gun into Virginia State and went nigger-hunting your boss would try to get the best of me, wouldn't he, Prince? "

" Shooting niggers? Yes, sir, I hope so," said Henry. He looked apprehensive. But Mr. Pratt nodded.

" That's the idea of it. I can't get down there to shoot niggers myself, so I aim not to have them come hunting in my town." It seemed logical to him. " I'll light you folks out to the barn," he said. " There's hay a plenty to sleep you. To-morrow morning I'll drive the nigger up to Bragdon's beyond Port Ontario. He'll put him on the ferry at Port Vincent."

" That sounds fine," Chad said. " But I don't plan to sleep here. I got to get back to the circus to-night."

Mr. Pratt stopped short. " You a circus man? " he inquired, lifting his lantern. " I wouldn't have guessed it. You look right down ordinary to me."

Chad grinned.

" Good luck, Henry," he said, shaking hands.

Henry shook hands diffidently.

" Good-bye, Marster Chad. You sho been good to Henry Prince." He swallowed. " I brung you a lot of trouble, boss. But I sho is grateful."

Chad said, " Maybe you brought me luck, too."

He shook hands with Mr. Pratt and walked out of the barn-yard. At the crossroad he looked back ; but the place was dark. There was no sign at all of any farm. It was a good stopping place ; and he felt that David Pratt would be equal to keeping Henry Prince away from Cisco Trid.

He turned towards town with nothing on his mind. He was a circus hand now ; but he aimed to be more. He hardly noticed that the rain was in his face.

Book II

THE LOCKET

SYRACUSE

Joe Duddy said, " By Cripus, it's a crazy business."

" What is ? "

" Why, hauling down the old rag here in Salina, pack the show complete, drag her a mile and a half, and set her up again in Syracuse. Why couldn't we just set one place or the other and let the people walk to us ? "

He rapped the last staube loose and he and Chad drew it together. Huguenine uttered a yelp and the round-top dropped, ballooning, so that the skinners had to find valleys between the swells to reach the centre pole. It made them look small, with the bare pole over them and the sprawled folds of canvas billowing at their feet.

Huguenine, who had trudged after them, grunted and said, " Now, Joe. You can't complain. The shorter the haul the quicker you get off to-night. Besides, we're going to stay over Sunday in town, and show again on Monday. You'll have Saturday night and all of Sunday to raise hell in."

Joe grinned. " That ain't too bad," he admitted. " So we're showing double again, like in this town ? "

Mr. Huguenine rubbed his beefy hands.

" You bet. Bisbee says we got to work for all the trade will stand before Burke and Walsh overhaul us. We had two over-flows here, didn't we ? Bisbee's had some wafers printed for Syracuse and Auburn : TWO PERFORMANCES BY POPULAR DEMAND. They look fine even considering the cost." He wiped his forehead. " If this business holds up as good, though, I'll get my money back for sure."

" That's fine," Joe said. " Maybe you could give me full pay this week."

" Now Joe, you know that ain't regular. Skinners get half pay on the road and the other half rests in the treasury wagon till the end of the season."

Stooping over the pole ring, Budlong said thoughtfully, " Show I was with petered out in Coosawhatchie. Us skinners kept the pay wagon in the middle of the line all night, but the gaffer had took the pay with him in his satchel. It was a mistake."

Bastock gave him a sharp glance.

" Where'd you say it happened ? "

" Coosawhatchie."

" I heard you say that. Where is it, you twerp ? "

" Eight miles south of Pocotaligo, six miles north of Echau."

Bastock gave it up, but Joe Duddy stopped to clean his thumbnail. " I heard of a gaffer had a secret vice," he said.

" Now Joe," said Mr. Huguenine, shifting his weight uneasily. " I ain't . . ."

" Oh, no," Joe said. " This gaffer though, he didn't drink, nor pull the feathers out of pigeons' tails, or nothing like that, not while he was tenting. It was worse. It was a lot worse. It was terrible, Mr. Huguenine."

" What was, Joe ? "

" This secret habit. Ever since I heard of it, I hardly trust to join out with any circus."

" My God ! " exclaimed Mr. Huguenine. " A grown man, was he ? "

" Oh, yes. Old enough to be my uncle." Joe Duddy picked his front teeth with the cleaned thumbnail and stared past the naked centre pole. " I'll tell you what it was. He just couldn't keep himself from sneaking off and depositing money in savings banks under the name of Purdy." Joe shook his head. " End of each season he'd go bankrupt. Skinners never got a cent of their due. One of them even felt sorry for him and the Missis. Then it turned out he'd get home and get a mortgage on the show and tell his wife he was going to scout around for backing and off he'd go, hell-raising around the circus route, staying in the best hotels, drinking French wines, flushing the best-looking pigeons, and collecting the deposits he'd made in the name of Purdy."

Mr. Huguenine's solid face puckered gravely. " My God, ain't he deceitful ? " he said. " Using that name that way."

Joe nodded. " That was the worst of it. It was his own legal name. The one he used in the circus was Oliver. Couldn't no one stop him drawing deposits as Purdy. He had references."

Mr. Huguenine's mixture of admiration and moral condemnation dissolved in an expression of hurt.

" I wouldn't do a thing like that, boys," he protested.

"Every cent of cash lays right in the treasury wagon." He glanced toward it self-consciously. Certainly nothing could look less like a vehicle for an absconder, what with Mrs. Huguenine resting her bulk on the rear step and batting off the mosquitoes with a turkey-feather fan. Chad had to smile, and Huguenine, seeing it, gave a grunt and walked off.

Joe said, "Can't you keep that damn face straight, Chad?. I'd have got A.D. feeling so mean in another minute he might have give us all a bonus. Go grab hold of the stay rope."

You could see he was feeling fine, though, as he and Budlong eased the centre pole down with Chad and Bastock paying out the stay ropes. Loading the stick was heavy work. The first time he tried it Chad had learned the importance of getting his grip exactly in the right spot; just as the tent had to be folded exactly if it were going to fit into the wagon.

The four men walked the stick up to the wagon and slid her home. It didn't look hard to a bystander, because they did everything so smooth, but the sweat was wetting through their shirts by the time they had the pole set.

The tent lay collapsed and dead when they came back for it. Folding it, they felt the weight of the canvas build up. Mr. Huguenine, moodily watching from the treasury wagon, saw them slide the rolls into the big wagon before he decided to start off. It was late twilight. The skinners stood together for a moment, blank-eyed, letting their muscles ease, as Mrs. Huguenine squeezed her bulk into the treasury wagon and closed the door. Chad saw the box tilt a little to the nigh side and guessed she had lain down on the bed.

"Gawd," said Bastock, "I wouldn't want to ride that way, without no real bed."

"Takes a broken axle to reach in where she can feel it," Budlong said.

Joe Duddy chuckled. They felt fine with two easy days ahead of them and pay day coinciding. "Come on," he said. "Let's get going."

They hauled out in their usual order, the tent wagon in the lead, taking the dip and roll to the road. The four-horse hitch wheeled smartly to make the turn, the wheelers holding up properly against the curve; and the reach groaned its heart out as the hind wheels came up level. The seat jacks in the second wagon banged against the side when the wheels hit the ruts, but the cage wagon rode light. They rolled along beyond the fence high on their small wheels, Budlong's shape hunched on the high seat, a lank silhouette against the last feeble shine of twilight in the west.

Behind Chad one of the led horses whinnied anxiously ; that would be Jerry ; he had no independence like the cream-coloured pad horse, none of Buck's courage. He turned to the back of the lot where they had been tethered to the fence. A dew was falling and it was near black dark, now ; but three small boys with hardier souls still lingered. " You going to take them, too, mister ? "

Chad grinned.

" Yes," he said. " There wouldn't be no show without them."

They came through the fence to lay grubby admiring hands on the shoulder of the cream-coloured horse.

" Gee, he's pretty," they said.

The littlest one asked, " Kin I have a hair from his tail ? "

" Sure."

" I got hairs growing from a black horse and a white one, but I never thought to get cream-coloured hair. Do they make cream snakes, mister ? "

Chad plucked a hair. " I don't know," he said.

" I use rain water myself," the little fellow announced. " You growing any cream snakes, mister ? "

Chad took the double lead and vaulted on to Jerry's back. The horses turned together.

" No," he said soberly. " Snakes don't grow on the road, because the wagon shakes the water in the bottle."

He told them to stand back. They came trooping after the horses across the lot, but stopped as they reached the trod circle where the ring had been. It was all that remained of the circus. When he turned into the road Chad glanced back. He could hardly see their small shapes, but one was shouting, " I'm the ringmaster, Ladies and Gentlemen. I'm the ringmaster."

" I'm the clown, I want to ride that cream horse. I'm funny."

The road led straight south from the town. The moon coming up from the low hills on his left shone like silver on the board covers of the evaporation sheds of the salt springs. They stretched in ranks over the ground, and looking down on them from Jerry's cushioned back was like looking down on the roofs of a sleeping town.

By now the performers would have settled in the hotel. They would have had supper, and probably the women would have gone to their rooms, to sew, or brush their hair, or do whatever a woman did to herself before she went to bed. Probably the Pamplons would be in theirs together. Chad wondered about Albany Yates. In Baldwinsville and Liverpool and Salina she had shared a room with Caroline Trid. Likely she would in Syracuse. It seemed strange that she should take such a fancy to a girl like Caroline. She had given her a dress of her own ; they were near enough of a shape for it to make over easily ; and Chad had to admit it had improved Caroline's appearance. Albany had showed her how to put up her hair so that she appeared quite womanish, the curls clustered free of the back of her neck, where the down was still soft. They made a pretty contrast together, though to Chad's eyes the benefit was all Albany's. He wasn't a man to hold with a team of off colours, like black and white or black and chestnut. But the contrast wasn't confined to colouring : it was the bright easy independent look on Albany's face and the constant adoration on the younger girl's that caught his eye.

Though Caroline was getting her keep from Huguenine, as far as the skinners knew she got no wages. But the Huguenines had adapted a costume of Mrs. Pamplon's for her and allowed her to appear in the ring with Albany during the Pamplons' act, and in Liverpool she had also appeared with Fiero, tossing him his balls. Fiero praised her ; he said she had a good eye and a sure sense of timing. It was rare to find them natural in a female. And yesterday in Salina he had purchased a small plank door and begun practising knife-throwing again. He used to be a knife thrower, he said, and, if the art returned to him, he would like to have Caroline act as his target. It was a great act, sure-fire, fabulous, he said. There was the lovely female, here was he, and she stood so still facing him, and he threw the knives, one above the head, one under each arm, one at each side of the waist, one each side of the knees ; and, as the grand frightful finale, one at each side of the neck. His eyes flashed as he told of it. It was superb ; and Caroline had said she was willing to try it. " You must learn to stand," he told her. " Still. So still. You must do it every night and every morning. You say a rhyme—

' Now I lay me.' Understand ? But first I must find how it goes with the knives and my eye. Then we shall see."

It had been Budlong's idea for Chad to lead the horses over the stages. He had made the suggestion in Baldwinsville, where their performance had been just about spoiled by rain. Bisbee had counted on the academy ; but the students had been forbidden the circus. Tempers were ragged when the show pulled out and it was a bad time to suggest anything to any one, but Mr. Huguenine had felt obliged to notify Albany Yates and Fred Shepley. The whole business came back clear as a picture to Chad.

The performers were all in the wagon except Albany ; she came picking her way through the puddles with Caroline and she paused, one foot on the wagon step, to look across the lot at Chad with that maddeningly impersonal expression on her face, as if he weren't an individual man at all. From the moment she had learned of his signing out she had treated him that way ; it didn't make it any better for him that she was still cool to Shepley. Her voice carried across the lot, clear as a bell, so every one heard it : " Do you think he can be trusted not to ride Buck, Mr. Huguenine ? "

Though the rain was still falling gently, she seemed oblivious of it. Fred Shepley was not. He hated wet weather like a cat. He threw one off-hand glance in Chad's direction and said, " Why not ? " and then, as if he had settled the matter, put his hand on Albany's arm and said, " For God's sake let's get started. We've had to wait fifteen minutes for you already."

She shook off Shepley's hand with a twist of her elbow.

" I'm interested in my horse even if you're not in yours. Buck shan't be ridden by anybody but me. That's to be understood, Mr. Huguenine."

As her eyes re-encountered Chad's, she did have the grace to colour up, as though, possibly, she recalled the ride they had taken together in Canastota. She had been friendly as you please that morning when she had known him merely as the stablehand at the Yellow Bud. " It would be tempting to a boy," she said to Mr. Huguenine.

Mr. Huguenine, who looked completely at a loss, as he always did when anything like a dispute among the performers started in front of him, said, " Why now, it was just an idea of Budlong's, Miss Yates. He says the pad horse is likely to get stumblefoot habits travelling blind in the back of the wagon, and I thought Chad here could lead the whole three of them."

" If Budlong thinks it's all right, I'm willing," she replied. " I can trust Budlong."

She dismissed the matter with a brief gesture of her mittened hand and at the same time managed to disregard Fred Shepley. She was light as a bird getting into the wagon, settling herself beside Caroline Trid and saying to Ike, " I'm sorry we kept you waiting, Mr. Wayfish."

Wayfish grinned at her and started the team smartly without much regard for Shepley, and when they had gone, Mr. Huguenine asked Chad whether he had heard what Miss Yates had said. Chad said he had. " Well, don't do it," said Mr. Huguenine. Bastock said it was nothing : skinners weren't performers, he explained. But that didn't make sense, either. She could be almighty pleasant to Budlong or Bastock and even smile at Joe Duddy as if she meant it. She would be as attentive to something Budlong had to say about shoeing as a prize-girl at school, bending over her head close to his hand while he showed her with his crack-nail finger how a hoof ought to be trimmed, or listening to Bastock's tales of famous fox hunts in England. Half Bastock's stories didn't make sense to Chad, but she would stare starry-eyed with her lips just parted and say, " Oh, Mr. Bastock, I'd love to try that sometime. Do you think Buck would hold up to that cross-country work ? "

" With you on him," Pete would say. " Why, you'd get the brush without half trying. Like birds, you'd be." Then he would explain the honour of receiving the brush, which sounded nonsensical, and she would say, " Do you really mean that ? " and smile till his ears turned red. She had all the pretty gifts when she wanted to use them.

Otherwise Chad found the life suited him. It had seemed hard work at first ; at night he felt his back was nearly broken ; but the other three skinners assured him it was easy. Wait till fall, Bastock said ; wait till the rain got into the canvas, doubling the weight of it, or you tried to handle the centre pole with sleet on it—supposing the show ran that long—or wait until they had to take the rag down with a windstorm worrying it. Budlong had a story about a man named Mussey who got his ankle fouled in a pig sty just when the tent dropped during a big thunderstorm. The wind lifted the round top a hundred feet, as if it were a balloon. Only the sustaining gas was lacking, and the round-top came down spang in the middle of the Mississippi River. The man was half-drowned when they recovered him, but the gaffer took no interest once he had got his canvas on shore. He said the man was lucky not to have got struck by lightning. The odd thing about it all was that when they untangled the canvas it was full enough of catfish to feed the entire company. But the one Mussey ate poisoned him and he died. It did beat all, Budlong thought.

While Budlong and Bastock seemed to have an accumulated experience of life to fall back on, Joe Duddy took the days and nights as they came. He was strong and not afraid of using his strength. He could if necessary handle the centre pole without Budlong's assistance; and considered his work as drummer an important road to success. His only worry was the health of the lion, Oscar, for whom he was responsible, except during parades, when Chad drove the cage wagon. He had, outside of becoming a musician, only one other ambition, which was to turn up in Albany one day with enough money in his pocket to patronise a real high-class house.

Chad kept the horses back as the three wagon lights took the rise of the canal bridge in turn, the stamp of hoofs and the hollow roll of the wheels echoing off the broad walls of the buildings. After them the hoof-beats of the led horses sounded light enough to be skittish. Chad glanced down the canal as he crossed over, seeing bow lanterns through the mist and one light still in a warehouse door where a line boat was unloading. The steersman of a boat passing directly underneath blew his horn to scare the horses, but they paid no heed. Chad yelled at the boatman as a matter of principle, and the boatman yelled back. Then he went down the ramp and passed into Syracuse at a trot to overtake the wagons.

The mist hung in the streets; he could feel it against his face, damp in the darkness, and smelling faintly of hayfields. They had been mowing somewhere out of town, he thought. The town was gone to bed, or was in the act of going, as candle shine from upper windows showed. A tavern door swung open and shut, emitting an uncertain pair of figures that walked side by side along the board foot-walk, then clove apart, migrating unsteadily by separate alleyways.

They had to wait at the corner for the night stage to pull

past them, and while the horses rested a window was raised over Chad's head. There was no light behind it, but he made out the man's shoulders and heard a woman's voice say, " What is it, Paul ? "

The man's voice answered from the sill : " Three box wagons. Looks like a circus outfit. Maybe it's the one you seen posted down at the hotel."

" Three wagons ? That don't sound like much. I bet it ain't at all."

Chad could feel the man's silence just above him, feel the dark in the room, the close stuffy dark, and the woman in the bed. Then the man's voice said abruptly : " It is, though. I can smell the lion."

As the man closed the sash, the wagons pulled ahead. Following them, Chad passed through into the rank jungle reek the lion's pause had accumulated in the roadway. There were street lamps here, their oil light like yellow blossoms in the mist. Then the triangular grass lot of the square opened beside them ; the wagons turned into it ; and Mr. Huguenine met them, yawning, his nightshirt stuffed into his pants. " Put the horses in the barn," he told Chad, pointing out the great brick bulk of the hotel across the street.

The bar was closing. Inside the office, Chad heard a clock measure eleven with successive wheeze and strike. A weary groom, roused out of the manger in the black cavern of the barn, fetched forth a lantern, showed Chad the stalls, and wordlessly watched him rub the horses down. He left them there, with a light feed, and came out again into the stable yard.

The back wall of the hotel rose up like a mountainside against him. It echoed the crack of his heel on a stone ; and a flavour of hot dinner buns still hung in the confined space between it and the barn. There were two lighted windows on the second floor. He wondered if one of them belonged to Albany's room.

2

TENT INTERIOR

WHEN Joe Duddy had taken up half an inch on the last peg stay, stepped back and looked around, he couldn't for once feel any satisfaction that the job was done. She was up, and it was circus weather all right—that damned piece of clown patter came into his head :—

> Weather it's cold
> Or Weather it's hot,
> We shall have Weather,
> Weather or not—

as it always did at this point of the morning and he had never seen anything funny in it, though it made him laugh the way it made the crowds laugh. People were pretty simple-minded. But this morning the weather stains stood out on the round-top like trace galls on a three-dollar mule ; and the tent, confronted by the imposing brick façade of the Syracuse House across the street, looked small, and insignificant, and timidish as if it had the idea that a show like Huguenine's Great and Only International Circus ought to have made its pitch on the outskirts of a town the size of Syracuse.

Not that Syracuse was much bigger than Salina ; but it had the air of a metropolis. Huguenine said that was how it was referred to in the hotel bar. Some of the stores, Joe had seen already, were brick all the way round, with no space between the side walls at all, just like genuine city construction. And Bastock said the place had a museum and an institute and the state asylum for idiots, and ten taverns and hotels, and the biggest brewery west of Troy. Greenway's Brewery, he said, turned out about 6000 barrels a year. To Joe Duddy it seemed that an honest drinker could hardly feel safe where the population showed such an extensive interest in beer. Possibly you could account for it by the proximity of the salt flats. Then he brightened up. Generally where there was plenty of thirst, pigeons were plentiful also. He would ask Bastock about that. The little man approached with a shoulder-load of seat boards.

" Sure," he said. " South Salina Street is the place for you,
Joe. Begin at the beginning and head south. The farther you go
the darker they get. Out in the Hollow towards the reservation,
the breed is genuine red."

" My Cripus," said Joe. " I ain't scalp-hunting."

" I didn't know." Bastock grinned. " There's plenty of seats
left to hog in."

Joe sighed and ambled up to the wagon. Chad had hauled
out a shoulder-load and was getting his shoulder under the
centre stripe. He was sweating. There was heat in the sun, early
as it was, and you had to hope not too many farmers had started
their haying. " Ready ? " he asked Chad.

Chad took his time. This always seemed to him the most
tedious part of the job, lugging in all the seats every morning,
and lugging them all out in the evening. He never sat on them
any more.

" You in a hurry ? " he asked.

Joe leaned against the tail gate.

" No, I just like to watch them bear down on somebody else,
Chaddy. I reckon those horses like it too. 'Tain't often they can
just stand easy and watch a man sweat, I guess."

Several teams were already fastened along the hitch rail
that entirely surrounded the triangular square. A few male
humans, looking about as lackadaisical but no more intelligent,
shared the interesting view. One of them, however, appeared to
be a wit.

" Hey," he asked raucously. " What you sell ? Liniment ? "

Joe turned red. He had to admit that was how the tent looked.
Set in the middle of the town like this, it did make a man think
of a medicine peddler's outfit ; but he didn't want to be told.
He started walking towards the hitch rail saying, " Sure—
liniment. Though generally a man like you ain't able to pay
us for it, so we give it away free gratis for the asking. How about
it rube ? Where'll you have it put on ? "

Out of the tail of his eye, Chad saw the bluster begin, the
nerve evaporate, and the sudden flurry of retreat. He didn't
have to worry about Joe and a rube of that kind ; they generally
showed up early ; they were a breed begotten by leisure out of
a disinclination for work. He passed into the tent with his load
and dumped it in front of the last tier where Budlong was driving
a toe pin to hold the seat jack.

It was a queer thing about the tent in the early morning—how the night's coolness hung on. Outside it would get hotter and hotter; but inside it would stay cool, even with the sun beating on the round-top; the dew would stay on the grass some days till nearly noon and there would be a smell of green in the green reflected light. Later, when the audience had been in it for a few moments, the tent would heat up like the inside of a bread oven; the soft earth and grass smell would be smothered by the smell of humans and the air would draw through the flaps with difficulty.

Mrs. Huguenine, who was inspecting the canvas for tears, jerked all over at the clatter of boards and exclaimed, " My stars and body! Are you trying to make kindling of them seats, young man?"

Chad said, " They slipped," and Bastock backed him up with a grin. " Yes, ma'am. I seen it."

Before she could fashion an argument out of it, Mr. Huguenine came hurrying in through the performers' fly. " Oscar needs his feed," he said excitedly. " Why ain't Oscar fed? I told Joe I had bought eight pounds of beef flank down the street. Where's Joe?"

Joe walked in then with a double load of seat boards. He dropped them with a crash and Mrs. Huguenine buried both hands in her bosom. " My stars!" she began. " You make my heart go bad. It's getting genuine flutters."

Mr. Huguenine said, " Anybody as fat as you is bound to get flutters, Bettina. Joe, that lion ain't been fed. Where's his meat?"

" I'll get it," Joe said. " I been disputing with a rube."

" You can't get it now. You got to clean that cage. Wayfish said they complained about the scent in Salina. He said they hardly let him into the hotel to change till he promised not to lay down on the bed. You give it a good wash."

" All right," Joe said. " But some crumby brisket stole my pail and mop."

" I've got them in the treasury wagon," Mrs. Huguenine said tartly. " A person has to keep clean. Can't you buy me a mop of my own, A.D.? Using the same one makes our wagon smell like the cage, too."

" No," said Mr. Huguenine. " If there was two it would get lost and then we'd be right where we started. It's cheaper to buy perfume. You got to buy it anyway for the show. A fat woman has always got to smell of perfume. It's part of the act. What do you want next? Violet?"

Mrs. Huguenine smiled thoughtfully.

"Violet is nice. I like violet. I'm partial to heliotrope too." She arched herself nicely. "But *you* say this time, A.D. It's you has to smell it the most."

"I don't care what you smell of," Mr. Huguenine said. "Chad, you get Bettina a double bottle of perfumery. Don't ask me what kind, either. Just so long as it's strong." He hauled out his pouch purse and untied the strings. "Here's some money for it. Any perfume smells good on Bettina." He turned a harassed smile on Mrs. Huguenine, who bridled in a puzzled way.

Joe asked, "When you going to pay us off?"

"After the show. You better hunt some water and get the mop. And don't ask me where to find water. But hurry up. Lillian wants to practise that grey with the pad horse and take Buck a few turns too, and I told Shepley he ought to do some practising himself. Bisbee thought he looked poor in Baldwinsville. Bisbee's going to come back to watch us here. As soon as you come back with the meat, get the horses over from the barn, Chad. Put pads on both big ones. Hurry up. Bettina—you found any holes?"

"Just a teeny one, A.D.," she replied. "I can't reach to fix it with the tent up."

"I wish it would rain, not much but enough to stop haying," Mr. Huguenine said. "Did Wayfish get drunk last night? Oh, there's Mrs. Pamplon. She'll know. And Bettina, I wish you'd ask her what she knows about Albany and Fred. Have they made up yet?"

What Mrs. Pamplon knew, Chad didn't find out. He was going across the square in search of the butcher and the perfumery. The meat was ready for him, and the butcher, whose name was Schultz, wanted to know whether the lion ate the eight pounds at one meal. Chad said so, which the butcher considered was an interesting fact. He laid his cleaver down carefully and leaned his red hands on the cutting block. "You don't give him nothing else?" he inquired.

Chad said no.

Aha, said the butcher. Then it went to show that the lion wouldn't eat a whole man possibly even wild. You couldn't

C.H.   F honestly say he was a man-eating lion, as advertised, could you?

Well, Chad said, probably the butcher, now, didn't eat more than half a boiled ham and a couple of pig's knuckles at one meal himself, did he? But it wouldn't be a lie, would it, to say he was a pig-eating Dutchman, either.

The butcher got mad too. It couldn't be much of a circus, he thought. Now the Association's Menagerie and Aviary had 47 wagons and 120 horses and 14 musicians. . . . Chad left him yelping and hunted up a drugstore. He found it a couple of blocks down, sandwiched between a jewellery store and a barber shop.

There were a good many different kinds of perfume on sale, and Chad enjoyed himself sniffing at the ends of bottles. The storekeeper was interested. He asked was it for a young lady? No, Chad said. The storekeeper said it depended also on the lady's appearance. For a dark brunette, you wanted something spicy, something to stir her up, he thought; for a blonde he liked the softer perfumes, like violette or Cologne water. Chad said he thought it had better be something spicy; and he selected a rose essence that, it seemed to him, would turn Mrs. Huguenine into something like a garden. Then the storekeeper tried to interest him in various notions; and one of them caught Chad's fancy. It was a small heart-shaped locket attached to a fine chain, but the point was that the heart contained a tiny sachet that could be impregnated with the perfume of the donor's choice. A drop would last for hours, the storekeeper assured Chad, and the chain was long enough to permit the heart to rest upon the bosom, "that interesting portion of the form." The sentimental aspect was obvious but delicate, and invariably appreciated by all ages of the sex.

Chad bought it. As soon as he had seen it, the idea had come whole into his mind. "I want you to write a card to put into it," he told the storekeeper. "Just put on it, 'From a Friend.'"

"Wouldn't 'From an Admirer' sound better?" asked the storekeeper.

Chad rejected the notion. He knew what he wanted. "Friend" was as far as he cared to go. If she liked it enough to wear it he could choose his own moment for letting her know who the friend was.

He delivered the perfume to Mrs. Huguenine and gave Mr.

Huguenine his change ; then he took Oscar's meat over to Joe
Duddy. Joe had raked out the cage wagon and was tossing pails
of water through the bars and rinsing it round the floor with
a mop. Oscar had shrunk his dingy carcass into a corner. Every
time the pail swung he winced ; and while Joe was mopping he
just stared with a hurt look in his dismal, yellow, weary eyes.

Joe finished the floor and then prodded him out of his
corner with the mop handle. He had to lean hard to get Oscar
to move off his little island, and when he finally did he walked the
wet floor gingerly, lifting his feet as high as the stiffness of his
joints permitted. He shoved himself into the opposite corner and
started to sit down ; but stopped in the act, and stayed there in
a kind of painful suspension.

"See that ? " said Joe. " He didn't quite dast. He never does
for a couple of hours. He don't walk, even. He just stays that
way." He put a pail into the dry corner and swabbed. " Some
day I'm going to let that poor durn cat out where he can dig
himself a hole."

" Why don't you give him a pan ? " Chad asked.

" A natural-born lion ? " Joe shook his head. " Naw. He's
too old."

Leaving them at it, Chad went after the horses. He lifted
his leg over the hitch rail, which was beginning to fill up on all
three sides of the square, and crossed to the hotel to deliver the
locket.

After the hot glare of the street, the office seemed almost
dark. He had to stop for an instant to accustom his eyes to it,
and standing there blind he could smell the faintly sour smell of
the overused chairs that were ranged round the huge boxwood
stove. Then a youngish man with pomatum on his hair said,
" Good-morning. Can I help you ? "

" I don't know," Chad said. " I got a package to leave for
somebody staying here."

" You can give it to me. I'll have it sent up. Who's it for ? "

" It's for one of the girls with the show," Chad said
cautiously.

" In Mr. Huguenine's company ? "

" Yes," Chad said. " It's for Lady Lillian."

" She's out now. I'll give it to her when she comes in."

" Well," Chad said, " can't you just put it in her room so
she'll find it there ? "

The clerk agreed with a patronising smile, and called a coloured boy.

It made Chad feel mad that a little snipe with slick hair could make him feel uneasy, but he was glad to get out. He marched round the hotel and talked loud to the hostlers, telling them to go easy with Jerry, and not to touch Buck at all. There was no sense in acting up about the cream pad horse ; a child could see that he knew everything there was to know about circus life.

He took the leads, the double in his left hand with the two pad horses on it, and Buck on the off side, and Buck made a few shies going round the corner of the hotel. A squad of small boys who had sprouted up out of nowhere came sifting through the wagons along the hitch rail, letting out shrill yelps as they vaulted it under the noses of the tied horses. Chad didn't pay any attention to them but let them answer their own questions while he got the pads out of Bastock's wagon and saddled up. Then, with the boys flocking like birds, he led the three horses to the hurdle by the performers' entrance and left them there swinging their tails in the small piece of shade. . . .

It was still cool in the tent, but the grass had nearly dried, foretelling the heat of the day. Close by, Fiero was practising knife-throwing, a scowl of concentration on his face. He had painted a crude silhouette of a human figure on his plank door and he was calling his shots to himself, and whenever he made a successful throw he would cry " Ha ! " and roll his eyes to see whether he had been observed. Chad had to admit he was improving. But he still kept piercing the forehead of the silhouette with unerring precision, and he said now, " I make him from Miss Trid drawing round with chalk as she stands and leaving the margin. But my God ! She is too tall ! " He started all over again : the flash of the heavy blades in the greenish light, the fine stance of Fiero, almost heroic in the bend of the forward leg, and the solid ominous *tunk* as the point bit wood and the blade twanged.

Fiero was the one active element in the tent ; all the other people seemed desultory, dimmed, like figures seen in an undersea dream. The Pamplons, testing the slack wire rig and passing remarks back and forth in French ; Budlong stretched out on a folded canvas near by with his hat over his face and his ankles crossed like a crusader ; Bastock splicing a length of rope ; Ike

Wayfish, the clown, sombrely limbering up with slow somersaults
and cartwheels and an occasional flip-flap, and the Huguenines
sitting at the end of the tent.

Mr. Huguenine was talking to Bisbee, who had returned
from somewhere or other, and was listening with his horselike
face bent down as if he expected a carrot. Mrs. Huguenine sat
two tiers above them—it was funny how she liked to hoist her
bulk to an upper tier, puffing while the seat jacks groaned ; " I
was a regular tomboy to climb," she once told Chad—while she
knitted a scarlet wool muffler. Now and then she threw a word
into the conversation of the two men, but most of the time her
bright eyes moved round the tent. She caught sight of Chad
immediately and said, before he could open his mouth, " A.D. !
Here's Chad wants to tell you he's got the horses ready
outside."

Huguenine said irritably without looking up. " I wish he
could saddle and bridle them two riders for me."

" Have they made up yet ? " Mr. Bisbee asked, lifting a casual
palm in greeting for Chad.

" Hell," said Mr. Huguenine, " how would I know ? They
quit talking in Vernon ; and they ain't been polite since. It
don't help his act any, either."

" They ought to get married," Mrs. Huguenine said.

There was a long pause, before Bisbee asked a question.

" How about this new girl ? The one Albany picked up ? I
can't remember her name.

" Trid," said Mrs. Huguenine. " Caroline Trid."

" Albany was dead set to take her along. She said she would
pay the girl's way if I wouldn't. I don't know why. Albany
is notional," Mr. Huguenine complained. " First she acts like
a fool with Shepley ; then she won't even be polite with him ;
then she picks up this girl."

" Kind of a chippy bit," Mrs. Huguenine said. " But maybe
she was just poor. She looks pretty enough now, except her bust
is puny. But she'll outgrow that, I dare say. And she makes
a good partner for Fiero. I always said there wasn't no sense
to a man tossing balls all alone. He's crazy about her. He wants
to throw knives at her too, now." Mrs. Huguenine switched
over her needles and started purling back across the muffler.

" She'd better stay thin, then," Ike Wayfish said, doing a
back flip and coming up with a mug on his face. Chad thought

he looked more comical without his paint than with it. The half-lost, half-sly look was there in nature, and his nose had its own red, too, a sadder, more reflective colour without the tendency to streak on a hot day.. " That girl could turn into something, I believe," Ike Wayfish said. " She's got muscle and she's full of whip. I hate to think of that Dago Italian taking pot shots at her with his hog-stickers. He's all right on the sides, I guess, but every time he tries to throw over the head he plugs that picture right between the eyes. It's uncanny."

" He said it was like a machine," Mr. Huguenine explained doubtfully. " He says it's just the way a piston has to make the stroke in a steamboat. He's learnt it one way. He said the woman he used to have for a marker was built close to a head shorter than this Trid girl. He's got to unlearn that one throw and learn it over. It's the only thing he don't like about her, her being so tall."

Mrs. Huguenine made a convulsive movement so that the seat jacks almost shook clear of the toe pins.

" It would be an awful accident, Mr. Bisbee, wouldn't it ? " Bisbee didn't answer, except with a smile.

" Well," he said, " Huguenine's Great and Only has been doing better than I figured, up to now. But Burke and Walsh is coming over the turnpike and they'll probably catch up to us after we quit Auburn. So I'm routing round north a little. We'll let them pass to Rochester and we'll skip it and take the towns along the ridge road and pick up what we can in Rochester on the way back."

" Rochester ? " Mrs. Pamplon had come over with her husband to join the group. " That is far west, is it not ? "

" Not so far," Bisbee said. He looked at her, then at Pamplon. " How's the leg coming along ? "

" It's fine," Pamplon said. He stood beside his wife. Their eyes were strained, but they wore the same smile, anxious, placating, half-shy. You could have told they were foreign even without hearing them speak. Mrs. Pamplon shivered briefly. " I do not like this so far west where we are going," she said.

" Can't help it," Bisbee said. " We've got to hunt our business. It's hard to find, even west of Rochester. I got hold of a paper—look here." He hauled a folded sheet of newsprint out of his poster-case and showed Huguenine. " That's the *Orleans American,*" he said. " From Albion. Look, A.D. The Menagerie's playing the ridge road but they won't hit it till August. But look what they're doing. Advertising in the newspapers!"

The advertisement was a two-column spread, and Mr. Huguenine began to read from it while the others crowded to look at the cuts of the Ichneumon, Elephant, Royal Tiger, Java Tiger, Cape Lion, spotted and striped Hyenas, Camel, one brown and one white, Horned Horse, 18 wonderful curiosities, nine down each side. In the middle was the print set off with two large cuts, the lower an elephant, the upper a great pleated creature that caught the eye and held it.

Bisbee read the lettering under it :—

UNICORN, OR ONE-HORNED RHINOCEROS

This animal has been a subject of much speculation among naturalists, it has been considered the Unicorn of Holy Writ as described in the Book of Job. It ranks next to the Elephant in size and many consider him as equal in bulk. This bull was taken in the Interior of Asia, and imported to Philadelphia at enormous expense in 1830 and he weighs upwards of 5000 pounds.

" My gracious," said Mrs. Huguenine. " He's heavy."
" Must be a load to drag. They can't lead him," Bisbee said.
Huguenine read the bottom print :—

This menagerie and aviary occupies 36 spacious wagons and the same are drawn by 113 splendid Grey Horses and 60 Men including 14 Musicians are required to complete its operation.

There was silence, in which, imperturbably, came the " Ha!" from Fiero, and the *tunk* of the striking knife. Chad was conscious of a sudden drawing together in the group of performers. They had got the hand-clapping in the country villages all right ; but here in this up-and-coming town, with its air of worldliness, when they read that advertisement, their own insignificance was borne in on them. Five wagons and round-top didn't look so good compared to 113 matched grey horses, 14 musicians, a rhinoceros of Holy Writ, and the money to put it all on the road.

The circus agent was watching them with an alert expression on his long intelligent face.

" I remember how we used to cuss the mud and wish for solid roads," he recollected. " Well, we're getting the roads, and look what they're doing to us. They've turned us into a little show, and a thing has to be expensive now before it can be a genuine wonder. People want to see a big display. Look at Burke and Walsh : they're supposed to be a ring show but they've put in animal acts. They've got a hyena too, besides the elephant. What has a hyena got to do with a circus ? "

" We've got a lion, though," Mr. Huguenine protested.

" Ah," said Mr. Bisbee. " How's Oscar, Joe ? "

" He's alive."

Mrs. Pamplon glanced at her husband, who shrugged his shoulders and turned his back. Her small colourless face was frightened. Chad knew why she was scared ; she was afraid her husband would break down and then get fired, so that they would be left stranded in a raw, tobacco-chewing stretch of country where the woods might contain Indians. But a little colour had come into her face.

She said suddenly : " These so big shows they do not have wire acts."

" Well, the Menagerie don't," Bisbee agreed kindly.

" But look, it has no one like brave Mr. Wayfish who lies down beside the lion ! "

Wayfish looked uncomfortable and modest ; he also looked as if he had never properly seen Mrs. Pamplon.

Bisbee said, " That's true. It's a great act of Ike's. I never saw the beat of it anywhere. It's about all we've got to advertise against these big shows with. I wish Oscar was healthier. He don't look savage enough."

" How about me, though ? I don't want to lay down with no savage lion," Ike said. " I know the garlic round my neck is a guarantee. But suppose he gets hungry for garlic ? "

Joe Duddy said, " There's plenty clowns."

Bisbee said, " I'm going to change our advertising some. Maybe I'll use the newspapers, A.D., and I will have to check the books. I wish we had something out of Holy Writ, by God, I do."

" There's Daniel in the Lion's Den, ain't there ? "

" Who said that ? "

Chad felt embarrassed. It had popped into his head. But Mrs. Huguenine clicked her needles. " Chad said it," she informed them, trying the length of muffler round her neck. " I didn't know he read the Bible, either."

" The modern Daniel, like him of Holy Writ as narrated in the book of . . . I've forgotten which book it is in. What's the name of that book, Chad ? "

Chad shook his head. " I just heard it oncet, Mr. Bisbee."

" It's in the book of Daniel," Mrs. Huguenine said tartly.

" That clinches it," Bisbee cried. He struck the sheet with the back of his hand, as if to erase the words and cuts of the Association's advertisement, and sonorously read imagined lines :—

MAN TO MAN-EATING LION
THE MODERN DANIEL IN THE LION'S DEN

Like him of Holy Writ, as narrated in the Book of Daniel (chapter and verse), this Modern Daniel will enter the lion's cage and make himself at home, reclining on the lion's bed beside the Savage King of Beasts in terms of intimacy and affability incredible to the beholder.

" How's that, A.D. ? Putting in chapter and verse that way ought to satisfy preachers a lot. It's Educational. Chad, that was a smart idea."

Mr. Huguenine agreed it was smart. " But I wish Chad could play a fife or something. We only got three pieces in the band."

He was thinking about the fourteen musicians. So were the others. In spite of Bisbee's new enthusiasm, the type of the Association's Menagerie and Aviary still remained on the paper. Their own parade would start in three hours—with three pieces. Burke and Walsh, even, advertised the New York Band of Seven Talented Musicians, assembled and led by that Impresario of the French Horn, Mr. Merwin Cleary of Bowery Theatre Fame. That was the kind of band Syracuse expected, or any town that Burke and Walsh had ever played to.

" Besides," said Mr. Huguenine, " Shepley ain't going to like Ike heading him in the posters."

" The hell with Shepley," Bisbee said good-humouredly. " Where is he anyway ? "

Mrs. Huguenine said over their heads, " Here comes Caroline Trid."

3

RING PRACTICE

SHE entered with a shy, apologetic smile. When Albany wasn't in the tent with her, she was apt to act shy, as though she knew that she was being carried by the circus through Albany's insistence. She would have gone over to one side, now, if Mr. Huguenine had not bawled at her to tell them where Lady Lillian had gone to.

" She's just got back," Caroline said. " She said if you asked for her, she'd be right along."

" Right along, right along," fumed Mr. Huguenine. " In how many hours ? Where's Fred Shepley ? Have you seen *him* ? "

" Not since last night, Mr. Huguenine."

Mr. Huguenine swore. They all heard the *tunk* of the striking knife, Fiero's, " Hah ! " and then, as he caught sight of Caroline, his excited shouting. " Miss Trid ! You please come over here. Right away." His voice vibrated. " I have nearly missed your head."

" My, that's nice." Mrs. Huguenine was beaming. She gathered up yarn, muffler, and needles, hoisted her huge hips, and lumbered down the benches to have a look for herself. It was obvious that Fiero could hardly contain himself for joy and pride. Caroline's thin face coloured as he led her to the board and made her turn her back to it.

" Please, Miss Trid, you take your cloak off, and lift your arms ? Look, the arms fit, the body fits ; and the head. Yes, yes, it just missed too." He stood aside so that the others might see, made a knee, and bowed to the Huguenines and Bisbee.

Caroline looked hopelessly embarrassed ; but the picture was effective. " Look at her, so young, with all the great big knives.

One mistake? She would have been dead. But no, Fiero has missed her. Clap hands." Without her cloak, in the faded lavender tights, her slim arms raised, her pointed face hedged in murderous blades, she would make a fragile appeal for the audience's breathless quiet, for Fiero's mercy. After he had stared at her a moment, Bisbee said, " You may be right, Ike. She might make something. Let's get Bastock. Chad, I want to talk to you."

He ignored Mr. Huguenine. But Mr. Huguenine didn't seem to mind. He hauled out his handkerchief, wiped his ruddy forehead and fat cheeks and said " Bettina, I want you to come with me to the treasury wagon. I got to practise some of the speeches. I got to get that *s* in gymnat—gysmant, I mean gymnsat. Oh, hell, I got to look it up."

" Why not say ' acrobat ' ? It's a lot thinner word," suggested Mrs. Huguenine.

As the Huguenines passed out of the tent, Bisbee called the little bowlegged skinner into conference.

" Have you paid any attention to that Trid girl, Pete ? "

" Some. She's a nice little piece."

" Ike thinks we might make something of her."

Bastock said, " Fiero says her sense of time is good."

Bisbee nodded. " That's something you can't teach. Same with horses, humans, and females. I've found talented performers in the damn'dest places, Pete, when I was agent for Buckley and Weeks. You wouldn't believe me."

" No," said Bastock. He sat quite still. Caroline Trid, unconscious of their interest in her, stood at the other end of the tent tossing bottles to Fiero as he called for them. He was working on three ; they were like bubbles in the green air ; and when he got his spacing worked out and yelped for the fourth, her motion was quick, easy, almost casual. Bastock's dark eyes brightened.

" You want her to ride ? "

" I thought of it."

" I bet." He studied Bisbee's long face.

Bisbee said, " There's no sense Huguenine feeding her just to fill Mrs. Pamplon's old tights, is there ? "

" How old is she ? " asked Bastock.

Bisbee turned to Chad.

" You know her," he said. " How old is she ? "

Chad said, "I don't know. I guess she's maybe fifteen, sixteen, maybe."

"I thought you'd seen a lot of her."

"Only once before she joined up with the show," Chad said. She run away from home, didn't she?"

"Yes. Cisco licked the hide off her."

"She's not apt to get to run for home then," Bisbee said.

"She don't look to me as if she'd run away from a fall or two," Bastock said. "But you can't train her on Buck, Mr. Bisbee. Not with him performing. It would mix him up. Albany's right about that."

"Who said anything about Buck?" demanded Bisbee. "I want a girl who can vault to a pad. There'll never be one that can somersault on a horse; there's hardly any men; but they tan do posing, or maybe even leap the ribbons. Maybe this girl could."

"Well." Bastock scratched his forehead. "I trained a couple of apprentices in the old country, but never taught no female. Maybe she ain't got ambitions to ride a pad. You can't teach 'em if they ain't got the ambition, unless they're terribly young to start with. They lose the ambition, but it comes back once they quit hurting themselves. But if she wants to try, I'll do what I can with her."

"Chad, you tell her to come over here," Bisbee said.

She was watching Fiero arrange his stuff for the show; she jumped when Chad touched her elbow, and flushed. "Come over back," he said. For an instant her eyes became estimating; they made him think of the way she had studied him that morning when she led him to Trid's house; as if she knew what he was thinking and what he was after, or thought she did. Her mouth turned sullen the way it had then. "Hell," he said. "I ain't asking. Bisbee wants to talk to you, and you'd better come along. He just about runs Huguenine."

"Mr. Bisbee wants to see me?" Her voice got husky with surprise. Then she suddenly lost colour. She didn't look sullen; she looked scared.

Chad said, "Hell, Caroline. He ain't going to throw you out. He wants to ask you something, that's all."

"Honest?"

She was looking at him. All the sullenness had gone out of her. She was young and she wanted help. He felt sorry for her.

" Honest Injun," he said. " I wouldn't lie to you."

She recollected herself then and turned silent beside him as they started across the ring. She was thinking about the nigger business : Chad guessed she still blamed him. Likely she had told Albany the whole story. He wondered if that accounted for the way Albany ignored him. It made him mad. How was he to know Cisco would take an honest trick of his out on a girl's back ?

They stopped in front of Bisbee and Bastock. Ike Wayfish was standing one foot up on a seat board and his elbow leaning on the knee and his receding chin on the heel of his hand. He didn't turn, but he watched Caroline out of the tail of his eye. Bisbee studied her a minute. He said, " Take the cape off, Miss."

Her hands went to the collar ; she hesitated for a minute ; then she let it slide off her shoulders, holding one corner of it in one hand, so that it crumpled shoddily on the green grass beside her heel, the left hand staying as if it were snared in the seeking gaze of the men.

Bisbee said, " You like being with the show ? "

She drew a slight breath, her lips trembling, and nodded wordlessly.

Bisbee made a sucking noise through his teeth. " Don't get scared," he said. " We think you might be able to do something of your own in the show."

She turned her eyes slowly to his. They had become large in her narrow face. Chad could hardly hear her say, " What is it ? "

" Did you ever ride a horse ? "

She nodded. Then she said, " Not much."

" Bastock thinks he can make you into a real rider, if you want to learn, Miss Trid."

She made a visible effort. " Like Miss Yates ? "

" No. We want you to try riding on a pad. It's hard learning ; you'll fall ; maybe you'll be no good at it ; but I think it would be worth trying if you've got the nerve. If you got any good, you'd get a place with the biggest circuses in the country, some day. Do you want to try ? "

" Oh, yes."

Bisbee nodded. " Mr. Wayfish and Pete Bastock will take hold of you. There's a lot to learn before you can begin trying to ride." He was tapping the grass between his feet with the end of his poster-case. " You'll be carried as an apprentice. No pay, you know, till you can handle an act yourself. But when you can

stay on your feet three times round the ring, we'll see about a
new costume for you. Lavender don't suit you." He smiled
suddenly. " White, I think. With ostrich feathers in your hair."
His voice lifted as it had when he was rounding out the Modern
Daniel. " Billed as the First Equestrian Artiste in America : the
Sylphide of the Upper Air. How does that sound, Pete ? "

Bastock grunted.

" You can play with them ideas yourself, Mr. Bisbee. We
don't even know yet if she can cross her legs when she sits down.
Missy, there's a lot of hard work, and there's bumps, and bad
falls, and you getting sick and crying because me and Ike make
you keep at it. You've got to learn to use your body, you've got to
learn to fall so you won't break your neck or legs—arms ain't so
important. But if you're willing to learn, I'll teach you what I
know. But I won't let you stop even if you want to, not unless
you're no good at all. Want to try ? " He cocked his eye at her,
and his grin was comical.

" Yes."

She smiled suddenly, the sullenness vanishing from her
mouth. It made her whole face alive ; it changed her ; if she
had been pretty to start with, Chad thought, she would be
something to look at. He saw that she was looking at him, too ;
and he couldn't figure it out. But he grinned and told her,
" Pete's said he would find out if I can do anything in that line
myself. We could try it together."

She kept on smiling. " That's fine," she said.

She looked straight at him for an instant, then glanced down,
hiding her eyes ; and he couldn't make her out at all. She seemed
a long way removed from the little chippy he had met at Trid's
house in her rag of dress that had nothing under it except her
bare skin, sitting on the kitchen table in all that raffle of confused housekeeping, swinging her bare foot and cocking the big
toe slowly at him.

If they had been alone he would have asked her straight
out what was on her mind, but Ike Wayfish, still holding his
Hamlet pose with his foot on the bottom seat, was watching
out of the corner of his eye ; Bastock and Bisbee were conferring
close by ; and the Pamplons had crossed the tent, talking rapidly
in their own language ; and it was at that moment also that
Albany Yates's clear voice preceded her through the performer's
entrance.

" Hallo, there, everybody," she called.

At the sound, Budlong took the hat off his face, sat up, and put it on his head. The others stopped talking, and Joe Duddy left off cleaning his thumbnail to grin at her. She came in quickly, holding the skirt of her habit in her left hand, and said, " Why, Mr. Bisbee ! I didn't know you were back with us."

Bisbee raised his palm in greeting, smiling at her ; and Caroline turning pink with pleasure and excitement, went quickly to meet her. At the same moment, the Huguenines re-entered, Mr. Huguenine muttering, " Gym-nast, gym-nast," under his breath and shouting when he saw Albany, " Where the devil have you been ? Where's Fred ? "

" Outside loosing the cream pad," she said. " I don't know where he's been. I've been shopping, though. I just had to find some things to wear or I wouldn't have been decent."

Her habit was the old one of dull green, reminding Chad of the ride they had taken together from the Yellow Bud barn. She must have known—she had an instant awareness of men's thoughts when they touched her ; for, inexplicably, after days of ignoring his existence, she smiled at him. Then, quickly, she put her arm round Caroline's waist ; and he could see Caroline talking to her in a low voice. She gave Caroline a little squeeze, and said in her clear voice, " Why, that's just wonderful, darling." They were standing together that way, prettily posed, when Fred Shepley entered the tent with the cream pad horse looking over his shoulder.

He saw them, but his blond face was impervious, except that his lips set in a small tight line. He stepped over the bank of the ring with the horse, who was moving his ears delicately at them and watching from his white-lashed eyes, stepping carefully over beside him. The horse wheeled automatically, presenting his off-side to the curve of the ring. Shepley dropped his robe outside and stood by the horse's shoulder, his green tights and leotard outlining his figure like a piece of sculpture, and a greenish luminance, like breathing light, on the spangles, while Bisbee and Huguenine approached him.

They talked in low tones, so that even in the small tent their voices blurred. For an instant the only other sound was the creaking of the seat jacks as Mrs. Huguenine climbed heavily to her perch on the fourth tier, sat down spreadingly, and remarked at large, " My, I do love to watch a ring practice go on. It makes me feel like a queen giving a command performance."

Nobody heeded her. They could all tell from Shepley's anger that Huguenine's attempts to soothe him were no good.

"Now, Fred, Bisbee don't mean you're scared or nothing. Do you?"

Bisbee shook his long head.

"What in hell does he mean?"

He just said you'd lost your style. He thinks something's on your mind. You ain't troubled, or anything, are you?"

"Why should I be?" Shepley demanded furiously. "It's none of your business anyway."

"Your act's our business," Bisbee pointed out coolly.

"Well, if you don't like my riding, you can get another principal," Shepley said. "And see what else you can get for twenty damn dollars."

Mr. Huguenine hastily raised his fingers to his pursed mouth.

"Fred, Fred. That ain't no way to talk. We don't want to lose you. It's for your own good just as much as ours." His voice lowered, carrying the tones of the others with it, and for a moment their talk was another indistinguishable murmur.

Chad, looking back towards the girls, realised that Albany Yates had been watching him. He saw the slight narrowing of her eyes; he could see the clear grey of them the length of the tent; and she had a half smile. But she turned her head at once and said something over the lifted curve of her shoulder to Joe Duddy. Joe listened to her, then came over to Chad, grinning at him out of his big face, and told him, "Albany says Buck sure looks dandy since you been handling him."

"Well, by God," Chad thought. He said, "That's fine."

Joe assumed a negligent pose with his shoulder against a stay of slack-wire rig, and wiggled the thumb he had left clear of his trousers pocket. "Do you want it in writing?" he asked out of the side of his mouth.

Chad was puzzled, but he told Joe he didn't need it in writing. He walked over the grass, which was now dry and beginning to acquire the peculiar limpness of tented grass on a hot day. The two girls had sat down on the bottom seat, in front of where Bastock was sitting, and their faces tilted as he came up to them. He noticed again the way Albany's eyes narrowed towards the outer corners, and he studied her throat for a possible indication of the locket; but her stock hid whatever might show and he could smell no perfume on her.

"Caroline's told me about you and her. I think it's fine. Pete says he'll begin you to-morrow." She paused, but Chad knew she was going to say something else. "You remember I told you I bet you could ride?"

She looked small and complete and perfect. She seemed to have forgotten that for a week she had chosen to ignore his existence. But he said, "Yes, I'm going to have a try at it," and felt foolish. God damn it, he thought, she's got all the tools in her own box.

"Fred looks mad enough to eat raw dog," Bastock observed.

The three men still confronted each other in the ring. Bisbee was the only one who looked at all cool. His dry voice reached them. "We've lost enough time. Let's see you ride, if you're going to."

The cream horse moved an ear. He was still waiting, imperturbable, keeping his weight under him, ready to move when the word should be given.

A whistling squirt erupted from Bastock's lips. "That horse," he said, "is worth the whole three of those grunts put together."

Chad knew that Albany was going to put in her finger. He could tell by the way she straightened up. The tight little flaring jacket showed off the pretty set of her shoulders, and she squared them cockily. But her voice, like her face, was composed and sweet as honey.

"Oh, Mr. Huguenine! I've got to change before the parade and I *would* like to work Buck, so if Mr. Shepley doesn't feel like riding this morning, could I have the ring?"

Mr. Huguenine's ruddy face was helplessly amazed. "Why," he said. "Why, I guess . . ."

"I'll ride now," Shepley broke in. His flush had fused on his cheekbones. "Bring the jump-up board, can't you?"

Joe Duddy unlimbered himself by a series of joint movements, picked up the board with its foot-high riser, and deposited it at random in the ring, leaving Shepley to set it for himself. He tested it, then backed across the ring, and Mr. Huguenine, taking his whip from the centre pole, cracked it. The cream pad gathered himself, tossed his head, and struck his gait.

Bisbee came over to the seats and sat down beside Albany.

' By God, you're a devil, aren't you ? " he said. " Sometimes I feel sorry for Fred."

Albany rested her chin on her fist, without looking at Bisbee, and laughed, not loud, but clear, so that Shepley could hear her if he cared to. He didn't turn his head. His hand on the horse's hip, he picked up the animal's beat, crossing the ring twice to verify it ; then made the indefinable pause and spring inside of the bank, saying, " Now," as he always did. The horse seemed to tighter. the arch of his neck. His ears swayed for a second, pricked again. Shepley marked the stride, matched his own, and came across the ring, striking the jump-up with his left foot, lifting into the air, and meeting the rise of the cream's quarters.

Bastock leaned forward. " Watch him, you two. I mean really watch. He was a hair soon on that one. He caught it too hard on his heels. But it weren't a bad vault."

Albany nodded, the curls on her right shoulder stroking the side of her neck.

" He doesn't often make that first vault to his feet."

Chad glanced at her and saw her eyes absorbed. Riding always took hold of her. She could be mad with Shepley for twenty-three and a half hours of the day, but she could love him on a horse. He thought ruefully that Shepley had a head start of him he would find it hard to beat, if it came to riding.

But watching Shepley's routine, he saw that Mrs. Huguenine was right in her excitement over a ring practice. The audience brought a lot to the riding, but it was also distracting. Now, with the round of the tent exposed to view, the billow of it motionless and sun-filled overhead, the thud of the pad horse's hoofs seemed shaped to the round. His cream-coloured hide and Shepley's green leotard matched in reverse the colour of the tent and grass ; and the performance of the two became elemental in its perfection of contact, a balance formed and broken and renewed. Horse and man were so absorbed that the members of the troupe seemed insignificant and were held motionless along the benches, caught like unaspiring ants in a grass-blade world, that has been touched with fire.

None of them had ever seen Shepley ride so well. Chad heard Bisbee suck in his breath once as his long face became intent ; then they were all still until Shepley had to call for the ribbons. Mr. Huguenine stuttered with embarrassment, and Caroline uttered an exclamation of dismay and hurried from her seat. Mr. Huguenine handed her one pole and took the other himself, and they lifted them after the horse had passed, the white cloth stretching between them, under which the horse lolloped at his perfect gait ; and Shepley, not noticing them, performed three leaps, clearing the ribbon wide, lighting erect, and on the third leap dropping from the pad to the ground, and without losing his stride coming over in front of Bisbee.

" Suit you, Mr. Bisbee ? "

Bisbee said, " That was fine, Fred. That's what I wanted to see. That was darned near great riding."

" Then Miss Yates can use the ring if she wants to," he said.

His eyes passed over Albany as if she were not there at all, encountered Chad's.

" He'll need a rub down. He's hot," he said. He walked off to the ring, picked up his robe, and passed out through the performers' entrance.

Bisbee got up. " You might have told him something, Albany. He earned it."

She rose also.

" It was good, wasn't it? " she asked.

" You bet your life," said Bisbee ; but she was looking at Bastock.

The little man nodded.

" It was good. If he could throw a somersault, he'd be a great rider, maybe."

Her face was thoughtful as she asked Chad to bring in Buck.

4

PERFORMERS' ENTRANCE

THE parade made a creeping progress along Salina Street, and Chad, driving the cage wagon, realised that it was not getting much of a turnout from the town. It was the beer wagon that got him mad, though. It had rolled out of a side street behind a mammoth team of matched bays that looked like Conestogas, and the driver had muscled into their line right behind Shepley. Now the big bezabor was standing up on his seat, snapping his whip, and bowing and kissing his hand like a God-damned monkey with a blister on his buttock. There wasn't a thing the circus could do about it either, except let him come, and smile their set audience smile at the waves of laughter and applause the teamster was getting.

Generally Chad enjoyed the parade down a main street. He liked to look at the faces of farmers and mechanics and store-keeps and drunks and womenfolks lined up in the sunlight while the boys broke free to tail the procession like a pack of rabbit dogs. He liked to see their expression of awe when Oscar's effluvia poured over their heads ; and he could hear their speculations as to whether it was a male or a female lion till he had gone by, and even then they could not always make out. Sometimes they looked as if keys had been turned in their minds ; as if what they saw were romantic and beautiful and had a kind of magic in it, the way they might witness a troop of goblins or fairies crossing the country where the wind blew, creatures that got their living with no waiting plough handles, no wood to split or cows to milk or butter to churn or cook-stoves to chain them.

But it was different here in Syracuse. Right from the start when Ike Wayfish turned the mule out of the square and bawled his dumb-fool question about where was the road to Syracuse, the heckler Joe had chased earlier in the morning began to blat like a hungry calf ; and Chad knew how it was going to be. The others had known too. Albany had flushed up bright and set her lips in a determined smile. Shepley had just set himself close on the cream's back and Mrs. Pamplon had moved over towards her husband. Even Caroline, whose job it was to sit with Mrs. Huguenine on the tail gate and hold the parasol over her (Bisbee said it made Mrs. Huguenine an interesting contrast), looked suddenly scared.

The hell with it, Chad thought. But it had to be done. They had made the pitch and you couldn't give a performance without a parade. He heard a woman say, " They look so poor, don't they ? " in a pitying voice, as if they were beggars. The only person who seemed to do well was Arganave with his microscope. He had pitched at the far corner of the square and had been packing the loafers in since nine o'clock. He had paid Huguenine his concession money at noon and said it was the best morning he had had since Utica. It seemed queerly immoral that a fake machine like that, which anybody with a bean of brains could tell was a fake, would get interest when a show, even if it was small, would be considered poor by the same class of people. Bisbee was right ; it was the money that people were interested in. They wanted to feel that their two bits was buying them a thousand dollars.

The beer wagon turned off east three blocks down, leaving a gap in the line, so that Fiero had to hurry to close it, and that got some more laughs. Then when he started a turn of juggling he dropped the odd ball and it went rolling over the curve of the roadway and a little boy let out a yell and grabbed it. If he hadn't yelled, Fiero wouldn't have known who had it.

" Oh, Cripus, the damn fool," Chad thought. " He's going to try to get it back. He's took right out after him, and he can't catch him. Nobody but a fool would try to catch a kid like that in a crowd. He's ducked in back of that mess of loafers by that notions store and they've closed up on him. They're laughing again. They ain't stopping Fiero, they're just looking at the circus. . . ."

Fiero was flushed and hot-eyed. He had forgotten every bit of sense he ever had, he couldn't even talk English and was yelling at the people in Italian, making gestures with his hands, each of which was still holding a ball. Now Albany was past him, and she didn't know what to do. She was looking over her shoulder. She expected Chad ought to do something.

" I can't," Chad thought. " I've got to mind the cat. There's that little rat holding the ball up down the street. He's tossing it up."

He had solemnly taken Fiero's place in the march, a little shaver with a gallus strap holding pants too big for him and bare feet solemnly stomping in the dust. He dropped the ball on purpose and scrabbled for it and that was when Fiero caught sight of it and came charging like a madman. But it was no use. Chad saw he would never catch the boy. He yelled at Fiero, " Leave him be." But Fiero cried desperately, " It's my ball, Chad. I can't juggle only two balls."

Fiero caught up to his place in the line with the bystanders all hooting and by that time he was so breathless and agonized and outraged that he could hardly hold on to the two balls he had left, let alone try to toss them. The boy, of course, had vanished. But he stepped suddenly out of the crowd beside the cage wagon and let out a shrill whoop. " Yah ! Butter tubs can't run."

He caught Chad's eye and Chad grinned at him and yelled, " Want a ride with me, son ? "

It confounded him. His face went slack and his eyes swelled.

" Come on," invited Chad. " You can set here beside me and ride the whole parade."

" Yah ! " yelped the boy. " Who wants to ride in a ten-cent show like yourn ? " But he began to walk along, keeping abreast of Chad. Chad said. " Who does ? "

That genuinely troubled the boy. His face got serious working at the idea. Chad said, " You could get a real close look of the lion from here."

If Fiero didn't spot the kid and chase him, Chad thought, he might bite.

" You mean it, mister ? "

" Sure, I do."

The kid reached up his right hand, remembered the ball was in it, and held up the left instead. Chad heaved him up. For a minute his bare foot rasped on the turning wheel hub, then he was sitting by Chad. He said, " If you make a grab for this ball I'm going to throw it to hell and back, mister."

" I ain't going to grab it," Chad said. " But if you give it back to Fiero when we get to the tent, I'll let you set in the show free gratis for nothing."

" Gee," said the boy. " All right, mister."

He squirmed round to stare at Oscar. " Is he old ? "

" Yeah."

" Has he ate humans ? "

" Sure has."

" Do you feed him human meat now ? "

" Not generally. It costs too much. Just horse thieves and such like," Chad said.

The boy froze. He stared into Oscar's yellow eyes for several minutes. Then the lion yawned, fraction by fraction, the final gape evolving suddenly, and ending with a deep grunting, coughlike sound, not loud, but throat-opening, so that the boy thought he could see the preparation of the digestive juices taking place. " Do you feed him ball thieves ? " he asked.

" Naw," said Chad. " Ball thieves generally die of gravel in the small entrails. They ain't healthy."

" Mister, if I give you the ball now will you let me see the show free gratis just the same ? "

" I said so."

The boy handed over Fiero's ball. Chad put it in his pocket, He grinned. After a minute the boy grinned. The boy asked, " Did you run away to join the circus, mister ? "

" I sure did," Chad said.

" Gee Crimus. I'm going to myself. But I'm going to wait till a real big circus comes, like Burke and Walsh. They got an elerphunt. I seen them last year so this don't seem like anything much, this show don't."

" Maybe it don't," Chad said, " But what we got is just as good or better than the big shows have. You wait and see."

Ahead, on top of the big wagon, Budlong, Bastock, and Joe Duddy whanged away at " Long-Tailed Blue " while the sweat poured off their faces on to the collars of their red jackets. The tune came back, thin, ragged, futile, but you couldn't help the words from popping into your mind :

> I've come to town to see you all,
> I ask you, how d'ye do ? . . .

The heat was stifling, the air dead. The apathetic faces on the sidewalks crawled back, the windows of the stores mirrored the heat. Flies crawled on them. Chad had never seen so many flies. He wondered whether a big brewery made flies come around a city. But there was nothing he could do about it except sit there and hold the lines. Bastock's team, which was hauling

the cage wagon instead of Joe Duddy's, knew all about parades,
and they eased the wheel over the bumps solicitously as if Oscar
himself had been driving them, supposing you could teach that
lion to sit up in a red coat with his legs crossed on the dashboard.
He envied Duddy's team left to stand in the lot. They were a
potbellied pair of scarecrows, one with a shoe boil as big as a
child's chamberpot, and they looked so bad that they couldn't
be used in the parade.

Time seemed interminable before Huguenine turned the big
wagon left at the canal bridge. Chad had a glimpse of him
glumly staring at his wheeler's rumps, of Mrs. Huguenine and
Caroline jolting on the tail gate and the Pamplons drearily
trudging after them. Shepley's face was sour and the cream pad
seemed to walk in his sleep. Fiero was paying no attention to
anything. Then as Albany reached the corner, a bunch of loafers
on the bridge raised a mordant cheer.

Chad saw her stiffen in the saddle ; then she touched Buck's
shoulder with the riding whip and he bowed, putting one knee all
the way to the road dust, and came up with a spring that brought
his haunches under him. Albany didn't acknowledge the loafers'
presence with so much as a glance, but they liked it and gave her
a hand.

By God, Chad thought, she could perform, and the little boy
beside him said, " My, she rides good ! " forgetting for a moment
that he considered this a ten-cent show. He glanced at Chad's
face and asked, " You married to her, mister ? "

" No," said Chad.

The boy stared at him.

" What do you do in the circus ? " he wanted to know.

" I tend the ring stock and lead them over the stages, and I
drive this wagon in the parade, and I put the tent up and tear it
down."

" Don't you ride ? "

" No."

" Ain't you going to, though ? "

Chad said he thought maybe, and that seemed to make the
boy feel better, for he said his name was William Frey. He came
from a house down South Salina Street. His mother was dead,
but the woman who ran the house called him son, and so did
most of the girls.

The procession drearily completed a loop of the north side

and recrossed the canal over the steep Clinton Street bridge and came out well along on South Salina and headed north once more. The whole troupe was tuckered out, just dragging their feet, horses as well as humans. A pig offered the only diversion, a thin sow with teats that looked as if they might sound like sleigh-bells when she ran. She took fright and headed up the street like a rifle bullet, and little William Frey let out a whoop and told Chad it was Mrs. Dempsey's pig and she would have to pay the five-dollar fine for letting her loose this time for sure.

Chad didn't pay attention ; they were getting back to the square, and presently Huguenine turned into it. Mrs. Pamplon stumbled dizzily when her feet hit the grass, so that her husband had to hold her up. Joe Duddy was in a blind and sweaty rage, and none of the rest had a word to say, except Mr. Huguenine, who said, " Bisbee told me to cover them streets."

" I bet that mulish twerp's been setting in the shade all morning," exploded Joe.

" Well, I won't parade again. Not in this town," Shepley said.

" Oh, yes, you will." Bisbee had entered the tent. " You'll do it Monday, just the same as to-day."

Shepley eyed him scornfully. " You think so. Well, think again. I didn't join out to be a laughing-stock."

Bisbee didn't turn a hair.

" I know you didn't. But you'll have a good crowd this afternoon. I don't say they'll be clever, but they pay twenty-five cents just the same. What do you care, Fred ? Why don't you put on a performance they'll remember ? So when Burke and Walsh stand here, they'll say, ' Well, you ought to 'a' been to that little Huguenine show. They had a high rider with real class.' And the same with the wire act and the equestriole," he added tactfully.

He was interrupted by a shout from Fiero, who had spotted William Frey. William, in spite of the contempt he had ex-pressed to Chad, was pretty well awed to be the only towner inside the tent with circus people. He yelped and bolted to Chad for protection.

Chad held the juggler off. " Leave him be," he said. " I've got your ball. I told him he could see the show free gratis for giving it back."

Fiero's anger evaporated in a smile that showed his teeth. He patted William's head and told him he was smart. Now everything was all right again. He flipped his balls into the air to prove it, giving William a fancy taste of his talents. The rest of the troupe, however, eyed him in distaste. It was the kind of behaviour you might expect from an Italian like Fiero, just like a jaybird hollering bad news on a rosy day and then forgetting the catastrophe before it happened.

Time pressed. Mrs. Huguenine hurried off to the treasury wagon, from which her husband had already started selling a few tickets, and shoved in past him for another dose of her new perfume. The other three women went over to Bastock's wagon, which, being empty, offered them a private place to spruce up in.

Working on the cream pad and Buck to get the sweat and dust of the parade off them, Chad could keep his eye on the wagon. Joe Duddy brought over the customary pail of water, handed it in with his head delicately half-turned, and then loitered round to the high rear wheel and leaned himself against it. Budlong was in sight by the curve of the round-top; Bastock, of course, was collecting the tickets. Nobody expected any trouble. There were a couple of constables hanging round, too. But whenever the crowd didn't feel just right the skinners were supposed to keep their eyes open, and tent pegs handy.

A splash of water glittered over the side of the tail gate close enough to make Joe jump, and then Albany's voice came out cordial and contrite. " I'm sorry, Joe. I didn't know you were there." She stood on the tail gate, smiling at him, making Joe grin like a fool. She looked like a fashion print in a lady's periodical. It was one of the things Chad never got to understand about her, the way she could get into that wagon with a pail of water and come out again looking as if she had just rigged herself new from the skin out. Beside her, Caroline looked as if she had washed her face and combed her hair; but she didn't look new.

Joe grinned sheepishly and held his hand up to steady them in getting down. It made Caroline bashful, but Albany stepped to the ground with her hand on Joe's as unconcerned as a bird.

" Always playing up to anything in pants."

Glancing over Buck's withers, Chad saw Shepley. He was standing bareheaded in the full glare of the sun; but he seemed oblivious of it. " What's the matter with that ? " Chad asked.

Shepley turned his head.

"Nothing," he said. "Nothing at all."

"Then what are you miyawling for ? "

Shepley's lip curled.

"Are you figuring to go with her ? Well, she won't fuss with a skinner long. Not her. A skinner ain't good enough, not even a fresh one who thinks he's going to be a principal rider."

"Yeah ? "

"Yeah," said Shepley. He watched Mrs. Pamplon get down ; then turned on his heel and started into the tent.

"It's natural," he said. "The female bitch."

Chad started to lay down his brush. But there wasn't time for a mix-up now. And Albany, with Caroline, had come up to the hurdle. She leaned on it now, poking Buck's nose with her whip handle, and the cream pad and Jerry edged over against Chad and tried to interest Caroline.

Albany said, "Buck looks fine."

Chad glanced at her but continued his work without answering.

"I'm worried about Mrs. Pamplon," Albany said. "She looks sick. I wish you'd keep handy to the wire when she's up, Chad."

"All right."

Mrs. Pamplon approached the performers' entrance rather unsteadily. Her face was paler than usual and there was a beading of sweat on her forehead.

"Have you seen my husband ? " she asked.

"He'll be here right away," Albany said. "Don't you want to skip this performance ? "

"No." Mrs. Pamplon shook her head. "He does not like to be on the wire if I am not there."

Mrs. Huguenine, who had sailed up behind a cloud of scent and sympathy, broke in : "You set right down on this bucket. in the shade, dearie. I know how it is to have a measly spell. Caroline can fan you, and I'll just skip back to the wagon for some whisky."

She thrust her turkey-feather fan into Caroline's hand and trundled away over the grass. Caroline waved the fan up and down in front of Mrs. Pamplon, who gave her a wan embarrassed smile. Albany turned back to Chad, resting her elbows on the hurdle and her chin on her fists.

"I don't know what's the matter with her," she said in a low voice.

"Maybe it's the sun," Chad said. "It was hot enough just riding."

"Yes. I can't think why we had to go so far. Those brick buildings make it twice as hot."

"That was pretty, the way you bowed with Buck to those roosters on the bridge. They surely liked it a lot."

She smiled thoughtfully.

"I wish this was a big outfit," she said. "There's a Burke and Walsh poster inside the hotel. It must be fine to travel with a company like that. Mr. Penny at the desk told me that last year all the Burke and Walsh top acts had dollar rooms. Think of it."

She stopped to watch Mrs. Huguenine, who had returned, administer whisky to Mrs. Pamplon and then ask Caroline if she felt at all faint. When Caroline declined, Mrs. Huguenine fortified herself. "It's lucky I don't have to climb a wire," she said with a giggle. "Oh, my stars. You'd better fan her some more, dearie. If I did it, she might smell my scent too strong. Ain't it a lovely one, though?"

She glanced at the round of the tent wall. Here and there small bulges appeared where boys on the top tier were sticking their fists against the canvas ; and a murmur, barely articulate, the strange audience noise of people settling themselves and waiting, issued from the performers' entrance. "A.D. says it's getting to be a good big crowd. My, it's a pity he never learned to short-change. The fellow who we bought the mortgage off said a good short-changer could earn a 10 per cent interest on the investment. But A.D.'s too honest. And anyway, his hands ain't the right shape for it, I guess. Now, I've done it once or twice. Well, it'll soon be time for the march around."

Albany was watching, her grey eyes turned from Chad. Budlong and Bastock came together around the wall of the tent, wiping the sweat off their faces. Joe Duddy was slinging his drum. Mr. Pamplon and Fiero walked up together.

Albany said to him. "I don't think your wife should try the stilts, Mr. Pamplon. She's had a faint spell."

Mr. Pamplon asked, "What is it?" in a strained voice, and had the matter explained to him. "It's nothing, Henri," his wife protested. "I am feeling better already."

" Maybe you better not do the march," he said, " then you'll feel better to go on the wire with me."

She shook her head, held her hand out to him, and let him pull her to her feet. They walked over to Bastock's wagon, where Ike Wayfish had leaned the three pairs of stilts against the tail gate. He was standing on it now waiting for them. He helped Mrs. Pamplon up and presently they mounted and came stalking back over the grass like figures in a heron's dream.

Chad saw that Mrs. Pamplon appeared able to handle the stilts. He said to Albany, " You've been mad at me about something."

If he had suprised her, she didn't show it. She returned her level grey gaze to him, again resting her chin on her hands, and drew her breath slowly, making a faint sound with it through her lips.

" Why ? "

" You haven't said a word to me till to-day."

" Oh," she said. " I didn't know whether I liked having you join out with us."

" So you wouldn't even say hallo ? "

" And I saw the way Caroline had been whipped. I had to bathe her back every night, you know. It still is livid."

" I didn't do that."

" She said it was on account of you."

" It wasn't, except in a way."

" Mr. Bisbee told me about you getting the negro away. But you might have guessed what would happen to her."

" I'm not that low-minded," he said angrily.

" I know that. I wasn't mad at you anyway."

" Then I don't see why."

" No ? " she said, half smiling. " Maybe it was just what I said, about not knowing if I liked you being with us. Maybe I just wanted to not talk to you." She took her elbows off the hurdle. Budlong and Bastock with their horn and fife had begun the tune, and then Joe Duddy explosively brought in the drum, almost in their ears. Albany slung the red cloak over her habit and picked her crown from the box Joe had earlier set handy to the flap and set it on her head in place of her stiff hat. Then she took the ball and sceptre from the box and returned to the hurdle to Chad.

" Why did you start acting nice to-day ? " he asked.

"Maybe because I liked you," she said.

"Long-Tailed Blue," had reached its closing bar. In the pause the quieting inside the tent, the stilled murmur, the concentration of eyes slowly finding the entrance, were felt by the group outside. Chad saw the doll-like blankness come over all of them, the Huguenines, Fiero, Caroline, the Pamplons, over Shepley running his hand through his yellow hair. He saw Albany Yates's smile stiffen, the inner warmth receding, the lips shaped like coloured wax. Only Ike Wayfish, in his lugubrious drunken make-up, remained unchanged.

Joe Duddy said, "What the hell?" and banged on his drum. Budlong and Bastock took up "Champlain," and one by one they passed into the tent, moving stiffly to the tune.

> Backside Albany stan' Lake Champlain—
> Little pond, half full of water . . .

Albany had been singing it one morning to demonstrate her unconcern to Shepley.

> Platt'burg dere, too, close upon de main . . .

Huguenine had disappeared inside. Putting the pad on the cream, Chad heard a single guffaw. That would be Wayfish trying to find a seat. Albany had entered the tent and the Pamplons were going in. Chad wondered whether Mrs. Pamplon would make it. She was biting her lower lip. If she fell she might bite it clear through.

> Town small, he grow bigger, do, hereafter . . .

Fiero and Shepley had walked in behind each other, and here came Ike Wayfish, running, to jump on the tail gate, mount his stilts. He made the entrance in long strides, ducked under, and the first actual snort of laughter issued from the tent. Ike was a real performer, Chad thought, maybe the best one of the bunch when it came to downright circusing.

> On Lake Champlain
> Uncle Sam set he boat
> And Massa M'Donough to sail 'em . . .

Chad cinched the pad on the cream and picked up the side-saddle. Wasn't anybody outside now. But it wasn't a country crowd. The laughing was kids' laughter ; they always did the most of it, but in a village pitch they put the high squeals in and you heard the steady under-mutter of talk and chuckles. It always seemed queer to Chad, the length of time it took to get around the ring.

> Bang ! bang ! bang ! den de cannons 'gin to roar
> In Platt'burg and all about dat quarter.
> Gubbenner Probose try he hand upon de shore,
> While he boat take he luck upon de water.

Chad could see Budlong's red jacket, as he came back to the entrance blowing away on the bugle, his adam's apple almost plastic in the exigencies of finding wind.

> But Massa M'Donough
> Knock de boat in de head,
> Break he heart, break he shin, 'tove he caff in . . .

They were out now, the three of them, with the rest of the procession emerging one by one, Mrs. Huguenine first, bathed in rose-imbued perspiration, then Albany, then the Pamplons ; and it seemed to every one that the performance might get off, for Mrs. Pamplon had made the circle.

"You done fine, dearie," Mrs. Huguenine said.

Chad had reached up for her, catching her round the waist, and she let the stilts go. She was quite white, but she smiled.

"She was wonderful," Albany said. "She certainly has the grit."

Pamplon beamed and said yes.

"But, oh, I don't *like* those people. They don't like us. They're dead, they don't care, they don't even feel foolish," Albany said. She came over to Buck and said "Honey" to him, kissing him.

The crack of Mr. Huguenine's whip and the wild yells from Ike told them that the performance proper had begun. . . .

5

THE SOMERSAULT

THE apathy inside the tent was like a fog. Pamplon got an occasional handclap, but for the most part the people just sat and stared. Mrs. Pamplon got through it ; but she didn't add anything to the act. She was clumsy making room for her husband's returns, and once she teetered so that Pamplon had to grab hold of her. But Chad thought he noticed a slight quickening of interest when Fiero started his act.

It wasn't Fiero that roused it, though. There was plenty of jugglers in the world, and Syracuse had seen its share of them. It was Caroline. A young girl in tights was something to look at ; Caroline was obviously young, and shy, and conscious of herself which gave a faint spice to her performance, simple though it was. A pair of youthful legs, however, didn't make a circus. After a minute or two, the audience became bored with the familiar routine and Chad went outside.

By the entrance Albany Yates was putting on her hat. The crown and cloak and ball and sceptre had been packed in their box. Beside the horses Shepley was rubbing the soles of his riding shoes in rosin. Mrs. Pamplon was lying in the shade while Pamplon stood with his back turned staring into the blank, blue sky. Ike Wayfish leaned on the hurdle and wiped his face with care not to disturb the make-up. He waved a hand at Chad and said, " Nothing's amiss, so money comes withal— Shakespeare. Or maybe Bisbee said it. They act as if they just don't want to laugh."

" Maybe you ought to try being funny," Shepley said. " Come on ; the leaping's due."

He loosed the cream pad from the hurdle. The band tootled a few notes to end Fiero's act and the juggler and Caroline emerged in the skipping run that carried them from the ring but turned flat-footed as soon as they reached the outside. Mr. Huguenine's voice was raised painfully for the next act. The Pamplons roused themselves and straggled in, and Ike and Fiero followed them.

"That was a mean thing for Fred to say," Albany said. "Mr. Wayfish tries harder than any one else."

Chad nodded. He felt tired and half drugged. He knew it was going to go bad right through to the end unless something or somebody happened to catch their interest. Even the lion act was sure to fall flat now, he thought, as he handed Albany up on Buck's back. He watched her moodily as she arranged her habit; it was a sin to send anything so pretty in to those bezabors.

She took the horse a turn round the wagons to settle him down; then waited beside the entrance, Buck dancing slightly with his forefeet, and pricking his ears for the pad horse's exit. He wasn't worried. All he wanted was Albany's approval, and he was sure to get that. Horses were lucky. "Here we go," Albany said.

". . . in their Equestriole, an act acclaimed throughout the Universe," bawled Mr. Huguenine. Barring only Syracuse, New York, Chad added to himself. But she got applause. Maybe it was the loafers from the Salina Street bridge; maybe it was because the two, horse and rider, had plenty of spirit; or maybe the audience had begun to get bored with their own silence. Fred Shepley listened with a smile. "Ain't it wonderful?" he said sarcastically, while Albany was reciting her little poem. When she came out, he said, "My, you were good. You just about floored them."

"Did I?" She cocked her chin. "I felt mad enough to choke them all at first." She flushed hotly as she met his eyes. "All right, high-rider. See what you can do."

"I'm going to."

The rest watched him go in, but Chad stared at Albany. He could see that she was mad as blazes for having forgotten herself and spoken to him. But he put down the fact that if she got excited enough she would do anything. It was something to remember. He heard Bisbee say, "Jesus Christ, watch Shepley."

Bisbee had stopped on his way out and his voice brought the other performers behind him to see what was happening.

Shepley was going through his routine with a fire he had never shown, but his performance was more striking because he seemed like ice. He didn't even pretend to smile; he was unconscious of the audience, of the ring, of everything but himself and the pad horse. And the horse felt it, Chad saw. He was going

C.H G

carefully ; his pace, perfect as ever, was not mechanical, but controlled as if he considered the individual play of every nerve.

Caroline had to call twice before Mr. Huguenine's blank expression of astonishment relaxed enough for him to take the ribbon standard from her, and then he nearly let go of the pole. Shepley took the ribbons superbly, clearing them high, and stealing an extra stride from the pad horse. He got a hand for each leap. " Burke and Walsh ain't got anybody to touch what he's doing now," Bisbee said. " And the crowd knows it. There's a newspaper fellow in there too from the *Standard*. I had to buy him drinks and give him a pass to get him to come."

Ike Wayfish said, " The piece won't come out till next week, though."

" I know that, but I can use copies of the paper. I'll give it to editors ahead of us. They'll print stories sometimes if they're wrote out to begin with by another paper. What's he trying to do now ? "

The first real wave of applause petered out. Shepley should have taken his spring to the ground. Instead of that he was riding the tail of the pad round and round, the horse keeping his gait as he would continue to do until led from the ring, and motioning Caroline off the bank. She stepped down after an instant, and Shepley, making another circuit, talked to Huguenine.

Huguenine shook his head, and Shepley spoke again with obvious impatience. The audience and performers were all still. The three bandsmen had forgotten to play. The tune ended after the ribbons ; they had no precedent to take them on from there. Then Huguenine automatically reached for his chewing tobacco. He got it half out before he recollected himself and restored it to his pocket.

" LAdies and GENTlemen. You are now going to see Fred . . . I mean Signor Rossello, attempt a somersault on the back of his running horse."

" Jesus," Bisbee said in a low voice. " No wonder A.D.'s buffaloed."

" . . . The acme of the riding art. It ain't been performed by half a dozen men in the Universe. Not by more than two, I think."

His solid face puckered uncertainly.

" It ain't advertised," he said, more to himself than to the audience, but his voice was audible enough over the soft thud of the pad horse's hoofs.

Shepley made two more circuits of the ring, straight as an arrow on the tail of the pad, with a little rise to the balls of his feet that gave him the full lift of the quarters.

"He's got their tongues hanging out," Bisbee said. "By jeepers, he's got mine. I hope he don't break his neck."

Mr. Huguenine folded and unfolded his hands helplessly round the whipstock. Bisbee had hold of the entrance flap, as if he had to hold himself on his feet. None of the others moved except Chad, who stole a glance at Albany. She seemed to be poised, one hand holding the skirt of her habit, the other the riding whip. Her lips were parted and her eyes followed the forty-two foot circle of the cream pad with the green figure riding him.

Chad looked back to the ring. "Suppose he does it," he thought. "What'll she do about it?"

Shepley was going to try it this turn. The action of his knees showed it, and the slow filling of his chest.

The green body rose; the spangles sprayed a green glitter on the air; it was a pretty somersault; it was perfectly timed; he came down facing the withers perfectly, meeting the pad with his knees, his hands grasping for the pad edges.

For an instant he looked like sliding to the inside; but the cream horse changed his lead, assumed the altered weight, and Shepley, his own face astonished in the instant of completion, rose to his feet, rode a half ring, leaped to the ground, and made his bow.

6

THE DEW FALLS IN SYRACUSE

THOUGH the sun had set, the grass in the square was still luminously green. A faint breeze carried the insistent flat notes of canal horns from the basin where boats were crowding in to beat the Sunday landing law. The few teams remaining at the hitch rail switched their tails languidly and at long intervals. A couple of dogs squeezed under the bottom rail and trotted across the square on some immoral peregrination. Back of the hotel in the twilight a robin liquidly announced rain.

Sitting by the main entrance of the empty round-top, Chad watched the lights coming on here and there in the upper windows as people went to their bedrooms : some went out again, but some stayed on. Now and then a wagon moved down the street, but its occupants saw nothing in the square except the white hull of the tent and the shadowy silent wagons. Saturday was pay day : the performers had all gone off long before ; even Mrs. Huguenine had locked up the treasury wagon and spurred herself down the street to look in the store windows. Chad fingered his own four and a half dollars and wondered how long Budlong would take to buy his whisky.

Budlong was a queer man. He wasn't interested in examining a town like Joe Duddy, who, as soon as he received his pay, had heeled off to try the liquor and flush a pigeon. Nobody knew where Bastock had gone to. Money in his pocket was like an Arabian ring on the middle finger of a wizard ; there it was ; and there Bastock wasn't. But Budlong seemed to lack such natural interests. All he cared about was a jug of corn and a horse blanket inside the tent entrance so disposed that he could lie on one, drink the other, and keep his eye on the treasury wagon.

Watching for Budlong's return, Chad was startled to see Caroline Trid come out of the hotel. She was alone, and she stopped irresolutely, glancing up and down the street. One of the men sitting on the porch left his chair and went over to her. He took off his hat, but Caroline shook her head. She began edging towards the street, turning a little all the time to face him, until she got out on the sidewalk. Then she started quickly across the roadway. The man, left standing, began to laugh a little louder than ordinary, Chad judged. He wondered what had become of Albany.

He didn't have time to do much speculating, for Caroline hurried. She came straight for the tent entrance, not seeing him, and he felt perverse enough to keep quiet, so that she walked briskly past him into the tent. The thud of her low heels on the packed ground was decisive and close to his ear ; he even heard the drag of her skirts across the limp grass. But she stopped just inside the entrance, as if the darkness were too all surrounding. He was aware of her hesitance in it. She said, " Hallo, there," in a low voice ; but there wasn't a sound even from Oscar, who for a wonder hadn't begun to snore. Then Caroline came back to the tent entrance, standing there, looking back to the hotel.

The man was where she had left him with his thumbs hooked in the waistband of his trousers. He had the appearance of a man trying to make up his mind whether to take after a girl or not. Caroline knew it, too. Chad heard her draw her breath slowly. He said, " Don't worry about him. If he comes over here we'll just tell him off."

She froze where she was. He could just make her out, for the dress was light-coloured, and she looked slender and tall, in that dimness almost like a *Lady's Book* pattern.

" Who's that ? " she asked.

" Chad."

" Oh." He heard the shiver in her breath. She was a nervy thing, he thought.

" I'm glad it's you," she said. And then after a minute, " Would you mind me sitting down with you ? "

" No," he said. " But you better sit on the blanket. There's some dew."

He made room for her and she sat down beside him. She smelled faintly of perfume. She didn't say anything for a moment or two, and Chad did not feel like talking. But then she started a conversation, suddenly making her voice sound bright.

" It's cooler out here."

" I guess it is," Chad agreed. She was watching the man across the street. He had eased off the porch and was sort of swinging his legs, like a man not going anywhere in particular.

" Albany went out after supper and it's still hot in our room and I came down for some air," she said. " I think it's a nice town, don't you ? "

" She went out of the hotel ? " Chad asked.

" Yes. She didn't say where, or when she would be back. It's funny, I thought it was an awful place, all during the parade, and the people looked awful, and then all of a sudden, after Mr. Shepley did the somersault, they seemed nicer. It was a wonderful somersault. Albany said she'd never seen anything like it. . . ."

Her voice petered out. The man had crossed the street and was now coming through the hitch rail, taking his time, still, and looking around.

Chad drew his feet back under him. " What do you want ? "

The man jumped.

" Nothing," he said.

" Well, mister, the next performance is Monday afternoon."

The man came forward a few paces.

" I reckon this is a public square," he said, with a shade of bluster in his voice.

Chad said, " Sure. But the wagons and tent ain't. Otherwise make yourself at home. There's plenty of damp grass to cool off on."

The man lingered a moment and Chad said to Caroline, " Funny the way the young ones like to hang around the tents, ain't it ? "

" Yes," she said. " They act just fascinated."

She giggled.

The man said, " Say . . ." But he thought better of it and retreated almost to the hitch rail. He stayed there a moment longer, then lifted his leg and hoisted himself over and went off, keeping out of the light from the hotel door.

Chad gave a low laugh.

" I guess that feller needs beans."

Caroline said gravely, " I'm glad you were here."

" You've got over your being mad at me ? "

" Yes," she said.

" It was a mean business," he said. " But I never thought of such a thing."

" I guess you didn't."

" You like being with the circus ? "

"Yes," she said. "I like it better, though, when we're on the road doing the little towns."

"So do I. We'll be roading after Monday."

She said. "This is the farthest I've ever been from home."

"I guess you don't miss it much."

She shook her head.

"I never knew what it would be like, being with nice people."

"Sure," Chad said.

"I like Mrs. Huguenine. She's nice," Caroline said seriously, "She's awful fat, but she's kind. Mrs. Pamplon is nice, too, but she don't talk much. She's gone to bed."

"How is she?"

"Mr. Pamplon said she was feeling better. He came and asked Albany for *sal volatile*. He doesn't know what's the matter with her."

It was desultory conversation, but it served to fill in the time; and Caroline seemed to think she ought to say something. She kept coming back to Shepley's somersault; and they discussed the off-hand way in which he had practically ignored the troupe's congratulations. When Wayfish asked him how it felt to do what only Hunter and De Forest were known to have done, Shepley said why not ask them. The clown had looked hurt.

Chad said it was bound to make somebody like Shepley big-headed; but Caroline said Albany didn't think so. She said Shepley came from a good family that had gone poor. He came from down at Fort Plain or near it and that was how he had got into circusing in the first place. The great menagerie man, Herr Driesbach, who now showed in the Bowery, came from Fort Plain. Shepley managed to get apprenticed to Westervelt, the rider, in Parsons' Circus. Later he had joined out with Captain Page and done the northern loop through Canada one season. He had quit Page to join Trimble, which was the show that had folded up on Mr. Huguenine's farm.

Caroline seemed to know all about Shepley's history, but when Chad asked what she knew about Albany, it turned out that she knew next to nothing. Albany had begun riding in equestrian melodramas and spectacles like Cataract of the Ganges, Bluebeard, and Siege of Montgatz. She had seen the famous white horse, Surrey, perform, and it was the sight of him that made her decide she would find herself a horse and train him to be as good. Then she found Buck. None of the big shows wanted her; the horse was too green for one thing, so she joined out with the first small show that would take her, which was Trimble's. She had thought of high-riding but had never tried it. "Do you think a woman could ever do a somersault?" Caroline asked.

"No," said Chad. They let it drop, Chad remarking that Budlong was certainly taking his time and Caroline saying dutifully that he certainly was. Then as if the mere mention of his name had been enough, Budlong loomed lankly out of the shadow beyond the treasury wagon with a jug swinging from his finger.

"You ain't been wasting your time, none," he said to Chad. "Who's your girl?"

"It's me, Mr. Budlong," Caroline said quickly.

"Well, I'm sorry I was so long a time. But I had to sample. Suppose a man's going to invest in a gallon, he's got to sample."

Budlong hauled a blanket out, sat down, elbowed the jug, and tasted it. He wiped his mouth and said, "I wonder was it milk came out of that there Roman wolf you see pictures of in school books. This-here's Bourbon. Bourbon is a good drink. It's good by daylight, and it's good by dark. It's good on a cold day and better on a hot one. You can take it standing up or setting down or lying on your back, and she'll swallow just the same. She's good with water, but she's better without, and a sensible man don't go to build a fire with wet wood anyway. I'll bet Bourbon would taste first-rate in a wolf's tit. Even Dagoes like it. Give me enough of it and I'll learn you the Constitution of the United States."

He sighed, making a faint hum in the mouth of the jug, and passed it over to Chad, who took a pull. The two men looked towards each other and Budlong said, "Missy, it wouldn't hurt you and we're all friends."

Caroline said in the darkness: "Bourbon is a man's drink, Mr. Budlong."

"That's so," he said. "That's so."

Then he took the jug back and said, "I'm obliged to you, Chaddy. You needn't wait up on me. You two run along and have a good time now."

You could tell he had fixed in his mind to be alone. Chad got on his feet and Caroline rose quickly beside him. "Good-night, Mr. Budlong," she said. They walked towards the gap in the hitch rail with the dew cool on their feet, Chad shambling through it and she lifting her skirt, her wrists curved, and her face down-bent.

Chad said, " What are you going to do, Caroline ? "

They were near enough the hotel lights for him to see her face, but she did not look at him.

" I guess I'll go in," she said. " I'm all cooled off. It was nice sitting out there." She smiled for him. " It's been real nice."

" Why, the evening's not scarcely begun," he said. " Don't you want to go to the stores or anything ? "

She shook her head ; and he remembered suddenly that she wasn't drawing any pay. She probably didn't have a cent in her little leather reticule. He could see that she hated the idea of spending an evening alone in a hotel room ; and he didn't blame her.

She stood looking at him, her face solemn and oval in the fanning bonnet brim. It was extraordinary how clothes changed a person. At Cisco's, in her ragged dress that left her half bare, she had looked older than her years and too full of knowledge for a nice girl ; but here she looked younger, on the nigh side of being timid, and he realised that he didn't know the first thing of what she was really like. Well, he had nothing to do on his own hook unless he tried getting drunk, and he didn't feel like that.

" Look here, Caroline. Maybe you'd come out with me ? " He could see her hesitate, and he said shrewdly, " I couldn't buy you no champagne wine. But we might go see the Museum."

" I'd like to," she said gravely.

7

IT RAINS IN NAPLES

A CONSTABLE told them how to find the Museum, and Caroline took Chad's arm. He found it pleasant to be walking along the street with a nice-looking girl. She had a light, carrying step ; and she was so excited at going to a museum that she lost a good deal of her constraint.

" I'll hardly know what to look at first," she told him.

" I don't know anything about it," he said.

" Mr. Wayfish said the exhibits were like marvels. He said there were waxworks, too. I've never seen real waxworks, have you ? "

" Not what you'd call museum waxworks," Chad said.

" Mother once saw a waxworks, before she was married. She said it even had figures of real living people in it."

" I don't know about this one," Chad said. " I imagine most of them are dead people."

Caroline nodded. He could see the beginning of the part in her hair under the flared bonnet brim.

" People generally get more famous when they're dead," she agreed.

They first heard the music more than a block away. It swelled out of a side street, and through it came the sound of bells. Chad said, " That must be it." But the music faded. When they turned the corner, however, they heard it again.

They were wondering which building it might come from when suddenly a door swung open, casting brilliant light across the roadway, and a man came out with a woman and the music filled the whole street. As the door swung shut, Chad closed his arm on her hand and said, " Come on, let's go right in," and she followed him up the steps and through the door. A man in a frock-coat that swelled over his hips said to them, " It costs two bits each." But he might as well have not spoken as far as Caroline was concerned, for the organ music was like a great wave engulfing her.

It filled the hall ; the lights seemed to swim in it. She could not see any one playing ; but confronting her were a line of wax figures all in real costumes, some with their arms folded on their breasts, some with their hands at their sides. Over their heads hung a line of bells, which Caroline felt sure must be the chime they had heard as they came down the street.

As they stepped forward together towards the figures, the bells started ringing. It was a beautiful sound, but the un-believable part was that the wax images were doing it. Every figure had a hammer hinged to the back of his or her head, and at the proper moment the hammer rose and struck the bell above it. The female figures rang the trebles, and the male figures the deeper ones. It was miraculous, to see those calm figures keep their pose and ring bells so, in tune with the organ. It was scarcely mortal.

After a minute the bells ceased, but the organ played on. Chad said, " Let's go in there." He indicated a door that had a sign, WAXWORK EXHIBIT, over it, and Caroline followed him with a feeling of impersonal reluctance, as if she dreamed.

The regular waxworks proved to be more interesting to look at if not as lively to listen to. Neither of them read easily, but between them they managed to work out who all the people were. The room was lighted by a gas chandelier of four jets that was almost fantastically bright in itself, so that all the details and features could be examined. By listening to a stout man who seemed familiar with the figures, Chad and Caroline learned that the hair was human and made in Paris, France. The eyes looked almost human at first, also, but after a minute or two they gave Caroline an odd feeling, and then she realised that it was because they never blinked, and she noticed another queer thing about them. The blue eyes were all exactly alike, and so were the brown eyes.

Thus David Lambert (the biggest man that ever lived) had a sort of family resemblance to Desdemona (being stabbed with an actual knife by Othello). But their costumes and all the rest of them were quite different. Caroline liked best the Sleeping Beauty, whose eyes were entirely closed, though the fat man assured his companion that she had eyes under the lids—it was a first-rate exhibit, he insisted. There was also Queen Elizabeth in a red wig with a crown full of jewels, and Lady Jane Grey with her head on the block and the headsman leaning on his axe like a man who had trouble in his home. He had a black cloth tied over his face and the sign said it could be viewed for the

price of ten cents.   Chad asked Caroline whether she wished to
see it, which she thought very gentlemanly of him, but she
said he oughtn't to spend money on her to that extent and looked
upset about it, so Chad did not insist.   Then, as if to reward them
both, the stout man summoned the proprietor, paid ten cents,
and demanded that the mask be lifted.   The proprietor tried
to get Chad to pay ten cents, and when Chad refused he could
not very well put them out of the room, so they saw the face
anyway.   After all the going-on, it was disappointing that the
executioner still looked like a plain man with trouble in his home.

General Washington and his Generals did not interest them
so much, so they crossed the hall to another room which was
labelled CURIOSITIES OF THE NATURAL WORLD.   It
contained a two-headed calf, a replica of the beating heart of
Byron, some remnants of the mastodon sea shells, stuffed small
animals, three parrots that never made a sound, and the Embalmed Head of a New Zealand Chief.

Caroline held Chad's arm again as they went from case to
case.   He seemed much more interested in the curiosities than she
was, but it was no more than right that he should study them
as long as he liked, since he had bought the tickets.   She did not
care to look at the beating heart of Byron so she looked at Chad,
and she thought he looked kind.   When he turned unexpectedly,
she blushed ; but he merely wanted to know what she thought
of the heart, and she said it seemed poetic to her.   She thought
it was a foolish thing to say ; it was the first thing that came into
her head.   Chad nodded approvingly.   " He was a poet," he said.
" I heard a man tell about him in the Yellow Bud.   He tried to
free the Greeks but he got drowned and they cut out his heart.
It went on beating till sunset, like a snake's, but they said it was
because he loved freedom so.   It sounds queer to me."

He wanted to return to the embalmed head, but the proprietor began announcing from the hall the evening's last Grand
Performance of the Italian Phantasmagoria, and they went into
a room with twenty or thirty chairs in it and a sheet hung
on the wall.   There were not many people so there was room for
them to sit down and they had just done so when the lights went
out.

They sat in complete darkness for a few minutes.   Nobody
said a word and Caroline could hear the breathing of other
people.   Then a bright light shot out and lit upon the sheet ;

colours appeared in it, and suddenly it turned into a picture as clear as day. It was a city, with a long street running right away from the bottom of the sheet, and buildings on each side, and green trees, and a closed carriage. The horse was thin and the driver's colour was not very good, but the proprietor said it was Paris, France. He rang a little bell. The picture disappeared, leaving white light, but suddenly another took its place. This, he said, was Westminster Abbey in London, England.

In that way, Caroline and Chad saw Vienna, and Athens, and Egypt, and Mount Ararat, and finally Naples, and it was in Naples that the wonder happened. First it was a clear day; in the next second a dark cloud had come over the whole top of the sky. The light faded like magic. Thunder roared, and all at once great flashing silver drops of rain slanted across the picture. After a minute the proprietor rang his bell and the lights came on.

The cool darkness of the street was a relief, for the Phantasmagoria had made the room very hot, and Caroline's head still rang from the thunder. It was not, of course, a real thunder. It had been produced by a ragged small boy with a summer head cold hammering on sheet iron. When the lights went on, every one saw him blowing his nose in a corner of the room. Yet it gave one a strange feeling to look up and see the stars clear in the sky.

As they walked slowly back towards the square, Chad was silent; and Caroline did not try to make conversation as she had on the way down. It no longer seemed necessary. She had the feeling that they had come to know each other well, as people do who have taken a journey in each other's company. It seemed scarcely possible that they had been in the Museum less than two hours. It gave her a dreamy feeling, so that it was a shock to realise suddenly that the lights ahead belonged to the hotel.

Chad stopped at the end of the porch, which was now empty of sitters. The chairs looked blind facing out at the street. It was quiet and nearly dark, since the dining-room lights had been put out. Only the bar-room windows and the main door were open.

Chad said, " Well, we're home."

" I had a lovely time."

They had been moving towards the entrance, their heels rapping together softly over the porch boards, and when he stopped she passed a step beyond him into the light. Her head was bent so that he could not see her face under the bonnet brim. The gauze scarf she was wearing had slipped from her shoulders, the ends hanging over her forearms, leaving her neck bare, and the light picked out the thin gold chain.

He recognised it at once, and following its course he saw that the storekeeper had been right about the length. The locket itself was hidden below the V of the dress. Then he saw that she was looking at him, her face flushing darkly. She started to pull the scarf back into place, let it go, and with a quick gesture pulled out the locket and showed it to him.

"Do you want to see it?"

"It's kind of caught my eye," he said slowly.

She said, "It's a perfume locket. We found it in our room and the black boy didn't know who it was for. Albany said to leave it till we found out, but it looked so pretty that I put it on after she'd gone."

She held it out to him and he took it in his fingers. It was warm, just as the storekeeper said it would be, and the perfume was sweet all round his face.

"I put in some of Albany's perfume," she explained. "I know I oughtn't to have worn it."

"I don't see harm in doing that," Chad said. "Did she like it?"

"Not as much as I did, I think. But I never had a real gold locket." She took it out of his hands and stepped close to show him how it worked. "I think the person that left it ought to have said who it was for, don't you?"

Chad said, "Yes."

"It wasn't right to wear it," she said. "I hope Albany won't be cross about it. But when I put it on I felt as if it might have been mine."

He watched moodily as she restored the locket to its place. It was ironical to think how he had planned for Albany to wear it and to pick his own time telling her who it came from. The plan had worked out, except to the person wearing it. What Caroline said about Albany having plenty of such things was probably true.

She was saying, "I wish we knew who sent it, though, and whether it was for her or me."

"I sent it."

" Oh." She turned white. " You wanted Albany to wear it, didn't you ? And I had to put it on. And then you took me out. I'm awfully sorry, Chad." Her lips quivered. " And talking about it like this. I'll put it right back and tell Albany the first thing."

" No ! " Chad wasn't going to be laughed at. If it hadn't meant anything to Albany it ought to be forgotten. " It wasn't for her," he said.

" It was for me ? "

Caroline was motionless : her fingers inside the front of the dress still touched the locket. He saw the colour returning painfully to her face, until even her neck was red. It made him feel foolish and helpless and angry ; and he couldn't evade her eyes. " Oh," she said again, and then, " Thank you very much," in a tight little voice. " I love it. I'll love wearing it. I had a lovely time to-night."

She turned quickly to the door. He had hardly time to say, " Good-night, Caroline." For she was running across the office and she looked as if she were trying not to cry.

Book III

THE TENTING SEASON

BURKE

THE week that included the last performance in Syracuse and the first in Auburn was the best of the season for Huguenine's. In Geddes, Jordan, Canton, and Weedsport, the tent was sold out. Of course, as Bisbee said, they were not on Burke and Walsh's advertised routing ; the big show would make the jump from Syracuse to Auburn by the turnpike, missing the canal towns, and it had not yet come close enough behind them to bleed the audiences. An advance agent, however, had made the loop, tearing down the Huguenine paper and putting up Burke and Walsh in its place. This did no harm because Bisbee had returned to Syracuse and started out ahead of the wagons, tearing down Burke and Walsh and tacking their own new sheets.

The new sheets were handsome—about ten by fourteen inches—and displayed two cuts. One was the MODERN DANIEL of Ike Wayfish standing nobly in the face of a charging lion ; but over it was the announcement of Signor Rossello's defying the laws of gravitation in his extraordinary somersault on the back of a galloping horse, as successfully performed for the first time in the Western Hemisphere at Syracuse on June 18, 1836—the attempt to be made at each and every performance. The cut was the original high-riding picture used in the big posters, showing the horse at full stretch and the rider poised on one foot. He had been made to do the somersault by the simple expedient of cutting him from the block and reinserting him, upside down. The result, as Bisbee said, was sensational. By the time the show reached Weedsport, moreover, the local papers were bringing out the story. Bisbee had secured proof sheets from the *Onondaga Standard* and was now winging over the roads well ahead of the show and handing a sheet free gratis to every editor.

The entire company reflected the prosperity. Shepley, naturally, was getting the advertising ; but any one who came to look him over was more than likely to watch the rest of the performance. It keyed them up to think that someone like Walsh or Burke himself might turn up for any performance. It put a kind of gaiety on all of them.

The chief trouble was that Shepley, though he made the attempt as announced, had missed the pad in both Canton and Weedsport. The thrill was there in the sight of the green body spinning over the horse ; the fall to the ring didn't rob it of any excitement—Shepley got a big ovation each time. What bothered Ike Wayfish and Bastock and Huguenine was when Shepley would hurt himself. Even without hurting himself, three falls might lose him his nerve.

Chad thought this was likely. He had been watching Shepley close since that first night in Syracuse and he could see, even while he was making those first three successive somersaults, that he was getting fine-drawn. The first time in Canton, he took it out on himself, saying he had been plain clumsy ; but after Weedsport, he claimed the pad horse had broken his gait. That was a lie, and every one knew it.

It didn't matter much, though ; for Albany and Fred had made up their misunderstanding. The news went out on Sunday morning in Syracuse when Mrs. Pamplon told Mrs. Huguenine that Shepley had moved over to the Syracuse House. They had had breakfast together in the dining-room. To Chad it seemed obvious that Albany must have done most of the making up ; he felt sure of it when she took pains later in the day to be nice to him. She said Caroline had told her about the evening they had had at the Museum and how it was Chad who had left the locket.

" It was a nice thing for you to do," she said.

She looked as if she meant it, too.

Oddly enough Mrs. Pamplon, who, in spite of her timid appearance, had such a nose for finding out details, acted pleased that Shepley and Albany should be taking up again. She thought it wholly proper—the two stars, they should marry. It would be enchanting, she said, and Ike Wayfish agreed. " A celestial conjunction," he called it.

Mrs. Huguenine disapproved of such language. She would rather see them wedded by a preacher. There was far too much gossip about the immoral lives of circus people as it was. She wished Mr. Huguenine would talk to Shepley about it, and Huguenine, looking like a farmer who has discovered glanders in his horses, said he would. But every one knew that he wouldn't. He hadn't said a word for a week.

Now he came round from the treasury wagon announcing that they had four hundred admissions. The tent was jammed. When Chad looked in he saw them packed together like pickled salmon in a barrel, even blocking off the usual alley to the main entrance. They hardly left room for the performers to get through ; and a couple of deputy sheriffs had to get to work to make space for the stilt walkers in the march around.

The march around had just begun when Chad noticed a buggy drive into the lot behind a spanking pair of light bays. The buggy wasn't extra special, nor was the driver. He was a small man, dressed in a black coat and waistcoat and dark trousers ; but he acted as if he knew what he was doing. In spite of the band music and the hollering in the tent that would have scared the average team endways, the horses merely slung hips and worked their ears at the ring stock ; and the driver wound the reins round his whip and sat there, first studying the round-top, which was popping boils in the breeze, then looking over the three horses, paying the most attention to the cream pad, and finally meeting Chad's eye.

When he did he raised his hand and beckoned.

" Sorry, mister," Chad said. " I'm minding the ring stock. You ain't supposed to tie in this lot anyhow."

The man stared. He had a thin, high-coloured face, and heavy-lidded blue eyes. For an instant they turned hard as porcelain. Then he climbed down over the wheel and came over to the hurdles.

He glanced into the tent for a second and said, " That's not a bad crowd, boy." Joe Duddy got ahead of the beat at the moment, and the stranger smiled. He counted under his breath, " Three windjammers, one, two, three, four five, six, seven, eight, three of 'em on stilts,"—his glance came round to Chad,— " and one punk." He went past Chad and looked at the ring stock. " Use the grey ? No. He's green. Two ring stock. I hear you've got a lion. What's the black do ? Academy act, I suppose ? " He kept nodding to himself as if he were quite capable of answering the questions for himself. " Have a cigar." He offered Chad one without looking at him, and Chad took it. " That pad horse looks pretty fair for a run-down show like this."

Chad said, "He's good enough. The black one's better, though."

The man made a small humming sound, his blue eyes shifting to Buck. "Not much of an establishment. I never expected to see it rolling again after it broke down with Trimble. No freaks?" His lips *tsk-tsked*. "Fat woman? I've seen fatter than her doing chamber work in the Astor Hotel. Well, where's Huguenine?"

"You can see him after the all-out," Chad said.

"I'll see him now."

Chad didn't like him. He didn't like orders anyway. He said, "Mr. Huguenine's in the ring. Maybe he'll see you after the show, if he feels like it."

"He'll feel like it," said the little man. "Give him this card."

Chad took it and read the name, Ovid T. Burke—in the corner was "Pres. Burke and Walsh Combined Equestrian & Acrobatic Circus & Menagerie." Mr. Burke had taken another cigar from his pocket and folded his lips over it. He did not light it, but when Chad looked at him, he let the cigar roll across his underlip and cocked it in the opposite corner. His china-blue eyes examined Chad carefully. His face was neither kind nor unkind. He looked as if he would be good at running a circus or any other project that he had in mind. Chad decided not to get too sturdy. He said, "Look here, Mr. Burke. Mr. Huguenine's got all he can handle in the ring I ain't going to give him your card till the show's out. But you can walk inside and watch the show if you want to."

Burke's eyes did not move from Chad's face, but his cigar rolled halfway over the lower lip before he caught up with it and brought it back.

"What you do here, son? Just punk?"

"I handle the ring stock," Chad said. "And Huguenine pays me for it."

"Yes. I figured that out myself. How'd you join out?"

"Mr. Bisbee offered me the chance. I took it."

"Too bad it's not a real show," Mr. Burke said. "You'd get along in a real show. Like mine."

Chad looked at him. "This one suits me all right."

Mr. Burke nodded.

"I know Bisbee. He's not a fool. When you see him, son,

tell him from me to leave off tearing my paper." He glanced at his horses. "They'll stand. I'll look this whistle show over."

He went into the tent as the band returned to the fly, let the tune drop, and came out, Bastock and Budlong knocking "Champlain" water from their instruments. It was Joe Duddy who noticed the team.

"What's that rig doing?"

"A feller came late. He's gone inside," Chad told him.

"Serve him right if his team runs off," Joe said, "leaving them there. Wish I had time to pull a couple of linchpins. Never pull more than two, Chaddy. Three makes it messy and four don't work half so good."

Budlong said scornfully, "Those horses won't run. They're clever. They've seen tents before. What's his name?"

"Burke," Chad said.

Chad could not tell whether Budlong caught the name, for Bastock was yelling for him and Joe to come inside. But Albany Yates had heard him and she said now, close to Chad's shoulder, "Did you say Burke?"

Her face was vivid with suppressed excitement.

Chad nodded. "Here's his card."

She took it, read it, and for an instant held it, tapping the corner on her gloved finger. Then she gave it back.

"Is he inside?"

"Yes."

"Have you told any one else, Chad?"

"Budlong. I don't know if he caught on."

"He wouldn't miss it," she said. She was looking at Fred Shepley. Her eyes had the clear impersonal hawklike glance he had noticed the first day he had known her, when she was riding Buck down to the wood lot.

"I wonder if I ought to tell Fred," she said quietly. "He might get nervous if he knew." She turned back to Chad and asked, "What do you think?"

"Suit yourself," he said.

Fred Shepley came over near them to get at the rosin box.

"What's the news?" he asked, staring Chad's way.

"Nothing, Fred. We were just talking. How do you feel?"

"I feel all right. I'll make it all right to-day if that fool horse doesn't start crossing his feet again. You saw him yesterday. It carried him right out from under me."

His eyes were defiant, and for an instant Chad felt almost sorry for him. He said, " I was out here. I didn't see him."

Shepley didn't press his question with Albany. They stood the way they were, saying nothing, each one of them in a separate mood. The Pamplons moved up to the entrance, ready to go in. Handicapping for the end of Fiero's juggling act broke out and the ring stock pricked ears, considering it, and then relaxed. Above, the round-top popped gently against the blue sky, and standing in its shade was like waiting on the outside edge of life. Within the canvas was the world : one step and you had to face it ; it took hold of you ; it was kind to you, or it bore you down. Time was not measured by any clock but was created by the impulse, displeasure, or applause of collected human beings.

They watched Fiero emerge, pleased with himself ; and Caroline Trid came as far as the canvas, her face slightly flushed, looked at them all, hovering a brief instant while Huguenine's voice shouted laboriously, ". . . Preemeer gymnats of Europe, in their first American tour . . ." and went in again behind the Pamplons. Chad felt Shepley's eyes moodily upon them as he stirruped Albany to her saddle.

The girl was light on the black horse. They waited their cue, controlled, poised, breathing like a single creation, eyes to the entrance. It seemed hardly an instant before they were going in and Chad and Shepley, the cream pad at their shoulders, moved up to watch.

She rode to-day as though she were in love ; and Buck responded to her mood, so that the two, horse and equestrienne, were like partners in a new flirtation. They acknowledged applause light-heartedly, delighted to take the world into their confidence ; and when Buck bowed it was as if she curtsied. Caroline Trid, who had joined them, said curiously, " Albany's made him bow twice in that one spot. I wonder why."

Chad had already picked out Burke's black-coated figure. The circus manager was following both the performance and the reaction of the audience to it. His china-blue eyes left the pair to swing round the tent and then came back to the ring. His face did not show at all what he made of it ; but it was plain to Chad that Albany had picked Burke out of the crowd and was performing for him.

It was plain to Shepley also. He had come out of his absorption when Caroline spoke and his eyes had immediately lit on Burke. He seemed puzzled for a moment ; then, as if the sight his eyes had taken in had just penetrated to his brain, he said, " That rig outside," and turned to Chad. " Did he come in that rig ? "

Chad nodded.

" That's what you were talking about," Shepley said.

" She wanted to know," Chad said.

" You knew. You told her, didn't you ? "

" Yes," Chad said. " He said his name was Burke."

Chad didn't know why he told Shepley, but looking at his face he could tell that the same thought was in both their minds.

" She didn't tell me," Shepley said slowly. " The bitch."

Caroline said angrily, " You've got no right to talk like that," but Shepley ignored her. He ignored Albany as she made her exit ; he gave Burke, who was clapping his hands perfunctorily, one look ; then he ignored him, too. " Come on, stumblefoot," he said to the pad horse.

Albany handed the reins to Chad but she followed him over to the hurdle to pat Buck. " Wasn't he fine to-day ? " she asked.

Chad said, " Both of you."

She rested her chin on the riding whip between her hands.

" I haven't seen Mr. Burke in years," she said. " Not since Parsons' Albany Circus. But he doesn't appear to have changed."

" He noticed you all right," Chad said. " You certainly played in his lap.

She glanced up quickly. " Do you think it showed ? "

" Well, Caroline noticed it. And Fred did, too."

" Fred ? Does he know Burke ? "

" I told him."

" Why did you ? "

" I don't know," Chad said.

Her eyes became curious. She stared at Chad, but she was listening to the tent. Then she turned abruptly towards the entrance.

Chad unsaddled, slapped Buck's rump, and went after her. She did not notice him when he came up, and he didn't speak to her, but looked in over her head. The crown of her hat just reached his eyes.

Shepley had finished the ribbons and Caroline had them bunched in her arms. Sweating heavily, Mr. Huguenine was announcing the defiance of the laws of gravitation in Signor Rossello's attempted somersault. Burke, across the ring, was looking towards the performers' entrance, but as Joe Duddy rolled his drum he glanced at the rider. Fred took a full circle of the ring before he somersaulted. He made the pad and he got a hand ; but Mr. Burke was already leaving his seat and edging towards the exit. He reached it before Shepley, touched his hat to Albany, saying, " How are you, Miss Yates ? " and saw Chad.

" Hallo, son," he said. " Don't forget to give Huguenine my card. I'll be back. I'm going to visit a little with Miss Yates." He took Albany's hand and placed it inside his elbow. " It's quite a while since I saw you," he said to her.

" I was just starting in then," she said.

" I said you were promising. Where did you find that horse ? "

Chad could hear her telling him as they started across the grass, following the round of the tent. Mr. Burke was carrying his cigar in his off hand, flicking the ash lightly with his little finger, and Albany walked lightly beside him, with her skirts held up in her free hand. They made a genteel picture ; but if Shepley thought so too, he didn't remark on it to Chad. He picked up a blanket, wrapped himself in it, and lay down on the grass.

Caroline was waiting by the hurdle when Chad went back to tie the cream pad ; she was looking for Albany. When Chad told her that Albany had gone off with Mr. Burke, she was excited. But she thought it was a shame Mr. Burke couldn't have stayed to see Ike Wayfish's act.

By now, every one knew about Burke's presence ; and after the tent emptied, the entire company waited inside for his return. He came in through the main entrance as if he owned the show. He looked cooler than frog water, Budlong said, walking up to Huguenine.

" Hallo, Huguenine," he said. " You got my card."

" Yes." Huguenine's solid face was troubled. His hands fidgeted. " I hope you liked the show."

" It's all right for a whistle show," Burke said. " But it's on my route and I don't like it. Get off it."

" The roads are public," Huguenine said, after a minute's consideration.

" Maybe they are," Burke said. " But New York State is

Flatfoot country. Any punk can tell you that." He pulled a fresh cigar out and lit it in Huguenine's face. "If you try to tie into me I'll bust you. It's a warning, see? So watch out."

Mr. Huguenine had to clear his throat.

"Seems to me Bisbee said something about the Flatfoots telling that to Raymond and Waring," he said hesitantly. "I ain't a circus man myself, but seems to me they made out all right. Joe, you keep shut."

Joe Duddy had started flapping his arms to crow. Burke paid no attention.

"You're not exactly the same class as Raymond," Burke said dryly.

No. But I've put my money in this outfit, and I ain't going to throw it away because you tell me to. I advertised my route and I aim to stick to it."

He looked solid as an ox in front of Burke and Mrs. Huguenine completed the delight of Joe Duddy by saying, "Don't hit him, A.D. He's too little."

Burke was unruffled.

"I've traced your dates," he said. "We're showing Lyons, June 30. If we find you there we'll take your show to pieces. That's all."

He turned to the performers' entrance, but he stopped as he reached it.

"And quit tearing my paper, Huguenine."

He stepped out. Presently they heard the buggy cramping as the horses wheeled. They were trotting snappily as they passed the main entrance, the little man sitting forward on the seat, holding his whip trailing like a mail driver.

"I wish to God I'd pulled them linchpins," Joe said. He picked the mop bucket off the cage wagon and started gathering horse buns from the ring. Ike Wayfish watched sympathetically, but the rest of them stared at Huguenine, who was leaning glumly against the centre pole, and after a few minutes Bastock said, "You sure stood right up to him, A.D." He spoke as if Huguenine instead of Burke had been the little man.

Mrs. Huguenine, however, wasn't a bit sobered.

"Don't worry, A.D.," she told her husband. "He can't do nothing, can he?"

"No," said Huguenine. "Not that I know of."

He looked up as Albany came back into the tent.

2

BASTOCK

IT was in Auburn that Bastock decided to look at Caroline on a horse. Till then he had refused even to consider it. Every morning, after the tent was up, he used the time before the parade putting her and Chad through a series of exercises. But the Sunday following Burke's warning to Huguenine, he changed his mind.

They didn't get any notice from Bastock. Chad was waiting his turn at the hand grips on the centre pole. Caroline was using them, standing straight upon her right foot and stretching the left as far and high behind her as she could while Bastock sat on the ring curb and whittled a plug in the palm of his hand. A slow rain was falling. The round-top showed wet and grey. Budlong was shaving himself near the main entrance. The mirror, propped on one of the blue seats, was turned to catch what light came in from a misty sky. Except for him, however, they had the tent to themselves. Joe Duddy hadn't shown up since supper time the day before, and Mrs. Huguenine had gone down to the hotel for a late breakfast. Oscar the lion was inside the tent because of the rain ; but he drowsed, taking his Sunday fast philosophically.

Caroline suddenly dropped her leg and twisted her body round without letting go the hand grips. " Do I have to do it again, Pete ? "

Bastock nodded. He stuffed his pipe and came over behind her. She made a face at Chad and slowly lifted the leg again.

Chad liked to watch, watching the curve of her back take shape, the hollow come into it, and the long leg in the faded tights reaching back. It made him feel sleepy, with the drip of rain in his ears, like one cat watching another stretch. Pete took her foot in the palm of his hand, as it came waist-high, and lifted it slowly until she said " Ouch ! "

" See, Missy ? There's a couple of muscles you didn't even know was there."

" I do now," she said, putting her foot down and rubbing

her hand up and down the back of her thigh. " But it does seem
kind of senseless to me just the same."

Bastock nodded. " You're limber enough, you turn cartwheels, and you can throw pretty back somersets, for a girl.
You could make a plastic all right, but we're figuring on horses,
Missy. You got to have strength. You don't want to tangle up
like a snarl of wool when you get on a pad. There ain't room."
His black eyes swelled solemnly at her. " If you was a kid, it
would be different. I could use a whip. Ain't nothing like a
whip used right to learn a human, just like a dog or a horse.
I ain't ever whipped a girl your age, though. Tads or women
is different. Chad here's too big for me to lick. I doubt if he'll
ever make a real rider anyhow. He changed his mind about
smoking, knocked the pipe into his hand, and stuffed the tobacco
into his mouth. " Chad, you get that pad horse, and we'll see."

" Me ? " Chad stared at him. " You want the cream ? "

Bastock spat disgustedly over the ring curb.

" My God," he said. " You two been yawping and blatting
about horses for a whole week and now when I say to get one,
you act like a couple of frogs. If you don't want to ride, say so,
and I'll resign right here."

" Oh, Mr. Bastock ! " Caroline, letting go the grips, turned
round. " It's only we're surprised. You said we couldn't start
riding for weeks ; didn't he, Chad ? "

" Months," Chad agreed. " He just wants to break my neck.
But I'll get the horse."

" Fetch the pad in here, Chaddy. If you saddle outside it'll
get wet."

" Can't I do anything ? " Caroline asked.

" You can set here and hold my hand for me," Bastock said
complacently. " I need it."

When Chad came back with the cream horse out of the rain,
they were sitting on the bottom tier of seats and Budlong,
finished with shaving, had joined them with a line of lather
drying down the wing of one ear. The rain made the tent
dim so the three figures seemed far away. It felt chilly inside ;
and a draught drew steadily through the main entrance, smelling
of raw dirt and wood smoke from the town fires. It hardly seemed
to Chad a comfortable day to start the active art of equitation.

But the horse accepted the pad tranquilly.

" Some day," Bastock said, " you're going to realise how

lucky you are to have a chance learning on a horse like him. He don't do anything wrong. If you fall, it's your own fault."

He looked the horse over for a minute before buckling on a longer rein. " Stand-up rein," he explained. " Budlong, fetch me that pratique strap, will you ? "

Budlong ambled over to where he had been shaving and ambled back with a long strap like a lunge strap, attached to what appeared to be a wide belt. Bastock accepted it dubiously. " There wasn't a pratique strap in this entire shebang," he said. " I had to have this thing made up last night." And Chad realised that Bastock must have made up his mind about riding some time yesterday. " Now, Missy," he was saying, " I got to buckle this on to you."

Puzzled, Caroline lifted her arms for him. " I had to guess the size," he said. " But we left plenty of allowance. Does it feel all right ? "

" Yes," she said. " What's it for ? "

" So you won't break your neck," Bastock said, eyeing her. " Maybe it's too high. I never pratiqued a girl. Well, we'll see." He put the end of the long strap through a ring in the pad pommel, took his place near the centre of the ring, and told Chad to mount the girl on the horse. " Set sideways," he said. " Like a lady in a picture."

Chad felt her slight shivering. He grinned at her, but her face was intent and pale. When she met his eyes, she started to smile, drew a quick breath, and turned to Bastock.

" Take hold of the rein, Missy," the little man said. Budlong had handed him a lunge whip, which he now cracked. The pad horse started easily. It almost seemed as if he knew what was up. He went like silk.

Chad stepped over the ring curb, but he didn't join Budlong on the seats.

" You don't need to grip. Set up straight. You've got the reins to balance with. You can't fall, Missy. Just think you're setting in a chair in your best dress on the Main Street Hotel porch and feel easy."

" I wouldn't feel easy there ! " Caroline said. " I'd be scared to death."

But it was surprisingly easy to sit the lolloping gait, with the slight inward slope the horse made following the curve. The colour began to come back to her cheeks. Presently one hand let go the rein, and Bastock, making a tiny inside circle on his bowed legs and watching her like a hawk, said, " Let it hang, if you don't need it, Missy."

She did, riding with her hands slightly raised, and Budlong said, " Pretty."

" Yes, she makes a picture, Bastock agreed. " Now then, Missy, jump down."

As she obeyed, Bastock set himself ; the strap tightened, and she was swinging by the horse's shoulder.

The horse stopped of his own acccord and Bastock let her down. " You see you can't hit the dirt if you want to when you've got a pratique strap, Missy. Did it set all right ? "

She was pulling it down in place, tucking her leotard into her trunks.

" It felt fine," she said breathlessly.

" All right, Missy. Now, up you get and we'll begin."

As soon as she was mounted and the horse in motion, Bastock directed her to get up on her hands and knees. " Hold on to the pommel if you want," he said. " Spread your feet some. That's it."

She looked unsteady, and she held tight at first ; but after a round or two, Bastock made her let go with one hand and take the reins ; then straighten up on her knees.

At the third stride she slipped and toppled, but the pratique swung her forward. This time, however, she hung by the middle, both ends down ; and she was completely out of breath when the horse stopped.

" Took your wind ? " Bastock asked.

She gasped, " Yes," and started to giggle. " I thought all my clothes were coming off."

Bastock grunted.

" Get up, this ain't a church picnic. You got to ride three rings on your knees."

Strangely, she did it ; and she was still erect when on her knees the horse stopped. Bastock said she was fine. Some riders, he explained, somersaulted from their knees. It gave you more spring. You took the horse on the rise and you were half over before you knew you had started. " But it don't look like so much, and you don't get high off the horse. Now then, back on the pad, Missy, and Chad, you hold that nag. Now, get up on your feet. Like this. Put your left foot just ahead of where his

hips are, and your right back of the pommel. That's it. You face
inward first. Facing out is harder. Don't stiffen your knees, or
you'll get throwed the first move he makes. Hold on to the reins.
Look at his ears. You've got your feet lined up with the reins.
Bring the left one nearer me. That's pretty. By God, that's
pretty. Look at it, you big bezabor," he said to Budlong.

Budlong lifted impersonal eyes and went on chewing tobacco.
But Chad saw what Bastock saw. She was pretty on a horse; she
had the right build. Long legs helped to make her look light.

She toppled; Bostock caught her; and Chad shoved her
back. She fell again, and again and again. Bastock gave over
talking to her about how well she looked. She looked worse each
time. And then, after half an hour, when Bastock had lost all
patience and suddenly roared, " Pull in that God-damned rump,
can't you ? " she made a circle of the ring, standing unsteadily,
her feet slipping and shifting and her knees like hammers; but
she stood up. And when the horse stopped, Bastock was triumphant.

" You're going to ride, Missy. You're going to ride high. By
God. Get down. Budlong, get her a blanket. She's valuable.
You'd get a blanket for a horse, wouldn't you ? Hurry up."

His black eyes stuck out at her; he beamed and wiped his
mouth. " My God, I'm tired," he said.

Caroline's knees turned to water as soon as she reached the
ground, but Budlong escorted her to a ringside seat, wrapped her,
and sat her down. " Now we'll set and watch the comics," he
told her.

Buckling the pratique on Chad, Bastock chuckled. They all
felt satisfied, as if they had all contributed to her ride round the
ring. Caroline herself looked proud, her eyes full of shine. Even
Chad grinned when Bastock said, " Remind me if I forget to
hold on to the strap, Chaddy."

" What do I do first ? "

" Get on the horse."

Chad started the cream pad, got him galloping, and put his
hand on the pommel. It was an easy vault, with the horse
leaning towards him, and the pad was big as a door to light on.

" My Crimus." Bastock was sarcastic. " He's a vaulter. Now
don't straddle him, set sideways, like Caroline. Gawd, ain't he
pretty ? Your feet are too big, Chaddy. Let your hands hang
but don't flap 'em, or you'll scare the horse. Get up on your

knees. There ain't no sense stopping for a master rider like you."

Sitting the pad was fine ; but as soon as his tail got off it, Chad lost his security. He had to grab the pommel, as Bastock pointed out with loud scorn to Caroline. But in a moment he got his knees where they belonged and spread his feet on the tail of the pad, making a sort of triangle of his shins, and tried to straighten. The tendency of his knees to lift surprised him. Twice he started to reach for the pommel and Bastock yelled at him to watch the horse's ears. " Look right through them. If you look down and watch the ground you'll see you're going in a circle."

Then he caught it ; and once he had it was easy to keep the position, for the horse's gait was regular as clockwork. Bastock stopped the horse after two circles and said he was all right.

" Maybe you'll ride, too," he said grudgingly. " But nobody'll fall in love with you. Now, we'll try standing up."

The first thing about standing that astonished Chad was the sudden decrease in the size of the pad. He took the position Bastock had described to Caroline, got a good grip on the stand-up rein, and nodded his head. At the first lift of the horse's rump he nose-dived. He had a flashing glimpse of Caroline's intent face, of Bastock's heels digging ruts through the grass, and then the strap caught him in the wind. He hit ground, but he was all right, except for a pain in his belly.

" You ain't doing much on that strap," he complained.

"I done enough to keep you from digging a hole. But we'll get Budlong. He's more your heft."

Budlong came over lazily and took the strap in one hand.

" What am I supposed to do with this-here ? " he asked.

" Pay it out when he starts swimming," Bastock said. " Now get up there and keep your behind inside your pants, Chaddy."

Chad tried it again, springing his knees more freely. He began to have some respect for Shepley. The idea of ever even trying a somersault was appalling. He tried to brace his right foot and take more of the rise in his left knee ; and suddenly he realised that he had made most of a full circle. It was the even gait of the horse that ironed out his troubles. As long as he followed the gait, he was all right.

Then he heard clapping, and looked over towards Caroline, but found he was on the wrong side of the ring to see her, and suddenly he fell off, and Budlong nearly cut him in two.

Budlong let him hang. " Do I let him down ? " he asked.

Caroline was still clapping her hands. " You went round nearly two times," she said. " You're lots better than me."

Bastock said, " I've seen one or two worse, but it's his big feet give him a head start, Missy." He unbuckled the pratique strap. " We done enough for to-day. You both feel sore to-morrow, probably. But maybe that will learn you that it's more comfortable to stay on the horse's back."

It was still raining. The drops formed on Caroline's hair, lit on her face. Watching her out of the tail of his eye, Chad thought she seemed a lot older. She was getting to be nice looking, he thought, she had a pretty mouth, the thin upper lip was short, and when she turned and caught him looking at her, it was quick to smile.

" I think it's awfully nice we two can learn riding together," she said. " Don't you ? "

" Oh, sure."

" I mean," she said quickly, " I'd be scared to death trying standing up on the pad if it was just me. But knowing you're trying it too makes it a lot easier."

" I feel that way, too," Chad said, " But you're going to be a real rider, some day, Caroline. Why, you hardly ever been on a horse."

" Isn't he nice ? " she said. " He's so careful. He tries so hard to go smooth and make it easy for us. I love him."

Stroking the peaceable cream-coloured nose of the horse, she blushed suddenly under the rain.

" I wonder why Pete wanted us to begin to-day. So sudden. He must have made up his mind about it yesterday, too. He had the pratique ready."

Chad said, " I been thinking about that, too."

3

FINDERS KEEPERS

HUGUENINE's CIRCUS began the week of June 27 with less than a hundred admissions. Overnight all their paper in Auburn had been torn down and a whole new series of Burke and Walsh tacked in its place. When he went to feed the ring stock in the morning, Chad found one on the livery-stable door. It had a lovely cut, four times the size of any of Huguenine's pictures, showing an elegantly draped tent interior with four male equestrians on four Arab horses facing as many similarly mounted female riders. The females all wore ostrich plumes in their hats ; their leotards were trimmed like grenadier uniform jackets except for lace ruffs at the throat ; and their trunks fitted the form.

MAMMOTH ARENA AND AMPHITHEATRE

Under the direction of Burke, Walsh & Co.

The above establishment will be opened in the City of Auburn on Tuesday, June 28, 1836. The arena is newly and completely fitted out, with a superior BAND OF MUSIC ; a first rate company of EQUESTRIANS possessing unequalled talent ; and a stud of HANO-VEREAN AND ARAB HORSES, which for beauty and management, excel all previous exhibitions ever offered such *a liberal and discerning community*. All patrons are particularly invited to view the Arena while fitting up to prove how comfortable they will be seated. It is likewise " proper to state that the strictest attention cannot fail to instruct as well as divert the genteel of society."

Upward of eighty men and horses are occupied in this immense establishment.

Boxes 50 cents ; Pit 25 cents. Performances will commence at half-past 10 a.m., and 2 o'clock p.m. Box seats for 2000 people.

Joe Duddy reported that along the store district the paper was twice the size of that one, with a picture of the elephant included, and a paragraph about the hyena.

"I wouldn't mind paying twenty-five cents to see it," he said. "I tore down some, and I drawed a bag and teats on the elephant, but durned if a feller who saw it didn't believe it was so. We can't beat a show like that, Chad."

Chad couldn't help feeling a hankering to see the big show himself. But he said, "Well, we'll be standing different towns till we get to Lyons."

"Yeah," said Joe. "But what do we do in Lyons?"

Chad hunched his shoulders. Mr. Burke did not seem to him the kind of man who would leave it open to plain competition. . . .

Riding Jerry and leading the other two horses, there wasn't any way a man could keep dry. The tent had weighed a ton taking down, and Bastock told them it would feel twice as heavy to put up. His belly was sore from the pratique strap. They had put in two hours that morning, and Caroline had made several turns of the ring standing up. Now and then during a flash of confidence she had given them glimpses of what she might turn into, and the way she looked then kept coming into Chad's mind. He himself hadn't done any better than he had on his first try.

But he had enjoyed himself during the first part of the practice. They all had. Caroline's face showed it; and there was a feeling of all of them working together, with Budlong, Joe, and Bastock all making remarks about Chad, and telling Caroline she was going to be a leading lady rider sure as fate. It was only after Albany Yates came into the tent that they began to go badly.

She had drifted in out of the rain, saying good-morning to them all, and hoping they did not mind her joining them. She stood close to Chad, watching Caroline thoughtfully, with her grey eyes, and giving her generous praise. But Caroline almost at once began to commit faults so badly that Bastock lost patience; and presently he took her off the horse and put Chad up and started to make savage remarks. The air of the tent changed completely. Only Albany seemed unconcerned. She said something pretty about them both and went out again.

But the practice had fallen all apart. Neither of them could do anything right. In fifteen minutes Bastock gave the thing up. " Take him back," he said. " Take yourselves away, too."

Walking down to the barn, Caroline said, " Why did she have to butt in ? "

" Why shouldn't she ? " Chad asked. " She didn't butt in, either. She was nice about both of us."

" It was fine before she came in." Caroline's face was set. " I hate her."

Chad was amazed.

" Why," he said, " if it hadn't been for her you wouldn't be with the circus, probably."

" Just the same, she's always after something for herself."

Chad kept quiet.

" First she wants Fred, and then she drops him, and then she takes up with him, and now she drops him again. She just turned him off."

" She did ? " Chad became attentive.

Caroline turned to look at him.

" She told him she didn't want to get married. She said there wasn't any sense in doing it now. What *does* she want ? "

" Well, I don't blame her not wanting him."

" Then she oughtn't to go with him," Caroline said fiercely. " If that's all she had done with him."

" Don't get spiteful."

" I'm not. Just because she does something open-hearted once. I don't see why I have to owe her everything all my life."

" She doesn't expect that."

" What does she expect ? " Caroline bit her lip. " You think she's just wonderful. So does everybody else. Go ahead," she said. " See if I care."

She left him abruptly, her cheeks flaming, and walked off towards the hotel. . . .

Just before dark the rain let up and the wind blew hard for a few minutes, clearing the air. To Chad's left a strip of pale yellow sky lay under the clouds. Ahead the road led over rolling land. He thought they ought to be coming to Throopsville before long, and he decided to stop at the first tavern for a drink. If they had a fire going, he would stay long enough to get partly dried out ; anyway until the wagons came along.

As the wind died, Chad smelled the wet meadowland. It was too dark for him to see much of the country, only the shapes

of trees and occasional farmhouses and barns against the pale
westward sky. The colour had drained from it and the light was
fading from the road. The horses splashed through puddles he
could not see, their hoofs spanking the water smartly. He looked
back for wagon lights, but there was no sign of them. Then,
facing forward again, he saw a small cluster of lighted buildings
stretching out along the level road and heard water falling in
Owasco Creek.

Throopsville was no more than a hamlet, and Clapp's Tavern
was easy to pick out. It had a liquorish breath, and a porch
along the roadside front. Chad turned Jerry round the corner,
hearing the voices inside peter out at the sound of horsehoofs
in the slop of the yard. A back door opened, shooting light upon
a sow with a spotted litter clustered against her mountainous
dugs and a wet-foot hen perched on her flank. An old man cast
his shadow over them. He stayed where he was, letting Chad
stall the horses in the dark. " Trading horses ? " he asked when
Chad had crossed the yard.

" No. They belong to Huguenine's Circus."

" Yeah ? There was a party of them come by in a wagon.
They stopped here for a while." He led the way into the taproom,
where six or seven villagers were sitting round the stove. They
looked at Chad when he said " Evening " to them and one of
them said " Hallo."

Mr. Clapp explained that Chad was with the circus. " Didn't
get the name," he said.

" Hanna," said Chad. " I'll have some whisky. You got any
Bourbon ? "

" Not here. Anyways, we call it corn. You ain't a ' dough-
face,' are you ? "

Chad grinned. " What is it ? "

" Demmycrat." A thin-faced man bit the word before he laid
it down.

" No," said Chad.

The thin-faced man nodded. " We had one dough-face vote
in this district last election," he said. " We thrown the other out.
How do you stand on the small-bills question, mister ? "

" I like 'em, but I like big ones better," Chad said.

" Yes. But how're you going to do business if banks can't
print no money less'n five dollars ? The dough-faces have got
the banks in their hip pockets and they're trying to put a mortgage

on the farmer so they can foreclose it. They hold up slavery to keep him down. They don't let him send abolition through the mails ; that little dough-face Kendall's close the Post Office against it. And what was they afore they got to Washington ? Oh, Andy Jackson was a soldier, I don't hold against him. But look at Taney and Kendall, two-dollar mules ! You put them kind of animals in power and right away you got a solid party twice the size you figured on. It's like putting fishworms in a box. In ten minutes they're all snarled in one big lump and then where are you ? "

Chad said, " Where ? "

" Yes," said the thin-faced man.

Mr. Clapp said, " I voted for Seaward and I'm going to keep right on voting for him till he gets elected."

A voice remarked from the corner, heavily, " Two-dollar mules can make manure just like horses."

" How do you stand on Masonry ? " asked the thin-faced man.

" I don't stand on anything but my own feet," Chad said. Someone laughed. As if he were reproving him the man who had talked about manure and mules said, " In France they say every other child is a bastard."

Nobody wished to dispute this statement. After a moment Chad asked, " How long ago was the light rig here ? "

Mr. Clapp said, " Couple of hours, I guess. They got some supper. They didn't appear like circus people. They paid up with cash money and they hardly talked at all. One of them's staying here now. She said she wanted to wait for the wagons."

" She ? "

" Yes," said Mr. Clapp. " She's in the kitchen with the wife."

He pointed with his thumb.

He didn't need to. The door was open. Looking through, Chad saw Caroline Trid. She was staring at him, her eyes large in her thin face.

He put his glass on the end of the plank bar and said, " Excuse me a minute," and went through the door.

" What did you stay here for ? "

She said, " Mrs. Clapp, let me make you acquainted with Mr. Hanna." The reproving formality of her voice embarrassed him. He turned to see a witchlike old woman in a corner take her hands from the dishpan and wring them and wipe them on her apron.

Her bright eyes shifted rapidly over Chad before settling on his face. She said, " These dishes are about done, thanks to you. I don't get much help. The glasses I wash ! Take him to the parlour if you want to, honey. Here's a candle."

Caroline, thanking her, took the candle, and led Chad through a door towards the front of the house. Another door off a musty stair hall opened into a dim little room that had a looking-glass, a bunch of dry flowers on a table, four chairs set facing, and a thin but blossomy carpet. It made Chad think of Elias Proops's remark about another place : " Only a ghost could chew tobacco there."

The candle shine pooled in the mirror and the blank windows equally. It lit Caroline's breast and face more brightly. Across the room, Chad had another view of her, her square shoulders with her bonnet hanging on them, her soft hair, and her own face above it, watching him. Beyond the door, now closed, the voices murmured in the tap-room.

" Why'd you stay here ? "

In the glass he saw himself asking the question and her head tilt to his face, and then he looked at hers, and he saw there were tears in her eyes.

" What's the matter ? "

" Oh, I just couldn't stand it in the wagon." Her voice gained strength with talking, but she kept it very low. " I didn't want to sit with Albany, and she and Shepley wouldn't say a word, and Mrs. Pamplon was so scared, and it was raining. And then Fiero tried to hold my hand." She smiled. " Wasn't it silly ? "

She was studying the candle flame, cradling the stick in both hands. " If it was raining, I planned to ride with Mrs. Hugue-nine."

When he did not answer, she raised her eyes.

" And I kept thinking about the way I was this morning. Getting mad and telling you I didn't care what you thought. But I did. We didn't speak all day because of it, and I wanted to tell you I was sorry. And if I'd gone on with the wagon, I'd have had to wait till to-morrow."

She stopped.

He said after a minute, " You waited here just to see me." " Yes."

She was looking again at the candle in her hands. In the mirror he saw the bend of her neck between the bonnet brim and the soft clustering of hair. She meant what she said; she had waited there for him. But she was telling him something else, making an offer; all he had to do was pick it up, and it would belong to him—like finders keepers.

Ever since he could remember he had had to take care of himself. He had always lived alone since he ran away from the orphanage. Even there, except for the little girl Marie, he had been by himself. He had never had a friend until he came to Canastota. Elias was a friend, but he was an old man; and Bobby Gray had been a tadpole. Ganting around like a lone fox, Elias used to say of him, and he had always liked the idea; he could put his foot in his pocket whenever he liked and light out.

And he had thought of Caroline as just a youngster, too; one who knew more than was good for her, perhaps. But now he wasn't so sure. He could see himself in the mirror like a colt put on a lunging strap for the first time, half scared, half interested, shying off and on. Then, realising they had been a long time there, he looked at her.

There was a patience in the way she waited, as if she understood what he was feeling, as if time were a candle in her hands. Catching two threads out of the light, the locket chain made links of them, and following them down to where they ended he could see the soft pressure of her breathing inside the bodice of her dress. It was a grey-blue dress, it must have been one of Albany Yates's; and it seemed odd that after chasing Albany in his mind so long, he should be on the edge with a girl in clothes of hers. But he hadn't thought of Albany lately, hardly at all; and the girl inside the dress wasn't Albany. He didn't know anything about Albany; but he knew all about how this girl was put together, seeing her in tights every day, watching her do exercises, putting her on the pad horse. He just hadn't bothered to think; and now he had only to put his hand on her shoulder.

He said, " If you keep holding the candle that way, I'm liable to get burned."

She lifted her face then, searching his.

" Burned ? " she said. " How ? "

" This way."

She dropped the candlestick, and the candle broke free as it struck the floor, rolled on the carpet, and went out. For an instant she felt like a rod in his hands. Then she melted. She didn't have to tell him she was in love with him, he could feel it ; and that she had been in love with him, storing it for him. It was something he had never had. It made him feel proud to kiss her.

It seemed to him as if it had been intended to happen ; he couldn't get over it. Each time he felt like kissing her again, she was ready. But she wasn't like the girls he used to pick up along the towpath. He was a person to her and she intended it to last ; she was in love ; he could feel it taking living shape beside the dried flowers on the table.

He looked over her shoulder after a while, at the blank windows, and saw four wagon lights pulling slowly along the road. He didn't say anything, but turned her so that they stood side by side in the dark window, looking out, her hip pressing his, and his hand on her waist.

She said, " I never knew, Chad, I never even guessed it."

" Are we going to tell them now ? " he said.

" I don't care."

" We've got to stop them anyway, before they get by."

" Let's not tell them to-night," she said.

He fumbled for the candle, picked it up, and put it in its stick upon the table. They went outside by the hall door. " I wish I could go with you," she said.

" It would take too long to get the saddle out. You can't ride in that dress anyway."

Huguenine's team pulled into the light and Mr. Huguenine regarded them with stolid amazement.

Chad said, " Caroline stayed over here to ride with you. Can she get in with Mrs. Huguenine ? "

Huguenine scratched his head.

" Why, I guess so. But what's the idea ? "

" It's her idea," Chad said, grinning at Caroline.

" Never mind. Let her get in with me. I'll find out fast enough." Mrs. Huguenine had risen from her bed ; the pay wagon rocked as she fumbled for the door. She opened it, standing there in a nightgown that looked like a tent, the hair upon her forehead sprouting a battery of curlers. " You come inside with me, dearie, and tell me what that Monkey has been doing with you."

"Where's the horses?" Mr. Huguenine asked Chad as the door closed.

"They're in the barn. I'm getting them now."

"All right," said Mr. Huguenine. "Geddap, you two."

He cracked his whip, and the wagon rolled along. Chad went after the horses. Mrs. Clapp was standing on the back porch, her eyes like a bird's.

"How'd it go, Mr. Hanna?"

"Fine," he said. "But we dropped the candle. There may be a grease spot on the carpet."

She nodded.

"Never mind," she said. "I liked that girl."

4

CATASTROPHE IN CLYDE

NOBODY but Mrs. Huguenine said anything about Caroline's staying behind at Clapp's Tavern. Huguenine had called Mrs. Huguenine out of the treasury wagon when they were raising the round-top on the Port Byron lot, and she had put her heft on one of the ropes. The canvas was like sheet lead to raise, still wet, but the sun promised to dry it out before packing time. Mrs. Huguenine raised her fat arms, with the rope wound round her wrists, and just sat down. The canvas couldn't resist her. And she said to Chad, "Well, so you're going to get married."

Chad was a little startled. "Caroline tell you?"

"Dearie, what do you expect she did, me and her in a wagon that size and I having made up my mind? Of course, she did. Cried some and said she had never dreamed of it. She said she had never known what it was to be happy in her life before. She said she wished she wasn't so ignorant and hoped she would make a leastways decent wife. Just like any other girl in love."

Chad said, "You think it's all right?"

It seemed pretty serious, getting married, now that Mrs. Huguenine was outlining the way a girl felt about it.

"I don't know how much money you've got."

"I've saved about twenty dollars."

"She don't make anything," Mrs. Huguenine said. "I don't

know. A man oughtn't really to get married unless he's saved up fifty dollars. In the old times, you didn't need cash money. You got a cow off your parents and you took up free land with an axe and a rifle. I wish I'd been born in that time. I'd have liked it. But nowadays it's different. Folks are trading in stores for their food and they spend money on their clothes. You're both young, though, and that's the time to get married. Especially for the girl, while she's got her looks."

She dropped the rope, which had left red trenches in her wrists, and watched Joe Duddy driving the staubes. Joe swinging the twelve-pound gimmix was something she liked to see ; the tent peg looked as if it were going down through butter ; and the crack of the sledge on the seasoned wood had an almost beautiful rhythm.

" I wish you joy, Chad," she said. " Both of you. And don't worry. I've not even told A.D."

She lumbered away briskly towards the wagon to clean up her breakfast dishes and get some washing done and Chad started setting up the seats and lugging in the boards. Bastock asked when he and Caroline wanted to practise and he said as soon as he had got Oscar's meat.

He went down the street towards the canal. Off and on during the night he had heard the boat horns, and after he had picked up the usual eight pounds of lean, and a salted mackerel for Mrs. Huguenine, he came back along the towpath, killing time to watch the boats. Early as it was, there were plenty of them, loading and passing through. Barrels of flour were being rolled on to one close by ; the flour must come from the mill, it was one of the biggest in the state, and the roll of its run of twelve stones was like a distant thunder over the noise of the basin. A line boat was dragging west right in front of him, carrying immigrants, with one young couple sitting side by side on the top deck, staring right and left, as if what they saw looked strange. It made Chad feel good to see it all again and hear the shouts, the cracks of the whips, the heavy blowing of the horses ; it took him back to the Yellow Bud ; it seemed mysterious to think of that same boat having hauled through Canastota. Maybe Elias Proops had seen it go by ; if he had he'd have noticed the immigrant girl. Her hair was like wheat and she wore it braided. It gave one a queer feeling too, to come out of the country at night, so far away, and find the same canal,

the same still ditch of water ; it was more impressive than
following its towpath, to come out on it that way and see the
boats hauling their slow pace. Another boat came by, more
immigrants on board. They were coming all the time, feeding
through, to strike out west from Buffalo. That country must be
filling fast. Illinois was a state, Indiana, and they said Michigan
territory would become one any time. They had spilled across
the Mississippi River, and Missouri was a state ; but when he
was in the orphanage most of that land had been Indian country.
Some day he planned to go out there and see it.

A boat horn droned by his ears, like a jackass bawling, din-
ning his head. He looked at the steersman, a thick-set man with
heavy hands and thickets sprouting from his ear holes. Chad
read the name on the boat's green stern : *Minnie L.*, Rochester,
N.Y. He had driven for that boat a while ; and he remembered
the man's strap, his drunken roaring coming towards the stable
to rouse him for the night trick. Now the captain's eyes, following the shore line, came to Chad and passed along with the even,
deliberate glide of the boat. He didn't recognise the shivery
little boy with freckles in a white scared face.

" There's your pay," the captain used to say, putting eleven
dollars on the table in the cabin. " Here's the receipt. Make
your mark here." And Chad would put a cross beside the ridged
thumbnail on the paper. Then he would stand aside, and the
captain would get the other hoggie to sign another receipt for
the same money. " There, boys," he would tell them, pocketing
the money, " we're all legal and businesslike. Now I'll just make
my mark " ; and he would pull the heavy strap from his pants.

Chad thought if he ever went west, it would be amusing
to take a passage on that man's boat ; it had four bunks in the
cargo space and the captain was always obsequious to passen-
gers. Then he remembered that he would have to get passage
for two. He was going to be married. It was something he had
never actually figured on until it happened ; but riding up the
road from Throopsville last night, he had got to thinking how
nice it would be to end that trip in a hotel room, in a bed already
warmed for him.

He hitched up his parcels and turned away from the canal,
wondering whether a girl thought the same kind of thoughts
before she was married. He didn't know about Caroline. Sometimes he thought she knew a lot ; and then at times she seemed

like a child. She had been that way for a minute in the dead little parlour ; and then she had suddenly seemed ready for anything.

Well, he thought, they were fixed for the summer, as long as the circus held out ; and if she got good enough to go on as a rider, they would both be making money. They would be almost wealthy if that happened. They could have champagne wine, even ; he wondered how much a bottle of it would cost and what it tasted like. He would like to buy a bottle the night they got married if it didn't come too high.

As he turned up the street he saw her ahead of him, and he lengthened his stride to catch up. " Hallo," he said.

It made her start. She turned quickly, seeing who it was, and blushed. Her eyes were shy.

" Good-morning, Chad," she said.

" You ready for practice ? " he asked. But he saw she was ; she was dressed in her tights ; her legs showed thin and long under the edge of the cloak. " Yes," she said, walking along beside him. But she kept her eyes straight ahead.

After a minute, Chad said, " I've been thinking about when we ought to get married."

She turned her eyes, then looked into his, saying nothing. " You meant it when you said you'd marry me ? " he asked her. " Mrs. Huguenine told me you'd told her."

" Yes. I didn't know if you'd meant it, though. My people aren't . . ."

He said, " I haven't got any at all, Caroline. I don't even know who they were."

" I had to tell Mrs. Huguenine. I had to tell someone."

" We won't be rich, you know," he said. " But we ought to get along all right this summer. I can get a job this winter."

She nodded. " I don't mind being poor. And we won't stay that way. Not when we learn to ride."

A little of the shyness had gone.

" I won't ever be much of a rider," Chad said. " But you will. I bet you'll be making more money than me in a year."

" Maybe you could get to be a circus agent," she said. " Like Mr. Bisbee. He makes nearly as much as a rider. I guess more than a female." She looked at him. " You'd be good at running a circus, I think. You'd have ideas, good ones. Wouldn't it be fun if we ever owned our own show ? "

THE TENTING SEASON 239

Chad agreed, thinking to himself that that wasn't likely to happen to people like them. "Probably, though," he said, "you'll want a house to live in."

She shook her head.

"I like travelling, Chad. I wouldn't mind it a bit. I was thinking last night how a person could fix over a wagon like that treasury wagon and make it seem a lot nicer."

They were getting near the lot. Under the sun the round-top had lost some of its soddenness. It was drying out fine. It was going to be a good day.

Chad found his tongue stumbling.

"Maybe we could get married Saturday, in Palmyra. Then we'd have Sunday, and I guess Mr. Huguenine would give me the day off. Would you be willing to do that?"

"Yes." She looked at him, her eyes again shy, and looked away.

Maybe he had smelled the fresh meat, or maybe the sun had got to him, warming his decrepit hide, or maybe Joe Duddy had left too much water on the floor of the cage wagon where he liked to sit down; anyway, the lion roared. The sound was heartening. It was the first healthy sound Oscar had made since the Saturday showing in Auburn. Both of them went to the cage wagon and watched Joe Duddy feed him his meat.

"He's taking hold pretty good this morning," Joe said.

"I think he's a nice old animal," Caroline said. "It must be pitiful, when you're old, being caged up that way."

Oscar, at the note in her voice, covered a free piece of meat with one paw, raised his yellow eyes, and coughed at all of them. . . .

Bastock was becoming excited over Caroline's progress.

"Once in a while you strike a natural-born rider," he said. "And she's one. Look at her, she's been up four times, but she can do straight riding and look pretty at it. She does the foot-to-pommel and we'll try her on the foot-around in a couple of days. She'll learn it. She knows how to handle her body, so when I tell her what to do she don't need a framed picture to figure it out."

He wasn't exaggerating. Every one who came to watch the practice saw she was good; and Mr. Huguenine said, "When she gets ready to go in the ring with it, we'll have Bisbee look her over. If he says it's all right, I'll put her on the pay-roll."

"It wouldn't hurt to put her on right now," Bastock said. "Suppose somebody who knew something about running circuses came around and took her from you."

"I wouldn't go," Caroline called, seeing Mr. Huguenine's worried face.

She was like a bird on the horse; she had confidence; and even in her plain circles of the ring she conveyed her own excited pleasure to the onlooker. It made Chad think of Albany's riding; Bisbee would call it "class."

They didn't see anything of Albany, except at show times; and little of Fred. Fred himself was not riding as well. He had failed twice on the somersault; he acted as if he had lost his ambition. Speaking about him, Bastock told Chad and Caroline: "You've got to love riding if you're going to be a rider. Take Fred. He don't. He can work himself up to ride if he's mad or feeling fine. A real rider can go in on a wet ring with leaks in the canvas and an ache in her belly and do a toe-to-mouth with water dropping down her back."

The haul to Clyde was the toughest one the show had had. They rolled down into the Seneca Valley after sunset, and passed through Montezuma village without stopping, to make the corduroy across the marshes before the light failed completely.

The treasury wagon got along well enough; but the tent wagon sunk the logs entirely under the marsh water, and before it had made a quarter of a mile, the team from the cage wagon had to be hooked on ahead of the four-horse hitch to bring it out of the slack, and then unhitched as soon as the big wagon was rolling and taken back for the cage. It was dark long before they got through; the horses were half wild with the bad footing, the threatening water, and the mosquitoes that swarmed into their ears. Their shoes dug at the slippery logs, tearing splinters out of them; they dodged holes by a miracle; and the only thing that kept them moving was the lantern Chad carried ahead of them. When they finally covered the four miles they had used up four hours; and dawn was breaking when they tugged into Clyde village.

It was light enough for Chad to see that the Huguenine paper had been replaced on the livery-stable door by one of Burke and Walsh's big sheets announcing their show at Lyons next day. A sleepy stablehand asked them what they expected to get out of showing in Clyde. Half the village had made plans to go over to Lyons, he said. Chad said he didn't know. It hardly seemed worth-while putting up the tent at all, let alone having a practice session. But Bastock insisted on working Caroline anyway. " Losing a day now she's started is enough to set her back a week."

The little man set himself on a bucket and drank water from a dipper while the other skinners just lay anywhere and went to sleep. Caroline had given Chad her cloak for a pillow ; he rolled it up under his head and lay on the canvas flap from the cage wagon. He could see the cream-coloured legs of the pad horse come by regularly as clockwork ; and if he squeezed his eye up he could see Bastock moving slowly round the pole, the pratique strap in his hand, his dark eyes red and half closed ; the grass smelled of dew, and the thud of the hoofs was like the ticking of a clock ; and he felt himself drifting down into the damp grass smell. But a sudden bugling note in Bastock's voice jerked him awake.

" She's done a foot-around. Just as neat, by Jesus," he was yelling. " Wake up, you big bezabors. She done a foot-around." He glared redly at them ; and then his face fell sheepishly. " Guess I must have got dozy. I wasn't hardly watching, and all of a sudden she done it."

Caroline's face was flushed. She was sitting on the pad, look-ing breathless, while the horse lolloped easily and tirelessly round and round. It was like a clock running down and Chad got a little dizzy. There was something queer. He said suddenly, " Where's the pratique ? "

Bastock gaped slowly. Then he looked at the circling horse, at Caroline on the pad, and then down at the bucket he was sitting on. The pratique strap lay on the grass at his feet. " Oh, my God," he said. " I had hold of it ; and then I got thirsty and I must have set down and forgot."

Caroline nodded.

" I wanted to try it without the strap. I saw you weren't noticing when you dropped it, so I unbuckled it. I wanted to see if I would feel scared."

" Did you ? " asked Chad.

She shook her head.

" Not after the first circle."

She smiled at him then looked quickly towards Bastock. He had hollered " Whoa ! " to the horse ; and as soon as the animal stopped he said, " Get down." His voice puzzled them both ; but Caroline obediently flipped her long legs and hit the ground. " Come here," Bastock said to her. " Pick up that strap. Give it to me." He doubled the leather, swung it suddenly, giving her a full cut across the backs of her thighs. The snap of the striking leather was like a pistol shot. Caroline stiffened and went white. Chad scrambled to his feet and yelled, " Hey there."

But the little man flung the strap away.

" Next time you get a notion to go off on your own hook, remember that." His voice trembled with rage. " If you want to learn, you'll do it my way. See ? Did I tell you you was ready to ride without no pratique ? "

" No," said Caroline. She looked as if she would like to rub her legs ; she seemed ready to cry. It made Chad mad.

" You got no business licking her whatever you say," he shouted. " Give me that pratique. I'll show him how it feels."

Bastock turned on his bowlegs.

" She might have broken her damned neck," he said. " It ain't your business anyway. I'm learning her. You keep your mouth shut."

" It is my business," Chad said grimly. " I'm marrying her."

" You're what ? "

" Marrying her."

" The hell you are." The little man's red eyes swelled. " Who told you you could do that ? "

Caroline had picked up the strap. " I did," she said. " Now who wants to lick who next ? "

The way she said it delighted Chad ; it wasn't what he would have expected of her at all, and he grinned at Bastock. But Bastock could not get the other idea out of his head.

" Well, I'll be bitched," he said.

" You're all of you tired out," Caroline said. " That's why you're mad. And I promise I won't do anything again without asking Mr. Bastock."

Bastock was mollified. " Maybe I was hasty," he admitted.

Budlong said, " For a hasty man you certainly did smack her. It woke Joe right up."

Joe grinned sheepishly. " I met a pigeon once and she liked . . ."

Pete turned on him. " Shut your mouth. In front of a girl ! "

"You done the smacking, didn't you? My God, I didn't dast use a strap."

They were getting steamed up again, like a bunch of steamboats, valves popping just about every so often. Caroline had never seen a steamboat, but she could tell pressure when she saw it.

"I ain't mad," she said. "Why should everybody else get mad?"

In the silence they could hear the *tunk-tunk* where Fiero was practising his knife-throwing back of the tent. He would throw the clutch of knives and then walk up to the board and pull them out. When he got to the board he would talk to himself, scolding or praising himself, as if he were two people. If things went too badly, he would complain about Caroline being so tall. It made Joe happy to hear him suffer.

"That crazy Dago," he said, and, as if he had heard it, Fiero stuck his head under the canvas, got up on the inside, carrying his knives fanwise in his left hand, and announced, "I make three perfectoes to-day. Maybe you lost a little hair. Phoo. What is some hair on a young lady?"

He beamed.

Bastock said, "That's fine, Fiero. But I ain't letting no rider of mine stand for them knives. Not till I know you're good."

Fiero showed his teeth.

"Yes, yes. You are right. But the trouble is I am too God-damn good. If I wasn't so good, I wouldn't put the knife in the head. To-morrow I do three more perfectoes and the day after I do three more, then I put the lady in. Yes? The great act, Fiero and Signorina Carolina. We get on the posters, don't you think?"

"I don't think. Go ask Bisbee. Anyway, she'll be Mrs. Hanna by the time you stick a knife into her."

"Mrs. Hanna? Signora Hanna." He shook his head. "The name is no good." He recollected himself and turned to Chad. "I felicitate you, you and Miss Trid both." He smiled tragically. Joe murmured, "I bet he was planning to marry her himself."

"Why not?" Bastock said, watching the juggler stride out of the tent. "He told me once it was a lot better to be married to your target because if you hit her she can't testify against you. Probably he's scared now." He wiggled his shoulders. "All the better. He won't be in such a hurry to start sticking her."

Budlong said, "That was a pretty name he called her,
Signorina Carolina. It would be a good name to bill her
with."

Chad shook his head.

"I ain't going to be married to a Dago. If I was managing
this shebang, I would turn all the names American. Then we'd
have a talking point against the big shows. I bet people would
like it. Americans for America; riding against the talent of
Europe."

Bastock nodded thoughtfully.

"I wouldn't wonder you were right, Chaddy. Why don't we
just call her Carolina? I never figured out why Albany didn't
go under her own name, playing New York State. How do you
like Carolina, Missy?"

"I think it's nice."

"Just Carolina," Chad said. "People will try to figure out
who she is and why she's named that. They'll start talking."

"Well," said Bastock. "I wouldn't wonder if she was using
it sooner than we planned."

"What you talking about?" asked Joe. "You mean a show
appearance?"

"I just got an idea of it, that's all." Bastock refused to be
worked on. He coiled the pratique strap.

"Will she wear a skirt or will she wear trunks?" Joe asked.
He stared frankly at Caroline. "She sure had a pretty leg, but
a buttock . . ."

"You shut up."

"Down in Virginia they come fatter," Budlong said. "It's a
queer thing. I always figured it was their partiality to smoked
ham."

"Bisbee and the gaffer will dress her," Bastock said.

Chad didn't enter the discussion. He took the pad horse by
the cheek strap and led him out of the tent with Caroline alongside. She said, "I wonder what Pete is figuring on."

"I don't know."

"I wouldn't dare to ride before an audience," she said. Then
she looked under the horse's head at him. "Would you like me
to wear trunks or a gauze skirt?"

He said, "I don't know. I like you in trunks. I think it
would be easier riding."

"Yes." She wrinkled her nose thoughtfully. "A skirt is

nore ladylike, though. Those gauze ones. Like what a dancer
vears. I saw a picture of one once. I'd like to look like her."

"You look all right whatever you've got on," Chad said.

She glanced sidewise at him, and looked away. She was
pleased.

"I'm going to be awful scared though." She reached up to
pat the horse. He arched his neck for her. "He's good," she
said. "He's nice. I love him. It's funny I never thought to ask
his name. What is it?"

"I don't know," Chad said.

She was amazed.

"Hasn't he got one?"

"No, they just call him the pad horse."

"But he's wise. He's so honest. He likes me, too. He likes
both of us. He ought to have a name," she said excitedly.

Her earnestness surprised Chad; but it pleased him too,
and he had to agree with her.

"Yes, he ought to."

"Why don't we name him? He could have a name with us
both, then. What would you call him?"

Chad said, "You want short names for horses. Like Dick,
or Prince or Buck."

"Buck," she said soberly. "When I joined out I thought he
was the most beautiful, loveliest horse that ever was. But now I
think—he is. He's got to have a name. It wouldn't be nice
otherwise."

"He is a good horse," Chad said. "He's handsome."

"He's faithful and he knows what to do. He wouldn't ever
go wrong with a rider, ever. I know it."

"You ought to name him."

They could see the barn ahead, the roof rising up behind the
hotel, and there were some people on the porch watching them.
Caroline said shyly, "I've thought of a name, but it isn't a short
one."

"What is it?"

"Jonathan."

"I don't know," Chad said. "What's it for?"

"He was a faithful friend," she said. "Once when Pa was
away, Ma took me and Andrew and Paul to the church picnic.
And a man told us children a story after eating. I don't remember what it was about, except battles and a king fighting against

savage people. I don't remember his name, but he had a friend
named Jonathan. And Jonathan always looked out for him, and
he died fighting for him. I've always remembered him."

"Then I think it's a good name," Chad said.

"Do you really?"

"Yes. We can call him John for short if we want to."

"I shall always call him Jonathan." She stroked the horse.
"Do you like that name, Jonathan?" He pricked cream-
coloured ears. "I think he knows it's his name," she said.

They had got used to people staring at them. Generally they
paid no attention; but the voices on the hotel porch were loud,
and one of them was Mr. Huguenine's.

"By God, you can't do it!" he was saying.

"Well, I am."

The second speaker was Mr. Burke. He looked just the same,
in his sober black clothes. His blue eyes were icily contained; he
studied Mr. Huguenine the way he would study a penned bull.

5

TROUBLE FOR HUGUENINE

HUGUENINE not only looked like a penned bull, he bellowed like
one. For a mild man it was extraordinary. Either he was in
bad trouble, Chad thought, or he was mad as hell.

Huguenine was both.

"For God's sake Mr. Burke, I won't have no show without
her."

Mr. Burke flicked a long ash off his cigar.

"I told you to watch out, Huguenine. I gave you warning.
But you decided to butt in anyway. You cut into our route. Of
course, it's going to ruin you. That's the whole idea."

He reminded Chad of Mrs. Mott picking beetles off her
front-yard flowers. She would take them cleverly by the head,
and pinch. The sweat rolled down Huguenine's face.

"We ain't hurt your business," he said. "We're a little
show. I took the mortgage just to help the feller out. I don't
expect to make big money out of it. I just want to pay up on my

own investment. You ain't got no legal right to one route any more than I have to another."

Any one but Huguenine could have seen it was no use arguing. " Sure, the route belongs to anybody," Burke agreed. " That's why I'm taking it. I've got the money to see it's mine, too. There just ain't room for any but Flatfoot shows here." He drew on his cigar, studied the ash, and pointed it the way a schoolteacher would his rod. " *I* can get along without Lady Lillian. But *you* can't. I can afford to hire her even when I don't need her. But she's a good act," he conceded graciously. " The horse is hers, too, so she brings him along. You haven't got a prayer."

So that was it. That was what they'd talked about in Auburn. Albany had known all week. Chad's eyes strayed over the porch. The circus people made a group at one end ; the Pamplons with worried eyes, translating what they heard in their French minds ; Fiero, flashing eyes and teeth uncomprehendingly and smiling hard at Mr. Burke ; Ike Wayfish, with the skirts of his clown coat hanging over the rails, and looking like a traveller in hymn-books. At the other end three or four hotel inmates tried to appear not to listen, and in the front door between them, the proprietor, leaning his hand against the jamb, estimated the likliehood of trouble.

Mr. Huguenine gulped.

" I got a contract," he said. " By God, I've got a contract."

" Sure," said Mr. Burke. " I don't doubt it. But she's breaking it."

" I'll get a lawyer," said Huguenine. " I'll bring you into court, so help me God."

" Go ahead," said Mr. Burke. " See where that gets you."

" I'd rather go to the poorhouse than be rode off by you."

" You probably will," Mr. Burke said, tilting his head. " Mr. Brewster," he said to the proprietor, " tell your groom to bring my rig around front as soon as the lady's bags are in. And hitch her horse to the lead ring. I guess she's about ready by now," he remarked to the company at large. His eyes caught sight of the cream pad and Chad and Caroline. " Hallo," he said.

Chad said, " Hallo."

Mr. Burke smiled evenly.

Chad said, " Suppose *we* start making trouble. You're quite a long ways from your show."

Mr. Burke continued to smile but his eyes chilled.

" I wouldn't advise you to try it." He tilted his head back and called for Mr. Brewster. " Sheriff inside ? Tell him I'd like to see him."

Even before the sheriff appeared, wiping Burke's whisky from his lips with his shirt sleeve, Chad saw there was nothing Huguenine could possibly do.

Mr. Burke said, " We've had kind of a disagreement, sheriff."

" Yep ? " The sheriff looked Mr. Huguenine over. " Yep," he said. He leaned against the doorjamb.

" This is a nice orderly town," remarked Mr. Burke.

" She sure is," said the sheriff.

He looked dubious, but he was willing to be told by a man of Mr. Burke's obvious importance.

" I guess you only allow moral shows here ? "

" I guess so."

Mr. Burke uncrossed his legs and recrossed them.

" Have a cigar, sheriff ? "

" Much obliged." The sheriff took the cigar, bit it, and examined Mr. Huguenine throughout the process.

Nobody said anything, and in the silence they heard the quick light heel taps of Albany on the stairs. She came out dressed for driving, her bonnet tied down snugly. She stopped for a moment, looking them over, and then she smiled.

" Good-bye, everybody," she said.

" Albany." Mr. Huguenine was hoarse. " You ain't just going to quit on me ? On all of us ? "

" I'm sorry," she said. She sounded sorry. Then she glanced at Mr. Burke and arranged the ends of her shawl. " Mr. Burke has made me a handsome offer. I accepted it."

" I know," Huguenine said. " But you might have told me. I got this town billed with you. I got Lyons and Palmyra billed. Why, I got you billed all the way out beyond Albion now. Besides, you signed a contract."

" Did I ? I'm sorry. But Mr. Burke asked me not to mention it." Her chin came up, bringing the bow of the bonnet ribbons with it. " Which one of you wouldn't do the same if you got the offer ? " she asked defiantly. " I want money, and Burke and Walsh are going to pay it to me."

She offered her hand to Mr. Burke, who had risen, and he tucked it in his arm and escorted her down the steps. A groom brought the rig round the corner from the barn and cramped the wheel while Mr. Burke handed her up.

Her bag was back of the seat. Another man led Buck out. She watched him fasten the lead rope. "Not too short," she admonished. "He likes to make play." She smiled at the man.

"All right, Miss Yates?" Mr. Burke asked.

"My saddle," she said suddenly.

"I've got a better saddle all waiting for you. Brand-new. English-made." He climbed in, settled himself, flicked the ash clean, and picked up the reins. He glanced back at Jonathan.

"Want to deal on that pad horse, Huguenine?"

Chad heard Caroline draw a sharp breath. But Huguenine said, "No."

"I'll make you a cash offer."

"Make me a dozen," said Huguenine. "And go to hell. I hope you break your neck."

Mr. Burke said, "Ready?" to Albany, and, when she nodded, started the horses. They went down the street at a smart trot, neither of them looking back. Jonathan lifted his head and turned it after them. He whinnied once, but Buck was straightened out by the lead rope and the dust was against his chest.

"Well," Chad said, "I might as well stable you."

He led the cream-coloured horse round the porch. Caroline said, "I wonder where Fred is."

Nobody knew where Shepley was, and nobody else seemed interested. Huguenine sagged off the porch and plodded away towards the tent; the Pamplons stared vacuously at Caroline for a moment before going inside to their rooms, and Fiero followed their example with a sad but encouraging smile for Caroline.

Ike Wayfish continued to sit on the rail, and when he saw that Caroline did not intend to follow the other, he cleared his throat companionably.

"You can't blame her. She's wanted a chance in a big show for years."

"I suppose not," Caroline said. "But I don't see why Mr. Burke had to do it."

"It's this syndicate, the Flatfoots. They dassn't let any

show get a following where they stand. Just like any other business."

"Are they so big?"

"They surely are. They've got four or five shows. Some they own and some they just rent stock to. They get wild animals in Africa and bring them over. They have to show a profit; they don't care what becomes of the people they ride out. If you get strong enough so they can't drive you out, they buy you in. With a show like this it's cheaper to ride you out. If Burke and Walsh don't want Albany next year, they'll find her another show or they'll drop her. But she's good enough to stick, I guess."

"What do you think Mr. Huguenine is going to do?"

Wayfish put his hands on his knees, found a loose thread on one, and picked at it.

"I don't know. He can't think of anything without Bisbee around."

The people at the end of the porch were watching them, the women drawing together to whisper, the men frankly looking at Caroline's faded tights, though the cloak partly covered them. Caroline felt better when Chad finally came round the hotel corner and joined them in the sun.

He asked, "Do you think we'll show in Lyons, now?"

"I don't know," Wayfish said. "A.D.'s a stubborn cuss."

"It won't do us much good, I guess."

"No."

Inside the hotel a clock struck eleven.

"Heavens!" Caroline exclaimed. "I'll have to get ready for the parade."

"I'll wait here for you," Chad said.

She gave him a quick grateful smile.

"Caroline's a real nice girl," Ike Wayfish observed. He boosted himself off the rail. "Want a drink?"

"No thanks."

Chad sat down alone, conscious of the stares of the porch-sitters, but ignoring them. He tried to figure it out. They had Shepley and they had the lion; if Oscar could keep healthy for a while, they ought to be able to get along somehow. He wondered how much money Albany's going would save the show in salary. If they broke down he ought to be able to get work somewhere. He could support himself easily enough; but getting married altered things. Still, Caroline wouldn't expect a lot, not the way she had been raised. They ought to get along. Maybe they better put off the champagne wine.

He noticed that the porch-sitters were still staring at him, and he wondered what they would think of a circus hand trying to figure how he could get married just the same as any young man.

6

LYONS

THE performance in Clyde was dismal. Though the town couldn't have known that the star equestrienne had quit, there had been not more than three dozen paid admissions, and the only applause came from a few small boys who had sneaked under the canvas. There had been no point in putting them out.

The only person who showed no reaction was Mr. Huguenine himself. He worked through his announcements with the same degree of perspiring uneasiness that he showed in a full tent. He stumbled over the " gymnats " exactly as he always did. His only pause came when Lady Lillian's act should have come on. He started to announce her, recollected himself, and for the first time actually got his chewing tobacco into his mouth. He bit hard and bawled to the three dozen confused spectators that owing to an unfortunate episode in Port Byron in which Huguenine's Great and Only International Circus's star equestrienne had broken both legs and a collarbone, the act had been temporarily discontinued. They would pass on to the even more startling performance of the world's leading high-rider, the great Signor Rossello with his death-defying disregard for the laws of gravity in his somersault on the back of his galloping horse. It was an improvisation to feel proud of and Mrs. Huguenine clapped heartily.

The main trouble was that Fred Shepley refused even to attempt the somersault. He had been sullen, speaking to no one before the parade and keeping moodily to himself before his entrance. Afterwards he stayed long enough to knock down some of the seats, and then without a word went off to the hotel. The skinners tore down the round-top and stowed it, and the rest of the company gathered at the lot to hear what Huguenine would have to say. They were waiting when he finally emerged from the treasury wagon, where he had been making a recount of the day's receipts. His face was glum.

"What's the matter with you?" he asked irascibly. "We ought to get started."

"We going to Lyons?" Wayfish asked.

"Yes," Mr. Huguenine bit the word and laid it down.

"We going to show?"

"We're advertised, ain't we?"

"Burke and Walsh will be showing the same stand," Bastock pointed out. "They ain't going to like it."

A kind of dignity settled on Huguenine's stolid face.

"I told that feller I wouldn't let him run me off the route. But he'll think he has if you don't get going."

"Suppose he tries to burn us out?"'

"Seen a show get burned out in Alabama," Budlong amplified the notion. "Gaffer was a stubborn feller. He got his warning not to show the next town. It was Point Comfort. He raised the tent and took tickets. They burned his tent."

"What did he die of?" Joe Duddy asked.

"Cholera morbus," Budlong said. "He caught it from the monkey."

"We'll show," said Mr. Huguenine. He climbed to the box of the treasury wagon and yelled over his shoulder, "You set, Bettina?"

The wagon lurched as Mrs. Huguenine moved from the small window and settled on the bed. "You bet your neck, A.D.," she called cheerfully. For once the treasury wagon rolled out ahead of the light rig.

Ike Wayfish shrugged. "Well, it's his money. We'll only get our heads broke. You boys and girls all ready?"

The Pamplons and Fiero climbed aboard; Shepley was already seated. Caroline said, "Can I come with you, Mr. Bastock?"

The little man shook his head. "No. If there's trouble, I'd have to take care of you instead of myself."

She got into the wagon without a word, taking the seat beside the clown. But when they started, she cast an anxious look back at Chad, telling him with her eyes to be careful. It made him feel good.

Bastock said, " It's my idea we better raise the rag to-night, if Burke ain't there to bother us."

" I believe in it," Budlong cheeked his spit. " If you got the rag all set, and the pegs all drove and the gimmix loose in your paw, all you do is knock at the heads butting in."

He mounted to his high seat, unloading his cheek on the way up. The tent wagon rolled heavily. The others followed. It felt queer to Chad, having only two horses ; and for the first time he actively missed Buck.

The cream pad moved up alongside Jerry as if he felt lonely also. He came in close, and the two horses started matching strides, arching their necks together as if they took pleasure in it. The notion came to Chad that they could be worked together in the ring in a two-horse act. They kept so even that it looked as if anybody could get up on their flat rumps and ride them standing. But he dismissed the temptation of trying it himself. A man who was going to get married in two or three days had no business risking a broken leg. . . .

Beyond Lock Berlin, the road crossed to the south side of the canal and headed due west ; but the canal came back again, with Lyons on the other side, and the wagons crossed the second bridge about seven o'clock and rolled into the village when householders were coming out on their porches after supper. Boys, playing backyard games, were lured forth by the sound of heavy wheels ; they stared a minute in disbelief ; then the cry went up : " It's the circus." For a short space it seemed as though good times had returned to Huguenine's. The boys were gathering a train ; and there was no better advertising in the world. " Look at the horses," they shouted, as Chad came along. They asked him what was in the cage. When he told them, those who heard became important. " There's the lion. Right in there" They ran boldly close, laying careless hands on the sides.

But a piercing voice rose at a cross street.

" I don't see no elerphunt."

Some tavern idlers turned their heads to tacked-up posters on the wall under the porch, looked back at the weathered wagons.

" That ain't Burke and Walsh. It's just a little show. It ain't got no elerphunt at all."

One or two boys, less sophisticated, still followed the cream-coloured pad horse ; but after the rest had melted away, they too dropped behind, and Huguenine's caravan pulled into the lot with nothing but the solitary treasury wagon to greet them. Budlong threw down the reins."

"A.D.," he yelled.

But Huguenine wasn't there ; only Mrs. Huguenine. The treasury wagon swayed as she came to the window. "I ain't dressed," she yelled back. "A.D.'s gone to the store. What do you want with him ? "

"Does he still figure to show, ma'am ? "

"I don't know. He didn't say different." She spoke with dignity. "A.D.'s stubborn, you know. He ain't likely to quit just because Burke tells him to." Her voice brightened. "You boys figure to lift the rag to-night ? If you do, I'll help as soon as I get this dress over my head."

She pulled the curtain modestly. As Bastock wheeled into the lot, Budlong said to him, "The gaffer's going to show."

"We might as well set her up," Bastock said. "I want to practise Caroline, anyway. Where's Ike ? Where's A.D. ? "

"Trading. I don't know where Ike is. I just got here," Budlong complained.

It was the third time that they had handled the canvas that day and the work went slow. The sun had set long before they got her raised, and they had to peg down the ring curb by lantern light. Mrs. Huguenine brought a stewpot into the tent for the skinners. She seemed anxious to please them, and she said they had had no time to get food and anyway she would like the stew cleaned up. It was rich in gravy, having been carried for two days, and they were grateful for it. They told her it was good. She beamed on them. "I wish I had my oven," she said. "Some nights I just keep thinking of a plate of hot biscuit with a teaspoonful of butter inside each and syrup over them. I keep thinking of that a mile to a time."

The performers came to the tent while the skinners were still eating. Caroline sat down next to Chad. Fiero set up his target board but the lantern light wasn't bright enough. The Pamplons looked lonesome and uneasy. Wayfish reported that Shepley had gone off after supper, without saying where he was headed for. "I guess he was looking for a sight of Albany," Ike said. "I went down to the other hotel and found she was staying there. The clerk told me she had the room next to Burke's and he was paying a dollar a day for it besides her food." It seemed wonderful to think of a circus paying out money like that on a single performer. Ike went on, " I seen one of their posters, too, a new one, and I took it off the board. There wasn't nobody round at the time."

He held it out. It announced Burke and Walsh's Mammoth Arena and Amphitheatre with the now familiar cut of the male and female riders posed before draperies. But as an added special extra attraction for the instruction and edification of the audience, it stated that the famous equestrienne, LADY LIL-LIAN, would appear in an important part of the performance, in her solo ride on the celebrated Arabian horse, BUCE-PHALUS. She would leap four-foot hurdles in the ring. (" They got room for jumping in a tent that size, I guess," Wayfish said.) " Her style of equitation is talented, graceful, and without parallel in any hemisphere, the march to the beat of the drum martial and spirited, and the waltz to the accompaniment of the full band of music undeniably sublime."

" She never done that with us," Joe Duddy said.

" We didn't have no full band of music," Budlong pointed out.

" Hell, I beat the drum all right, didn't I ? "

" What is it, anyway ? " Caroline asked. " I mean the waltz."

Chad said, " I guess she sidesteps him and makes him change lead." He thought of that early morning ride, back in Canastota, when she rode out patterns through the trees. " I don't know if it would look much like waltzing."

Anything would look good if you have a full band of music," Bastock said.

They passed the poster from hand to hand, regarding it gloomily. " She ain't got a picture of herself the way she had in our posters," Mrs. Huguenine pointed out, but no one else seemed to share her satisfaction. They clustered wordlessly in the ring, their faces lit dimly by the lantern light, which threw glum shadows of them on the under-curve of the round-top. In the silence outside they heard one of the horses hopefully blowing in his feed box for a stray oat.

Bastock said suddenly, " No sense in just setting here. Do you think you could practise, Missy, if we hung some lanterns on the pole ? "

Caroline said, " I'll try."

" Bring in the pad, Chaddy."

Caroline went out with Chad to get Jonathan. She held the bridle while Chad saddled him with the pad. The horse craned his head towards the feed boxes of the wagon teams ; he could not understand why he had not been fed ; and his mane drew over Caroline's face. It was still in the lot. The new moon lay on its back above a tree shape in the west.

Caroline said, " I made a wish on the moon last night."

" Did you ? " Chad was working on the pad, his head under the flap. His voice was muffled and short.

" Yes. I always try to wish on a new moon, seeing it over the right shoulder. That's luck. They say if you wish for money and say money to yourself, you'll never lack cash, if your wants aren't too much. I don't want a great deal."

" Is that what you wished for ? "

" It spoils the wish to tell it."

" Well, I hope you wished for money."

" Chad, what do you think's going to happen ? "

" I don't know."

" I wish Mr. Bisbee was here. He'd know what to do. Do you think Burke and Walsh will do anything to us ? "

" How should I know ? What do you want to ask questions for all the time ? "

" I'm sorry. I didn't know I was."

" Well, you was."

" It seemed so lonely in the tent. All of us seemed lonely. I had to talk. But I won't ask any more, I don't want you to be mad at me."

" I ain't mad," he said, coming round Jonathan's shoulder. He could make her out faintly, her hand on the arch of the horse's neck, her cheek against his mane, one knee bent. " Give me a kiss," he ordered.

She put up her face obediently through the horse's mane, but Chad caught hold of her, pulling her tight against him. He felt her shiver and kissed her hard.

When he let go of her, she asked, " You haven't changed your mind ? "

" No." He jerked the horse's bridle impatiently. He felt fine again walking with her towards the dark tent. There was something almost humble in the way she came with him that made him forget the labour of raising the canvas a second time in one day. She belonged to him. If he wanted to tell her to do something, she would do it.

The pad horse pricked ears at the entrance. He wasn't used to night practice and the tent looked strange to him with the lanterns hanging from the centre pole. The ring seemed to be sunk into the grass, the round-top to float high.

The performers had moved over to the seats, except for Wayfish, who with Bastock talked to Mr. Huguenine in the ring. Huguenine had his hat off. The light glistened on his perspiring forehead. He listened to them stolidly, watching the shadows of Bastock's hands moving on the grass at his feet.

" She won't be ready to ride by herself for a month," Bastock was saying. " But Ike can carry her through. He's willing."

" I'm glad to do it," Ike said. " She's got gifts."

Chad touched Caroline's arm, and she started and smiled a little. But her face was pale and intent.

Huguenine grunted. " If she's any good I'll have to pay her. And I'll have to pay for new paper."

" You've got to do that anyway, A.D.," Mrs. Huguenine called, fanning herself on the top seat. She was enjoying the novelty of the whole business.

" Sure, sure," Huguenine complained. " But where's the money coming from ? I ain't no Flatfoot. I ain't no syndicate. God damn it, I'm just a farmer, and what I know is farming."

" Well, you've got you a circus now. She'll die unless we get another act going. The show wasn't anything in Clyde."

" I get the knife throw perfectoed," Fiero broke in eagerly.

" Wait till you do," Bastock said.

" Only now and then I miss not hitting the head," the juggler said. " It is a little inch."

" Sure, you're fine, Fiero." Bastock caught sight of the three in the entrance. " Bring him in," he said. " It won't hurt you to watch, A.D. Let's see how the horse goes in lantern light."

The pad horse stepped high over the ring, put down his head, and blew softly when Bastock started him. But he fell into his trained gait once he was moving and the light shone on the pad, picking it out brightly, an island floating over the ground.

Ike Wayfish took off his coat.

" I ain't got my tights," he said. " But I don't mind trousers."

" No vaulting to-night," Bastock said. " You ain't used to it.

C.H.

I

We'll put Caroline up." He called Caroline over, helped her on to the pad. " Set back, Caroline. Now, Ike."

" What do we do, Pete ? "

" Try making your feet, first you, then her. You ain't got no pratique on, Missy," he reminded her.

Ike rose easily, turning to face Caroline. He gave her his hand, riding backwards, the look of astonishment he always assumed automatically covering his face. They stood rather unsteadily on the moving pad, then caught their balance.

" Let go of him, Missy. You all right ? If you feel you're going, jump clean. Turn around, Ike. Now take his belt, Missy ; that's fine."

It was a fumbling business ; but with Ike's assurance, and his belt in reach, Caroline gained her own confidence, and a picture suddenly came out of the riding—the red-nosed lout and the graceful, long-legged girl. Chad saw it at once ; and even Huguenine's face brightened. Bastock, flashing a glance at him, nodded.

" It's got comedy," he said.

Chad said, " You could start her alone, and then Ike could run out and vault in front of her and pretend to be falling off, and she would try to catch him. We could call it courtship or something."

" Courtship of the Lout Lubin," said Ike ; " we can work it out. In the end I take my clothes off and show my expensive costume and she lets me kiss her hand. It would be pretty."

Bastock agreed. " When he's in tights, then they can do their posing. It's a good idea, Chaddy. Now, try changing places. No. It ain't safe. You get off, Ike, and mount back of her."

Before they had thought, Caroline was left alone, riding the pad on her feet. Standing close to the curb, looking up at her, Chad saw how absorbed she was. He wasn't in her mind at all ; she smiled at him, but she smiled the same way at Budlong and Joe and Mr. Huguenine.

" Set down ! " bawled Bastock.

She came out of herself, then her smile widening.

" You didn't tell me to, Mr. Bastock," she said maliciously.

" I thought you had sense. Look out."

Now that she was seeing their faces, her balance deserted her. She went over the off side, jumping just in time, and striking on her hands and one knee. " My stars," cried Mrs. Huguenine.

She had torn her tights over the knee and the knee was scraped. It made her limp. Bastock was swearing frantically. " Can you walk ? " he shouted.

" It's just a scrape. It's not stiff." She showed him. " When I started looking at all of you the lights seemed to look queer. I just wasn't paying attention."

" Well, get up again," he said. " Stop that horse."

The pad horse stopped, moving his ears.

" Why don't you give her a chance to catch her wind ? " Chad asked.

" Damn her wind," said Bastock. " She's had a fall. The only thing is to work the notion right out of her as long as she can move. If she wasn't a female I'd give her a licking to take her mind off it." He was angry at himself and her.

Ike acted anxious at her unsteadiness when they had mounted again in reverse positions. " Take her by the waist," Bastock said.

" Now, you, you feeling all right ? "

Caroline said, " Yes."

" All right. Begin doing your exercises."

He watched while she did her leg stretches backward past Ike's middle. Ike held her steady. She had nothing to hold on to herself, and her arms were poised for balance. It had a kind of fascination, watching the girl's legs and body adapt themselves to the problem of balance. At moments, when the poise was perfect, she seemed almost afloat in the lantern light.

There was not much to it, but it made a routine of sorts, and to the little audience of tired performers and skinners it was new. As Bastock said, there was a lot to be added to it. The toe-to-mouth, the leg-forward, the foot-around, with Ike and Caroline changing hands. " We'll try putting her on in Pittsford," he said.

7

THE ELEPHANT COMES TO TOWN

CAROLINE was not destined to make her bow to the public in Pittsford, but they did not know that then. They were all hopeful after that night practice ; it encouraged them to think that they might be building a brand-new act. There weren't many female riders who could pose on a pad. It made Chad excited and proud to see the notice they all took of Caroline.

" I don't feel like sleeping yet," he said. " Do you ? "

Caroline shook her head.

" Aren't you tired, though ? "

" No. Anyway, with the old rag all set up, I can sleep late to-morrow. How about going down and seeing if the big show's come in yet ? "

" I'd like to," she said.

" Then go change your clothes while I put up the horses. I'll meet you at the hotel."

He watched Caroline through the front door and saw the people in the office look after her as she crossed to the stairs. He could imagine that happening in times to come, when she was famous. " I'll probably still be raising canvas," he thought. She would be bound to grow ambitious. The first thing he knew she wouldn't want to hang around with a one horse show ; she would want a full band of music ; and somebody like Burke would turn up to offer it to her. Chad would just be tagging along. He knew he would never have the ambition or the talent to become a first-class rider himself.

When he finished with the horses, he ambled round to the porch, standing quiet in the darkness, the way he used to scout for Mrs. Mott at the Yellow Bud. There weren't any lights. The only illumination came from the hotel windows.

Caroline was waiting for him in her print dress, her head bonneted, her reticule swinging nervously in her fingers. She was watching for him, but she hadn't seen him ; and he stayed still enjoying the look of her, all feminine, and much younger than she seemed riding, and he saw she was anxious for him to get there.

" Here I am," he said, enjoying her start. She ran at once down the steps and took his arm. She was wearing the locket ; he smelled the perfume as she walked beside him down the street. She kept close up to him, matching her steps to his. She was fun to walk with that way, quick, and light, and full of life.

They stopped on the canal bridge, to stare eastward along the dark thread of water. There was a bow lantern so far off that it seemed stationary and they studied it a long time before they made out which way it was moving.

Chad heard her draw her breath slowly.

" What is it ? "

" I was thinking how you must have gone by our house," she said. " When you were driving. And I never knew it."

" Knew what ? "

" That I was going to be your wife. Maybe I even saw you." She turned her head. " What did you look like, Chad ? "

" Just like any other hoggie. Pretty dirty. Half naked, probably." He grinned. " I knew your place. Lots of times, when we were hauling past Canastota on the night trick, I'd think if I could keep awake past Trid's house, I'd be all right."

" Maybe you even saw me," she went on with her thought.

" I might have."

" I didn't look like much, either." She was silent. Then she said in a low, fierce little voice, " If you and me . . . if we have children, I won't let them run around the way I did, being dirty, hearing dirty talk."

" Even tenting ? " he asked. " Not even if I got to be like . . ." He caught himself. ". . . If I turn out lazy and no good, just projecting after easy money, never doing no work, getting drunk all the while ? "

" Like Pa ? Why don't you say it ? But you won't. I won't let you. But even if you did, my children wouldn't live dirty."

He had to admire her ; she had seemed so young ; and now she was talking this way about him and her and the children. Children seemed a long way off for him. He didn't think of them, getting married. But he didn't mind her talking of them if she wanted to ; it aroused pleasant speculations. He let himself hang over the railing, watching the black water and the bow lantern coming along it towards them. He could see its reflection now, even though he couldn't yet make out the horses.

" Suppose I got to be tough and started knocking you around ? "

She took the notion calmly.

" You won't. Because I won't let you. I made up my mind about you a long time ago. Do you think I'll let you change it ? "

She didn't lean against the rail ; she was erect. He imagined he could make out the line of her small jaw under the bonnet brim. And he found he was believing her. She was chock full of wanting to live ; she aimed to make herself a good life ; and she had picked him to help her. She was so durned serious about it.

He grinned to himself.

" I wonder why they make bonnets like that ? "

" Why ? " He could tell from her voice that he would always be able to startle her.

" Because if a feller wants to kiss a girl, he just about has to make a full dive and come up underneath to do it."

She put it back off her head with one quick sweep of hand and arm.

" Oh, Chad."

After a minute she said, " You keep talking about marrying and raising children. Have you stopped to think that two days from this minute you and me *will* be married ? "

" What do you think I've been thinking about ? "

" Well," he said. " Maybe getting to be a female star per-former."

Her voice was sarcastic. "A lot you know. What do you think a girl would think about just before she's getting married ? What do you think I'm like ? " She moved quickly to him, putting her arms hard round his waist and lifting her face. " Don't you like me ? "

" Yes," he said, saying the word into her mouth.

She loosed herself.

" I think we better go look for Burke and Walsh."

" All right." He started off the bridge but she touched his arm with the tips of her fingers.

" I want to be married right, Chad. I wish I had bed linen, and china and some glass and even clothes to bring with me."

" What would we do with chinaware ? " he asked.

" It's what a girl ought to have. I'm not bringing anything."

" Well, I'm not either. I never even knew who my father and mother were. We're starting out from scratch. Maybe we'll have more fun that way."

" Yes, maybe. Trousseaus is what they call them. Rich people."

" Is it ? " Chad ambled along easily in one rut, letting her pick her way along the other, the fishbone of sod dividing them. " Ain't that light on the road, Caroline ? "

She stopped and stared.

" I think so. It's not a house light. It's moving. There's another one, behind it."

" Must be a roll in the ground. They're coming over it. There's number three."

" Four," Caroline counted.

" They must be the light wagons. I guess that's the lot, down there. It's been mowed. We can stand under that tree and they'll turn in by us."

They entered the lot where the bars were down and moved along the fence towards the tree. Its shadow hid them. It had low branches and made fingers against the sky.

A man was carrying a lantern across the lot, and Chad saw now that there was a wagon by the far fence. The man wished them good-evening. " You come to see the circus pull in ? " he asked.

" We have," Chad said.

" You want to come and see it to-morrow and bring the lady. The tent will be up then. She's quite a sight. You can see the show for a quarter of a dollar, twenty-five cents. You want to see the freaks. Greatest concourse of human oddities ever seen in this state."

" What is there ? " Caroline asked.

" Well, take Ella, the girl without any limbs. Ma'am, you would certainly like to see her. Drinks, sews, cuts paper with her mouth. She's got beautiful features, sir. Yes, sir, cut the legs and arms off all the women in this country and Ella McChesney would still be the belle of the ball."

" Got a fat lady ? " Chad asked.

" Sure. Only she's a child. Five years old."

" How much does she weigh ? "

" Two oh five in a silk kimono. This here's a moral enter-tainment. You ought to see the dwarfs, mister," he said when

Chad made no comment on the fat child. "And the Living Skeleton. All for ten cents, mister. I'll be looking for you."

He passed them, going through the bars and taking a stand in the road, where he started to swing his lantern. By its light, Chad and Caroline made out a group of figures coming down the bridge from the village. They picked out Bastock and Budlong in the forefront, and then realised that practically all of Huguenine's company had decided to see the show roll in. Caroline called and waved her arm, and they all congregated under the apple tree.

They were just in time. The first wagons were rolling along the straight stretch, the horses quickening stride as they saw the lantern being swung. The rolls of wheels, the stamp of hoofs, gained volume. The lantern swinger started bawling, "Right in, Jed. Right in and clear across. Solid going all the way. Had a good trip?"

"Sure. Roads are all right. Had to shore up a crick bridge for the tent wagon."

The teamster swung his team through the bars and the eveners crashed as the tugs slacked going off the road shoulder, and then snapped up the weight as the horses levelled out.

Mrs. Huguenine put back her shawl. "Hunh! That wagon don't look nothing extra. Look at its paint."

The second wagon rolled in close. The lantern caught a scroll of gilt paint. BURKE, WALSH & Co. A couple of light rigs followed it, drawn by single horses.

"Lucky boy rigs," Bastock said. "Here's two more." He spat. "Moral show, hey?"

Then another heavy team, dragging a bigger wagon, went off the road and the load banged heavily. Seat jacks. It was followed by another just as big, and then a third smaller one loaded just with planks.

Across the field the wagons were lining along the fence, their lanterns making a glow. The man with the hand lantern ran into the lot and marked off where the seat wagons were to stop.

"Plenty of figuring to a show with this many wagons," muttered Bastock. Nobody else said anything. It was being borne in on them that this was the kind of concern that could roll right over Huguenine's Great and Only International Circus and hardly feel a bump.

After the seventh wagon had driven in, the ring stock came along the road and they seemed to make a herd. One of the teams in the lot started whinnying ; they were answered down the road ; the Huguenine troupe heard a spatter of hoofs ; a man yelped by the bars, and the ring stock trotted through, heads up in their cloud of dust, and were driven to a corner where men caught them and haltered them and tied them to the fence.

Someone had started a bonfire, feeding it with a bag of straw, so that the flames leaped and threw a light all over the lot, even on to the road. A rig went by the bars, keeping on the road for the village, and was followed by two more. " They got coaches," someone said under the apple tree. " Look at that. They can let down the curtains when it rains just as if they'd bought tickets."

Then the tent wagons, two of them, each with a four horse hitch, rolled heavily along the road, turned off with groaning reaches, and headed for the bonfire. The horses were beauties, matched Conestoga Chunks, fat and strong.

" I guess that's all," Ike said. " I'm going to bed, myself."

He started for the road, the others following him. But as they neared the bars, Bastock cocked his head suddenly.

" Wait a minute. Look."

They hadn't heard anything from the road; the voices in the field had settled into a steady current of sound, like the noise of water ; and the shape rocked down towards them, deliberately treading the dust, with a gentle, almost wistful rumbling in its inside. It was enormous.

They saw it first over the rails in the faint outer zone of fire-light : a bulging, thoughtful looking skull and swaying ears, dark grey, with a hypnotic sway of its high shoulders. But as it drew abreast of them they saw the small eye caught in firelight, the sagging lip and hanging trunk, and the tired man who tramped beside it. They could read no expression in the beast's face ; intelligence in anything so huge would be incredible. But it had seen them by the fence. Suddenly its trunk reached sidewise, straightened, so that the end travelled with a tiny hook along the upper rail, pointing to one after another of the people. When it came to Mrs. Huguenine, the hook raised, straightening, still sideways, and from the end of it came an unexpected brief little puff of hay smelling wind. The ribbons on Mrs. Huguenine's bonnet stood straight up. She cried, " My stars and body ! " And the trudging man seemed to wake himself.

" Hey there, Grace," he said sharply, striking the trunk with the palm of his hand, a dry, harsh, rasping sound. The trunk immediately fell into its former pendent posture, coiled on itself above the dust in the road. The great solemn stride was uninterrupted ; the ears, however, sailed forward for a moment. Then only the hindquarters were visible. Somehow they looked queerly out of place, and they reminded Chad of a snotty old woman passing Sunday loafers on a hotel porch.

" I thought I was going to be killed," gasped Mrs. Huguenine. " What was it ? "

" The elephant, ma'am," Pete said.

She gave herself a shake.

" I thought it was. But when it stuck that thing out at me and let it off, I didn't know what to think. What do elephants eat ? "

" Hay," said Bastock.

" I'm glad to hear it," Mrs. Huguenine said.

8

BURKE AND WALSH

IT was Caroline's idea that they should have breakfast together, and sitting down at Mrs. Denby's table that morning, Chad had to admire the idea. Mrs. Denby ran a quick store beside the canal : the front held her counters ; the back was her kitchen ; and she had laid the places so that Chad and Caroline could look through the door and enjoy the view of canal and fields. Framed by the doorway was Burke and Walsh's tent already erected. Even at that distance it seemed colossal.

" It went up so quick," said Mrs. Denby, swinging the coffee, eggs and fried potatoes on to the table. " I wish I had sausage for you. I make the loveliest sausage."

Caroline said, " This looks awfully good, Mrs. Denby."

" They had the elephant in Cheever's shed back of the relay barn," said Mrs. Denby. " He came right by this morning when I was sweeping my steps. Swinging his head just like a creature in the Bible, and his little eye was so knowing. I've baked you some biscuits, though. I hope they're good. Oh, did you ever see such *gorgeous* biscuits ? "

The pan came from the oven in a fine vapour of hot baking.

" He went over the bridge so careful," said Mrs. Denby. " A mouse couldn't have been delicater. I hate mice, they're so dirty in their habits. The poor thing rumbled, though. I think he had a bead of wind in his inside by the sound. I suppose he's old. Wind does overtake persons so when they get older. I make my own butter. It's delicious. I think I'll have to see the circus after all."

Caroline and Chad let her follow her spasmodic thoughts. Her food was good, at any rate, and they were hungry.

" Are you going to the performance ? " Mrs. Denby asked. " I want to see the performers. Especially the female ones. I suppose circus people don't get married much. It's funny the way you can't really tell whether a woman's married or not, isn't it ? Do you think Mr. Van Buren's going to be elected President, Mr. Hanna ? "

When Chad said he did not know, she nodded. " They say he's not married," she said. " My word. Did you read about that canal woman they found murdered over near Newark ? Two months ago. She was young, too. I read about it in the *Western Argus.* I think murdering is dreadful, don't you ? Because you can't tell who did it half the time." Her angular face became entranced. " I wonder why creation arranged for women to have children ? Did you ever think of that ? "

Chad said, " No. But somebody had to have them. It must have been a toss up at the time."

" Oh, heavenly days ! " exclaimed Mrs. Denby. She went into the front of the store to deal with a canal cook who had come in with the determined face of a woman who has resolved to forget nothing. Mrs. Denby quickly fixed that. She had the cook floundering after the second item. " Flour, eggs, pitcher of milk. You want to have that covered. No telling what might get into it. Frogs, maybe." She brushed a stray lock off her cheek, and the canal cook in desperation did likewise. " Frogs spit, or is it spiders ? And men, of course. I don't know about elephants."

" Elephants ? " The woman brightened. " Coming down the towpath this side of the relay barn I kept seeing it laying right in the road. And I thought it must have been a horse and I couldn't understand the fact. You hain't got any Salvinie's Colic Elixir ? "

" No. But I have a powder for bugs and roaches, and horehound candy, and peppermint oil. Peppermint is good for colic. But it ain't no help with roaches so you'll need some of both, probably."

" I guess I will."

" Hogs sometimes eat roaches. I'm always noticing things like that. Maybe you ought to have some salt pork."

" Lard ! " exclaimed the canal cook. " I made up my mind to get some lard."

" I've got some preserved gooseberries," Mrs. Denby said. " Now you've bought lard, you could make a gooseberry pie, seeing you have the flour. Of course it ain't rhubarb pie."

When Chad stepped out to pay Mrs. Denby, the canal cook was looking rumpled, weary, and utterly distracted. Outside a boater was blowing the guts out of his horn. " Men like to make a noise when they're angry, or when they're happy, or when they're drunk. I read in a book ostriches don't do it," said Mrs. Denby. " I hope I see you folks at the circus."

" I hope so," said Caroline. She had to stifle her giggles as they went down the steps. They could see the boatman stamping up and down his boat. Caroline put her hand inside Chad's arm. " My, you were awful. That business about the Lord having to toss a coin."

Chad was grinning. He had enjoyed himself, Mrs. Denby, the breakfast, which was the best he had had in a long time, and the discovery that Caroline was fun to do things with. A couple of times, while Mrs. Denby was holding forth, he had only had to meet Caroline's eye to make her buckle.

" I wonder if Mr. Huguenine really plans to show," she said as they walked up the street from the canal bridge.

The town was filling already with farm rigs. It was a real circus day, blue sky, white clouds, and just enough wind blowing to make people restive. Chad and Caroline overheard several groups talking about the mammoth arena, and some had had a glimpse of the elephant. The luck boys were working the side-walks ; a watch and spoon artist, a thimble rig, the seven sights of Pagan Rome. A block farther on they encountered Professor Arganave sadly packing up his solar microscope under the menacing scrutiny of two thick-jawed gents.

" I been moved on three times," he complained to Chad. " You talk to them, will you ? "

Chad examined the two gents and decided he wouldn't.

" I offered them two dollars," said the professor, " but they want five. They say you got to be with Burke's show here. Ain't I got a right ? Look at the crowd. I could do good business."

On the porch of the big hotel a collection of men and women were looking things over ; they were a noisy, laughing crowd. Even if Chad and Caroline had not been a month with Hugue-nine's they would have known them for circus folks. They had the friendly, confident aspect of performers who know they are travelling with a going concern.

" It must be exciting to be with a big show," Caroline said. " I wonder where Albany is."

She was not in sight, though Fred Shepley was. They saw him standing in the bar-room door. His face was pale, and he was talking in a loud, unsteady voice to a man in a blue coat and flashy polka-dotted waistcoat. When he caught sight of

Chad and Caroline in the crowd on the sidewalk he turned his
face away.

They pushed their way along through the throng to the
small hotel where Huguenine's company had put up. While
Caroline went in to change to her ring costume, Chad went
round to the barn after the horses. The stable hand was inside
sucking a straw. He said, "'Morning," and stuck the dry end
of the straw against the cream's rump.

"I been down to look at the big show's horses. They ain't
got any ring animals any better than yours."

"There isn't a better one than that cream anywhere," Chad
said.

"It must be tough being a good horse in a bum show,"
observed the stable hand.

Chad didn't argue. He said, "We got better riders than they
have, even if we ain't got an elephant."

"Yeah. That makes a difference. You take a rich bastard
and he can spit on anybody's stove; but you and me we got to
use the spittoon, and if it's the wrong one we get throwed out of
there." He put the straw back in his mouth.

Chad took the horses out to the street and waited for Caroline.
She came along in a minute, wearing her cloak over the tights.
They turned off the main street, going by back ways towards
the lot.

Ike Wayfish and the skinners were inside the tent, so Bastock
started the ring practice immediately. Chad stayed long
enough to see that Caroline was all right. On the way up she
had told him that she wasn't worried about falling again. It was
the lantern light that had made the ground seem out of place,
deep down, she said, like the earth in a dream. Moreover, Ike
had stopped handling her as if she were a hot iron, and he was
solid himself on the pad so that she did her poses with confidence; and Bastock kept saying, "Oh, my God, it's going to
be an act."

When he emerged from the tent the first thing Chad saw was
Mr. Huguenine in the act of shaving. It was a regular domestic
sight. Mrs. Huguenine sat on the top step of the treasury wagon
with a towel hung over her knees and held a basin of hot water
on the towel. A small mirror was hung by a cord round her
neck. Her bosom gave it the proper tilt to throw the light upward on Mr. Huguenine's face, crimson from the effort of

bending over. Neither said a word, but her eyes were eloquently solicitous as they followed the course of the razor and her lips kept moving as though she conned a charted course like a pilot working a boat down river in a fog. As Chad approached, she moved her head slowly so that the mirror did not move and warned him with her eyes. He stood still, listening to Mr. Huguenine's short breathless grunts until he paused to wipe the razor.

"A.D.," Mrs. Huguenine said sharply. "That's my petticoat."

"So it is, so it is," said Mr. Huguenine. He erected a hair on his wrist by the simple method of bending the joint, cut it off, said, "You wait a minute, Hanna," and went to work under his nose.

He worked the razor in little strokes, like a turkey pecking crumbs from a bucket of hot mash. In spite of himself, Chad became as absorbed as the man and his wife. None of them paid the least attention to the smart clop of hoofs coming down the packed dirt of the street till the rig spun into the lot and the two horses came down on their pasterns with a quick stop, stamping and blowing.

"Hey there, Huguenine!"

"God damn it," said Mr. Huguenine.

"Did you cut yourself, dearie?" Mrs. Huguenine asked.

Mr. Huguenine swept the lather off his lip with the ball of his thumb and looked at himself. "Smarts but don't bleed," he said, and looked up at the horses. It was Mr. Burke's rig, and Mr. Burke was sitting in it with another man beside him.

This second gent was considerably bigger than Mr. Burke, but his clothes weren't as natty and one loop of his string tie had loosened.

"Hallo," said Mr. Huguenine.

"I brought my partner along. This is Mr. George Walsh. Huguenine and Mrs." He ignored Chad. "Did you make a good tent in Clyde?"

Huguenine's eyes stuck out for a minute. "Good enough," he said. "I expect to pick up business here."

"You do?" said Burke. "You're feeling kind of cool."

"Yeah," said Mr. Huguenine. "I was."

"My partner ain't," Burke said. "He wanted to tear your tent down."

"Kick them out on their fat . . ."

Mrs. Huguenine rose up with the basin in her hands.

"Young man," she said, threateningly.

Walsh worked his jaws as he stared at her ; he let go a spit over the wheel.

"George isn't feeling so friendly," Burke said, his blue eyes wandering round the lot. He listened to the thump of hoofs from the tent. "Working on a new act, Huguenine ? "

"You can find out for twenty-five cents," said Huguenine.

"Thanks. If you want to see our show I'd be glad to offer you and your missis a free pass."

"Couldn't use it," said Huguenine.

"You plan to show ? "

"Yep. And you ain't going to stop me here, Burke, nor your dumb-faced partner neither. I seen the sheriff and the town board and they say I got plenty of right to show when I want to in this town."

"Go ahead," said Mr. Burke, in an affable voice. "But I warn you not to break in on our parade, see ? "

"I'm parading at twelve," said Mr. Huguenine.

"Then keep off the main street."

"I'll parade where I choose."

Mr. Burke studied the reins in his fingers.

"All right," he said. "See what the public thinks when your run-down, two-dollar rigging runs up against ours."

Walsh was still eyeing Mrs. Huguenine. His spit was high and promiscuous.

"Kick their fat . . ."

"Young man," said Mrs. Huguenine, "I warned you."

Her face blazed. She swung the basin and let the contents strike where they would. Part hit the horses and part hit Mr. Walsh, and Mr. Burke had a share of the floating lather. The horses were not as accustomed to shaving water ; they bolted. They made a wild circle of the lot and hit the opening by a miracle.

"What did you do that for ? " Mr. Huguenine asked gloomily " Now I got to get me more hot water."

"I'll get it," she said, stamping her foot so that the wagon bucked. "I'll boil it for you. By Jerusalem, if you was men you'd have clawed them two monkeys right out of that wagon."

Chad had to grin. " I don't believe I could've run fast enough."

She began to smile.

" Them horses don't like wet when it's hot," she agreed. " Oh, A.D., you've begun to bleed ! "

" Well, I can't see if you go jumping that mirror that way."

Chad didn't see much use hanging around. A.D. had made up his mind to show ; not even an elephant was going to move him.

He went back to the tent and told the others.

While they were talking it over, Fred Shepley came in with the Pamplons, and Fiero.

" I was talking to their top-rider," he said. " He don't somerset from his feet at all Just from his knees. What do you think about that ? You'd think they'd give me a job."

" I ain't seen you somersetting much at all lately," Budlong said dryly.

" Well, I'll somerset to-day."

Bastock gave him an eye for a brief instant.

" Better pick out the right horse when you're coming down," he suggested.

" They're making a star place for Albany," Shepley said, as if he had not heard. " And we had her below me, too, here. God knows how she got her job."

Chad had had an idea rolling around his head for some time and he said now, " Wouldn't it look good to let Caroline ride the cream in the parade ? "

" No, she can't," Shepley said. " A top-rider can't walk in a parade."

" You could ride Jerry. He's a handsome horse. But Caroline hadn't ought to ride him till he's used to it."

" I could ride him all right," Caroline said quickly.

" Sure she could," Shepley said. " Besides, my tights look better on the cream."

Bastock considered it.

" I'll have to ask the gaffer. But it's a good idea. It's one more piece to our parade. God knows we need them. Maybe some will look at her."

Mr. Huguenine said he didn't care. He was busy nailing huge sheets of paper to the tent wagon. They had been lettered by hand. They said :

HUGUENINE'S GREAT AND ONLY INTERNATIONAL CIRCUS

See Daniel in the Lion's Den.

See Signor Rossello, in his somerset on a galloping Horse.

See Mr. Wayfish, the Buffo, who makes Children laugh.

See all the great acts, wire artists, refined Juggling.

ALL CHILDREN will be admitted free if escorted by 1 adult.

FOR THIS DAY ONLY

" I thought it up last night," he told Bastock. " It cost me fifty cents, but by God I'll have a good tent here if I pay for it."

9

FULL TENT

Up ahead there was confusion. Ike Wayfish was trying once more to force his mule through the crowd that blocked off the entrance to the main street and a tough-looking bezabor was making passes with a tent peg at the mule's nose. She was parrying nimbly. Chad saw Ike's top hat rise high as she reared to strike with her forefeet, and the crowd swayed and jammed towards the corners.

On top of the tent wagon the three skinners were anxiously banging away at " Long-Tailed Blue," but their notes were already being smothered by the approaching fanfare of Burke's full band. Their music was electrifying. Their drums were magnificent. The brasses echoed all over town and the leader with his French horn made notes beautiful enough to stir the heart. " Hell," thought Chad. " We'll have to turn back again."

They had tried three times to get on to the main street, but each time a posse of Burke's canvasmen, armed with tent pegs, had made the entrance ahead of them and it would have been pure suicide to work through the line. All the way up the length of the town this had happened ; then as Burke's made the loop and started back, Huguenine had bawled to Ike to cut in ahead.

Chad gave Caroline a glance. She was dressed in Albany's former historical costume of crown and cloak and sceptre. She certainly looked pretty sitting on Jerry. And the horse was behaving well, keeping close behind the cream pad. He merely jigged a little when the band came close.

As Chad expected, Ike turned back. He looked defeated. Huguenine bawled to him to try again farther along. The skinners clambered off the roof to take the horses by the head and back the tent wagon round in the narrow street. The crowd re-formed across the street, laughing. As soon as the wagon was headed back, Huguenine shouted to Fiero and the Pamplons to get up and ride. All three of them looked completely terrified.

"And don't start playing till we get out on the street," Huguenine said to Bastock. The skinners went up to the roof ; the wagon rolled around the corner and they started again parallel to the main street. Out of the tail of his eye, Chad saw the opposing roustabouts yell and run down the street.

"A.D.," he yelled.

"Yeah ? "

"Why don't we turn around again ? They've pulled foot."

Huguenine looked over his shoulder.

"God damn and Maria," he roared.

Laboriously the entire process was repeated. This time they came to the street with only the country people in front of them. Over their heads, Huguenine's caught sight of the passing procession. It was worth seeing : the plumes on the lady riders, the spangles on a dozen men ; a buggy in which side by side rode the giant and the dwarf in identical uniforms. The dwarf was driving. It was comical, even to the Huguenine troupe. Chad edged the cage wagon forward till it was right beside the tent wagon. He could hear a mutter up street. "The elephant's coming." And he looked at the crowd. They would be moving along to follow the circus in a moment.

But there was a gap in the procession. Nobody seemed to know why and the people on the walks started hooking forward into the main street to see what the elephant was doing. Perhaps the cessation, perhaps the smell of the elephant, roused Oscar. He hoisted his old hips shakily and roared. In that narrow space between houses he made a furious din. The bystanders melted away in sudden panic ; it had never occurred to them, till they stopped trying to see the elephant, that a man-eating animal was right there in their midst.

Chad saw it all then.

He jumped off the cage wagon and yanked Mr. Huguenine's paper sign off the tent wagon. Caroline saw what he was doing and moved Jerry up to the other side. Huguenine never knew it had happened till the paper was being trampled in the dirt. He started roaring as loud as the lion, but Chad said, " Go ahead ! "

Ike also had caught the idea. Burke's procession would be confused and in a hurry to fill up the gap. He raised in his stirrups. He could see Burke's tough tent-peggers still galloping down the main street to the next intersection on the side from which they had driven back Huguenine's. " Good work, Chaddy. I'll turn off the other side."

Budlong also was getting the drift. He put his hand over the bugle mouth and grabbed Joe Duddy's drumsticks.

" Will somebody tell me the road to Lyons ? " Ike bawled, and the mule, waggling her ears, pranced into the main street and started after Burke's first half. She was magnificent now, handling Ike's hat. In her excitement she took a piece clean out of the brim and had to grab again. The crowd, which this far uptown was mostly from the farms, yelled and cheered. They hadn't kept track of the wagons on the way up. It all looked part of the original parade. The tent wagon wheeled in, then Fiero, juggling, the Pamplons, Caroline, and Fred Shepley. Caroline got a hand. Any one would have. People just wanted to be amused.

As the cage wagon made the turn, Chad craned round to look back.

He could see the swinging ears of the elephant. She had her coiled trunk high. She trumpeted and came on towards Oscar.

The trumpeting took the fight out of the old lion. He crouched right down and started moaning like a tomcat up a tree wondering if his bowels would hold out till the dogs got tired of waiting.

There was still a good line of performers behind the elephant. There was the rig with the fat girl and there was a clown in white face working away at a droning hurdy-gurdy while a couple of tumblers threw flips in front of his wagon, and there were some more riders tailing the whole shebang together with the monster tent wagon which was placarded with signs saying :

"FOLLOW THE PARADE TO THE MAMMOTH ARENA. BURKE & WALSH'S STUPENDOUS MORAL ESTABLISHMENT. SKILL, BEAUTY, AND FUN FOR ALL. ADMISSION 25 cents, CHILDREN at half price."

The crowd was already coming along after it, thronging the centre of the street, talking, laughing, shouting, eating dust, as happy as hogs hitting home at mash time.

Ike Wayfish made the second turn off the main street ; the tent wagon followed suit. The crowd, seeing people up the street already on the move, started moving with the wagon. Chad turned the cage wagon and saw that the elephant was turning, willy-nilly, after Oscar. Oscar was making catarrhal noises and holding fast to the bottom of his cage. The others naturally followed the elephant. If there had been any doubts in the minds of the crowd, the children couldn't have been shaken off from the elephant, no matter what. Where it went, that was the place to go.

The elephant's driver may have had some curiosity, but he was thankful enough to have his charge moving again not to be upset by turning one corner more or less. The back of the cage wagon anyway looked pretty much like any circus wagon, having no bars ; and because he was on foot, the driver couldn't well see beyond. Back of the elephant, nobody had much chance to see ahead.

Way down the street, the big band banged away. On top of the tent wagon, Joe Duddy suddenly grabbed his sticks and rolled his drum. It didn't matter now. The uptown crowd was coming after Huguenine's. The elephant-keeper caught on when the show doubled back across the main street once more. But Grace, the elephant, found this procession moving nicely. She was rumbling her bead of wind happily in her inside ; no mere hook was going to turn her away now. And the horses and riders and drivers behind her effulgent rear were too used to being in that position to think much of the direction she took.

They attained the Huguenine lot half an hour before show time. But Mrs. Huguenine didn't wait. She rolled across the lot like a ship under heavy sail, unlocked the treasury-wagon door, paid off the constable retained to guard it, opened the window, and beamed happily on the first-comers.

" This way for your tickets, gents. Have your quarter of a

dollar ready. Twenty-five cents. The first ten children will be admitted free by the courtesy of the management."

Never had she made change so rapidly. The customers streamed into the tent. By the time the harassed elephant man had persuaded Grace that the hay was not for her, Burke's rig came galloping in.

There wasn't time for him to do damage. His own show was starting and he had to have the elephant ; he had to have the clown. Some of the horses had to appear in the grand entrance. But his face was blanched. His eyes looked like blue frozen glass. Even his cigar was dead. He passed Chad as he followed the elephant through the crowd, and to Chad's surprise he nodded.

" I warned you folks," he said quietly ; and then he added, " By Almighty God, I warned you."

But there was no use worrying. The show was in hand ; the tent was nearly full ; Huguenine, doffing his hat in the ring, showed a red, perspiring, satisfied, but wondering face. His voice was hearty. " LAY-dies and GENTlemen . . ."

10

BACK ROAD

MR. HUGUENINE's all-out-and-over was hoarse but triumphant. Ike Wayfish, who had come running out to the performers' fly, turned back with the rest of the troupe to admire the audience filing out. It had been a good show. Fiero's juggling had been lightning fast ; the Pamplons had worked like grease on the wire ; best of all, Fred Shepley had done his somersault. They all complimented him on it and for once he was willing to accept their praise.

It was Budlong who pricked their bubbling exaltation.

"You want to be setting here admiring yourselves when Burke's roustabouts come in like a bunch of hyenas ? Or do you want to have got a couple of miles between ? " He wasn't wasting time himself. Already he had knocked loose the toe pins. Bastock and Joe Duddy were shoving Oscar outside. "Fred, you and Chad get the boards out. You Pamplons ought to have your wire down. Fiero can pack loose tackle. We need every man."

There was something grimly convincing about the way Budlong took over. The only person who didn't feel it was Huguenine. "I got to count my ticket-take," he said.

"You'd be lucky to be able to count after Burke gets through with you, A.D."

Bastock, who had begun carrying out the seat boards, said, "Yeah. It's tough enough when rubes start pitching into you. But when another circus gets on your tail, it's nasty. They know how."

Budlong said, "I'd rather have a Mississippi township hunting coon up the leg of my pants."

"They wouldn't dare come in here in daylight. The sheriff told me . . ."

"A.D., do you think any sensible sheriff is going to come around when there's about thirty hyenas loose ? What's more, when they're sorting us out for our coffins, he won't even know what happened. Neither will Burke. His show will have moved."

Don't make me laugh," said Bastock. " Where do you think you're going, Fred ? "

" I'm going to change at the hotel and get my clothes."

" Like hell you are. You come here and try lugging seats."

" Well, I don't want my show ruined," Huguenine acknowledged. " What'll I do ? "

" Hitch up the teams," Budlong said.

" Say," said Chad, " let Caroline take the light rig down and pay the hotel off. She can get the men's clothes."

Caroline said, " Of course. Mrs. Pamplon can come with me."

" Yeah. A.D., you hitch up for her."

Fiero, lugging out one of the chests, yelled to Caroline to bring his laundry, which was hanging out the window. " Backside window," he shouted.

Caroline waved her hand.

With Shepley, Fiero, and Pamplon all lugging seats and jacks they cleared the tent in record time. But Budlong wasn't satisfied. " I won't feel right till we get the wagons rolling. Wish to God they was rolling now. Suppose he decides to send his hyenas up here before the tear-down."

Bastock shook his head.

" He won't. You got to run a circus like a habit. You got to all-out, and you got to tear down, and roll the wagons. You start doing different and you're bound to get stuck, just like trying to eat with your back end. Besides, he'll want to get his wagons out of town before any trouble starts. Then he won't know nothing."

Shepley stopped to catch breath.

" I wonder what Albany would think if we had bad trouble with them."

" Never does no good to wonder what a woman would think —not unless you got her right where you want her," Bastock said.

" Yeah," said Joe Duddy. " And when you got her there, if you can't keep her from thinking at all, you might as well buy bird seed."

The canvas came down in a billowing cloud. They dashed in to squash the wind out of it and brought the pole down with a run. The four skinners loaded it and folded the canvas and stowed it, while Fiero, Shepley and Pamplon pulled the pegs.

By that time Huguenine had the horses harnessed and hitched to the proper wagons. They were ready to go. Budlong stood back from closing up the tent wagon and raked the sweat off his chin. " Where's them women ? "

" They're a coming," Mrs. Huguenine called. She had appointed herself an armed sentry, with a wagon spoke in one hand and a claw-hammer in the other. Now she hiked up her skirt with her little fingers and fairly skimmed the grass to the treasury wagon.

Caroline drove the team into the lot at a resounding trot. Her face was flushed and her eyes bright with excitement.

" We're ready to go," said Huguenine. " Which way do we head ? The Newark road's t'other side of the canal. The bridge is close enough to the main one so Burke will see us go over."

This was something that had not occurred even to Budlong. He was stumped. He turned to Chad after a second and asked him what he knew about the country. Chad had been doing his best to remember ; but it was astonishing how little of the country a canal hoggie came to know.

" I think there was a road on this side of the canal," he said. " I remember a couple of bridges between here and Newark."

Caroline came up to them.

" There is. I asked the clerk at the hotel. He acted like a real gentleman and helped me pack for Mr. Fiero and Mr. Shepley. He says there's a back road leads off the end of this street. It follows close along the canal through East Arcadia and Lockville. He says it ain't much good, but it's been dry now, so we ought to get through."

" You got a think-piece," Budlong said, but he didn't waste time praising her. He climbed up to his high perch with a tent peg, which he laid under his feet. " Ike, you take the rig. But keep back near us. Put them extra pegs in handy. Get aboard, folks."

Caroline hung back.

" I'm going to ride Jonathan," she said.

Chad noticed then that she hadn't changed from her ring costume. " I can ride him 'stride," she said.

Budlong said, " We can't be hampered by no woman. Get on that wagon."

" No," she said. " If there is trouble, Chad can't just turn Jonathan and Jerry loose. I'll be there to hold them."

"All right," Budlong said, saluting her with his whip. It was a little past four when they hit the road.

The Newark road forked left over the canal bridge on the west side of town ; their own road was an alleyway leading back of a canal barn and a small ramshackle building that reeked of peppermint. Budlong told Chad and Caroline that he could see Burke's tent between the buildings. "They're tearing her down. Some of their wagons are rolling up to the bridge. They'll come by here in twenty minutes."

He glanced ahead. The light rig, the treasury wagon, the seat wagon, and the cage wagon were all in plain view, heading straight as a string along the canal bank.

"Ain't there no bends in this road ? "

"I don't know," said Chad. "There's some trees ahead, though."

"Looks like a meeting grove," Budlong said sourly. "Hardly enough underbrush for a rabbit to be decent in."

The light rig, however, trailing dust up from its tyres, turned beyond the trees and dipped down. Budlong brightened a little and shook up the four-horse team. He wouldn't work a trot out of them ; he didn't dare, with the loaded wagon and the uneven ruts. The road was already dwindling. Its grass backbone was high.

Turning the corner, Budlong glanced back.

"Hain't showed up yet," he reported. He looked south over the canal. "That main road's right in sight. This is the God-damnedest back road I ever saw."

Beyond the grove, the road swung west again, then dipped into a low fold of the ground, and came out on the bank of Mud Creek. Here at last were trees. The piers of the canal aqueduct stood solid in the current to their left ; but Budlong said that none of the main road was visible, and the wagons, one by one, rolled through the shallow ford roiling the water, and leaving two tracks of frothy bubbles.

Caroline and Chad were the last to cross ; and they stopped a moment to let the horses dip their noses and watched the bubbles drift slowly with the current. The spot was deserted except for a pair of teeter-birds, skittering along the sunny bank. The leaves hung motionless on the trees, and the sun poured a still heat into the creek bed. The groans of the tent wagon laboriously working up through the trees dwindled. A hot-weather bird unwound its heat screech. For a moment it seemed that such a thing as Huguenine's circus had never existed at all.

" I'd like to stay here for ever."

" You'd get bit awful," Chad said, slapping a deer fly on Jerry's shoulder.

" I mean just to stay. Not to have to eat, not to think of money, not to think of what's going to happen to me ; just to be here, like now, in the sun."

"It's a hell of a idea. Where'd I be? How'd we get married?"

" You'd be right here, just the way it is. There just wouldn't be any time. There wouldn't be any good and bad and the hurts people can do to each other. I'd rather heaven turned out that way than all marble and gold."

" Ain't you curious about what's going to happen to you ? "

" Not now, not this minute." She turned her face and looked at him and blushed. " Well," she said, " time's gone by, after all."

" We ought to move," Chad said, and she obediently turned the cream through the ford. She had let the cloak slip back from her shoulders. Her legs were shaped to the barrel, and as the big horse stamped powerfully through the ford, his motion showed in her thighs. She sat him with a straight back but with her head bent a little. In the tight-fitting lavender costume, against the green of the trees and the desertion of the stream, there was an outlandishness about her that prickled Chad : it was almost as if the horse were carrying her off.

Then they were among the trees, riding upward through a green tissue of shade ; and they saw the tent wagon ahead and the outlandishness evaporated. She was just a small circus performer riding the stage between stands. Budlong was swearing at them for hanging back. " Get up front where I can watch you," he said.

" All right," Chad said, meeting his eye. Budlong figured they had been muzzling up to each other, but he didn't mind that.

They crammed the horses round the wagon and saw the others ahead, travelling slowly across a stretch of flat country. Somewhere to the left a dog was barking cows home ; they could hear a bell or two. The sound kept pace with them in the levelling sunlight, and after a few minutes they saw a house and barn beside the road. A man with a milk pail stood near the road.

He eyed the caravan suspiciously.

" You can't camp here," he greeted them.

" We don't want to camp," Ike said angrily. " Does this road take us into Newark ? "

" It will, though you'd better cross over Buxsted's bridge to the main road. Whyn't you take the main road in Lyons ? "

" We must've missed it."

" Nobody but a durned fool could miss the main road," said the farmer. His cows were coming down his lane, followed by the barking dog and a couple of children. The nearness of beef on the hoof roused old Oscar's ambitions. He started coughing to himself inside the cage wagon, and the cows stopped suddenly and began to mill in the lane, driving the dog to distraction.

" Move on, get out," shouted the farmer. " Damn gipsies."

He shook his pail at them.

" Snooty galoot," Bastock commented. Budlong said nothing. His eye had lit on a few chickens ahead. They had been prospecting the roadside grass and the high weeds and bushes held them close to it. " Chaddy," he said softly. " Is that bastard watching us ? "

Chad looked back.

" No. He's all mixed up with his milkers."

Budlong whistled round his spit and let the last of his black-snake drop close to the ground on the side nearest the chickens. It quivered, twitching up the snapper like a snake held by the tail and forking his tongue. As it came abreast of the first chicken Budlong lifted it. It shot out in a line, the slender end popped softly, and the next instant the chicken was being raised by the neck. The neck was broken. Budlong fished him up and laid him next the tent peg under his feet.

" Got to be gentle," he said to himself. " Got to be gentle."

He snaffled a second, a rousing fat hen. It was like magic. The rest of the chickens just stood and admired. But like other credulous beings, time and the inexorable passage of events preserved them. The tent wagon had gone by and Budlong was contenting himself with delivering a homily on the art of snaking poultry. " Got to be gentle. Got to flick the wrist. You get ambitious and you take the head off. But go gentle, Chaddy, and your pot's bound to be full. That hen will make good gravy."

He prodded his thumb into her. " Too fat to lay, anyhow ; she's no loss to that snotty bastard. And that little rooster couldn't tread a strawberry. I'm just saving him feed."

Bastock bawled back, " How many'd you get ? "

" Two," Chad said. " One's a fat hen."

Bastock yelled up ahead to Joe. " Two, Joe. One's a fat hen."

Budlong's was obviously an old and tried accomplishment. Somehow it heartened Chad. It gave him the feeling that in a riot those three bezabors would turn out better than gold. He eyed the sun, which had begun to sink towards the horizon.

" If it starts up sudden anywheres," he said to Caroline, " you take the horses through the nearest fence. And you keep off, see ? Look out for yourself. In the dark, like that, in tights, a man might mistake you."

She looked at him, her face filled with tenderness.

She said, " All right, Chad," humbly.

And he thought, " Christ ! " without feeling profane.

II

BETTINA ON THE BRIDGE

NOBODY had thought of asking the man with the milk pail how far it was to the next farm, or whether the next farm was Buxsted's, where he had said the bridge was. They struck rough hauling. For a quarter-mile the tent wagon had to be eased over rocks and into holes an inch at a time if there wasn't going to be a broken reach or axle. When they got through the bad piece, the sun was a red ball in the western haze, a balloon balanced on the lip of space.

The glowing light it poured across the land seemed to enlarge distances. The track was leading them out into a big farm. The left side of the road was screened now by an apple orchard ; but they pulled beyond it, the road mounting a slight grade towards a hayfield where a few left-over cocks sat on their long shadows. The picture of the land grew familiar to Chad's eye. A kind-hearted woman here had given a skinny driver-boy a

drink of switchel from a pail. He remembered how the field
sloped over the roll of ground clear to the towpath ; that day
a line of men had been mowing the top of it ; he had seen them
against the sky. Beyond, now, would be the bridge, sixty, seventy
rods away, and the house and barns were back a hundred yards
on this same road. He turned to tell Budlong to look south
towards the main road. But Budlong was already looking,
watching the crest of the hayfield as his head slowly rose with
the grade. He made a quick hissing noise. " Stop them up
ahead, Chaddy."

Chad thumped Jerry with his heels ; the first couple of jumps
brought him up with Bastock. "|Stop," he told him, and went
by. Joe Duddy happened to be watching. He had stopped the
cage wagon already. Huguenine, however, kept right on. He
had pulled out eighty feet, with the light rig still ahead, before
Chad got to him. Chad risked a yell to Ike and pointed left.
Ike pulled up and stared, as did Fiero and the Pamplons, but
from the way Fiero flashed his teeth, Chad knew that he had
caught them in time. When he came up to them, he saw that
the road had levelled out and the rise of the hayfield still kept
them out of sight.

" Budlong said to stay here," he told them. " I guess he's
seen Burke's show. I'll go back and find out."

Caroline had dismounted. She was standing by the nigh
front wheel of the tent wagon, staring up at Budlong's lean
brown face. She was shivering a little. " Don't get scared,"
Chad told her.

" I'm not. I'm just excited. Budlong says they're hauling
past the bridge road."

" They could have seen my head," Budlong said. " But
there's a line of boats on the canal. They probably thought it
belonged to one of the boats."

He raised himself inch by inch to look once more, this time
ahead.

" This wagon's too high. If it was a foot shorter we could
get right past the buildings. There's woods on the other side.
People on the farm must be eating supper. There's a couple of
kids, though, but they're crossing the bridge. They've gone to
watch the big show."

Chad's eyes lit on the haycocks.

" We can get by," he said. " You go ahead," he told Caroline. " Tell the rest to pull right by the farm and wait for us when they get into the woods."

He gave her a leg up and sent her off. Presently the wagons started ahead. Budlong said, " What you plan to do ? "

" Your lines are long enough so you can drive standing on the roof, ain't they ? "

" Yep."

Chad said, " I'll hand you up three or four of them haycocks. It's far enough off so the hay will make you look like a decent farmer. "

Budlong grinned. " Start pitching, sonny."

Chad forked the fence. He dropped four cocks over it and then started handing them up. It was quite a job, without a fork, but the more that stuck to the sides of the big wagon the better. Budlong spread it with artistic appreciation. " It sure will look like one hell of a big hayload," he said.

" Burke's people won't know the road's low down. What are they doing now ? "

The tent wagon was rolling along now and with perfect unconcern Budlong watched across the canal the procession on the other road.

" Must be a dozen wagons gone by the bridgehead," he reported. " There's three coaches and the rest look like luck-boy outfits. The tent wagons are coming along. They've got five box wagons. It certainly is a big establishment," he said admiringly. " Maybe Burke thinks we've been scared out. By Cripus, there's his rig ! "

They were bearing down on the farmyard now. The bridge road coming in from the left was in sight.

" Think you better haul in behind the barn ? "

Budlong shook his head.

" I don't think he noticed. The bridge will block his sight. He was talking to the kids. Once we're by it, we're all right for a while."

The barn hid their own view now ; then the wagon rolled across the road from the bridge. A battered signpost said : Lockville 2 miles. Chad, riding in the ditch, saw the bridge bare against the sky. Then they had passed two corncribs and a shed and were in the woods, and the rest of Huguenine's were waiting for them.

They were grouped close together beside the treasury wagon,

and the lay of the ground now allowed them to catch glimpses through the trees of the procession passing on the other side of the canal. " They're hauling by," Ike said. " By holy, there goes the elephant."

" Yep," said Mr. Huguenine. " They play Palmyra to-morrow. I guess they've give up looking for us."

It was quiet in the woods. They imagined they could hear the roll of the wagons along the other road. Then with the startling clarity of clapping thunder, a team and wagon banged over the bridge. It was Mr. Burke's rig. He was pointing his whip towards the barn, and the two children, obviously torn with a desire to see the elephant, were pattering along beside him.

" God damn it," said Bastock. " He seen you and he's asked them something about their Pa and they've told him Pa was eating supper. We ought to have moved on."

Budlong said, " Get going."

There was a good chance, with the big show already past the bridge and travelling opposite them. If they were out of sight by the time Burke came to the crossroad, he would have to follow along to find them. If he did that, he would have to go back to the bridge, overtake his own show, get his canvasmen, and return round the whole loop. That would give Huguenine's a head start. By the time they were caught up with, it ought to be dark. They might have found a place to hide. Burke couldn't spend the whole night looking for them ; he would need the gang to make the pitch in Palmyra early in the morning. And if he didn't come after them now, Huguenine's would wait the time out in the woods until near sunrise before moving on themselves.

It seemed fool-proof. While the small wagons forged ahead rapidly, the tent wagon slammed through the low branches and not even Huguenine bothered to think of lost paint. Keeping to the rear, Chad watched the diminishing spot that marked the road entrance of the woods. It was getting darker fast ; he doubted if they could be seen, even before they turned the corner. Then he shouted to Budlong to stop. The groaning of the wagon would be a dead give-away.

They waited ten minutes without Burke or any one else showing up. Budlong began to feel hopeful. " Maybe he wasn't sure he seen me at all." He unloaded his old quid and got himself a fresh-starter. "Bastock's always imagining things. He had me believing Burke had asked those kids about their Pa. Probably he just went to the house to ask if they'd seen our circus. They said, No. They ain't seen anything."

Chad forked his fingers up and down in Jerry's mane.

"He ought to know we took that road," he said. "Somebody was bound to tell him and he wouldn't have left without asking."

"That's so," said Budlong. "What you think we better do?"

"Well, we can't turn around," Chad said, eyeing the bulk of the tent wagon. "We might as well go ahead and get out of these woods before it's black dark."

They got rolling again, but for a while it looked as though they had fixed themselves even if Burke hadn't. The road wasn't made for a rigging the size of the tent wagon. In one place they scraped the boles of trees on both sides simultaneously, and there were about a hundred yards where Chad had to get up on top of the wagon and chop branches as they came to them. But they pulled out of the woods shortly after and found smooth tracks.

Both sides were pasture. They could tell, in spite of the darkness, from the silhouettes of the thorn trees which had waists sculptured by the browsing of cattle. Caroline said they looked like ladies in a fashion plate, promenading; and the notion delighted Joe Duddy, who said that the one on the left must be wearing quite a corset. He didn't see how the pigeons managed it, anyway. It was funny the way most genteel ladies and the fanciest pigeons wore the tightest corsets. He remembered one he had cut the strings of and it was like. . . . Chad and Caroline let the cage wagon roll ahead, carrying Joe's memoirs with it. The only thing to listen was Oscar, who was making pleased, snuffling grunts at the smoother going.

A fleece of cloud had risen in the west. They saw the moon through it for a moment; then it dipped under and the blackness settled. In the space of comparative light, however, they were made aware of the opening up of the countryside. And after a little they heard a boat horn and saw the bow lantern approaching not two hundred yards away.

Calling a halt, Huguenine suggested getting out lanterns, but Chad and the skinners argued against it. While they were discussing round the treasury wagon, the gliding light on the boat disappeared, and in the next moment Chad saw it again, in an aura of reflected glow. Then it emerged into the night once more, a point in darkness.

He said, " There's a bridge, there."

" Where ? "

Chad pointed.

Bastock said, " Let's cross it and get on to the main road."

" It's just a farm bridge, probably."

" If it is, it was built to cary a hay-load."

" The tent wagon weighs more than that."

" Hell," said Budlong. " We'll get over. I want to get on a decent road. I get tired snaffling this wagon through all them trees. It wears my nerves down. I knew a skinner went crazy taking a wagon through a woods trace. Started tracking right off into the bushes."

They didn't let him tell what the skinner died of. Suddenly they felt fine. Burke's show had gone by, or the lights would be in sight. Burke's show was way ahead. They had thought they would be forced to keep to this track all the way into Lockville. But with the bridge handy, the main road had become feasible.

Chad and Caroline, leading the procession, scouted for the turn-off. It proved merely a pair of ruts. There was a small hay barn close by, but no house. The farm buildings, they judged, would be on the other side of the bridge. They crossed together, the two horses sniffing the bridge and then stamping over nobly. On the far side the ramp sloped more gently on to the meadow-land. Chad handed Jerry's bridle to Caroline and walked back over the bridge. The wagons were lined up on the north side, waiting for him.

" It looks all right," he reported.

" We ought to have a light on the bridge," Huguenine said. " There ain't nobody after us now and the horses will go steadier with the wagons if they have a light to look at."

After a moment they decided it was all right to have a light on the bridge. The whole land was quiet, and the canal, except for the boat that had already passed, was a black and empty trench. Chad took the lighted lantern and laid it on the planking next the rail. The bridge top became an island in the darkness, just enough light reaching out to shade the two ramps.

Budlong got down and stood on the bridge to feel the timbers as the wagons went over. They shook somewhat under the seat wagon, but he said they were sound enough to prop Jerusalem.

He climbed up on the tent wagon and started his four horses. They had a stretch before they hit the grade, and then they started digging. For an instant the wagon seemed to cock against the sky, and Budlong on his high perch reared in darkness. His voice came down in syllables, encouraging the horses. Their bellies were taut and hard with straining. Then the front of the wagon came down ; the whole bridge quivered ; the reach gave an excruciating groan ; and the wagon levelled and started rolling down the other ramp, bucking its pole up to the wheeler's chins.

Budlong relaxed and looked behind. They could see him curse, but what he said was drowned by a wild yell from the road they had left.

" Burke's, by God."

It was Bastock.

" Tent pegs ! " he shouted.

" I'll be back," yelled Budlong. " Get up on the bridge."

They had no time to think. They grabbed for the tent pegs and ran pell-mell to the bridgehead. They could see the rig coming at a gallop ; it was coming from the west along the road they had just quit. It carried two lamps, and the vent-holes sprayed light enough for Huguenine's little group to see the load of Burke's hyenas cramming the open box.

Chad tried to count them, a dozen anyway ; they all looked tough. His mind went hastily over Huguenine's : four skinners, Huguenine made five, Fiero six, Pamplon seven, Ike eight, Shepley nine. But Burke's gang would all be fighters. It was just God that had put the bridge there, or maybe it was the canal commissioner, or the pig-headed farmer who had stood up for his rights, or the Democratic vote. It gave them a chance to make a stand. He felt a small cold spot in his smaller entrails enlarging rapidly. If they had had a minute more they could have ripped the planks out of the bridge.

But they had barely time to beat the gang to the top. Chad's feet pounded up the planks with Joe Duddy's and Bastock's. Huguenine, blowing in his wake, was crying, " That God-damned foxy bastard." Then Budlong burst through them and hollered for room. He dropped his tent peg and took the light sledge in both hands, and as the opposing gang milled up the ramp roaring, he swung it from behind his calves, underhand, and let it go. It spun into their legs like a cartwheel lacking the rim. It mowed down three. They heard it cracking on shin-bones, and an ugly shout burst from the men.

"Kill the bastards."

Budlong spat into his fist and grabbed his tent peg. The Burke men crashed into them. Chad was spun around by a glancing knock on his head ; and he saw Fiero galloping away. Damn the Dago. Out of the mess a thick-built man materialised, jabbing at his guts with the end of his pole ; he felt it and then a resounding hollow pumpkin sound from the man's head surprised him. He dropped the pole and covered his skull, and Fred Shepley, white as fish belly, gave him a shove and the man's thick middle buckled uncannily and he went tail first through the rail, his splash shooting water nearly to the bridge floor.

The fight became completely snarled. It made no sense. A head showed up and you brought your peg down, and as like as not you hit another head. Pamplon was dropped early. Chad tripped over him where he lay. He looked completely dead, but the blood was coming from his nose. He heard Ike yelping, and then Joe Duddy bellowed just above him. He knew it was Joe from the size of his legs and the faint smell of Oscar on his shoes. He heaved himself up to see Joe and a red-faced mug wrestling for the same peg. Their faces were absorbed. They weren't doing any damage. They might as well have been counting cats. Chad swung his boot into the man's rear end with all his might and felt it bounce. The man belched like a steamboat, straightened and turned, and Joe Duddy brought the club down on the top of his head. The man fell against Chad and sat down hard. It was Walsh himself. To Chad it seemed beautiful. Then a stone hit him on the arm, and he saw Fiero poised on the bridge above, with rocks at his feet. His left leg was extended, his right hand back, he heaved, said, "Hah ! " and let her come. Chad ducked. He heard Mr. Huguenine yelp, and whirled to see Shepley standing off two men.

Shepley had lost his peg and was using his fists. He was doing fine. But a third man hit him with the haft of a sledge and he went down like a post, full length. Chad took the rush of the three men. Budlong appeared with a bloody mouth and cracked one of them. He heard Joe Duddy's call for help. A great wet mass hit him in the back ; he felt the weight like a bear's all over him and a pair of hairy arms took him round the waist, squeezing the juices in him, and he knew it was his thick-built antagonist climbed back from the canal. He butted back-wards with his head, and the man banged him on the planks and fell on top of him. They started rolling. Fiero shouted, " No rocks ! " in a piercing voice and leaped for life. His splash coming up met Chad and the thick man going down, and they all three tangled in the water. " Drink, bugger," grunted the thick man, jumping on Chad's neck. Chad ducked under water and clawed for his legs. He caught the waistband of the man's trousers and yanked. He felt the fly open and kept pulling. The trousers came down and Chad let go. The man stood there hobbled. He couldn't kick free. Chad reached out and pushed him over as easy as a rotted fence post. He went full length, mouth open, making a wide swell that lapped Chad's wishbone. Heaving a minute to get his wind back, Chad de-cided that he needn't bother about him. He could smell mud roiled from the bottom. As he started wading for the bank, the thick man rolled up through the water desperately hoisting his trousers, and floundered towards the other shore.

An enormous upheaval of water on the upper side of the bridge announced a new arrival. Chad waded to see who it was. It was Mr. Huguenine. He was making feeble paddles with his hands. He kept saying, " God damn Walsh."

They were in pitch dark under the bridge. The light from the lantern lit only the water on the lower side. Chad grabbed Mr. Huguenine and started laboriously to tow him out.

Overhead the stamping ceased.

They heard Walsh say, " I guess they're licked. Let's get the wagons."

Mr. Huguenine groaned in Chad's hands. Chad felt himself getting sick. He was thoroughly surprised when Mr. Huguenine suddenly and completely vomited. It seemed as if somebody had made a mistake. He started to grin. He was getting silly. And they were licked. In just a second now Walsh would set fire to the tent wagon and the whole Huguenine show would be done for, for good.

There not being anything else to do, he kept on towing Mr. Huguenine to the shore. It was difficult getting him up the slope of the berm, and at the top he dragged him round so his head hung down to the water, in case there was any more draining in prospect. He would be all right there.

Chad started stumbling towards the wagons. He wanted to find Caroline and get her out of the way, if possible, before Walsh's hyenas reached the horses. But he was stopped short by Mrs. Huguenine's voice.

" You stay right where you are, Mr. Walsh. If you move, I'll let it off and so will Caroline. I don't know who she'll hit, she ain't never fired a gun before. But I'm bound to get you."

There she was, just short of the top of the bridge, with an enormous shotgun in her fat hands. Her bonnet ribbons shook as she emphasised her words. Beside her, pale and intent, Caroline pointed a small rifle at the victorious remains of Burke and Walsh's gang.

Mrs. Huguenine continued, " Sundays I set on the porch with the rifle and shoot woodchucks, Mr. Walsh. With this spray gun I can just about pucker you. No, don't go back. Just your tough boys. I want you to come up here."

The gang showed no intention of moving. Mrs. Huguenine's snapping eyes and complete determination could not be misread. It wasn't the idea of the gun that scared them so much as that it was in Mrs. Huguenine's hands. To their eyes, the opening of its muzzle must have taken on some of the woman's own width.

Mr. Walsh didn't like it either.

He said, " I guess we've had enough, ma'am. We'll go now."

He couldn't keep the satisfaction from his voice. It was fairly obvious that Huguenine's was in a bad way, even if their equipment did remain.

" Maybe." Mrs. Huguenine drew a snorting breath. " But I don't trust you. I want to be told plain you're through. Come here, mister. Come closer. I want to see you, when I talk to you."

It was fascinating. The red-faced Walsh looked as if his mind were leaning backwards. He approached her up the bridge, a step at a time, across the top, and stopped three feet in front of her. " That's enough," Mrs. Huguenine said sharply. " Now, Mr. Walsh, you give me your word as a gentleman you won't bother us here again ? "

" Yes, ma'am, I do," said Walsh.

Quick as lightning she lifted the barrel of the gun. She brought it down. She pole-axed him completely. He fell on his face. His chin bounced just once from the planks.

" I believe him," Mrs. Huguenine said complacently to

Caroline. "Now you fellers can put him in the wagon. And get going. Tell Mr. Burke I think he is a skunk. And don't get funny. Me and this girl are staying right here."

She watched them steadily as they took Walsh by the arms and travoised him down the bridge. After a minute the wagon started. Mrs. Huguenine put the gun butt solidly on the planks. It thumped, and in the same instant the barrel belched forth a thunderous report.

"Oh, my stars!" she screamed. "It went off!"

12
MR HUGUENINE IS BLED

How Huguenine's managed to get to Newark was a puzzle to them all for a long time afterwards.

Chad had rushed up on to the bridge; at least he had thought he was rushing till Caroline pulled his arm over her shoulder and said, "You lean on me."

"I ain't hurt," he told her. "I'm just sore."

But it was pleasant to let his weight lean on her and feel her slim body using all its strength to hold him up.

She said, "I saw you fighting that man and go off the bridge with him. I was sure you were killed. But you licked him, Chad."

With Mrs. Huguenine, they took stock. Joe Duddy was sitting up and rubbing his head. Budlong had a nose-bleed as well as a broken mouth and had lost two teeth. Bastock had a lump on his head as big as Chad's, and when he got on his feet he had to sit down again, suddenly. Shepley had been sick; he was weak and giddy; but he had no broken bones. Pamplon seemed the worst hurt: he was still unconscious. Caroline found somebody's hat and fetched water in it while Mrs. Pamplon who had rushed from the wagons now that it was over, ministered to him with a wet small handkerchief and wailed.

Budlong came over to examine him.

"He'll be all right," he pronounced. "Frenchmen stun easy."

He sat down with his back to a rail upright and said he

wished he could chew. Fiero returned. " My rocks were all gone," he explained. " I look all over but there are no more rocks."

Chad said, " We better fetch A.D."

He and Fiero went down to the canal bank and dragged Huguenine up to the road. Mrs. Huguenine said, " Is he bad ? "

" I don't know," Chad said.

She nodded.

" You got to expect it when you go jumping off bridges at his age. Take him up to the treasury wagon and lay him on the bed."

It was a hard job, but Fiero and Chad and Joe managed it. Huguenine lay on the bed like a bundle of wet wash. But when they lit a candle, he groaned and opened his eyes.

Closing them again, he asked, " Did they burn the wagons, Bettina ? "

" No. It's all right." Mrs. Huguenine poured whisky into him till he choked. " He's liable to get a stroke, but he'll be all right to-morrow, I guess. But you and me will have to get the show to Newark. Bastock and Joe can drive, and I'll take the treasury wagon. I guess Ike or Fiero could drive the light rig. But you'll have to handle the tent wagon. Can you ? "

" I guess so."

" Any man who's been hit on the head like Budlong or Joe or Pete would get dizzy that high up," she said. " Caroline will have to bring the ring horses. I think myself the sooner we get started the better."

It was a painful procession that finally rolled into Newark. Caroline helped Chad stable the horses and get the other performers to the small tavern. It took some time to persuade the proprietor to let them in, and longer to get him to give them beds after he had seen their condition. Chad was all played out when he got back to the lot. The three skinners were asleep under the tent wagon and Mrs. Huguenine was sitting on the steps of the treasury wagon in the early light of dawn.

She held her fingers to her lips.

" He's gone to sleep, Chaddy," she whispered. " I set down here to see if he would, and now I dassn't get off because of shaking the wagon. But I brought a blanket out for you, and here's some whisky. Take a good drink and go to sleep. When you wake up we'll figure what to do."

She was still sitting there when he closed his eyes.

Four hours later he was wakened by small boys talking excitedly outside the cage wagon. They could smell the lion and they were trying to see him.

Chad chased them out of the lot before going over to ask for Huguenine. The rocking of the treasury wagon showed that Mrs. Huguenine was busy inside ; so Chad sat down to wait in the sun with his back to a wheel. He had a good deal on his mind and nobody to talk to. Budlong, Bastock, and Joe Duddy were still snoring under the tent wagon with a few sun-stirred flies exploring the eddies over their faces ; they ought not to be wakened until it was necessary. In the meantime, however, somebody would have to get Oscar his meat ration and find out how Shepley, Ike and Pamplon felt. Fiero, of course, was all right. It would have to be decided whether they would show. He hadn't had time to look around the town to see if any of Huguenine's paper remained—probably none. As he turned the prospects over in his mind, he could find just one good point : Burke and Walsh had had to haul through Newark in the middle of the night. Probably nobody had seen the elephant. Oscar might have some attraction after all : he had had for those little boys. Chad wondered how small boys managed to get up and get to the right place, no matter how early. This bunch had still had sleep grit in their eyes.

A basin of water arched through the window of the treasury wagon and Mrs. Huguenine, as usual, looked out after her throw to make sure she had hit nobody.

" My stars," she said. " I didn't wet you, did I ? "

" No, ma'am. How's A.D. ? "

She came out of the door, closed it behind her, and beckoned Chad away from the wagon. She sat down on the pole of the cage wagon. " Set alongside," she invited. But, noticing the bend of the pole, Chad said he preferred solid ground. " Well," said Mrs. Huguenine, " A.D.'s pretty bad. He's miserable and he thinks he feels worse. I think he's got some fever and I'd like you to bring him a doctor."

" What do you think's the matter ? "

" I don't know. He might have hurt his insides. Falling off the bridge that way. If he'd only let them hit him on the head," she said. " Moses on the mountain ! "

Chad didn't try to figure out what she meant by that ejaculation. He said he needed money for Oscar's meat.

"I'll give it to you. I clear forgot about that poor old cat. I don't know what I'd do without you."

"Well, I been figuring. Do you think we'll show here?"

"Show? We've got to." She nodded at him. "I know you boys feel mean. We all do some, ourselves." There were dark pouches under her eyes. Her face didn't look solid this morning, but sagged, as did the rest of her. "A.D.'s an old man," she said suddenly to Chad. "You boys probably don't figure how old he is. He's near seventy. When I married him twelve years ago, my mother thought I was throwing myself away. She said I'd bury him inside of five. But I didn't, did I?"

"No, ma'am." Chad picked a grass blade and sucked the tip. "We can get the tent up all right. I'm thinking about Shepley and Pamplon. Pamplon got a real lick, and Shepley took a beating too. I don't believe he could even vault, let alone somerset."

"We got to show, Chad." She folded her hands in her lap, leaned towards him, staring. Her eyes looked large. Chad had never noticed before how good-looking they were. She said to him, "Here's how it is. We have to show to eight hundred and fifteen people a week, Chad, or a hundred and thirty-five every day, just to pay expenses." She stopped. "No, that was before Albany quit on us. The number of full tickets we have to sell is seven hundred and twenty-five now, or about one hundred and twenty-one. Her board and salary come to $23.25. Eighteen dollars for salary—we can't pay like a big show."

Chad looked at her with admiration.

"How do you keep all those figures in your head?"

She lifted a plump hand.

"Land of Goshen! The way poor A.D. worries his head and talks figures, I've got them all by heart."

Chad was interested.

"I'd be curious to hear what they are," he said.

"I don't mind telling you. We pay out $124 a week for salaries—that includes me at $5. Then board costs $47.25. The stock costs $10 and Oscar $1.50. We generally have to pay something for lots and we allow $20, but Bisbee generally gets them free. The $20 covers all his expenses, and we allow a dollar fifty a week for paper. Now if we miss a day's show, you see that throws the whole business off, and we have to borrow for that week against the last good one. We been making money; but lately we've been losing. It comes pretty close, and it's getting closer, and it makes A.D. fret so."

She looked at Chad.

" You see why we got to show ? "

He said, " Yes. I hope we can. I'll see how Shepley is."

He got up and roused the skinners. They complained. They were all sore, and Budlong's face had swelled out of all recognisable proportion. Chad told them that Huguenine was going to show, and that when he returned with meat for Oscar, they would haul the rag up. Bastock and Budlong merely grunted, but Joe Duddy's lamentations followed him all the way out of the lot.

The tavern was open for business and Caroline was waiting on the porch.

" I wanted to go up to the lot, but I was afraid I'd miss you. Are you feeling all right ? " she asked anxiously.

" Kind of tired, that's all," he said. " Have you heard anything about Shepley or Pamplon ? "

She shook her head.

" Well," he said, " I'll have to find out. You know where their rooms are ? "

" Yes." She took him upstairs. The sleepy clerk at the office desk eyed them without comment. The upper hall was a dark channel smelling mustily of bedding. She showed him the door.

The Pamplons were awake. Mrs. Pamplon in a ragged but lacy dressing-gown, her hair still in papers, answered Chad's raps. She said her husband was just getting up ; his head ached, but he was all right, possibly. Could he perform ? Oh, it was impossible. Such a blow ! Pamplon heard the discussion and came to the door himself. He had been shaving. His face was white and his forehead showed an ugly swelling. He shrugged his shoulders. He would perform ; maybe not the manual of arms. " Silence," he said to his wife. And she wilted away from the door.

Fiero answered at the next door and Chad went into the room. Shepley was sitting up on his side of the bed, his feet on the floor, his hands braced on the mattress. He would ride, he said, grinning wryly. But he didn't know whether he could vault standing. The show had to be put on. " We won't expect a lot," Chad said. " You took a beating." He felt embarrassed at having to change his opinion of Shepley so completely. " I want to thank you for cracking that feller's head, Fred."

" That's all right," Shepley said. " I guess Ike's all right. He went out early." He heaved himself off the bed and began stepping gingerly round the room. " It's funny what a lot of places you can get hit without knowing it at the time."

Fiero said importantly to Chad, " I get him fixed. Me, I am all right. If I had had rocks enough I would have spoiled the attack."

" That's right," Chad agreed.

" With the knives, I miss, because that is how I learn. With the rocks, never. I throw, I leap, I dive."

He flashed his smile.

Chad closed the door and found Caroline still in the hall.

" Is Fred all right ? "

He nodded.

" What about eating ? "

" Just a minute, Chad. It's so warm, I think I'll leave my shawl." She walked down the hall to her own room, pausing at the door to look at him. " Do you want to come in ? " She was shy. Both knew what her words meant. And Chad, curious, felt some of the same shyness. " I was lucky," she said. " I got the room all to myself."

Chad stared round ; to-morrow night he would be sharing a room like this. The bed stood in the middle of the wall ; there was a wash-hand stand with crockery that had brown mottles. The cake of soap was thin. Her nightdress was hung over a chair to air. In spite of its mustiness, the room still contained a faint, young-woman scent.

Chad stood uneasily while she hung the shawl under the gingham dress-curtain, picked up the nightdress. It must have been one of Albany's. Practically everything Caroline owned must have come from Albany. He wondered whether it disturbed her, too."

" You are ready ? "

" Yes, Chad."

She had had no time to find an eating-place, so they hunted one together. As they ate Chad revolved in his mind the feelings he had had in her room. It must be hard for a girl not to have anything of her own.

After they had paid their bill, he said, " I ought to make you a present before we get married. A man ought to, when he gets betrothed. I don't know what a girl would want to buy, but here's two dollars."

He had figured the amount out carefully. He handed her the bills without looking.

" Oh, Chad," she said. " It's too much."

" No, it's not."

" What do you want me to buy ? "

" Something for yourself." He couldn't tell her outright. " Something pretty, with lace maybe."

She said nothing. When he looked at her he saw tears in her eyes. " You're so good," she said softly.

" Lord knows what the show will be like. A.D. can't move out of bed, Mrs. Huguenine says. She wants me to get a doctor. I better hurry up and find one."

They found a doctor's sign on a porch rail. It was a good enough name, and Dr. Jos. Danvers looked like a good enough man and he came along with them. There wasn't room for him and Mrs. Huguenine together in the treasury wagon, so she waited outside with Caroline and Chad, fidgety as a hen hatching eggs. After a few minutes the doctor opened the door and asked for a basin.

" What for ? " Mrs. Huguenine asked, turning putty-coloured.

" To bleed him into," the doctor said shortly.

" It's under the bed," she said. " A.D. thought he was going to be sick. I put it there. Is he all right, doctor ? "

" Yes." The doctor closed the door. Pretty soon he opened it once more, to emerge with his hat and bag in hand. " That will be fifty cents," he said.

He was a youngish man and he looked curiously at them and at the other wagons and the skinners.

" Keep him lying quiet for a week and he ought to be all right." He put his hat on. " What happened to him ? "

Mrs. Huguenine had climbed into the wagon for the money, so Chad told him that Huguenine had fallen off a canal bridge. He had to explain how Burke and Walsh had tried to run them off the road. The doctor nodded. " I got home late last night and they were passing through town then.

" Chad ! " Mrs. Huguenine sounded faint. Chad went into the wagon and found her sitting on the edge of the bunk with a fifty-cent bill in her fingers. She said, " Take that basin away. It makes me sick. Poor A.D. All that blood. Oh my."

Chad took the basin up. It looked as if there were a quart of blood in it. But Huguenine wasn't particularly pale. He opened his eyes and told Chad to offer the doc a free pass. " Yes," said Mrs. Huguenine, cordially. " If he ain't bled A.D. to death, he's welcome."

Chad delivered money and invitation to the doctor and handed Joe Duddy the basin to dispose of. " What'll I do with it, give it to Oscar ? You suppose that old man-eating cat would drink it ? " Joe asked. " It might tonic him some."

The doctor smiled. " I'd like to come if I'm free," he said. " A lot of people have got over to Palmyra. But I hope you folks run Burke off the route yourselves."

He shook hands with Chad, lifted his hat to Caroline, and stalked across the lot towards his house.

" He hadn't even had his breakfast," Caroline said sympathetically.

" Oh, he'll eat it all right," Joe reassured her. " Doctors never throw up."

" Chad," Mrs. Huguenine called. " A.D. wants to see you."

" How are you feeling ? " Chad asked him.

Mr. Huguenine opened his eyes and said, " Thirsty." He closed them. " Doc says I can't have no likker. What I want to tell you is you've got to take my place. You've got to till I get up."

" I couldn't do that."

" You got to, Chad. There ain't nobody else. If Bisbee was here he could. But he ain't, damn his hide. That feller's always somewhere you don't know where," Mr. Huguenine said blurredly. " I can't argue. Doc said so. You do it."

" I ain't got the clothes."

" Wear mine. I got the speeches all wrote out. Bisbee done it. You can read if you've got to. You got to act up with Ike——"

" Couldn't Bastock ? Or Budlong ? "

" They'd look like skinners just the same. No, I'm depending on you. Get my coat out, Bettina."

The coat went on, but it hung pretty loose and Chad's arms showed all of the wrists. But Mrs. Huguenine said he was handsome. The hat was tight, however. " Hold it in your hand. I'll give you twenty-five cents extry a day," said Huguenine. "I got to rest."

The idea appalled Chad. In the first place he did not know how Budlong and Bastock were going to feel about it. They were older hands and by rights it seemed to him they should have been chosen for the job. In the second place, it was fun to listen to Huguenine's confusion, but it was going to be a lot different being out there himself in the ring. His instinct told him that he would have just as bad a time with " gymnast " as the gaffer had. He felt like a fool coming out of the treasury wagon with the coat on his arm and the hat in his hand. But Caroline caught on instantly. Her whole face lighted.

" Oh, it's wonderful, Chad."

" No, it ain't."

" You'll be fine. I know it. I always thought you could handle a show. Mr. Huguenine thinks so too, or he wouldn't ask you. I'm proud."

Well, that was nice, he thought, but he ignored her, crossing to the three skinners. They eyed him and his garments, and Bastock grinned and said, " 'Morning, gaffer."

" You ought to get the job," Chad said.

Budlong said, " We wouldn't want to miss the fun. Besides, we're musicians. The show can't get along without us."

Joe Duddy grinned.

" Got any orders, Mr. Hanna ? "

Chad felt better.

" Yes, put up the rag," he said.

The tent went up slowly. But they got her raised and the ring pegged and the seats in about eleven o'clock. They were exhausted. Ike showed up apparently able to ride, so Caroline had a ring practice and by noon, when the parade started, they all felt a little more limber.

13

THE RING

As soon as Ike Wayfish started to make his exit on stilts Chad knew that the job of equestrian director suited him. For one thing, he could handle a whip better than Huguenine. He didn't miss a snap. He could even get gradations of sound and expression out of it, so that people could tell how he was feeling. He found himself becoming a young, self-important man, with a great notion of how things ought to be run, and this built up Ike's part better than Huguenine's obvious confusion and lack of ease. Every now and then the audience was inclined to sympathise with Huguenine.

That was all wrong. The equestrian director ought to be a man you instinctively disliked, and the whole show ought to be built up to the moment when he was confounded by the man and the man-eating lion. In other words, every one should see how fine and efficient the equestrian director thought himself so that they could gradually come to share with the clown the exquisite ecstasy of making a monkey of the boss.

Ike began to play up almost from the start. The back chat had more whip to it ; Ike looked less mechanical and more scared ; and that by contrast made his determination to get into the show funnier. It wasn't long before a little girl in the front row, noticing one of Ike's attempts to get back into the ring, screamed, " Look out, Mr. Clown ! " at the top of her shrill voice.

Chad hadn't had much time to memorise the speeches. Bu once he had worked through the opening address, it didn't matter. The acts carried him along. He had been listening to Huguenine for nearly a month, and the words were all in his brain and seemed to come out of themselves.

The smallness of the audience helped. It was easier to attract their attention, to make them listen. A big tentful often bolted off on some track of their own, like a batch of calves finding a hole in a fence. A little boy might get sick, and the high-rider could throw a somersault and break his neck, but the whole tent would be looking to see what the little boy was going to manage next. With a small audience, also, it was easy for Chad to estimate the reaction to the individual performers. For instance, the faces turned to follow Caroline almost as much as to watch Fiero during the juggling act. And she had almost nothing to do there. On the other hand, while the Pamplons were at work, they paid no attention to Mrs. Pamplon. They were only interested in Pamplon, but they weren't sympathetic, the way they were with Caroline. Fred Shepley fascinated them, and of course they loved Ike. Chad decided that Caroline, if she managed to become a good rider, would pull the crowd with her as well as or better than Albany had. He studied her to see why. She was pretty ; she was a lot prettier than she used to seem ; and she had a good build. The men watched her. With Mrs. Pamplon, the tights just meant tights ; but with Caroline you thought of the girl in the tights. And she didn't do any of the things Mrs. Pamplon did, like bending her knee, or tiptoeing one foot, or smoothing her short skirt, or pirouetting. Whatever Caroline did, however, showed that she put her heart into it. She seemed to like the people ; she wanted them to like the show ; right now, she showed by the way she looked at Chad that she thought he was being wonderful. At first, it seemed like a mistake. Then he realised that it helped him to build up the picture he was giving them of the cold, exacting ring-boss. It would work out even better when they reached Palmyra and she did her first public riding with Ike.

The show itself went surprisingly well, considering what Huguenine's troupe had gone through. People forgot the bruised faces of the band players. Though Budlong's swelled mouth choked the fife notes pretty badly, Bastock was clear enough with the bugle, and Joe Duddy had never gone stronger on the drum. Pamplon had had to give up his manual of arms ; he was giddy on the wire ; but he managed the rest of it. The great surprise to Chad was Fred Shepley. He vaulted well and he rode, though stiffly, with the kind of fire he had showed during that first ring practice in Syracuse. Chad wondered how he had misjudged the fellow so badly ; Shepley was the kind who lifted when the rest of the world was going down. He said now, as Fred leaped the ribbons, " Don't clear those garters so high, just clear 'em. You're making the rest of the show look like monkeys anyway."

Shepley grinned. " You forgotten the spiel about my somerset ? "

" Don't try it."

" You say it or they won't know what's coming."

" You're a damn fool," Chad said, really alarmed.

Suddenly he became aware of the fact that the audience was listening to them both. He had fallen out of character. He snapped his whip. He had better announce the somerset before Shepley made a complete monkey of him by making the attempt.

He saw Shepley's face draw tight as he lifted himself for the somerset ; it put a drag on the front muscles and it had got him where he was sore. But Shepley stayed on the horse. He didn't try to make the somerset to his knees. He spread his legs coming down and lit to his fork. Then he leaped off and took a bow stiffly and said out of the corners of his mouth, " What an equestrian director ! "

Chad let him go. Ike Wayfish was making his rush, shouting, " Let me ride ! "

" That ain't a pullet," Chad shouted in excited relief.

There was a moment's silence. This was supposed to be a clean show. But suddenly the men guffawed, and Ike spread his arms and crowed and hit the horse and fell comically enough to carry the rest of the audience by. But Chad was sweating when he roared the " All out and over."

They congratulated him, Mrs. Huguenine the first of all, crossing the ring kerb with a rise and fall like a ship on a billow. She kissed him. " My, I wish A.D. could have seen you, Chad."

Chad felt embarrassed.

" We want to tear down early," he said. " We ought to get to Palmyra before dark."

" What's the hurry ? " Ike asked.

" I'll tell you," Mrs. Huguenine said. " The equestrian director's going to get married. Him and the new lady rider. We'll all have supper after the show in Ludlow's Hotel. Maybe Ike will arrange it."

" Sure," said Ike. " I'll be pleased. Get out of here, you two, so the rest of us can make arrangements right now."

Caroline was flushed bright and near tears. Mrs. Huguenine and Mrs. Pamplon kissed her ; and the men were shaking Chad's hand. When Ike and Fred Shepley broke away to come over and wish her happiness, her heart overflowed. She had never had any friends of her own, but now she was going to be allowed to share Chad's with him. She felt so proud. Trid's house and Canastota seemed a long way off. . . .

The show pulled into Palmyra to find Bisbee waiting on the lot. His intelligent eyes took them in with one embracing survey.

" My God, folks, I'm glad to see you. Where's A.D. ? "

He clicked his tongue as they told him. His long face became thoughtful.

" I guessed there'd been trouble when I saw their new paper. They got Albany advertised with *their* show now."

" We knew that two days ago," Mrs. Huguenine said tartly. " While you was still gallivanting through the west."

" There ain't a scrap of our paper left here or in Pittsford," Bisbee said calmly. " A couple of Burke's men chased me coming out of Pittsford. They acted mad, so I guessed there's been some kind of trouble on the road."

" Mrs. Huguenine opened Walsh's head with a gun barrel," Bastock told him.

" Purty," said Bisbee, swinging his eyes admiringly to the fat woman. " I wish I'd seen it happen."

" Did they chase you far ? "

" They had rigs. I cut into a pasture. Nothing to it." He sat down on the grass. " It sure is hard luck, working a girl like Albany to the top and having her stolen. But that's business. How's the show going ? "

" We nearly paid in Newark. We had ninety-four. That's without Albany on the pay-list," Mrs. Huguenine explained.

Bisbee nodded.

" There won't be no profit here, though. It's hardly worth showing. Now we got to figure . . ."

" We'll show here," Bastock said. " A thin tent's all the better. We're putting on Caroline, the female high-rider, in her first public appearance."

Bisbee stared. They had to explain, and then his face brightened and he looked at Caroline.

" By God, I'll see her to-morrow. If she goes well, we'll do better than we did with Albany. You put a female in tights on top of a horse and every man in the place will get dirt in his eye trying to watch her. Carolina," he caught right on, " the

American equestrienne, riding against Europe's best. It means new paper. It'll have to be drawed special. What's the act ? "

Bastock explained.

Bisbee nodded. " We'll have to work her in with Fred too. It'll be more exciting, her in tights, him in tights, and Ike trying for a toe-hold, just like every man in the audience would want to. How old are you, missy ? "

Caroline said in a low voice, " I'll be seventeen in a month."

" ' This young and beautiful and talented American girl, the sylphide of the upper air.' You remember I said that ? I know a printer here that has an apprentice can draw. We'll get a block and have the posters printed by to-morrow night. There's no use showing Pittsford, though. We'll try Penfield with the new paper. ' Unique, unequalled attraction.' We can't show Rochester either. Burke's would burn us out for sure this time. But there's a lot of interest out in the west about Oscar and Ike. How is Oscar doing ? "

" Not too sassy," Joe Duddy reported.

" That cat," Bisbee said in a worried voice. " I hope he don't peter out now. He's our only card against the menagerie, out west. Who's doing the ring announcing ? "

" Chad is," Shepley said. " He's good."

Bisbee stared again.

Chad saw that Bisbee felt the same thing. There was a new friendliness in the troupe.

Fiero bustled forward.

" My knives are all right. To-morrow I can throw them at Miss Trid. Superb."

" No, you can't," Bastock said. " She's too valuable."

Bisbee agreed. " We'll maybe pick up a boy, cheap. It ought to be a good act too."

" No, no," Fiero protested. " I throw missing Miss Trid. I miss hitting some other girl."

" Listen, Fiero. You happen to hit a girl and you'll get hanged. You hit a boy, and maybe we can get you of town."

Fiero spread his hands.

" Such country, such people. So backside."

" I better talk to A.D.," Bisbee said. " As soon as I get the paper printed to-morrow I'll light out for Penfield. We'll show there July fourth. We ought to have an American flag for Carolina."

" I'll get one," Mrs. Huguenine promised. " But you'll miss the wedding."

" What wedding ? "

They had to tell him about that. " I've been missing things, all right," Bisbee said.

" I guess you have, all right," Budlong said dryly, trying a chew.

14

THE WEDDING

" My heavenly days," said Mrs. Huguenine. " I wish A.D. could be here to see it. Poor dear silly man. To fall off a bridge that way and miss out on this-here champagne wine."

She raised moist sentimental eyes to look at Mr. Bisbee. Bisbee was, it seemed to her, exactly like a horse her grandfather used to have, a brown horse with a long nose and a very intelligent face. His name was Prince, and if you could have brought him to Palmyra and sat him down right there at the other end of Ludlow's Hotel table, with a black coat on, and a spotted tie round his neck, he would have looked just like Mr. Bisbee. She leaned her elbow on the cloth, inclining her fat red cheek to Mrs. Pamplon, and whispered, with her eyes still on Bisbee, who was getting to his feet, " It don't seem possible Granpa could have sold him to the glueworks, does it ? "

" It is a pity," Mrs. Pamplon agreed politely, watching her husband. It was obvious that he was only drinking the champagne out of politeness. Mrs. Pamplon wondered how these strange Western people made their champagne wine anyway. It lay down in one's stomach as if it never wanted to get up. Henri would have a headache most positively. She would have no sleep, because Henri's headaches were savage ; she would have to tend him with cold towels. If he would merely pretend to drink. But Monsieur Wayfish kept asking him to say it was good. One had to please. She shuddered, as a dizzy image came into her mind of wild hogs trampling out grapes in a vat while they chewed apples and a careless wine-maker spilled molasses.

" What do they do to him in the glue factory ? " she asked Mrs. Huguenine.

" Why, I never asked. They grind bones and fry fat, I think. It smells terrible. It doesn't even smell like glue. . . ."

Mrs. Pamplon stared at Mr. Bisbee in bewilderment, as Mrs. Huguenine proceeded, " He never kicked, even when I pulled hairs from his tail. Shhhhh ! He's going to make a speech."

Bisbee was on his feet. He arranged his wine-glass and his brandy-glass neatly in their places. " Ladies and gentlemen, my good friends . . ."

He raised his face. The table in Ludlow's dining-room had been tastefully arranged. He and Mrs. Huguenine faced each other down the length of it. On one side sat the three skinners, new-washed, new-shaved, their coats brushed. On the other were the bridal pair, flanked by Ike Wayfish and Shepley. Mrs. Pamplon and Fiero kept Mrs. Huguenine company. Pamplon was next to him. Everybody was wearing his best clothes. It was astonishing, he thought, that Chad could look so respectable. He wore a blue silk necktie round his neck, and a pink rose in his lapel. Caroline, as was proper, looked enchanting, with a bit of white gauze round her head and pansies in her hair. Bisbee cleared his throat ; he would make his speech short.

" It gives me great honour, on this nuptial occasion, to have been voted the chair. I appreciate my inadequacies. The one sad note of this matrimonial engagement is that the man who should properly preside is now in bed, I am thankful to say, not suffering, and soon, I trust, able to resume his accustomed sphere of activity in the great world of entertainment exemplified so happily by Huguenine's Great and Only International Circus. I refer "—Bisbee bowed the length of the table—" as you may suspect, to our respected proprietor, equestrian director, and shall I not add universal good friend, A. D. Huguenine. Shall we drink his health ? "

The tears rolled out on Mrs. Huguenine's cheeks, as she rose with the others, to drink, at a public gathering, her own husband's health.

" Wasn't that elegant, though ? " she asked Fiero. The Italian nodded. " I should have brought my knives. So I could have framed the head of that stag. It would divert extremely, I think." He gazed at the mounted head upon the wall over the fireplace, a deer of good horns, with an appearance of having caught cold, for there was a slight leakage of sawdust from the nostrils.

Fiero was feeling fine : such food, the brandy free, this champagne wine. He was glad he had been seated at the ham end of the table. Though the turkey was all right when some of it managed to filter past those horse-skinning men who drove the wagons. There had also been two ducks, a large whitefish with a sauce of cream and eggs, and a piece of beef à la mode. The ice-cream was vanilla. Now the cake had been set down before Mr. Hanna and Miss Trid ; but no, he should say Mrs. Hanna. Signora Carolina. He had thought of the name, or had someone else ? It was on the new posters, however, and to-night, even before that small crowd, she had ridden like a blessed virgin. That was not to be said aloud, but he had not intended profanity. If he thought about knife-throwing maybe he would not say such things even in his thoughts. Ah, virgins, he thought. He had never thrown his knife at a virgin ; probably he never would now.

" Mr. Fiero, do you feel all right ? " asked Mrs. Huguenine. He smiled.

" I feel so sad and so happy," he told her.

" Shhh," she said, loudly, feeling the small occasional bubbles in her nose. She had better say " hist " next time, she decided ; no telling what this champagne wine might do to a woman if she wasn't accustomed to it.

Bisbee rapped on his glass, and the kitchen door swung open and one of the tavern help, a girl lacking a front tooth, bawled, " What do you want ? "

Bisbee was flustered. " Nothing, thank you, my girl. Nothing."

" Oh," she said. " Well, it's out back, to the left, in case you want to know."

Bisbee hemmed a moment before he regained his stride.

" It is auspicious," he said. " An auspicious occasion, that our acting equestrian director and our new and unique star, Carolina, the only lady high-rider now travelling New York State, should on the night of such a happy debut also, in the more sentimental if not wider field of matrimony, make another debut, which I am certain will be even more happy, if such were possible. May these conjoined careers continue as long one as the other and both be pursued as they have started under the benevolent and celebrated ægis of Huguenine's Great and Only International Circus."

" What's an ægis ? " asked Joe Duddy.

" It's a bird, I guess," Bastock said. " I've heard it before."

" Like a pigeon, maybe ? "

" Bigger . . ."

" Hist ! " said Mrs. Huguenine, with a horrid feeling that the proper consonants had eluded her.

" Mr. and Mrs. Hanna have already damped their toes in the sea of matrimony. They are about to wade in," said Bisbee in a loud voice. " It is a sea some of us are lucky enough to have adventured in ourselves. And those who have not had parents who embarked before them. I wish to propose a toast to matrimony . . ."

He raised his glass, motioning the others to their feet.

" To matrimony ! The immemorial institution of mankind —its foundation is the female form divine—its support is love— it's consummation joy ! "

He drained his glass.

" He don't include the pigeons," Joe Duddy started to point out.

" Shush ! " said Mrs. Huguenine.

Mr. Bisbee remained standing over the applause.

" To the happy couple, Mr. and Mrs. Chad Hanna ! "

Every one shouted.

The kitchen door swung open.

" Mr. Ludlow says to please be careful with the glassware."

The door closed.

" Now," said Bisbee, with a fine disregard of the interruption, " the bride must cut the cake."

" Oh, dear," said Mrs. Huguenine, rising again like a rubber ball. " I must see Caroline make the cut. It reminds me of my own wedding so."

Caroline's hand was shaking. Chad whispered to her to bear down. He wished the dinner was over. He had drunk a lot of champagne wine and it wasn't what he thought it would be like at all. It made him feel heavy ; he longed for the end of the dinner, when they could escape, get into the light rig, and drive to Fairport. It was eleven miles to Fairport. They wouldn't reach the tavern till ten o'clock, if they started this minute. It would be terrible to get there and find themselves locked out.

Bisbee had suggested their going to Fairport.

"You'll like it better, going away. That's what you do at a wedding, anyhow. You take the bride away. She expects it. It makes her feel excited to leave home like that. It's a dandy little tavern, too. Not costly but real comfortable. If you tell Mr. Lusk you know me, he'll give you a room on the back if you'd rather not face on the canal."

It was a good idea, Chad thought, if they ever managed to reach the place. Besides, Fullam's Basin was only a mile farther west on the canal, and at Fullam's the Penfield road crossed north. They could rejoin the circus there at eleven o'clock on Sunday.

Caroline made the first cut, blushing as she said, "I want Mrs. Huguenine to take this, so she and Mr. Huguenine can eat it together."

"Now, ain't that sweet?" demanded Mrs. Huguenine, reaching for the plate. "I'm going to take it right up now so I can tell A.D. what Mr. Bisbee said and what you've just said. I'll say good-bye now." She hugged Caroline with her free arm, the other holding the plate and cake safe from harm. "I got to kiss you both. My, my, my. It's worth it travelling two hundred miles just to have a thing like this happen. I got to kiss you, too, Chad." Her cheeks were wet.

Caroline took up the knife. "Now, Mrs. Pamplon," whispered Bisbee.

Chad watched her cutting the cake. It made him self-conscious to have to stand beside her. He glanced apprehensively at the skinners, but they were all eyeing the cake, fingers ready on the plate rims. Cakes didn't come often, not cakes with white icing and made with raisins, currants, citron, nutmegs and lemon brandy. "Got to chew a wedding cake good," Budlong admonished the company. "Knew a feller choked to death eating one. Wedded by the minister one day, buried the next. Double money for the church. I carried the coffin so I heard the funeral speech. Minister got mixed and called him the currant Mr. Boffle. Nobody else laughed . . ."

Fiero frowned thunderously.

"Has everybody been helped?" Caroline asked, glancing round the table. "I—Chad and I—want to thank you all. It's been a wonderful wedding supper. I hope you're all as happy as I am."

" Bravo ! " exclaimed Mr. Bisbee.

Chad wondered whether this was the time to go. Caroline seemed waiting. She was wearing the same light print dress, but it seemed to him that she looked older in it, more fashionable. Her waist was narrower and her hips and breast fuller. He wondered whether getting married changed a girl's appearance. Looking at her now, one would hardly suspect that a few hours ago she had been making her first public appearance on a pad. She had ridden well, too ; but now, when she met his eyes, the colour flooded her cheeks, and her eyes dropped ; and standing close to her he could hear her shivery intake of breath. She was pretty. He thought of all the time he had hardly noticed her, with Albany Yates around the show, and he wondered for an instant what it would have been like to have stood where he was now, with Albany. He and Caroline had just seemed to drift to this ; but he wasn't sorry. He was excited.

Shepley touched his elbow. " I've got the rig ready," he whispered. " Your things are in it. Come on."

Shepley's face was pale. As Chad shook hands with him, he suddenly knew that Fred also was thinking of Albany.

Ike Wayfish gave a shout. " Come on, folks. We can finish the cake and champagne after we've got rid of these two."

They made a stamping, trouping out of the front door. A stable-hand, grinning, held the heads of the odd horse and Ike's mule, hitched to the light rig. Shepley helped Caroline over the wheel.

She said, " Why, Fred ! What's this ? "

" Surprise," bawled Joe Duddy. " Surprise, surprise, surprise ! "

It was a huge carpet satchel, with a great medallion of flowers on one face. The colours showed red and yellow and blue in the light.

" It's from the members of the troupe," explained Ike. " Wishing you all well."

Chad didn't know what to say, but Caroline called in a choky voice, " I think you're all sweet people. I love all of you."

She burst into tears.

" Get going, you fool," Shepley muttered to Chad. Chad took the lines.

Somebody threw a handful of rice, but the horse and mule were already trotting. He glanced back ; he saw Fiero, in the middle of the road, left leg extended, right arm back. " Duck," yelled Chad. The shoe whizzed after them, but Chad had been too late. The wheeling toe caught Caroline's fluttering veil, tore it off her head, and the whole mess hit Alice, the mule, square in the rump. She gave an exclamation, and broke into a gallop.

" Did it hit you ? " Chad asked.

" No." Caroline shook her head.

" I'll certainly never let that Dago throw a knife at you," Chad told her grimly.

15

FAIRPORT

It was half-past ten when they came along the road into Fairport. They had been following the canal bank for several miles, seeing few boats, but moonlight traced the water for them. Then it picked out the low belfry of the church ahead, even before the village came into view. A dog was barking, working up a hatred with the moon.

Neither Chad nor Caroline had said a thing for some time past—the faint coolness in the air, the stillness of the road, their own wheels, making a mutter in the sand. There was one loose felloe that had a small rattle when it came around. It made them realise how tired they were ; and for a while Caroline had leaned against Chad's shoulder when he raised his arm suggestively. But she acted shy ; he could feel her holding herself to stay there, and after a bit he let her go. Now she straightened up on her side of the seat, her eyes ahead, on the belfry, and the upraised ears of the mule.

" I guess this is it," Chad said. " It's been far enough."

They saw a small cluster of houses along the canal. It was easy enough to find the tavern, which fronted on the towpath, with a small section of second-storey porch over the front door. As they rolled up to it, they saw a faint light from one of the windows.

" Thank God," Chad said. " Somebody's awake."

" You're lucky people," Mr. Lusk told them when he opened the door. " I was just going to get to bed."

" Mr. Bisbee said he thought you could give us a room to-night."

" Horse-faced feller ? " asked Mr. Lusk. " He's been here before. You from the circus ? "

Chad said yes ; and Mr. Lusk examined them, breathing hard. He had a round face full of pale fat ; he sounded asthmatic.

" Yes," he said, " I'll give you a room for fifty cents, a fine feather bed." His eyes creased. " There won't be anybody else coming into it either. This place is empty, only me and my coloured cook. You'll have to put up your own horses, mister. But will you sign the book first ? "

He went slowly, carrying his lamp, to a small desk in the hall under the stairs, squeezing himself behind it, opening a thumb-marked ledger, dipping a pen, holding the feather towards Chad, and placing his forefinger, with a long exhalation of breath, on an empty line.

Chad wrote, " Mr. and Mrs. Chad Hanna."

" Now," said Mr. Lusk, " if you'll fetch in your bag, I'll take the lady upstairs while you stable the team."

As Chad went out he heard the stair treads creaking, Mr. Lusk breathing hoarsely, and he saw Caroline, following, her face lifted towards the light. When he had put up the horse and mule, though, there was light on the towpath from the upper window. He looked up at it and saw Caroline pull the curtains shut.

" Turn that key, will you ? " Mr. Lusk asked as Chad came through the front door. " The missus likes the room all right. You new married ? "

Chad said they were, sheepishly.

" Come into the bar and have a drink on the house," said Mr. Lusk. " 'Tain't often I get a bridal pair. I always feel like wishing a man luck. It's the least I can do for him."

He poured two small glasses of whisky.

" Well, here's to haying weather," he said. " It'll make me roar some, but you won't hear it ; I sleep downstairs. You can have breakfast at eight o'clock."

" Thanks," said Chad.

" I'll hold the light for you going upstairs. Good-night."

" Good-night."

The hall was dark, but Caroline had left her door open a crack. He pushed it open slowly. She was sitting in a big bed, wearing a nightdress with small frills round throat and wrists. Her eyes looked large. She said, " Isn't it nice ? " in a queer tentative voice.

Chad said it was. It was the nicest room he had ever been in, with gold-bordered crockery and a picture of a shaggy bull and cow and calf by a river under a castle wall.

A boat horn blew way down.

He put his hand over the candle, and in the darkness undressed, standing by the window, with the cool air drawing over his skin. He saw the bow lantern creeping along the endless thread of water. He could hear the slow hoofs of the horses. A driver boy's voice said tiredly, " God damn you lazy devils," as if the boy were close to tears. Poor kid, he had an hour on his trick. But Chad could go to bed, with his own wife, in a hotel room. He climbed under the coverlet beside her, feeling her tremble. She was his wife now ; he felt a pride of ownership, of having got somewhere, of beginning. He wondered if she was scared, but she came right into his arms, the rising feathers behind her walling her in against him.

" Oh, Chad."

He knew then how she had wanted to be married ; she made him think of the way he first remembered her, sitting on the kitchen table back in Trid's house, slowly raising her bare leg as if for his inspection.

" Bridge," came the driver boy's thin cry.

The horn answered.

" I love you so, Chad."

Her face following his in the darkness.

I

FIRST ALARM

CHAD stopped the mule and horse under a shade tree beyond the bridge at Fullam's Basin. It was a blistering morning, without wind enough to blow the dust. The leaves hung heavy and the canal teams struggling on the towpath were wet to their fetlocks with sweat.

Chad looked lazily at Caroline. It had been wonderful, waking up at seven and knowing they did not have to get up till eight. He had waked Caroline so she could enjoy the fact, and she had, and they had made love to each other all over again, lazily and slowly, the way you supposed the people did on Quality Hill. About half-past eight they went downstairs to find the coloured woman ready to take their breakfast orders. They chose sausage and fried eggs, and fried potatoes, and bacon cut thin and cooked crisp, and cuts from a peach pie. They ate in the small dining-room. The windows opened on the towpath, so that passing canal teams blocked off the entire view, even darkening the room, and the drivers looked in on the couple eating at leisure like gentry. It was a wonderful feeling. Afterwards they went upstairs and Chad, smoking a cigar he had bought from Mr. Lusk, sat out on the porch while Caroline packed their new bag. He could hear her humming, light and soft. She sounded happy ; and it made Chad feel satisfied with himself to hear her. She brought out the bag, carrying it open with both hands for him to see their things packed together, explaining to him, " My nightdress is on top of your things, so it won't get mussed so badly. Isn't it a beautiful bag, Chad ? "

" It's not too bad," he agreed, knocking the ash of his cigar over the porch rail, and seeing her, all eyes, watching him.

So they paid their bill and got out the rig and took their time coming along to Fullam's. But this was the end of the honeymoon : they would be getting back to work now ; and Chad said, " I wonder how much pay Huguenne will offer you ? "

C.H. 321 L

"Probably not much," Caroline said. ·

Alice, the mule, lifted her big ears a few minutes later and squalled. They got out of the rig and went up on the bridge to see the caravan crawling towards them through the glare of sunlight : the treasury wagon in the lead with Mrs. Huguenine and Mrs. Pamplon on the front seat ; the cage wagon, with Pamplon riding beside Joe Duddy ; Bastock and Ike on the seat wagon, and the great bulk of the tent wagon in the rear.

Then they made out Bisbee, trotting his brown horse beside the treasury wagon. He drew way ahead of the procession, riding up the bridge ; and, stopping beside them, he looked down with his long face sober and only a slight glint in his eyes.

"How are you ? " he asked.

"Fine," Chad said, grinning.

Caroline blushed.

"I bet," said Bisbee. He fished in his poster case and pulled out a slightly rolled sheet. "Here's the new paper," he said. "I got to get on to Penfield and post some. Then I'm going out along the route. Mrs. Huguenine's taking A.D. on to Rochester right after the show to-morrow. She wants to give him a bath at the springs. But you'll camp in Gates. Then the rest of the route is Parma, Spencer's Basin, Brockport, Clarkson, Murray, Gaines and Albion. I'll meet you there."

"Do we show in Gates ? "

"No. We'll show in Parma the sixth. You can kill time in Rochester, and A.D. can get a double dose of bathing. So long," Bisbee said. "A.D. will talk to you about pay. But one thing : Caroline ought to keep right on practising."

"Oh, yes," Caroline said. "I know that."

Nodding to them, Bisbee kicked his horse in the ribs, and moved off through the village. He was well out along the Penfield road by the time the wagons reached the bridge.

Mrs. Huguenine hollered greetings as if Chad and Caroline had been away from the show for at least a month's time. But the performers were equally glad to see them, and especially the light rig, for they were tired of the lumbering box wagons. They climbed in beside Caroline with their bags. Before Chad had unhooked the ring horses from the treasury wagon, the rig was rattling ahead along the road. It looked just the same as any other stage they had made ; except that Caroline turned to wave to him. Chad mounted and moved up beside Mrs. Huguenine to ask for A.D.

"He's some better, but he's so terrible stiff. You let a heavy man like him get knocked around and he feels worse than London Bridge." Mrs. Huguenine adjusted the cotton stocking she had wound round her neck for a dust-cloth. "Mr. Ludlow showed me an advertisement in the paper, though. About them Rochester baths. They only cost fifty cents to get into, and Mr. Ludlow said some of these springs, if they're genuine mineral, can do a lot of curing. We're going to try it."

"You too?"

"Do you think I'd let A.D. try something I hadn't?" she asked. "They let in females. I got the advertisement right here." She fished a clipping out of her shelf-like bosom. "Listen to what it says :—

'Ladies and gentlemen can be accommodated with a warm or cool showering. Ladies are respectfully informed that a number of rooms have been fitted up especially for their use. For better accommodation of those who may not be acquainted with bathing, and for those who may need assistance, arrangements have been made to have female attendance in readiness.'

"There ! Seems to me that ought to do him good." She shoved the clipping back into her bosom. "Don't mention it to A.D. He'd get balky. I ain't told him yet."

There were quite a few people on hand when the circus rolled into Penfield. Being Sunday, and past noon, people were ready to turn out, and quite a few came along to the lot to watch the tent being raised. Some of the younger men were ambitious enough to help lug seats from the wagon ; in that way they could see the inside of the tent before any one else. Joe Duddy was good at organising such volunteer efforts.

"You boys done fine," he said. "But you'll have to clear out now. The lady performers have got to practise."

Dressed for practice, Caroline brought the new poster into the tent. Chad had observed people studying it on the inn porch, but this was the first chance he had had to see it close to.

The poster showed Fred Shepley doing his somersault on the right top, but in the left top, galloping towards him, poised on one toe, arms delicately raised, was a female figure whose one defect was a blot on the left knee. " It's me," Caroline said, tense with excitement.

CAROLINA, the American equestrienne, the only female principal rider now performing in New York State, will appear in every performance, equalling the most difficult feats of equitation now performed by the leading equestrian females of Europe and Asia. Already her talents have earned for her the Universal title of *The Sylphide of the Upper Air*. Her beauty, grace, and talented mastery of this difficult art, as well as her modest and refined manners, both in and out of the ring, have made her a favourite in all the cities in which she has appeared.

Bastock interrupted them.

" That don't mean a thing," he said. " It's time you got practising. Ike's here and Shepley's coming. The gaffer wants to talk to you, Chaddy. But bring the cream in first. And you better bring in Jerry too. It's all-fired hot out there."

Mr. Huguenine had heaved himself out on to the steps of the treasury wagon, from which post he had been watching the 'erection of the tent. His face was blotchy and he breathed hard in spells. But when Chad asked him how he felt, he said, " I'd feel better if Bettina quit fluttering all the time. You got that tent up fast. Seems like good times again to be off the main road and people anxious to see the show. Maybe we'll do better now. If I had a drink, by jeepers, I'd drink it."

He ruminated over his wrists.

" Bettina says you done fine. We raised your pay. But Bisbee says we'll have to pay your wife." He paused again. " You got to know we can't pay her much. She's just 'prentice riding, really."

" She ain't bad," Chad said.

Huguenine pursed his lips.

" Bisbee says she's pretty good. We put her on the poster, that's something. A lot of young girls would be proud just being on the poster."

Chad sat down on the grass. He said, " Most of the proud people I ever saw made good money."

Huguenine eyed him.

" Ain't it hell the way it works out ? " he asked petulantly. " You needn't act so chesty. I'm going to pay her. But you could give me time to work up to it. It's just as hard to work up to paying out money as it is to work up to get paid. Bisbee says maybe she's worth five dollars a week. That's what Bisbee says."

"He's kind of a funny feller," Chad said. "First he puts her up with Shepley on the paper, and then he offers her five dollars. What do you say to that, A.D.?"

"I ain't said. I'm telling you. Five dollars is a lot of money. Specially when you think how I carried her along, feeding her, free gratis for nothing. *And* let her use my horses *and* allowed a man to teach her when I was paying him for other work."

"Well, she's equal to what Shepley is on the paper," Chad said.

"That's just to fool the customers," Huguenine said testily. "My back hurts. Say, did you marry a girl or did you marry a top-rider with money ideas?"

"The girl suits me." Chad dug his knife into the grass between his legs. There was a worm there; he held it up; and Huguenine looked at it, too, and said it was a puny kind of worm. "Five dollars is puny," Chad said.

Huguenine groaned.

"Bettina only gets five," he pointed out.

"Yes. But she shares the show's profits. Caroline don't. You make another offer and maybe we can talk."

"Talk? You mean you'd quit?"

"Oh, I'll stay. But Caroline, well, it might not be worth while her risking her neck for five dollars. Would you risk yours for five dollars?"

"There's no call to talk that way. My neck's just about bent off anyway."

"Then she's my wife. I got to think about her that way. Suppose she broke her neck, I wouldn't have no family."

"That's one trouble. You'll probably fix her so she can't ride. That happens to a lot of married people. Women especially," said Huguenine, driving the point home.

"Well, if you've promised Bisbee to not pay her more, why don't you pay me two dollars extra? That makes seven dollars and a quarter a week."

Huguenine swore at him.

"A.D.!" cried Mrs. Huguenine. "The doctor said you wasn't to strain yourself."

"He wants seven dollars. God damn it, that hurt," said Huguenine, straightening his neck. "As soon as I saw your face, Chad, I knew you was going to give me trouble. I can't argue. But I'd rather pay her seven dollars."

"Either way," Chad said, grinning. "It's cheap enough."

"Well, you'll have to run the show then. Bettina's taking me to see a doc in Rochester, so you'll have to bring the treasury wagon. You'll have to sleep in her. Tell the boys I want to talk to them. Tell them to come right out. I want to lay down."

Fred Shepley was practising vaults with Caroline on the pad. It was something that Bastock had not dared let Ike Wayfish attempt. He was fine with his comedy mounts, but he was used to using the entire pad.

It was exciting enough with Fred Shepley working. His face was intent. He had to time the vault exactly to a hair or he would knock her off like an apple in October. She could not wear the pratique as the strap would have got in Shepley's way.

The tent was completely silent, only Bastock in the ring, his eyes anxious. Chad didn't dare interrupt, but standing beside Ike and the other two skinners, he saw that Bisbee had the right idea. Shepley and Caroline were handsome together ; their builds matched nicely ; they made much more of a picture than Caroline and the clown. Ike's crazy doings would be used merely to set off the top-riding.

Shepley had his heart in the business. He was taking chances himself to make sure of Caroline's safety, hitting the pad so far back that it looked as if he might miss it altogether. They were so completely absorbed in their work that neither of them had noticed Chad's entrance. It was only when Bastock called for a rest that they saw him.

When the others had gone out of the tent, he sat down on one of the seats, waiting for her to come over to him.

"Did Mr. Huguenine speak about my pay, Chad ? "

"Yes," he said. "You're going to get seven dollars."

"Seven dollars ! "

"Yes."

"Aren't you glad ? "

"Of course I'm glad."

"You don't sound so." She studied him a moment. Then she said, "We've got a real nice room at this hotel. It's not as nice as Mr. Lusk's. I don't think we'll ever have one as nice as that."

"You can't tell. You and Shepley were certainly doing good."

"He's wonderful. I feel a lot steadier with him than with Mr. Wayfish."

"That's fine."

She said, "It's hard to smile. I feel funny trying to, but Pete said I'd have to learn. He said male riders don't have to, but female riders have to smile all the time. He said people expect it."

Chad said, "You look fine up there. You both do. You make Fred look better." He kicked at the grass. "A.D. says I have to run the show until he gets better. We're taking the treasury wagon into Gates for him. I got to sleep in it. Maybe you'd rather go to a hotel."

"Oh, no. I've wanted to sleep in the wagon ever since I saw it. It'll be fun. Just think, it will be like having our own show. And we'll be making twelve dollars a week, fourteen, I mean. How much is that a month?"

"Fifty-six dollars," Chad said, after some figuring.

"We're rich, almost."

Chad hadn't considered it in monthly pay. It was a lot of money. He began to feel better. He figured it out—suppose Huguenine's managed to keep on the road to the middle of October, that would be three and a half months, nearly a hundred and ninety dollars. They could live a year on that much money; they could stay in a hotel.

They could go back to Canastota and put up in the Yellow Bud, and Mrs. Mott would have to take his orders for a change, and wouldn't he run Diney ragged? He saw it all: he and Elias Proops sitting out on the front porch when the weather started to get warm—they'd take the corner room next to the old man's, the one Albany had been in. The recollection stopped him short.

"What's the matter, Chad?"

He turned to Caroline.

"I was wondering about Elias Proops, how he was. I thought maybe you and me could spend the winter in the Yellow Bud. Would you like that?"

"What would you do there?"

"Nothing," Chad said. "Just have a good time. You wouldn't have to work, either. We could hire a horse and go over to Syracuse once in a while. We could take Elias along. I guess you never saw him."

"He looked something like an old goat, didn't he?"

"That's him. Regular old goat. Just about as knowing."

It would be fun, all right. He could imagine himself standing off Elias's comments every morning.

"Well, you better get riding," he said. "The better you get, the more we'll make Huguenine pay." The others had come back to the tent, Bastock saying facetiously, "Can I get back on this practice, gaffer?"

"Go ahead." Chad made his voice sound important. Then Fiero spoiled it all by coming up to congratulate him sincerely. "Now you are the boss, now maybe I can begin throwing the knives, hey? I have not killed her for three days, expect one hole by the arm. I am good, superb," he said humbly.

"We'll see, Fiero. Maybe when we get to Rochester we can pick up a boy for you."

"When do we reach this Rochester?"

"To-morrow."

Fiero turned pale. "So soon. Oh, it is wonderful. I get on the poster. You wait."

"What's troubling you, Joe?"

Joe coughed into his hand.

"Maybe you'd step outside, Chaddy?"

"Can't you tell me here?"

Joe rolled his eyes at Caroline. He performed another cough. "It's something I got to show you," he said.

"All right," Chad said. "I'll come along."

He followed Joe out into the sunshine.

Joe said, "I wanted to tell A.D., but he said he couldn't be bothered. He said you was running the show for a while and to see you. You just come over here and look at it."

He led the way to the cage wagon, lifted the panel off, and, putting his face close to the bars, beckoned Chad forward to do the same.

Chad looked in. The old lion was stretched out on his side, panting in the heat.

"I don't see anything," he said.

"Don't you see nothing? Nothing at all?"

" No," said Chad.

" I couldn't mention it in there with Caroline. That's the whole trouble. There ain't anything."

" What are you talking about ? "

" Just that. I ain't cleaned his cage since yesterday morning. There ain't anything in it. That old cat ain't moved his bowels all day."

" You sure ? " Chad looked back in.

" Well, smell."

They stood cheek to cheek, inhaling.

" I guess you're right," Chad admitted. " But I don't see it means much."

" Don't you ? I guess you never been troubled that way. But if you was, just imagine how a cat his size feels. I been nursing that old animal," Joe said. " I been swamping out his place. I know him. Maybe he ain't so active, but he never missed doing his business. I guess it was the most fun he had. No, sir." Joe wiped his forehead. " That-there's a sick animal."

" What's the matter with him ? "

" I don't know. He don't show nothing special outside of what I showed you. Maybe he's just old. He was old when I see him first, and he ain't got younger. Maybe a doctor could tell us."

" I don't know what a doctor would know about a lion," Chad said. " Probably all he needs is a physic."

" Yeah ? What kind of physic you going to give him ? He ain't no horse, Chaddy. You don't even know how many stomachs he's got."

" Maybe Budlong can think of something for you to give him."

" I ain't putting no physic into that animal," Joe said.

Chad studied Joe for a minute ; but it was obvious that Joe had passed a law.

" Well," he said, " he may come round by to-morrow. We'll wait and see. There's no sense worrying till then."

2

PENFIELD

CHAD hadn't discussed Oscar's puzzling condition with any one but Caroline. As soon as he came to their room in the tavern that night she saw that he was worrying over something. It was easy enough to tell Joe Duddy there was no sense in worrying ; he couldn't help it himself. Any time an animal went wrong a man had a right to get upset ; animals' insides were something one took for granted. With a lion in a cage, whoever, nothing any one knew about dosing seemed to have a reliable foundation. The problem spoiled his whole built-up notion of how it would be coming into a bedroom at the end of the day to find Caroline waiting for him. He was more like an old married man whose best cow has developed a milk fever. He hardly looked at Caroline, who was waiting up beside the airless window in her new nightgown. He said, " Hallo there," and sat down on the bed and started taking off his shoes.

She watched him for a minute without speaking. Last night he had told her the nightdress was pretty ; he had said she was pretty. The nightdress had ruffles round the throat and at the cuffs of the sleeves ; it made her feel dainty ; it made going to bed with Chad an exciting thing, feeling nice like that, knowing she was nice, because she felt nice. She had spent some time extra combing her hair, so that it curled from the centre part, softly, over her forehead. She had fixed up the room a little, cleaning the old soap from the soap dish and the fingermarks from the wash-bowl, and moving the chair to the window, so that he could see her sitting there the minute he opened the door. But he had hardly looked at her.

" Chad," she said. " What's the matter ? "

" Nothing."

" Yes, there is."

" What makes you think there is ? "

She flushed. She couldn't tell him why. She couldn't say, " Last night you liked me so, you practically ate me up, like a lion eating a human, but I like being eaten. I was fun, wasn't I ? You said so in the morning."

She said, instead, " You look all tired out. You're frown-ing."

" Can't a man feel tired ? "

" Of course he can. So can a girl." She came over to the bed, sitting beside him, so he could feel her with his shoulder. With an appreciation of her own artfulness, she made the touch light, and his reflex, putting his arm round her, was automatic. " Something's worrying you. I can tell it. Why don't you tell me ? Maybe it's not so bad, if you tell me."

" It's Oscar," he said, and he told her what Joe Duddy had told him. He had been to look the last thing.

She gave a low laugh. It was a relief to know Chad wasn't just used to her in one day.

" Men are funny," she said. " As soon as anything goes wrong with their insides they get scared to death. Maybe lions are the same. Why, he'll be all right in a day or two. You'll see."

Chad had to grin at her grown-up tone. She was trying to look grown-up too, she was fetchingly womanly, sitting upright inside his arm, long and slender with the nightgown shaping her.

" Poor old Oscar," he said. " I wonder if he ever got married before he was taken ? "

Caroline had a smile, the inward-knowing feminine kind of smile, that made a man wonder whether he ever got inside of her at all. She let her head tilt a little, so he could kiss her mouth if he felt like it.

" I wonder," she said. " I wonder how a lioness would feel."

She knew she could handle Chad, a while anyway. She wondered how long it would last. He was a roamer by nature. It still seemed incredible that he had found her roost at all. A foot-loose man, she thought he was ; and she had the instinctive knowledge that he liked to be, and must be, kept guessing all his life. It was all right now, anyway.

The first firecracker for the Fourth woke them in the pre-dawn. They lay in the bed, whose old cords rolled them back downhill into a mutual valley whenever they tried to move at all, and listened to the tentative bangs, let off by small boys at the risk of parental wrath, spreading like a mild disease across the village. There was no point in trying to sleep after that. Daylight brought courage to small boys. They got up in time to see the tavernkeeper raising the American flag on the liberty pole, with a soiled British pennant underneath it, and a ragged squad of militia loosed a stuttering rifle salute practically in their faces.

After that the Fourth of July took form with the increasing heat. The militia trooped into the bar to reward themselves for their patriotic early rising. Firecrackers gained force and frequency. The local company appeared before the tavern and rested their rifles against the porch rail waiting for the officers and the inevitable parade.

Chad had to go to the lot. He looked at Oscar, who had been roused by the noise and was nervously shifting round the cage wagon. Joe Duddy said nothing had happened. "But maybe he'll get something scared out of him anyway. You going to tell A.D. ? "

Chad shook his head. He didn't want to worry Huguenine, who was worried enough about his own condition ; and he doubted whether Huguenine would have any worth-while ideas about a lion anyhow.

Caroline and Shepley practised riding for two hours, and afterwards they worked Jerry with the cream. The grey was getting a good gait ; he went steady even when some boys loosed some crackers outside the tent.

Then, having stabled the horses, the circus troupe returned to the tavern to watch the drill and listen to the oration.

The oration was properly hoarse, loudly patriotic, and mostly concerned with saying what a low article the British nation was. The pauses were frequent and times for applause that allowed the orator to refresh himself from a glass handed out of the bar window. He wound up at a sort of hand gallop after three-quarters of an hour, evoking considerable admiration with his finishing powers, and then reviewed the militia, who presented arms, shouldered them, did the manual, formed squads, and marched away down the main street behind drums and fifes. They looked spirited as they went off, they returned dogged, dusty, and dry ; and the whole adult community adjourned to their porches, leaving the streets to the younger generation, who started loosing the more expensive crackers.

Every now and then during the meal hour the shout of " Runaway " brought the porch-sitters to the sidewalks to cheer or screech advice to a farmer sawing the mouths of a wall-eyed team as they pelted down the street, the womenfolk clutching the smaller children on the bucketing seat, the wheels spinning a glory of dust. The village was in fine humour for the circus.

They liked everything. For once Pamplon, doing his manual on the wire, received so much applause as almost to put him off balance. Even Fiero got a loud hand. Caroline was followed round the ring with an almost tender anxiety. Chad thought she and Shepley would practically bolt an audience like this one to their seats once they had perfected their double act. Shepley's ride was perfect. This audience might have read about Burke and Walsh's mammoth arena, but never having seen such a thing they thought Huguenine's round-top was immense.

Ike Wayfish, of course, was the life of the whole show. Penfield loved him. He was what every man felt like but didn't dare act like, and the womenfolk could laugh because Ike was no relation and it was all make-believe and nonsensical.

His surreptitious attempt to bandage the lash of Chad's whip was greeted by roars of laughter ; his rendering of the ballad, " Sally of the Green," moistened eyes visibly ; he had a good voice and he had done some mellowing of his own.

" My girl wants to marry a banker, instead of me," he confided to Chad sadly at the end of the song.

" Does she ? " Chad was cold.

" Yes, sir. Do you know why ? "

" No ; why ? "

" Because when she deposits a kiss, she expects to get some interest." Ike clambered out of reach of the lash. " And do you know what she says, Mr. Equestrian Director ? "

" No, I don't know what the person you call a ' girl ' says."

" She says——"

" Well," impatiently, " what *does* she say ? "

" Wouldn't you like to know ? "

The old saws went wonderfully. Ike's final emergence in his stars and stripes brought down the tent, and as he climbed in with Oscar, Chad could hear the indrawn breaths. He watched closely.

Now that the firecrackers had died down, Oscar was logier than usual. He wouldn't even lift his head. He just lay there, panting and slitting his eyes at the audience, and Ike even lifted his head aside. But Penfield thought it was wonderful. It was something they would obviously remember for a long time.

A man lying down with a lion was one sight nobody had ever seen.

But after the all-out-and-over Ike came over to Chad.

" What's the matter with that cat, Chad ? "

" I don't know," Chad said.   " He's got indigestion, I guess."

Joe came horning in.

" Chaddy, couldn't I let that critter out of his cage ? "

" No."

" My Cripus ! He wouldn't hurt nothing."

" Suppose he run off and fell in the creek ? "

" He wouldn't. He hates water. Just think, that cat's probably never had sand between his toes since he was captured alive in Africa. Maybe if he ate some grass, it would help. I've seen genuine cats eat grass."

" Try it. Put some in."

" A cat can't eat mowed grass," Joe said scornfully. " That's why I said let him out—so he can browse it."

" They've probably got different grass in Africa," Chad said. " This might just make him sicker."

" I hadn't thought of that," Joe admitted. " Maybe some spring lamb would digest easier with him. Or maybe some venison. It's a wild meat. It might activate something in him."

" No," Chad decided. " Lamb costs too much. We got to tear down now, so we can get to Gates before dark."

" Why don't you tell Huguenine ? " Ike said, and there was a murmur of agreement from the company, who had realised that something was wrong with Oscar.

" Him and Mrs. Huguenine have left for Rochester in the light rig," Chad pointed out.

At the name of the city, Joe pricked his ears. " Rochester is a good place. You can flush pigeons up and down both sides of the river for nearly half a mile." He eagerly closed the sides of the cage wagon, his mind already on the pursuit of pigeons. " If I could take that cat along with me to-night, maybe that would make him feel better."

It was a wonderful notion. All during the tear-down he and Budlong and Bastock worked on it. Taking Oscar into some of those Water Street Houses would make a sensation, probably. Even a cross-eyed man without a nose could get action taking Oscar with him.

Chad made a count of the day's take. They had pulled in 157 full tickets. Sitting in the treasury wagon, Caroline helped him with the count. Then they locked the cash in the chest and shoved the chest under the bunk.

Every one else was ready waiting. Chad said, " I'll drive between Bastock and Joe. Rochester is a pretty tough town."

Sitting on the seat of the treasury wagon, with Bastock ahead of him and the sound of the other wagons rolling the dirt behind, he was conscious of his responsibility.

" How does it feel, Mr. Gaffer ? " Caroline's face was pressed against a small aperture right behind his ear.

Chad grinned.

" I just found it," she said. " If you lean back I can kiss you."

He did, after making a survey of the road, and she kissed the edge of his ear.

" I wonder if Mrs. Huguenine ever did that to Mr. Huguenine," she said.

Chad nodded. He wished Oscar would manage something, even only a little. It was a stony road. That might help some.

3

LADY LILLIAN RIDES FOR BURKE

CHAD looked through the bars of the cage wagon at Oscar. The dingy old lion was lying on his belly as if he still felt in it the jolting of the eleven-mile haul from Penfield.

" You think it would do any good to make him stand up ? " he asked Joe

" No. He won't get on his feet till he's sure he's quit moving. If you lit a fire under his tail, he'd just lay there and let the smoke come out his mouth."

" I wish it could," Chad said. " You don't suppose he could have picked up something that's got lodged in him ? "

" Pick up something ? " Joe asked.

" I mean a stone or a rag or something."

" Listen," Joe said indignantly. " I swamp that cage just as carefully as they do the bar in the Astor Hotel. You couldn't find a better-swamped lion cage in seven counties than this one is. If you ain't got anything better to think about I'll just pull my foot for town."

Chad looked round. Up a slight slope he saw the back-side of the post office at Gates, an apple tree, a privy, and a small hog pen. It wasn't much of a place to stop in, but the postmaster, an inquisitive man who said his name was Sturgis, had told them they could use it for nothing if they would let him and his kids look at the lion. They were all staring at Oscar now.

" Boys," the postmaster was telling them, " that's a genuine lion. And you wouldn't have seen him, either, if I'd took you to Rochester." He looked pleased with himself.

His oldest son, a replica in small size, swayed his jaw like his father, and said, " Could I bring the Tomlin boys to see it, mister ? "

" Go ahead," said Chad. " Only don't pester him."

As the boy scuttled off, his father said, " *I* wasn't going to wear out horseshoes going to Rochester. No, sir. Nor pay out eighty-seven cents seeing a God-damned circus. My Pa didn't allow me no nonsense, and I don't figure I'll allow my boys any. You feed him pork ? "

" No," said Chad.

" That's too bad. I got a half pig hanging up side of the house."

Chad left him. Bastock was coming back from putting up the stock. The tavern stable, he said, didn't look like much more than the tavern did, but one night wouldn't hurt them. The weather didn't look too threatening.

Chad told him, " I guess I ought to let Huguenine know about that lion. Maybe I'll go back to Rochester to-night."

" Might be a good idea, Chaddy."

" Will you stay here ? Joe's going off. I wouldn't want to leave Caroline alone with the treasury wagon."

" Sure, me and Budlong will stay, and I'll keep sober."

Chad went to tell Caroline. When he had broached the idea, she had agreed that it would be better for her to stay with the treasury wagon, taking his place, since he was responsible. " I'll be back before midnight," he said. He felt a little mean, for she had picked up some cold meat and a jar of pickles and planned a picnic supper for them. " Bastock will look out for you," he said.

As he walked out to the road he heard a familiar *tunk*. Fiero had set up his target against the wheel of the tent wagon and was employing the last minutes of daylight in industrious practice. Caroline's silhouette was completely hedged with knives, except for the finishing one above the head. Fiero caught sight of Chad and brandished his last blade in greeting. "All perfectoes," he shouted happily. "Now you go to the big city to find me a little boy, or a little girl, hey, Mr. Chad?" He wheeled back magnificently for the throw. He let the knife fly. It glittered in the air, and the point found home square in the forehead.

For an instant Fiero stood transfixed. Then his chest heaved and he spun round and pointed an accusing finger. "The sun!" he shouted. "See how it gets low too."

At the sound of his voice, Joe Duddy, who was already out along the road, turned, and seeing Chad, waited for him to catch up. He said companionably, "That crazy Dago will kill somebody yet. You coming to Rochester?"

"Yes," Chad said. "I've got to see Huguenine about Oscar."

Joe nodded. They started walking the three miles back to the city. They had pulled through it about half-past six, crossing the river on the Buffalo Street bridge. Then, the sight of the trim streets and all the crowded houses had depressed them. It didn't seem possible for even as big a show as Burke and Walsh to exhaust the patronage of a place that size. But it would have invited complete disaster to have pitched in open competition with them now.

Grunting a little as he walked, Joe kept up a snappy pace. He was anxious to hit town before all the pigeons had found roosts. "I wish we could get a ride in," he said. He had put on a coat and had a cravat round his neck. His face was earnest and his thick legs plugged away at the road purposefully. Seeing him, no one would have thought that he could raise the devil. But the devil raised in him within a hundred yards.

"You know, if somebody picked us up, Chaddy, we could make town before eight, maybe."

Chaddy grunted.

"Yes, sir," Joe said after another hundred yards. "I think I'll just go to Burke's lot. The pigeons ought to be plentiful there. And if I found a purty, I might take her in to see the last half of the show."

"They showing at night?" Chad asked.

"Sure. I seen it in the posters in Palmyra. 'For those unable to attend our exhibition here,' it said. It's too bad you're a married man," Joe said virtuously, " or we could find two purties and have a real party. I bet you and me could straighten out the street corners if we got started right. Well, Caroline sure is a nice girl, Chaddy. But you take a pigeon and you can make progress before you get started."

"Yes, I guess you can."

Chad's voice was non-committal, but Joe had planted the seed of an idea. He could take in the rest of Burke's show and still get to see Huguenine before half-past nine. And there would be an opportunity to watch Albany—if she was riding in the last half. Caroline wouldn't have to know about it. He had the idea she would be upset.

"I'd kind of like to see how Albany's doing too," Joe chatted on. "They've got her placed in the last half. I read that paper right through. Wait a minute. I hear a wagon coming."

He suddenly went lame.

"Hurt yourself?" Chad asked.

"It's the sciatica," Joe said, seriously. " I had it ever since I got shot in the knee at Plattsburg. If you'd kind of let me lean on you, maybe I could get along better."

When the wagon overtook them, Joe was in a bad way. The driver pulled up. " Don't look at him," Joe hissed. " Just keep on going. If you ask for a ride, nine out of ten won't take you on."

The man said, " You two·going my way? "

Joe looked up innocent as a spring lamb.

" We're going to Rochester, mister."

" Well, so am I. Climb on. You've got a bad leg? " asked the man, when he had his team going again.

Joe turned bashful. " Kind of," he admitted. " It's a ball wound I got to Plattsburg. Seems like, when I hear the guns going off again on the Fourth, she always acts up on me."

" Oh, you're a veteran. I'm proud to lift a veteran."

It was a quick and pleasant ride.

" Where'll I drop you? "

Joe, who had been listening for the music, said, " This is fine. I can get to my sister-in-law's in half a block. She wants me to see her own doctor. Thank you, mister. . . ."

Chad was wondering how he would get away from Joe, but

he needn't have worried. As soon as the man who had given them the lift had driven out of sight, Joe's bad leg limbered and he started full steam ahead for the circus lot. "We can walk along till we get to the Rensselaer House," he said. "You'll want to turn off there to find A.D." He took it for granted that Chad was not coming to the circus. "I'm just as glad you ain't going. A married man among pigeons is worse than cinders in your pants at a camp meeting."

He waved as they came near the hotel.

"So long, Chaddy."

Chad let him get well ahead before he went on towards the lot. It was out of sight behind the baths, or what Chad took to be the baths, a building back of the hotel.

The Amphitheatre was a wonderful sight. The banner on its centre pole appeared to wrap the stars. The canvas glowed with the light inside, like a palace, and the music from the big band issued stirringly and strong, with a clear sweet note of the French horn over it all.

The lot was nearly empty ; three or four women and a few small boys hovered near the entrance. Joe Duddy had obviously made his choice. He was stamping into the tent with his hand buoying the elbow of a female in carnation-coloured silk. Chad had to grin. Joe had often said he liked them curvy, and this one certainly filled the bill.

The three or four women fluttered towards the entrance as Chad approached, but he shook his head, grinning at them, watching their faces fall. A constable stepped up to him. "You meeting any one, mister ? " Chad shook his head. "All right, you," growled the constable. "Get back where you belong."

The ticket-seller looked at Chad. "You're coming late."

"It's the only chance I've got."

"Reckon you'll have to stand."

Chad didn't care. He didn't want to sit where he could be seen. "I've got a reserved seat, though." Chad shook his head again. The ticket-seller took back the ticket and waved him on.

He went inside, feeling the music enwrap him. It was like going into a fairy meeting-house. The audience up on the highest tiers looked larger than life. There was only a narrow alleyway ahead glowing smokily from rings of tallow candles. There were hundreds of them, they seemed like thousands, and as he looked at them, the candle flames seemed to Chad to fuse and become one solid breath-taking illumination.

The roll of the drums over his head deafened him. It brought a dead silence. Out of it, the voice of the equestrian director announced the scenic rider.

" Ladies and Gentlemen . . . It is our honour to present . . . for your attention . . . and applause . . . the great scene rider . . . Charles Ainsworth . . . appearing successively as Don Quixote, the crazy . . . Robert Macare, the pickpocket . . . the Monk of Mexico . . . and Andrew Jackson, in full uniform, bearing the American Flag . . . Old Hickory Never Surrenders . . . Lad-ies and Gentle-men . . . your attention. . . ."

Craning his neck, Chad saw an aisle half-way round the tent where only one or two people stood, and stepping under the seats he made his way to it. He reached it just in time to see the scene rider galloping round the hippodrome. In this enormous tent there was a wide space outside the ring, and the horse had plenty of freedom. It was a good horse, a bright bay, and the scene rider rode him standing in the saddle. But after the first change of costume, Chad let his eyes roam. He picked out Joe Duddy on the opposite side : Joe's pigeon had a plump face with a crimson small pursed mouth that opened egg-shaped when she laughed. She laughed continuously and it was plain that Joe was wasting no time at all. In the midst of their palaver, the band broke into " Yankee Doodle." The Monk of Mexico was shedding his robe ; . epaulettes flashed on his shoulders. From the breast of his tunic he drew a peaked hat, donned it, and from his sleeve an American flag which he waved with stirring, patriotic yells. Chad wondered if General Jackson yelled that way at New Orleans. But it did not matter. Roll upon roll of applause deadened the fifes and drums. In spite of himself Chad felt a thrill at Mr. Ainsworth's stern eye, set face, and gallant bearing. Still fluttering the flag, he galloped off, through the draped red hangings of the performers' entrance, and the equestrian director was soliciting their attention for the unique, graceful, talented riding of Lady Lillian, unparalleled equestrienne, the toast of Europe, the wonder of Asia, the delight of the United States. . . .

The band struck up a dance tune, the curtains lifted, a whole troupe of lady riders entered, horses prancing, once round the hippodrome, and then, taking stations inside the ring, faced out towards the audience. They all looked handsome in their costumes and tights, and at a pause in the tune they suddenly in unison drew fans from their saddles, opened them, and began to fan themselves like ladies sitting out a dance.

Then the curtains parted, and Albany appeared on Buck. Chad's critical eyes went over them. Buck was in good shape. He looked beautiful with his white saddle and bridle, and he made the entrance waltzing.

But Albany was a vision in white. Her whole costume was white. Even the high hat with its ostrich plumes. She wore white gloves, and the toes of her boots showed white when the white habit swung off them with Buck's changing step. The only colour was in her face and in her black hair. Black hair, black horse; the rest was white. He had to admit it was beautiful.

He lost sight of her behind the posed equestriennes; then she came round to his side, the smile bright on her lips, and he studied her close. Her face, he thought, had changed. There were lines at the corners of her eyes. The wide mouth showed the smile, but it wasn't excited.

And Chad saw suddenly what it was. The lovely music, the big tent, the costumes of the other pretty girls. It was an act, all right, but it wasn't Lady Lillian, the titled English equestrienne, who struck wonder to village audiences with her mastery of a horse. Here only a few of the better-dressed were moved to applaud; the rest of the audience sat still, stoically accepting what seemed to them a pretty interlude that was interrupting their real fun. Albany wasn't the top class after all. He realised suddenly that Caroline would have gone better, beginning though she was. A girl pad-riding, a long-legged girl in tights who might fall, was exciting. Here there were too many girls sitting on horses.

When Buck lay down dead and Albany made her speech, her voice sounded small, and the rhyme, ending with General Jackson, was an anti-climax. It ought to come before Ainsworth's ride. He felt suddenly angry and hurt: angry at Burke for not knowing better, for not seeing that he was bleeding her act; and hurt because the crowd did not see how good she was, how exciting and beautiful it was for a girl to control a horse like that. He remembered the manœuvres she had performed with the horse in the maple grove that Sunday morning. She brought back for him the same feeling of something more in it than merely horseback riding.

She was making her circle of the ring for her applause. Though he knew that she had seen him, he couldn't clap his hands. They felt too empty. He just stood there and let her ride off.

A minute later the buffo came on astride a little donkey, doing the Tailor Rides to Brentford . . . "Your old friend, Cabbage MacPickle, sometimes designated as the Shakespearean clown, for which appellation he is indubitably indebted to the Bard of Avon . . ." And the audience howled with delight to have finished off the lady rider. Chad lost heart for the show. Let them laugh. He went back to the canvas, lifted the flap, and crawled under. He wished he had not come.

4

SYMPTOMS

CHAD walked moodily to the hotel. He felt mean. But he could not have helped himself for a month of Sundays. After all, Albany Yates had left Huguenine's without warning. There was no sense saying Burke had bribed her. It was her own choice. It was what she had wanted to do all along.

He walked up on to the porch, found the office, and inquired whether Mr. and Mrs. A. D. Huguenine were staying there. The clerk glanced at him and finished some unimportant business, and then made a show of consulting his book. Yes, there was a Mr. and Mrs. Huguenine. Did Chad want to see them? Chad felt like knocking his head off his neck, but he said he did want to, and after a few minutes he was taken up a carpeted stairway of dark wood.

It was quite an establishment; he had never been inside a building like it; and he could not imagine people like the Huguenines staying there. It must cost plenty of cash merely to sleep there, let alone taking baths.

The clerk tapped on a door down a long corridor and Mr. Huguenine hoarsely bade them enter.

"A young man says he wants to see you." The clerk spoke

through the door without bothering to look inside. " He says
his name is Hanna. Do you want to see him ? "

" Yes," said Mr. Huguenine. " Come in, Chaddy."

He was lying on a big bed in a flannel nightshirt, with three
or four extra blankets. Just lying there he was sweating. He
waited till the clerk had closed the door before he started swearing. From the sound of his voice, Chad judged that Huguenine
had been keeping right at it, too.

He caught his breath and told Chad to sit down. " Bettina's
gone off into the city. She figures she's got a relative, a half-
cousin or something, living here. There's a whisky bottle under
the mattress under my feet. Get it out, will you ? There's a
couple of mugs on the wash-basin and they say the water in the
pitcher is all right to drink if you want water."

" How are you feeling ? " Chad asked. " You look kind of
hot."

" Got to do it," Mr. Huguenine said. " It's part of the baths.
I got to go out there every morning and every afternoon and let
them pour water on to me out of some kind of nozzle or something. It sprays like a cow's tit you take too low down. God
damn it, and then they bring you back here and they make you
sweat it all out again. I tell you, Chad, it's a tough business.
First time I walked in there a man took hold of me and told
me to get my clothes off. I thought he wanted to look at my
back, but he said drawers too. Yes, sir, drawers and shoes come
right off. Even my hat. Honest to Christmas. God damn it,
they put the water right on to your head. You stand there and
you hold your breath so you won't get drowned, and they just
lean on it and douse you. Think they'd ease up ? No, sir. And
the steam comes off your feet. And then when you begin to
feel like a boiled oyster with your shell off, they give it to you
cold. And then they walk you out naked and running water on
to a table and wrap you up in the God-damnedest big towel. I
was pretty scared. The first time they put the water cold, I just
about wetted. But I figure they couldn't see. Now," he said,
his voice sounding hardier as he downed his drink of whisky,
" I'm getting used to it. Yes, sir, I don't hardly wince when the
water hits me. I guess I've got it pretty well beat now."

" That's fine," Chad said. " How's Mrs. Huguenine ? "

" She's only had one bath. I heard her holler in the female
quarters when they hit her. But it stands to reason when you

wet a woman like Bettina she feels it a lot. She's been cantering round the city and spending money and having a fine time. She even went to Burke's show. She didn't see Mr. Walsh, but you know what she did see ? "

" No," said Chad.

" Albany. Says she looked pretty, too. They got her rigged out all in white. But she thinks Albany ain't doing so well, notwithstanding. It's too bad. She was fine for us."

" She's probably making money," Chad said.

" I guess so." Mr. Huguenine quickly changed the subject. " You got to Gates all right ? "

" Yes."

" Say, who's minding the pay wagon ? "

" Caroline. Bastock and Budlong are with her. I wanted to see you."

" What for ? "

" It's about that cat. He ain't well. I don't know what to do with him."

Mr. Huguenine's face sobered as Chad told him the details. He demanded a second drink. " Put the bottle back under the mattress," he said absently. " No telling when she'll get back ; and I ain't supposed to drink liquor. Just that God-damned water. Inside and outside. Rinse the mugs out, and if she smells whisky say you been drinking. Does he act bad ? "

" He don't do anything but just lay down," Chad said.

" Don't bloat up when he eats ? "

" No, but he don't eat much. Joe wants to try him on lamb."

" That won't do any good. If he ain't bloaty, though, he hasn't a colic. Wish he was. I'd put a teaspoon of turpentine down him. Turpentine sure does bore the gas loose from man or beast. Perhaps he'll be all right when you get back."

" I don't think so. He looked bad when I came over. The road must have shook him up, too. It was rough."

They confronted each other from chair and bed with the same bafflement on their faces.

" Oh, lord," Huguenine said finally. " If it ain't one thing, it's another. If I could get him in here, maybe we could fix him. I had a drink of that water and I felt it flowing the minute I swallowed. Say, Chaddy. I'll buy a bottle of that water for him and you give it to-morrow if you see he ain't better."

Chad was dubious.

" You think it's all right ? "

" Why not ? I took it, didn't I ? It's natural water, too. The Lord made it and he made Oscar, didn't he ? Seems to me if he ain't fixed to cure him, we ain't. You pull that wire in the corner and they'll fetch us a bottle." Mr. Huguenine's face brightened. " Ain't it wonderful what they do in a hotel ? That invention rings a bell somewheres and after a while a feller shows right up. But you pay for it, too."

Chad pulled the wire.

" Don't hear a thing, do you ? " asked Huguenine.

" No."

" That's it. Now you just come and set down and it will happen."

Chad did so, and sure enough, in about three minutes the door opened. But it was Mrs. Huguenine, all breathy from coming upstairs. " Why, Chad Hanna ! Ain't this a pleasant surprise ? " She sniffed. " A.D. ! " she said sharply.

" Yes, Bettina."

" You been sneaking likker again ? "

" I guess maybe Chad has had something."

" Yes," said Chad. " Mr. Huguenine said you were hunting relatives."

Huguenine cast him a grateful glance.

" Oh, yes. I saw my name, Billings, over a little store when we were coming into town. So I went down there to-night and found it. It was a little place where they make clothes-pins. You know what I found ? " She giggled. " Can't guess ? Coloured folks ! I walked right in and said my maiden name was Billings and I'd come looking for my cousins, and this female coloured woman came out and said I was welcome ! " Mrs. Huguenine giggled all over. " She was nice as can be, too. She said Mr. Billings worked here. I visited there quite a while. She showed me her baby. And you know what ? The little thing was just as black as she was. Only two weeks old and coal black. My, I wish I'd had a baby ! "

Someone knocked on the door and Huguenine shouted to him to come in. It was a waiter, coloured. Huguenine looked at Chad. " I been telling Chad about that wire," he told his wife.

She said, " My stars. You been pulling that again ? They complained at the office to me about you pulling it just to see these fellers show up."

Huguenine breathed heavily.

" I want a bottle of that spring water," he said to the waiter.
" Yessuh."

In her relief Mrs. Huguenine felt chatty.

" Your name Billings ? "

" Yes, *ma'am* ! " The darkey showed his teeth.

" Mine is too, and I saw the name on your wife's store and
went to visit with her. I saw your baby. My, she's pretty ! I just
loved her. Don't you ? "

" Yes'm. Which one was it, ma'am ? "

Mrs. Huguenine looked baffled.

" Mrs. Billings said she was two weeks old."

" Oh, that one. I ain't ha'dly got accustomed to her yet,
ma'am. But I guess she's nice, all right." He beamed duskily
at Mrs. Huguenine. " They comes so often I don' get cotched
up with them till they's one or two years old."

" Say," Huguenine exclaimed. " You ought to know something about lions."

" Lions, suh ? " The darkey stared at Huguenine and
scratched his head.

" Well, you come from the same country, don't you ? You
ought to know. Mine's constipated."

" I done come from Virginny, suh. Ain't no lions there."

Well, I thought maybe you'd have some kind of instinct or
something."

" The onliest instinct I got about lions is to stay away from
them, suh."

Huguenine lay back on the pillows.

" Well, we'll try some of that water on him. You fetch it."

Billings rolled his eyes as he departed.

" Seems funny one African don't know about another,"
Huguenine said. " If he don't, we don't, that's sure. I guess
we've just got to kind of feel our way. You take it back, Chaddy,
and you give him half a bottle before his meat to-morrow. If
he's all right you can maybe give it to someone else. It costs
money."

It was pitch dark when Chad started out of town. Burke's
show was over long before, and he got no lift. He had an hour
of walking before the smell of pigs identified the Gates post office.

He saw the candle shine from the treasury wagon faintly.
Caroline had tacked some muslin over the window to keep the

mosquitoes out. When he went in, she was lying on the bunk, fast asleep, the blanket half-thrown off. He put the bottle on a small shelf, watching her as he undressed. She turned in her sleep, as if to meet him, and said his name. It made him feel guilty, thinking of Albany Yates. He wondered what she would think, if she knew of his going to see Burke's show.

He pinched out the candle and she said his name again as he let himself down gently on the bunk beside her.

5

OSCAR GETS TO GAINES

It was astonishing to Chad how Huguenine's troupe revised their opinion once they understood that the old lion really was sick. Though Joe Duddy, in spite of his complaints, had always felt a kind of sentimental attachment and interest in his doings, nobody else had had much use for him. It was natural enough for the skinners and Huguenines to show interest ; but Caroline reported that Oscar was practically all the performers discussed in the light rig between towns. When the cage wagon rolled into Parma on the afternoon of the fifth, it looked like a reception committee waiting for him in the lot to see if he had accomplished anything.

Ike Wayfish had volunteered to administer the spring water that morning in Gates. But it had proved no trick at all. Oscar had been lying on his side at the time. They had worked nooses round his feet and a strap round his neck, tightening them simultaneously and feeling like a bunch of fools when Oscar made no fuss at all. Ike had gone in and stroked him, holding the bottle behind his back with his free hand so as not make him wise before they hauled his head into position. Ike looked a little like a doctor called out on an early morning case the day after election. He slid the neck of the bottle between Oscar's slack jaws and the old lion took a swallow. He just about had to if he didn't want to strangle ; and he opened his eyes and looked at Wayfish like Julius Cæsar in the play. When Mrs. Pamplon admired Monsieur Wayfish's bravery out loud, Ike said shortly, " *He* done the swallowing," and walked away from her. Later he confessed to Huguenine that he had done some mean things in his life, but he had never felt sorry about one till he saw Oscar's eyes. " He trusted me. He must have thought we was friends."

Joe Duddy drove carefully so as not to shake the lion up. At noon-time, he drew the wagon into the shade for an hour to let him rest, and the other wagons stayed by for company. They took off one flap to give the cat some breeze, and he lay there, with the side of his head against one paw, sniffing it.

Huguenine said, " I wonder how long it takes to work through something like him."

Nobody knew. That evening in Parma he was just the same. They put up the round-top and held a practice in the ring, as usual ; but during rests, instead of just standing around, they would go over to the cage wagon and visit with the lion.

That was another thing. They had stopped thinking of him as the cat. He was Oscar—almost the way, for instance, that Fiero was Fiero. Looking at him, the Italian said sadly, " What a pity. I have just this minute thought. If a lion could be trained to stand for a knife-thrower ! But now he is too sick." Fiero said it was his worrying about Oscar that had turned his eye.

The queer part was that Joe thought Oscar appreciated the concern they felt for him. He would lie there watching Caroline and Shepley double on the pad, his eyes unwinking while they rode, only closing them again when another halt was called. " You see, he feels anxious like. The way you might, Chaddy, being married to her and all."

Caroline had made a big step forward in the few short sessions she had worked with Fred Shepley. " I feel a lot more confident. It's easier to learn what to do with my feet when I'm on the pad with Fred. I was always scared to lean in enough with the horse, before."

Fred said, " You've got an instinct for it."

He was walking back to the tavern with her and Chad.

" Do you think I'll ever be really good ? "

" You're good now," Fred said. " But I think if you keep on riding you'll be known all over this country some day."

His evident admiration for her seemed to fluster Caroline. She turned red, trying now to turn it off.

" Let's go and have supper together. Will you come, Fred ? "
" I'd love to."

Chad, who had been wondering if there wasn't anything that could be done about Oscar, realised that Fred was looking towards him.

"Yes," he said, "come along."

When they were alone together in their room, Caroline told him that he hadn't sounded friendly at all. She spoke stiffly. "It's only decent to ask Fred sometimes," she said. "Now he and I are working together."

"Well," Chad said, "I don't care if he does come."

"Don't you want me to ride well? Wouldn't you like it if I got to be the best female rider in the country?"

"Yes," he said. "It would be fine."

"You don't think I will, though, do you? Well, Fred does. He said I could."

"When did he tell you that?"

"To-night," she said. "You'd have heard him, too, only you were so busy thinking about that old lion."

Chad said, "If Oscar dies we won't stand a chance to draw in Albion. That's where we meet up with the Menagerie. We've got to draw there."

"We did all right in Penfield. And it looks as if we were going to do all right here."

"We've got to draw every day this week, or the show will break down. We've got to get a crowd in Albion. That's a big town. Huguenine's counting on money there." He turned on her. She was standing in her underclothes, her dress limp in one hand. "I don't doubt you'll get to be good. You're good already, just as Fred said. But the show don't hang on one act. Not on yours, either. We could get along without you. But we've got to have that lion act."

"I believe you don't care." Her voice was muffled by the dress. She had got caught up in it somewhere. In trying to get it up again she hiked up her petticoat with it. She was helpless inside the bundle of clothing with her long legs in their snug drawers entirely exposed. "I believe you think more of that lion than you do of me. I hate him." She sounded near tears.

Chad started to laugh.

"I hate you, too," she said.

He took hold of her, bundling her, petticoat, dress and all.

"Let go of me," she cried.

But he wouldn't. It struck him as a delightful novelty. He picked her up off her feet.

"Chad!" she said desperately. She started to kick. "Chad."

"I bet you think more about Fred than you do about me," he said, imitating her voice. "But Fred can't do you any good now."

He could hardly hear her voice.

"If I could get my head out I'd bite you."

"All right."

He set her feet on the floor and with one sweep of his hands drew dress and petticoat over her head. He dropped them on the floor. "Now bite," he said.

Her face changed. She started to smile. Then she moved up close, saying, "I can't reach you like that. Bend down. I dare you to."

He did so, grinning. And she suddenly clamped her teeth on the lobe of his ear. It made him jump. "You bitch! I bet you drawed blood," he said, feeling of it.

She nodded. "I tried to."

With a quick stoop she had picked up her dress and slid it over her head.

"By God, you're vicious. I ought to take it out on your hide."

"I feel vicious," she said, pursing her lips. "Real vicious. No, you don't. I'm dressed now and probably Fred's waiting for us this minute."

"You ought to be punished, though."

"All right. You can after we come home." Her smile widened. "I'm nice to punish, aren't I? You can spend the evening thinking about it." She picked up her shawl. "Get your coat on, Chad."

When he joined her at the door, she put her hand in his arm. "Does it hurt?" she asked. "Really?"

"You bet it does."

"Well, I *was* mad. We've only been married three days and you had to go off and stare at Albany Yates and spend the rest of your time thinking about poor old Oscar. I didn't like it."

"I'll remember you for a while," Chad said, making his voice grim. "How did you know I'd seen Albany?"

"Joe Duddy told me. But he says she's not doing well a bit. I feel sorry for her. Was she riding bad?"

"No," Chad said. He would have liked to twist Joe's neck.

He glanced sideways at Caroline, but her face was sweet. He decided to tell her the truth. " That tent's just too big for Albany."

" Well, don't tell Fred. He still thinks she's wonderful. He told me yesterday they had planned to get married once." She sounded almost maternal to Chad. " Why don't you ask Fred what he thinks about Oscar, Chad ? He's been with other circuses. He might know something."

But Fred Shepley said he hadn't ever paid any attention to the lions. He wished he had, though. He couldn't see how the show could get along without Oscar.

They had come back to their own tavern as the only other place in the village looked dirty to Caroline. Parma was a tiny place. The keeper of their own tavern told them that since the canal had been put through he had lost a lot of trade. He had to depend now on the farming people. It was a good township though, more than two thousand people in it ; and the farmers were benefiting from the canal, so he supposed if he hung on he would do well enough in the long run. Mostly, though, he was interested in telling them of William Morgan's abduction and he swore he had heard the death carriage going through. What was more, he claimed to have heard it on September 12 several times since, driving like mad through the middle of the night towards Niagara. He said he had heard the ghost of Morgan calling for help. It showed Thurlow Weed was right. He had no doubt Morgan had been drowned. Was either Chad or Shepley Masons ?

When they said they were not, he said he was glad to hear it. He said he didn't believe in Masonry or the Democratic Party. He said some people knew how to make money and some did not, and the thing was to let those that could make it, like Nicholas Biddle, make as much as possible or it wouldn't be made at all. That made sense, didn't it ? Unless somebody made money it stood to reason there wouldn't be money, didn't it ? Now the country was getting throwed out on the dump heap. They'd see. Or their children would, if they had children—he didn't suppose circus people did have many children. It stood to reason that a woman doing queer things all the time wasn't going to be much of a breeder, didn't it ? He supposed that was their business though. He heard they had a sick lion. If he had a sick lion he would give it ginger. He would dissolve ginger

in pure whisky and see what it did. Ginger was an almighty
tonic and what it didn't reach, whisky would. It was getting to
be impossible to buy good whisky cheap around here any more
now that farmers were drawing all their wheat to the canal.
Distilleries were going out of business. The whole country was
getting changed all around.

When the tavernkeeper finally left them alone, they moved
out on to the porch. It was too hot to walk, and anyway there
was nothing to see in Parma. Ike and Fiero joined them, but
Fred Shepley did most of the talking. Even Chad had to admit
that Fred made good company, and he had a lot to say about
circuses and riding. It was Fred's theory that the day of classic
riding was over. You could never develop great riders travelling
round the country the way Huguenine's did, or even the way
Burke and Walsh did, for all their huge tent and the money
they had. Good riding demanded a permanent ring, where the
equestrian could always go for practice.

Ike broke in to say that Mateer was first-class, but Fred
pointed out that Mateer, though travelling the west with Brown's
Circus, played exclusively in theatres and circus barns. It
amounted to the same thing as the Pearl Street Theatre in Albany.
Moreover, he said, look at the way the taste of the country
people went. They were as much interested in menageries as
in riding. Burke certainly would not have bothered himself
with an elephant and hyenas if it hadn't been necessary. But
city crowds had the chance to go again and again and so learned
to appreciate the fine points.

While they were sitting there, a creaking wheel in the
direction of Rochester caught their attention. It came on
slowly ; and after a few minutes Professor Arganave appeared.
" Is this Parma ? Where is Parma ? " he demanded before he
recognised them. His relief was intense.

He had had a bad time in Rochester. Burke's tough boys
had driven him out of town. He had set up three blocks away and
shown the man-eating lion blood as belonging to the man-killing
elephant. He had made a great spiel about the tusks of the
big bull dipping through a man's ribs when the creature was
amok. This was the only slide of amok elephant blood in the
world. The dangers of procuring it had been incalculable. . . .
Amok meant mad, like a mad dog on the one hand, and a
rutting buck deer on the other. The professor said he had gone

to the Athenæum and read a piece about elephants, so it was nearly all correct. The trouble was that a little boy who saw the slide happened to ask Mr. Burke himself what they had done with the elephant's tusks. How did Arganave know the elephant was a cow? He hadn't dared to go see himself for fear of being recognised. Now his microscope was all bent up and he would have to straighten it out. But it was good to be back with the lion. How was he?

His face became dismal when he heard that Oscar was ill. He inquired the price of a bed, but when he learned he could get nothing for ten cents, he sadly drove his creaking wheel off down the south road towards Spencer's Basin to find a convenient field.

" Poor man," Caroline said softly.

" We have to take Burke's leavings, and he takes ours," Ike said. " I wonder who takes his."

" His wife, probably, if there are any," Fred said.

" Is he married? " asked Caroline.

" Yes. He showed me a miniature of her once. Sometimes he rigs his microscope so he can look at it life-size. He told me once he didn't think she was faithful. She works for an umbrella-maker, who boards with her." Fred smiled. " She re-covers Arganave's umbrella every season when he leaves home. That's what makes him suspicious."

At eight o'clock they broke up. Chad said he was going over to the lot to see that everything was all right for the night. Caroline went up to their room. Shepley asked Chad whether he wanted company.

Chad told him to come along.

They had gone only a few houses down the road when they met Joe Duddy pounding along towards them.

" Chad! " he yelled, waking echoes. " That you, Chad? "

Chad said it was.

" Oscar," Joe said. " He's begun . . . Caroline ain't with you? "

" No, just Fred."

" That water's working."

Fred Shepley whistled.

" Maybe he'll come round then."

" He's coming round all right," said Joe. " Hurry up."

When they reached the lot, they found Bastock and Budlong

holding lanterns up to the cage wagon, and Huguenine, with Mrs. Huguenine's assistance, moving painfully towards it.

"He's quit now," Bastock said.

The old lion was on his feet. It was the first time they had seen him so in days, and though he wavered a good deal it was an inspiring sight.

"He ought to feel better," remarked Mrs. Huguenine. "A.D. did."

"Yes," said Budlong. "If he can feel anything."

Mrs. Huguenine ignored him. "I could take hands and dance," she said. "And I'd kiss Bastock if he'd let me."

Bastock blushed.

"Nobody can't say I'm not a lion doctor," Huguenine said happily. "Joe, you better clean up."

"I didn't know when I was lucky." Joe sounded mournful.

Chad had heard a preacher or two tell about miracles, but this was the first one he had ever witnessed, and it seemed to him to beat hollow anything he had ever heard of. He walked back to the tavern with a real feeling of friendliness for Fred Shepley. They went into the bar and bought each other drinks, and only parted in the upstairs hall, shaking hands for the first time since they had encountered each other.

Chad turned from backing through the door to find Caroline waiting for him in bed. Her face was studiously meek. But she didn't interrupt when he told her the good news; she never mentioned anything about their dispute earlier in the evening. She treated him exactly like a good wife who had a respect for woman's place in the world   When Chad said, "I guess he's going to be all right now," she smiled, and he said, "Blame it, you sure look pretty."

"Do I?" She sounded as if she had butter on her tongue. . . .

Oscar continued the good work in Spencer's Basin and Brockport. He went off the track one day in Clarkson, but he came round again Sunday afternoon in Murray. He seemed almost lively there and while Fred and Caroline were holding their practice he took a walk up and down the cage wagon, swinging his head on the turns in the old way. It seemed like a good omen to Caroline; the double act was due to open in Gaines on Tuesday.

Gaines was full of posters of the Menagerie and Aviary. Nobody in Huguenine's had ever seen advertising of such magnitude. Some of the posters were six feet high and the rhinoceros was as big as a man's head. But in spite of them, Huguenine's showed to their first full tent in a long time.

The act was a sensation. It was a threatening afternoon ; there had been thunderstorms working up along the marshes all day, and the lights kept changing. But the cream pad worked perfectly, and when Chad saw Fred vault the first time he knew the act was all right. He felt proud, watching the rings of staring eyes. Fred was right about Caroline. They were watching her ; they would go home talking about her. He got the idea right there that people talking did more than posters could. Some day Caroline was going to be famous.

To finish the whole performance off, Oscar acted up a little with Ike. He even tried to lick his head. And when Ike backed out of the cage wagon, the old cat heaved himself up and turned round and padded after him. He moved pretty slow, and he showed the audience his chafed side. But he covered that up by letting out the first roar they had heard him make since they reached Port Byron.

It had been such a success that Huguenine had the whole troupe down at the tavern to celebrate before hauling out. They returned to the lot in a body. They stood round the cage wagon while Joe Duddy fastened the side blinds. Oscar was lying peacefully on his side, the chafed side uppermost, but he lifted his head, blinking at them, and twitched the end of his tail. They all agreed that he was a real trouper. Mr. Pamplon, a little unsteady from another attempt at drinking American brandy, called for three cheers, in which Mrs. Pamplon joined shrilly. They all felt that they were bound to make a showing in Albion, Menagerie or no Menagerie.

6

DEATH IN ALBION

It was good to see Bisbee again. All the way down from Gaines
Chad had been worrying about how they would manage to
show in a small place against an establishment the size of the
Menagerie. But the sight of Bisbee, quietly walking the white-
nosed horse through the long shadows, inspired confidence. He
looked just the same as the first time Chad had seen him riding
up to the Yellow Bud porch—his long, horse-like face was
thoughtful, his clothes dusty from the road, and he sounded
brimming with confidence.

" Heard about Caroline and Shepley's new act. A man
came into the tavern just before I left to meet you. He told about
it. He said it was beautiful. I deposited a dollar for him to drink
with, and I guess he's still talking. Best advertising you ever
heard "

Going through the village he pointed out to Chad the more
interesting features, the female seminary, the log jail, the court-
house, with as much familiar pride as though he had lived in
Albion since it was settled. There was Menagerie paper everywhere, but Chad saw none of their own. He asked Bisbee whether
he had had much trouble.

" Not to signify, trouble. I didn't try to tack up again. I
worked the newspapers. I had pieces in the *American* and the
Republican. Part of it's about Carolina, how the big circuses
have tried to buy her away." He rolled his cigar over his lower
lip. " ' Only the high sense of honour, not surprising to those
acquainted with this lovely star of the upper air, with which
she regards her contractual obligations has made possible
Albion's viewing of such unparalleled grace, modesty and talent.'
I saved her a copy. Thought she might like to preserve it."

Chad thanked him.

" There's our lot," Bisbee said as they crossed the canal. " It's
small, but it's this side of the Menagerie's. They need acreage.
I hear they show in three pavilions."

Chad eyed the lot unfavourably. It was low and it looked
wet. And Bastock was dubious also. " We can't risk any soft

bottom with this double act," he told Bisbee. "It's too dangerous."

"There's footing for the ring in the corner," Bisbee said imperturbably, watching Bastock verify the fact.

"How about that big show? Won't they make us trouble?" Chad demanded.

"I don't think so," Bisbee said mildly. "I've handed out free passes to the town board and the sheriff. I gave the sheriff ten free passes in case he wanted to swear in some deputies. A man likes to hand out free tickets if they don't cost him anything. And I told him that Albion was probably the first town its size to have two shows running the same day. I said it was bound to get into the papers and advertise the town. He could see that." He drew on the cigar. "I hear Oscar's been sick," he said to Huguenine, who had sat down on the top step of the treasury wagon to watch the erection of the round-top.

"Yep," said Huguenine. "He has. But I guess I've cured him. I gave him a bottle of that bath-house water. It cost fifty cents but I guess it was worth it."

Oscar was lying down. When Joe took off the side blinds, however, he swung his head to face the mild south wind, his yellow eyes unblinking. He looked like a brown-stone statue, except for the slight stirring of his stringy mane.

"You know," Bisbee said, "I've got to admire that cat. When I heard he was sick, I felt kind of sad."

"We all did," Mrs. Huguenine said. "And he's been so nice, in all the time we went through. It was a time, too, Mr. Bisbee. I give my word it was."

She climbed down the steps past her husband with the blankets in her arms and hung them over a tree limb to air.

"Oh, Caroline," she called. "Would you mind whisking them before you bring them in? I found a moth bug on them."

Caroline, holding the cream at the tent entrance, waved her hand in reply and smiled.

"Her and Chad have been sleeping in the wagon," Mrs. Huguenine explained to Bisbee. Her fat face puckered up with sentimental tenderness. "They're just like two loving-birds in it. And she's so neat and clean I love to have them. Doc told A.D. he had to sleep in houses till his back limbered. You feel the dew in here. But those two!" She rolled her eyes. "I guess they just love dew."

As Caroline entered the tent, Bisbee looked after her thoughtfully. " Yes, she's nice. So's Chad," he said cautiously. " I guess you can trust them."

Mrs. Huguenine bristled.

" I guess we can," she said indignantly.

Huguenine grunted.

" Chad knows a lot too," he said. " He's pretty near as good as I am."

" Well, he's different," Bisbee said tactfully.

" Maybe that's it. But he's run this circus pretty well," Huguenine said. " He acts responsible."

" Getting married does that," Mrs. Huguenine said. " A nice girl like Caroline settles a boy."

Bisbee nodded, lipped his cigar, blew smoke, and followed it with slow strides towards the tent. He watched the practice with approval, made Bastock grin by nodding his head slowly, and went out through the performers' entrance to examine Oscar.

Chad and Joe were shutting him in for the night.

" How's he eating ? " he asked Joe.

" Pretty fair. He didn't eat so good this morning. I think he's still gassy here and there," Joe said. He closed the blind against the wind.

An hour later, near dark, the practice was over, and Chad was carrying the blankets into the wagon when he heard Oscar roar.

He stopped short at the steps to listen. The lot was still, there was no sound even from the canal basin. Joe Duddy was in the village somewhere, and except for themselves only Bastock and Budlong remained. Maybe the lion had had a dream, Chad thought, or maybe he had imagined the sound. But Caroline appeared in the door to ask what was the matter with Oscar.

Then Oscar roared again, his voice filling the evening. In the succeeding silence they now made out the pad of his feet. Something had excited him.

" Here, take these blankets." Chad stuffed them through the door and hurried across the lot. The two skinners emerged from the tent at the same time. Bastock said, " I never heard him make no noise like that."

" Listen a minute."

Budlong's lean face was lifted.

Far down the road they heard an answering roar, faint and far away, but unmistakably a lion's.

" It's the Menagerie coming," Budlong said.

From the cage wagon they could clearly hear the pad of Oscar's feet. He was moving rapidly back and forth in the narrow space. They heard his hide rasp against the slats.

" That excitement ain't going to do him good," Budlong said. " Knew a man got excited on top of a flux . . ."

" Keep quiet," Bastock broke in. " Hear that ? "

It was a sound that none of them had ever heard. High-pitched, weirdly gibbering, almost like laughter. It brought a light thud of feet and Caroline ran down to them.

" What is it ? It's awful. I'm afraid."

" Better light a lantern," Bastock said. " Maybe light will quiet Oscar."

" This feller," Budlong said, " saw ghosts."

They put the lantern by the cage wagon so Oscar could see the light through the cracks, and he paused in his walking.

Chad said suddenly, " I'm going up to the lot. I bet it's a wild animal."

" I'm coming with you," Caroline said.

The idea relieved them all.

The roars had brought some people out of the village. They paused at Huguenine's lot, then hearing another blast from down the road, with a renewal of the high-pitched insane laughter, they moved ahead.

Chad, Caroline clutching his arm, went with them. In the darkness, with the increasing wind in their faces, it was almost like walking to the world's ending.

A man was standing by the bars, swinging a lantern. Into its light tramped four heavy grey horses, rolling the first tent wagon. As the laughter broke out close at hand, Chad raised his voice to ask the man what it was.

" Hyenas. They carry on like that before a storm. They always do. You can't stop them. They're crazy."

Behind them, towards town, Oscar started his roaring once more.

" That's a lion," said the road-marker. " He's from that little one-horse rig down the road. He's probably smelled these hyenas."

It was a queer experience, the wagons hauling past into the

lot, full of sound and inner movement, and a strange covering smell from the foreign animals one could not see. It impressed Chad, but he was more impressed by the team upon team of matched horses, all greys. In daylight, he thought, the sight of that caravan of greys tramping the roads would be something a man would remember. They made Huguenine's little assortment pitiful to think of.

He jerked Caroline's arm.

" We better go back," he said.

They reported to the skinners.

Budlong said, " It does smell like a storm." He had lit a second lantern which he had inside the round-top. " Oscar quieted a few minutes ago. Probably smelling Africa worked him up."

" If it's going to storm, we better get him inside," Joe said.

In the soggy grass, the cage wagon was hard to handle. Even Caroline had to push. She bent her slim body between Chad and Budlong at the tail gate. The wind was blowing hard by the time they had wrestled the wagon through the performers' entrance, and Bastock said, " It's a real blow coming. We better lace the canvas before the wind gets underneath. It's lucky we're low down."

They worked fast lacing the flaps. Budlong went round the pegs, setting them all with the sledge, while Caroline carried a lantern for him. The wind was yanking her skirt, wrapping her. It felt warm for all its force. But it took her breath like a winter wind. The wild hyena laughter from the Menagerie lot whipped brokenly over her head, like torn leaves. The first roll of thunder broke just as the men finished work. She and Chad pelted for the treasury wagon through the first rifling drops of rain.

The thunder lasted only a short time. They watched from the window in the treasury-wagon door, seeing the round-top spring out at them and vanish in the lightning flashes. Great valleys appeared in it, and sudden bubbles. But it held.

Then as the rain gained force and steadiness, the wind settled to an even blow. The thunder rolled northward, faded, and died.

Chad lit their candle.

" It's all right," he told her. " It's a good thing we had the tent up, too, or the ring would be like mush by now."

In the close space of the wagon, all they heard was the rain.

By the time they were undressed, that, too, had slackened; there was only the drip from the roof. Chad said suddenly, " I wish I'd taken another look at Oscar."

" He'll be all right, Chad. I'm sure he is all right. He'd quieted down before the rain came."

What Caroline said was true. Oscar had quieted down. He had stretched out, his nose to the crack through which the wind drew the scents of Africa. Joe Duddy found him that way in the morning, his worn old carcass unmoving. Joe looked a moment at the armpit tufts ; it always seemed strange to him to find a creature haired the way a man was. Then he poked the mop handle against the slatted ribs. " Hey you, Oscar," he said. " Wake up."

Budlong wandered into the tent.

" What you doing to the cat, Joe ? "

" Rousing him," Joe said. He poked again. It came over him then that Oscar wasn't breathing. " My God," he said. " Get Chad. Get the gaffer. And you better tell Bisbee."

" Tell him what ? " asked Budlong.

" Oscar's dead."

It was a catastrophe far more serious, they realised, than Albany's defection. It seemed worse, because they had expected something of the sort to happen, and then their fears had been lulled.

" He was the only lion we had," Huguenine said miserably. " Now we ain't even got him."

Even Bisbee showed defeat.

" By Harry," he said, " I just don't like showing here without that cat act. I don't like doing it at all after all the stories I got printed in the paper."

" If we announce he's dead, there won't nobody come," Huguenine said.

Ike said, " Maybe if we screened the wagon in the back and put a strap round Oscar's neck, Joe could wiggle it to make him look alive. I could do a lot of things. Maybe I could put my head in his mouth, like Van Amburgh."

Bisbee shook his head.

" We'd lose all the seat space at the back of the tent," he pointed out. " We can't afford that, even if Joe made Oscar act up. But Joe couldn't. Have you looked at Oscar, Ike ? "

" Not to study him," Ike admitted.

M 2

"Well, he's the deadest-looking lion you ever saw. You wouldn't believe a lion could look that dead. You could put a fireworks display in his inside and he would still look dead."

Ike gave it up. He sat down on the step of the treasury wagon, to which Bisbee, the Huguenines, himself, and Chad had adjourned. Over the lot by the entrance of the round-top, the other performers and the skinners stood in a group watching them.

"We couldn't buy a lion, maybe from the Menagerie?" asked Mrs. Huguenine.

"They wouldn't sell," Huguenine said in a despondent voice.

"If they did, they'd ask more than this entire show is worth," Bisbee said. "Besides, I don't know how Ike feels, but I wouldn't want to be the Modern Daniel with a brand-new lion."

Ike didn't bother to answer.

"I guess we're licked," said Huguenine. "Do we announce it, Bisbee? Or do we go ahead and take a chance?"

"You said yourself they wouldn't come in," Bisbee reminded him. "Not even a punk's going to pay to see a dead lion when he can see four or five live ones at the same price."

Chad scratched his head.

"I don't see that, Mr. Bisbee. You can't get so close to a live lion. But I don't see why we couldn't advertise Oscar being dead. Kind of a curiosity, see? Like seeing the mammoth's bones in Rochester. Lots of people can see a live lion. He began to warm up to the idea himself. "Hell, they can see four or five of them right here. But they won't have many chances to see a dead one. He's the only dead lion on exhibition in the United States."

"By God," said Bisbee. "Say in North America."

Chad grinned.

"The Western Hemisphere."

"The world," suggested Bisbee. "They may kill 'em in Africa, but they don't exhibit them in a cage wagon, I'll bet a hat."

"You might take a chance on the Universe while you're about it," Ike put in wearily.

Huguenine grunted.

"The United States sounds good enough for me. But it's an idea, Chaddy. That's something none of us else have had. Bisbee, can you get a poster drawed in time?"

" I'll do it myself, if I can't."

Bisbee was off.

He was back at noon with two huge sheets of heavy paper, announcing the exclusive exhibition of the only dead lion in captivity in the United States. The larger, to be fastened on the round-top itself, could be read from the road. The smaller, to be affixed to the cage wagon in the tent, announced that for an additional ten cents the spectator could have the unusual experience of entering the cage wagon with the lion and examining the king of beasts as closely as his curiosity impelled.

Bisbee was enamoured of this refinement of Chad's idea. Before long he had worked himself up to the idea that the whole scheme had been his from the beginning. " Somebody like you puts the idea into my head, I don't know how, you don't know how, but there it is." He tacked the sign to the wagon himself. " There," he said, " you see if that don't draw them in."

It did. It was astonishing how many entered the cage at the end of the performance. It was as good a stand as the circus had enjoyed since Lyons. But all during the preceding performance, Chad, with the rest of the troupe, had been conscious of the dead, slitted eyes behind the cage-wagon bars. A dead lion might draw all right, but live lions lasted longer.

Book V

THE RETURN SWING

HARD TIMES FOR HUGUENINE'S

In death, as in life, old Oscar endured phenomenally. He drew fair business in Batavia, LeRoy, and Stafford. Entering each town in solitary state, the cage wagon, draped in black and driven by Joe Duddy with a crape rosette on his hat, never failed to attract attention. But by the time the show reached Caledonia a mild bloat had appeared in the carcass. It was the first time any one had ever seen Oscar looking thrifty, and for that one day he was a handsome animal. In Avon, however the odour became noticeable, and in Mud Hollow it was so powerful that half a bottle of Mrs. Huguenine's perfumery barely dented it. They buried him in Honey Falls.

Joe Duddy dug the hole. Chad, Bastock, and Budlong dragged the body to it. Ike Wayfish's eyes were moist as he watched the earth dropping in. " Alas, poor Yorick," he said. It made one sad to think of an African lion lying under the Black-eyed Susans.

Huguenine's wasn't the same show without Oscar. Without the Modern Daniel's great finale, the whole performance seemed to lack point. Going south from Canandaigua, moreover, they were following the route of both the Menagerie and Burke and Walsh. It was Bisbee's theory that the two big shows would have hit the haying season. " They're going to play the big towns," he said. " They'll miss the farmers. We'll roll in on the heels of the wheat when folks feel rich. Maybe we won't do quite so well in big places like Penn Yan and Elmira and Ithaca, but we'll just sweep up the country towns." If he had been all right, or all wrong, things wouldn't have been so bad ; but he was right about the big towns and wrong about the country villages. Eighteen thirty-six was a bad year for the Russian midge ; rust and a burning drought had cut what survived of the crop in half. Both Huguenine and Chad figured that out after their second day of travel through the wheatfields, but by then lord knew where Bisbee was. The circus had to follow his tacking of the paper.

Gorham's Corners paid them eighty-six admissions. In Potter they performed in what amounted to panic before thirty-nine full tickets. They did better in Penn Yan, and the show would have gone well, except for Huguenine, who made his first appearance in the tent. If it had done nothing else, the hot, dry weather had served to bake the soreness from his back. He sat on an upper tier, leaning forward on his knees, his stout face intent upon the ring.

At first Chad felt pleased to see him there ; but before the Pamplons were half-way through their act, the gaffer's presence began to get on his nerves. He missed a cue from Ike and except for the clown's quick pantomime even the audience would have caught the error. It shook his nerve for a minute or two ; the pace dropped off ; and Caroline had to check her entrance for his introduction. When he looked up again, Huguenine's face was heavy with disapproval.

" He just sat there like a damn-fool owl," Chad said angrily to Caroline. She had offered to ride the stage with him to Milo Centre. " He acted as if he didn't like a thing."

" He's probably worrying about the money, Chad."

She sounded unconcerned.

" I know that. So am I. If things go on like this, we'll have to lose our pay or the show will have to close up entirely. But nobody can do a decent job if he's going to sit there like that."

He brooded, leaning his hands on Jerry's withers. Caroline, half a length ahead of him, was looking over the country as if she enjoyed the sight.

" It's beautiful," she said. " Look at it, Chad, and stop worrying so."

He said sourly, " It's dry."

It was dry everywhere. Even the wind felt dry. Far ahead, dust snaked by the light rig's wheels stretched for a hundred yards along the fences. Behind them the caravan was strung out against the evening sky. It was clear in the west, but to the north thunderheads were piled above the high, parched fields of wheat.

" The crop's burned out," Chad said. " People here don't want to spend money on a show like ours."

The wagons looked small and faded under their dust ; at the tail end the empty cage was like a mockery. Two boys in a farmyard stared listlessly at them. Probably they could not even read the lettering on the tent wagon. As he had again and again in the past few days, Chad realised what an animal attraction would mean to the show. A lion's roar, now, would have those boys bare-footing half a mile along the ditches. Even without a roar the jungle smell would have attracted them. But what would make the show would be an elephant. That was what a circus needed. He could imagine how the elephant would look, swaying behind the cage wagon. As soon as chores were done, those boys would be off telling half a township of the wonder they had seen. It would make them feel big. All the children in the neighbourhood would be stirring up their parents that night for the admission money. An elephant was better than five dollars' worth of paper.

Chad had no idea what an elephant would cost—too much for a show like Huguenine's to buy, he felt sure. It would be impossible to find one anyway. He wrung his brains trying to think of a substitute, and as usual, when anything was going badly with the circus, he wished for Bisbee.

Bisbee always had some idea with which to distract Hugue-nine. He could talk the kicking hind foot off a mule. And Chad could not get rid of the feeling that Huguenine was laying for him.

" That must be Milo Centre, Chad."

Caroline pointed to a tiny cross-roads hamlet down the grade. It looked small enough to cover with a handkerchief, hardly two dozen buildings scattered along the main road. It was so small it seemed incredible that they would show there at all. Caroline giggled suddenly.

" Where'll the parade go ? " she asked. " Just up and down ? "

The whole length of the village was not more than two or three hundred yards with an empty field facing the tavern. A parade in such a place would be ridiculous.

Chad said, " We won't have a parade."

He glanced back at the caravan. Huguenine was driving the treasury wagon in the lead. Over his shoulder, Mrs. Huguenine's fat face peered through the little window. Chad wondered what they made of Milo Centre.

Huguenine made his opinion clear as soon as the wagons had wheeled into the lot. " This is a hell of a place for a stand," he shouted to Chad. " Who picked it ? " His eyes were bloodshot from the dust.

" I suppose Bisbee did. I'm not paid to route the show."

Chad was willing to have a row right there if Huguenine wanted one. But the gaffer swung off on his heel. " Get the rag up," he said over his shoulder.

The business of raising the tent went slowly. Joe Duddy wanted to leave it till morning. " I'm drier than a tadpole in a snake's inside," he complained. " Where do we parade ? Round the cemetery ? "

" There won't be a parade," Chad said.

" Well, that's something."

Budlong and Bastock worked in silence.

" I got to lug these seats in, and to-morrow I got to gaffle them back into the wagon," Joe said. " But who in hell's going to sit on them ? Milo Centre's ghosts ? I bet they get free passes, too."

" You ain't funny," Bastock said. " Same time for practice to-morrow, Chad ? "

Chad said yes.

He paused in the dark, under the shadow of the empty tent. The ring was laid and the seats in. He agreed with Joe that it showed a lot of work for what would enter it to-morrow.

" What's the matter with this show, Pete ? " he asked.

" It's no damn good," Bastock said promptly.

" It's the same show we've had all along, except for Oscar."

" Yes. Caroline's better than she was, but the show's no good. It ain't got any ending, for one thing, Chad." Bastock leaned against the centre pole.

" We haven't got a lion," Chad pointed out.

" I know we ain't. We got to get something else."

" You got any ideas ? " Chad asked.

" Well, people used to go out laughing. Now all the laughs for Ike come in the middle of the show. Maybe he could work up something better at the end."

" I don't know what."

The little man stared at his feet.

" I don't know either. But one thing's sure. If something don't happen pretty soon, Huguenine's is going to break down right on the road. I bet the gaffer will hold back pay next Saturday."

"If he don't pay, I quit," Joe said.

"Who asked for your two cents?" Bastock said scornfully. "Go on and quit. But you won't get your season's half-pay at the end, see? The gaffer's got you by the scruff, Joe. You ain't a performer. Soon as a circus starts going bad a skinner finds he's got an interest in it, like me. I been thinking about that Jerry horse. What're we lugging him round the country for, hog-fatting him? We don't get nothing out of him but wind."

"Too bad he ain't a trick horse," Chad said. He thought a minute. "How'd it look if, when Ike starts peeling those fool clothes off, he started acting up—snot with me? He could holler for another horse. Then when he got down to his striped tights he could finish with a Roman riding act."

"It ain't much," Bastock said. "It's better than what he does, though. But you'd have to break in Jerry and the cream to working double. The grey goes pretty fair alone, and the cream ought to steady him some."

"How long would it take to do that?"

"Two weeks, maybe. You can't learn an animal the way you would a human. If you get him tired, he'll quit on you; and once he's quit, he'll always quit if he can. And he has to be trained right. Ike can't hold two horses' rumps together with his feet."

"Two weeks is a long time."

"It's the shortest I'll promise for. And he'll still be green."

"I'll talk to Ike about it," Chad said. He wandered toward the tavern. Mrs. Huguenine, who was cooking supper on the lot, waved to him; but Huguenine did not turn his head.

In the tavern Chad found Caroline, Shepley, and Ike Way-fish sitting round the dining table in silence. The Pamplons and Fiero had gone upstairs. They had started keeping company, like strange people in a hostile land. Caroline said, "I told them there'd be no parade to-morrow, Chad."

He nodded, sat down, and pulled up the plate Caroline had saved for him. A disgruntled serving maid appeared with a damp rag which she wiped over the table round his plate. He waited till she had made up her mind to quit before describing the new idea for Ike's finale.

Ike said he could manage the Roman riding if the horses went steady enough. Shepley thought it was a good enough idea. "But," he said, "you and Ike have worked the clowning up so it's twice as good as it used to be, Chad, and it hasn't drawn people in."

They knew the new finale wasn't likely to do that, either ; but anything was worth trying.

The tavern porch offered no attraction ; after fifteen minutes of staring up the dark and empty road and the houses whose occupants showed no more interest in the tent than they might have in a pile of straw, Caroline announced that she was going to bed.

" I'll leave you gentlemen to talk," she said. " Good-night."

" Me too," said Ike. But instead of following her in, he stopped beside the door in obvious amusement, felt in his pocket for a match, struck it, and read the poster tacked to the clapboards. " ' Huguenine's Great and Only International Circus,' " he exclaimed, " ' . . . . presents Signor Rossello, talented equestrian, in his death-defying somerset . . .' " The match fizzled close to his fingers. He dropped it, lit another, and pushed his red-nosed face closer to the paper. " ' . . . Carolina, sylph of the upper air . . . and Ike Wayfish, the celebrated Buffo . . .' My, my ! Let me see, ' This dazzling but moral entertainment of skill and mirth commingled will be offered for the approval of the enlightened citizens of Milo Centre at one o'clock Thursday July 28th.' Boys, we're in luck ! "

He passed into the tavern darkness.

Shepley grinned.

" Ike's kind of a card," he said. He paused a moment. " I wish I got the fun out of it he does."

" He has to keep in practice," Chad said. " He don't get any more fun than you or me."

" Maybe not," Shepley agreed. He put his feet up on the rail. " I wonder how Albany is making out."

Chad was silent. It was the first time he had heard Shepley mention her name.

Shepley, however, did not seem to mind his silence.

" You know," he said, " it's not just Oscar dying that made a change in the show. It's never been the same since she left. She could get around anybody she had a mind to. Huguenine used to act worried sometimes before you joined out with us, but she always wheedled him back into shape. She used to talk about you quite a lot," Shepley added after a pause.

" Did she ? " Chad sat quiet. If Albany had felt an interest in him, she had concealed it pretty well. But that morning in Canastota she had acted friendly, as if something had happened there in the barn to excite her. And Shepley was right enough about the way she made life exciting for other people. It made Chad wonder how things would have turned out if she had given him a hint . . ."

Shepley was saying, " You're lucky to be married. When I see you going up nights, it starts me thinking, though. Did you know Albany and I were agreed to be married ? "

Chad said, " Yes," There wasn't much you could say to a man who was talking the way Shepley was.

" She'd get as mad as I did, and just as quick. She didn't care what she did. But she made up wonderfully when she wanted to. I get pretty sick of the show since she's gone. If it wasn't for riding with Caroline, I'd be ready to quit."

Chad said, " You done a lot to help her. She's grateful."

Shepley said quickly, " That's nice. She's done a lot for me, though. She's ambitious. Albany was too, but it was different with her. She was ambitious to get rich. Caroline's ambitious to be a famous rider. I bet she will be. But that's why it's fun to work with her."

Chad didn't say anything.

Shepley went on, " I bet you don't know how ambitious she is. Riding, her whole mind's on it. I can feel it in her when I take hold of her waist. She's using every nerve she's got. You get the feeling she won't let anything stop her, not even if she broke her back."

Chad thought there was a lot in what Shepley said. He hadn't thought of it himself ; but there had been times lately when he felt that Caroline had changed.

Somehow she had taken hold of her own life. She no longer depended on him for ideas. She had gone off without saying a word when she drew her first full salary, and bought herself new clothes, and the clothes Albany had left her she gave away to the girl in the tavern. Sometimes, though she was smiling when he told her something, he would have the feeling that she was keeping back part of her mind out of his reach. And once or twice she had had strange spells of independence, when she seemed to resent his being in their room.

" I guess you want to go up," Shepley said. He took his feet off the rail, rose and leaned against it, looking out. His face and fair hair showed in the light. He did not look as much sorry for himself as just bored.

" I guess I will," Chad said.

Shepley said, " I might as well, myself. This isn't much of a place, not even to get drunk in."

The village lay silent in the darkness. The thunderheads they had seen in the north that afternoon had come to nothing. They had sunk beyond the skyline, a feeble glimmer of heat lightning showing where they hung.

A spotted sow ticked slowly up the road, studied the two men with reddish eyes, and lay down, grunting solidly as her teats squattered in the dust between the ruts.

2

MILO CENTRE

CHAD lay on the bed watching Caroline do her hair. She always brushed it the same way. She took a strand and ran the brush through it a regular number of strokes and then studied the strand against the light. Then she cleaned the brush with the comb and started on another strand. She sat a little forward in her chair, like a man playing a fiddle, one long leg extended, the other tucked back. It was an oddly masculine posture for such a feminine occupation ; but her legs in their snug drawers had nothing masculine about them.

Chad's eyes wandered back up the smooth line of the pelisse to the curved motions of her arms and travelled from them over her head to the small mirror. He could see her face in the dim glass, young, oval, and absorbed. One corner of her mouth was pointed in a half smile. The brush made an even, soft, bristly whisper in the room. He thought she could sit there brushing her hair till doomsday.

" You're like a cat licking her paws," he said. " Just like."

" Oh, am I ? Thanks." The point at the corner of her mouth deepened a little towards her cheek. " I do it so I can look nice for you, mister."

" You look nice."

" It's taken a lot of brushing to make you say so."

She wouldn't hurry a single stroke, and he felt too lazy to pester her. He liked just to lie there. A girl had a way of putting her person in a room; it stayed there even when she was not in it; the scent of her hair, her skin, her clothes, the perfume she used—Dr. Bonfils's *Rose Subtile*. He wondered idly what she would seem like wearing a different scent, like violet, for instance. Violet was for blondes, too; a spicy perfume like *Rose Subtile* was preferable for dark brunettes. Suddenly he recalled who had told him that: the storekeeper in Syracuse from whom he had bought the locket he was going to give to Albany.

Letting his eyes nearly close, he watched Caroline through the slits. Her taking the locket and wearing it as soon as Albany had left their room was a child's trick. Sometimes it was easy to forget how young Caroline really was—just a kid. Raised up at Trid's house she must have seen things going on girls didn't as a rule; it made her seem older than she was. Inside she was no older than her age.

"How old *are* you?" he asked abruptly. The question startled her. She let the brush rest on her knee.

"Why, going on eighteen," she said. "Don't you remember? That's what I said when we got married."

"I didn't ask what you said, but how old you are. The first time I saw you you looked only part-way grown." A faint colour rose in her cheeks. He saw she didn't like being reminded. "Remember?" he said. "You was bare-foot and bare-legged, and your dress didn't amount to much of anything. I guess you didn't have much else on, either. You sat on the table and swung your legs at me." He had to grin.

She looked hurt. "I don't see what difference it makes how old I am. I'm all right for a wife, aren't I?"

"Sure," he said. "You're fine. I just asked how old you are. It don't make any difference to me." He felt bored with the whole discussion. He had been a fool to start it in the first place. Caroline took pride in her marriage. He could see the thoughts building up in her head. She probably had been thinking of vaulting; imagining an applauding full tent and Chad's expression of delighted pride. At that point he had had to remind her she was only a kid, and now she was wondering why.

Suddenly her fingers became more active. She finished braiding her hair, stood up without looking towards the bed, and let the pelisse slide off her shoulders and arms, revealing herself in chemise and drawers before she blew the candle out. She wanted him to see that she didn't look like a child. " Hell," he thought, " don't she know colts are born with long legs too ? "

He had started the whole business because he was fed up with Huguenine, with the show, with Fiero's pestering for a living target, and the thin tents, the parched fields, the dull villages, Mrs. Pamplon's nameless dreads—with himself, if it came to that.

Maybe he was with Caroline. She always had to ask his opinion of her day's work in the ring. Bastock knew twice what Chad did about it, but that made no difference to her. If Chad praised her she would practically purr all night and wake up beaming at him. If he criticised her she would listen with just as close attention, and she would do everything she could to please him. She probably thought he was mad with her about something now, and she was going to try to please him. She wouldn't let him go to sleep until she had found out what the matter was. He could tell by the quiet way she slid into bed, straightening herself beside him, slim and cool, and bare as a trout. She was right about one thing ; she was a pleasant article in bed. But it almost made him laugh : two months ago he had had no more idea of getting married than a flea in a pickle jug ; and here he was now with a wife inside his arm, and he was trying to think of something that would satisfy her so she would let him go to sleep. To-morrow wasn't going to be any picnic, considering the tent they could expect from Milo Centre, and Huguenine not fit to speak to. . . .

Chad tried to take no notice of Huguenine next morning during the practice ; but he kept thinking all the time how bad times could change the temper of the show. The morning coolness had left the tent early. Already you could feel the heat on the round-top. Outside the rear wall, the *tunk* of Fiero's indefatigable knife practice went on and on. Most any time they could expect the cry, " Perfecto ! " and the seed-brained Dago would lug in his heavy target to show them the pattern. It was too bad he couldn't throw knives at himself.

The Pamplons weren't there, but everybody else was. They stood round the narrow ringside watching Caroline practise vaulting. It was to be only a half-vault, striking the pad in a sitting posture ; but she had plenty of spring in her long legs to do that ; and when she had it perfect the mount would start her act in flying style. The old business of the hand-up had always seemed a clumsy interlude to Chad. Even with Ike's clowning, it made a halt in the performance. Audiences hated to be kept waiting ; they liked things to snap at them ; the whole secret of a circus was to keep them guessing as to what would happen next. That gave him an idea for building up the act still further. His mind worked rapidly on it, like this :

Chad as equestrian director commences spiel for Carolina's act. He's all alone in the ring—not another performer in the tent. Just a line for her—" Attention, Please ! Huguenine's G and O is honoured to introduce the only lady top-rider now performing in N.Y. State—on her beautiful horse " . . . Hanover-Arabian ? It sounds fine. Chad orders horse brought in. Ike lugs in scrubbiest of the cage-wagon pair, that one with the bad eye and the pumpkin-sized hock. That's a laugh. Chad shouts, " Hey there, thistle-chin," sends him out, apologises to audience, and begins talking about horse again and his sumptuous costly harness. Ike comes in again, with the mule this time, and she's got a bag of hay instead of a pad. " What do you mean by this impertinence, sir ? " Ike says, " Didn't you say, ' Hay, thistle-chin,' to me, Mister Equestrian Director ? " That's a laugh. " I can do you the *haute cole*," Ike says. Grabs hold of bag to mount. Alice high-kicks at *haute cole* and Ike comes down holding handfuls of hay. Chad chases both of them. While he is doing that, cream pad enters by main entrance all alone and commences circling the ring as band plays. Audience has a good look. Horse all alone in the tent ought to make a novelty. Chad returns and commences the pretty spiel about Carolina, America's toast, sylphide of the upper air . . . but turns towards the main entrance as Ike sticks his head in. While his back is turned, Carolina runs in the performers' entrance, makes her mount from the jump-up board alone, so that by the time Chad finishes spiel, she is standing on the pad posing, lovely as a bird. It seemed sure-fire.

Probably Huguenine wouldn't think much of it. It seemed like a waste of effort with the show falling in pieces. But if Bisbee ever got them something to take Oscar's place, everything they did to slick up the main performance would pay back. The first thing to-day, though, was to put the new idea for Ike's finale in a Roman riding act up to the gaffer, and it was better to feed him only one new idea at a time.

Chad glanced towards the top tier of seats. Huguenine's solid face showed some approval. Caroline, running to meet the horse's curve, was a pretty picture. She ran well—quick, light, springy, like a boy. She hit the board perfectly, and though she had to grab for the hand-holds, she managed to stick on.

Chad looked round for Ike, and spotted the clown's moonpale, red-nosed face peering from behind the centre pole. As Chad jerked his thumb towards Huguenine a gleam of intelligence showed in Ike's eyes. He stalked across the ring. Whenever he had a proposition to make, Ike became portentous. Now, in his frock-coat and rusty hat, he had all the unctuous dignity of a Bible salesman.

Chad said to him, " You better do the talking."

" Leave it to me, boy. Leave it to me." Ike showed his easy confidence by placing a foot on the second tier of benches directly under Huguenine, raising his hat an inch, and saying, " Good-morning, A.D. I only just seen you this minute. Had a pleasant night ? "

" I been setting here since practice started," grunted Huguenine.

But Ike wasn't to be upset. He passed his fingers down his nose and said, " My eyes ! They've bothered me since I lost my glasses in Nashville three years ago. I always intended to go back and look for them. Without them I am exposed to these little awkwardnesses." He pulled a cigar from his pocket. " Twopenny stick ? " He offered it apologetically. " I'm economising," he explained. " Cutting down the luxuries in favour of the necessary elementals."

Chad had to grin. Everybody knew what Ike's necessary elemental was. But Huguenine, looking baffled, seemed to see nothing funny. He accepted the frayed cigar and disposed of his chew.

" By God, it's time we all done that. I ain't seen more'n seven rigs pull into this dogyard all morning. This circus gets crumbier every day."

Ike looked grave. He lit himself a second cigar and offered the light to Huguenine. The combined vapour swirled round their heads.

" As a matter of fact," he agreed, " I and Chad were just saying you were right about the show. We better sit down, maybe. Sit down, my boy," he said to Chad. " Will you share the weed ? " He offered Chad the butt end of his own cigar, his fingers curled enticingly. Chad declined. " Now," Ike said to Huguenine, " you're right about the end of the show. It peters out. It's got no bang at all. So I and Chad put our heads together yesterday and here's the idea." He outlined it. " What do you think of that ? " he asked.

Huguenine puffed his cigar and watched Shepley and Caroline practising. As far as Chad could tell, Ike had hardly made a dent in the gaffer's intelligence. Outside the tent they heard Fiero shout, " Perfecto ! " He'd be in in a minute. Mrs. Huguenine cocked her head. She had been listening to Ike's outline. " I think it sounds just wonderful," she said. " Don't you, A.D. ? "

" Maybe," Huguenine said. " How long does Pete think it'll take to work that grey horse in ? "

Chad said, " Two weeks."

" He'll still be green."

Mrs. Huguenine said, " It's just as easy to fall off two horses as one, after all," as if that made the whole act simple.

Ike bowed his head to her.

" You're right, ma'am. How about it, A.D. ? "

" Sure. Go ahead. The show's going to hell anyway. In two weeks' time there probably won't be any show at all."

" A.D.'s feeling discouraged," said Mrs. Huguenine. " But everything's going to turn out all right. You'll see. It's always daylight after dawn."

Fiero entered with his target. His teeth flashed in his face. " See, boss ! All the time perfectos now. You get me the little girl, and then the circus is fine again."

Chad said, " Yeah. It took you a long time. How many knives did you put in the forehead this morning ? "

" Only two. But I have thought it out with my brain," Fiero said. " I practise two or three times. The knives go bad. Yes. Then I come quick and put the little girl on the door. I do the misses outside and the perfectos inside."

Chad felt as if he were going crazy.

" Oh, get out and shut up, Fiero. I don't know who you killed but you can't kill anybody here."

The Italian showed his hurt feelings. He picked the board up without a word, and took it out of the tent. Huguenine said to Chad, " That ain't no way to talk. Fiero's doing the best he can."

" He'll never be any good with those knives," Chad said.

" Maybe not. But you can treat him decent. You ain't God Almighty."

Ike broke in tactfully.

" Well, if you think the act's a good idea we'll get to work on it."

" I didn't say I thought it was good," Huguenine said. " Maybe it is, maybe it ain't." He raised his voice. " I'd like to know what's the matter with this show. That's what I'd like to know. It costs me just as much to run and it don't pay anything."

Chad said, " We're doing the best anybody can with what we've got. We get more laughs, but the people don't come into the tent."

" Laughs ain't enough. Maybe that act will get a laugh. But what's a laugh ? People want something wonderful. Riding two horses don't seem wonderful to me. It ain't like a lion, that's sure."

" There's no use talking lion if you haven't got one," Chad said.

The ring practice had stopped. Caroline and Shepley were standing beside the cream's head. Pete had let his whip-lash drop to the ground. Joe and Budlong were sitting on the kerb. All of them were listening with their eyes on Huguenine's red face.

" I don't need you to tell me, Hanna," Huguenine said. " He was all right till I got sick, wasn't he ? "

" What do you mean by that ? "

" I said he was all right till I got throwed off that bridge. You can't deny that."

Caroline's hand covered her lips, and her eyes, on Chad's showed her apprehension. She was trying to warn him. He thought angrily that she'd rather have him back down ; she was afraid of losing her job if he lost his. The freckles stood out on his face, but his voice quieted.

" You ordered that bottle of water for him, yourself, Huguenine."

" I did after he was taken bad. Somebody had to do something, besides gallivanting round getting married and . . ."

Chad interrupted him. "You're trying to say I neglected Oscar, Huguenine?"

"I ain't trying to say nothing. I'm saying that as soon as I got sick something went wrong with that animal. You were supposed to be in charge, Hanna."

Chad started to get off the seat, but Ike rapped the top of his head smartly with his hat brim.

He said, "A.D., you know what was the matter with that cat. He was just too old. Chad done fine with him."

"He knows it God-damned well," Chad broke out. "If he got out and bought a new attraction instead of sitting around here bull-frogging at everything everybody tries to do to save his God-damned show for him, we might get somewhere."

The utter silence in the tent stopped him. Even the cream pad's ears were quiet. Then he heard Ike telling him to go outside and cool off. He was going outside anyway. If Huguenine wanted to fire him, all right ; he could come outside and do it.

He walked into the heat-hazed sunshine and looked at Milo Centre and the small line of wagons hitched in the church shed. He hated to think of all the work he had put into the show ; but the business had crept up on him. When he joined out he had had no idea of sticking with it any length of time. It had seemed a handy way of getting himself out of Canastota, and Albany's being with it had made the notion of tenting a month or two seem worth while.

And now look at him. Married to a girl who hadn't amounted to a bean seed in a pumpkin patch. She'd soon be making more money than he was, though he had to work all day and half the night just to keep a worn-out rigging from breaking down completely. And getting blamed for what he had done. It would certainly have made old Elias Proops laugh to see him.

Well, if he was going to quit, Milo Centre was as good a place as any. Inside the tent he could hear Ike and Huguenine wrangling. Caroline was staying inside there too. You would have thought A. D. Huguenine was the Emperor of Russia the way they were carrying on.

He went over to the tavern porch, sat down, and waited to see what would happen. Huguenine didn't come out. Nobody did for quite a while, and then it was Joe Duddy. He took the grey horse from the hurdle and led him in.

Twenty minutes later, though, all of them came out together—Ike, Shepley and Caroline first, then the Huguenines, then Budlong and Bastock, bringing the ring stock. The Huguenines went into the treasury wagon. He could hear Huguenine's heavy voice still grumbling and he saw Mrs. Huguenine throw some water out the window and then look to see if she had hit anybody.

Chad watched the three performers heading towards him—the long-legged girl flanked by the spangled rider and frock-coated clown. They had the road practically to themselves. Joe Duddy had been right about the place feeling dead.

Chad could see the expression of relief on Caroline's face clear across the lot. She smiled at him as they came up on the porch.

" My, it's nice not to have to hurry. Mr. Huguenine doesn't think there's any sense parading."

Shepley seemed pleased also, but Ike looked solemn.

" It would have been a good idea to tell the gaffer about there being no parade, Chaddy."

" Did he get mad about that ? " Chad asked.

Shepley laughed.

" He was mad at you in general. If Ike hadn't talked him bat-faced, he'd have come right after you, I guess."

" I was going to tell him, only he started acting rough first," Chad said. He was conscious of Caroline's standing close to his shoulder. Out of the tail of one eye he could see her knee beside his elbow, the tights wrinkling at the back as she let it rest.

" Have you washed for dinner ? " she asked. She made an invitation of it. But he didn't want to talk his row with Huguenine all over with her. He lied.

" Yes, I washed out back."

He knew she didn't believe it, but she went upstairs without urging. Shepley followed her in. But Ike, leaning his hands on the rail, looked the village over.

" This is about the fourth poorest village I ever made a stand in."

" Fourth poorest ! " Chad was incredulous. " Name the others."

Ike didn't hesitate. " Spain's Stand, Georgia, and Oakfuskee and Burtborn or Bornburnt, I don't recall which, but both of them were in Alabama. That was a lean season. I remember when a tavern gave us credit in Fort Hawkins. My Criminy! We used the credit up before they got the pie on the table and they had to take it back to the kitchen till after the show. But it proves that things can always get a little worse than they are." Ike blew his nose like a trumpet. He didn't notice that he was using his six-foot comedy handkerchief, and Chad didn't see any reason to point it out to him. " Likewise," said Ike, " things generally get better."

Chad said, " Maybe you're right. I don't think this show's going to pick up much ; but I know one thing. Huguenine ain't going to use my back to do his high-riding on."

Ike pulled a sigh.

" You're young. Young people always look at the dark side. Those things blow over, too, Chaddy, if you give them time."

3

DUNDEE

FOR a while it looked as if Ike Wayfish had been right. The circus showed to only forty admissions, but it showed ; and the tear-down kept to time, the wagons were loaded, and the light rig started off for Dundee just as usual. Huguenine acted as if Chad didn't exist at all, and Chad returned the compliment ; but at least Huguenine dropped no complaints either about the gate or about the performance. On the surface things seemed about the same as usual ; Mrs. Huguenine even remarked on the fact. But there was a subdued electrical feeling in the truppe.

Chad felt it in half a dozen ways. Fiero's sullenness during his act : he took his cues but managed to keep his back to the ringmaster. And the Pamplons were palpably nervous both with Chad and with Huguenine, as if they had not made up their minds what was expected of them. The three skinners kept blank faces ; they didn't say an unnecessary word. Chad had expected things like that ; what made him mad was the way Caroline seemed inclined to keep company with Shepley and Ike, as if she were afraid that Huguenine would feel annoyed if she showed Chad any attention.

It didn't come out during the performance. In the ring she

went through her act with an exact duplication of every nod to him, or smile. But she disappeared from the tent as soon as the double act was over. When the tear-down started she was safe in the tavern, though she usually waited to see the crowd file out. And when the light rig was starting, she came out with Mrs. Pamplon and climbed right in. She was full of talk, to which Mrs. Pamplon listened with a kind of amazed politeness. Chad was hogging seat-boards out of the tent at the time ; he had a load on his shoulder when he saw her, but as Joe Duddy was close behind, he couldn't stop without slowing up the tear-down. What made him madder was the sight of Huguenine looking on from the treasury wagon.

He didn't know whether Caroline was just deliberately getting back at him for not going upstairs with her before dinner when she had wanted him to, but it didn't make any difference if she was. She had no right to behave so. She was making it seem as if his own wife were against him. He slammed the boards into the wagon and went back towards the tent. Ike had picked up the light rig's reins. He waved his hat as he always did and Alice, the mule, cocked ears and brayed.

Ike was the only person in the troupe who had acted natural with Chad, but that didn't make things much better. He went around as if everything were happening for the best, exactly like an undertaker at a funeral.

Dundee, however, was a much more promising town. They hauled in during twilight and picked up the first tail of small boys they had had in a week. The lot was near the bank of the creek, on good sod, and they put up the rag before black dark. . . .

Chad was still mad when he finished bedding the ring horses ; he asked for Caroline as soon as he came into the tavern. The tavernkeeper's wife was in the office, a starchy-looking woman with a squeak in her corset. She asked him what his business was with the lady.

" I'm Mr. Hanna," Chad said flatly.

" Are you ? " she said and consulted the ledger. Finding the names Mr. and Mrs. Chad Hanna there, she sniffed. " I didn't see you when the party came," she said, as if she didn't believe him. " I understood the light-haired gent was Mr. Hanna."

" He's Signor Rossello. This one. See ? " Chad pointed impatiently to Shepley's handwriting. " Where's my room ? "

" If you're Mr. Hanna, as you say, your room's at the end

of the hall on the back," she said maliciously. "But you won't find her in it, *Mister* Hanna. She's had supper and gone out with the gentleman."

"Where'd she go to?"

The woman tossed her head. "It's not my business keeping track of circus females. Why don't you find her for yourself? You ought to have better ideas than me where to look."

Chad went upstairs just the same to make sure the woman wasn't lying. Caroline, however, was out. The dress she had driven down in hung over a chair. The satchel bag they had been given for their wedding present was open on the floor. She must have got dressed up in a hurry to go out. He leafed through the clothes she had hung up, figuring what was missing. She was wearing the printed muslin with the full skirts, her white shoes, and her cottage cloak, probably using the hood, since she had left both bonnets.

There was no use expecting to find a note, as she had only just learned to write her name. He went to the window which faced against the next house. The other window was only a small grille through the face-board of the tavern, opening into the room at the floor level. Chad went downstairs. He had to pass the woman in the office, and he could hear her corset squeak as she craned to see where he was going. He headed for the bar.

Ike was there, setting up a drink for Budlong, who had brought his jug for refilling. Chad got himself a drink and asked Ike whether he had seen Caroline.

Ike pursed his lips at himself in the mirror.

"She went out after supper. Before you hauled in. She waited round a while but you didn't come so she figured there might have been a breakdown."

"She go alone?" Chad asked.

"No. Shepley offered to escort her. So you needn't worry, Chaddy. Have one on me." He didn't wait for Chad's nod. "Set 'em up, John."

"Sure, mister." The bartender was affable. "My name ain't John, it's Frank." He cleared his throat. "Frank B. Doty."

Ike's clearing of his throat made the bartender's effort seem puerile.

"I always appreciate frankness," he said, pausing for his

laugh and getting a snicker. " I'm frank to say myself I wouldn't mind if I was drinking gin. But when I drink whisky I always find the bartender's name is John. If it ain't I try another house."

" My father's name was John."

" It's always gratifying to know one's father's name," said Ike. " I'll buy you a drink, sir."

The bartender said, " Thank you, but the boss said I wasn't to give you credit above three rounds."

Ike drew himself up, stared at the bartender, slowly reached for his purse, put in his fingers, withdrew them, closed the purse and paid fifty cents on the wood.

The bartender took it. " That don't cover one of these last three drinks."

" Don't it ? " said Ike. " Well, Frank, withdraw your own. Now, Chad, we were talking about Caroline. Mr. Hanna's wife," he explained for the benefit of the room. " Charming young female, beautiful. She wears tights in the performance of Huguenine's Circus. She is, as a matter of fact, the famous Carolina." He laid his hand on Chad's shoulder. " What did you want to know, my boy ? "

" I want to know where she went to ! " Chad said in a lowered voice.

" I told you," Ike said. " She went out with Shepley. Signor Rossello in public life." He turned back to the room. " The Signor's death-defying somerset on the back of his charging steed is something Dundee has never seen before nor will, in all human probability, again, gentlemen." He drained his glass, took Chad's arm, and escorted him to the porch. He wasn't exactly drunk yet, Chad thought, but he was beginning to be.

Outside, Ike's manner sobered somewhat. " You must pardon my digressions in the cause of public advertising. What are you so hot after Caroline for ? "

Chad said, " I want to talk to her. Did you see the way she was acting in Milo ? Just as if I was a dog."

" She's young," Ike said. " Likely she didn't know how to act. She's just a little girl. You have to be kind to little girls, Chad. You haven't got a dollar, have you ? "

" By God, she's married to me," Chad said.

" Yes. So she is," Ike said. " But she thinks a great deal of you, Chaddy. So do I. You couldn't make it fifty cents ? "

" Now she's cleared out as if she didn't want to see me. I ain't going to stand for it."

" She's probably out looking at the stores. A harmless female foible. If I had twenty-five cents, even I could make inquiries for you along the street, seeing you're worried.'"

" No," Chad said. " I'll hunt her up myself."

Ike sighed. " Extension of credit don't seem to be a habit in this town," he observed. " I dare say there may be some open-minded private citizens, however."

He readjusted his high hat and drifted back towards the bar-room door as a man came down the street. " Good-evening," he said blandly ; but Chad didn't wait to see how the experiment proceeded. He headed down into the town.

It was dark. There were few people on the main street, and most of the stores had closed their doors long ago. He didn't really expect to find Caroline in a store, but he gave them a try, looking through the windows as he went along. At the end of the street, the roadway came near to the creek and a little way down he found a boy fishing a run.

He asked the boy whether he had seen a man and a girl come along the road. The boy said he had seen some. What did the girl look like ? Chad described Caroline's clothes and the boy showed interest. " Handsome ? " he asked. Chad said she was. " Kind of acting up to him, do you suppose ? Holding hands, like that ? " Chad said it was possible. " That's the way they all act once they get beyond the houses," the boy said. " I seen lots of them. Walk along as neat and nice and ladylike when they're coming down the street, but soon as they get in the dark they'll side up like heifers."

" How about this girl ? " Chad asked.

" No, she didn't come along here. I been fishing since after sunset. That's the time to get here." He snickered. " Watch 'em go down and watch 'em come back. They always stop about here to fix up. No, I didn't see her. Wish I had. She must be a looker."

Chad didn't comment.

" Why don't you hang around ? " asked the boy. " When Aggie Meigs comes back, I bet it will be fun. It's the first time she's gone out and that mechanic didn't figure to miss any tricks. Her people are strict, too." He dabbled his grasshopper and snickered.

Chad left him abruptly. He had no desire to see a scared girl coming home from her first kick at the whiffletree. Returning through the village, he kept along the creek shore. There were sawmills and a gristmill and three factories. Dundee ought to make a good circus town. But he didn't see anything except one couple coming from behind the woollen factory. The man gave him a hard glance.

He reached a brickyard and turned back towards the lot. But he saw no one there either except Huguenine, who sat on the steps of the treasury wagon and stared at the embers of a small fire. Joe was probably off smelling out a pigeon, and the other two skinners would be in the tent. Chad skirted the lot and passed beyond the tavern through a district of nice houses that led him into the open fields. He turned back there, having seen nothing at all.

It was late when he reached the tavern. In the bar-room Ike was talking to three townsmen. From the interested expressions on their faces and the satisfaction on Ike's, Chad judged that the clown was earning his way.

" You're late," Ike said. " You missed Shepley."

Chad nodded and started to pass through, but Ike lifted a pale detaining hand.

" Allow me," he said. " Gentlemen, I want you to have the privilege of meeting Mr. Hanna, our manager and equestrian director. Mr. Drown, Mr. Frailey, and the gentleman in black is Mr. Packer." Leaning back in his chair, he beamed upwards at Chad, so that his face resembled a red-nosed moon reflection floating on a duck pond. " Mr. Hanna," he went on glibly, " is a man of wit, humour and ability. His duties, in an establishment the size of Huguenine's, are, I may say frankly, enormous. Besides his work in the ring, gentlemen, he supervises the daily practice of the artistes, and the care of the valuable ring stock, and is also responsible for the moral conduct of our younger artistes. I might say truthfully, gentlemen, that Mr. Hanna is the veritable *deus ex machina* of Huguenine's Great and Only International Circus."

The townsmen stared at Chad with respect, but there was a glint in Ike's eye. However, now that he had dug in his spurs in return for Chad's refusal to loan him a quarter, Ike was anxious to be rid of him.

" Mr. Hanna looks tired," he said. " So we had better bid

him good-night." He smiled and waved his hand, and as Chad left, Mr. Packer was saying something in a low voice and Mr. Drown was replenishing Ike's glass.

Upstairs there was a light under Caroline's door.

4

CAROLINE

SHE was hanging up the cottage cloak when he opened the door. Her hands were raised towards the clothes hook, her waist arched and slender above the wide, flowered skirt.

" I wondered where you were," she said over her shoulder.

" All over town."

She turned quickly to face him.

" Chad. What's the matter ? "

" I was looking for you."

" Looking for me ? "

" Yes. That's what I said."

" What for, Chad ? "

" Ike said you'd gone out with Shepley."

" Wasn't that all right ? "

" How do I know ? "

He saw her lips tighten. " I thought you must have had a breakdown. So Fred and I went for a walk."

" You certainly made up your mind in a hurry. We got here on time and I came straight in as soon as I was through work."

" I don't see what was wrong about my going out. We just went for a walk."

" It must have been quite a walk. I looked all over for you." His voice rose. " A married man has got a right to find his wife at home, where I come from."

" I suppose you mean the orphanage ? " She was sorry as soon as she had said it ; but Chad said, " It was a damned sight decenter house than the one you came out of."

" Perhaps it was. I'm sorry I said that, Chad."

He didn't look at her. He could tell by her voice the way she looked, her eyes solemn and large.

He said, " Back there in Milo you acted as if you didn't want anything to do with me. That's no way for a wife to act."

" I didn't mean it that way, Chad. I just didn't want Mr. Huguenine to get any worse tempered than he was."

" You're taking his side then."

" No, I'm not. But we don't want to get him mad. I'm just learning to ride. It would be foolish to quit now."

" There's other shows."

" If they'd take me. But they mightn't have anybody as good as Bastock to teach me, Chad. Don't you see ? "

" All I see is that Huguenine said Oscar died because I wasn't doing my job, and you act as if you think he's right."

" You know that isn't fair."

Her own voice had lifted a little.

" And besides that, you'd rather go around with Shepley than with me."

" That's not true either. I won't have you hinting things like that. You've got no right to."

" I'm not hinting. I'm saying. If it ain't so, why did you sneak off with him before there was a chance I could get here ? "

" We didn't sneak off at all. Mr. Wayfish saw us go. It was way after supper. You're just being nasty. Talk about acting the way I do, and the way Mr. Huguenine does ! You're trying to blame me for the way Mr. Huguenine acts."

" Huguenine's got nothing to do with you and Shepley. He wasn't here any more than I was when you two lit out for the woods, or wherever you did go."

" Stop saying that ! "

Her foot stamped under the wide skirt. He looked at her, grinning a little. Her face was dead white and small and angry and frightened, and determined too.

" Chad, the trouble with you is you've got to thinking the show can't run without you."

" Is that so ? I took this job without no warning, and not much more pay, and I did it a darn sight better than he did, didn't I? Didn't I ? "

" You don't need to yell so." Her voice had quieted. " Of course you did. But that's no reason you have to feel so touchy all the time, Chad. Don't you see that all that's the matter with Mr. Huguenine is that he's worried ? "

" He better be worried. If he don't do something pretty

quick his show will buckle up right underneath him. If I had any sense I'd quit it now and take up somewhere else."

" You'd quit just because the show was bad off ? " she asked.

" Yes. Why not ? "

The colour came back into her face.

" Well, I wouldn't. Albany Yates might do that, but I won't."

" You'll do what I say ! "

" I won't do that, and you can't make me. The Huguenines have been good to us. He carried us along when we weren't anything to him."

" I was earning *my* keep," Chad said. " And he's getting you for less than half what you're worth to the show. We don't owe him anything."

" I'm not talking about dollars," she said.

" Well, I am about sense."

" You're not so funny."

" Well, you aren't funny either."

They stared at each other, at a loss.

Chad got his wind first. " Talking about big heads," he said, " you needn't think just because you've got top billing you're the en-tire circus. Not even Huguenine's, my girl. You're just a girl with long legs the customers like to see in tights. Being as you can stay on a pad, it makes the looking better, that's all."

" Don't say *my girl* to me."

" Why not ? " He was staring at her, his eyes half closed, and she saw the freckles stand out as they had the day before when he tangled with Huguenine. " Maybe you don't figure to be my girl, though. Maybe you're hoping I'll quit so you can be Shepley's. Then you won't have to run out as quick as you get to a new stand, like to-night."

Her eyes darkened in her white face. Suddenly she slapped his mouth.

Chad took it unmoving.

" I guess that's the Trid blood coming out in you."

She didn't say a word, but he saw her breast rise and fall in the bodice of her dress. She didn't stop looking at him. She made him think of the time he had found her in the tent in Canastota. She was no longer sure of herself. She was frightened and her eyes showed hurt. She was on the point of tears. She looked smaller, somehow, facing him, and it was an obvious effort for her to shape her lips to speak to him.

" Do you mean what you're saying about me and Fred Shepley, Chad ? "

" What do you think ? "

" Oh, stop hinting and saying questions ! It's not true. I've told you, I tell you now, but I won't say it again." Suddenly she bent towards him and reached inside her dress. " Do you remember when you got me this ? " she asked, pulling out the locket. " I've never told you what it did for me, have I ? But when I knew you'd given it to me, I stopped feeling like a chippy girl, I planned to be somebody. Whoever you wanted me to be. I was proud to marry you. I'll still be proud I did. I've been a pretty good wife, haven't I ? I've tried to be. I've never looked at any one else than you. But if you want to spoil it you can go on saying things like you are now."

Remembering whom he had bought the locket for, he felt a twinge of shame. But she had him by an unfair hold. It was her fault she had figured it out so, though. Suddenly he felt sick of the whole business.

" All right," he said. " Let's forget it. I'm going to bed."

He passed her towards the bed but she turned to face him.

" If I'd known you wanted me to be here, I would have waited, of course. But you know you've been late before."

" I said, let's forget about it."

She bit her lip, turned towards the mirror. He lay in bed while she undressed. The crockery had a gold stripe but the soap dish didn't match, and there was a pink garter under the chest of drawers. He wondered how it had got there and whether its former owner had hunted for it. He couldn't get it out of his mind and he was looking at it again when Caroline blew out the candle.

She came to bed without a word, staying very quiet on her side of it. He knew she was awake. She stayed awake a long time, but even after he was sure that she had gone to sleep some feeling of her offended hurt stayed in her, making him think of a self-righteous-looking spinster lady who used to bite her lips whenever she passed him and Elias Proops on the porch of the Yellow Bud.

It got on his nerves so after a while that he finally slid out of bed and put his shirt and trousers on, and went outdoors and round to the tavern barn. The groom was snoring away in his room behind the feed-room ; the cream pad's gentle whicker of greeting didn't wake him. Chad went up into the loft, and made himself a bed in the new hay. It felt fine to be sleeping in a barn again. He rolled over two or three times, feeling the green stalks buckle under his shirt, and kicked out his legs. He went to sleep almost at once.

5

HUGUENINE SPEAKS HIS PIECE

WHEN Chad woke, the stable-hand was close by, forking hay down on to the mow floor. Beyond his spindle-shanked figure the cracks between the east boards showed grey daylight. There was a sound in the roof, as though thousands of mice were fingering the shingles. Chad rolled over on his back and then sat up to listen to it, and the stable-hand quit forking and sunk his tines and leaned on the handle.

" By Cripus, you sure come up a fluking when you woked," he said. He had a sorrowful and nervous set to his mouth, and after a little study Chad decided that he had painful teeth. But when the stable-hand asked whether he had been in the mow all night, Chad made out that practically all his teeth were gone. The nervous expression came from the continual gum-running of his tongue.

" Yes," Chad said. " It was hot so I come in here."

" 'Tain't bad, sleeping in a mow. But 'tain't legal, neither. You'd ought to have asked me."

" You was asleep," Chad said. " I hate to wake a sleeping man."

" Me too. I durn near forked you this morning, but it seemed mean, so I figured to use the handle when I done throwing down the hay." He paused. " Where'd you come from ? "

" Milo Centre was the last town."

" Oh, you're with the circus. I thought you was one of these-here fellers says they're looking for work. That's what they tell you anyway. They come from all over. I tell them, how do you expect to find work if you're on the road all the while ?

C.H. N2

Sometimes I leave them stay here, though. I offer to let them lug manure or something, but it's queer how seeing a fork and the hind end of a horse will make some of those fellers change their minds about getting a job." He paused to work his tongue round his gums again, and Chad felt obliged to inquire whether he had tooth trouble.

"Well, I look at it as yes and no. A teeth doctor come here a while back ; he had a lot of little picks and a kind of pincher to gaffle on to your tooth with, and he done some pulling on me, but she kept right on paining. I said to him, ' Doc,' I said, ' this costs me fifty cents a try and it don't seem to get us nowhere.' So he took out another clutch of teeth but it didn't do no good. I told him so right up and down. And he said, ' Hell, you don't cut a tree down with one lick, do you ? ' But on account of I was a good customer, he reduced his price. But when it come to the last one, I held out. God damn it, I say, a man's got to have something to show for his money."

Chad agreed. He got to his feet, listening to the noise on the roof.

It was raining.

"Sort of a mizzle. But the wind sets south-east," said the stable-hand. " I don't look for it to stop till night."

Outdoors Chad decided the stable-hand was right. The rain was light but there was a fresh earth-smelling wind drawing across the town. The roofs of the houses glistened and a couple of ducks were slapping their feet in the puddle under the burdocks by the corner of the barn, and there was a hollow musical drip in the rain barrels.

It was late, too. The tavern help was up ; he could hear the cook still sleepily missing her distances in the kitchen.

He hurried across the yard to return to the bedroom before Caroline woke.

She was up, however, washing her face in cold water. She said good-morning through her wet fingers and grabbed blindly for the towel. He handed it to her and she dried herself. When her face emerged, her cheeks were pink and her voice sounded natural.

"You must have gone out early," she said. Her eyes did not show that she had started crying last night as soon as he had closed the bedroom door.

He said, " It's raining."

"I heard it as soon as I woke up," she said, nodding. "I thought when I heard it that we hadn't had a drop of rain since Oscar died." She checked herself. "Since we left Albion. That's more than two weeks ago, isn't it?"

Her voice was bright and cheerful. She was trying to find them something to talk about besides themselves.

"Sixteen days," Chad said. "But it might have held off till Sunday. This town looked as if it might have given us a decent tent. It won't now."

"Maybe it will clear, though. It's not raining hard."

She was dressing for practice. He watched her button on the little military jacket. It fitted the hollow of her back, snug as a glove's finger, the flared little tails emphasising her sex.

"You'd better put on something over that," he said. "That woman downstairs don't think a lot of circus people anyway."

"I was going to wear my pelisse," she said. "That makes me respectable-looking, doesn't it? Nobody but you needs to know what's going on underneath."

She smiled so cockily that he grinned back out of habit. And they went downstairs like that to the dining-room that was dim and stuffy from having its windows closed against the rain. Ike Wayfish was pressing his red nose to a pane and the others looked up wordlessly from their plates as Caroline said good-morning to them. It was easy to tell from Mrs. Pamplon's curious expression that she had overheard their quarrelling last night. Probably she had already spread the word, Chad thought, for Shepley looked embarrassed.

Ike said, "It's getting harder," and started to pursue a fly up and down the frame. His hand was uncertain. He gave it up, watching the insect settle in undisturbed impertinence, and came over to the table. "No egg, madame. No sausage, please. Just tea." He forked the tails of his coat over the chair seat to sit down. "I talked to the gaffer this a.m.," he announced in a hollow voice, stirring sugar into his cup. "He says if we don't draw decent tents here and in Havana there'll be no pay on Saturday. He claims he's been losing money since Lady Lillian abandoned us in Clyde. He says the good tents we've had haven't made up for the others. I haven't kept track of figures. Has anybody else?"

Shepley said, "You can't count people turning somersets on horseback."

" *No!* " Fiero agreed vociferously. " You cannot do it, not juggling, nor walking on the ball. Impossible."

" That's the trouble," Ike agreed. " There never was no performer with sense enough to keep track of the admissions. And he couldn't if he had the sense. You haven't kept any count, have you, Chaddy ? "

" Mrs. Huguenine told me what we had to draw if we were going to pay," Chad said slowly. " I figured we were holding even before Oscar died. But I ain't sure. She never told me what the count was."

" That's it," Ike said. You never heard of a gaffer who'd give the ex-act figures. They only tell you they're losing money."

" I believe what Mr. Huguenine says." Caroline's cheeks were bright. " I'm sure he's honest."

" I think so too," Ike said to her. " But that only makes it worse for us. If he can't pay, he can't. And now when we're in a decent town, it goes and rains.

> The universe is full of thieves,
> And mud is all the clean rain leaves."

Mrs. Pamplon stared at him painfully.

" Oh, this country, it is wicked ! " she exclaimed. " All the time it rains, rains, rains ! " She turned to her husband. " Oh, Henri, I wish I was 'ome, in my beautiful France."

" Beautiful France ! Pah ! " Fiero turned glittering eyes on her. " All the time you complain. You say it is wild, there are too many Americans, there are not enough people, it is too dry, too hot, it rains, rains, rains ! Why did you leave your France for if it was so beautiful ? Hey ? "

" You are talking to my wife, Juggler ! "

Mr. Pamplon had risen to his feet. Fiero's hand automatically grasped a table knife.

" Wife ! " he said. " Hah ! A rabbit complains less."

" Getting mad won't stop it raining. Mrs. Pamplon's nervous, Fiero," Ike said soothingly. " It's natural in females. It's the chief charm of the gender."

Pamplon was breathing hard.

" Throw it," he said. " I am no piece of wood in a door with paint.

Fiero, however, was rapidly cooling off.

" I was hasty. I apologise. Mrs. Pamplon is correct. This country is abominable. There is not one person in it of the right size to be my target. Besides, it rains ! "

It kept on raining. It fell during the parade, softly, insistently, heartlessly. By the time the troupe had made the half-way mark and started back for the lot, their costumes were bedraggled, sodden, sad affairs, and Chad thought that even an idiot with fifty dollars in his pocket would not have bought a ticket.

From the ring he watched the audience damply take their seats. They showed no enthusiasm when he gave the word for the grand entry, but followed the march around its mechanical circle and let it go without a single handclap. For once Mrs. Huguenine showed a sense of defeat ; she failed to blow a single kiss. Huguenine looked in for a few minutes and vanished. The performers went through the motions of their acts under the rain-streaked round-top like wax automatons, and as soon as the all-out-and-over had been given, they huddled back to hear what Mr. Huguenine might have to say.

He came in through the main entrance, his shoulders soaked from the rain, and demanded in a peevish voice what they were waiting for. " It's fifteen miles to Havana," he said.

For a minute nobody moved. Then Budlong reached for a sledge, tapped loose a toe-pin, and pulled it smoothly. His lean face was like an Indian's as he cheeked his tobacco and followed his spit leisurely towards the next pin. Joe Duddy and Bastock began to remove the seat boards and the tear-down got slowly under way.

It didn't satisfy Huguenine, however.

" What the hell's got into this circus ? " he demanded. " Performers are paid to pack their own things. This ain't a funeral."

He started to leave the tent ; but Fiero surprised them all by shouting, " Hey, you wait a minute. You say I get paid. Do I get paid to-morrow, hey ? "

It stopped Huguenine dead, and when he turned back his head and shoulders were hunched like a cornered bull's.

" It's none of your damned business."

Fiero turned to the tent and raised his hands.

" Not my business ! For what is it I walk on the ball ? For what I juggle little balls, and bottles, and knives?" He swung back on Huguenine. "For what I pack my things and get all wet in this damn rain, hey?"

Huguenine looked over the Italian's head.

"Did you put Fiero up to this, Hanna?" he demanded.

"No, I didn't," Chad said shortly. It made him mad to have Huguenine pick on him. Caroline's worried eyes were watching them both, and Chad saw her relief when Ike Wayfish stepped up to Huguenine.

Ike said, "I told them what you said about the show this morning, A.D."

Huguenine gave a defiant sort of grunt.

"Well, you saw what kind of a tent we got to-day, didn't you? And you ought to know what kind of a show you put on. It was terrible right straight through. There wasn't hardly three entire laughs. Not one of you was any good, except maybe Caroline and Shepley together. But they weren't riding good either. Pamplons were terrible. So were you, Fiero. Ike, I could hardly hear what you said. Maybe it was funny. It didn't sound funny to me. You can't expect to make a circus pay with that kind of a performance. God damn it, every one of you was laying down. The band was full of crumbs."

Joe Duddy glanced up hotly.

"You can't do nothing when your drum gets wet. By God, I whaled the tar out of it."

But Huguenine's anger had suddenly abandoned him.

"Maybe it's the audience, I don't know. But the show ain't going like it used to go. It's just paying expenses and a little over. I can pay you folks half-pay to-morrow, or I can hang on to the money in case we don't make expenses next week. I didn't want to get into this business anyway," he said in a moderate voice. "But it seemed all right when we started out. We had just a good simple show and the folks liked it. Everybody was friendly in it too. Now it just ain't doing anything." He raised his eyes. "Well, you can take your pick to-morrow."

"Me, I want my pay," Fiero said defiantly; but Huguenine had turned and was already walking heavily out of the tent.

Joe Duddy looked at the Italian scornfully.

"My God," he said. "Ain't that just like a Dago?"

But the rest of them went to work in silence. The performers finished their chores, and Chad and the skinners wrestled with the soaked canvas. Huguenine came over to help them shove it into the tent wagon.

"We won't get into town till ten o'clock," he said. "Hanna, I want to talk to you to-morrow morning. You better bring my coat back to the treasury wagon to-night. My wife will have to let it out again."

That seemed to be all he had to say. For a minute Chad didn't take in the full drift of it. Then he walked rapidly after him over the soft grass. "Huguenine," he said.

Mr. Huguenine had climbed up on the seat. As he looked down the little door behind his shoulders opened. But Chad didn't pay any attention to Mrs. Huguenine. He was feeling a queer sick creeping in his insides.

"Yeah," said Mr. Huguenine.

"You said something about that coat. You mean you want me to quit?"

"There's no sense in me paying you to be equestrian director now I can do it myself."

"I've done a lot for the show," Chad said.

"Well, look at the way it's going. You and Ike been monkeying around with it for five weeks and there's less laughs than there used to be." Mr. Huguenine fingered the reins. "Maybe I've been short on you," he said. "I don't say you haven't worked pretty hard on it. But when things get as bad as they are a person has to do something, Chad. And I can't afford to keep on paying you seven dollars. That's all."

"You never done that," Chad said. "You ain't paying my wife what she's worth, either."

Huguenine said, "Listen here. Caroline's lucky to be getting anything. Generally a rider gets apprenticed for a year. I'm letting her practise on my ring stock and letting Bastock train her and I'm paying her too. Something. Twenty-eight dollars a month is good pay for a girl. Anywhere."

"You're blaming me for Oscar dying."

"I ain't blaming you for nothing," Huguenine said patiently. "I guess you was just too young to handle the job, but there wasn't anybody else to do it, that's how it was. I don't say you didn't do it better than a lot of young fellers would have. But you got to know more about circusing before you can expect to get carried steady in that job. Not when I can do it myself."

"You can do it!" Chad cried. "Go ahead and try. Somebody ought to tell you what you sounded like. Hell, you couldn't even remember your speeches. You're just a farmer in the ring. What are you going to do with all the patter I and Ike have worked up ? You'll be all mixed up before you begin."

"Chad," Mrs. Huguenine's broad face was pressed in the small door, "don't talk like that. We think a lot of you. You and Caroline both. We want you to like working for us."

"It's a funny way to go about it."

"Bettina's right," Huguenine said. "I don't blame you for feeling bad. But you aren't going to help yourself talking that way. I can't hire anybody who talks to me the way you just done."

"You haven't hired anybody. I quit. Here and now," said Chad. "I'll take the ring stock down to Havana. But I ain't going to go back working for a roustabout's pay and nothing else just because you've got wind in your pants again. I've quit."

Mr. Huguenine sucked a short breath. "You damned, trouble-making canaller," he said. "You ain't quit ! I've fired you ! I tried to tell you decent, but you've acted up-snot once too often with me. I'm sick of it. You're fired. You can draw your pay to-morrow and get the hell out of this circus. Understand ? "

"All right," Chad said. "I told you I'd take the ring stock down. I'll do it. Then we're through."

As a parting irony he started to lift his hat to Mrs. Huguenine. Her face was puckered in the tiny aperture. She opened her mouth, but Huguenine gave her no chance to say what she was going to. He started the horses with a jerk, and the nigh hind wheel lifted a slice of muddy sod against Chad's shoes.

He kicked it back. The tent wagon was lumbering up to him through the rain. Budlong looked down.

"Had a argument with the gaffer ? " he asked.

"Yes," Chad said. "I told him I'd quit and he says I've been fired."

Budlong offered no comment beyond a pretty figure eight of his long lash. It didn't pay to let the tent wagon stop in rainy weather once you had her rolling. The horses were buckled into the collars, their feet thrusting for holds. The other two wagons wheeled into its tracks. Chad went to get Jerry and the cream. It was still raining.

6

HAVANA

COMING down to the level of Seneca Lake in the dark made the prettiest piece of driving Chad ever saw Budlong perform. As soon as the ring stock went over the edge of the grade, and he felt the steepness of the pitch, he knew the wheels would need chaining ; and though Huguenine's had no further calls on his services, he put the horses off the road and waited for the wagons to come.

The treasury wagon came first and went down the drop with the brake shoes rubbing noisily. Then in about five minutes the mass of the tent wagon loomed up on the crest behind the thin glow of its lantern. The four big horses stopped, pricking their ears, and blowing out their nostrils. The wheelers laid their ears back as Budlong's weight hit the pole between them. He jumped clear of the eveners and came forward past the horses.

Chad said, " It's a steep drop."

Budlong showed no surprise.

" I see it is. There's probably shelfs, though "

Chad said, " I guess so. Huguenine's brakes went off a couple of times."

" We'll chain the wheels."

" Both sides ? "

" Yep." He kicked the dirt. " The rain's loosened the top," he said. He brought the four horses forward till the front wheels were on the roll and stopped them. The wheelers were already sitting on the breechings. " Chain your side," Budlong said.

Chad threw the hook between the hind-wheel spokes and wrenched it up to the side ring on the box. Budlong repeated the operation on the other. " Get up, a step," he ordered, and the wheelers gingerly eased their weight off the breeching. The wagon came after them for a couple of feet, then settled where it was.

" They'll drag her all right," Chad said.

Budlong climbed back to his precarious perch in silence and sat there a moment, looking down. Then he took his cud of

tobacco from his mouth and laid it on the roof of the high box
behind him.

" If I can find it when I get to the bottom, I'll know I'm
right side up," he said to Chad.

" Why don't you drive her from the road ? "

" Well, Chaddy, if she goes, either I'll fall on top of her or
she'll fall on top of me. Up here I've got kind of a head start."
He had picked up the lines and shaken out the long lash of the
whip. He eased the wheelers back, fingering in the top lines,
and then let all four horses out together. The horses had to dig
to get the ponderous wagon started. The chained wheels ground
on the gravel, slid forward, and Budlong's head dipped out of
Chad's view under the tilt of the box.

Once going there was no stopping it. By the time Chad had
swung up on Jerry's back and brought the ring stock on to the
road, the big wagon was rocking at a half trot fifty yards ahead.
He couldn't see Budlong, but he saw the team, all four in hand,
all four on their nerve, playing their ears, now forward for the
road, now back for Budlong's voice. But at one sharper curve,
when the chained wheels slewed, peeling the surface to the road
shoulder, Chad had a glimpse of him leaning forward, hands
raised to shake the lines, and the team, the strain puckering their
haunches, buck-jumping like one. The wagon dragged at an
angle for half a dozen yards, spraying small stones out of sight
over the bank ; then the hind wheels ground into line again,
and the whole rigging straightened out for the valley floor.

When at the bottom, Chad jumped off the grey to take the
chains off, the horses were lathered, but Budlong was working
on his chew, and saying that the God-damned thing was wet.
They waited a minute until they saw Bastock's lantern light
leafing out the trees up the hill behind them. Then Chad said,
" I might as well get going," and Budlong said, " So long," and
that was all there was to it. But the warmth of excitement the
hill had raised in Chad gave way to the soaking touch of rain
as the ring stock plodded beside the long black reach of the lake.
There was nothing to see, nothing to hear except the sudden
echo of hoofbeats as an outcropping of rock came close to the
road. He felt lonely ; he knew he was going to miss the circus ;
but there was nothing in Huguenine's for him. He thought of
Burke and Walsh. In Auburn, Burke had practically offered him
a job.

Jefferson Village at the head of the lake was dark except for the light of the treasury wagon, which was just pulling out of town. Chad slowed the ring horses to match their pace to it. He didn't want to pass the Huguenines; so they came into Havana in that order.

The treasury wagon stopped in the roadway, but Chad went by it to the nearest tavern. Let Huguenine find the lot for himself. The performers weren't staying at the tavern he picked first, but the bartender told him that they were down a block at Twombley's. He put the horses in the barn; it took almost an hour to get them into shape and he punched the cream pad's ribs when he was through. Bastock would probably handle them, but even Bastock wasn't a man to fuss over them.

Then he went into the bar, for the office was dark, and asked where his wife's room was. The proprietor was corking some whisky bottles.

He said, " Mrs. Hanna? You mean the girl? "

Chad said, " Yes."

" First room on the right. Faces the street. The lot's just over the way a hundred yards beside the crick." He laid his palm on the cork. " Have one on the house? "

" No thanks."

" Take a candle off the bar. Help yourself."

Chad opened the door to find the room dark. Caroline was in bed. She turned her head sleepily and said, " Oh, it's you," which for some reason made him angry.

" Yes, it's me. Where's Huguenine's coat? "

" I hung it up. What do you want it for? " She started to sit up.

" Huguenine wants it to-night," Chad told her. " He's taking back the job with it."

She said, " Oh! " as he took the coat down.

He laid it over his arm. " I might as well take the hat while I'm at it," he said.

She was sitting up now, but she didn't say anything as he went through the door and closed it.

When he returned half an hour later he found her still sitting up in bed, and for a minute or two while he undressed she just watched him with her hands folded between her legs. But he ignored her, and finally she said, " Chad? "

" Yes."

"Don't act so mad. Tell me what happened."

"I told you. Huguenine took the job back. I quit."

"But couldn't you go back to your old job?"

He said sullenly, "Do you think I'd go back to be a roust-about and hang around while you made the money, and got top billing and all? I don't want to look like a fool."

"I don't see why that would make you look like a fool, Chad."

"Maybe you don't. I do. Besides, I told you I'd quit."

"I'm sure Mr. Huguenine would let you go back if you asked him."

"He won't. After I quit, he fired me."

She said slowly, "You wanted to quit."

He looked at her then. Her face was miserable.

"Why did you?" she asked. "Are you mad at me? Just because I went out with Fred Shepley last night? There's no reason you should be." She picked up the blanket with her finger-tips. "But it must have started before that. What did I do? What difference does it make who makes the money? It belongs to both of us, doesn't it? Suppose we weren't circus people, and you got sick, and I had to go to work. That would be all right, wouldn't it?"

"There's no use talking about it," Chad said. "I'm quitting. If you want to come with me, you can. But you don't want to, do you? You said so before."

She shook her head.

"No. I don't want to. But I'd do it in a minute if I thought it would do any good. Chad, don't just stand there with your back to me. I mean it when I say I'd go along with you." Her voice faltered. "This is the first time in my life I've had a chance to become somebody worth being. I thought that was what you wanted, and now it seems to me I ought to go ahead. Besides, Chad, what are you going to do?"

"Oh, I don't know. I haven't made up my mind yet. Maybe I'll go back to Canastota. I don't know. I'd like to see old Elias before he dies; he's going to some day when he ain't thinking about it. Maybe I'll just ramble round the country some, though. I've never been down this way before."

"If you do that you wouldn't want me along. I'd be in your way." She had gained control of her voice, as if she had made her mind up. "I've been thinking about you and me since last night, Chad. I think you're getting tired of me, maybe more than you are of Huguenine's Circus."

" I'm not tired of the circus, or of you either," he said. " But I won't stand being kicked out of my job when I haven't done nothing bad."

" Just the same, if you hadn't felt like leaving, you wouldn't have let Mr. Huguenine get you so mad, out of reason, almost. Maybe it's better for you to quit. Maybe you'll want to come back. If you get work somewhere else, though, you can let me know." She had her womanly look on now, her forehead slightly puckering. . " I'll tell the Huguenines where I'm going to be after we close and you can send me a letter to their place. I'll come wherever you are if you want me. And if you want to find the circus, probably Mr. Bisbee can tell you where it's going to be from now on."

Chad looked up quickly from untying his boots.

" Is Bisbee here ? "

" Yes, he was here this afternoon. He sat on the porch with me after supper."

" I can see him first thing in the morning."

Bisbee ought to have some idea of where Burke and Walsh would be standing. . . .

Caroline saw that Chad had something on his mind to ask Bisbee, but she didn't ask what it was. She had, as she said, sat out with Mr. Bisbee on the porch after supper, and somehow— perhaps it was the disinterested kindness of his long, horsey face —she had started talking about Chad. Before she knew it she was telling Mr. Bisbee about the row with Huguenine, and a little about the quarrel she and Chad had had.

It seemed as if she could see Bisbee nodding this minute.

" Probably he'll quit," Bisbee had said. " He's a roaming sort of cuss, and his kind have got to high-tail about every so often. You think a lot of him, don't you ? "

" Yes," she had said.

" Then let him go. You can't keep that kind tied, horses, dogs or humans. They'll go mean. But if you let him go, and he comes back, he'll always come back if you give him time."

It was something she had foreseen vaguely weeks ago, soon after her marriage. She watched Mr. Bisbee lighting himself a fresh cigar. He had blown a long drift of smoke.

" If he don't "—Mr. Bisbee dropped an absent-minded hand

on her knee—" why, I'll look out for you. And I'll make you the most famous female equestrienne in all North America." He smiled. " Maybe I'll do it anyway, Chad or no Chad. So let him go. . . ."

It had been hard to do.

Chad said, " I'll keep track of you and see you in the fall anyhow."

She said rather pathetically, " I'm your wife, Chad. I'll always be."

He kicked the second shoe off, looking at her now.

" Sure," he said.

" You're not mad ? " Her lips trembled for a minute, but she shaped a smile with them.

" No, I'm not mad at you, Caroline."

" Then come and prove it to me."

She was half-laughing and half in tears.

7

BISBEE ON THE ROAD

CHAD had done some figuring on how he was going to talk to Bisbee, but Bisbee didn't give him the chance. He was sitting out on the porch, smoking his morning cigar, with his feet on the railing and his high hat cocked forward to keep the balance perfect.

" Hallo, there," he said. " I hear you and Huguenine have made a pretty complete mess of things between you two. He claims he's said his say, and you look as if you wouldn't back down for gold or glory."

" No," Chad said. " I won't stand being frogged around all the time for doing what I never done. He's fired me, and that's enough."

" Yes. That's the way it always is. I don't blame you or him. Poor old farmer, he's feeling meaner than a lop combed rooster getting dug by a bantam cockerel." He grinned to himself under his long nose. " Is your wife going along with you, Chad ? "

" No. She's going to stay."

Bisbee nodded without comment.

" Any idea where you're going ? "

" No. That's why I wanted to ask you . . ."

But the agent interrupted him.

" Then you might as well come with me, and you can ask me what you want to after we leave town. I've got a rig ; I bought it for a song. I'll tell you about it. It's down in the stableyard. You hitch the horse to it and we'll light out at noon. I've got to see A.D. now."

That was how Bisbee always was, Chad thought ; you had to take him or leave him. He had never known a man, except old Elias Proops, who managed to do so exactly what he wanted to do. Elias, however, used to accomplish it by doing nothing at all ; while Bisbee was always on the go.

Chad collected his pay a little before practice time. Huguenine wasn't in the treasury wagon. Mrs. Huguenine said he was talking to Bisbee in the tent. But she said he had left Chad's money in a paper.

" He said half the pay you earned when you was just a skinner would be waiting for you in Herkimer this fall. You can get it there, or we'll give it to Caroline."

" Give it to her," Chad said. He had to grin at Mrs. Huguenine's fat anxious face. She had both hands buried in her bosom. " You've been nice to both of us, ma'am," he told her. " You might kind of keep an eye on Caroline."

Tears rolled out on her fat cheeks. " I will," she said. " But I hope you'll come back before then, Chad. A.D. always gets over his mads. He's so fiery, sort of. Always blazing up or going out, or something."

Chad went back to the tavern porch to kill time. Most of the performers had gone over for practice. Caroline was late. She must have been lingering in the office, for she came out as soon as he sat down.

" You won't leave before I get back, Chad ? "

He told her no ; and she crossed the roadway towards the tent with her quick, long-legged, easy stride.

Joe Duddy came out of the stable alley with the two ring horses, and Chad noticed that the cream pad was striking his nigh fore toe. It was none of his business now ; the shoes had been reset this morning ; but he couldn't help pointing it out to Joe.

Joe seemed flustered. He had to admit, though, that Chad was right. " Darned if I know why he does it," he said.

" Probably the blacksmith spread the heel," Chad said. " You pick up his foot and see."

Joe said, " You're right. I watched that God-damned blacksmith close, too. But I didn't see nothing wrong."

" Maybe it won't bother him, but if it does it'll show up in practice and you'd better fix it before show time. Somebody might get a fall."

Joe gave him an understanding nod. " I'll do it during dinner," he said. " You needn't worry, Chaddy."

The only trouble with Joe was that his head was all fluttered up with pigeons. Chad hated to leave the cream pad to a man like that. He had never seen a horse he fancied better except Albany's Buck.

Feeling foot-loose, he went to the tavern barn and hitched Bisbee's horse to the rig. It was a high-wheeled spring carriage built to carry four, but he could roll it with one hand. He left the animal hitched to it in the shade and returned to the tavern, going upstairs to his room, where he packed his few clothes. He made a bundle of them with an odd yard of calico Caroline had. She would need their wedding-present bag.

She saw the bundle as soon as she came in, but she didn't mention it. When he asked how practice had gone, she said, " All right. Jonathan seemed kind of rough-gaited."

" He's got a bad shoe on," Chad said. " I told Joe to get it fixed."

He paused ; then told her about collecting his due pay, if it ever proved to be collectable. She wanted him to take a share of the money they had saved up from her salary, but he wouldn't touch it, and she accepted his decision quietly. She seemed quite calm as she got out her pelisse to wear down to dinner.

" I'm not going to dinner," he said. " Bisbee and I are pulling out in a few minutes."

" Then I'll say good-bye now." She lifted her face for a kiss, and when he had kissed her, she said, " Let's shake hands."

" All right."

It moved him more than kissing her had. He said, " You're a good girl, Caroline."

She stiffened, staring at him, and to his surprise he saw the tears rising under her lids. Then she brushed her eyes and turned and ran out of the room, tying her pelisse as she went. He had meant to give her good luck, but she had gone too quickly. . . .

It felt queer to be on the road, to look back and see the parade forming up on the lot—Joe Duddy knocking odd thumps on his drum, Caroline mounting Jerry from Ike's hand, Huguenine heaving Mrs. Huguenine on to the tail gate of the seat wagon—and to know that he was not going to be in the procession at all. They wouldn't miss him in the parade ; with no lion they didn't need to use the cage wagon anyway.

"I aim to put something into that cage in a week's time," Bisbee said. "That's what I'm after now." He snapped his whip, getting a raised tail from the horse. "What do you think it is ? "

"I don't know," Chad said. "You haven't found a lion, have you ? "

"Nope," Bisbee said. "It's no lion."

"'Tain't a lioness, is it ? " Chad asked to humour him.

"It's got nothing female about it," Bisbee said, "but he ought to be a wonder just the same."

"I guess there's not much you could find around here, except a bear, or a wolf, or a panther."

"None of them. Besides, I don't lay much stock in a natural animal," Bisbee said. "And this-here's going to be a wonder for Huguenine's." He seemed to be in his best form, tickling the rump of the horse, and staring far ahead down the road. Chad could practically see his brain turning over ideas like the spinning of the wheels under them, and he realised that the agent was already working out the advertising. In spite of himself he began to get interested.

"I've heard tell of a three-headed calf," he said.

"Nope. It ain't a freak, though I always wanted to handle one. I'd like to do a story about the different ideas such an animal would have to contend with while operating on one single body. Talk about a man and wife. Sometimes I think I ought to have been a preacher."

The rig spun nicely on its yellow wheels. The springs, set high on the axles, rocked the body over the jounces, and the way the seats were set, low to the floor, gave one the feeling of flying. The white-nosed horse, moreover, had a fine long raking trot.

"I always planned to try him in harness," Bisbee said.

" Then I heard of this wonder and I happened to be in a card
game at the time with the gent who told me about it. So I played
the cards with buttons on them and I won the wagon off him
because I wanted to bring this attraction along with me when I
got it."

" Then it's human," Chad said sharply.

" Yes, sir. And I'll tell you what he is. He's a strong man.
But he ain't just a wrestler. He's a regular slam-bang gigantic.
This feller I played with was a young engineer; he's working on
the Erie Railroad. And he'd seen this feller working on the
tracks. Hell, they didn't blast regular boulders, they called for
this feller to lift them out by hand. He can carry six rails on his
shoulders, and he can carry two kegs of liquor, one under each
arm. He weighs three hundred and sixty pounds, but he ain't
fat. I'm working out the paper for him, and it ought to sound
good. Listen."

Bisbee cornered his cigar.

WORLD'S LARGEST MAN ! NOT WAX. HE EATS
AND BREATHES. A MAMMOTH LIVING SPECIMEN
OF HOMO SAPIENS, INTACT.

He must be seen to be believed. Ladies need have no fear of
him. He is as affable as he is tall. $10,000.00 is offered by
the management for the equal of this LUSUS NATURAE.

" He sounds costly," Chad said.

" He does, but he won't be. They tell me he's simple, sc
we'll hire him out for a skinner and he won't know the difference.
He'll be tickled because he'll have a costume. I think we'll dress
him in an Oriental rig-up. Then he can wear pants and no shirt.
And the turban will put a foot on to his height."

" I thought you said he had a job on the railroad."

" He had, but they fired him, because he wanted to drive
spikes and he hit so hard he made dents in the iron rails."
Bisbee whistled a bar through his teeth. " Imagine that feller
walking down a street in the parade. They say he's seven foot
high. We'll have Ike fall off his mule and this feller can pick
him up and put him on and pat the top of his head, easy."

" Where's he live ? "

" In the town of Candor," Bisbee said. " That's where
we're going now. This engineer didn't know whereabouts, but

the feller has a farm. I've got the name, though. It's Clinton Cronk." He became thoughtful. " He won't have any tattooing on him, probably, but I hope he's hairy."

He fell into such a complete brown study that Chad didn't care to interrupt him, but after half a mile or so he roused himself.

" What was it you wanted to ask me, Chad ? "

Chad thought a minute ; then he decided to come right out with it. " I thought you'd know where Burke and Walsh would be standing now."

" Take the lines," Bisbee said. With both hands free he pulled a little note-book from his pocket and turned the pages. " To-day's Saturday, July thirtieth," he said after a minute. " Burke's in Albany. They stand there through August first, then play two days in Schenectady and two in Amsterdam. Then they go to Ballston, Saratoga, Mechanicsville, and Waterford. They play Troy three days and two in Hudson City. Then they go to Clermont and Rhinebeck and play three in Poughkeepsie—August 19, 20, and 22." He turned back through the book. " On that day Huguenine's ought to be in Truxton, if we ain't broke down."

" Thanks," said Chad. " How'd you figure all that out ? "

" Oh, I got Burke's man drunk one night and went to bed with him. He wore boots but hung his coat on a chair. He didn't know who I was." He put the book back. " Aiming to try Burke's ? " he asked casually.

" I'd thought of it. I think he nearly offered me a job in Auburn. He hinted, sort of. I didn't want it."

" It's a big show. I don't think you'd like it as well. I'd hate to see you stay with it. I don't want to lose track of you."

" How do you mean ? "

" Some day I'm going to have my own circus. I want to run the business end and I want some fool, quick-tempered, freckled feller to handle the show end. Kind of a canaller type like you. I'm not rich enough to buy it myself. I got some money saved but not enough, and I'm figuring Huguenine will want to get rid of this outfit cheap when he's through this year. Maybe I'll have to give him a share in it, but I'll be running it." Bisbee let his voice tail off.

" You don't think Huguenine's will break down ? "

" It may."

" What'll you do if it does ? "

" That's the trouble. If it gets attached by a sheriff some-where I may be out of luck. I can't buy in all the wagons or the horses. That cream pad might get picked up by some fool farmer. God, think of that ! I've got to keep it alive."

Chad said slowly, " I'd kind of like that job."

" Well, keep thinking about it. It may take time. It's taken me sixteen years to get this far since I got the hankering to own a show." He laughed. " I bought into one once. We were down in Virginia and it broke down the same week. For a sack of feed. The horses had ate it. They allowed the other per-formers some money to get away, or they had some of their own, but they didn't leave me a cent. My partner had cleared out the day I bought in, so there I was."

" What did you do ? "

" Well, I had some paper left, so I started out. I papered that circus all the way to Philadelphia, getting my room and supper every night for tacking up the sheet in some particular tavern. The way I did in the Yellow Bud. That's one thing I've learned. If he's got paper enough, a circus agent can go clear across America without a single cent in his pants." His eye slid round for Chad's appreciative grin. " But I don't think I'll take a show of mine over that Pennsylvania route. Those Dutch remember like elephants."

Chad thought that the possibility of Bisbee's getting control of Huguenine's Circus was slight ; but if he ever managed it he would be a first-rate man to work for. Bisbee made good company ; he liked the sights along the road ; he saluted every woman they met, and if she proved to be a pretty girl when they got opposite the opening of her bonnet, he was in high delight. He talked a lot about circus life ; and he believed that its future lay on the road. " Out west," he said, " they're mostly permanent shows. They move, but they've got buildings in the cities. The roads are too soft to count on for heavy stock. But they're getting better all the time and when B. D. Bisbee gets his circus that's where he's going to strike for. Why, there's stretches out there where you could sell a full admission to the cows. Those county towns are first-rate places. A small handy show could fill two tents a day if it could manage the travelling. They've never seen nothing like a circus since they moved there, and now they've broke the sod they're getting circus-hungry.

A circus reaching a place like that stops it being just a backwoods settlement. When he goes out around, a man's able to say, ' Bisbee's Combined Circus, Menagerie, and Equestrian Establishment played my home town. . . .' And it sounds as if he came from somewhere."

The fervour faded from his voice.

" Well, everybody has to do a little dreaming. Right now my job's to keep Huguenine's from dying. Maybe this Cronk will do it. A.D.'s always wanted a strong-man. But I don't mind saying, I wish he was an elephant."

They reached Horseheads early in the afternoon and stopped at a sway-roofed tavern for a short drink and some cold roast pork. Then they struck east for Spencer.

" I've routed the show north," Bisbee said. " From that town, they'll head back to Catherine's and then across to Ithaca and then come down through Slaterville, and Richford to Owego. I've tacked my paper all the way to Homer, so I've got nothing on my mind."

Late in the evening the brown horse rolled them over high ridges down to Spencer, where they spent the night, and they started again next morning about six o'clock, pulling out of town through the Cattatonk Valley with the steep hills swathed in mist. The horse was fresh and the air was cool and the sun was a golden haze.

Bisbee drove with an intent eye, as though he were already nosing the trail of his strong-man.

" It's nine and a half miles to Candor," he said as they walked the horse up a short stiff grade. " I've got no idea where he is. I'll have to ask in the settlements." He pulled out his notebook. " Candor Village is the first place we come to. I'll begin there. It's a post office, too."

Candor Village, near the border of Candor township, was a small place with a single store that had a few open pigeon-holes in a dark corner at the back. In one of these was a letter, so it was easy to see it was the post office. In front of the pigeon-holes, seated on a keg of salt fish, was the postmaster.

8

THE LEGEND OF CRONK

THE only customer in the store was a middle-aged woman who seemed to be divided between a case of needles, a new pickle firkin, and a pair of spectacles.

Bisbee doffed his hat to her and stood respectfully to one side so that she could complete her choice. She appeared flustered by his courtesy. " Oh dear, Mr. Gaffin," she said to the storekeeper " making up my mind's so hard. I need those needles, but if I get them, I won't be able to use them, the way sewing makes my head ache. And if I get the spectacles, I'll see good but I haven't got but one blunt needle in the house. And the hens have just about quit laying, too, and I ought to have that firkin against pickling time. You won't have more firkins later ? "

" I might and I might not," said Mr. Gaffin, eyeing Bisbee with a good deal of suspicion.

The woman tried the spectacles on and giggled.

" I bet they make me look *awful*."

" I assure you they do not," Bisbee said gallantly.

" And I do see so much better," she said, colouring slightly. " How much are they, Mr. Gaffin ? "

" I said they was three dollars. That's the price. And that's going to stay the price. They're Almy and Wilcox glasses, they just come in, they ain't marred nor bent. And they're good for persons from 5 to 105. It says so. What do you want, mister ? "

" Let the lady make her choice," said Bisbee.

" She'll be all day at it, most likely."

" Oh, Mr. Gaffin ! Such a thing to say. But don't let me delay the gentleman."

Bisbee bowed to her. " I'm looking for a man named Cronk. I understand he lives in Candor."

" There's lots of Cronks in Candor," said the storekeeper. " What's his front name ? "

" Clinton. Clinton Cronk."

" What's he look like ? "

" I've never seen him myself. But I hear he's about seven foot tall. A powerful man."

The woman said, " He certainly sounds like a Cronk. They grow mostly to body."

" Yes," Mr. Gaffin agreed. " But I don't know any Clinton Cronk. How old a man ? "

" I don't know. I should guess around the middle thirties."

" That wouldn't be old Thomas Jefferson's boy ? " The woman seemed anxious to be helpful.

" Tom Cronk didn't have no boys," said Mr. Gaffin. " He has one girl. She was a big heifer, though, weighed close to two hundred when she was sixteen. Burt Atherton married her. He said he might as well stanchel her before she got too big to handle. She was tee-total and she used to come chasing down here after Burt. Pick him right out of his chair and throw him on the floor. They had one baby born dead and Burt always laid it against her being so tee-total."

Chad said,

" We're looking for a man."

" I know you are," Mr. Gaffin said irritably. " I'm just trying to recollect the Cronks we have around here. Daniel Cronk was a cousin of Thomas's. He bred a lot better. He had a couple of boys but they was just middling size, for Cronks. About two hundred pounds."

" This Clinton Cronk's supposed to be over three hundred."

" Yeah. A real Cronk. Let me see. Didn't Roxy Ann Wolsey marry one of them Cronks ? "

The woman tossed her head.

" She had to, poor girl. That was Snyder Cronk. He was built rakish-like." She hesitated. " I mean all teeth and handle. He wasn't so strong. They moved, and the last I heard they was settled in Ketchumville."

" He had asthma," Mr. Gaffin amplified. " Come August, and he'd set here whistling and roaring like a steamboat, so weak he couldn't lift three hundred of flour into his wagon. Had to heave her on to the hub and take a fresh holt every time. Snyder ain't the man you're after, mister."

Bisbee said patiently, " This Clinton Cronk's been working on the railroad."

" Doing what ? "

" I don't know. Laying tracks."

" Oh, you mean the Erie Railroad." Mr. Gaffin was scornful. " Likely that won't never get built at all. I thought you meant the Ithaca and Owego. Got a station on it right in this village. You can see the cars go through pretty near every day unless it's icy, or snowing, or raining real hard, or something."

The woman said, " All the men is crazy about railroads. Why can't the state build us a canal ? "

" Where'd they get the water from ? " Mr. Gaffin said acidly.

Bisbee coughed diplomatically.

" Speaking of Cronk," he said.

Mr. Gaffin scratched his head. " Well, sir, this is how I see it. You might try West Candor, that's west of here on the other road. If that don't do nothing, there's South Candor and East Candor, and lastly there's Willseyville, north up the railroad. The only other place is Weltonville on Doolittle Crick. But it ain't even got a post office."

" Let's try West Candor first," Bisbee said. His enthusiasm had gained considerable force. " That engineer wasn't lying. These Cronks appear to be quite a bunch and Clinton ought to be a giant just the way he said."

Chad thought it certainly seemed so. And in West Candor it looked as if they had struck a trail of sorts. There was one Cronk man in residence and he was down at the sawmill. When they entered, he was feeding 28-inch, 12-foot hemlock log to the saw by himself and he wasn't even using a peavy as far as Chad could see. He was only about six feet tall, but he was built out like a canal boat and he had a good-humoured stubbly face and a coating of blond hair. He said his name was Jason Cronk.

" Clinton Cronk ? Well, sir, he might be one of old Uncle Waxworth's whelping. He was a tearer. Him and my Pa inherited our house and being twins neither one would move out for the other. I remember they got argufactious about a cow and both took holt of her, and Uncle Waxworth pulled the tail right off her and she took on so the horns broke off in Pa's hands and she left the country." He guffawed. " Them two was always fighting. It made things hard on the womenfolks after they married, the way they was always throwing tables and beds at each other. Pa would get mad and throw his bed at Waxworth and it didn't matter who was in it, either. Ma stood it just about so long and finally she set fire to the house one night after them two weasels had been at it for three or four hours. She took us children outside and Waxworth's woman took hers out and the two of them lit her off." He started laughing again. "They thought them two men had had enough, but it seems they must have been in the cellar or somewhere, dead or unconscious, because they never showed up. Waxworth's woman blamed it on Ma and she moved over to East Candor. She had a baby born about seven months after and 'pears to me his name was Clinton. But I don't know for sure."

Bisbee quivered like a dog catching a rabbit scent.

"Would he be blond like you?"

"Naw. All them Waxworth Cronks was black as skunk pups."

"Well, I'm obliged to you."

"Sure," said Jason Cronk. "That's all right."

He turned the log with a heave of his hands and shot her at the saw.

Outside, Bisbee brushed the horse up and they spun back to Candor Village, passing through in a whirl of dust and taking a small rutty road straight across country.

"I figure we've picked up his tracks, now He's better than I figured. If he's real black I'll make him a Malay executioner maybe. He'll look savage all right. I hope he don't shave."

Chad himself was catching the excitement. He couldn't help it, being with Bisbee.

In East Candor they had a bite of dinner and got word of Clinto Cronk's youth. He existed all right. They heard how at the age of fourteen he had pulled the bell out of the church steeple while ringing it. It had almost hit him on the head. It would have killed him if he hadn't caught it, their informant said, though those Cronks were a tough family. He had been 'prenticed to the blacksmith when he was sixteen, but the blacksmith had had to get rid of him because he kept tearing the shoes off the horses with his fingers. "He wouldn't work them off easy-like with the pinchers." But he had moved away to Weltonville about fourteen years ago.

It was three o'clock in the afternoon when they got to Weltonville and, though Clinton Cronk wasn't living there now, the memory of him was still fresh.

Yes, he was seven foot tall, perhaps better than that. But he couldn't ever seem to do good work. If he was sawing a board he was always wearing the teeth off the saw. If he was chopping wood, he broke the axe helve the first lick. He had gone down to Owego for a ploughing match and won the thing before the other contestants were three-quarters through. But he didn't get the prize because one of the judges noticed that the traces were slack all the time, the horses being just able to keep ahead of the eveners ; Clint, they said, was shoving the plough himself.

"He moved up on a farm thirteen years ago," the innkeeper told Bisbee. "He married. A little, thin, puny-looking girl from Weltonville named Nance Clagget." An only child and she had inherited a small farm, he had heard. He had gone to the wedding and she came only up to Clinton's wishbone. "It's funny," the innkeeper went on. "All those Cronk boys married little active girls, and I've heard the Cronk women generally wed smallish men. Kind of unnatural till you consider it from the brainy angle." He gave them road directions.

Bisbee was practically seething with suppressed enthusiasm, but the pace they had been travelling all day had slowed the horse down.

The late afternoon sun was shining full in their faces as the weary beast hauled them over the brow of the ridge, and the narrow track led straight across the upland. It didn't look like much of a place for a farm. There were a few weedy sheep and some dinky cows. But at sight of them, Bisbee grabbed Chad's arm. "Look at their teats, will you ? " The teats hung long and thin as if they had been shaped by an inexorable hand.

Bisbee said solemnly, "We're going to make history here, Chad."

A rickety contrivance of a house sided the road and a queer-looking thick-legged boy skittered out of the back door towards a slat-walled barn as if the appearance of a carriage had terrified him. Then, as they walked up to the porch, a woman began clamouring. It was a sharp, annoyed, hectoring voice, and it said, "You going to be able to get up for supper or do I have to lug you in your food again ? "

Chad whispered, "He must be sick."

Bisbee said nothing, but his hand was shaking as he knocked on the door.

" Who's there ? What you want ? I got no money and I don't want to buy nothing. Peddlers ain't welcome here."

Rapid steps came from the back bedroom. A small, thin, quick-moving little woman jerked round the door at them. She had on a faded dress. Her feet were bare.

Bisbee took off his hat.

" Are you Mrs. Cronk, ma'am ? "

" I am," she said belligerently. " What of it ? "

" I came to see your husband. I represent Huguenine's Great and Only International Circus. We need a strong-man and we're prepared to do business with him."

" Is that so ? Well, that nail-brained buck rabbit couldn't do business with a tin woodchuck. You better talk to me. What'll you pay ? "

" Ma'am, I've got to be assured Mr. Cronk is as large as they say."

" He's large. That's about all he is though, the big misery."

" May I be allowed to see Mr. Cronk ? "

She gave a scornful laugh.

" Go ahead. Look him over. He's in bed."

She looked as if she hated the hair of every man that ever lived. Bisbee tried to pacify her.

He said apologetically, " You understand, I have to be sure he's as gigantic as they tell me. I know he's strong."

" Strong ! " She fairly screeched with laughter. " That article ain't got the strength of a half-growed girl." She caught Bisbee's sleeve and shook it. " Listen to me, mister. All the time he comes home saying he can't work because he's too strong. He spoils the saw, he breaks the axe, the horses don't pull the plough fast enough so he can't win the prize. But does he work here ? Does he make any money ? Does he pull a pigweed out of the squash, even ? " She laughed again, savagely. " He goes down to work on the railroad. ' Railroad cars are more my size,' he says. But back he comes on Monday saying they won't let him work because he spills the rails. ' All right,' I says, ' if they won't hire you, I can. You can begin carrying out that tub of wash water.' And what does he do ? He picks it up—that tub I been lugging out and emptying since I was thirteen years old—and suddenly he lets out a yell and drops it all over my kitchen floor and grabs his stomach. And now the doctor says he's ruptured himself ! Strong-man ! You tell *me* he's strong ! Laying in bed, moaning like a frog with a bee in his belly ! Go and look at him if you want to. Go ahead. Don't stand there. Go look at him. Go on. I tell you, look at the big mustard."

Bisbee gaped at her and suddenly, losing all patience, she shoved him with both hands, prodding his back, jolting him. There was nothing to do but walk in as she said. Chad went through the door with Bisbee, being pushed in his wake.

They found a small room almost completely filled by the biggest bed they had ever seen. Chad judged it was nine feet long. Lying flat on top of it, his feet sticking up below the covers like a monumental duck's, was an enormous man with a thick black growth of beard and miserable, shamed eyes. He must have been nearly eight feet tall. His hands, like two scoop shovels, were folded on his middle. He hardly noticed Bisbee and Chad ; he stared guiltily at his little wife.

" Chewing tobacco again ! " she cried. " Soon as my back is turned in my own bedroom. Shame on you. Shaming me before gentlemen ? You spit it out. You wait till I get the pail. You nasty lump."

She skittered out and in again, and Cronk obediently deposited the bale of barely-worked leaves into it.

He turned hound-dog eyes on Bisbee, who swallowed once or twice before he was able to say, " I'm sorry to find you like this, Mr. Cronk."

" Who'd expect to have a washtub do that to a man ? " Cronk asked in a small hoarse voice. " That comes of trying women's work. Doc says I can't move off my back for a couple of weeks. It'll be a year before I can leave home, he says. Every time I move it comes out in my middle just like a cabbage. I shove it back but it comes out again. It's the most powerful rupture doc ever seen. He said that. Nance, you got to admit he said that."

" I don't care what he said," cried the woman. " You make me sick. All you ever done round here was build that bed for you to lie in. And me too ! And look at what come of it. Where's that crazy boy of yourn? Claude, Claude, you come here ! " She was out of the room.

Bisbee said, " I'd hoped to make you a proposition, Mr. Cronk. But under the circumstances, I can't."

" I heard you telling Nance. I guess you're right, mister. I'm down licked for a while. I got to be careful now all my life, doc says."

Bisbee was backing from the room and Chad followed him. In the kitchen they encountered Mrs. Cronk, breathily pulling the thick-legged boy by one ear.

But at sight of the boy's face, Bisbee stopped short.

" Mrs. Cronk," he said, and Chad saw the familiar gleam returning to his eyes. " Maybe you and I could do some business after all. Have you considered sending your boy with the circus ? "

Chad looked round the lady's shoulder and saw the boy. His hair was nearly white, he kept his head lowered. He looked to be about thirteen but he was big for his age, built broad. He didn't look special to Chad.

" Lift up your head like a man," Mrs. Cronk said, and turned back to Bisbee. " You want Claude ? What for ? "

" His teeth," said Bisbee. " Chad, look at his teeth."

" Them ? " asked Mrs. Cronk, wonderingly. " I always thought they marred him."

Chad could see the boy's face now. It was pathetically dull. His eyes were whitish, like his hair, and ran a little from the red lid corners. But the wonder was there, all right ; from the upper jaw two unbelievably long teeth extended over his lower lip.

" Those teeth may make his fortune, and yours too, Mrs. Cronk, if you let me take him with me."

She looked muddled and confused. " You mean to say a Cronk man can make me some cash money ? "

" Seven dollars a week, clear and net," said Bisbee. " If you'll just sign your name to a paper in front of a lawyer."

" Seven dollars ! " She shook her head " Mister ! If you just take him off my hands a while, you could have him for fifty cents. The trouble he makes me. But I'll settle for seven dollars," she caught herself quickly.

" I'll be up to-morrow and drive you to the nearest lawyer."

" There's one in Weltonville. I'll fetch Claude down to-morrow morning," she said. " Do I get any money to start with ? "

" A week's advance ? " said Bisbee. " And the rest at the end of the season ? "

" You'll fetch him back ? I got kind of used to him."

" Yes."

" We'll be there to-morrow," she said.

Bisbee made his departure with a flourish.

On the way down the hill he said, " Claude's not what I came for. But think of him in the cage wagon ! "

He turned words on his tongue for a few minutes, then broke out :—

" THE WORLD'S LIVING WONDER. UNPARAL-
LELED. THE ONLY DOG-TOOTHED BOY IN CAP-
TIVITY. HE EATS RAW MEAT."

Chad wasn't so sure. The sight of Claude, for all his peculiar-
ity, or because of it, made him uneasy. But he didn't want to
spoil Bisbee's fun, so he said nothing.

Bisbee spent a long evening working over an idea for a new
poster that would include the dog-toothed boy. Watching his
absorbed, horse-like face, Chad wondered what Bisbee ever
did with his private life. He might have a wife ; for all any one
knew, he might have a dozen. More likely he had none. But if
he did have one, Chad thought, she probably knew no more
about B. D. Bisbee than he did. Bisbee was as independent as a
dog carrying a bone across country.

About nine o'clock, though, he looked up from his paper and
smiled at Chad. " I'll call this a day's work," he said. " You've
brought me luck, Chaddy. This boy might even beat Oscar as
an attraction. There's something about a genuine freak makes
plain people feel lucky." He started rolling his notes into his
poster case. " You plan to pull out to-morrow ? "

" I guess so."

Bisbee nodded. " I was going to offer you a ride back to
Elmira. But if you're going after Burke, you'll want to cut
north to Ithaca. You can take the steamboat there." He shook
hands. " Good luck, boy, and don't forget what I told you,
yesterday."

Chad said he wouldn't. He could see that Bisbee wanted the
triumph of his return with Claude Cronk undiluted. It would
be a shock to Huguenine, who had made up his mind to hiring
a giant. But that was Bisbee's look-out.

Chad himself had no desire to return to Huguenine's ; even

supposing Huguenine had cooled off so soon, he didn't want the job back unless Huguenine was ready to beg. Once he had got work with Burke and Walsh, Huguenine would realise what a fool he was. It would be pleasant writing Caroline what life was like in a real circus.

The only bed had a peddler in it, so Chad relinquished his third of it to Bisbee and bedded himself in the stable mow. The hired girl lit him out to it with a lantern ; she seemed willing to stay if he passed the right word, but Chad patted her on the head as he started up the ladder, and told her to be a good girl.

9

FAST TRAVEL

CHAD didn't see Bisbee in the morning. No one was down except the hired girl, who gave him his breakfast and informed him in a lugubrious voice that it was queer but she hadn't hardly slept a wink all night. Chad said it was, and stepped out of the kitchen door into the early mist.

The creek bottom was still in a half-dark, but the mist was roofed by light streaming across the uplands from the rising sun, and when Chad had climbed through it, it was like stepping into a clear new world with blackbirds singing and the dew beading on the mullein leaves.

He pushed along rapidly, for he wanted to reach the Ithaca road at Candor while there was still a good chance of picking up a lift. During the night he had figured that he might be able to catch Burke and Walsh while the circus was still playing Amsterdam. According to Bisbee's notes it was scheduled for the fourth and fifth ; and if he caught it there, he would save himself the trip overland to Ballston Spa. To-day was the second of August. That gave him three full days and two nights, and it was just possible, with luck, to cover the distance, though he couldn't afford to buy passage on a packet boat.

He made good time across the upland and came out on the Cattatonk Valley half a mile south of Candor about seven o'clock. The ruts he was following dropped steeply through the woods and headed northerly towards the village. He was going along the bottom land when he heard a horn blow behind him on his left. It blew three or four toots in rapid succession as though the man on the business end were feeling mean. It sounded like a canal horn, but there wasn't any canal in the valley. It puzzled Chad until, beyond a sharp bend, the road pitched up about two feet sharply and he came out on the railroad track.

He hadn't thought of the railroad, but if a brigade of cars were going towards Ithaca, he didn't see why it wouldn't be a good idea to take them if the tariff wasn't too high. There was no doubt about the cars coming. He could hear the metallic rumbling of the wheels on the iron rail strips edging the wooden stringers. He couldn't see anything, because the road-bed itself curved off into the woods, but the train was getting pretty close. The horn whooped again, a long blast, and he judged that must be to warn a wagon that might be coming along the road. He stepped nervously to one side ; he had never seen a train in operation and he didn't know how fast this one might be driving. He hadn't much idea of how you stopped a train, either, but he thought of his red bundle. If he put that on a stick and waved it, probably the driver would see it.

He found a stick in the brush and had just stuck it under the bundle ends when the horses came into sight round the curve. They were drawing a single car at a full trot and the driver was using his whip freely. Chad swung the bundle. The man reached behind him for his horn and blew it again. Chad swung the bundle out over the tracks once more and the off horse, which had a white eye, snorted and shook his head.

" Put down that God-damned bundle," roared the driver.

Chad yelled back, " I want a ride on the cars."

" Go to the station ! You got to get a ticket at the station."

Chad said, " How can I if the cars have already gone by ? "

By this time the off horse was throwing out his front feet and doing some fancy plunging. The driver had to pull him down to keep him from throwing himself off the track entirely. He started swearing and sawing at the reins. The horn dropped out of his hands, bounced over the footboard, and rolled to Chad's feet. Chad picked it up and blew it nastily as the car rolled by.

The car was built like a squarish heavy coach and there was only one passenger inside, an old man with a frozen look of

" I don't know. Ever see anything of Cisco Trid ? "

" My," said Elias, chuckling. " That man was mad. The nigger got away. I figure that was your doing." He waited for Chad's nod. " But he was madder because his girl had run off, too."

" She joined out with the circus," Chad said.

" Did she ? What become of her ? "

" I married her."

Elias squawked. " You married ! "

" Yes."

" No."

In the silence, Diney drifted through the bar-room door and handed Elias his drink. She didn't pay attention to Chad till he reached up and pinched her. It made her buck up standing.

" For mercy's sake ! " she squalled.

Her eyes rolled.

" Hallo, Diney. How are you ? "

" I was all right. You come back here to stay ? "

" No," Chad said.

Diney turned and bolted through the door. " Oh, Mis' Mott," they heard her calling. " That Chad Hanna's back home, but he ain't stayin'."

Elias said, " Now you'll have them all out. What did you marry her for ? "

" I don't know. It happened that way," Chad said. " She's begun riding. She's pretty good. She's pad-riding."

" Does she get paid ? "

" She's getting five dollars a week."

Elias was impressed.

" That's durn near as good as a pension. The way I've always looked at marriage it's all right except you've got to live with a woman. But if you've got one that can make money it's worth putting up with. I wish I could recollect what she looked like."

" She looks all right," Chad said.

" Pretty ? "

" Kind of."

Elias said solemnly, " Seems to me you're taking an awful chance, coming away. A pretty girl that can make money's liable to get snapped off by any man. *I* wouldn't have let one go by before I had my pension."

"I bet you wouldn't." Chad grinned. "Mrs. Huguenine's looking out for her."

"Well, maybe that's all right. Just the same I don't see what you're running off for. Just to get work."

"I kind of like the business," Chad said. "I don't want anybody telling me I'm no good at it."

"Well," said Elias, "it's wonderful. I never figured on you being married, especially to a sensible girl that can make money. I thought you was too easy-going for that. When you went off I figured you was chasing that black-haired, heiferish Lillian woman."

He tailed off as they heard Mrs. Mott come downstairs, and Chad was glad to let the talk drop entirely. Mrs Mott came out and stared at him without much favour and asked how he was and went back. Later Chad saw Mott in the bar-room, but Mott was non-committal.

It seemed to Chad that the flavour of the Yellow Bud had somehow changed. Business was all right, but the place looked smaller. The fusty smell of the front stairs seemed to have got all the way to the bar. Maybe it was just Elias ageing faster that made it, or maybe Chad himself had changed. He certainly felt different from the morning when he had walked past the porch to go riding with Albany Yates. He had a whole world in his pants pocket that morning.

It was something of a struggle for Elias to get moving, but once he had motion up he could creak along pretty well, and he walked down to the landing with Chad about noon where there was a Traders' Line boat ready to haul east. His neck looked more like a turkey's than ever ; talking brought out strings in it ; and he had to move his lips once or twice before he could talk.

"I'm getting old, Chad," he confessed. "I hate to see you go. I always kind of valued you. But I'm glad you're married I wouldn't leave her too long, either." He shook hands. "Chad," he whispered as the driver hooked the rope to the eveners, "she ain't got a secret for you yet, has she ? " Some of the old goatish gleam came back to his eye.

Chad grinned

"She's got long legs," he said. "She ain't like Fanny."

But it made him uneasy, and he was glad when the team picked up the slack and the boat got going. He stood on the cabin deck, raising his hand to Elias. Somehow, in the midst of all that active basin dock, the old man looked so forlorn that Chad almost wished he hadn't stopped at all.

Such a business hadn't entered his head, either. It would take old Elias to think of that question. He wondered if Caroline was the kind of girl that hid things like that. She wasn't exactly like Fanny Preston Lovell. As he had said, she had long legs.

" Get down, you God-damned fool," roared the captain.

Chad threw himself on the deck.

The shadow went over him and he looked up comically at the captain's blazing eyes and white face.

" Haven't you ever rode on a canal boat ? " demanded the captain. " Didn't you hear me yell low bridge ? Or was you aiming to knock it down with your head ? "

Chad sat up cross-legged and laughed at him.

" I didn't want to miss the view," he said.

Just the same, he figured he would keep on going to Amsterdam.

II

BUCK

THE line boat was hauling through to Albany, so it made good time. Chad was put ashore at Port Jackson a little after three o'clock, two days after leaving Canastota. In three days he had covered over two hundred and thirty miles, travelling by railroad, steamboat, and canal. Even with the time he had taken visiting at the Yellow Bud he had arrived in time to catch Burke and Walsh in Amsterdam.

As the line boat slid towards the village, he picked out the giant round-top on the far side of the Mohawk, its white peak reflected in the glassy water. Now, crossing the river, he could hear the thumping music of the band. Rigs, carriages, and people on foot met him as he turned up the road. The main performance was over and the concert in progress. From the numbers passing him, Chad judged that Burke and Walsh had played this afternoon to probably as many admissions as Huguenine's had drawn in the last six days. He was impressed, and he lost some of the confidence he had felt about getting a job.

The lot was still full of clamour. The luck boys were making their final appeals to the common sense of the citizenry of Amsterdam. Chad's one glimpse of the show had not prepared him for their numbers : weight-guessers, thimble artists, soap salesmen, who stuck one or five-dollar bills inside the wrappings of cakes of scented soap, dropped them into a bag hung from their necks, and offered the customer his choice of any cake in the bag for ten cents. Close to Chad a man in a frock-coat stood on a box and bawled through cupped hands that the gentlemanly management had requested him to warn the populace that pickpockets had been reported on the lot and every man who couldn't afford to lose his money had better keep his hand on his wallet. That was an old one : Chad grinned at the fellow and held up a ten-cent piece and put it back in his side pocket.

As he rounded the big tent, he was jostled by people coming out of the freaks' pavilion, and, feeling for his handkerchief, found that the ten-cent piece was gone. The fakers were thorough on Burke's lot. It gave him a new idea of the show. Huguenine, for all his stupidity, would have chased a pickpocket ; but then in Huguenine's crowds there was less chance for a pickpocket to work.

He stood a while beside the great bow of the big tent, watching the activity. Inside the tent the band was playing the chorus :—

> W'eel about and turn about,
> And do jis so ;
> Eb'ry time I w'eel about,
> I jump Jim Crow.

Some of the performers were moving in and out of the line of parked wagons packing their paraphernalia. The ring stock was lined up at the far fence. The horses were good, several of them greys and whites, and one light chestnut that looked above average. Their bulk obscured Buck ; but suddenly Chad saw his head lift as he reared against the halter rope. His ears were back and he struck with his front feet and a man yelled.

There was a cry of " Send for Mr. Burke ! " and then a roustabout came forward from the line of horses, holding his wrist with one hand while blood dripped through the tight fingers. He stopped a couple of men carrying foot stands and seat stringers. Apparently part of the main tent was dismantled while the concert was in progress. The concert wouldn't draw a full crowd.

Chad turned his face right and left looking for Burke or Albany Yates. He wanted to find Burke before Walsh saw or recognised him. He knew he wouldn't stand a chance of joining out if Walsh laid eyes on him first. But Burke, he thought, was an impersonal kind of man. If he considered that Chad was any good at all, he would hire him, no matter what. And that noon in Auburn he had been willing to praise Chad.

Inside the tent the black-face tenor was singing two-thirds of the way through " Jim Crow " :—

> O den I go to Washington,
> Wid bank memorial ;
> But find dey tork such nonsense,
> I spen' my time wid Sal.
> W'eel about, and turn about . . .

Some of the audience were taking up the chorus with laughter by this time, and the tenor lifted high and nasal through their handclaps :—

> I tell dem dere be Old Nick,
> W'at want de bank renew ;
> He gib me so much money,
> O lor', dey want it too.

The audience liked that. They yelled at " Ole Nick," and they could hardly quiet themselves for the familiar verse to come :—

> I den go to de Presiden',
> He ax me w'at I do :
> I put de veto on de boot,
> And nullefy de shoe. . . .

The roustabout with the cut wrist reappeared round the tent wall with Mr. Burke striding quickly along beside him. Burke was mouthing a cold cigar ; and his blue eyes were icy. The top of his hat did not reach above the roustabout's ears, but it was obvious that he was giving the man a raking over and the big fellow was feeling meek about it.

"If you can't handle horses you've got no business on the horse-line," he said.

"I can handle them all right. I got along all right with this bugger till that accident in Albany, didn't I?" He opened his good hand and looked at the gash in his wrist. "I wasn't even looking at him," he said. "He reached out for me and he knicked me with a calk. He's turned ugly, that's what he has. Why, Ainsworth had a terrible time just to get him into the tent."

"You let Ainsworth handle his end and you handle yours," Mr. Burke said shortly. "If you give him a trimming you'll just make him uglier. Any uncut horse is liable to have bad spells. This one's too valuable to risk turning savage for good."

Chad picked up his bundle to follow in their wake. Buck's turning ugly seemed queer to him. He couldn't figure it out. The horse had always required some handling, but he had never shown a mean streak with Huguenine's.

Burke and the roustabout wove their way through the crowd and turned up the end of the horse-line. A couple more handlers were standing near the far end of the line, looking Buck over, and the horse was standing perfectly still, looking back. His ears were neither up nor down, but poised, Chad saw, like every square inch of him, and ready for what was coming. Burke took his stand just out of reach and lit his cigar.

Moving up close behind Burke, Chad had a good look at the horse. His hide showed marks of spurring; Chad couldn't think what had got into Albany. She had always used the spur lightly. Then he realised that he was looking at the off-side of the animal, and he realised that a man had been riding Buck. Albany always rode side-saddle.

The roustabout also was pointing it out to Burke. "See where Ainsworth's worked on him? That don't do him no good, Mr. Burke."

Burke said coldly, "That's the way Ainsworth rides. He fights the horse. It makes the audience take notice. It's exciting. The way Ainsworth rides isn't your business, George. Bring him off the line and see what he'll do now."

"I won't touch him now," George said sullenly. "Not unless you'll let me give him a clubbing."

"If you can't handle him, I'll get someone who can. Come on, you two."

One of the two handlers made a half-hearted move, but

Buck's lip lifted and his head went up. The handler changed his mind abruptly. "He ain't my horse," he said. "He ain't used to me like he is to George."

George gripped his wrist and cursed.

Mr. Burke said, "The tear-down will be over in an hour. If you haven't got him in hand by then, you can come and get your money."

"Yes," said George. "I will. And then what will you do, Mr. Burke?"

Burke paid no attention. He turned sharply on his heel and saw Chad. His eyes didn't change a particle. "Hallo," he said. He was obviously working on Chad's face. "I remember you," he said. "You were with Huguenine's whistle show. What do you want?"

He was neither hostile nor friendly.

Chad said, "I want a job."

"Huguenine's broke down, did it?"

"No, I got fired."

"What for?"

"I quit. I'd been equestrian director, and then he put me back in my old job. When I quit, he fired me."

Burke puffed smoke.

"I got one already."

The horse-handlers guffawed.

Chad didn't bother with them. "I want work," he said. "I didn't figure to be equestrian director with you."

Burke said, "Do you think you can handle that horse?"

"Maybe. If I can have him alone for an hour."

"Go ahead." A covered smile came into Burke's china-blue eyes. "If you can bring him round gentle, I'll hire you at regular pay."

He walked off. George looked sourly at Chad. Luckily neither he nor the other two had been in the shindig at the bridge.

Chad glanced round for a spot to drop his bundle and one of the handlers told him to put it in the feed wagon. That showed the importance of Burke and Walsh, hauling their own feed wagon. It stood at the end of the line, so Chad tossed the bundle inside.

"I ain't after anybody's job," he told George.

"Did you handle that horse with Huguenine's?"

" Yep."

" Well, if you can handle him now and I don't get fired it's all right," George said. " I don't want anything to do with that animal now. As long as that girl rode him he was easy enough. Since Ainsworth took him over, it's been just about my life's worth to breathe in the same county with him." He slammed his hat on the ground. " Oh, it's all right for the scene rider to rough him. But me, can I protect myself ? No, the horse is too valuable. He costs money. Handlers come cheap."

Chad said, " Why ain't Lady Lillian riding ? "

" Got throwed and broke her arm the last stand in Albany," George said. " I don't know where she is. She wanted to ride with her arm strapped. She claimed she could do it. But Burke wouldn't hear of it. He didn't want damaged goods in his show. She never went so well, either. I got to admit, people like to see Ainsworth ride. He's a regular cut and ripper and has the horse on his hind end every other second."

" Where does Lady Lillian ride in the wagons ? "

" I said I don't know where she is. Burke said he had hired the act, and if she couldn't ride he'd take the horse and put someone else on him."

" He ain't sorry," one of the handlers said. " I think him and Walsh been working on her anyway. They had the clown in her act, and he was always scaring the horse."

George said, " You better stop that talk, Benny."

Benny said, " Well, God damn. Burke wasn't sorry."

Chad made no comment. He had got the idea in Rochester that Albany wasn't up to a big show. Now he was beginning to see that Burke might have been trying to kill the act from the start. He had wanted the horse, not the girl. Chad remembered how he had thought that Burke would be a good man to run a show ; Burke would know what he wanted to do and he would do it. Horse-handlers had a way of talking something up till it swelled like a balloon, but Chad thought there was probably something in this talk. He wanted to see what it was. If Burke was trying to cheat Albany something would have to be done, and as far as he could see, in a show run like this one, he was the only man who would do anything.

He remembered her old confidence in herself. It made him mad to think of her being licked unfairly, if it was unfair. He took another look at Buck. Buck was the first part of the job.

Buck's mishandling alone would have been enough to make him join out.

He said, " You fellers go back to your crochet and let me work on this animal by myself."

He waited till they had moved off, George to get a bandage for his hand and the other two to start hustling out the seat boards. From the big tent the band was playing the comic duet of " What a Beauty I Did Grow." Being a white-face act for the two clowns, that probably marked the end of the concert. The round-top would be coming down any minute now. The familiar preludes to the road travel to the next town might help to distract Buck. During that time Chad had to get the horse to remember him if he could.

The first thing he did was to pick out the chestnut horse, and using him as shield put him into the line on one side of Buck. Then he got a grey that resembled Jerry slightly and tied him on the outside. All the time, he came near, he talked to Buck in an off-hand voice, telling him to move over, to pick up his feet, pull in his ears, go blow his nose in a bucket of beans, anything at all so that the horse could listen to his voice. Buck could smell Chad close on the other side of the chestnut but he couldn't reach him, and Chad knew he wouldn't make a try unless he was dead sure. He was too smart for that. Chad's idea was that if Buck were standing quiet and listening to his voice, he would begin to get used to it, even if he didn't remember. And after about ten minutes, Chad decided he was making some progress. Buck's ears had started playing. They pricked when Chad moved off down the line ; the horse had begun to take an interest in what he was doing. But the ears slanted back whenever he came close, and he knew enough not to make a real move yet.

But with each little degree of progress he felt he was making, Chad's anger against the fool who was willing to spoil a good horse increased. Buck used to rear at the lightest touch of a spur when Albany was riding him, and this show-off had been regularly raking him. Burke and the crowds might like it, Chad didn't ; and if he was going to handle the horse, he would make good and sure that it was stopped.

He spotted a small freckled boy on a nearby fence who was watching him with open-mouthed concentration, and it gave him an idea.

"Hey, freckles," he said.

The boy half slid off the fence.

"You talking to me, mister?"

"Who else is freckled round here?" Chad grinned.

The boy turned grey. He stammered, and then with a rush of blood to his face said, "You are, mister. Kind of, that is."

Chad laughed out loud.

"That's right. You thought I was talking to myself, didn't you? I ain't. I'm trying to tame down a misused horse."

"Yes, I seen that, mister. I was watching. He's taming down all the time."

"Don't you want to look at the elephant?" asked Chad.

"Naw. Little runts like elephants. I like horses."

"Well, you could help me, if you wanted to."

"Could I? What is it?" The boy was off the fence, tumbling over himself in his eagerness like a bag of potatoes.

"Know a place where you could steal maybe ten or a dozen carrots?"

"Yes, sir. I'll have 'em here quick."

He was gone through the burdocks like a rabbit. Chad went on talking, fussing up and down the line of horses. After about ten minutes the boy came back breathless with a bunch of fair-sized carrots. "I didn't wash them," he said.

"That's all right. Give them to me."

"Ain't you going to give him one?"

"Not yet."

Chad walked in front of Buck, letting him see the carrots and smell them, but keeping out of reach. He started feeding about three horses off down the line and came back, taking plenty of time over each one, so that the horse reached for it, whickered, or took on somehow.

At first Buck didn't let on. But after a minute he took a step forward, easing the strain on the halter rope for the first time. Then he took another step so that he was leaning his chest against the hurdle. His ears went back as Chad moved up to the chestnut, but they pricked up again as the chestnut took the carrot with a sensual prehensile grab of his lips and solemnly muched it down.

Chad stood where he was, seemingly careless, but watching Buck's eyes. "Don't move at all," he said to the boy in the same tone of voice he had used to the horses.

" No, I won't."

" And don't talk, sonny," he said, seeing Buck's ears slide back. He fed the chestnut another carrot and walked in front of Buck. Buck's head followed the carrots. He was interested all right. Chad fed a couple to the grey and Buck sidled over until he was touching shoulders. He looked at Chad and then angled his neck and head and caught a piece of the top. Chad held out a carrot. He had judged the distance and was safe, so he deliberately looked away from the horse. He felt the distrustful blow from the horse's nostrils on his hand and from the tail of his eye saw Buck reach out twice, watching his head all the time. The third time he angled his neck and took the carrot.

Chad looked round and saw Burke watching him from down the line. Burke nodded, and Chad made up his mind. He walked past Buck's head, close enough to give the horse a chance if he wanted it, but Buck was too interested in his carrot.

Chad said, " Look here, Mr. Burke. I'll get that horse into shape. But if I work on him, whoever's riding him has got to quit using spurs like that. I heard what you told George. Well, it don't matter to me."

" I'll speak to the Equestrian Director," Burke said.

" He better do something about it. If he don't, I will, myself."

Burke looked at him steadily.

" I said I'd speak to him," he said coldly.

" Another thing," Chad said. " I'm taking him over the road myself this evening. I'm going to wait until the show starts, and I'll ride that grey and take Buck and the chestnut on a double lead." He saw Burke stiffen up. " That's the way I took him with Huguenine's," he explained. " He's got to get used to me again."

Burke said, " All right. You can wait. I'm starting after the show myself and you can trail my rig."

" Then you better tell George," Chad said.

As he came back down the line he saw both Buck and the freckled boy watching for him. The boy said, " Gee, is that the boss ? "

Chad nodded.

" You surely back-talked to him," the boy said admiringly. " Could you get me a job with the circus, mister ? "

" No. I'll tell you why. I've only just joined out here myself. You wait till next year."

The boy looked sad, but luckily the elephant came swinging along behind the line. In spite of what he had said about little runts, the boy's feet got restless and a moment later he was pelting along the road after the beast.

Chad went up to Buck and fed him a carrot, reached out while he was munching it, and caught his halter. The horse didn't even jerk his head.

"You monkey-shining fool," Chad said.

He felt happy.

The horse felt it too, for he dropped his head and let Chad rub between his ears in the old way.

12

BIG SHOW

BURKE and Walsh's tear-down was worth watching. Three months ago Chad wouldn't have appreciated half of what was going on. To the untrained eye it was all hopeless confusion : the fakers picking up their belongings and skedaddling, all in a hurry to find the best pitches on the next lot ; the roustabouts lugging out the last of the seats, stringers, and jacks on the heels of the concert audience while others were already loosening the stays and tent pegs. From the performers' entrance the concert artistes emerged in a group ; the musicians packing their instruments into a wagon and hurrying back to lend a hand with the canvas, which was already quivering at the peak. The two clowns, costumed as soldier and hayseed, with sword and ox whip, strode straight through the lot, and in their wake the high soprano picked her way in a flowered satin dress, lilac velvet pelisse, and rose-coloured gloves. They acted like lords and lady, expecting lesser folks to step aside.

The shouted orders blended into a seemingly senseless hubbub, and the seat wagons, now loaded, sliced through the middle of it. The horse-handlers returned to the line and cut out the ring stock, leaving the three at the end for Chad. "Burke says you're bringing them. You can have them," George said. They herded the horses back of the feed wagon and pulled out behind the seat wagons, crowding on to the road like cattle and raising a cloud of dust, in the mist of which, to more shouting, the canvas came ballooning down. When the dust cleared, Chad saw midget-looking men racing up the valleys of it to the centre pole.

It took a lot of hands to work that fast ; it took someone like Walsh to keep the men driving ; red-faced and swearing, he was everywhere ; but the man who organised the whole shebang was the one who counted, and Chad's respect for Burke went way up. Smoking a fresh cigar, Burke drove his pair into the lot and sat there watching the canvas being folded and wrestled into the tent wagons. The centre pole was marked with stripes to show where it should hang in the side brackets. Not a minute was lost that human ingenuity could contrive to save.

Chad realised that it was time for him to get moving. He had bridled the grey. Now he buckled the lead to the chest-nut's halter ring and with the other lead walked in beside Buck. The horse shivered and sprang back against the halter rope, but Chad stroked his neck and buckled on the lead.

He unhooked the other two, loosed Buck, and swung on to the grey's back. Buck plunged wide on the lead and came back spraddle-legged and dancing ; he was more scared than ugly, however. Chad worked the three horses round the outside of the lot and had them pretty well lined up when he came back to the road. There Burke and Walsh were waiting in their rig. Chad told them to go ahead. " He'll behave all right if we let him move."

Burke drove out smartly. His pair were roaders and kept an even trot. It was a bit fast for the grey and the chestnut, but all the better for Buck. They rattled through town ahead of the tent wagons. In front of the taverns, the performers were getting into their rigs. Chad looked them over as he went by without seeing hide nor hair of Albany. He wondered whether she had been worse hurt by the fall than George had said. He couldn't imagine her staying behind just for a broken arm ; Buck, he thought, meant more to her than anything else in the world ; she had found him and trained him ; she couldn't afford to lose sight of him.

Buck had settled down in the first mile, and by the time they overtook the ring stock he was going peaceably enough. Noticing it, Burke ordered Chad to keep his place. Then he let out his pair, taking the road shoulder, and whipped past the whole procession.

Moving slowly down the valley, the circus line at first stretched out for over a mile, but as the sun fell lower behind them, the line shortened. First the elephant was overtaken by the tent wagons and the ring stock. When Chad passed her, she was treading somnolently along on one side of the road with the hook swinging in one ear and her handler looking as bored, tired, and dusty as she did. Then one by one the performers' rigs overtook them and went on ahead after Burke's and those of the fakers. Looking back as they moved up on the higher ground out of Glenville, Chad saw the elephant behind the tent wagons, so that the procession had finally sorted itself into the order in which he had seen it haul into Newark more than a month ago.

It moved more slowly than Huguenine's small show had; but there was something in sitting up on a horse's back and having the small boys in the farmyards yell if the elephant was coming. After dark, however, the slow pace began to drag. Chad began to feel tired. A couple of times he barely saved himself from rolling off the grey's broad back, and he had to do some figuring before he worked out that Huguenine's, about this time, would be half-way to Catherinestown from Spencer. Then he wondered what on earth had started him on such a thought and he recalled Elias Proops's last words on the canal dock at Canastota. It made him feel like a fool to wonder whether his own wife was going to have a baby. It didn't make sense to start speculating about it at eight o'clock at night on the road between Glenville and Ballston, anyway.

They made a right-angle turn into a narrow road about half an hour later and Chad saw that the turn had been railed to show the way and a line of hay laid across the main road. They were now heading east towards Charlton. All the small roads after that were railed off. The whole route must have been taken care of. It reminded him of the consultations Huguenine's three teamsters used to hold at some of the back-road forks.

He didn't see why he kept thinking of Huguenine's all the time. He didn't owe Huguenine's anything, but he couldn't help wondering whether Claude had made any difference in their business. He guessed he was just getting sleepy.

He fairly rolled off the horse's back when the ring stock pulled into Ballston. A man with a lantern guided them into the lot. Fires were already burning on it. He placed his three horses at the end of the line and brushed them down. He was working on them when a man said behind him, "Is your name Hanna?"

To Chad's surprise, Walsh appeared to have forgotten his part in the clem at the bridge. He seemed almost good-humoured.

"You've done a good job on that animal," he said. "But I can't control Ainsworth. He's high-class and he rides his own way. You can try to persuade him if you want to." He leaned against the hurdle. "It took you quite a while to catch on to Huguenine's, didn't it? Well, you're in a real show now. Burke says you're all right, and if you do your work you're good enough for me. First thing, I want you to show up when we put up the tent to-morrow. Everybody works here. Or they get out."

Chad said all right. He asked whether the ring stock were left out all night.

"We move the ring horses into the freaks' pavilion," Walsh said. "The hostlers put that up."

That was where Chad slept. As the new hand he was deputed to go into the village with Benny after food. They got a couple of loaves of bread and some neck of lamb which Benny stewed with onions and greens, and later they bedded down the horses in the tent.

Other roustabouts weren't admitted. They had to sleep in the open. "They're just plain hoggies," Benny explained. "Leave them wallow."

Chad gathered that Burke and Walsh was constructed of social levels. After the partners ranked the riders; after them other ring performers, with the wire artiste at the top; then came the boss windjammer, then the windjammers, then the hostlers, and finally the plain roustabouts. Chad was lucky to work right into the horse-handlers' society, but Benny admitted that he knew his business. Even though you were a hostler, however, the riders didn't seem to know you were around.

After the tent was up, Benny said they had an hour or so unless some of the stock were wanted for practice. There being no call for Buck, Chad decided to cut into the town. He made inquiries at several of the smaller taverns—he didn't think Albany would have money enough to put up at an expensive-looking house like the Sans Souci Hotel—but he found no trace of her. He had to give up before finishing his round of the town.

Parade time came early with Burke and Walsh, and the horses had to be ready saddled. Benny said they used practically the entire string, as one of Burke's main points of interest was the troop of equestriennes.

Chad asked whether Buck was used in the parade, and Benny said that Lady Lillian had always ridden him but that up to now Ainsworth had preferred his spotted horse. That turned out to be the case in Ballston. When the parade was ready to form and the riders showed up for mounting, Ainsworth came down the line to see how Buck was making out. He was a lightly set man with straight dark eyes so widely spaced that they gave his face an almost blank expression His shoulders were made to look broad by the tight waist and full skirts of his riding coat.

As soon as Buck saw him, he went back on his halter rope, and Chad had to jump in and grab him to keep him from damaging one of the equestriennes.

Ainsworth made no move.

"You're the new hostler Walsh was telling about," he said. "You don't like having a horse spurred."

"You'll turn him ugly," Chad said.

"I'll turn him any way I like. All you have to do is get him to the tent. No horse ever threw me and no horse ever will. If he wants to turn ugly, so much the better. As for you, you mind your own business."

Chad's hands were too full of horse for him to answer. But the girl who had nearly been mashed by Buck's plunging made a small outcry. "My! I think Mr. Ainsworth's wonderful. He's such a gentleman. Even riding that horse he looks gentlemanly. He can ride anything!"

Bitchy little fools, Chad thought savagely, couldn't they see that turning a horse half wild and making him jump and cavort wasn't real riding? The secret of riding was to get horse and equestrian as nearly one being as possible ; it couldn't be beautiful unless both were liking it.

The bank was tuning up. Now the boss windjammer lifted his French horn and, at a sign from Burke, blew three rising notes. The girls all went to their horses. Chad and Benny followed down the line to give them leg-ups. Benny said, " I used to like this part of the job when I was young and bullish. But hell, it's just beefsteak after all."

He shambled off to lie down in the shade of the main tent. Chad remained with Buck until the procession had pulled out of the lot—clowns, band wagon, equestriennes, elephant,

jugglers and acrobats to turn flip-flaps, cartwheels, and somersets; equestrians, and the wagonload of freaks; the armless girl
sitting in a chair and holding a parasol in her teeth; the fat
lady, and the male midget sitting on the giant's lap. The tattooed
man had to walk in a turban and Oriental trousers, and in spite
of the sunshine he looked cold.

The band music drifted away towards town, and presently
the lot was a deserted place except for the few hands left and the
suckerless luck boys. One of these drifted up to Chad while he
was saddling Buck and held out a dime.

Chad said, " Don't come too close."

" Don't worry," said the luck boy. He was the fellow who
had announced the presence of pickpockets. " I just wanted to
give you this. I didn't know you was joining out. We don't
touch kinkers or hands. It's the rules."

Chad grinned in spite of himself. The man's small-chinned
face was all drawn down with conscience.

" Hell," he said. " I was asking for it."

" Well, you was," the other said. " And let me tell you, a
dime is a darned sight harder to whittle off than a hundred
dollars." He paused, swallowing, and looked round him. " Say,
there's a female wants to talk to you. She's back of the freak
hotel." He raised his hand palm upwards, blew on it, and
wheeled off.

Finishing with Buck, Chad moved round the freak pavilion.
It stood to one side of the main tent. The back corner behind it
contained nothing but the tackle wagon. Beyond that a growth
of sumac came right up to the fence. Against the sumac leaves
a woman was standing, and Chad didn't need to see her arm in
a sling to know who it was.

" Albany ? " he said.

" Oh, Chad, I'm glad to see you ! "

He stared at her face. The grey eyes had the same direct
look, the wide smile was there, but her lips seemed shaky and her
eyes were frightened and hurt. " I'm glad to see you," she said
again. " How did you happen to join out here ? "

He told her, " I and Huguenine had trouble." He let it go
at that. Just now she wasn't interested to know more. She
touched her arm said, " Did you know I got hurt ? "

" Fell off Buck," he said with a grin. " Sure, they told
me."

"Yes, I fell off. Now Burke's put that Ainsworth on him," she said. "He can't ride. He'll spoil the horse."

Chad said, "He's started. But I've quieted Buck down considerable."

"Ainsworth will make him hate everything human," she said. She laid hold of his arm. "Mr. Burke's trying to steal Buck from me, Chad. He's been intending to from the first, only I was too big a fool to see it. I thought he was in love with me and I could play with him." She glanced quickly round. "I must tell you about it, when you get off."

Chad nodded. "I don't know when I get time off except at night. Are you tailing the show?"

"Yes. I haven't too much money left. I find a boarding-house. I'll be in Saratoga to-night. Have you been there?"

"No."

"Well, there's a little road runs west out of town towards Rock City. I'll be on that somewhere, close to town. Will you come when you can?" She started to smile. Then she touched his arm again. "I haven't any one else to depend on, Chad. I thought I was as good as any man. I've found a woman by herself hasn't any chance at all."

"I'll be there. But I may be late."

The band music burst out louder as the procession passed a street opening. Then there was a whistle on the lot behind them, an unmelodious rendering of the chorus of "Jump Jim Crow," and it seemed to Chad that the whistler put the accent on the *Jump*. Albany caught it too.

"I don't want any one to see me," she said. "They think I'm still in Albany."

Chad said, "I'll show up."

He watched her till she was screened by the sumacs, then walked openly back past the tackle wagon in time to encounter Mr. Walsh coming round the freaks' tent.

Walsh's eyes were suddenly suspicious.

"What are you doing here?" he demanded, glancing towards the wagon.

It was still locked, however, and Chad said, "I just went into the bushes," and had the satisfaction of seeing Walsh look foolish.

On the other side of the freak tent, the luck boy with principles was leaning nonchalantly on the horse hurdle, still whistling. Chad said, "Thanks" as he walked by and the luck boy said, "Any time, friend."

There was nothing to do until show time, but that arrived so quickly that Chad hadn't had a chance yet to sort out his ideas. The main thing was to get Buck over this performance.

Now and then during the first part of the performance he got calls from Benny or George to cut out one, two, or six horses and deliver them at the entrance. Changing saddles or putting on pads had to be done fast. Chad saw that all the theories he had tried to work out with Huguenine's little show were right ones. Burke was a successful showman, and he ran his performance on the jump.

Chad's spare moments were all spent with the black horse, talking to him, petting him, making much of him. He had to get the idea into Buck's head that being with Chad Hanna was being secure and comfortable. It was the only chance of keeping a horse like Buck from turning into a regular man-killer, but he wasn't sure of having succeeded when George passed the word for Ainsworth's high-school horse.

Chad led him to the performer's entrance. The horse began to nerve up the minute they started. He was lifting and throwing by the time they reached the canvas. His ears went up and he blew when Ainsworth appeared in uniform.

"Come up on his side," Chad said. "And treat him easy."

Ainsworth never said a word. His wide-spaced eyes took on a slight shine, however; he caught the reins, got his toe in the stirrup, and was up. It was a wonder, Chad thought, that he hadn't had to call for two more men to control the horse. He stared up at Ainsworth. He was ready to say please, for Buck was standing still and shaking in every nerve. He saw Ainsworth looking down at him as he gathered the reins. Then he reached over and struck Chad with his crop across the face.

"You God-damned roustabout," he said. "Get out of my way."

Chad jumped and saw the spurs sink, and Buck went way up and was clubbed between the ears and came down, and bombed through the entrance as the bugle sounded. It made Chad sick with rage, but he watched every inch of the performance while George said over his shoulder, "Didn't I tell you? Look at that. He likes it. He wants to crazy him. He . . ."

"Shut up," Chad said. "You don't need to tell me."

Ainsworth didn't even approximate Albany's act. But he didn't want to. He put Buck over jumps. He made him side-step ; but it was only a step or two at a time, and then the horse broke and reared and the audience stormed applause as the rider fought him back. It was sheer savagery, and Chad felt himself getting savage watching it, so that he didn't even feel the blow on his face. He could only think of one thing. A man like Ainsworth ought to be killed, Burke and Walsh ought to be killed for allowing it, the whole audience ought to be killed.

The horse was throwing froth ; his chest was white with it ; he was drenched with sweat, and blood showed where the spurs were raking. He had been turned into a mess and the fool people were calling for an encore.

Chad didn't have time even to make a pass at Ainsworth. He hopped to the ground and threw the reins, and Chad had to lunge for the bridle.

Buck carried him way to the end of the lot before he dragged him down, and then he stopped, shuddering, with his head to his knees, and Chad found himself blubbering like a small boy.

He finally got Buck back to the line and went about the rest of his work slowly. He made up his mind to make another plea to Burke or Walsh, though he knew it would be no use. They expected him to keep the horse manageable out of the ring ; what Ainsworth did inside the ring was good business. But they didn't know.

He was washing the horse down when Walsh came along looking for him. " You're supposed to work on the tear-down."

Chad looked up with the stick in his hand.

" Mr. Walsh, I'm trying to keep this horse from going crazy," he said quietly. He had to be quiet now. He had made up his mind that he and Albany would have to steal the horse from the show. But he couldn't do that if he lost his job. And he couldn't keep his voice from heating, either. " That Ains-worth's crazy," he said. " If he don't drive the horse mad, he'll break him down so he won't be good for nothing."

Walsh didn't take it.

" Ainsworth rode him harder than I ever seen him," he said. " But he told me why. He said you got impertinent. You're not supposed to tell a top-rider what he's to do, Hanna. If you don't like the way Ainsworth rode, you can blame yourself." He seemed to measure off his words. " You know too much.

You better keep it to yourself if you want to stay with this show. I guess, though, Ainsworth may have learned you."

"I won't forget that," Chad said, and bent to his work before Walsh could answer.

13

ALBANY

PULLING into Saratoga Springs on Saturday night, the big show settled itself for Sunday. Buck had picked up a little spirits on the seven-mile trip, and he bedded down quietly in the freaks' pavilion. The show was paid off on the new lot, the performers and circus hands lining up in order of rank. Chad drew his two days' pay. Two dollars wasn't much, but every dollar would count.

Benny was in the tent. He asked Chad whether he had planned to see the town. Chad said he had thought of it.

"Well, being as you're the newest handler you ought to stay here, but being as I am the oldest, I don't find much pleasure in picking around a town like this. A roustabout don't get far here anyways. I'd as lief stay as not. You go along."

"Thanks, Benny."

Benny raised one hand. "I'll tell you, though," he said. "If you was to buy me twenty-five cents' worth of whisky, and if you was to lay the bottle with the stopper to my nose when you come in, I wouldn't say I wouldn't dream pleasant."

Chad asked seriously whether he should loosen the cork.

"Are you crazy?" Benny asked in alarm. "Suppose I drank it in my sleep?"

The high-pillared hotels on the main street made a man feel small. As Chad went along he heard summer guests chatting behind the screens of clematis vine. The lights from the huge windows silhouetted their heads and made a green and gold pattern in the leaves. Dance music was playing, and now and then the passer-by could get glimpses of men and women swinging past the windows.

But Chad didn't linger to watch. He had to ask twice to find the Rock City road. It was a narrow thoroughfare, offset at one corner so that he almost missed it, but after crossing the railroad track it led straight west.

He walked along under the elms, looking for a female figure. There was no light except from the scattered houses, so he slowed his pace and started to whistle softly " Long-Tailed Blue." He thought he must have passed Albany before he heard her call softly, " Is that you, Chad ? " and he crossed the road to where she waited by the trunk of a tree.

She took his arm at once and said, " Let's walk on out till we get to the country. Then we can talk. Hearing that tune made me feel homesick for Huguenine's. It was fun there."

He didn't answer and they walked without speaking till a meadow opened out on their left. She said, " Let's cross the fence."

" Don't it hurt your arm ? "

" It won't."

He had to help her over, though. He took her in his hands to lift her down, and she stood a moment when he had set her on her feet, without moving . It was one of those instants that catch time ; Chad could still feel her in his hands. It left him confused, and it was she who made the first move. She bent over and brushed the grass.

" There's no dew. Let's sit down."

He could hear her spread her skirts on the grass and he sat down close to her.

" Tell me what happened. I know Buck threw you."

She said, with quick anger, " It wasn't Buck's fault. Mr. Clayton—he's McPickle, the clown, in the posters—waited till I was making one of the jumps and then he fired off a shotgun. Buck half-turned and we smashed the hurdle and went over. That's all."

" Hadn't they warned you ? "

" No. Though I ought to have known what would happen," she said bitterly. " Mr. Burke was trying to spoil my act from the beginning. He wanted Buck. So did Mr. Ainsworth. At first I thought he was friendly. He kept telling me I ought to get more style, more excitement, into the act. He said I ought to spur him up." Her voice lowered. " *You* know, I couldn't do that."

" Yes," Chad said.

" Then after the doctor said my arm was broken, Mr. Burke

came to the hotel to see me. He said he was terribly sorry. I believed him even then. I told him I would be able to ride with my arm strapped, but he said he couldn't mar the programme with an injured female. He said I wasn't really cut out for a big circus, and what I ought to do was sell him Buck. He had the bill of sale ready in his pocket. He gave it to me, and I tore it up."

She stopped for a minute, and the voices of the crickets came against them like a wave in the darkness. It made speaking an effort when she started again.

"He said he was sorry. But I had agreed to work the act in the show. As I couldn't appear, he would be compelled to use a substitute for me. He didn't have to tell me who it was."

"Why didn't you take Buck away?" Chad asked.

"How could I? I said that was what I would do, but he said I couldn't. I'd been staying in the expensive rooms the way Mr. Ainsworth and Mrs. Dester did, but he said my contract called for regular keep. I'd never bothered to read it. He showed it to me. He said he would keep the horse until I had paid what I owed and that any court in the country would allow him to. He said a female by herself wouldn't have any weight against a well-known, moral establishment like Burke and Walsh. I had begun to see that for myself."

Chad was incredulous.

"Didn't you have money to make up the difference? I thought you were getting big pay. I thought that was why you left Huguenine's."

She shook her head in the darkness.

"I was going to get a two months' trial on Huguenine's pay. Then I was going to have twenty dollars a week—he said. If the act went well. It didn't. I knew that. But I thought it didn't matter so much, Mr. Burke seemed so "—she hesitated— "so interested."

"You quit Huguenine's for that?"

"Every one has to learn once, I guess." She drew a long breath. "I've learned, anyway." Her voice resumed a narrative note. "Mr. Burke left me in the hotel. He said since I was *deserting* the show, Burke and Walsh naturally couldn't be expected to pay my expenses. I think he thought I'd be laid up there for a while, but I moved out next morning. I've kept out of sight. I know they're treating Buck badly. I couldn't do anything myself. But I hoped something would turn up—he might kill Ainsworth or something and I could get him back. And then you turned up ! " She leaned towards him. " Tell me how he is."

Chad rested his knuckles on the grass between his knees. She might as well know. He told her. She didn't make a sound. " I ain't the only mad one," he said. " The handlers are pretty mad about it too." It sounded foolish to say that. It didn't mean anything.

She said softly, " I found him myself. I broke him and trained him and I never used a harsh word to him. It's hard to see him go like this."

" He won't go."

He hadn't worked it out in his own mind, but he knew it was true as soon as he said it.

" What do you mean ? " Albany waited a minute. " Mr. Burke won't sell him."

" No. I haven't money anyway."

" You mean, steal him ? "

" It's not exactly stealing. He belongs to you anyway."

" They'd make it stealing, Chad. Nobody dares steal horses from a circus."

" You scared ? "

" No." He could hear her pulling grass. " Chad, if they caught you, it wouldn't be like the sheriff catching you. Even horse-thieves leave circuses alone. I haven't got any right to ask you to do that for me."

" You're not asking me, and I'd do it if you weren't round, just the same. Burke isn't so awful smart. He can run a circus, but I bet he's no better chasing a horse-thief than Cisco Trid was at chasing a nigger."

He was beginning to feel hardy about it. It would be like old times.

" I've got to figure the thing out," he said. " And I'll have to do it while the show's laying over here. I'll do it some way."

" Where'll you take him, then ? "

He thought a minute.

" This'll be as good a road as any. How much money have you got ? "

" About thirty dollars," she said.

Chad figured. " I've got about five. That ought to be

enough. We'll have to buy a rig somewhere, if you don't mind skedaddling round the back roads with a roustabout."

" It would be fun."

He said, " Will you trust me with twenty dollars ? "

For answer she fumbled with her purse in the dark.

" I know which is which, because I always fold them the same way." She gave a little laugh. " I'm an orderly kind of person, you know."

Chad took them, feeling her fingers inside his.

" I'll strike across country into Broadalbin, come down to Johnstown, and meet you in Fort Plain. Do you think you can get there ? "

" Yes. What day ? "

" Give me three days. They may push me close. You put up at the American Hotel so I can find you without asking round. I'll have a rig by then and you can ride with us."

It sounded fine and she said " I'll be there " almost gaily. But he saw a hitch in it.

" How will you get out of this place without them seeing you ? As soon as they miss me and Buck they'll be watching every road."

" Don't worry about me. They'll be looking for the horse and you, not for a female in a veil and mourning. Besides, I'll take the railroad. No one would hunt a horse-thief on a railroad car ! "

14

THEFT

HE left her at a small house on the edge of town, and she shook hands. " Good luck," she whispered. She went in with a quiet swift drawing of her skirts across the door frame. He had a glimpse of her figure, small and erect, against the dim light in the hallway. Then the door closed, but her voice came out to him, almost gay : " Here I am, Mrs. Daggett, safe and sound."

He walked down the street with his spirits rising. It was going to be fun, once they shook loose. A girl with Albany's nerve would turn the business into a regular high time. Sneaking Henry Prince round Casastota would be nothing to it.

He stopped at a small bar on a back street near the railroad to buy a bottle of whisky. " Make it a fifty-center," he said and watched the keep draw it. Benny would be the goat, if he got Buck away, so the old man might as well have some comfort for it.

The lot was dark and looked deserted. He couldn't hear a human sound through the racket the crickets were making. The complete darkness was a good thing for him, but now he would have swapped it for a little wind. The wagon stock were mostly lying down ; he saw the shadowy blots their bodies made beside the wagons and felt that their heads turned silently to watch him pass. As he came up to the freaks' pavilion, though, he could hear Benny's snoring.

The old man had a slight roar in his windpipe, perhaps of asthma, for he was using a long stroke of breath. There was less danger of waking him than of his waking himself. His breathing climbed way up and hung there with a kind of bubbling and then broke downhill like a wagonload of cobblestones, and he would hesitate and fight for a minute. He kicked one foot like a sleeping dog when Chad's hand touched him. Chad found the location of his face by feeling the draft and laid the bottle in the hay as Benny had suggested. It was uncanny. For a moment Benny's entire breathing system seemed to be suspended. Then he gave a groan and went on again with a good steady snore and no more wind fighting.

Leaving the old man lying, Chad picked his way over to the horses. Most of them were lying down, but, as he had expected, Buck was still on his feet. The horse scented him and blew softly, and Chad went in beside him and patted him for a minute. Then he untied him and the other three horses attached to the same hurdle and laid the hurdle over on its side. All four took it quietly. Two didn't bother to get up. The third one did, but he was just curious. Chad waited a minute to make sure that Benny hadn't been disturbed.

By this time Chad had figured out pretty well what he was going to do. He didn't have much time to waste for the hostlers were apt to be turning up before long. He took his knife, and timing the rips to Benny's breathing, slit the wall from top to bottom. He had to stoop a little and he knew there was a chance that Buck would refuse to use the opening. If that happened he planned to bull through the entrance.

But before he could try it, he had to get a bridle. He had never been on Buck's back, and the way Ainsworth had mistreated the animal, it was likely that he would put on a show. Chad ducked through the slit and went over to the tackle wagon. It was locked up, so he went round to the side and picked one of the team's headstalls off the harness hook. It felt near enough Buck's size for him to use. He could adjust it later on. Working in the dark, he cut the end of one of the reins from its fork behind the stitching and buckled the free end to the other bit ring. It wouldn't look like much, but it would make a bridle rein. He was about ready to try now. All he had to do was to make out who was in the treasury wagon and whether he was asleep. He knew that Burke and Walsh wouldn't leave the wagon without a guard.

There was no light in the wagon ; there was no one under it, and he couldn't hear any one breathing inside ; but the crickets made so much noise that he couldn't have heard anything short of a production like Benny's. He would have to take a chance on getting past the wagon and out of the lot before any alarm started. It wasn't likely he would have a better chance than now.

He sneaked in past Benny—he didn't want to use the flap for fear of scaring the horses—and came up beside Buck the way he had the first time. The horse shivered when he slid his hand up to the crest. He unbuckled the halter and let it drop and slipped the headstall over his head. Buck took the bit kindly, but the headstall seemed over-sized. He would have to use a tight rein.

Benny was still snoring comfortably against the bottle cork. Chad drew in his breath deep and let it out, and it was odd to hear Buck do the same thing. He took hold of the rein and whispered, " Come, boy." The horse took an obedient step forward. Chad could feel the tent wall with his fingers and brushed his palm along it till he found the slit and put his hand under the beginning of the cut and pushed up.

There was some play, but not much. He widened the slit by turning his elbow up, and the noise of the crickets seemed to boil into the tent. It didn't disturb Benny, however. So Chad went through and got Buck's head under. The horse stopped there. Chad didn't dare pull for fear he would haul back or rear and bring the whole tent down with himself inside it. He waited a minute, whispering to the horse, and then pulled lightly. Buck took another step and then tucked down his quarters and came out with a sort of buck jump.

The canvas rubbing on his hide made a sound like tearing cloth. Beyond it Chad heard Benny flounder in the hay and roll over. One hand must have hit the bottle for he said, "Hey! You're back."

Chad stuck his head back through the slit and said, "Yeah. Just looking at the black horse."

Benny grunted. He made no other sound and Chad thought he was probably wrestling over the problem of having a drink now or waiting till morning. His self-control must have won out, for after a minute he rustled back into the hay and his breathing almost at once started lengthening out.

Chad decided to give him time to settle down ; but it was a mistake. He had barely started to edge Buck along towards the lot entrance when voices broke out along the road. He recognised George's voice among them. The hostlers were coming back.

He thought quickly. If it was just the hostlers they would come straight to the tent, go inside, and then Chad would have about two minutes in which to make his move with Buck. But if there were other roustabouts with them, they would scatter all over the lot to their wagons and one would be bound to see him. It would be just luck if he got out. Benny had waked up once more, also, and was fishing round, complaining, and asking Chad where the lantern was.

Suddenly he said, "Hey!" Then he gave a yell, and at the same moment one of the horses whinnied and a white shape burst through the slit. Buck threw up his head and snorted. The second horse wheeled, trotted up to them, sticking his nose curiously up to Buck's. Chad remembered that the spotted trick horse had been hitched to the hurdle with the other three. He swung his hat in the animal's face and yelled, "It's Ainsworth's horse."

The horse snorted, wheeled, and bolted for the lot entrance. Chad grabbed Buck's mane and swung himself on to his back. His heart stood still with the horse. He said quietly, "Come up," and touched him with his heels.

Buck leaped forward. The spotted horse had scattered the returning hostlers and as Buck made the entrance Chad heard George yelling, "It's Ainsworth's horse. Come on."

Back in the tent, Benny started to roar, "Horse-thieves!"

The treasury wagon door swung open, but Chad was past the fence. One of the hostlers jumped out in the road ahead of him but Chad yelled, " I'll catch him ! " A gun went off, and Buck fairly flattened out between Chad's legs.

The man didn't dare stand his ground. He fell to one side as the black horse came up, and then the dark shapes of George and a couple of roustabouts scurried for the fence like rabbits. " I'll get him," Chad shouted to them.

Ainsworth's spotted horse had a good turn of speed, and he used all he had straight down the main street. Some dogs picked him up near the United States Hotel and carried him straight on through the town. Fighting Buck down to a trot, Chad followed through the dust looking for his corner, and he made it before the hullabaloo had got too loud behind him. It was too much to hope that no one had noticed him, but as the confusion mounted he hoped what witnesses there were might have forgotten a quietly moving horse and rider.

To that end he slowed Buck down to a walk. The street was quiet and completely dark. The yelling on the road from the circus lot was deadened by the huge bulk of the hotel, and in the dust Buck's hoofs made almost no sound.

Chad held him to a walk all the way to the railroad tracks. He had just worked up on to them when he heard the pursuit coming past the hotel, and he stopped Buck dead to listen. If they went on down the main street he had nothing to worry about ; and if they turned after him, he doubted whether there was another horse in the establishment to match Buck's speed. The spotted horse might have, but he was pretty well out of the picture by now, having his own private race with the dogs.

Voices broke out in the blackness back of him. He could hear shouts echoing off the hotel walls. Then some of the horses started ahead down the main street, but two turned in with a sudden precision of hoofbeats that told Chad they were on his street.

He lifted the reins ; then, on a sudden impulse, he turned Buck south along the railroad track. Albany had said that no one would think of finding a horse-thief on a railroad car. They wouldn't be any more likely to hunt for the horse along the tracks. He kept Buck walking quietly half a hundred yards and stopped him again. He had only a minute to wait before two horses stamped upon the track behind him, dipped down beyond, and went off on the Rock City road. They hadn't even stopped to listen down the railroad.

As soon as their hoofbeats had died out, Chad started Buck again. He kept him to a slow trot for he didn't know the condition of the road-bed. But the wide-spaced cross-ties were well buried, the dirt packed and smooth, and the horse had easy footing.

Coming out of the town, he saw a big fire on the circus lot. Burke's rig stood in the middle of it, and Burke himself was listening to the stories of half a dozen different men. They all kept pointing to the side of the freaks' pavilion and to the town.

Chad was too far off for their voices to reach him, but he could imagine them yelling and Burke asking questions. From that distance Burke looked cool as a cucumber. After a minute Burke waved them away and drove out of the lot, but instead of heading back to town he turned south. Chad saw him take the whip and the road pair leaned out, and he knew that Ballston would be blocked off for him.

Now and then when the silhouettes of trees against the dark sky gave a clue to the railroad's direction, he was able to let the horse out a trifle. But it seemed to get darker as they went along, and in a little while they were forced to keep at a walk, the horse picking his way between the twelve-inch scantling on which the rail strips were mounted, and long before they reached Ballston Chad knew that Burke must have arrived.

Burke, travelling a road with a lantern on his rig, could keep the horses at a full trot. He would have had time to rouse the sheriff, secure deputies, and post the roads round the village. Chad saw that his original plan of abandoning the railroad, circling the town, and rejoining the tracks on the far side would have to be abandoned. The darkness was too black to make such exploration of back lanes feasible, even if he could have expected no watchers.

But along the six miles to Ballston there hadn't been a living soul on the railroad track. It occurred to Chad that the chances were against finding any look-out on it here in town. And the notion of riding the horse quietly right straight through the village appealed to him. Burke, capable, calm, spinning his complete web, and Chad riding the stolen horse in at one end and out at the other without rousing a single suspicion. It would probably convince Burke that he had headed north after all.

Moreover, it was beginning to rain, and if the rain held till morning, even Buck's tracks would be washed out. If they figured out the railroad business by that time, it would be just a guess. They couldn't be sure about it.

"Just keep on walking, boy," he said. Buck had a quick, springy walk that covered ground. His hoofs made almost no sound except when, occasionally, his shoe calks dug a tie. They were half-way into the village before Chad made out a house window. A pane of glass reflected the light from a lantern a hundred yards off down a side street. The lantern was quickly covered, but ahead he saw another light moving rapidly across the railroad, heard the rattle of wheels on the plank crossing, and guessed it was Burke ferrying a last watcher to some unknown road.

The rain was coming hard when he and Buck reached the main crossing by the station. The station itself was dark. A lone white cat was crouched on a window-sill and Chad saw it faintly as he went by. It was all he saw in Ballston Spa. Even the dogs had taken cover. As the rain soaked into him he comforted himself with the notion that the watchers were getting wet as he was, or if they weren't it was because they didn't care whether the circus lost a horse or not.

After he had travelled twenty minutes, he figured he was through the town and he had nothing more to worry him. From now on he was sure he would be ahead of any watch that Burke could set up for him. All he had to do was to stick tight to the railroad until he reached the Mohawk River. Then he would turn off, take the main bridge over, and disappear into the city. He doubted whether Burke could afford to take the time to hunt as far as that for him. And if he did, Chad figured that he wasn't likely to be stopped. In Schenectady he would buy some kind of a rig and, with Buck in shafts and harness, drive out in broad daylight.

15

MR. AND MRS. SEAVEY

AT noon two days later, driving into Fort Plain, Chad inquired the way to the American Hotel. He had spent the night in Fultonham, so there was plenty of roading left in Buck, and the more they got out of him that day, the better pleased Chad would feel. The horse was becoming accustomed to travelling in harness. He was smart and made no real difficulty ; and he only lost his temper on a downhill grade when the breeching caught up with him. It meant going down at a rattly clip, but that was all right except on stony roads.

Then the horse didn't worry Chad as much as the rig. It was a high-slung, two-wheel chaise. He had bought it, with an antique harness thrown in, for fifteen dollars in a livery barn in Schenectady. It hadn't been driven in years, and Lord knew when it had been built. At a smart trot on level stretches the wheels stood up well enough, but at a walk they would waver like a mule's ears, and when the wheel lifted for a cobble, the spokes rattled like false teeth.

However, it had a high top that rose up straight and black as a minister's hat and gave the contraption an air of respectability. Inside it Chad looked like an earnest back-bush farmer who had inherited direct from his grandfather. He saw a friendly kind of amusement on the faces of the people in the American Hotel's front porch as he got down, and he felt like grinning when Albany rose from the corner and walked slowly to greet him in her mourning veil.

Her voice sounded faint and tired.

"Oh, Mr. Seavey," she said, taking his arm. "It's been so tiresome waiting for you."

He knew she was up to some game by the tremulous pressure of her fingers.

"Mother died day before yesterday. She just passed away. (My name's Samantha Seavey and I'm married to you and you've got to pay my bill.) She asked for you three times during the last hours. I wish you'd have gone."

"I had to sell those cows," Chad said heavily. She was shepherding him to the office.

"Mr. Jones has been very kind to me," she said in a low voice, and the interested-looking young clerk raised a blush over the points of his collar.

"It's been a pleasure to have Mrs. Seavey stay with us," he told Chad. "We'd hoped to entertain you."

"We got to get back to . . ."

Albany squeezed his arm.

"Yes, I miss my little girl in Richfield so. She'll comfort me."

Her bag was ready packed. Chad picked it up after paying the bill and they walked out. On the porch every one looked at them and then looked sympathetically away. He could feel Albany shaking on his arm, and he started to give her a jerk before he realised that the other guests thought she was weeping. So he handed her in over the wheel, climbed up himself, and with a glum face started Buck off on the road to Stark.

As soon as they were out of the village she put back her veil. Her face was bright pink and her eyes shining. "I thought I'd suffocate under this veil," she said. "They'd all been so nice and you came up the steps looking so puzzled and sour and mixed up—*just* like a man with a weepy female on his hands!" She went into peals of laughter, and he looked at her sidewise.

"Well, maybe I was funny," he admitted. "When you called me Mr. Seavey I didn't know what to do. Why'd you have to pick on that name?"

"I don't know. It doesn't sound made-up, somehow. Jones, or Smith, or White, or Snell: they might be made up or they might not. But nobody would think of saying her name was Seavey unless it *was* Seavey. And I thought if Mr. Burke or someone did happen to come there, they'd never find my own name. So I said my name was Mrs. Thomas Seavey and should I put my own name, Samantha, down? And they said just my husband's name—so I *had* to have a husband because I'd just thought of my poor mother dying and I didn't want to kill every one at once. I told that nice Mr. Jones all about how it was going to be such a comfort to get back to my family and have my child and husband to comfort me. It made me sound so respectable. Where *did* you ever find this carriage?"

Chad told her. " I used up fifteen dollars for this rig. Take the lines and I'll give you back the rest of your money."

" No, you keep it. A wife shouldn't pay for her husband at the tavern. I think you ought to act more bossy with me, too. Tell me to hurry up, or fetch your hat (we'll have to get you a hat to go with this buggy top). You don't want to look so bashful, Chad. You're to be the honest kind of man who thinks his female relations ought to step quick when he speaks to them." Her laughter was infectious. He grinned at her and she met his look with her hand smoothing the black hair back from one cheek and her grey eyes suddenly turning thoughtful.

" Now let me see what kind of a woman I am. I think maybe I like being ordered round. You see, we haven't been married two years yet and I think you're such a fine man. You're cross with me, but that's for my own good, and I think you can do anything you set your mind to. Doesn't that sound right ? " She giggled. " And we've got one child, a lovely girl, eight months old, but you're apt to blame me because it isn't a boy. I'm being terribly silly, aren't I ? But I feel so fine, Chad. Tell me how you got away. I could hear them galloping out along the street but I never heard you."

" It was what you said about hunting a horse-thief on the railroad that made it so easy," he said, relieved at the change of subject. He told her everything as it had happened. " Burke's not going to catch us now."

" I don't know," she said. " I don't think he'd ever give up going after something he wanted. He makes me afraid."

" Buck's one thing he won't get."

He was glad that she had sobered down. She sat beside him, silent for a long way, her grey eyes staring out along the road ahead.

" Buck goes pretty well, doesn't he ? " Chad asked.

" Yes," she said, absently. " Chad. Where are we going to ? "

" Right now to Stark, and then to Springfield. I'm going to push Buck hard to-day. I want to get across the Great Western Road to-night."

She said, " Yes. Then what ? "

" I haven't thought it out altogether," Chad said slowly. " But the way I look at it, we ought to keep going south a while, and then reach off on a side road and find a small place and just stay there for a week. The less we move around the less chance Burke has of hearing about us."

She nodded, a little impatiently, he thought.

"That sounds like a good plan. But Chad, we just can't stay in one place for ever. We haven't got much money."

"How much have you got?"

They figured out that they had about nine dollars left between them.

"Even if we go to cheap taverns, that can't last us much more than a week," he pointed out. "And we've got to feed Buck as well as ourselves. I'll have to find work somewhere."

When she looked at him, he saw that both of them had the same idea.

"Huguenine's is due to play Sherburne in about two weeks," he told her.

"Do you think he'd take me back?"

"He's crazy to have you come back. The show hasn't gone right since you left. He won't be able to pay you what you used to get, though. He had to cut down the pay before I quit. But you can live on it."

"I don't care." Her buoyant spirits returned. "It's going to be wonderful to get back," she said. "I felt homesick for Huguenine's almost as soon as I left it. I never appreciated them."

"Oh, Huguenine's all right, I guess," Chad said.

She turned quickly to him.

"So are you, Chad. You've been wonderful. I don't believe anybody else would have got Buck away. They wouldn't have even tried to."

He saw she meant all of it.

"You've done so much for me, for both of us," she said. "Buck looks fine."

Chad shook the lines.

"He's just putting on style. He knows you're riding back of him, that's why."

The horse shook his head and blew out his nostrils. Albany smiled, and a little later when Chad stopped to let Buck drink she got out and went round to his head.

Chad stayed in the rig, watching a couple of cows and a woodchuck on a bare wind-blown hillock. He glanced at Albany as she climbed in. The front of her black dress was dribbled with moisture from Buck's lips and her eyes were shining. After that she didn't talk about themselves but looked out at the country.

They crossed the Great Western Turnpike a little later, and took a road south from Springfield. About eight o'clock they came to a small settlement named Middlefield. The tavern was a tiny place and the only bed was one that Albany would have to share with the proprietor's mother-in-law. Albany tossed her head, and Chad, smothering a grin, told her sharply to stop her foolishness, and she made a face at him over the man's disconsolate shoulder. . . .

The next day they started off in a south-east rain. Though Buck had freshened up nicely, Chad drove him at a walk most of the time. They kept dry enough ; it was pleasant to sit back against the mouldy-smelling leather and feel the rain drumming against the top. The damp, forest-smelling air drew in against their faces. Albany's cheeks were pink and her grey eyes shone.

" We'll have to work on Buck while we have the chance," she said. " Heaven knows what he's got to be like.'

" You can't ride him," Chad pointed out. " We haven't money to buy you a side-saddle, and you oughtn't to ride him bareback with that broken arm. How long will it be like that ? "

" About a month, the doctor said. But I don't mean to ride Buck. You'll do it."

" Me ? "

" Yes. We can find a piece of woods, like that one in Canastota. Remember ? And I can sit down and teach both of you. It will be fun." She studied the horse. " He'll come round fast."

At Cooperstown Chad decided they had gone south far enough. If they were tracked that far, a pursuer would expect them to keep on along the southern branch of the Great Western. He turned round the foot of the lake and took the first western road. In the afternoon it brought them to a small village named Oaksville, on the outskirts of which was a tiny tavern.

While Chad was putting up the horse, Albany talked to the woman who kept the house, and when he came in she reported that they could stay there for a week at five dollars for both of them. " She wanted to know about us and I told her we'd just been married and that you lived in Sherburne and we wanted to stop some place cheap for a honeymoon. But we're still Mr. and Mrs. Seavey, Chad. And I said you'd be willing to help with some of the chores. Her hired man quit last week.'

"That's all right," he said. "But . . ."

She raised her hand.

"Hush," she said. "She's coming back."

She was a lean little woman with sparse white hair, and her name was Mrs. Hussey. Her eyes, going over Chad from head to toe, were knowing as a chipmunk's. Pursing her lips, she said, "I'm pleased to meet you, Mr. Seavey," in a dry thin voice. "Will you bring your bag upstairs?"

She led them up the narrow staircase. It ascended between two walls and opened on as narrow a hall with doors to right and left. One, she said, was the attic. "There's rats or squirrels, or bats in there," she said. "They're all the time dragging bodies or something over the floor. I hear them from my room, the cruel little creatures. But I leave them alone as long as they don't come out of it. Live and let live." Her head twitched as she opened the other door on a small room under the slope of the roof.

Chad's one impression was of an enormous bed. He didn't see how it could have been got into the room at all. It couldn't have got up the stairs or through the window. "The roof," Mrs. Hussey explained dryly, when he asked. "It was hit by lightning, so before he mended it, Mr. Hussey brought the bed in. The Lord disposes." She eyed Chad. "Mr. Hussey was a joker too," she observed, touching the bed foot with one finger. "Well, I guess Mrs. Seavey wants to dob up some, so if you want supper, Mr. Seavey, you'd better come down and split me some wood."

Chad met Albany's eye and grinned. But he went down meekly after the little woman and dutifully split wood. "Is there anything else?"

"Anything else?" she said. "There's water needed. Then you could rake the yard and hoe the beans and clean the stable, to begin with."

Wondering what kind of jokes Mr. Hussey used to spring, Chad compromised on the stable. He cleaned the stall of dry manure, swept the carriage floor, and then groomed Buck. In spite of all his roading, the horse was in good spirits. He took on generally, arching his neck against the brush, and throwing his head when Chad went over his withers. Both of them enjoyed it.

"He hasn't looked like that in a long time."

With all their snorting, stamping, and hollering, neither horse nor man had heard Albany come in. It gave Chad a start to see her compact figure standing there outside the stall, reminding him so of the barn at the Yellow Bud, and her smile was for both of their turned heads.

" I'll sit here on the bucket," she said. " You go ahead so we'll be ready for supper." She picked up her skirts with her good hand and sat down on the up-ended pail. " Buck always fancied you from the start," she said.

" I fancied him."

Chad went to work again, but now Buck, under Albany's eye, was decorous as a deacon.

" Isn't that the way? You can always hear men taking on for a big time, but as soon as a woman shows up, they sober down. I don't mind swearing." She stretched her back, beaming at them. " You two ! Oh, I haven't felt so happy for so long. You've done so much for me, Chad. I think I'd have died, if you hadn't got Buck back for me."

" You wouldn't die," he told her. " You couldn't."

It was true. She wasn't the kind. Caroline might, but not Albany.

" You're so wise ! " Albany said. " Maybe you can figure out what we're going to do to-night."

" You started this Seavey business," he reminded her.

She met his eyes with a laugh, but her cheeks coloured in spite of her, and suddenly she looked down.

" I hadn't figured it quite so far," she admitted.

" Well, you better begin figuring now. We're supposed to be married, you know. What's more, you're just a bride. You stuck that in yourself. What'll she think if I stay out in the barn ? "

She looked up at him, half laughing, half rueful. Then she looked down at her bandaged arm. The evening light coming in against her cheek made her pretty as sin to look at, and Chad's lip lengthened a little as he wondered how far she had played this Seavey business in her own mind. She had played him up before, that day in Canastota, and then had stood him down after he joined out with the show. He enjoyed paying her back a little for it now.

" It wouldn't look very convincing," she admitted in a low voice. " But I could say you were coming in later, or you'd had to go to the post office, and she could help me undo my dress."

Chad snorted. " Do you think I look like a man who'd get a woman to undress his wife ? "

" No-o-o," she said faintly. Then she looked up quickly. " What put that in your mind ? "

She took him by surprise. Without realising it he had been thinking of Caroline. He hadn't told her about Caroline ; he didn't intend to yet.

" Well, isn't it true, anyway ? "

" I'm sure it is. Chad, did you marry Caroline Trid ? "

" What makes you think that ? "

She laughed at him.

" I'm sure of it. I thought you might. Though I thought for a while you were in love with me."

" Did you ? "

She nodded, still watching him.

" You remember ? That day when we went riding. And after-wards once or twice. Caroline was in love with you and she used to be jealous of me. I wondered why you didn't catch on to her. She's a fine girl, Chad. She's the kind of girl you needed to marry. Not somebody like me. I'm lazy. I'd never keep you going ahead, you know. She will. And you'll get somewhere, I'm sure of that. Once you know what you want."

He rested the brush on Buck's quarters and looked out the door. There was nothing to see except the evening and the tavern chimney laying a drift of smoke across the sky. He couldn't work up any steam about Albany ; and a week ago it wouldn't have seemed possible for him to feel like that. But he knew what he wanted. He wanted his old job back. He had made something out of the circus ; even though Huguenine had stopped it, it still wasn't dead. It was something he had made ; it was in him ; he could start it going any time he had a chance. And Caroline was part of it. He felt a quick unsettling wave of longing. In Albany's place now she would not be laughing, probably ; she was so young it made her serious. But she could be gay in strange, odd, electric flashes, gone as soon as they came. She had not come with him perhaps because she knew he wanted to come back.

" I married Caroline in Palmyra," he told Albany.

" I'm glad," she said. She turned her face towards the door

for a minute. " It makes me happy for you both." She turned to him again with her frank smile. " But we're still Mr. and Mrs. Seavey and we haven't got Mr. Seavey out of the bedroom."

" That's easy," he said. " I'll just drop out the window. It ain't far, and it's the other side from Mrs. Hussey's room."

" She might hear you, though. You can make a rope of the blanket and I'll pull it in afterwards. Like Rapunzel, you know. She let the Prince down with her hair. Did you ever hear that story, Chad ? "

" No."

" I'll tell it to you," she said, " while you finish, Buck."

And she told the story in her warm voice while the brush whispered over Buck's hide. Mrs. Hussey, surprising them there, must have thought they were a crazy couple.

" Your supper's been ready for fifteen minutes," she said. " How long did you say that girl's hair was ? "

" Oh, yards and yards, Mrs. Hussey." Albany got up.

" I'd have Rapunzelled her ! " said Mrs. Hussey, skittering back across the yard. . . .

Chad unfastened Albany's dress in the little room, an hour after their supper.

" Thanks," Albany said. " I can wriggle out of the rest after you've gone."

She watched him tie the blanket to the bed. " I hope it holds." She leaned out of the window to see him go down and giggled suddenly. " Look out for the witch," she whispered.

For eight days they stayed with Mrs. Hussey. Every day they took Buck out to a wood lot on a neighbouring farm and worked him through the trees. Albany, sitting on a log, told Chad how to use his weight. He had to learn to ride all over again—he had never ridden a horse that was bridlewise ; and sometimes it seemed to him that it was Buck who was training the rider, not the rider getting Buck back into training. He began, after the second day, to understand some of the spellbound feeling he had seen in Albany's eyes that morning in Canastota. She had been right after all when she had told him that losing Buck would have killed her—a part of her anyway.

After the practice they spent hours talking about Buck, or about Chad's ideas for running the circus. " You must have made it exciting. Poor Mr. Huguenine never had any idea of how to run the show," she said. " I don't see why it went so badly."

" They're bad times, I guess," Chad said. " Money's tight, and the poor crops make it worse."

Even a tiny backwoods town like Oaksville was beginning to feel the pinch. Mrs. Hussey was always complaining about the cost of eggs and flour and meat.

Chad said, " People won't spend money just for a show. You've got to catch them with something wonderful. Oscar didn't look like much to us because we were used to him, but people who had never seen a lion thought he was terrific. Maybe this Claude Cronk I told you about will help."

She kept him talking. It seemed to him he had never talked so much about anything in his life, or would again. He told her about everything that had happened since she left the show : the clem at the bridge ; Caroline's riding ; Oscar's slow sickness and his death in Albion and his posthumous exhibition through five towns. But she always brought him back to the work he had done in the ring, and he began to plan more for the show, like his ideas for Caroline's entrance. Albany thought that would be entrancing.

Both of them felt homesick for Huguenine's when they said good-bye to Mrs. Hussey. " Well, I won't say I won't miss you two," she told them, eyeing the store of firewood ready split in her shed. " But why a married man would want to fuss with a horse so much just beats me."

They started laughing as soon as they were out of earshot. . . .

" You don't remember the date Huguenine's plays Sherburne ? " Albany asked.

" Not exactly."

They hadn't much money left and they might have to push on to meet the show. Chad wondered how Mr. Huguenine would greet him. He was willing to ask for his job back at roustabout's pay, and Albany was sure it was the thing for him to do. " You want to be around if anything turns up," she said. " Never mind what Huguenine says—he'll come around. Some of the company are going to act queer with me, too, I expect."

Chad wondered if she was thinking of Shepley. She had hardly mentioned him in all their time together. He wondered if she would ever fall in love with any man.

" I'll always remember this week," she said.   " Not just getting Buck back, either, though it's part of it."

" It's been fun."

" Do you think Caroline would mind, if she knew ? "

" I don't know," he said slowly.

" Some day I'll tell her, maybe. Mr. and Mrs. Seavey . . ." Her voice softened.   " I think they were a nice couple, don't you ? So well-behaved."

He said, " That's Sherburne, I guess."

He pointed out the little town ahead, dry and dusty in the noonday. The roofs showed over a patch of trees into which the road was leading. Albany was quiet as they drove into the shade. Then she said, " No woman could have a better friend than you, Chad. I won't forget it."

He turned to look at her and found her leaning towards him, her grey eyes tender. With a quick gesture she raised her mouth to his.

Buck chose that moment to shy. The chaise wheel struck a log beside the ruts ; the dry felloe dished, and all the spokes fell out. It was as magical a coming-apart as any man ever saw. The chaise lurched on the splintering spokes. The top swayed slowly, wavered, and settled like a sighing cow. Buck pulled up short and stood there, surveying his accomplishment round his shoulder.

Albany gave a choked cry as Chad picked himself off her and hauled her from the wreckage.

" Are you hurt ? "

" Not bad." She gave a rueful laugh. " That seems to be the end of Mr. and Mrs. Seavey."

He looked at the wreckage. Even glue wouldn't help it much. " We've got to walk," he said.

They looked ridiculous coming down the street. Chad led the horse and carried the bag, and Albany walked abreast of them on the footpath. It meant they would have to wait in Sherburne for the circus to come up to them, and that meant getting credit somehow. Getting credit nowadays was worse than pulling teeth. Chad eyed the group of men on the tavern porch with genuine misgiving.

16

BISBEE

THEY were discussing a poster freshly tacked beside the bar-room door. It was a small sheet, but the print on it was imposing.

The WORLD'S
UNPARALLELED *&* ONLY
LIVING WONDER
Claude Cronk, the DOG-TOOTHED BOY
HE EATS RAW MEAT!

Huguenine's Great and Only International Circus will Exhibit the said *Lusus Naturæ*, at each and every performance, *inside the main tent*.

☞ Public Statement addressed to the populace of North America :—

To those who may esteem it a cruelty keep a Boy so closely *confined, as in a cage*, the Proprietors deem it their obligation to inform them, that it is done OUT OF CONSIDERATION OF THEMSELVES, and OTHER OWNERS OF POULTRY AND FOWL. *Cronk's* nature impels him to pursue the feathered Valuables, *once he gets loose*, with the undiscriminating perseverance, as well as with all the SAGACITY OF THE POINTING DOG, which his physiognomy so closely suggests to the AMAZED BEHOLDER.

A small man with a piercing voice broke the silence :

" If you ask me, it's a lie. I ain't going to see a lie nor pay no twenty-five cents for it, either."

Inside the bar-room a chair scraped slowly over the floor. Chad saw a tall hat emerging over the heads of the men.

" Friend," said a calm voice, " did I hear you say I was a liar ? "

The group split beautifully apart, leaving the small man

alone in front of Bisbee. Bisbee was holding a full glass in one hand. He extended it now to the small man. "Hold it while I roll my sleeves up. I ain't used to being called a liar," he observed, beginning to turn back the cuffs of his shirt. "*I* say Claude is the world's only and unparalleled living wonder. *I've* seen him. *You* say he isn't. *You* haven't seen him. You better drink my likker, mister. It'll help to deaden the pain."

The small man was completely buffaloed by having to hold the glass. He started to put it to his lips, then checked himself. Such publicity was something he hadn't counted on.

"Now, mister," he began, using his hands like a crawfish, "I ain't saying he ain't a living wonder."

"Ah?" Bisbee was all attention. "Then what's your objection?"

"I was only objecting to the 'only' part. Take Andrew Jackson. If he ain't a living wonder, who is?"

"How about Nicholas Biddle?" someone said.

Bisbee lifted his eyes.

"Nicholas Biddle," he said. "If I had him in a cage wagon I would make my fortune. Sir, your point is well taken. Claude Cronk is really an *unparalleled* living wonder. *Only* may put it just a mite too strong." He put his sleeves back into place and reached for his glass. "I'm obliged to you for holding my likker, sir. But see Claude for yourself. If you're not satisfied, ask for your money back." His eye had caught sight of Chad and Albany and the horse, and the lid quivered. "I see some old friends of mine. Excuse me, gentlemen."

He shoved his way to the street with long strides and took his hat off to Albany. "You here! And Buck and Chad!" His intelligent eyes went over them, taking in her broken arm, and the harness on the horse. "You're coming back to us?" he asked Albany.

"If Huguenine's will take me back."

"Take you back! My dear, there isn't a soul that wouldn't kiss your feet, if you asked them, in all *Huguenine's immense establishment*." He raised his voice for the benefit of the men on the porch. "Come inside, my dear. Come in. I'll give you dinner. This calls for a celebration. They've got a private parlour in this house and we'll have dinner in it. Chad, you come upstairs as soon as you've put up Bucephalus. I'll take the bag."

He bowed as he ushered her through the office door. Fifteen

minutes later, Chad was shown upstairs to the tavern's private parlour. The room was so small that if a fire had been lit in the Franklin stove, the skirt of Bisbee's coat would certainly have been ignited. He sat at the end of the table, Albany on his right, and an empty place was waiting for Chad. Both of them smiled as he came in, and Bisbee said, " Sit down, sit down. Albany's been telling me the whole story. The complete, infamous and dirty deal." His long face sobered. " Burke's a tiger : we have to remember that. But I don't believe he'll bother us now till we strike the Hudson Valley. I've ordered a bottle of champagne wine. Here it is. Waiter, fill the glasses. Maybe Lady Lillian will save Huguenine and Bisbee's neck. I hope so. God bless you and knit your arm like sixty, my dear. Stand up, Chad." He raised his glass.

Albany sat beaming at them both.

As soon as they had drunk, she rose and raised her own glass.

" I want to drink to you. To both of you, and Huguenine's, and to everybody in the world that comes to see it. I'm so happy."

Chad turned his eyes from her face to Bisbee's.

" You just said Huguenine and Bisbee's neck," he said. " Does that mean . . ."

A shade of embarrassment crossed Bisbee's face.

" I'm afraid it does," he admitted. " I hadn't intended to do it, but since you left, the show went right downhill. I don't understand it. Claude doesn't draw the way I hoped. I thought it was only a temporary condition, and it seemed like a good moment in which to gain a half-share at a price I could manage." His grin was wry. " I seem to be destined to buy into folding concerns, Chad. But by God, now I'm in it, I'll run it till it falls apart. And right now I'm appointing you equestrian director."

Albany exclaimed, " That's fine ! Chad's told me all he did. You watch what he'll do now, Mr. Bisbee."

" I hope so," Bisbee said. " Huguenine's all crippled up again and he'll be willing to take you back. He thinks I'm ruining the show by buying all this new paper, but you've got to advertise. Maybe we can pull her through. Lady Lillian ought to help, as I said." He smiled at Albany again. " I don't mind saying I was feeling discouraged till you showed up. It's given me hope, though. This morning in this hotel bar, I happened to pick up a last month's copy of the *Ulster Republican*. I didn't put much stock in the notice I saw then, but now you've made me think my luck has changed."

" What is it ? " Albany asked.

" I'll raise no hopes but my own," said Bisbee, shaking his head. But Chad saw the old light shining in his eyes.

" Is it a lion ? " he asked. " Or a tiger ? "

Bisbee shook his head once more.

" I won't tell you. You can't wheedle me. But you can look at the notice if you want to."

His smile at their bent heads was almost benign. Albany read slowly, " Deceased last Wednesday, at his home between this town and Woodstock, Albert Hanson, at eight o'clock in the morning, suddenly, of a flux, in the seventy-first year of his age. He is survived by his bereaved widow, Mrs. Susan Lent Hanson, who submits the above notice . . ." She looked up. " What does it mean, Mr. Bisbee ? "

" Exactly what it says, I suppose. I'll say, though, that Hanson was once a sailing master. He was a cantankerous man and sometimes quarrelled with his wife's relations."

Bisbee took the paper back, folded it, and stuck it in his poster case.

" It's just a chance, but every chance is worth taking. I've got a notion that my luck has turned, and I remember telling you, Chad, that if B. D. Bisbee went ahead, he wanted to take you with him. You won't get any extra pay now. But there's new country next year for a little show if we can keep alive that long, and when times get bad, that's the time B. D. Bisbee wants to expand. Now, I'm going to post this Cronk paper as far as Athens. That's where I'll meet the show. I've got some of the old Lillian posters and I'll put them up here and there. It will take care of Albany and Buck. The rest is up to you."

" We'll come along," Chad said. " Where's the show now ? "

" In Virgil. Day after to-morrow it should be in Homer. You better meet it there. I saw you had a harness on Buck. Have you got a rig ? "

" We did have," Chad said, and Albany laughed.

Listening to their explanation, Bisbee sighed. " I'll have to give you mine and fork my own animal again. But have them drag that rig behind the cage wagon. It's too good to lose. Need any money ? " His face saddened. " Well, everybody

does." He gave them two dollars, and after lunch Chad hitched
Buck to the yellow-wheeled rig, and he and Albany started east
along the Smyrna road. Bisbee, astride his white-nosed horse,
waved his hat in farewell.

17

THE PITCH IN HOMER

It was a windless afternoon when they drove into Homer, and
as they neared the lot they could hear the playing of the band.
The music didn't sound like Burke and Walsh's, but to Chad and
Albany it had a friendly ring. Nobody but Joe Duddy could
thump a drum like that, and to hear the fife was as good as seeing
Budlong's face with walnut cheeks of wind.

"It's circus weather," Albany said. "There's the round-top.
I wonder if it's full."

The grass in the lot didn't look to Chad as if there were a
full tent. It had none of the threadbare juiceless look one liked
to see. The round-top sitting on it was the only worn thing in
sight. And he had not noticed many rigs.

"I don't care," Albany said. "It's just like coming home. I
was a fool to quit. Look at Buck. He knows it's Huguenine's."

He had pricked his ears at the tent-wagon team. Now he
whinnied. They answered, and then from the tent came another
answering neigh. A loud "Hurrah!" was followed by a small
burst of applause. Then with a cry of "America for ever!"
the cream and Jerry burst out of the main entrance at full gallop
with Ike in striped tights on their backs waving an American
flag and cursing wildly as he hauled the reins with his free hand.

"Whoa, whoa," he roared. "God damn you, whoa."

They stopped short in front of Buck and dumped him neatly
between them. He lit with an arm over each neck and stared
unbelievingly at Buck. Then he saw Albany and said, "My
God."

"Hallo, Mr. Wayfish. How are you?" she said, smiling at
his red-nosed wondering face.

"Fine," he said, as intelligence slowly dawned. "Have you
come back?"

"Yes, I have, and I'm glad to be here."

"You brought her?" he asked Chad.

Chad grinned.

"I better get Buck out of the way of the crowd," he said.

"Yes, said Ike. "They're likely to come out stampeding after me. All four dozen of them. It's the first time we tried this act and they're just about wild. I noticed a woman crying." He let go of the horses and led them to the hurdle, Chad driving Buck behind them.

The band was issuing from the performers' entrance. Fiero, who was following them disconsolately, uttered an ecstatic cry, caught Albany's hand in both of his, and kissed it. Then he rushed into the tent yelling to Huguenine that Signorina Yates had returned.

Looking up from hitching Buck to the hurdle, Chad saw Caroline. "Hallo," she said, and he said, "Hallo, Caroline."

Every one else was crowding Albany into the emptying tent to see Mr. Huguenine.

Chad picked up Caroline's cloak and handed it to her and she put it on, watching him all the time.

"Did you want to come back?" she asked him.

"I didn't know till a week ago," he told her. "Ever since it's seemed a long time getting here."

"Really, Chad?"

"Yes, really."

She fastened the cloak in front and looked into the tent.

"Is *she* coming back, to stay?"

"Yes. Do you mind?"

"No." She looked into his eyes again, and he saw a kind of shyness in hers. It made him feel shy himself.

"We talked to Bisbee in Sherburne," he said. "He wanted Albany back, and he told me I could have my job back again." He felt cautious as a cat on quicksand.

"That's fine, Chad. The show's been bad."

"I've been thinking up a new entrance for your act. It's a real build-up." He glanced sidewise at her. He didn't want to tell her the idea had occurred to him before he had quit Huguenine's. "Ike's in it, too."

He was rewarded by the deepening corner of her mouth. Her eyes were still on his face. And suddenly she seemed to break all over and had her arms around his neck.

" Oh, Chad, it's good to have you come back. It's seemed so long. So awfully long."

The tears were running down her cheeks ; he could feel them on his own as she kissed him. Then she let go as an apologetic thump of the drum warned them that Joe Duddy wanted to come out. Caroline gave a little laugh, putting her arm through his, and turned him to confront the rest. He said quickly, " Will you ride over to Truxton with me ? "

" Yes," she said. " Here's the Huguenines."

Mrs. Huguenine enfolded him, arms, bosom, and rose perfume.

" I never been so glad in my whole life," she said; but Huguenine looked glum. He stumped painfully in her wake, his solid face puckered.

" Hallo," he said. " Will you come over to the wagon with me ? "

Mrs. Huguenine patted his shoulder.

" Now, don't take on, A.D. Everything's turned out so lovely."

" She's got no ideas of anything," Huguenine complained to Chad. He sat down on the treasury-wagon steps. " She thinks money blooms like daisies. Albany said you'd seen Bisbee in Sherburne."

Chad said yes, they had.

" Well, maybe I was hasty before," Huguenine said heavily. " This show ain't done no better. Bisbee's got that crazy boy, paid money for him, but it doesn't do no good. Nothing Bisbee does, does good, but I can't tell him. You see how it is with me, I'm all crippled up again. Bettina wanted me to take a bath in Union, and this is what it done." He paused, staring at his beefy hands. " What I mean to say is, I'd be glad to have you come back. Bisbee thought it would be a good idea if you showed up. He owns half this circus now, so I got to consider him."

Chad said, " I'll take the job back."

" I can't give you no extra pay. But I can give you part of seven dollars, maybe."

" That's all right."

" You'll take the job back ? "

" Yes."

Mr. Huguenine breathed noisily for a minute.

" I hope there ain't no bad feelings," he said finally.

" Not with me."

" Oh, isn't that just lovely, though." Mrs. Huguenine had padded up to them. " Now, A.D. can get some rest. Poor man, he's been so miserable, Chad." She beamed as Mr. Huguenine glumly stared at Chad.

It was almost like old times. The tear-down went rapidly, the skinners piling extra loads on Chad whenever there was a chance. " He wants to make up for lost time," Joe said. " We ought to help him out."

Bastock had to have the details of stealing Buck from Burke and Walsh, and Chad gave it to him in pieces. The little man was delighted, but Budlong was serious.

" That Burke won't quit looking for him. He's a stubborn cuss." He dropped his chew on the grass and wiped his mouth with a free hand. " So's Huguenine. Look how he got crippled again. I heard of a stubborn cuss like him once, but he got a bone eating shad. He started to choke but he said he wouldn't let no shad down him. He got his throat so full of bones that the doctor had to go right in after them."

" I suppose he died."

" Yes, he did. He died of blood poison," said Budlong.

Joe Duddy hooted.

" He'd have strangled first, you dumbhead. Don't you know it takes time to die of blood poison ? First your foot swells up, and then your legs get hard and you get red lines on your belly . . ."

" Who said anything about a foot ? " Budlong demanded. " The doc got stuck in the thumb by a shad bone while he was trying to get it out of the stubbron fool's neck. That's the way it is with stubborn cusses. They don't pay attention."

They gave Chad their own idea of how the show had gone, and all of it was bad. It was a good thing he had come back, Bastock said ; he thought Caroline was ready to vault in public. She was riding better all the time.

" Have you had much bad weather ? "

" No, it wasn't the weather. It was just the show. Shows went bad, the way some things mildewed, and some rotted. That Cronk hadn't done them any good. He was just a trouble to everybody.

Joe Duddy said, " Aw, Pete. He ain't so bad."

Joe, it appeared, had been able to teach Claude more than any one else in the show.

"It ain't because Joe's so smart," Budlong said. "It's just because they think so much alike. You ought to see him listen while Joe tells him pigeon stories, shaping his mouth and slapping his knee, just like two frogs on a mudbank."

There was a good spiel for him though. He was announced as the wild boy. "While he is becoming accustomed to the more civilised bedding of wheat straw, he prefers to make himself a nest in grass, ferns, or any of the wilder herbs." It had taken a week to teach Claude to climb up on the shelf they had fixed for his bed in the cage wagon. But he had finally learned to do it and worm round and round like a dog before lying down. During the performance, also, he wore a sort of sack of deer-skin, dressed with the hair on, and it was Joe's final duty in the tear-down to make sure Claude was dressed in his own clothes. "It's in the contract we treat him like a civilised human," he said. "I got to do it."

They lined the wagons up to start. There were low clouds in the west and Huguenine thought they looked like rain.

Budlong shook his head.

"We won't have no bad weather till we start getting near the mountains. The rain's sure to hit us then." He had never known it to fail for the roads to go bad when a circus was mixed up with mountains.

Chad had the cream saddled for Caroline. He now brought Buck up close on the lead beside the grey. The light rig was hauling away from the hotel, Ike as usual driving, with Fiero beside him, the Pamplons in the middle. On the rear seat Albany was sitting beside Shepley.

Caroline waited for Chad on the porch. He gave her a leg-up, and they rode off behind the wagon. Behind them the caravan rolled slowly out of the lot.

Caroline nodded ahead.

"They've taken up about where they left off," she said, and turned to look at Chad. When she smiled he thought that none of all the equestriennes in Burke and Walsh could touch her.

"Do you want me to tell you about her and Buck?" he asked.

"Do you want to tell me, Chad?"

He thought a moment before he said he did, and then told her the whole business.

After a time, she said, " I should think you'd have fallen in love with her."

" I started to think so," he admitted. " Only it worked out the other way."

He was thinking of·Elias's proposition, and he kept studying her. But if she had a secret to confide in him, she gave no indication of it.

He started telling her his plans for her entrance, growing so absorbed in them that he did not notice the preoccupation on her face. " We ought to practise to-morrow, even if it is Sunday."

She said, " Yes. Do you think the show can keep running, Chad ? "

" I guess so. Do the others think it won't ? "

" Mrs. Pamplon says her husband talks of quitting when we reach the Hudson River. He plans to take a steamboat to New York."

" Bisbee's going to meet us there, in Athens," he said. " He's got some new kind of idea."

Book VI

THE BAND BEGINS TO PLAY

THE MAN IN THE MOON

It took five days before the show began to shape up to where Chad had left it. He called the entire company to practise every morning, seeking ways in which to dress up Fiero's act and brighten up the Pamplons'. He split Shepley's appearances, making a finished act of Caroline's riding ; her new entrance, as he had planned it that dismal morning in Milo Centre, through her solo riding, to the double act with Shepley.

Albany followed her with Buck. She carried her crop jauntily in her slung hand ; one hardly noticed she had been hurt. Then Shepley had his final solo act and did his somersault ; and Ike completed the programme Roman riding from the tent.

Claude's appearance was the main problem, and he made up his mind to try it between different acts on different days, combining the exhibition with some pantomime from Ike and the trick mule who drew the cage wagon into the tent and round the ring.

Huguenine kept out of things for the most part, and the only suggestion he made was to express a suspicion that Joe Duddy allowed the half-witted boy to ride on the seat with him during the night hauls. Chad promised to keep his eye on Claude.

By the time the circus pulled into Sherburne, he felt that they had a real performance to offer ; the company were trying hard ; their spirits had improved. With Albany back, some of the easy-going atmosphere that had existed when he first joined out returned. Fiero, for instance, had found a new sympathiser for his knife-throwing problems, and Mrs. Pamplon found a fresh interest in trying to follow what she had come to call " that affair."

Shepley and Albany were right back in the thick of it. They had their first quarrel Monday morning in Truxton, and their first making-up next day in DeRuyter, and that night Mrs. Pamplon listened at Albany's door for fifteen minutes and said she was sure Shepley was inside the room. She forgot all about her beautiful France in condemning such abominable conduct.

It made no difference to Chad except for the havoc it played with Shepley's riding.

"Why don't you marry her?" he said after the performance. "She'll never settle down till you do."

"She'd never settle down if I did, either," Shepley said with a wry smile. "I guess she's made that way, and I am too, and we'll always chase each other, one way or the other. The show's all right, isn't it?"

"When you ride decent, it is."

At night, however, when he got the day's count from Huguenine, his satisfaction evaporated. They were doing better, but not enough to cover salaries. He couldn't make it out. Putting big signs on the cage wagon to advertise Cronk was something to try, but it made little difference in the ticket sale. Huguenine said gloomily, "I'd have done better just to pocket my loss when I bought that mortgage."

"We've got to hang on till we get to Athens," Chad said. "I promised Bisbee we'd do that."

"The show's getting better." It was a handsome admission for Huguenine to make. "But it don't make no difference. What can Bisbee do? I'll have to pay off part way and then I'll have to take out a mortgage on my own farm. I never owned a cow that wasn't clear in all my life. What do people want?"

There seemed to be no answer.

Chad went back to the cage wagon and watched Joe Duddy overseeing Claude's dressing.

"Don't let him ride outside," he told Joe.

"Me! I wouldn't do a thing like that. I know when I got orders." Joe's face was printed all over with virtue.

Chad swung up on Jerry and took the double lead. Caroline had refused to ride down to Norwich with him. She hadn't been looking well, the last two days; he wondered whether she had picked up Fiero's autumn cold. It was comical to see the Dago practise knife-throwing, getting his arm way back, poised for his cast, and then sneezing like a blast of powder. It was a wonder he hadn't killed someone, the way the knife flew wild.

Chad had tried to persuade Caroline. He had pointed out how nice the ride would be along the Chenango River. But she said, "I feel tired. Besides, it gets dark so early now." He wondered if she were angry because he had suggested that she and Albany share a room. He could sleep out with the skinners.

It would save the show seventy-five cents a day. Albany, he told her, was perfectly willing, but he knew Caroline didn't like the idea, and neither did he.

He felt tired, starting out, and to keep himself awake he repeated some of the new patter he and Ike were working up for Claude's exhibition. Some of it was sad . . .

"Didn't he have a Ma?" asked Chad, and Ike would say, solemnly, "Not to call her mother."

Caroline was right about the early dark. Before Chad had covered half the distance, the sun went down. Only a faint leaf-patterned gleam showed where the water was. The bed of the nearly completed Chenango Canal was a trench of shadows. It seemed extraordinary for boats to cross the hills from the Mohawk Valley and come down again to the bed of this south-flowing stream.

The three horses went briskly. The air had sharpened; a mist hung along the riverside fields. At times Chad rode with only his head above it, and the dark shapes of the trees seemed to stand in a white floodwater, and he smelled the hay breaths of the horses.

It magnified the solitude; he had left the wagons far behind. Looking back, he saw nothing that moved except the moonlight spreading silver on the mist. It was a white moon for August, it felt close to frost. And he thought it would be pleasant to reach the hotel and find Caroline in a warm room waiting for him.

The moon was clear of the hills when he rode into Norwich. He was surprised by the size of the town. The houses stood close, sharply echoing the beat of the horses' hoofs. But the street was deserted except for a dog who turned his head without bothering to lower his leg and then lurched off behind a barn wall.

After two more crossings, however, Chad met an old man. The old man had a basket on his arm, and through the covering stuck the white head of a goose. The goose hissed as Chad stopped to ask for the hotel and the old man stroked the curved neck absently while he gave directions.

Caroline's window faced the east. She was sitting by it, in the darkness, watching the moon, and humming a nursery rhyme.

> The man in the moon
> Came down too soon,
>   To ask the way to Norwich . . .

Chad said, " I learned that in the orphanage. I had to get up and say it when the ladies' society made its inspection visit."

She turned quickly.

" Oh," she said. " I was wondering if you had seen him."

Chad grinned.

" I saw an old man, but he had found his way to town. He told me where you were. He had a basket."

Her voice quickened.

" Did he, though ? "

" You ought to have seen him. I wish you'd been along, Caroline."

" I wonder what his business was ? " she asked. " Didn't he say ? "

" No, he only told me where the hotel was."

" But he knew ! " she exclaimed. " It makes it seem nice, Chad."

" What does ? "

" The man in the moon, coming too soon. I wonder if I ought to keep on riding."

Chad stared at the shape of her head. Then he felt on the bureau for a candle, lit it, and, as the light grew, looked at her face. Her smile puzzled him.

" Keep on riding ? What are you talking about ? " He felt stupid. " You want to quit ? " he asked incredulously.

She shook her head.

" We'll have to last the season out with the show, because we'll need the money. Next spring, anyway. I'm going to have a baby, I think."

" Think ? " he exclaimed. " Don't you know ? "

" I'm pretty sure. I've been thinking so for a week."

Chad sat down. He knew Caroline was looking at him and he realised that she was scared and upset. But he couldn't think of anything to say. All the way down from Sherburne he had been feeling fine and foot-loose ; and in that time he had been making out to be a father.

" What do you think ? " Caroline asked.

" Think ? About what ? "

" About my riding." She sounded cross.

" I don't know," he said. I don't know anything about it."

She was making her voice sound rational, but it was a little strained. It seemed to him that her eyes had grown larger.

"Of course, it's not very far along." She smiled again, rather apologetically. "You know I'm not very old, Chad. I'm not really quite eighteen and I don't know much, about . . ."

"Why don't you ask some woman? Mrs. Huguenine."

"She's never had a baby. She wouldn't know." Caroline wasn't exactly scornful, but it seemed to Chad that she was putting Mrs. Huguenine on one side of the barn, so to speak, the way one sorted out a dry cow. Cows were snotty creatures anyway. He jerked himself in his chair, bringing his mind back to the subject.

"You ought to ask someone, I guess."

Caroline said, "Mrs. Pamplon told me once she'd had a baby. Maybe I'd better ask her."

"We ought to find out before to-morrow."

"To-morrow?"

"Yes." He felt irritable. He had the feeling that he was tired and that Caroline was shoving off women's business on him. "If you ought not to ride, you ought to quit right now. Though I don't see what harm it could do, unless you fell." He looked at her. "You feel all right?"

"I've felt mean in the mornings, but I feel all right by show time. I feel kind of dizzy in practice. Do you think I ought to ask Mrs. Pamplon?"

"Well, there doesn't seem to be anybody else. Where is she?"

"Just down the hall."

"Well, go ahead. You won't learn anything by sitting here."

"Chad." She looked at him, biting her lip. Her eyelids puffed as if she were going to cry, but she did not. She got up without speaking, crossed the room, and closed the hall door behind her. He was alone. He felt that he had acted like a fool. Probably she was feeling more scared than she let on. He got up abruptly to join her in the Pamplon's room; but Caroline and Mrs. Pamplon were hurrying towards him down the hall.

Mrs. Pamplon was holding a wrapper tight round her. Her hair was in curlpapers, but her eyes were excited. She swept past Chad with an assurance of manner she had never shown before. And as soon as Caroline was inside and Chad had closed the door, she said, "Congratulations, Monsieur Hanna. I am so glad. My husband will be so glad too when I tell him. Oh, we tell no one else, but I tell my husband everything."

C.H.

Q 2

" Chad ! Mrs. Pamplon thinks it's all right for me to keep on riding."

In her relief, Caroline looked like a changed girl.

" You're sure it's all right ? " Chad asked the Frenchwoman.

" But, of course. She must be a little careful," Mrs. Pamplon said. " But she is healthy. When the baby gets heavy, it is another thing. But by then the circus it will have stopped. Madame Lautrec rode every time with all seven of her children and she was very famous. Having babies is not so much. Pretty soon it is all over, and, see there, it is only an infant after all."

Her thin face had lost its frightened, tired expression. It was only a little sad.

" My own babies they have grown up. I do not know where they are. But you will have a baby now for eleven, twelve, fifteen years."

She kissed Caroline and did a jerky sort of curtsey to Chad that fluttered her curlpapers. When she had gone, Caroline said, " She's a funny person. But she was so nice. She said she had been sure I was having a baby, and she was awfully pleased because I'd told her. She knew I was going to have one by my eyes. I don't know how. Can you see anything in them ? "

She came close to him, looking into his.

Chad tried to smile ; but he was thinking that Elias was right. The old man had an instinct for such things even for people in a magazine. It was different for the Lovells, though ; Wilbur Lovell could always make a hundred dollars in the next instalment, while in real life all the Hannas had to bank on was B. D. Bisbee's last idea.

" What are you thinking about, Chad ? You look so solemn."

He looked at her ruefully. " I was thinking that having long legs didn't make much difference after all."

2

RAIN

FROM Norwich, Huguenine's Circus worked south to Bing-hamton ; then it began a long eastward haul for the Catskills and the Hudson River through Delaware and Greene counties, and there were a few miraculous days when everything seemed to blossom for them. For no reason that Chad could discover, they drew good tents from Coventry to Unadilla. Though the grain crops were in, the weather fine, and the roads good, he couldn't explain the increase in business. But the troupe and Huguenine asked for no explanation. Their spirits rose miraculously. The performances went off with a shine you could see reflected on the faces of the audience. Caroline rode like a bird ; Albany and Shepley fell hard in love, behaved scandalously, and outdid themselves in the ring ; Fiero discovered that Claude Cronk, the dog-toothed boy, was just the height to be safe for his knives and painted a new, fresh-coloured silhouette on his board. Huguenine decided that half salaries could be paid in Unadilla, and then the seat-wagon team both fell ill at once.

Bastock diagnosed it as a running kind of colic, but Budlong said it was horse cholera. There was no cure for it, he claimed. All through the good week he had been smelling bad weather, so at first his opinion was discounted. Then the off horse died and Huguenine had to use most of his profits to buy a new team. The dealers skied their prices for the circus ; and the team they finally bought was second-rate. The performers all had to take a dollar on account. Chad thought he saw their bad luck closing down, and in Franklin it began to rain. That was September fifth, and before night every one felt sure that what Budlong had said about mountains, circuses, and rain was going to prove correct.

Chad went to the post office that afternoon to ask if there were any letter for A. D. Huguenine or Chad Hanna. He thought that Bisbee might possibly have some good news to send. But there was no word.

It was still raining next day in Meredith and the canvas,

which had gone up like lead, came down like a wet and dirty mop. They had to use all performers to help get it loaded. Chad asked at the Meredith post office without success. Next day in Delhi, Huguenine's was lucky enough to have one clear day and a three-quarters crowd, but to make up for it, Fiero's juggling went way off, and Caroline came down with morning sickness for the first time. She had to give up practice, and she looked washed out by show time, and scarcely got through her act. The Italian was upset by a return of his cold and Chad's refusal to let him try Claude Cronk as his target. He made a speech about it !

" You want for me to go all over the American States throwing my knives behind the barns ? Hey ? I will not do it ! I must have the living model or I must stop throwing knives, absolutely, without doubt. I lose my art ? Who cares ? The Great Mr. Huguenine's Great and Only Circus boss ? Even Rome she toppled down upon the tops of such blocked heads ! "

Chad didn't bother over what Fiero thought. It was a relief not to have to hear the *tunk-tunk* of the knives and shrill suggestive " Perfectoes ! " Getting the show moved and the canvas up was all that mattered to Chad now.

. During the eighth and ninth a north-west wind blew stinging showers across the hills, and the wind added to their difficulties with the canvas. After the show in Prattsville, Chad saw Caroline into the light rig, wrapping her in two blankets and an oilcloth he had bought to keep her warm. She had developed a hopeless, sullen streak ; she didn't want anybody's help ; she liked to consider herself independent. Mrs. Pamplon kept saying it was natural and drove her mad with prescriptions of warm milk, or camomile, or essence of rhubarb. It was a relief to get her off. Even in the light rig it would be ten o'clock before she reached Cairo, and the rest of the show would be lucky to make the town by daylight.

It was six o'clock anyway when the tent wagon sucked out of the lot and lurched sidewise into the turnpike ruts. Huguenine bawled to Chad, " Keep with the wagons. We may need help." He eyed the sky. " The wind's dying out, though. Maybe it will clear."

He was right about the wind. It stopped blowing entirely about six-fifteen and shortly after the sun dropped out of the clouds at the horizon and seemed to pause there in a colourless, watery strip of clear sky. Its light stretched along the rolling country to the mountains and the red-brown, mushy trough of the road leading to their feet. Directly overhead a cold, slate-coloured blanket of clouds hung motionless.

The tent-wagon wheels lifted two crusts of muck and the hoofs of the four-horse hitch sank fetlock deep and sucked out, balling mud. Glancing up at Budlong's lean face, Chad was reminded of what the skinner had told him in his first days after joining out. "You ain't seen any circusing till you've handled the rag in a rainstorm."

Well, he had been seeing circusing this past week. He was seeing more of it now. Already the sweat from tearing down the round-top had turned clammy on his back. He looked at the hammering heads of the treasury wagon team, and Huguenine driving them, his big wrists resting on his knees.

Back of the treasury wagon Bastock came with the seat wagon. He was bundled up in a thick red shirt with a sheepskin waistcoat over it. The cage wagon brought up the rear.

Joe Duddy leaned his shoulders against the box, as if he were talking to Claude Cronk. Chad thought, "He'll probably get him out as soon as it's dark," and he made up his mind to catch Joe at it to-night.

Just before dark the wind suddenly began to blow again, this time from the south-east. Their last glimpse of the mountains showed the crests capped in storm, and a quarter of an hour later the rain hit them. Though the first driving drops felt almost warm, there was no way they could protect themselves against it. A teamster on that road had to see where he was going. Half the time Budlong was forced to stand on his high perch to follow the feeble glimmer of his lanterns that reached only a few feet beyond the leaders' heads.

At ten o'clock a single lighted window told them that they had pulled into Windham Centre, and luckily the light belonged to the tavern. They left the wagons in the road, not daring to risk what might be even softer ground, and had quick glasses of hot rum ; Chad, Budlong, Bastock, and both Huguenines, for Mrs. Huguenine declared she hadn't dared undress. "Suppose a bridge falls through," she said. "I don't want to drown barelegged."

The tavern keeper and a couple of workmen who smelled of tan-yards eyed her without favour ; in fact the way the tavern

keeper turned to address Budlong was almost ostentatiously un-
pleasant.

"Where you hauling to ? " he asked, as if afraid they might
say Windham Centre.

"Cairo."

"What you got ? "

"Huguenine's Great and Only International Circus, you
peaked little whip-snap," said Mrs. Huguenine. "This-here is
A. D. Huguenine himself. Now what do you think ? "

"I think you're crazy in the head." Serving liquor to
females must have been contrary to his principles, and Mrs.
Huguenine had swallowed hers just like a man.

Budlong, however, wasn't interested in any one's reactions.
He wanted to know how the bridges were.

"The bridges are all right if you hit them," the tavern
keeper said.

"I'll hit the bridges," Budlong said. "How far is it through
the mountains ? "

"Better than seven miles to Acra," replied the tavern keeper.
"*I* wouldn't bury my mother-in-law in Acra to-night."

Huguenine kept peering through the sluiced window panes.
"No sight of Joe anywhere," he reported.

"Where's anywhere ? " demanded the tavern keeper.

Bastock banged his glass on the bar. "Come out and I'll show
you, mister. We can't let the stock cool out, A.D. Joe'll get
there all right."

Budlong agreed.

"Joe can always get from one bar to the next."

"I hate to think of him breaking down to-night, though,
with that Cronk and all. That boy ain't too healthy."

"Don't you mind about Cronk, A.D.," said Mrs. Huguenine.
"All he has to do is lay in bed."

Huguenine agreed reluctantly. They couldn't wait and it
was asking too much to make a team backtrack with one of the
wagons. Besides, when two wagons met, it might be impossible
to turn the searching wagon round again. The ruts were deep.

Chad saw it coming, like other thoughts that Mr. Huguenine
had had. He cursed under his breath. "All right," he said. "I'll
go back for Joe."

He waited to see the big wagon start. It made such slow
progress that it was five minutes before Bastock's lantern faded

out. The ring horses stood in the window light, their tails turned to the wind. Chad stabled Buck and the cream pad in the tavern barn, mounted Jerry, and headed him back. The horse didn't like it, and Chad had to use the whip to get him moving. Even so, for half a mile he kept turning his head and whinnying. That was the only sound except the rain.

Without wagon lights, Chad had to ride blind, letting the horse pick the track at his own gait, a dismal, plodding walk. Once they crossed a roaring brook, but he could not see it. Most of the time he spent inventing curses for Joe Duddy. But when, unexpectedly, the wagon lantern showed up through the drenched branches round a curve, he forgot to swear. When the grey whinnied, instead of an answering whinny from the cage-wagon tea, a high-pitched jibbering sound broke out, reminding Chad of the hyenas in Albion.

He realised suddenly that, in spite of the mud, the horses were coming at a fast pace. Yanking his own horse off the shoulder of the road, he had no time to wonder whether Joe had lost his mind. The lantern light swung towards him ; he saw the wild eyes of the frantic team and heard their heavy blowing. The scrawny little beasts were bucking their collars as if the devil held the reins and they had lightning in their bits.

Jerry floundered into the ditch. Chad had a glimpse of the man jumping excitedly on the box, slashing away at the team, and taking a sudden wild lunging cut at the grey as he swung by around the corner. He was jumping up and down on the footboard and yelling like a crazy man.

When Chad managed to get Jerry pulled up and turned to look after the wagon, he felt a kind of jolt inside. The driver was peering back round the corner of the box. The lantern shone on his head, on his two strange teeth and the whitish hair plastered like a faded handkerchief on his uneven skull. His eyes were gleaming like a roadside animal's. Then abruptly, with a jolt of the wheels, he lurched out of sight and all Chad saw was the blocky box of the cage and the whip lashing to one side and the other. Claude Cronk was at the reins.

" Joe ! " shouted Chad. " Hey, Joe ! "

He heard an answering bellow from the cage.

" Help ! Help ! Help ! "

Even without the mud and darkness it would have been hard to make the big grey run. He had learned his gait and how to keep it. At the crack of Chad's whip, the horse arched his neck and broke into a methodical rocking canter. Chad swore. He didn't like to shake the ring horse up and run him wild. But he had to stop Cronk. Let alone foundering the little team, let alone smashing the cage wagon against a tree, or a bridge rail, or driving right into a creek and drowning Joe Duddy, Cronk was valuable stock and had to be saved for his own sake.

The team had to haul the wagon through the mud. Crazy with fear though they were, they could not make any better time than the grey horse cantering. Little by little Chad drew up behind the cage wagon. Inside, Joe Duddy started shouting, " Whoa ! Hold up ! So, boys. So ! "

Instantly Claude's face appeared over the top of the cage. He hammered on the roof with his whip butt, yelped at Chad, and then ducked out of sight and whipped the daylights out of the horses once more.

" Whoa ! " Joe went on roaring hoarsely. " Oh, my God. Whoa ! Whoa ! Whoa ! "

Chad had pulled up close to the rear. He shouted, " That don' do any good."

" I know. I been yelling at them crazy horses since an hour. I didn't know they was so tough. Help ! " The wagon had pitched into a sink pot. The front off-wheel bucked up with a screech of the reach, and a tremendous crash sounded inside the cage.

" You hurt, Joe ? "

" I'm durn near killed. For God's sake stop them horses. Who's that ? "

" Chad."

" Well, stop them ! " Joe raged. " My God, if I was outside I'd stop them ! "

Cronk was up on top hammering the roof again.

Joe yelled, " He does that every time I talk."

" He's crazy," Chad yelled, and choked as a wild dollop of mud broke on his front teeth. " He won't let me by."

Claude Cronk was sawing the team in front of Chad whenever the grey pulled past a rear wheel. Chad edged the ditch, but the ring horse kept his feet. Jerry was roused at last ; he was throwing his head and snorting. He was willing to go.

Chad started yelling, " Claude. Claude, boy. Good boy. Claude want a piece of candy ? I got candy in my pocket . . ."

The only reaction was a bellow from inside the wagon.

" I tried that on him. Get up and grab the headstalls, can't you ? "

" You shut up ! " shouted Chad.

" By God, I won't. I'm sick of being apple-smashed in here."

" Shut *up*," Chad bellowed. " You God-damned fool. You started this." He lost his temper entirely, cursing Joe from teeth to toenails. He had some canal language that kept up with Joe's, and it came up into his mouth like genius.

Joe yelled right back.

" I always thought you had a frog-spotted snooty mug," he bellowed. " By Jesus Christ, when I get out of here I'll pull your rump out through your teeth."

Chad glanced suddenly at the top of the cage. Absorbed, his arms spread out for balance, Claude Cronk was listening to every word. In his strange face there was a fascinated, approving gleam of near-intelligence. And as Chad caught his breath and Joe quieted after a thunderous bump, he spoke the only rational word any one had ever heard him make.

" Race me ? "

It was Chad's first chance. " All right, Claudie." He tried to make his voice sound as if it were just a game. It was hard with wet mud still between his teeth. " Let's go."

He gave Jerry a vicious cut, and charged up beside the wagon. The big grey went wild. His broad hoofs hammered along the harder shoulder of the road. He drew up abreast the eveners. Too late, Cronk saw what had happened and yanked the team against him. It brought their heads in reach of Chad. He grabbed the cheek strap of the nigh horse, hauled back on Jerry, and set his knees. The whip curled once around his shoulders.

Then, like running into a dead wall, the little team stopped, dropped their heads, and started shuddering. A silence of falling rain seemed to rush up the road behind them. Chad said, " Whoa," quietly, and he stopped too.

Joe bellowed, " Let me get my fingers on that God-damned idiot."

" Shut up," Chad said. " Now, Claude, you got to go back to bed. Make your bed, see ? " He gave the order they used in the show.

Cronk stared at him. His face had turned dull. There was just a hinted flicker of understanding. He showed his dogteeth for a moment. He looked pathetically earnest. He climbed off the seat. And suddenly he jumped into the woods.

" Cronk ! " Chad said sharply. " Come back here."

He heard the boy flounder through the brush, and felt this crazy night would never end.

" Can't you let me out now ? " Joe pleaded huskily.

Chad stood beside the cage wagon, listening for sounds from Cronk. They started again presently, a faint scuffling noise. Opening the cage-wagon door, he said to Joe in a low voice, " Come quiet. He's ducked into the brush. We've got to find him."

Joe obeyed with meekness. One leg of his pants was torn from hip to knee, and he had scraped his face.

" He's up in there," Chad said, taking the lantern off its hook. " You keep right and I'll go left and we'll try to corner him."

But they had no trouble at all. The dogtoothed boy was only trying to do what he was told. When they found him, a hundred feet away, he had gathered a little pile of sticks, wet ferns, and broken brakes and was solemnly turning round and round on them, making his bed. All Joe's rage evaporated at the pathetic, wet, cowed spectacle.

" It ain't his fault. He just don't know nothing," he said, picking him up in his arms. " Cripus, he's wet. I bet he'll take sick. I better dry him off."

As they sheltered inside the cage wagon, the boy whimpering softly like an outrun dog, Joe explained. " He kept on making them dumb noises at me all the time. I told him to be quiet, but it didn't do no good. So after a while I got down and opened the door to see what was the matter, and he jumped right out." Joe shook his head. " I don't know what gave him the idea. I'd never let him loose, you know," he said, popping his eyes in an attempt to appear honest. " But he wouldn't let me touch him. No, sir. I tried everything. He'd run off a little way and then he'd stop. Pretty soon I thought of teaching him to chew tobacco. That was a good idea. He wanted to see if it was candy. I chewed some and then I give him just a pinch. Then I put in a good load to my own mouth and I held him out some more. When I spit, he acted interested. So I backed off to the cage and he come after. Then I got into the cage and spit some more and he looked in, but all of a sudden he reached back and slammed the door and hooked it. Jeepers, he acted quick. I hollered, but he just went around and around the wagon. I heard him talking them funny noises and patting on the wagon with his hands. I tried to make him come in but he wouldn't. Honest to Christmas, I got scared. I didn't know what he'd do. And then he got up on the wagon seat after a while and I heard him making noises at the horses, and then he got the whip. I wasn't ready for that. I was up at the front and arguing with his dumb wits and the first jolt knocked me clean to the other end. My pants caught and look what it done to my face ! " Joe breathed hard. " If he wasn't so dumb I could have killed him twenty times."

There wasn't much Chad could say. What with fixing Cronk, locking him safely inside, and picking up the other horses, they never overhauled the wagons. It was nine o'clock in the morning when they finally pulled into Cairo.

3

ATHENS P.O.

THERE was a row that morning before practice. Huguenine was waiting under the bedraggled entrance of the tent and the first thing he wanted to know was where Bisbee's carriage was.

Neither Chad nor Joe had thought of it. Somewhere during Claude's wild drive it must have broken loose. It might be anywhere from fourteen to twenty miles behind them, perhaps careened into the ditch, perhaps wrapped around a tree ; worse yet, it might have stopped just standing in the road for the mail coach to pile into. Chad had to explain the business and Huguenine rose up like a bear at Joe.

Joe shouldered the harangue aside.

" All right, all right, you can fire me if you want to," he said. " But you've got to pay me first. I ain't quitting without that and you can't make me, neither, Mr. Huguenine."

He walked off to help lug in the seats, took one on his shoulder, and stood there with it, eyeing Huguenine ; then, passing him, he spat to the other side as if he wouldn't even soil the Duddy spit with impure contact.

Huguenine was helpless with fury. Mrs. Huguenine tried to get him into the treasury wagon to lie down ; she feared a burst blood vessel. Chad tried to soothe feelings all around, but gave it up as a bad job and went about mechanically lining up the troupe for practice.

Mr. Pamplon announced that he was going to quit in Athens and warned Huguenine to have his money ready. But Huguenine wouldn't even talk about money any more and the Pamplons refused to turn out. They would perform, they would not practise. Besides, Mrs. Pamplon felt a female obligation to attend Mrs. Hanna. It took all of Chad's persuasion to get the women out of Caroline's room. The tavern was a dingy place, close to a tannery, and the smell, after the long cold ride, had completely defeated Caroline. She lay in bed limp as facecloth in a washtub, grey to the very eyelids, but she tried to smile at Chad when he closed the door on the Frenchwoman's offended back.

" Do you think you can ride this afternoon ? " he asked her. All she could do was nod.

It was a terrible performance. Ike had caught a cold and his nose dripped with the clouds. Chad, while he and the clown hitched the mule to the cage wagon before the show, thought grimly that they were pretty close to the end. He would get the establishment to Athens, that was all.

But he didn't want to quit. They had made a good show. It needed just one thing to get it going again. Both he and Ike knew what it was, but there was no use mentioning it.

In the afternoon they pulled along to Catskill and made a pitch near the docks, where there was also a cheap hotel. Late in the evening Chad and Ike made the rounds of all twelve other hotels, searching for B. D. Bisbee's name. They found one house in which he had spent the night of the twenty-fifth of August and asked if there was any mail for Huguenine or Hanna. There wasn't.

" He said Athens," Ike reminded Chad.

Chad said, " I've got a mind to go over to-night and see."

But he didn't go to Athens. Huguenine had sent word to Caroline for Chad to come back to the lot. Claude Cronk was taken sick. In the first emergency, Budlong returned with a female nurse who said they should consult a doctor. The poor creature had pneumonia in at least one lung. There was nothing she could do except to charge fifty cents and offer Chad her card :—

MRS. OLIVIA DANGLE

MIDWIFERY PRACTISED

* * *

Mrs. Dangle offers herself to the public in the above profession, which she has practised for twenty years in a principal city of England. Her practice there is well known. Also a few Lucky Visits in this country.

" He's out of my line," she said to Chad. " I shouldn't ought to have been called."

A doctor came who told them the boy must be got into a house. He had pneumonia. He had never heard a more mortal bubble in a human chest.

The hotel proprietor refused to admit the freak. He said he had to consider his guests, so after carrying Claude back to the lot, Mr. and Mrs. Huguenine were forced to give up the treasury wagon and get a room for themselves, an additional expense which reduced Huguenine to utter silence.

Chad and Joe Duddy spent that night and all the next day watching the poor boy to make sure he was kept covered. He lay on his back in the bunk, making strange sounds, only opening his eyes to stare bemusedly at his watchers.

Ironically, that Sunday was a lovely day and so was Monday, when they showed, and a fair crowd turned out for the performance. Caroline struggled through her act successfully ; Albany made her usual dashing appearance on Buck ; and Shepley was working his solo act when the first calls began to rise for the dogtoothed boy.

At the start, Chad tried to pass them off, but the clamour grew so insistent that he was forced to halt Ike's hayseed ride to announce that owing to an unfortunate and desperate illness, the world's living wonder could not be exhibited that day.

It was the first time that Chad had seen an audience turn ugly, and this one contained an infusion of dock hands who looked as if they wanted trouble any time. After the all-out, they took their time in leaving the tent. The skinners, backed up by the male troupers carrying tent pegs, finally managed to work them out, but they kept hanging round the entrance, demanding their money back, and shouting that they had been cheated. Gradually the noise picked up a crew of idle men from uptown. Looking them over, Chad ordered all the female troupers to keep inside the tent ; it was all he could think of to do. Huguenine had locked himself into the treasury wagon with Cronk and the money and it was up to Chad to get the circus rolling.

In that situation, Joe Duddy proved himself pure gold. He spat on his hands and said, " Give me them seat boards." He loaded up enough on his thick shoulders to make two ordinary men stagger and bulled out of the tent into the waiting gang as if he didn't see them. " Come on," he hollered. " There's nothing out here except some lot fleas." The very motion of his buttocks was belligerent.

Chad told the troupers to finish tearing down the wire and ring properties and he and the other two skinners loaded up and went after Joe. They could look tough, particularly Budlong, but they didn't invite respect as Joe did. They were jostled by three or four, but Joe was back with a sledge handle. " Get out of my way, you crumbs," he grunted, and bulled back inside. It seemed miraculous that they had made the trip, but by the time they had got inside the tent again, the river hands were fortified with additional numbers. It would have been suicide to make another attempt to pass through them and the circus people and the town gang confronted each other at the entrance.

Any one could tell that a clem was building up, but for a few minutes more the thing hung fire. It lacked only a word, a gesture, to set it off, when the constabulary arrived. There were four of them, including the sheriff, looking as if they wished the whole shebang were in the river.

The sheriff sided with the river hands. All he wanted was to get the circus out of town. He routed Huguenine out of the treasury wagon and compelled him to refund thirty full admissions, though there had been less than fifteen river hands to begin with. The sheriff hung around during the tear-down and rode to the town limits with the show.

" Keep going," he said, " and don't come back. You're lucky you're not in jail, you and your whole dirty outfit."

Chad rode in the treasury wagon that afternoon. The boy's breathing had become more rapid and his skin was hot and dry to the touch. He lay there, staring at the ceiling, his squat body jolting, his white hair plastered to his forehead with sweat, and babbled half-articulate words. He seemed to think he was being punished for his misbehaviour two nights before and he kept saying he hadn't meant to be bad. " Claude's not bad boy," he kept saying. Then he would shake his head. When Chad touched him, he stiffened like a dog, holding himself still and making whimpering noises. Chad felt sure he was going to die and wondered how Huguenine and Bisbee would settle up with the Cronks. It didn't seem right to have taken a boy like that away from home in the first place ; but it was the kind of thing Bisbee was likely to do. Lord knew where he was now.

The wagons pulled in to Athens in the evening and the tent was raised just before dark and the treasury wagon drawn inside as an additional protection against the rising wind. The lot again was close to the river. When Chad came out of the tent to get some supper, he could see white teeth on the waves.

Mrs. Huguenine had volunteered to share the watch on Claude with Joe, so Chad was able to spend the night in Caroline's room. They ate supper gloomily. Ike had been to the post office only to find it closed for the night. The Pamplons, sitting in a corner, debated with Fiero whether they would quit entirely and pocket their loss of salary.

Caroline, in bed, watched Chad undress with anxious eyes.

" What will we do, if the show stops here ? We haven't much money, Chad."

He got their money out of their bag and counted it. Altogether they had less than twenty dollars.

" I shouldn't have bought so many clothes," she accused herself. " But I didn't know . . ."

" Neither did I ! " said Chad. " There's no use worrying now."

" Could you get work here ? "

He shook his head.

" There's loose men all around. We'd better get back to Canastota. There might be work on the railroad."

" I won't be any good at all. I just seem to be able to ride at show time." She stared at the dark window. She could hear the noise of the river against the dock pilings. " Chad, wasn't Mr. Bisbee going to join us here ? "

" He said he was going to try to," Chad said gloomily.

She sat up in bed, hugging her knees, and fetched a smile.

" My mother said that day you came to our house that if I sat on tables showing my legs to strange men that way, I was bound to get into trouble. Isn't that funny ? I bet she never expected it would be in a hotel in Athens, though. Are you scared, Chad ? "

" Scared ? No, I just don't know what to do next."

" Maybe there'll be a letter to-morrow."

It kept boiling down to Bisbee's last idea.

But at the post office next morning there wasn't a word. The postmaster turned out a bag of unclaimed letters and let Chad run through them for himself. " Help yourself," he said.

When Chad walked back along the river, he noticed that the wind was getting chancy. It came in gusts and the pattern of them could be traced across the greyish water by the lines of whitecaps. A dock hand informed him that it smelled like a blow coming.

4

BLOWDOWN

CHAD kept his eye on the round-top. There was more sway to the centre pole than he liked to see. He knew that Budlong had reset the pegs after practice, but the wind had been building up steadily since then. He would have liked to ask Huguenine whether he should stop the performance, but Huguenine had gone down to watch the presses bailing hay in the great barns by the river, and all Chad could think of was Budlong's fool remark. Budlong supposed that any man who had married a woman like Mrs. Huguenine would feel fascinated by a hay press. But to send the audience out would probably mean another refund, and they had a fair tentful in spite of the placard announcing Claude's withdrawal from exhibition. The show was half-way over, and the audience didn't seem to be aware of the way the wind had risen. They were absorbed in Carolina and Rossello.

Caroline wasn't going any too well ; she was pale and uncertain ; but there was no sense worrying about her. Shepley was aware of her condition and was taking pains. He dropped Chad a reassuring nod as he went round. Half her trouble to-day was probably the wind.

A queer thing about the wind was the way it worked inside the tent. The canvas seemed to leak air outwards until one could almost feel the weight of atmosphere on top of the round-top. Then with a report, a great gulp of rain-smelling windy air would suck under the side wall, pushing back the contours, to vanish slowly again, until Chad himself had a dizzy sense of walking in a vacuum.

It was natural for Caroline to feel it even more. She minded stuffiness of any kind, even heat. She wanted her windows wide open every night, no matter what the weather was, and sometimes when Chad came in fresh from grooming the ring stock, he could see the distaste in her eyes.

Mrs. Pamplon said it was to be expected. Five weeks, a month, three weeks even, and *pouf !* she would be eating like a lady wolf. She would feel magnificent. Her face it would become all pink and fat, all filled out with colour, so handsome, yes.

Now, as Fred Shepley nursed her through the act, her face was clay-white, but she included Chad in her acknowledgment of the applause. " Don't look so worried. I'm all right. I'll see you at the hotel."

The wind defeated her, however. A moment after she had left the tent, he saw her re-enter and take an empty seat on the back row.

Chad passed the word to Albany to cut her act and he himself eliminated her introduction. As she rode Buck through the entrance, the wind stiffened her veil and the horse's mane, like weather vanes. She immediately returned as Caroline had, taking the seat beside her. But Chad had Rossello on his hands now, and the show had only two more acts to go. Fifteen minutes after announcing the somersault, he would be able to give the crowd the all-out-and-over. But he wished that he could do it now. He kept one eye on Shepley and the other on the canvas, seeing Shepley make a perfect somersault and the weight of the wind bearing the round-top down. He could hear the wind pouring over the canvas ; rain was coming with it. The first drops struck like hail, showing black spots where the tent was mildewed ; and the ring began slowly to darken. A Hudson River squall, the dock hand had told Chad, sometimes blew hard enough to gut a sturgeon. The blow he had predicted was bound to bring squalls in it. Chad glanced at Budlong, who was weather-wise. The lean skinner's cheeks had apples of wind, as he blew, but his eyes travelled the centre pole from peak to foot and stayed there.

It was time for Ike's hayseed ride.

> And when she walks de streets around,
> De hollow of her foot makes a hole in de ground,
>   So clare de kitchen, young folks, old folks,
>   Clare de kitchen, young folks, old folks.
>   Old Virginny never tire !

Chad watched the foot of the pole while he bawled to Ike, " All right, if you think you can hang on ! " The foot of the centre pole was shifting, very slightly, not steadily, but now and then ; intermittently, as the peak bore off, the sod stirred, and the pole loosened. It did not seem at first glance to amount to much ; but when the strain slacked, the base of the pole did not return, either ; and watching it, Chad got the impression of something stealthily on the hunt, moving one foot at a time, making no noise, choosing its moments with untamed patience.

He cracked his whip twice as Ike came round. " Make it faster, hayseed. We haven't time to watch you all day long." He let the lash curl on the base of the pole and saw that Ike had caught his drift.

Ike's shedding of his clothes was almost fountain-like. He bawled for another horse. Shepley sent Jerry in out of what seemed uncannily a dim twilight. For an instant there had been a lull and the grey horse appeared to step right out of the grey sky. Then the wind came back, and estimating the minutes left, Chad listened to the sound of it. The air in the tent, thinning again, had grown colder, but in spite of that he felt sweat on his face. He heard Ike's voice dimly yelling, " Hurrah ! America forever ! " The clown was riding off. He hadn't made his three circles of the tent, he was giving up his applause entirely, and Chad thanked God the horses were out.

He didn't use the line about hoping you have enjoyed our show. The centre pole had renewed its shifting. He bawled the

" All-out-and-over ! " at the top of his lungs and started for the
seat on which the girls were sitting.

The voice of the wind attained a higher pitch, as though it
scraped the corners of the mountains. The inside of the tent
grew almost dark. The fife and bugle faded out, but Joe Duddy
in a kind of hypnotism continued thumping the drum, and
suddenly the audience became aware of the wind's force, and
started beating each other for the entrance.

Afterwards Chad wondered whether it would have been
wiser to keep the audience inside. For as they spread the entrance, the wind found the vent it had been working for and
the entire round-top seemed to umbrella outwards, the centre
pole slid from under, and the canvas cascaded down in thunder-
ing billows. Chad heard it flap the earth as he yanked Caroline
off the seat and threw both of them under the edge of the side
wall. They didn't make it. The canvas snuffed them to the
ground. He tried to shield her by lifting with his hands and knees,
but he felt as if a million pounds were on top of him, and he
gave up, lying flat beside her on the dank grass.

" All right ? " he asked.

" Yes," she gasped. " Where's Albany ? "

He yelled and heard Albany's half-strangled voice. " I'm
all right."

" Then lie still."

There was nothing else to do until someone could get the
canvas off their backs. He realised what must have happened.
The wind had folded the canvas back over them, carrying some
of the seat jacks in the fold, and they were pinned inside.

Round about they could hear people yelling, calling for
friends, issuing wild instructions. Someone was shouting through
a speaking trumpet, "Stand back everybody. Don't trample on
the canvas." Chad figured that Athens must have a fire brigade.
Then someone stepped in the small of his back, fell over him, and
lit on Caroline. Chad bucked and felt hands feeling for them
through the canvas. " My God," Joe Duddy bellowed, " I got
a pigeon here." He abandoned Chad immediately, and went
to work on the edge of the canvas, rolling it back over their
bodies.

In three minutes they were out and Chad could look over
the mud-smeared trampled mass of the tent. The fire brigade
in leather hats were doing manful service, hauling people out

from under. The top of the centre pole protruded from the canvas close to where he and Caroline had lain. A doctor was bandaging somebody's head.

Though the wind still blew in fitful gusts, the squall had chased itself across the river, a blurred, receding blot above the hills.

" That surely must have been a blowdown," remarked a nasal voice.

Chad swung on his heel.

It seemed incredible that Bisbee had showed up, but there he was on his white-nosed horse, the faces of both intelligently examining the foundered round-top.

" I guess I only just missed it," Bisbee said. He watched Fred Shepley hauling Albany to her feet.

" Yes, you just missed, it," Chad said, and felt Caroline catch his arm.

" Chad ! " Her voice broke out. " Oh, look ! Over there, Chad ! "

She pointed a mudstained arm.

" Yep," Bisbee was smiling soberly at them both. " He moved a little slower than this horse."

From the street that led down to the lot, a grey shape was emerging. As it came closer to the canvas, two fans of ears swung forward. A smallish, crooked-shouldered man hung a hook in one of the ears and, halting beside the elephant, surveyed the outlook with distaste. But the elephant seemed as unperturbed as Bisbee ; rocking gently on its feet, it hung a curl in its trunk just above the grass.

" I got him," Bisbee said unnecessarily.

5

THE ELEPHANT WALKS AROUND

" His name's Van Buren. I don't know why he's got no tusks. But Pollock says he's easy to handle. Pollock's been with him ever since Captain Hanson brought the animal to this country."

Bisbee was enjoying himself. He had invited the entire company, including the skinners and the crook-shouldered little Pollock, to dinner in the tavern at Coxsackie Landing. The weather had finally cleared. Across the road, the lot was visible from the dining-room window, and in the lee of the tent wall the grey shape of Van Buren swayed amiably above a pile of hay.

Pollock nodded his head.

" Easiest-handling bull elephant you ever see. I've tooken him out as far as Pittsburgh and north clear to Augusta, Maine. Tooken him alone for exhibition and worked him with Hanson's circus the three years he had it." He rubbed himself behind one ear and rocked a little on his chair. " Just only, he's thievish with sweets. You got to watch him."

Mrs. Huguenine said admiringly, " My ! I can imagine it."

Already the effect of having an elephant in the troupe was making itself felt. The tavern keeper seemed a good deal more respectful than others they had lately dealt with ; he offered no objection to their moving Claude into the house.

Mrs. Pamplon said that as a child she had toured with a circus possessing an elephant, a larger beast she thought, but not so amiable.

Bisbee nodded towards the window. A regular congregation of children were lined up round the beast, and the constable who had volunteered to act as guard through the noon hour was kept busy fending them off with his truncheon.

" Pittsburgh was where I first saw him, eleven years ago. I didn't know if he was still alive, but as soon as I saw that piece about Hanson dying, I thought I'd just go see. Hanson had brought him over on speculation, figuring he could sell the animal to his wife's relations. She was a Lent, and they're mixed up with the Flatfoot crowd. But the Flatfoots refused to meet Hanson's price, so he started showing the animal himself. That

was all right till he made up his circus. Then the Flatfoots rode
him off the roads, the way they tried to ride us off, so I knew
if the animal was still alive, he wouldn't have been sold to the
Flatfoots anyway. , There he was, when I got there, playing in
the front yard with a piece of scantling. Mrs. Hanson was
willing to do business." Bisbee paused to light a new cigar.
" Well," he said, " he's ours now. I've paid a quarter of the
price down, and we've got a year to meet the rest. The Flatfoot
shows have all come east. There's nothing to bother us from
here to Herkimer, and next year we can head west ahead of the
big show and clean the country. West," he said, turning to Chad,
" is where I told you I was going to go. Why, there's places
out that way where they've never even *heard* of elephants ! "

" Then I come too. Out there, they are not so much afraid of
knives as all these people here. If I go, I can find myself, perhaps,
a little woman, nice and thin and poor so she is glad to marry the
great maestro, Fiero. I take my board along and measure her."

" You're hired," Bisbee said seriously. " I'd like to think
you were all coming out next spring with Huguenine and
Bisbee's Great American Circus and Gallopade. That's what
I've thought of calling it, if it suits my partner . . ." Huguenine
gave a pleasant grunt and Mrs. Huguenine patted his hand.
" I've thought out a new line for our paper, too." Bisbee cleared
his throat. " AMERICAN BEAUTY, BEASTS and BRAINS
BEFORE THE WORLD ! How does that sound to you ?
We'll start out clean, new paint, new costumes, new wagon
stock, and we'll have Van Buren. We've got two months left
this year. We ought to draw election crowds."

Ike said, " Do you think it's a good idea to call that elephant
Van Buren? I'm no Whig, but I know some places where they'd
peel the eyeballs of a skunk with that name."

Joe Duddy flushed a fiery red.

" How about Daniel Webster for a name ? "

" How about him ? " demanded Bastock scornfully.

" Well, I knew a pigeon from Boston, Massachusetts, once,
and she said all the pigeons there would vote for Daniel Webster
supposing they was men. She said she might vote for Jackson,"
Joe admitted candidly, " only twice was enough for any man . . ."

Bisbee raised a tactful hand. " We don't want to discuss

politics here, Joe. A circus isn't a political party and it's not the planks that count in its platform, it's the cracks." He smiled. " We'll think of a better name for him."

" Like Oscar ? Maybe ? " Joe suggested.

" That's bad luck. Oscar died," cried Albany.

" He hung on, though. He was a good old cat."

" How about Columbus?" suggested Caroline. " He discovered America, and this one's going to discover some out west."

Pollock swung forward on his chair.

" That's a good name," he said, staring at her favourably. She flushed.

It was the first day she had felt like herself since the rain started. Chad glanced at her face beside his shoulder, remembering suddenly the way he had first noticed it, walking up to Trid's. She met his eyes and suddenly her hand found his under the table. Next year they'd have to find a way to carry a baby with them, but he figured he could leave the business to her. It was time for the parade. He called the company out.

They lined up at the edge of the lot : Ike on his mule, the tent wagon with the three skinners, Shepley on the cream and Caroline on the grey, Mrs. Huguenine with a new dose of rose perfume on the tail gate of the seat wagon ; Fiero, the Pamplons, then Albany on Buck ; and lastly Columbus, towering with amiable concern over the diminutive figure of Pollock. Only Claude, the dogtoothed boy, was missing, but Chad could see them all in that line, walking the streets from Herkimer to the Mississippi River.

But a circus did not play for to-morrow, it played for to-day.

He lifted his hand, and Joe Duddy struck the drum. At the *boom* the elephant swayed its ears and its dry hide rustled as it swung its foot. Ike started on the mule. There was a real street crowd waiting for them, all down the block.

" Is this the way to Coxsackie Landing ? " Ike asked courteously.

Chad climbed up to the seat of the tent wagon. Behind him the fife and bugle let go for glory :—

> I've come to town to see you all,
> I give you how d'ye do. . . .

THE END